THE COVENANT OF MALTA

What's Past is Prologue

A Novel By

G. J. DALENTINI

The Palo Alto Press
New York

The Palo Alto Press

With the exception of obvious, historically documented events and public figures depicted as the backdrop to this narrative, all other aspects of the story, and all other people places and events contained in this book, are fictional and are solely the products of the author's imagination. Any similarities to actual people, places, or events are entirely coincidental.

ISBN 978-0-9894233-0-4

ACKNOWLEDGEMENTS

My sincere thanks for your comments, insights and suggestions. Even the ones I didn't like… especially those.

Thom
Kim
Barbara
Jerome
Carole

For Kimberly.
The most courageous woman I know.
Real or imagined.

"You cannot exaggerate it. The Order of Malta is a hidden government or the most mysterious government in the world."

- Jordanian MP Jamal Muhammad Abidat -
"The Knights of Malta – more than a conspiracy"

"Do not stint on your attacks, Egyptians, either with car or truck bombs. These are photos of the Order of Malta embassy in Cairo. I ask Allah to have it closed down or blown up, along with those inside it, who hate Islam and Muslims."

- Message posted on Islamist Websites -

PROLOGUE

"The Ambassador answered us that it was founded on the Laws of their Prophet, that it was written in their Koran, that all nations who should not have acknowledged their authority were sinners, that it was their right and duty to make war upon them wherever they could be found, and to make slaves of all they could take prisoners and every Muslim who should be slain in battle was sure to go to Paradise."

- Thomas Jefferson –

"The policy of Christendom has made cowards of all their sailors before the standards of Mahomet."

- John Adams -

BOSTON

April 25, 1980

The old man's eyes, cool blue pools lost in a jungle of hot red tendrils, searched from face to face in the dimly lit bar. If he found what he was looking for it would bring him some comfort. But he soon realized that he was searching in vain. There was anger, frustration, even confusion in their faces—but no fear. None. He knew it would be there someday, but by then it might be too late.

The young man sitting opposite him tapped his fingers impatiently on the sticky surface of the tabletop. "Penny for your thoughts."

The old man returned from his musings, smiled, and took a sip from his mug.

"Come, Victor", the young man insisted. "We're supposed to be getting drunk and raising a ruckus, not moping in our beer, old boy."

"I'm not moping, Thomas, just thinking."

"About what?"

Victor pointed to the television over the bar, and his young companion turned towards the screen and watched as an angry mob of Muslim men shook their fists at a burning American flag. Then the screen flashed to a scene in the desert containing the smoldering wreckage of aircraft, and in the sand around them, a black oily residue left by the machines during their death throes the night before. What the audience in the bar couldn't see were the incinerated remains of the US Air Force and Marine Corps servicemen who were aboard the ill-fated C-130 Hercules transport aircraft and the RH-53D Sea Stallion helicopter that had collided during the aborted mission. The news anchor informed his viewers, "It's been 173 days since the beginning of the Iranian Hostage Crisis, and America's prestige continues to be battered by this latest debacle, an aborted hostage rescue attempt that cost the lives of eight brave Americans."

"I was thinking about that," Victor said.

Thomas shrugged.

"And I was thinking about this." The old man waved his arm in a graceful arch.

Thomas responded this time with a confused stare.

The old man stared back at him and then inquired with intensity, "Why is this here? Why are we here? Why do we wear these clothes, speak this language, and drink this beer— or any alcoholic beverage, for that matter?"

Thomas Lancaster belched. "This isn't Sunday, is it?"

Victor's passion subsided, and he smiled. "No, I don't mean *that* kind of *why*," he said, poking his thumb towards the ceiling.

"I'm talking about history, my good man!"

"Oh for God's sake, Victor, not more shop talk, not tonight. The whole point of getting drunk is to forget about work, not relive it."

"Sorry, I can't help it. I am an historian, after all, as are you."

"My field is linguistics," Thomas slurred.

"You are an historian, Thomas; you just don't know it yet."

"Here we go again," Thomas Lancaster said, throwing his hands up in surrender. "Okay Victor, you win! Now let's change the subject. Let's discuss, perhaps, that gorgeous waiter over there."

"Stop being juvenile," Victor said as he resumed staring into the space over Thomas's left shoulder, his fingers tugging rhythmically at his white beard.

"Okay, okay, out with it!" Thomas exclaimed.

"I found something today." Victor replied in an almost inaudible whisper.

"Yes? What? Speak up man!"

"Do you remember that legend I was researching?"

"Which?"

The old man recited a passage from memory. "Turmoil and war over the expanse of time, but you shall know his love when you see the sign."

"Oh, you mean the one about that chap from Malta, or was it Sicily?"

"Both, actually."

"Isn't that the research being funded by your mysterious friend? What's his name?"

"Barella."

"Right, Barella. No first name."

"He has a first name."

"Yes, but you have no idea what it is."

"What I do know is that the funds are deposited in my account every month. Like clockwork."

"You can be such a mercantilist sometimes." Thomas said frowning.

"In this economy? You bet I am. How else can I afford to pay your stipend, young man?"

"True."

"I knew you would understand, if I put it that way."

Thomas grinned. "And he is rather attractive, in a caveman sort-of-way. Nice body under those expensive suits, but a little too ethnic-looking for me."

"I'll tell him he's off your man-menu."

Thomas snickered. "You think he might be….?"

"No, Thomas. He's straight. In fact, he's so straight it's frightening. And he carries a gun, so I suggest that you keep clear of the man."

"A gun? How deliciously sinister. Who is this man, Victor? Some sort of secret agent? CIA? Or perhaps he's from the Mafia?" Thomas beamed.

"He has high-level contacts at Harvard University, so the Mafia is off the list. Well, maybe. It doesn't matter, in any event. The work is interesting, and the funding is quite good. Besides, it is historical research, not weapons research, so what harm could it do?"

"So, why would a spy want you to research a medieval legend?"

"Actually, more Renaissance than Medieval. Do you remember the story?"

"Yes, of course. How could I forget? The madman who would do anything to satisfy the demands of a pope. What about it?"

Victor shook his head. "Well, first off, that's not what I told you. That may be your interpretation, but it is not mine. Second, there seems to be a great deal more to the legend than I originally thought. I'm just not sure anymore."

"You're not sure about what?"

"I'm not sure it's merely a legend."

"Well, that just makes the story even more troubling, doesn't it?"

"Perhaps, from your point of view, it does. But you have to put it in the context of the time and place."

"Yes, yes, of course, it's all relative. Right?"

Victor shrugged. "History is drenched with filicidal blood, from Abraham and Isaac in the Old Testament, to modern accounts, during the American Civil War, for example."

"But Abraham did not go through with it, Victor, did he?"

"He would have. That's the whole point of the story. It was an act of faith, of devotion to an idea. But it was not the act of a *madman*. Jesus, the son of God, was sacrificed for an idea. The entire Judeo-Christian ethos is based upon the notion that certain ideas or beliefs are far more important than living flesh, even that of our own children."

"The geopolitical ambitions of the Bishop of Rome hardly qualify as such an exultant and noble goal," Thomas retorted.

"That's not what we're discussing here," Victor snapped. "It wasn't about ambition, it was about survival; survival of the very idea of Christianity, as well as this world we now live in," Victor said, again waving his arm at the room.

The waiter noticed Victor's gesture and approached their table. "Can I get you gentlemen another round?"

"Yes, please!" Thomas exclaimed. "Two pints of Guinness, my good man."

Victor placed a hand over his half-filled glass and shook his head.

"Very well then, bring both pints for me." Thomas declared.

Thomas followed the waiter's departure with his eyes.

Victor followed Thomas's gaze. "Do I have your attention, Thomas?"

Thomas turned and replied with a wry smile.

Victor picked up his story. "From the moment Islam emerged from its desert obscurity it began to consume the world around it. The Arabian peninsula, North Africa, Persia, India, large swaths of Southeast Asia, as well as regions in what is now the Soviet Union. Then into Eastern Europe and the Byzantine Empire, where fell the last of the Roman Empire. All of these civilizations had existed for thousands of years, but virtually overnight, the Muslims engulfed and digested them, and like that," Victor said, snapping his fingers, "these places were transformed into worlds that were alien to their surviving inhabitants. Finally, only a handful of kingdoms in what is now Western Europe remained free from subjugation. Then even those began to fall victim to the sword of Islam. Christianity, which at one time dominated Europe, the Middle East, North Africa—the entire Mediterranean basin—was suddenly on the verge of extinction."

"Yes, yes, I know all of this. What is your point?"

"My point is, is that *they* don't know it," he said, bowing his head towards the other patrons in the bar. "But someday they will, just like the man in my story knew it. He was afraid for the survival of his family, his people, his entire way of life, and it was this fear of cultural extinction that motivated him to act. It was this action that helped him to slow Islam's advance and ultimately stop it. If it were not for him, and men like him, we would be living in a very different world, one I do not believe either of us would recognize, and a world in which people like us could not long survive. And now they're back," Victor said as he returned his gaze to the television.

The screen filled with the image of a bearded man wearing a black turban. He stood in a window and solemnly waved to the jubilant, cheering crowds. Then more file footage, showing bound and blindfolded American hostages being led away.

Thomas watched Victor's face, as Victor watched the screen. The man sitting across the table from him was, until recently, lively, light hearted and happy. But in the past few months he seemed to darken to the point of being nearly unrecognizable. His erratic mood swings were sometimes almost as alarming as the change in his physical appearance. Thomas replied sympathetically. "Oh, come now Victor, you're not equating what's happening in Iran now with what happened centuries ago, are you? That is ancient history. These are current events, my friend, and it is the contemporary version of the French revolution, a spiritual reawakening. They are tired of waiting for liberty to be delivered by their imperial Western masters, so they are going to take it for themselves."

"You are doing the same thing, Thomas: equating current events with our history. Unfortunately, you have chosen the wrong history. The French Revolution? My God, man, you're starting to sound like your crazy friend Foucault!"

"I happen to agree with Michel."

"Not even Foucault agrees with Foucault!" Victor grunted. "People like him have deluded themselves into thinking that the violence in Iran, and other places in the Middle East, is politically progressive, that it's the beginning of a new era of western-styled democratic enlightenment in the Islamic world. But those people on the screen despise us, and everything about us, especially our liberal democratic institutions. Their revolution is not about moving forward into the twentieth century, it's about moving backwards into the fifteenth, and this is just the beginning."

Victor took a breath and continued, "Why do otherwise intelligent people keep making the same mistake? Every time they see something that looks like a revolution, they compare it with the first one, and the last one that succeeded, the American Revolution. Every other one since has been a disaster: French, Russian, Chinese, Cuban, etcetera, etcetera. And the people that these revolutions consume first are the ones who are actually trying to do the right thing. Then, inevitably, the monsters take over. With Iran, they're at that point already, and in record time."

Thomas placed his face in both of his hands and let out a groan. "Victor, can we talk about something else, anything else. Please?"

Victor ignored his protest and continued. "The last Islamic Caliphate, the Ottoman Empire, fell only fifty-five years ago, after dominating the Mediterranean region for nearly seven hundred years. In our arrogance, we assumed that the Islamist threat to the world was gone. But I do not believe that - I do not believe that at all. And if I'm right, the twentieth century will not be remembered as the end, but merely as a brief respite in their relentless holy war of terror and conquest. You will see it for yourself, one day. I might not live that long, but you will. Mark my words, we are living in the deceiving calm found in the eye of a hurricane, completely ignorant of the fact that the second half of the storm is nearly upon us. And this man from our distant past, the one whom you deride as mad, is precisely the kind of man we will be needing if America and the West, as we now know it, are going to survive."

The old man fell silent and placed a bony hand on his forehead. *I might not live that long? No, I will certainly not live that long.*

"Are you okay?" Thomas asked gently.

"I'm fine. Just a bit of a headache." Victor reached into his shirt pocket and withdrew an amber drug vial, popped off the lid and tossed two large capsules into his mouth, then washed them down with a gulp from his mug.

"What did your doctor say today?" Thomas inquired.

"What they always say." Victor responded with a dismissive wave of his hand. "They need to do more tests. If they continue to extract my blood at this rate, they'll fix me all right. They'll bleed me to death," Victor said forcing a smile. Then he considered again what his doctor had actually said. '*No one has any idea why your immune system seems to have suddenly shut down. There's nothing we can do.*' It was all the information that Victor needed in order to come to the correct conclusion about the terminal state of his health. But it was how the doctor said it that confirmed the death sentence. It occurred to Victor now, sitting there in a dark Boston pub, contemplating the end of his life, that perhaps his body and his country were afflicted with similar diseases. Neither was capable of defending itself against a threat it couldn't recognize. And as long as that remained the case, death would be the inevitable outcome.

"Victor?"

"Yes, yes, where was I?"

Thomas was tempted to probe further, but he knew that it would be pointless. He wasn't going to get any more details tonight about his friend's obviously declining health, so he played along and returned to the previous subject, this time with a little taunt. If he wasn't going to cheer his friend up, at least he could make his heart race a little faster. "Well, I was about to say something to the effect that those people in Iran don't give a damn about America or Americans. If we leave them alone, they will leave us alone."

Victor dropped his hand to the table with a slap and looked at his young friend in astonishment. "Oh honestly, Thomas? You can't be serious. They've never left any Christian nation alone, and they've never made an exception for America. After gaining its independence, our adopted country had only one concern: to peacefully coexist and trade with other nations. It had absolutely no interest in international affairs. On the contrary, it did everything possible to avoid European-styled international intrigues. Do you think that saved us from the Islamic terrorists? Of course not! Our ships were attacked, and our people enslaved, without provocation. Why? Because in the eyes of their assailants, they were inferior Christians who owed their Islamic masters tribute just for the privilege of existing. The first war the fledgling United States of America fought was against the reign of terror of North African Muslim raiders who infested the waters of the Mediterranean and the Atlantic."

Thomas watched with some alarm as Victor's face turned red, and his veins pulsed with anger as he spat out his next sentence. "And the Europeans, to their eternal shame, paid protection money to these bastards for hundreds of years. They thought they could buy peace, but they were attacked anyway. In addition to seizing their ships and crews, these bloody pirates engaged in constant assaults on European coastal towns and villages: Italy, France, Spain, Portugal, England, Scotland, the Netherlands, Ireland, and as far north as Iceland. They captured thousands of ships and raided countless seaside villages and towns. The populace became so terrified that long stretches of coastal regions in Spain and Italy were almost entirely abandoned by their inhabitants and remained so for hundreds of years, even into the nineteenth century. How do you think many of the once magnificent coastal cities of Europe became sparsely populated, poverty stricken villages?"

"The Muslims raided Ireland and Iceland? I've never heard that before," Thomas said as the waiter returned with the two pints, placing them next to the empties in front of him. Thomas gave the waiter a wink. The man responded with a tight smile and left.

Victor rolled his eyes and shook his head impatiently at his friend.

Thomas grinned, picked up the mug nearest him and took a long swig. "Sorry old chap, where were we again?"

Victor continued. "The main purpose of the Islamic raids was to capture Christian slaves for their markets in Africa and the Middle East. Did you know that there were millions of Europeans in slavery by the time the United States was founded? And several eyewitness accounts of these slave markets have survived: men, women, and children stripped naked and poked and prodded like cattle by their prospective purchasers. Our children are taught about these unspeakably barbaric scenes in grade school, but what they are taught is that the slaves for sale were Africans and the buyers Europeans. This was true, of course, in the Americas, but in these Islamic markets the situation was reversed. The buyers were Africans, and the human goods were white Europeans. Our history is deafeningly silent on these events, despite the fact that they took place over a period of hundreds of years and started long before the English settled Jamestown, and also well before the first slave set foot in the New World."

"Good lord Victor, are you drunk already? You're only on your first pint!"

"No, I'm quite sober, but I do believe you are," He said glancing at the empty mugs sitting on the table in front of his young antagonist. Victor asked, "Do you know why I became an historian, Thomas? I spent my boyhood in a little Irish town, in western County Cork, called Baltimore. Every spring, the old people would sit around the fire and recount a shocking tale about how, in the middle of one dark June night, the entire village was sacked by Islamic raiders. They claimed that almost every person was captured and subsequently sold into slavery. Everyone except the old people. They were of no economic value as slaves, so they were slaughtered on the spot. Then, years later, a handful of these people, who managed to survive and return home from Africa, told tales about how they watched their family and friends being worked or beaten to death in the stone quarries, or behind an oar in a galley ship, or worse, being used as sex slaves. When I first heard this story I was a child, and it terrified me. Later, as a know-it-all university student, I dismissed it as a fanciful tale conjured up by generations of creative Irish minds. But then, one day, I discovered a poem written by a man named Thomas Osborne Davis. It was called 'The Sack of Baltimore'. And in it he recounts exactly this same seventeenth-century event. It was only then I finally and fully appreciated the importance of history, but most of all I realized that the history we forget, or ignore, is often the most important history we have. You see, we have sanitized our history. We tell our children a version in which they are never the victims, only the victimizers. We have raised generations of arrogant, self-flagellating, people who have forgotten our history, Thomas. But those people on the television screen have not. To them, those were the good old days, and now they want them back!"

"Victor, enough with the apocalyptic visions, already. Let's talk about something a little lighter. How about those Red Sox. How do you think they're going to do this season?"

The old man shrugged. *Who gives a damn*! "Great, now let me finish my point. This Islamic terror lasted well into the nineteenth century when, one day, a man by the name of Thomas Jefferson, a pacifist and a slaveholder, of all people, sent a tiny American armada to Europe to put an end to the Muslim terror once and for all. Then, just like now, Europe was too busy appeasing their Muslim tormentors with tributes to do it themselves. And now, just like then, it will be up to America to end the terror. But first she must once again reawaken to the enormity of the danger."

Thomas wagged a thumb at the television screen and said. "I think we just got the wake-up call, Victor."

"No, that's exactly the problem, America is still sound asleep. They just don't get it. Look! You can see it in their eyes. No fear! Fearlessness is a characteristic Americans pride themselves on. But we will pay a terrible price for it. Even this thing on the screen that's happening right now, to other Americans, hasn't roused them. It is like during the early days of World War II; it was a million miles away, they thought. As far as they were concerned it might as well be happening on the moon. Why worry about it? Then came Pearl Harbor. Someday, what you are seeing on that screen won't be over there, it will happen here, in Boston, or New York, or some other American city or town. And by then, it will be something much more terrible, and it will have happened on American soil, in a place where they live, or visited recently, to people they know—their families, or their neighbors. And when the bodies are piled up in the streets, or buried under the rubble, then and only then will they finally fully understand the threat."

"Victor!" Thomas protested, "Somehow this country has managed to defeat the Japanese, the Nazis, and we're doing a pretty damn good job boxing in the Soviets, as well. I think we can handle a few Mid-Eastern fanatics."

"It's not the same type of threat!"

"So, you're suggesting that they'll be worse than the godless commies?"

"Yes I am," Victor replied, ignoring Thomas's sarcasm. "A Russian, who doesn't believe in God, has no illusions about heaven. If he dies in battle, he knows his next destination is a hole in the ground. If they start a nuclear war, they know that they're just dust in the wind. But these people? They think they're going to paradise. And there are billions of them. The Americans, and the Russians too I think, are going to miss their polite little Cold War, someday."

Victor lapsed again into silence.

Thomas propped his elbow on the table, rested his chin in the palm of his hand, and sighed.

"I had no idea you were such a patriot, Victor."

The old man smiled. "Me neither. I'm starting to sound like my old da." Victor's smile faded and he swallowed hard. "I remember one of the last things he said to me. He was lying on his deathbed and, for no reason I could comprehend, he suddenly confessed that there were two women in his life. Naturally, I was stunned. As far as I knew he never had anyone other than my ma. All I could think of was thank God she never lived to hear of it. When he noticed the stunned look on my face, he held up a hand and said, 'Let me finish my story, boy-o.' So I bit my tongue and let him. 'Both of these lovely ladies,' he said, 'took a poor wretch like me in when no one else would have me. And not just that. They treated me like I was someone. No matter how unworthy I was they never turned me away or treated me poorly. In their eyes, I was always a man worthy of respect. Now, I won't tell ya that they were perfect, or without flaws, cause they had 'em. But you know, I loved every one of those flaws, every wrinkle, and every scar. My ladies were both all beauty to me. Your ma, of course, was one, God rest her mighty soul. The other is this land we call America, boy-o. Don't ever forget that, for the rest of your life, always remember it.' And I guess I did."

Victor took a napkin and wiped his face. "I never told anyone that story before. In fact, I can't remember the last time I even thought about it. Strange isn't it? The things we remember, the things that touch us the most, we don't ever realize it at the time, but we do in the end."

Thomas wiped a tear from his cheek, "So what was that other story you were going to tell me?"

"Which?"

Thomas smiled slyly. "The one about our savior from Malta."

Victor, again ignoring the sarcasm, reached across the table for the spare mug of Guinness, and patiently began telling his tale. "Well, it all seems to have started in a place called Segesta, on the Island of Sicily..."

BOOK I

"I intended to conquer Rhodes and to subdue Italy."

- The Tomb of Mohammed II, Sultan of Turkey (1481 A.D.) -

"Amid the turmoil and tumult of battle, there may be seeming disorder and yet no real disorder at all; amid confusion and chaos, your array may be without head or tail, yet it will be proof against defeat."

- Sun Tzu, *On the Art of War* –

Chapter 1

SEGESTA, SICILY

May, 1510 A.D.

The journey had begun in the dark hours of the morning, and he was exhausted. Now, with the sun low in the western sky, it required the gentle encouragement of his mother's hand to keep him going. His small legs ached, and his feet were covered with patches of caked mud where the road dust had mixed with the blood seeping from the raw flesh around the thongs of his sandals. If he could just sit down and rest for a little while, he thought.

"I'm very tired, Momma," he said, struggling up the steep slope.

She brushed aside her long, wavy, dark hair and looked down at him. "We're almost there, Sebastiano. Be patient for a little while longer. Can you do that, my little one?"

He responded with a little shrug and continued to place one foot carefully in front of the next. He thought about the word his mother had taught him before they began their journey: "Sacrifice". His five-year-old mind didn't understand what the word meant, but he knew that this word and today's journey were somehow connected.

On finally reaching the top of the hill, a broad, verdant valley came into view. It was edged by blue-green mountains and stretched a great distance into the haze framing the horizon, and the entire landscape was blanketed by tiny, brightly colored wildflowers that trembled in the gentle breeze. A sweet smell wafted to his nose. In the center of this majestic scene stood a solitary Greek edifice on a small, round promontory.

Sebastiano's mother pointed to it and said in a half-whisper,

"Look Sebastiano, it is as beautiful as I remember it from when I was your age."

"It is very nice, Momma, just like you told me," the boy said without conviction.

"Yes?"

"Is it old, Momma?"

"Oh, yes, it is very, very old."

"As old as Grandpa?"

She laughed. "It is much older than Grandpa."

The little boy thought about that for a moment, then said, "But not older than our church at home, right, Momma?"

"Oh, yes, much older than San Domenico too. This temple was here long before any building in Sciacca."

How could this be possible? The boy wondered. How could it be here even before his hometown? Then, as they began to make their way carefully down the rocky slope and towards the temple, Sebastiano suddenly stopped and smiled as a thought formed in his mind. "But it is not older than Jesus! Right, Momma?"

"Yes," his mother replied. "It is even older than Jesus."

The boy gave his mother an incredulous look. "Older than Jesus, Momma?"

"Yes, Sebastiano. So many questions for such a little boy," she said, gently patting his head.

They continued walking for what seemed to Sebastiano to be a long time, and yet they still had not arrived at the base of the temple. He also noticed that what had originally appeared to be a smallish, rather ordinary-looking structure from the distance had grown to a size that exceeded anything he could remember seeing before. When they at last stood at its base, Sebastiano traced the height of one of its golden-brown columns with his eyes, up and up until it reached the remnants of the roof's structure, which stood so high that it seemed to touch the clouds that drifted in the sky above.

Crumbling pieces of marble were strewn across the temple's floor, along with other debris that had accumulated over the long centuries. As they proceeded to walk its length, Sebastiano noticed small patches of green shoots that traced the cracks and borders in the dirt-covered limestone beneath his feet. After they reemerged from the far side of the structure, they proceeded down yet another steep slope. The warmth and light of the sun soon faded as they entered the shadows of a deep and rocky chasm.

For most of the day his mother had marveled at how strong and brave her little boy had been. But she could see the exhaustion and fear growing on his face, now. He stopped and tried to pull away. "I do not like this place," he said.

When his mother thought about what waited for him at the end of their journey, she couldn't keep her tears away. She wiped her eyes, leaned down, and whispered into his ear. "Sebastiano, we are almost there, be brave."

He looked up at her and noticed that she had been crying. His mother had told him many times that this journey was a very important thing for him to do, and that it would make her happy. But she did not look happy now, he thought. She looked tired and sad, and perhaps afraid, just like him.

She pulled him gently along. "I know you are tired, but soon this will be done, and then we will both rest."

Descending ever deeper, they followed the twisting path until a stream appeared at the very bottom of the ravine. The ground leveled off, and they proceeded along the slippery bank until it lead them to a cave. The clear, gurgling water flowed into its black entrance, nearly filling the entire width of the opening, all except for a narrow ledge. His mother carefully picked her way along the ledge as she led Sebastiano into the small opening. The low ceiling to the entrance caused her to stoop until the cave's height increased to a point where she could stand upright again.

In a few moments Sebastiano noticed that the sound of the stream had disappeared, and the air suddenly felt colder. He shivered. Other than the sounds of their footsteps, and his breathing, there seemed to be no other sound or movement at all. His mother led them deeper into the cavern. The air became colder still. Sebastiano could now see the mist of his breath in the dim light that was barely filtering in from the now distant portal behind them.

His mind was suddenly filled with an overpowering sensation of danger. His instincts seemed to beg him to stop, and his fear kept building with each and every step until it reached the point where his mind's pleading seemed to grow almost audible. He desperately wanted to turn around and run for the light.

But just as his fear seemed to peak, he sensed something even worse. It was waiting for him in the cold, dark, silence, and seemed to reach out and touch his heart, causing it to flutter between the rapid beats. He tried to pull back, but his mother's hand tightened around his and keep him from fleeing. He finally gave up his struggling and his mother led him on.

The light from the cave's mouth then faded altogether. But his eyes, now adjusted to the darkness, began to perceive tiny flickers of light in the distance ahead. His mother pressed on, towards the lights and, as they got closer, the shadows around them began to yield strange shapes and patterns in the cave's rocky interior. Soon he recognized the flickering lights as candles; they were placed upon a rough-hewn stone altar that had been carved out of the living rock of the cave. All around the altar were strange symbols and stone figures, some of them life size, and they seemed to stare back at him as he approached.

"Momma!" he said, now sobbing, "I want to go home. Please Momma, take me home."

Then one of the figures appeared to move, and his feet froze to the ground. His hand began to tremble within his mother's grip.

"Just the boy." A sharp, merciless voice echoed in the chamber. His mother suddenly released his hand and pulled away from him. Sebastiano grabbed for her, but she stepped back out of his reach. When he turned to run to her she gestured for him to stop and walk towards the altar. He took a long, deep breath and obediently turned back. He could feel tears leaving cold streaks on his cheeks as they ran down his face. He tried to be brave, just as his mother had told him, so he stifled his sobs in order to prevent them from becoming uncontrollable. With quivering lips he resumed his approach towards the dreadful figure at the best speed his unsteady legs would allow.

As he moved closer, the stone-like figure became clearer. It was only an old woman. But his relief was fleeting. Her white face stared down at him with lifeless black eyes, and as soon as he came within reach, her hand darted out like a striking viper. It happened so fast that he did not have time to react, and before he could retreat she had a firm grip on a handful of his hair. He tried to squirm away, but her grip was too strong, and it hurt him to struggle. She lifted his face up towards her's, and the pain increased. He winced at the foul smell of her body and breath as she examined him the way a hunter examines a fresh kill. Then, just as suddenly as he was captured, she released him. He tried to run, but his legs seemed paralyzed, and without a word, she poked a bony finger into his face and then steered it towards the stone altar.

Having been prepared for this moment, he understood the meaning of the gesture. The boy regained the control of his legs, but rather than do what he knew he must do, he instead retreated a couple of steps. Again she grabbed his hair, harder this time. He let out a gasp that echoed in the chamber. She pushed him toward the altar. Somewhere within his young, terrified mind he understood that there was no way to escape, and so he finally resigned himself to his fate.

Placing his small feet into the steps carved into the side of the altar, he lifted his body onto it and lay down on the cold surface. Now, staring into the darkness above him with his hands placed at his side, his fingers felt a wet, sticky substance. He didn't need to see it to know what it was. It had the same smell as the urn that his father used when he slaughtered a goat.

He began to weep again. "Momma?" He was answered by his mother's sobs, echoing off the hard walls to his right.

Then the old woman reappeared in the darkness over him, the light from the candles illuminating a sharp, creviced face covered with dark blotches and enormous moles. She lifted a large stone mace high above the boy's head. He closed his eyes and tried to escape this place, at least in his mind. But there was no place to go.

It was over quickly.

Chapter 2

THE ISLAND OF RHODES

December 1522 A.D.

His eyes fluttered under closed lids.

He felt his legs trembling with fatigue as he moved quickly through the cold and dark towards the bright light at the cavern's entrance until, at last, he was free again. A series of fast breaths, the sweet scent of the flowers from the hill, and the feeling of his mother's hands on his shoulders made the last of his sobbing stop. A warm, gentle breeze dried the tears on his cheeks.

For a long time after they left the cave, Sebastiano and his mother did not speak. But he could still hear the old woman's words in his head. They seemed as vivid now as when they were spoken, as if they were somehow seared into the very substance of his brain.

As he lay on the altar, the old woman moved the stone mace above his head in strange patterns, all the while muttering words in a language he could not understand. She brought the mace down, gently touching his left and then right shoulders. She raised it again, high this time, and froze, as if she had actually become stone. Then he watched in stunned silence as her body shook and trembled, and she began speaking in a voice that sounded like a chorus of many voices.

Bastards' blood united, house of Hohenstaufen and Hieron benighted.

Sleeper now awaken, lest your people and your kingdom be forsaken.

An island fortress shall you be, and save them all from their enemy.

Two fathers, brothers, sons shall be the price, all to guilty hands less one by your own device.

No more shall any suffer this fate, for a holy shield shall defend them from evil's hate.

Through the blood of the princess shall they be divided, as through the blood of the prince shall the One be provided.

A line reborn and destinies repeat, on the New Island where the waters meet.

One king lost and one king saved, the truth of their fates buried in the grave.

Visions of time shall the Chosen provide, with the gift of second sight as his mentor and guide.

Turmoil and war over the expanse of time, but you shall know his love when you see the sign.

Tears of the Father and tears of the Son, the children of Abraham shall again be one.

Then his great name shall resound in the ears of all, until the world again shall forever fall.

His mother stopped and sat down in the wildflowers beside the ancient Greek temple, pulling him down into her lap. They both watched in silent wonder, as the colors of red and orange from the setting sun seem to set the sky ablaze as the last traces of the glowing disk disappeared beneath the horizon. The towering limestone columns of the temple stood above them like protective sentinels against the brilliantly colored sky. Physically exhausted and emotionally drained, she still found the strength to turn him gently in her arms and regard him with smiling, moist eyes. Then, lifting his little body to hers, she held him so tightly that he could hardly breathe. Easing her grip, she began rocking him slowly as she kissed him all over his face. The kisses made Sebastiano giggle. She began tickling his sides and started to laugh with him.

"You were so brave, my little Sebastiano!" she exclaimed as

she hugged him tightly again. "Tomorrow we go home. But tell no one what the old woman said, understand?"

"No one? Not even Poppa?"

"No, not even Poppa. This will be our secret, forever. Yes?"

The boy responded with a cautious nod.

His mother retrieved some food and water from the pouch on her shoulder and they both ate and drank as the fiery sky ebbed, quenched by the flow of the cool shade of evening. When they finished their humble meal, she withdrew a heavy wool blanket from the same pouch and wrapped it around them as they lay down on the soft, aromatic grass. Then she began to gently move her fingers through his hair where the old women had gripped him, and continued to stroke his head until he fell asleep.

It would be the most peaceful and joyous moment he would ever know: lying safe and warm in his mother's arms, her gentle touch caressing his head, in that strange and beautiful place, at the end of that unforgettable day.

But then a hand appeared—a dark, disembodied, disfigured hand, like that of the old woman, beckoning him away from his place of peace. He instinctively turned and began to run. The hand moved swiftly. His mother disappeared. He screamed as the hand came for him. He ran as fast and as far as he could, while the flowers around his feet wilted and all of their beautiful colors faded to gray. "Momma, Momma!" he cried as the hand closed around his throat.

Sebastiano's eyelids suddenly opened, his eyes squinting at the glaring morning light. His makeshift pillow of sand and coarse gravel stung his cheek, making him wince. Despite the discomfort he kept his weary head still as his eyes focused; first on the tip of his nose and then on the sand and gravel just beyond it. He noticed that the small grains of sand were dancing, and then larger pebbles joined them. The motion was rhythmic: short and sudden followed by stillness. He leaped up from his dirt bed and wiped the sleep from his eyes and the grime from his face.

"Not again, Holy Father, please, not again," he said to himself. Then turning, he yelled as loud as he could from his perch on the wall, "We're under attack!" He heard another voice in the distance answering his and further spreading the alarm. "We're under attack, to your stations!" Moments later the whole fortress began shuddering under the weight of the enemy, as if massive fists were striking a flimsy door.

Sebastiano retrieved and loaded his bow with his last arrow, as the lingering memory of his dream and the sweet smell of that faraway hillside was replaced by the smell of the blood and the filth and the decay that now surrounded him. Bow now at the ready, Sebastiano watched from the citadel's shattered walls with a combination of awe and terror, as the massive Muslim army pressed its attack.

His prospects of surviving this day were remote; he knew that. He also knew that the remaining moments of his life, however many there may be, would be neither glorious nor merciful. His superiors long-ago informed him that, as a mere squire, the enemy would afford him neither an opportunity to surrender, nor ransom, as would be accorded to a nobleman. The best he could hope for would be a quick death: perhaps an arrow in his heart, or a swift sword blow to his neck. It was more likely, they told him matter-of-factly, that he would spend the last moments of his young life watching parts of his body being hacked off and his entrails being strung out in the rays of the sun above Rhodes, as he was systematically butchered like an animal at the hands of a vengeful enemy.

Sebastiano was flanked by others, all equally terrified, and scattered among them were a few of his fellow squires who, like Sebastiano, no longer had a knight to service. Among this pathetic roll call were also a handful of soldiers, a few knights, and even a professional mercenary or two, all now too sick or wounded to raise a shield, wield a sword or mount a horse. Most of the rest were locals: farmers and fishermen who just months ago found themselves trapped between the hammer of the invaders and the anvil of the defenders. Hastily assembled and poorly trained, not one of them was fit to replace the men who had already found the peace of a shallow grave. But none of the training or skills of a professional soldier were required now, and in any event, it would make no difference. Regardless of their skills as warriors, their health or their courage, nothing would affect the outcome now. Any man with an arm capable of drawing a bow and launching an arrow would almost certainly find a target in the mass of enemy that now swarmed over the ground in every direction. But the enemy's numbers were so great that the volley would not even hinder their advance, much less halt it.

The looks on the faces around him revealed all Sebastiano needed to know about their thoughts. They were the same as his: fading memories of homes and families that they would never see again. Most managed to stifle their tears and focus their silent attention, waiting for the order to release their last remaining volley of arrows.

From the moment the siege had begun in July, the battle was lost. Even the legendary Knights of Saint John and their massive fortress on Rhodes, which had previously repulsed the terrific attacks of their Islamic foes, were no match for this army. The enemy force of 140,000 men dispatched by Suleiman the Magnificent was without precedent. It had always been just a matter of time before they all joined their comrades in the grave. Now that time had finally come.

A frail, young friar clothed in a filthy, bloodstained cloak, staggered through the ranks, whispered hasty prayers, and heard abbreviated confessions from each of the men and boys on the wall. When he approached, Sebastiano waved him off. The priest stopped in astonishment. "Will you forgo your confession at this moment of reckoning and condemn your soul to eternal damnation?"

Sebastiano glared back and said, "Look at this damnation of hell that, in God's name, you and your ilk on the other side have brought to us in this life. Leave me; I have made peace with my Maker and do not need or require your blessing, forgiveness or council." Sebastiano surprised himself with the fury of his own words.

The monk's face contorted and his baldpate seemed to glow red with anger, but he said nothing more as he moved on to the next man in line. The others around Sebastiano stared in wonder at his outburst, but he ignored them and returned his attention to the advancing enemy.

Finally, the order to loose their arrows came, but it was barely audible over the raging sound of the attackers. Their volley flew out from the top of castle walls in stuttering, irregular waves toward the swarming mass covering the field before them. Hundreds of the invaders seemed to melt away as the arrows found their marks. However, just as quickly, others filled the voids and the army surged forward without even a moment of hesitation. Seconds later thousands of Muslim archers, stationed behind the advancing front line, answered the Christians with a massive barrage of arrows of their own. The swarming projectiles filled the air so thickly that the bright light of the sun was momentarily dimmed by their flight. The arrows, buzzing like vicious insects, sailed towards them, finding none but a few targets among the thin ranks on the walls. As the last of the arrows fell to the ground, the air became clear once again.

"No!" Sebastiano said to himself. "I will not meet my end here, waiting for these savages to slaughter me like a goat."

He dropped his bow and, ignoring the murmured protests of his fellows, turned and ran along the wobbly planking that lined the inner boundary of the walls. Sebastiano stopped at the first ladder he could find and slid down the rails without touching a rung. One of the knights called weakly from the top of the ladder ordering him to return to his post, but Sebastiano quickly left the sound of the man's voice in the distance and ran, dodging the wreckage and refuse-covered cobblestone alleys, until finding the familiar chapel that served as a makeshift quarters for about fifty men. He entered the building and slammed the heavy oak door behind him. A few small windows set high in the thick masonry walls partially illuminated the cool, dim interior. Mercifully, the same walls shielded him from much of the sound of the battle that was raging outside.

His sleeping quarters were comprised of a few square feet of stone floor that occupied a corner of the chapel's former oratory, and was furnished with a crude bed constructed out of a rough-hewn wood frame and covered by a thin, straw-filled mat. He sat on the bed and tried to catch his breath and clear his head.

"What am I doing?" He said aloud as he placed his face in his hands, trying hard to suppress his tears. He knew he was going to die here as surely as on the wall, but now he would die like a frightened old woman.

Then it came to him again, the memory of that day with his mother, the time that the oracle had recited the prophecy of his future greatness. Was it all just the ravings of some crazy old hermit? Surely, it must be so, because now his life was just minutes from ending, and none of those great deeds would ever come to pass. Suddenly, the thought of that silly poem, the so-called prophecy, that he and his mother had kept secret as if it were some sacred promise from God, filled him with anger. What a fool he was for believing it! And what would his mother think of him when she heard the story of his end, when she was told how his body was found alone, hiding in his bed like a coward?

Sebastiano felt the heart in his chest begin to pound and his skin flushed with rage. He suddenly stood, turned, grabbed the ends of the bed frame and heaved it to one side. Concealed beneath it lay a long wooden chest. His hand reached beneath his shirt and felt for the object that hung from a lanyard around his neck. A strong pull parted the lanyard. He examined the tarnished yellow-green brass key and noticed that his hand was trembling. He steadied himself, inserted it into the first of the three locks on the chest, and turned until it caused the latch to snap open. Two more and the steel-banded lid of the box was freed. But before opening it Sebastiano looked carefully around the room. When he saw no spies, he lifted the lid and quickly removed the contents of the chest, laying them out on the floor.

It was his master's armor. Don Guillermo della Palermo had made a gift of it to Sebastiano from his death bed a month before. Sebastiano remembered fondly the weak smile on the Don's face when he commented how close in size and build the two of them were. Then the dying man made a startling revelation.

Sebastiano had served as a page to the Don since the age of seven and then as squire since the age of fourteen. He was taught to read and write and was trained in the arts of armed combat. This was a very strange thing to happen to a peasant boy from the small southern village of Sciacca, but as he would find out on the day of the Don's death, it was not so strange a thing after all.

One of the first gifts Sebastiano received from the Don after he began his training was a book called *How a Man Shall Be Armed for His Ease.* It was, in essence, a knight's instruction manual that provided the names of all of the pieces of armor and, most importantly, the order and manner in which they were assembled on the knight's body. As part of his training, Sebastiano was required to memorize every diagram and recite every word in the book, which he now began doing again. He knew it would be for the last time.

"He shall have no shirt upon him except for a doublet of fustian lined with satin, cut full of holes." Sebastiano removed his filthy shirt and then slipped the white doublet over his head. *My Don was the direct descendant of Frederic II.*

"And he should wear a pair of hose made of worsted wool. Around the knees should be wrapped bulwarks of thin blankets to reduce the chafing by the leg harness." Sebastiano tugged the hose high on his legs and then tore strips of cloth from his bed linen, wrapping his knees with them. *Frederic II was the King of Sicily and Emperor of the Holy Roman Empire.*

"He should wear a pair of thick shoes, provided with points sewn on the heel and in the middle of the sole to a space of three fingers." He lifted his master's shoes from the chest and put them on his feet, feeling with satisfaction how well they fit. *Frederic II was a great man who ruled a vast European empire from his beloved city of Palermo.*

"First you must set the sabatons and tie them to the shoe with small points that will not break." Sebastiano placed the armor coverings over his shoes and tied them tightly. *My Don told me that Frederic was a man so widely admired by both his subjects and by his contemporary monarchs that he was given the name Stupor Mundi — The Wonder of the World.*

"And then the greaves and cuisses and the breeches of mail." Sebastiano placed first the greaves on his lower legs, and then the cuisses over his thighs. *The blood of Frederic II, descendant of the great Norman warriors who had rescued the island of Sicily from the Arab invaders nearly five hundred years ago, flowed in the veins of my beloved Don. Those same Normans ancestors would repeat this feat of conquest a few years later on another island, this one in the North Sea, Britannia.*

"Then place the tasset upon his hips. And then the breastplate and gardbrace and vambrace." Sebastiano's body was now covered in armor, from toes to chest and from shoulders to wrists. The etched band across the top of the breastplate depicted the Virgin and Child in the center, Saint Paul on the right, and Saint George on the left. A Latin inscription below the images read, "*Christus Res venit in pace et Deus homo factus es*": "Christ the King came in peace and God was made man". The inscription across the top of the backplate read, "*Iesus autem transiens permedium ilorum EST*": "But Jesus, passing through their midst, went his way". In the very center of the breastplate was the Don's coat of arms, the fleur de lis.

Sebastiano then allowed himself to think about what the Don had told him that day, when the great secret that Sebastiano had never even suspected was at last revealed. *The blood that flowed in my Don's veins is the same blood that flows in mine. My Don, who treated me with the kindness of a father, was my father in fact.*

"And then the gauntlets." Sebastiano placed the gauntlets on each of his hands. He opened and closed his fists and looked in wonder at the gloves of steel. *Hands like these had defeated the Muslim invaders so many times before.*

"Hang the dagger on his right side, and his short sword upon his left in a round ring that it may be lightly drawn. And then put his surcote upon his back." The dagger and the sword made a gentle clanging sound as he placed the cote around his neck. The weight of the steel strapped to his thin frame should have made Sebastiano feel heavy and fragile, but it seemed to have the opposite effect, as if he were being held up, lifted up, and strengthened by, and in, the arms of his ancestors.

"The basinet follows, laced in front and back so that it sits just so." He lifted the great helmet and placed it carefully on his head, lacing it firmly in place. He was now no longer a mere man of flesh and blood; he was now a fortress of Christendom.

"And then his long sword in his right hand, and a small pennant bearing the figure of Saint George in his left." Sebastiano turned the sword in his hand and watched with delight as the glistening, razor-sharp edge reflected the beams of light coming in through the windows. He then brought the hilt of the sword down on the klappvisier of his helmet. The sharp-nosed visor, designed to protect his face, came down with a clang. He lifted his pennant in his left hand and held high the figure of the patron saint of his ancestors: Saint George, the Roman warrior and martyr who sacrificed all for the love of Christ.

"Now he is ready to take to the field." He walked stiffly towards the chapel door, carefully steadying his footing under the weight. By the time he emerged into the sunlight he could hear the howls of the enemy nearing the tops of the walls. For a moment, Sebastiano watched as the men on the ramparts dropped stones on their heads as they climbed up siege towers and ladders towards the defender's positions. "Not much time now," Sebastiano whispered to himself.

He walked across the square towards the stables, unnoticed in the chaos.

Chapter 3

As Sebastiano approached the stables, he noticed two boys, Paulo and Stefano, both pages of about fourteen years of age, standing just inside the doors of the stable and peering out at the mayhem. He knew them well, and they knew him. This would be his first test; his knightly career might end here, and now, with these two.

However, Sebastiano noticed that they looked confused and scared, and not the least bit suspicious, so in his deepest and most authoritative voice Sebastiano said, "Bring me my mount, *Stupor Mundi*." Then he waited anxiously to see if they would comply with his order. They did, and without so much as a questioning look. In fact, they seemed relieved to have someone giving them direction.

At the first sign of the impending attack, the pages had prepared the horses in their care for battle, as was their duty. Sebastiano watched as several fully armored horses milled about restlessly, tugging at their tethers as the sound of battle approached. But they would go unused today, because their masters were either dead or dying at this very moment.

Paulo and Stefano returned with a giant white Percheron stallion, the product of Norman war horses crossbred with Arabian steeds captured from the Muslims who fled before the Norman advance across Sicily centuries before. This same noble line had been tested in battle again and again, from the coldest northern territories to the furnace-like heat of the eastern and southern reaches of the Mediterranean. The Percheron's size and power, combined with its agility and intelligence, made it the envy of all of the kingdoms of the Mediterranean basin. But this particular stallion was remarkable even for this breed. He seemed to have all of its best traits magnified. Sebastiano's former master had named the stallion Stupor Mundi in honor of his great ancestor, Frederic II. If it was his time to die, Sebastiano thought, he could think of no better companion to share his end with than this great, brave beast.

The pages brought Stupor Mundi up to the mounting platform as Sebastiano stiffly climbed the stairs to the top of the four-foot-high wooden structure. Stupor Mundi, fully outfitted in his glistening armor, peered at Sebastiano through the opening of the chanfron, a steel plate that was shaped to fit over the front of the horse's head and nose, and moved his head up and down in excitement at the sight of his master. The movement of the horse's head made the armored crinets on the stallion's crest and neck scrape and chatter. The pages, holding onto either side of his bridle, were nearly lifted off their feet as the horse reared slightly and then, on returning to all fours, Stupor Mundi began pumping his massive hooves up and down in powerful thrusts, rattling the other steel plates on his chest and hindquarters.

Sebastiano looked down and smiled at the sight of the boys struggling to hold onto the massive animal. How many times, he wondered, did his same struggles bring a smile to the face of his Don? He considered the man for a moment as he began to take his mount.

Though the direct descendant of the great and successful warrior, and emperor, Frederick Barbarossa, the Don seemed to enjoy neither the charismatic leadership abilities, military experience, nor the good fortune of his ancestor. Misfortune had dogged their expedition from the moment they left the port of Palermo. First, they were nearly wrecked in a storm in the Ionian Sea, which claimed the lives of several of their party. Then, they narrowly escaped the Suleiman's fleet off the coast of Saria. However, the worst was yet to come, following their arrival on Rhodes.

As the weeks and months went by, their cohort was decimated, succumbing to combat or to the effects of starvation and disease, until only two of them remained, Sebastiano and his Don. Looking back at their misadventure, Sebastiano wondered if any man's experience or luck could have changed the inevitable outcome of their doomed mission.

Then, about four weeks earlier, Sebastiano found himself at

the bedside of his master as he lay dying of dysentery. It was then that the Don confided his secret to Sebastiano, a secret that in turn answered a question that he had long held: Why the special treatment?

As a child, Sebastiano had been among the very few of his townspeople to receive an education. His tutor, sent from the great Norman capital at Palermo, taught Sebastiano to read, write, and speak Italian, Latin, and Greek. These were the languages of the nobility and the clergy. He read the great Greek and Roman philosophers—Plato, Aristotle, Socrates, Cicero, Seneca, Epictetus—and studied the works and inventions of great scientists, like Sicily's local son Archimedes and his contemporary from Alexandria, Euclid. He was even introduced to some of the great Islamic philosophers such as Averroes and Avicenna. This type of education was rare, even for nobility, but it was unheard of for a fisherman's son.

Sebastiano remembered frequent encounters with the Don as he passed through his small village. Kind words and sage advice seemed always to follow with these visits, along with generous payments for the smallest of deeds performed by Sebastiano at the Don's behest. When the time came, the Don took Sebastiano as a page. And then finally, the ultimate honor was bestowed upon Sebastiano nearly a year prior. Summoned by the Vatican to help defend Rhodes against the impending attack, the Don invited Sebastiano to join him and his small army of Sicilian volunteers that he had assembled to answer the call.

It was on the Don's deathbed that Sebastiano learned that he was the product of a brief but passionate love affair between his master and his then-unwed mother. The revelation came as a shock. Sebastiano loved and respected the man that he thought was his real father, so the news that he was a bastard was painful and embarrassing in more ways than one. The Don told Sebastiano that he knew it would be so, which is why he nearly took the secret to his grave. But he had other reasons for disclosing the revelation. As the Don's eyes welled up with tears, he told Sebastiano what he already knew, that his two other sons, Sebastiano's half-brothers, were dead. The eldest, Guillermo, had died in a riding accident three years ago. Then the youngest, Frederic, had perished just a few weeks before, during one of the many assaults on the citadel.

Following the death of his second son, the Don's spirits were broken and his health rapidly declined. But there was one more son that he might be able to save, he said, and thereby save his family line. So on that day, Sebastiano found himself mourning the passing of his master and, as it turned out, his real father. He was a man Sebastiano had already grown to love as a son loves a parent.

As his last official act, the Don lifted a weak hand, touched Sebastiano firmly on his head and declared, "From this day forward you will be known as Don Sebastiano della Sciacca." Then he placed a ring bearing the family crest on Sebastiano's right index finger. The Don went on to order Sebastiano to abandon the hopeless cause in which they were now engaged, any way he could, and find his way back to Palermo. He then handed Sebastiano a letter containing his last will and testament, bequeathing all of his worldly possessions and hereditary rights to his last surviving son. He made Sebastiano promise not to disclose this information to anyone before he returned safely to Sicily, for fear the young man would fall victim to the ambitions of the many ruthless foreigners, from the ranks of both the invaders and defenders, now assembled on Rhodes.

The Don's last words before he passed away that night were the barely audible ramblings of a man in feverish delirium. "The Oracle was right. His Mother told me about how brave the little boy was in the darkness. So brave. He will save us all, he will save us all. My brave son will save us all."

After Sebastiano buried the Don, he secretly gathered up and hid his inherited possessions, locking them, along with the letter, in the large wood and iron chest beneath his bed.

It was all for nothing, Sebastiano concluded as Stupor Mundi chafed against the bit. Adjusting his position in the saddle, Sebastiano realized that he would soon die in this remote, cursed place, like the Don and his half-brother before him. And when he did, no one would survive to tell Sebastiano's story, or any other story for that matter. No one would tell his mother how much he loved her, or how much he loved his adoptive father, or how thankful he was to be raised by two such good and caring men.

The Oracle was wrong. He would save no one, least of all himself. He would ride to his death in a matter of minutes, and the rest of the Christian defenders would be slaughtered with him. Then the Muslim infidels would invade Sicily, because Sicily had always been the gateway to Europe. And then and there his mother, and the rest of his family and friends, would be wiped out, or worse, taken as slaves to end their bitter days in the bowels of a galley behind a massive oar, or in the case of the women, sold and used as prostitutes.

These thoughts began to make Sebastiano's head swell with rage. A fire seemed to rush along his veins as he drew his sword and retrieved his shield from its stand. He spurred the stallion forward, but the horse did not move. Sebastiano struck with the spurs again, but still Stupor Mundi stood his ground. Finally, Sebastiano remembered one of the peculiarities of this beast, and said to the horse forcefully, "Come Stupor Mundi, it is time for battle." At the sound of the words, the horse began marching out of the stable and across the courtyard to where all of the surviving defenders were formed in line before the ramparts of the citadel and the great Tower of Italy, which already flew the colors of the enemy.

They took their place in the very rear and at the center of the line. Only a final pair of wooden doors stood between them and the vast army on the other side. Soon the doors would yield to the onslaught and the enemy, in their tens of thousands, would flood in through the breach. He did not have long to wait before his rendezvous with death, Sebastiano thought.

Chapter 4

The gates of the Citadel rumbled and bulged with each shattering impact from the enemy's siege engine. Inside of the gates, a line of five hundred week and starving soldiers stood silently by, shoulder to shoulder, in ranks five men deep. About one hundred mounted knights took their positions on each side of the infantry, protecting their flanks and preparing to repel the invaders. Less than six hundred remained of the more than three thousand knights, soldiers and local volunteers who had originally held this forlorn citadel on this godforsaken island on that first day, when the masts of the Muslim fleet darkened the horizon like some primeval floating forest from a terrifying nightmare.

The assembled defenders spoke not a word, not even a muttered prayer or farewell to their comrades in arms. All had already been said. The army, from Sebastiano's vantage point at the very back of the line, seemed like little more than an assembly of the dead simply awaiting delivery to the grave. His eyes then turned out and upward towards the massive gates and the steel bands that held the hinges to the walls of the castle's entrance. He could hear the heavy oak timbers starting to split and crack. Then the hinges finally gave way, and with a last plaintive groan, one door and then the other fell to the ground with a crash, both disappearing beneath a cloud of dust.

There was a brief moment of perfect stillness as the air cleared, and then, like a river from the bowels of hell, the invaders came on.

They attacked in a formation ten men wide, driving themselves like a spear into the heart of the defenders' ranks. They made short work of the first and second lines of infantry, who seemed to melt away as the enemy advanced through them. Nevertheless, the Christian defenders maintained their discipline and filled the center with the reserves from the back and the flanks as they were trained to do, and as they had done during so many previous battles. This time, however, it seemed like such an obviously futile effort, as the replacements were transmuted into dead flesh almost as soon as they filled the ranks of their deceased comrades in the center.

Then it happened. Sebastiano could see, as well as feel it. The last shred of hope and faith, and with it the last vestige of honor, drained from the men before him. He watched in mute horror as the army was transformed from a disciplined body of warriors into a mob of terrified individuals, each desperate to cling onto the most remote possibility of survival.

First to flee were the soldiers at the extreme right and left flanks. Then the mounted knights began to waver and break before the onslaught. Stupor Mundi and Sebastiano stood their ground and waited as the line before them thinned, and then parted, like the sea before Moses.

Stupor Mundi began to snort and kick, not in retreat but in an effort to advance. Sebastiano pulled back hard on the reins to hold the stallion in his position and chided his mount, "Not yet, my friend; let death come to us." But the animal was impatient with waiting and he began to spin and kick as Sebastiano held on tightly with his arms and legs. "Give me one tenth of your bravery and we will meet our end in a way that will be worthy of a song," Sebastiano said through gritted teeth.

As the faces of the enemy drew closer, Sebastiano could see the victory in their eyes: like a predator tearing at the back of its dying prey. The vision initially filled him with fear. Then a sudden upwelling of rage came, drowning the fear. *I will never again see my mother and father,* he thought as his rage built. *I will never see my home or walk the streets of Sciacca with my friends again.* He let the tension slip on the reins. *I will die here in defeat, and then these bastards will invade Sicily*. With a sudden gnashing of his teeth, a shrug of his shoulders, and the straightening of his back, Sebastiano bid it all farewell: farewell to his family, his home and his life on this earth.

Now, all of his thoughts became focused on the present, on the moment before him. The scope of his vision seemed to narrow to a few degrees, as all else became a dark and blurry tunnel. His hearing faded as well, causing the battle to become mute, replaced by the sound of his heart pounding and the air rushing into and out of his lungs. He could feel Stupor Mundi's beating heart and pumping chest through the sides of his legs. In a moment, they seemed to synchronize - his heart and mind with that of his mount, as though they had linked together, as if they were now one animal, one terrible being, advancing towards the neck of its tormentor. Then another massive surge of rage filled this beast's chest, and was set loose.

As the thousands of advancing enemy soldiers parted the formation of the Christian defenders from the front, a single white stallion and its rider approached from the rear. At first, the advancing Muslims were so focused on those fleeing that they did not even notice the lone horse and rider. Then the Christians' ranks evaporated entirely, leaving only Stupor Mundi and Sebastiano standing defiantly before them on ground littered with the dead and dying.

At that moment, Stupor Mundi snorted and reared, and as he did, both the horse and rider released through their mouths a combined sound that immediately refocused the attention of the invaders. The sound, at first, seemed as though it was not coming from living flesh at all; beginning as a deep, bass noise, like the rumble of thunder, it then ascended into a terrifyingly high shriek, like the sound of storm-driven winds blowing through a ship's rigging. It was a sound belonging to no living person or beast; but rather an ancient, primitive chorus conjured from eons past. It seemed to rip through the air of the courtyard like an explosion. It echoed off the walls of the fortress and then, as it filled the ears and hearts of the attackers, their attention was instantly drawn away from those fleeing and up to this single, unearthly apparition.

Stupor Mundi immediately returned to all fours and began

pumping his legs up and down like massive pistons. The rhythmic sound of hooves striking the ground, armor clanging armor, the bellows-like blast of the horse's breath, and the clouds of dust kicked up and into their faces, caused the front line of attackers to instinctively pause to reassess the risk of making the kill. And with that pause, the entire charging front of the Muslim army froze. It was only for an instant, but their momentum was lost. And in that same instant of time both Sebastiano and Stupor Mundi were convinced, with the carelessness of the condemned and the bravado of the insane, that the entire army before them, all 140,000, was theirs for the taking.

Stupor Mundi charged. The stallion's iron peytrel armor slammed straight into the unfortunate foot soldier in his path; the screaming man went down under the charger's hooves and abruptly fell silent. Meanwhile, Sebastiano slashed downward with his sword to the right and then the left. Five more Muslim infantrymen were thrown back as Sebastiano bludgeoned them with his shield; several were flung aside by Stupor Mundi's armor, or else trampled beneath his hooves. Some tripped over the feet of their confused comrades and found the same fate. Then the horse charged again as Sebastiano rained broad and powerful sword strokes on the enemy, like a farmer with a scythe in a field of ripe wheat. Each arc of Sebastiano's arm brought a sickening harvest: heads, parts of faces, fingers, arms — all severed from their owners. Pieces of flesh, hair and bone filled the air around them, along with an almost continual spray of blood. Soon the sword, the shield, Stupor Mundi and Sebastiano were drenched red as they swung and turned and dipped together in this terrible dance of death.

Amidst the chaos of the battle, Sebastiano thought he heard a faint, small voice in the dim recesses of his brain, screaming at the horror all around him. However, the voice was quickly silenced by the brutish roar coming from his throat as he brought the sword down again and again, the sensation of steel slicing flesh and bone carried through the blade, the gauntlet and into his fingers and hand. It should have made him sick. He should have been repulsed. But all he could feel was an unrequited hunger, an unquenchable thirst for more.

The invaders tried several times to regroup, but Sebastiano and Stupor Mundi gave them no time to reform their lines. The warrior and his steed kept pushing the enemy ranks, driving into the densest mass of men they could find.

Ironically, the rider and his horse had an unexpected advantage over the vast army before them: they presented a small target that no more than a dozen men could attack at once; the ranks of thousands could do little more than stand by and watch, waiting their turn as their companions were consumed by this flailing machine of death.

As this wildly implausible scene was unfolding, a handful of the fleeing Christians slowed, stopped, and turned, becoming spectators to this incomprehensible play unfolding on this gruesome stage of slaughter. A moment later, one of them brandished his sword and shield and, with a whooping battle cry, waded back into the enemy. He was quickly cut down after gaining only a few steps. But then a small group of perhaps twenty Christian solders fell in line and charged. Confusion began spreading through the invader's ranks as this cohort of Christians slammed into their left flank. Then the cavalry turned, regrouped and, led by the war cry of the Knights' Grand Master, threw themselves at the right flank of the invaders. A moan of stunned surprise rose from the Muslims as fear of annihilation raked the courage from their hearts. Soon the entire retreating Christian army had turned and began fighting with a ferocity reserved for warriors who, having narrowly evaded the disgrace of a complete rout, were determined to regain their lost honor at any cost.

The reversal staggered the invaders. Initially their lines held, but the narrow, spear-like formation, which moments before had been the source of their powerful thrust through the defending lines, suddenly became a deadly liability as it was flanked on both sides and came under concentrated attack by the enraged

Christians. The front of the Suleiman's army began to waver and then they broke. Dropping their weapons, they began to flee for their lives, back through the breach from which they came. Thousands more outside of the walls joined them, until nearly half of the army was now in full flight. But those towards the back of the ranks, who could not yet even see the spectacle in front, continued to rapidly advance toward the citadel. As a result, the half of the army in panicked retreat collided with the half that was still advancing; thousands of the invaders were trampled under the feet of their own comrades.

Sebastiano and Stupor Mundi lead the Christians' pursuit out of the gates of the citadel, directly on the heels of their enemy, like a pack of ravenous wolves, trampling over a grizzly carpet of mangled flesh and blood-drenched mud, hacking and slashing as they went until they could no longer raise their swords, shields or their legs. By day's end, when nearly all of the Christians returned victoriously to the citadel, they carried with them a hoard of captured food, water, and weapons, but mostly they bore the satisfaction of having turned a disaster into an unimaginable victory.

It was a complete rout for the Muslim army. The enemy's number was reduced by nearly a quarter; more than thirty thousand men lay dead or dying on the field. The ranks of the Christians, on the other hand, were reduced by less than one hundred during this counter-attack. It was a miraculously small price to pay for such an epic victory.

The clear blue sky of that morning was replaced by a uniform gray ceiling of clouds. Then orange rays of light pierced the heavens and illuminated a part of the field where the dead were piled in a great circular heap. At the center lay Sebastiano's motionless body. Suddenly his body began to move. He blinked his eyes, trying to clear the blood and grime, and then struggled painfully to his knees, groaning against the weight of his armor. Sebastiano removed his gauntlets and helmet and surveyed his surroundings. He was relieved to see that the citadel, which stood about 300 paces away, had gates standing in its entrance and the flags of Christendom were once again flying on the ramparts and the Tower of Italy.

He rubbed his eyes as he tried to comprehend the carnage between him and the gates. The air was filled with the sound and smell of the thousands of dead, bloated bodies around him. Now and again he heard a muffled cry in a foreign tongue, or a pathetic moan of hopelessness. The ravens, gulls, wild dogs, and swine were feasting on the flesh of the fallen men—some of them still alive.

The pain in Sebastiano's body, and the sights, sounds, and smells of the battlefield overwhelmed him, and he began heaving against an empty stomach. As he lifted his head, his eyes fell upon the lifeless mass of Stupor Mundi, less than two paces away. Sebastiano crawled to his companion's side. The brave creature had taken three or four armor-piercing lance thrusts to his chest and two arrows in his neck before finally collapsing. His rider had gone down with him, receiving multiple blows that pierced his armor and mangled his flesh as well. Sebastiano brought his hand down and slowly stroked Stupor Mundi's mane as tears filled his eyes. He would have surely broken his back and been killed or paralyzed, Sebastiano thought, but for Stupor Mundi's final service to him, cushioning his fall with his body.

Suddenly there was the sound of horses approaching from behind, but before Sebastiano could turn to look, a bolt of pain seared the base of his skull and his vision faded to black.

Chapter 5

Three robed men stood over Sebastiano's body. They were alone in the tent, except for one undetected woman who hid behind a screen and silently watched the solemn gathering with her bright green eyes.

"He looks very young. Are you sure this is the one?" the Sultan asked as he looked down at the unconscious Christian.

The older man standing to the Sultan's right said, "Our reports have been confirmed by several of our most reliable men and also by what I have witnessed with my own eyes. But he does look young, even for an archangel."

The Sultan, wearing a stern expression, turned toward the speaker. The old man continued, "A rumor, your eminence. The Christians believe that he is the archangel Michael, who came down from heaven and delivered their army from certain defeat."

The Sultan's face softened. "He appears to me to be made of flesh and bone. And what rumors are circulating in my army?" He inquired.

The old man looked nervously off into the distance. "I have heard him called the Narasimha by some of the Persian mercenaries."

The Sultan responded with a puzzled look.

"It is an Eastern deity, my lord: half man, half lion."

"This is blasphemy!" said the third and younger man, standing to the Sultan's left. "I will take the heads of these Persian barbarians myself. Then I will take his." He said motioning to the Christian on the bed.

"You will leave the Persians' heads on their shoulders, my nephew," the Sultan said in a sharp voice. "We cannot afford the loss of any more able-bodied men. And you will not lay a finger on this man. He is my guest and he will be treated so."

The Sultan turned abruptly back to the old man on his right as the younger man tried to regain his composure. "What else does my army say about this Christian?"

"Their counter-attack was led by a small group of about twenty men. Our army has taken to calling them the Pride of Lions. And this one, the one on the white stallion, was their leader. I have heard them call him the Jaws of the Lion."

"Yes, I have heard this as well," the Sultan murmured. "At least this is not blasphemy," he said, giving his nephew a wry grin. The young man, now barely containing his anger, bowed curtly, turned and paced quickly out of the tent.

"Continue," The Sultan commanded of his older companion.

"Based on what I was told, and what I saw, lion would be an apt description, my lord. They were not the actions of a man that I witnessed, but those of an enraged beast. I do not believe I've seen his equal, at any age."

The Sultan shot an angry look in the direction of the speaker.

"I meant, my Lord, that I have not seen his equal among our enemies."

The Sultan returned his attention back to the unconscious stranger, shook his head and repeated, "But he is little more than a frail boy."

"Frail boy or not, my lord, since that debacle two days ago our army is filled with fear, and this one they fear most of all. Your nephew may be correct. Perhaps it is not wise for us to permit him to live."

"Perhaps. But what would the army think of their Sultan if he slaughtered a lion like a goat? Would such behavior please Allah? Besides, perhaps this boy warrior can help us in other ways," the Sultan said thoughtfully, "assuming he survives his wounds."

After a few moments of reflection the Sultan commanded, "I want him secretly moved to the tent of the women, and I want one hundred of my personal guards surrounding that tent and protecting this man. I am sure there are others, besides my nephew, who would like to see him dead. But he will not be touched unless you hear an order directly from me. Allah will determine if he will live or die. And if he is spared by Allah, he will not be touched by any man among my army. Do you understand?"

"Yes, my lord."

Chapter 6

When he opened his eyes he found himself surrounded by beautiful young faces; they were floating about everywhere in the haze and they were touching him and whispering to each other in a tongue he could not understand. Angels, Sebastiano thought. They must be, and they were bearing him to heaven. One of them looked into his eyes and smiled. She touched his face gently with a soft, warm hand. Her eyes were a beautiful emerald green, like the sea near his home on a summer's day. It was the last thing he remembered seeing before his vision faded to black again.

When he woke the second time, he found himself alone in the darkness. He struggled to move his limbs, but they would not obey him. But he was able to move his head slightly. A moment later he heard movement and saw a light, and then the angel with the green eyes appeared over him in the golden glow.

She was so beautiful, he thought. He smiled at her and she returned the smile. Then she very carefully took his head in one arm and gently placed something into his mouth. It felt warm and soft against his lips and he instinctively began to suck on it, as if he were an infant again. The fluid that flowed into his mouth tasted sweet, like goat's milk, but a bit more salty. Then he felt himself slowly drifting away.

When Sebastiano awoke the third time, he was looking up at a white ceiling that seemed to be moving. A gentle, warm breeze was blowing over his bare chest, and the air was perfumed with the scent of flowers. Had it all been a dream? Was this a dream? Or was he dead? If he was dead then surely this was heaven, he thought. He tried to focus on the undulating surface, but his eyes kept losing their focus and he began to feel sick. He sat up, trying to prevent himself from vomiting, and he felt every inch of his body scream with pain. No, he could not be dead; it would not hurt this much.

He sat motionless for a moment and waited for the agony to subside. Only his eyes could move freely, and they began absorbing the sights that surrounded him. The walls were the same color as the ceiling, and they were moving too. His brain finally made sense of the images, and he realized that he must be in a great, white tent of some kind, though it was larger than any tent he had ever seen. Sebastiano began to regain command of his other faculties and further examined his immediate surroundings, and his own body.

He was lying on a large bed covered with white, down-stuffed pillows. His armor and clothing were gone and he was covered by a blanket made of a very fine cloth. He thought, at first, that it could be silk. But that was absurd, silk was much too rare and expensive to be used for bed linen.

The blood and grime were gone from his skin also, along with the smell of death. His wounds had been cleansed and bandaged and the scent of flowers was everywhere—even on his skin. He sniffed his hand; he smelled like the field flowers in spring.

Moving like an old man, he stood. He waited for the haze in his head to subside and then tried to stretch his limbs, but the pain stopped him cold. Sebastiano let the blanket drop to the floor as he examined the many bandages that covered his body. He placed his hand on the back of his head and winced with pain as his fingers touched a large, tender lump.

Then he heard the sound of murmuring voices, and when he looked up, he saw several young women staring back at him with amused curiosity. He came to the sudden realization that, except for the bandages, he was completely naked. Moving as quickly as he could, Sebastiano grabbed the blanket from the bed and covered himself as one of the women approached.

She was older than the others, perhaps by three or four years, he estimated. His eyes locked on her. She had a slender body and delicate arms and hands. With a deft motion she tucked a strand of her long, glistening, midnight-colored hair behind an ear.

Nearing him, she placed her hands on her hips and smiled. Sebastiano realized that he was staring at her, but he could not help it; her brilliant green eyes were somehow familiar to him, and they pulled at his attention with an irresistible force.

He began to feel lightheaded again and his legs weakened; he slumped back down on the bed. The woman went to a nearby table, lifted a large silver chalice and brought it to him. He looked at her and then down at the drink. He suddenly realized that he was very thirsty, and he took the chalice. Just as he was about to bring it to his lips, he hesitated and began to study the contents.

"How long have I been here?" he asked in a raspy voice.

"Six days," she replied in a hesitant, heavily accented Italian.

He sniffed at the chalice and looked suspiciously at his hostess.

She smiled. "It is safe; it will help make the pain small. It is from a most-high man of Islam, Ibn Sīnā." She said struggling to remember the Latin pronunciation.

Sebastiano interrupted her. "Avicenna, the great Persian philosopher and physician?"

"Yes! You know of him?" She asked with a puzzled look.

"Of course. Your prisoner has read the works of many Muslim scholars."

"You are the honored guest of the Sultan, not a prisoner. If you want some other thing, tell me, and you will have whatever you wish."

Sebastiano took a sip from the chalice. It tasted at first like the juice of an orange, but it had a very bitter aftertaste. He removed the cup from his mouth, making a face.

"Yes, it is bad to the taste, Green Eyes said with an easy laugh. It is always so with such drink, yes?"

Sebastiano nodded, but he had no idea what she was talking about. The woman reached out towards Sebastiano's face, but he pulled away.

"Let me show you what to do," the woman said as she gently pinched his nose between her fingers. "Now drink." She commanded.

Sebastiano gulped down the remainder of the liquid as her fingers held fast to his nose. When he lowered the cup, he could taste nothing. The woman smiled at him. "It is good, yes?" Sebastiano smiled, "yes, it is good."

They both laughed at the nasal sound of his voice. Then he reached up and gently removed her grip from his nose. As he did, she began to protest. "No, no, no."

Sebastiano soon realized why, but it was too late. As soon as her fingers left his nose the taste came back, but it was much worse than before.

She quickly lifted a plate of food from a nearby table and pushed it towards him. "Here, this will help."

Sebastiano tore off a piece of the still-warm bread with his teeth and chewed quickly. Green Eyes covered her mouth and began to laugh again.

Sebastiano frowned at her as he reached again for the plate, this time taking a chuck of the cheese. He took a greedy bite and then repeated the same with the meat. He recognized this taste, at least. Both were from a goat, which brought back memories of home. The last meal he could remember had consisted of moldy, hard bread and rancid water.

He stopped eating long enough to take a breath. Then he remembered his vision of the angel, the beautiful one with the green eyes, and he realized that she was standing right in front of him, still laughing as she watched him eat like a starving wolf.

"I have been here for six days?"

"Yes." She nodded.

Green Eyes handed him another chalice filled with liquid. He pushed it away. "No." He said forcefully.

"It is only water," She said.

He sipped it to confirm it contents, then gulped the cup dry.

Green Eyes brought another tray and Sebastiano drank and ate still more. At one point, he belched, causing the women across the room to giggle at his rude manner.

When he was finally sated, Green Eyes took away the empty plate and chalice and brought him a robe made from the same delicate material as the bed sheets.

"Stand, please," she said to him.

Sebastiano hesitated, looking over at the giggling women. Green Eyes followed his stare across the room and suddenly barked an order in a language he could not understand. The room was emptied in moments, leaving only the two of them. He stood up cautiously, covering himself with the blanket as he rose.

She placed the long robe around his shoulders and he slipped his arms into the garment. He noticed that his skin began feeling warm and tingled slightly, but most noticeable of all was that the pain in his body had started to subside.

"What is this?" he said, holding up a piece of the robe. The woman was at first confused by the question. Then she smiled in understanding.

"It is made from cloth brought from Asia."

"What animal produces hair that is so fine?"

"It is not an animal's hair," she said, "it is from . . ." Her brow furrowed as she searched for the proper word. ". . . An insect," she said, finally.

Sebastiano looked at her skeptically.

"Yes, really, it is from a small—what is your word? A worm."

Sebastiano thought for a moment, and then realized it must be silk. He knew his island home of Sicily was one of the few places in the world, outside of Asia, that produced and exported this fine material. It was a skill brought to the island by their former Muslim conquerors, hundreds of years ago. But it was such a rare and expensive product that none but the wealthiest and most powerful nobility and clergy even knew what the material looked like, and few of them ever felt it on their skin. His Don, one of the wealthiest men in Sicily, could afford to buy a few pieces as embellishments to his finest clothing, and to reduce chaffing under his battle armor, but Sebastiano never remembered hearing of anyone so wealthy as to be able to afford to make bed sheets and robes from the material. How amazingly decadent, he thought.

He returned his attention to his beautiful hostess. "What will you do with me now?" he asked.

"Your presence has been requested by the Sultan, this evening for dinner, if you are strong enough."

"Do you treat all of your prisoners so well?"

"You are not a prisoner." She insisted. "As I said, you are the honored guest of the Sultan."

"So, then I am free to decline the Sultan's invitation and walk out of here?"

"You are his guest, not his prisoner. But I cannot imagine why anyone would want to return to that place of disease and death behind the walls of the citadel."

Sebastiano could not think of a reason either.

"But please," she went on, "if you must return, first let me bathe you and feed you again."

"Bathe me? I am already clean."

"You are no longer filthy, or smell like a dead animal, but you are not clean."

She took his hand and led him through the tent past a draped partition. Behind it was a large tub carved from a fine brown wood that felt smooth and oily to his touch. She made a motion for him to get in and then she began to gently remove his robe. He held the robe closed against her attempts and looked at her with a stern face.

She smiled and said, "Don't be shy. I have come to know every part of you."

She gestured again towards the tub, but he hesitated. "Are all Christian men so?" she said, rolling her eyes. "I will turn while you undress."

She turned and he quickly dropped his robe and got into the warm water. He had not bathed for months, and then only in the seawater from the harbor. He looked around at the strange and exotic surroundings, and his beautiful companion, and wondered again if perhaps he had indeed died and was in heaven.

She began to wash him with soap that smelled like roses, removing his bandages as she went. Her hands were soft and thorough and he felt himself relax as she gently kneaded his shoulders and his back. Then she slowly moved her hands around to his chest and carefully washed around his wounds. When he flinched, she stopped.

"I am sorry, did that hurt?" she asked.

"No, I'm fine."

"Shall I continue?"

He gave her a hesitant nod, and she did.

She said, "As I watched you in your bed, I was wondering if you would ever come back to the world and speak again. Many thought you would surely die, or perhaps that you would live, but without your mind. I am very happy you have returned to me."

Sebastiano did not know how to respond. She was a stranger, but he somehow felt a bond with her and she seemed to have the same feelings towards him.

He said, "I had dreams of an angel. She was very kind and very gentle. I remember her green eyes, like yours."

She continued the bathing and massage, moving down his chest and passing her fingers over each of his ribs. "You must have nearly starved to death," she said. "How could someone so frail fight so furiously?" Sebastiano did not reply and she moved her hands down further to his abdomen and to another wound. "I fed you milk, but you will need many weeks of meat and cheese for you to fully recover."

"I remember this, you feeding me. It is like a childhood memory. I remembered sucking on a . . ." He stopped and blushed.

Green Eyes giggled. "No, it was not my breast. It was a goat's udder, and the milk of a camel. My people have used it for many centuries to cure the sick and heal the wounded. I think it is why you have survived."

"Thank you," he whispered.

"Thank the camel. She is the one who restored your life. You can meet her later. You have already met the goat." She laughed.

She worked in silence for a while and then said, "You have no wounds on your back, only on your front. The Sultan says you are the bravest of your warriors... perhaps, the bravest of any warrior."

"My bravery is common among my people," he said, smiling at his private joke. He wondered how the Sultan would treat him if he knew just how common Sebastiano was. Well, there was no need to discuss that, was there?

"The men of our army whisper when they speak of you," she continued. "They call you…" She hesitated trying to find the words in his language…"*Mascelle del Leone.*"

Sebastiano's brow pinched in confusion. "Jaws of the lion?"

She nodded. "They say that your small army was cornered and crippled and about to die. Then it turned and attacked them like a great, desperate, lion. And they say you were at the very front, leading this ferocious beast, tearing and ripping apart flesh, like the lion does with its jaws."

She moved to the other side of the tub and turned her attention to his feet. "The Sultan does not like this talk among his army, and if men are caught saying such things they are flogged."

She began to move slowly up, massaging his legs. As she moved towards his groin, he felt himself becoming aroused. He placed his hands on her's to stop her further progress. She stopped, looked at him, and then down into the water between his legs. She smiled and said, "Ah, I see everything is still working. I feared that you might have been more severely injured."

She freed her hands and moved up further. As she did she brought her face close to his and kissed him gently on the forehead, once on each eye, and then fully on the mouth.

Sebastiano tried to move his head away, but she reached up and gently laced her fingers through the waves in his brown hair, looked into his pale-blue eyes, and kissed him again, this time exploring his mouth with her tongue.

Then she suddenly released him, stepped back, and with a single agile shrug let her clothes fall to the floor, revealing a smoothly curving body that was brown at the extremities but nearly white from her breasts to the bottom of her legs. She stepped into the tub as a confused Sebastiano protested.

"What are you doing?"

"It is good," she said as she kissed him again, this time touching her tongue to his. Sebastiano pulled away. "It is not good. You are a slave and under the command of the Sultan to please his guest. A Knight of Saint John does not take such advantage. I may not accept such gifts."

"So you think I am a gift from the Sultan? A slave?" She smiled at him with her gentle eyes. "No, I am Basilah, and the Sultan is my father. And if he catches us he will not be happy with you or me." She made a slashing movement across her neck.

Then, smiling gently at him, she opened her legs and folded down toward him. Sebastiano felt the smooth insides of her thighs caressing his body and felt her hand deftly working between them. He slipped inside her without resistance; she closed her eyes and began to move her hips gently up and down. He placed his hands on her shoulders and feebly tried to stop her again. She took his hands away from her shoulders and placed them on her hips. Then she held his head between her hands and brought his face to her breasts. The sweet, musty smell of her skin filled his head and his resistance evaporated.

She then placed her mouth close to his ear and whispered, "It is I who take advantage of you. You are *my* gift. The same warrior who would not yield to my father's greatest army, yields to me."

Chapter 7

The Sultan and his entourage were seated on a wooden platform raised slightly above ground level, and it was covered with thick, richly woven carpets. He watched Sebastiano crossed the broad expanse inside the tent, escorted by his most beautiful and most favored daughter, Basilah, and noticed that her arm was entwined with the Christian's as though he were a prince. Her prince. The others sitting around the Sultan probably noticed the same thing, but if they did, they dared not comment.

The last time Suleiman remembered seeing his daughter this content was before her marriage to that miserable bastard Mahmud. He had not deserved Basilah's hand in the first place. Then, after years of cruelty, he left his young daughter a childless widow within the first week of the siege. Publicly, Basilah and the Sultan mourned his loss, but privately Mahmud was missed by neither of them. The Sultan had hoped that one day his daughter's vivacity would return, but he hardly expected this now, especially with this Christian. She should still have been in mourning for her late husband, at least for the sake of maintaining appearances. *I am not sure what troubles me more: that our army is so fearful of this boy, or that my daughter is so fearless. We have all been on this accursed island too long. This was to be a brief stop on our campaign into Italy. We were to capture this hellish mound of rock within a few days and then move on to Sicily. We should have been in Rome by now, with the city and its treasure at my daughter's feet.*

Basilah brought Sebastiano before the Sultan, interrupting his contemplation, and released her arm from his. Then bowing before her father she announced, "I present the Christian warrior, Sebastiano della Sciacca." Then she quickly added, in nearly perfect Italian, his newly acquired name of legend: "Mascelle del Leone".

Sebastiano stood there in his best warrior stance, but said nothing.

The Sultan frowned. "I see you have been studying your Italian, my beloved daughter. Your language skills have improved considerably. Strange; last time we discussed this you seemed to have little interest in learning a foreign tongue."

Basilah smiled. "Father, you know how stubborn your daughter can be. But I always, in the end, see the wisdom of your words. I am my father's daughter."

The Sultan returned the smile and shook his head slightly. "You are your mother's daughter."

Basilah bowed as the Sultan turned his attention to Sebastiano. Having long had ambitions of annexing Italy to his empire, he was well versed in the Christian's language. He said to Sebastiano, "I bid you welcome. I hope you have found your accommodations adequate."

"I have found every comfort that could be afforded a prisoner."

"A prisoner? You are a guest, not a captive. You are free to take your leave of us at any time. But first I request your company at this evening's dinner, which is to be held in your honor."

"Why would an enemy who has slain so many of your warriors be treated as an honored guest?"

"You are so honored for precisely that reason. My people honor brave warriors who fight so ferociously in the name of God, even if he is their enemy. It is the same God, no?"

"There is only one God," Sebastiano replied.

"Yes, there is only one God. Your people and mine at least agree on that point."

"Your eminence, I cannot, in good conscience, be your guest while my fellows are under attack by your army."

In a slightly impatient voice, the Sultan said, "There has been a truce since the last battle so both sides may bury their dead. There is no attack planned this night; at least, none will be initiated by my army."

Sebastiano did not know what else to say. He glanced at Basilah, and she smiled in return and gave a small nod. He was in no hurry to leave her company, in any event. "Very well, your majesty. With that assurance, I will accept your invitation and return to my army in the morning."

The Sultan watched the silent exchange between the Christian and his daughter, now with some discomfort. "It is done, then. Tonight we shall meet again and break bread like civilized men of God." He turned and spoke to a very fierce-looking man standing behind Sebastiano.

"Hafiz, please escort our guest back to his quarters and see that his every need is met."

Hafiz placed himself between Sebastiano and Basilah and escorted them back to their tents. Hafiz did not know how to speak the Christian's language, but he communicated his feelings very clearly just the same. Hafiz had no interest in treating this barbarian as a guest; he would have killed him in an instant if it were not for his uncle's intervention.

Sebastiano glanced over at Hafiz and he could see the man's hatred for him in every gesture and every look. Sebastiano turned away but took care to keep Hafiz in his peripheral vision. Basilah, on the other hand, paid no mind to her cousin's feelings or intentions. She was too busy trying to formulate a strategy to successfully rendezvous with Sebastiano after Hafiz's departure.

And succeed she did. Basilah came to Sebastiano within the hour, bearing his dinner wardrobe and the offer of another bath. The woman was insatiable. The two of them spent hours with their bodies entwined in his bed and then again in the tub, until finally she left Sebastiano exhausted, to prepare for dinner.

Chapter 8

The extravagance of the venue amazed him. The decor seemed more like that of a royal palace than a tent, decorated with beautifully carved, gem-encrusted furniture and floors that were covered by intricately woven carpets containing patterns and shapes Sebastiano had never seen before. In the center of the room, and stretching nearly its entire width, was a knee-high table covered from one end to the other with a feast the likes of which he was sure had never been imagined, much less witnessed, by anyone from his home town.

Sebastiano noticed that only men were in attendance, and all of them were dressed in royally colored robes similar in style and appearance to the one that he was wearing and, like him, they all wore headdresses made of the same fine silk that Basilah had recently introduced him to. She was standing by his side again and, as she gazed up at Sebastiano's stunned expression, she whispered in his ear, "It is all in your honor."

She deposited him onto a seat at the right hand of the Sultan, and near many important looking men. Then, to Sebastiano's chagrin, she retreated to a place out of his sight.

The men at the table immediately subjected Sebastiano to an intense crosstalk. Of course, he could not understand anything except for the occasional translation provided by the Sultan. Hafiz was seated across from Sebastiano, and on occasion shot a look in his direction that required no translation. Nevertheless, the Sultan and the rest of the men near him seemed genuinely friendly.

Servants suddenly converged, surrounding him with plates of food, and a goblet with drink that he supposed to be wine. He noticed that the large glass decanter, containing the rich red liquid, was served only to him. He was momentarily suspicious, until he remembered a conversation he overheard between two of the knights in the citadel. "Muslims do not drink wine," he recalled one of the men explaining. "For Christians, drinking wine is a requirement of our religion, but for Muslims it is forbidden." "That", the other knight said responding with a laugh, "is the reason I would rather die than be forced to convert to Islam."

Soon the effects of the food and drink subdued any of Sebastiano's remaining anxiety. Most of the talk, as nearly as Sebastiano could discern, was related to the subject of the recent battle. While Sebastiano did not know the exact details, he did know it was a significant victory for his army. However, he was also sure that the victory could not possibly prevent the knight's inevitable capitulation. It was just a matter of time before the Sultan's forces overran the fortress. In light of this, it was still a mystery to him as to why he was here at all, as a guest, rather than dead on the field where they found him, or in chains. The Sultan interrupted his thoughts.

"I hope you are enjoying your stay with us?"

"Yes, your majesty. But I will take my leave of you and return to my army in the morning."

"Yes, and then the truce will be lifted and we will once again be enemies in battle."

"As it pleases your majesty."

"It does not please me at all. I have no wish to slaughter you and your army, but that is what it must come to."

"Neither I nor my army has any wish to slaughter or be slaughtered, but we must do our duty in the service of God."

"This is true," the Sultan replied, "we all must do what is honorable, but I can't imagine any purpose to this end, and I cannot see how it would please God to have such brave warriors' blood spent for no purpose."

"I cannot see any other way. You are a great and wise man.

Perhaps your majesty knows of a way to avoid this end."

"Yes, perhaps I do."

The Sultan turned to the group and spoke briefly to them. The comment caused the other conversations to end abruptly and all eyes turned towards Sebastiano. Then the Sultan spoke once again. At that point, Hafiz stood up, made a terse comment in Sebastiano's direction and then left.

The Sultan turned towards Sebastiano and said, "All of my generals agree that the slaughter of your army would be a disservice to honor. Let me propose that we would permit your army to leave this island, in peace, if you give your word never to return."

Sebastiano thought about this for a moment. It immediately occurred to him that it might be a trick. On further thought, however, it seemed to him that this proposal was the only logical reason for him being here. The Sultan must be tired of spending his treasure, and his army's blood, in order to capture this useless rock in the middle of the sea. But at the same time, he was stuck here just like the Christians were, because he could not retreat without losing face.

Sebastiano replied, "My army would never agree to surrender their arms or their possessions."

"They would not have to. Take your arms and all of your possessions with you."

"How would we leave the island? Our ships have been captured or destroyed."

The Sultan took a deep breath. "We will provide you with ships and crew, if necessary, for your departure."

Sebastiano considered this. He was being offered his life and the life of his army. All they had to do was agree to leave.

"I will take your proposal to my army in the morning."

Sebastiano then considered his own words. *My army? They are not mine to convince. Would they even listen? And if they did, would they believe this unbelievable tale, or would they hang me for impersonating a knight, or worse, as a traitor?*

"I will need your answer by the setting of the sun," the Sultan informed Sebastiano.

Sebastiano nodded with faux confidence. "You will have it, your majesty."

When Sebastiano returned to his tent that evening, his head was swimming with the thought of leaving the horrible citadel on this terrible island and finally going home. His head was also swimming from the feast. Most of all, his mind and his body were focused on the thought of Basilah returning to his tent and his bed.

He considered that the risk of being with her now was much greater than before. Before dinner he thought his life was worthless, so the prospect of being caught with her and dying at the hands of Basilah's enraged father, or her cousin Hafiz, seemed a more pleasant prospect than returning to the citadel and dying in misery behind its walls. Now, he and his army had a new lease on life… at least it would if they believed him. Would he risk it all if he saw her again? Yes, he thought, he would.

Sebastiano paced back and forth most of the night, waiting for her. He wanted to touch her and tell her that her father had granted his army safe passage. He also wanted to ask her to come away with him, back to his beautiful island of Sicily. He had no idea how he would accomplish the task of stealing her away, but he knew that if she agreed he would arrange it. Somehow.

She never returned to him that night. Perhaps, he thought, he would see her in the morning on his departure; in fact, he was sure of it. But when that time came and passed without her appearance, he turned his attention to the matters at hand. He bade the Sultan goodbye and promised, once again, to have an answer by sunset.

Sebastiano, dressed again in his battle armor, which had been repaired, cleaned and buffed to a glistening shine; rode a new mount. It was a black Arabian stallion, a gift from the Sultan. At his left side was the shield bearing the coat of arms of his late master and his sheathed battle sword.

Sebastiano turned and gave a shallow bow to the Sultan, who watched him from a distance. He looked for Basilah again, but was disappointed by her absence. Then he rode out across the field between the Muslim camp and the citadel's walls.

The ground was covered with shallow graves and the stench of death, along with clouds of insects, hovered in the warm air all around him.

The men on the walls of the citadel did not know what to make of the lone knight, riding towards them in glistening armor across the empty field. A trick? The sound of the tower bells suddenly began peeling, signaling to the inhabitants behind the walls to man their battle stations.

Sebastiano watched the frantic activity with detached interest and also with a bit of fatalistic amusement. After all that he had survived, he thought, wouldn't it be strange to be killed by his own army just as he was about to deliver them all from certain death?

A man called from the tower. His voice seemed confused. "Who are you and what are your intentions?"

Sebastiano pulled back on the reins, bringing his horse to a stop fifty yards from the gates. "I am Sebastiano della Sciacca," he called back to the man on the wall. "I am one of you. I was taken captive after the last battle."

"Why did they release you?" the man inquired.

"To bring a proposal of peace from the Sultan."

Chapter 9

Peace? The man heard the word, as did many others on the wall who were listening to the exchange, but none of them could comprehend it. Surely, it must be a trick. Sebastiano spurred his stallion and renewed his approach when suddenly an order was barked out from another location on the wall.

"Halt where you are!"

Sebastiano stopped the horse in its tracks. After a moment of silence, he heard the same voice ask, "Whose shield do you bear?" Sebastiano scanned the wall looking for its source. It was the Grand Master.

"It is my shield, Grand Master, as it was my father's before me. I am the son of Don Guillermo Della Palermo."

Sebastiano heard the Grand Master bark a few orders and then watched as the doors of the citadel began to open.

"I shall greet you at the entrance of the gate," the Grand Master called down to Sebastiano.

Sebastiano resumed his approach toward the gates as more people gathered on the walls to watch. By the time he reached the entrance it was lined on both sides with men who stared silently at him as he rode by.

Standing directly in his path was the Grand Master. Sebastiano handed his shield and sword to the nearest man, dismounted, and bowed.

The Grand Master studied him. "A knight bearing a shield with that coat of arms was seen leading the counter attack in our recent victory. That knight brought us great honor that day. But I do not know you as a knight—and you seem little more than a boy. Do you claim to be that man?"

Sebastiano silently nodded.

"We found your horse dead on the field", the Grand Master continued, "but we could not find your body or account for you among the known living, before or after the battle. Some of us were beginning to wonder if you were an apparition. Then we heard a rumor that the Turks had captured a great warrior they called Mascelle del Leone."

Sebastiano blushed. "My Lord, I cannot claim to be this great warrior of whom you speak, but I have been addressed by this name during my captivity."

"If you are the one I watched wade alone into the enemy ranks that day, then I will claim it for you."

Sebastiano silently bowed his head.

"Tell me about the offer of peace," the Grand Master inquired.

"It is an offer directly from Suleiman himself, my Lord. He will permit us to leave this place with our weapons and our property and will provide us safe passage, if we promise never to return to this island again."

The Grand Master was taken aback by the news. "This is a difficult thing for me to believe. It must be a trick."

"I do not think so, my Lord. I cannot understand why else they would spare my life, treat me as an honored guest and then release me with full armor, and this mount, if this were not a genuine offer. I spoke a great deal with the Sultan myself. He seems to be a man of honor."

"It still seems to be an impossible offer."

"Why?"

"Because we have found a traitor among us. He has been providing information about our depleted condition to the enemy for weeks. If the Sultan knows this, then why would he offer us safe passage when he knows that we are about to collapse from disease and starvation?"

"The Sultan made no comment about such information," Sebastiano replied. "He seemed preoccupied with the morale of his own army, following the last battle. I think he may even fear a mutiny among some of his men."

The Grand Master thought about this. Then he smiled.

"Why are you smiling, my Lord?"

"I am smiling because I think I may know now why we have received this offer."

"Why?"

"I believe I am looking at the reason."

Sebastiano was puzzled.

The Grand Master continued. "For the past several days, both sides have been retrieving and burying the dead under a flag of truce. And there have been many conversations between the common soldiers as they go about this work. Many of the reports have been about the enemy's fear of this Mascelle del Leone. Some have even commented that, in the last battle, the invading army was tricked into attacking. Or as they claim, lured into the lion's den to feed this beast with their flesh. We thought these reports were the ramblings of a few cowards. But perhaps, they reflect the minds of many. In a strange way, the traitor may have done us a service. The Sultan may have concluded that the traitor's reports were a ruse to lure them into the recent disastrous battle. Perhaps he released you as a means to be in turn released from this untenable siege."

"Perhaps. But then, we should use this to our advantage, my Lord."

"And to what advantage would you use this, if it were true?"

"We should attack them and drive them all from the field."

The Grand Master looked at Sebastiano with amused

bewilderment. "Perhaps young lion, but we older, less noble beasts know that sometimes discretion is the better part of valor. We will indeed use this to our advantage, but we will do so by accepting the Sultan's offer and leaving this place while we still have enough strength to move under our own power."

The Grand Master turned to a knight beside him and said, "Our hero, the Mascelle del Leone, has returned, and he has brought us deliverance. Tell all the men to chant his name, bang their shields, and pound their staffs as loud as they can, very loudly, so as to convince the enemy that we have the will and the strength to follow him again into battle."

The knight smiled and nodded with understanding and then turned to pass the word. As news of a potential peace treaty spread through the ranks, it was met with a deep and genuine thanksgiving towards the mysterious young messenger. It did not require much cajoling for the men to celebrate the return of this hero. No subterfuge or pretense was required to welcome the man that had saved them from certain death. In moments, the air was reverberating with the clamor of swords against shields, the pounding of staves against the earth, and then chanting: "Mascelle del Leone! Mascelle del Leone! Mascelle del Leone…"

Within hours, the Sultan's offer was brought before a hastily convened council of knights representing the eight Tongues of the Order, each one signifying a geographical and cultural sub-order of the Knights corresponding to the language spoken in each region in Europe from which they originated. The council reviewed, considered and accepted the terms without objection. It was the eve before Christmas and the air was filled with a sense of celebration.

Sebastiano was summoned before the council and given the task of bearing the message back to the Sultan. The honor of being given such a great responsibility, directly by the Grand Master himself, filled Sebastiano with pride. But just at that moment, one of the council members loudly objected to bestowing such a responsibility on a boy who was not even a

Knight of the Order. The objection began a murmured discussion among the council members. The Grand Master rose, and raised his hand. The room fell silent.

Addressing Sebastiano directly, the Grand Master said, "Some members of the council believe that such an honored task should not be entrusted to you because you are not a member of our Order. I must confess to you that I agree with this view." The words of the Grand Master made Sebastiano's knees feel weak and he bowed his head in shame and disappointment.

"That being the case," the Grand Master continued, "I have no choice but to bestow upon you the rank of Knight of the Order of Saint John." Again, there was discussion among the members of the council, but this time louder and mixed with objections and moans of protest.

The Grand Master then turned his attention away from Sebastiano and to the council. "This man", he said in a loud voice, "just days ago gave us such an example of bravery and martial skill that many of us doubted our own eyes. Some of us even believed that only an archangel sent from on high could have performed such an unimaginable feat and brought us such a great victory, just at the moment when we were in the midst of losing, for all time, our personal honor and that of our Order. If any of you can make the case for not repaying him with this recognition for his magnificent service, stand now and you will be heard." The Grand Master looked around the silenced room and found no further objections from any of the council members.

"Very well, then." He turned back toward Sebastiano with a regally stern face and said, "Hand me your sword and kneel before me, Sebastiano Della Sciacca." Sebastiano complied. The Grand Master placed his right hand on Sebastiano's head. He recited a prayer of thanksgiving for the Order's deliverance from destruction and asked God for the strength to continue in the service of his will. Then he welcomed the newest member of the order by reciting the litany of responsibilities and deprivations expected of him in his service to God and the Order of Saint John. He asked Sebastiano if he accepted the oath and he received a quivering "yes" in reply. Finally, he grasped Sebastiano's sword by the hilt and held it with the blade pointing straight down, so that the hilt and down-turned blade, crossed by the hand guard, made the shape of a cross. He kissed it and then told Sebastiano to rise and do the same.

"From this day forward you will be known as Sir Sebastiano della Sciacca, and by your brothers of the order you will be addressed as Le Mascelle del Leone. All rise and embrace our new brother." Each member of the council filed by and did so. Then the Grand Master placed his hand on Sebastiano's shoulder and said, "And now, young knight, take our acceptance back to the Sultan, before someone there —or here—changes his mind." The Grand Master slapped his shoulder and smiled at him. Sir Sebastiano returned the smile and left immediately to fulfill his mission.

Chapter 10

It was the first day of the New Year. Sebastiano, along with the entire surviving Christian army, had packed their belongings and boarded the ships provided by the Sultan to begin their permanent exile from the Island of Rhodes. The newly homeless Knights of Saint John left with mixed feelings. On the one hand, they were grateful to be leaving their months-long trial of death and misery, but they could not help feeling sad about departing the fortress island that they had defended so well, for so many centuries. To make matters worse, they had no other place to go, at least not as an intact order. They would have no choice but to disperse their numbers among all their countries of origin until they found, or were granted, a new post to defend.

For his part, Sebastiano also had mixed feelings, but they were for a different reason than the others. He was happy to leave Rhodes behind him, and did so without hesitation. His only regret was leaving without seeing Basilah again. He wondered about her and why she seemed to have disappeared. She was absent the day Sebastiano returned to the Sultan bearing the Order's acceptance of the peace terms. He was tempted to inquire about her at the completion of the meeting, but decided that this might arouse the suspicion or anger of the Sultan at a time when it could be least afforded. So, he simply thanked the Sultan and the members of his council for their generous hospitality, and returned to the citadel alone and disappointed.

It occurred to him that, given the victorious disposition of her father's army and her royal privileges, if Basilah had wanted to see him or send a message, she could have. He certainly could find no way of contacting her without risking the truce upon which thousands of men's lives depended. He considered that perhaps, for her, their affair might have been simply a matter of passing interest, or something for her royal amusement. Nonetheless, he wished he could see her one more time, if only to say goodbye. In the weeks and months to follow, the thought of her would make him depressed, and perhaps a little bitter.

Before the army's departure and dispersion from Rhodes, the Grand Master offered Sebastiano an opportunity to accompany him back to his home in France as his deputy. It was position of responsibility that would provide a young man of humble beginnings great opportunities for advancement and, eventually, the power and influence that came with high rank in a powerful and respected institution.

It was a very great honor, to be sure, but Sebastiano's interest in living the life of a Knight of Saint John, with its dedication to duty, honor, poverty and celibacy—especially celibacy—had little attraction for him.

His Don, a knight and nobleman by birth, once told him that obeying the code of an ordinary knight was difficult enough without adding the special clerical burdens of poverty and chastity required by the Order of Saint John. In fact, Sebastiano was beginning to have doubts about even being selected by his Don to undertake the responsibilities of an ordinary nobleman.

Both honors had been suddenly and unexpectedly bestowed, and the last one was even more intimidating than the first. However, Sebastiano had been so overwhelmed by the momentous occasion of his christening before the council of knights; he gave little thought to the long-term ramifications, at least at the time.

The more he thought about it now, however, the more his doubts grew. At least as a nobleman in Sicily, he could have a relatively normal life. As a Knight of Saint John, he would have to live the life of an armored monk.

He ultimately informed the Grand Master that he would have to decline the offer with great regret. He explained that he was the only surviving son of Don Guillermo Della Palermo and that his father made him promise, on his deathbed, to return to Sicily to look after his subjects' welfare. So Sebastiano returned to the island of his birth to live out the remaining days of his life in peace… or so he thought.

Chapter 11

SCIACCA, SICILY

June 20, 1527 A.D.

For he left his pretty boy, father's sorrow, father's joy.

-Robert Greene-

Sebastiano stood on the balcony watching the crescent moon rise above the calm Mediterranean Sea. More than five years had passed since his triumphant return from Rhodes. And, as with many of his fellows, it took months following the truce with the Sultan for him to finally find his way home to family and friends.

Sebastiano spent the first few weeks after his arrival traveling to the homes of his dead comrades in arms. He told many stories of the heroic deeds performed by the men whose bodies would remain forever on Rhodes. He was determined to make sure that every one of them was remembered as a hero by their mothers, wives, fathers, siblings, and children, whether they were in fact heroes or not. As for his story, he never spoke of it, but even after five years he often thought about those grim days on Rhodes, and just as often he thought about Basilah.

He wondered what had become of her, and for years, he made every effort possible to discover her whereabouts and to get a message to her. But she was somewhere behind the walls of the Muslim world, and the gates into that world were closed to Sebastiano and his kind.

As time passed his longing for Basilah slowly ebbed, but it never entirely faded. At long last, four years after he arrived home, he took a wife. Her name was Lucia, and he had grown to love this woman, so there was no doubt in his mind that he had made the right decision. However, there always remained that part of his heart that was occupied by Basilah, and he thought that it probably would remain so, whether he wanted it to or not, for the rest of his life.

As he stood peering at the distant horizon, he had no way of knowing that a small boy was looking back from another shore, and this boy was also thinking about him. Sebastiano did not know the boy even existed, but the little one knew him, and even at the tender age of four, he was already being taught by his uncle to hate his Christian enemies, and Sebastiano especially.

Sebastiano's thoughts were interrupted by the sound of a door opening behind him. He turned to see his mother standing with a small object in her arms. It was wrapped in a blanket and it was moving. Then it began to cry.

His mother said. "Your firstborn is a son, Sebastiano."

Sebastiano approached cautiously and asked his mother a question with his eyes. She responded by lifting the baby and placing him in his father's arms. The child was impossibly small. The first, strange, sensation of holding his son was hard to describe. He somehow felt complete even though, moments before, Sebastiano had felt no part of himself missing.

The infant's arms waved in the air as he cried, until one tiny hand met Sebastiano's lips. Sebastiano kissed his son's infinitely delicate fingers and the word "perfection" came to his mind. His son was perfect, flawless: not a mark or scar of any kind on his body, his mind or his heart. He was fresh, new: another opportunity for a perfect life.

Then Sebastiano's happiness and pride were suddenly replaced by a sense of intense fear, more intense even than the fear he felt on Rhodes. He suddenly knew, with every fiber of his being, that he would never be safe or free from fear again. For the rest of his life he would be fearful, not for his own existence or safety, but for the safety and happiness of his tiny, perfect, son.

Chapter 12

THE ISLAND OF MALTA

September 11, 1565 A.D.

"If the Turks should prevail against the Isle of Malta, it is uncertain what further peril might follow to the rest of Christendom."

- Queen Elizabeth I -

The sound was silence. It was the first time such was heard on this island for many months. Then it was broken, for an instant, by the clang of a sword hitting the ground. Then silence again. After a long pause, Sebastiano lifted his helmet from his head and let it fall next to the sword.

The wind rustled his long gray hair and beard as he removed and dropped his gauntlets. Tears appeared in his eyes and they began to stream down his face at the sight of the bloodied, lifeless body at his feet. A soundless word formed on his lips: "Sacrifice."

Sebastiano sank to his knees and turned his attention out towards the horizon where the blue sky met the sea in the distant haze. A strong morning breeze was building from the north, but instead of carrying the fresh smell of the sea, it carried the overpowering stench of the dead lying in shallow graves, along with the smell of the filth of the trenches surrounding the fortifications, and the foul odor of putrid ships' holds filled with diseased and rotting flesh.

It seemed to Sebastiano like a terrible, recurring dream, a nightmare that he was cursed to keep reliving. Forty-three years had passed since his victorious day on Rhodes. But that sweet victory, he now realized, had put in motion the events that led directly to this unspeakably painful moment.

Four decades of continuous conflict between Christians and Muslims had ensued following the Knights' retreat from Rhodes, a seemingly unending war of destruction between his people and Basilah's people. Hundreds of thousands were dead and millions fatherless, son-less, husband-less, homeless, or enslaved. Yet, in all of that time his yearning to see her again, to touch her, was neither quenched nor fulfilled. More than ever, he longed to see her now, to hold her in his arms again and to beg her forgiveness for all of the sorrow he had brought to her—especially that which he had brought to her on this day.

He closed his eyes and tried to picture Basilah in his mind, but all he could see was the sight of the horizon filled with the ships of the Muslim fleet and the long-ago fields of Rhodes covered with the dead, just like the scene that appeared when he reopened his eyes. It was the same play, but the stage had changed from an island in the eastern periphery of the Mediterranean to one in the center, a location very close to the beating heart of Christian Europe.

And Sebastiano was now an old man. Most of his former comrades from Rhodes were dead. Here on this new battleground of Malta he fought alongside new men. Their names and young faces recalled memories of their fathers or uncles, now gone. But to their surprise, and his, this old man could still fill the armor of that much younger man from Rhodes.

Sebastiano's legendary victory on Rhodes had saved the Christian defenders from certain death and had shaken the confidence of the Sultan and his army in their belief that the conquest of Europe was within their grasp. So a peace was made, and for a brief period, Europe was safe from the invaders.

However, without their island fortress-sanctuary, the Knights of St. John found themselves scattered across Europe. And without the constant pressure that the seafaring knights placed upon the Sultan's Mediterranean supply lines, the armies of Islam were once again able to roam the region without challenge. They soon resumed their ambitious plans to take all of Christian Europe, and succeeded in conquering large parts of it: Austria, then the Hungarian cities of Buda and Pest, and finally Transylvania fell under their yoke.

The Holy Roman Emperor, desperate for some relief, gave the Knights a temporary home on Sicily and then a permanent one on the island of Malta. Within months of their arrival, they transformed the small, barren island into another impenetrable fortress, even more so than their former citadel on Rhodes. The Knights of St. John now became known as The Knights of Malta, and with their new base of operations secured, they resumed their attacks and harassment of the land and sea supply lines of their ancient Islamic foes, bringing them once again to a standstill in their conquest of Europe.

The Sultan had to crush the Knights of Malta if his plans to conquer Europe were to succeed. The Knights knew this and anticipated his next move. They were prepared when the Sultan's fleet arrived on May 18. The Great Siege went on for months, one bloody engagement following the next, until the Knights realized that the cause, eventually, would be lost without reinforcements.

So, the word went out from Malta to all of Christian Europe and to all of the remaining Knights, wherever they were, that help was desperately needed. As was usually the case, most of the kingdoms of Europe ignored the call. But a few brave ones, such as Sicily, answered it with fresh armies. The Sicilians would be led by the legend of Rhodes himself, Sebastiano Della Sciacca, or as he was known by friends and foes alike, Le Mascelle del Leone.

When the messenger from Malta reached him with the desperate news, Sebastiano was at first reluctant to leave his family and his quiet Sicilian home. War was a young man's business, after all, and this old man had already done his duty in the service of Christendom. But the message from the Grand Master was soon followed by a summons directly from Rome, and there was no mistaking it as a request for volunteers; this was a command from the Pope himself, ordering Sebastiano to report for duty. The summons made clear that his service was essential to the survival of Malta, and Europe, and that his refusal was not an option.

After many sad farewells to his family and friends, none expecting to see the great man again in this life, Sebastiano set out to again face near-certain death in the company of his comrades in arms.

It was not until his arrival on Malta that Sebastiano came to fully understand the reason why his service was so essential to the Knight's cause. The leader of the Muslim army, who was so ruthlessly directing the systematic destruction of Malta, was the grandson of the very same Sultan whose army Sebastiano had met and defeated on Rhodes. And this man had demanded Sebastiano's presence as part of a temporary truce.

His name was Ghazawan Hafiz. His men called him Al Asad— *The Lion*. The Grand Master explained to Sebastiano upon his arrival that it was this man who had fought the Knights to exhaustion, and just as he was about to complete his conquest of Malta, and the destruction of the Knights of St. John, he unexpectedly withdrew his army from the walls of the citadel. Then Ghazawan demanded a contest of single combat between himself and Sebastiano - the result of which would determine the fate of Malta, and by extension that of Europe as well.

At first, the Grand Master thought that the proposal was the ramblings of a madman. Who would propose such a duel when victory was in his hands? Now he had the answer. But before revealing it to Sebastiano, he once again reviewed the desperate condition of his army. Their supplies were nearly exhausted and the men were starving. This two-man contest, while seemingly insane, was the last and perhaps only hope for Malta, the Knights and Christendom. He begged Sebastiano to understand that it was the only way, and that it was his Christian duty.

Then he told Sebastiano the truth, a truth that nearly everyone from the Grand Master to the Pope in Rome now knew, and it struck Sebastiano as if he was physically attacked.

"Ghazawan is the son of Basilah, daughter of Suleiman the Magnificent. He wants vengeance for his mother's shame, a shame that he says you visited upon her in his grandfather's tent on Rhodes, forty years ago."

Sebastiano staggered back with shock. Until that moment, he did not even know that Basilah had had any children. With his heart breaking with the revelation, he became livid in his refusal. His brothers of the knighthood had betrayed him. How could they propose such a thing? How could they even consider it? What they asked of him should be asked of no man.

It required the intervention of the Pope himself to finally force Sebastiano's hand. Indeed, his refusal had been anticipated, even before he was summoned to Malta. Therefore, a council of Rome was convened and an envoy from the Vatican traveled to Malta for the sole purpose of delivering their ultimatum.

The envoy was the same priest whom Sebastiano had mocked on the walls of Rhodes before he abandoned his post and ran to meet his destiny. This young, zealous priest, now a bitter old cardinal, stared coldly into Sebastiano's eyes as he recited the Council's directive. It would be excommunication and disgrace for him and his family if he refused this challenge. On the other hand, if he fought and won, an unprecedented guarantee of protection from the Pope himself would be granted to Sebastiano and all of his sons and their sons, in perpetuity.

Sebastiano had no choice but to agree.

And so, a covenant was made on that day, on the island of Malta, between Sebastiano and the Bishop of Rome, a covenant that would change his life, the lives of his descendants, and countless others as yet unborn.

Sebastiano met Ghazawan the next morning on a barren, flat

field, and before the eyes of both armies, he defeated the Muslim champion. Now that it was over, Sebastiano was overcome with the shame and sadness of what he had just done. He gently touched his opponent's face with trembling fingers. He could see Basilah, he thought, in Ghazawan's nose and mouth. But the eyes that now stared lifelessly into space belonged to the dead man's father. Sebastiano lifted Ghazawan's body in his arms and rocked him slowly as sorrow swept over him in shudders and sobs.

After all of his years of sacrifice, it was the first time in Sebastiano's life that he clearly comprehended the meaning of this word. He finally understood that it was the essence of his creed. That though he could never make recompense for the pain of the One at Golgotha, his mission, the true purpose of his existence, was to conduct his life in a way that might, to some infinitely small extent, assuage the depth-less anguish borne by the Father, his Lord God. Because, despite his Creator's limitless power to safeguard his beloved Son from any and all pain, he was required to watch and endure his Son's crucifixion, his sacrifice, for the sake of the world's salvation.

How intensely Sebastiano now felt the mass of this obligation upon his shoulders. How cruel was the taste of that revelation in his aching heart, as bitter tears of sympathy for his Creator's incomprehensible pain rolled down his cheeks.

The audience of tens of thousands, from both sides, watched this scene of sorrow in rapt attention, and in complete silence, until a single old soldier in the front of the Muslim ranks started to weep at the tragic sight before him. Then he whispered something. It was barely audible at first, even to him. But with each repetition he said it a little louder. The stone-faced man standing next to him joined in. Then the next man, and the next, added their voices. With each repetition the volume grew, as did the number of tongues in the chorus, until it finally expanded into a shattering, repetitious chant that spread across the field and throughout the entire Muslim army before the citadel. Then the Christians within the citadel joined in.

The men from both armies, with tears now flowing freely from their eyes, chanted as with one voice. "Mascelle! Mascelle! Mascelle! Mascelle!" Over and over the word came, louder and louder. Then some began to pound the ends of their spears into the earth. Others beat their swords against their shields. Some dropped their weapons to the ground and began pounding their chests with empty fists. The very earth beneath their feet shook with the combined effect.

The sound was filled with an odd combination of despair and joy: despair for the sacrifice of blood made by the two lone warriors before them, and for the fruitlessness of the bloodshed over the previous months by all of their brothers and friends who would never see home again; and joy at the thought of their salvation and delivery from death. And when some permitted themselves to think again about seeing their homes and their children and wives, they began to wail.

Only two men on that desolate island did not join in the chorus of thanksgiving that day. One was lying on the barren field, no longer among the living. The other was the man who killed him, and who now clasped the dead man's lifeless body to his chest: Sebastiano della Sciacca, Le Mascelle del Leone, was on his knees mourning the death of his and Basilah's firstborn son.

BOOK 2

"We all were sea-swallow'd, though some cast again, and by that destiny to perform an act whereof what's past is prologue, what to come in yours and my discharge."

- Shakespeare -
The Tempest

"The extent of your impotence and weaknesses has become very clear."

- Osama bin Laden -
1996 Declaration of War against the Americans

Chapter 13

THE ISLAND OF MANHATTAN

April 6, 2001

The prophets of doom did try to warn us. They said that the turning of the new millennium would bring unimaginable calamities: plague, sudden extermination by asteroids, alien invaders... Y2K. They were nuts, of course. The new century came and went, and absolutely nothing happened. Or at least that's what we thought. Who knew that some of these turn-of-the-century cataclysms came equipped with time-delayed fuses?

When I woke up on that cold spring morning I was greeted by three things. The first was the lingering memory of a bad dream. Actually, I wasn't sure that it was bad at the time, but I'd figure out that part a little later.

Second, I was greeted by the ruins of the first turn-of-the-century disaster, an economic extinction event known as the dot-com bomb, and I happen to be one of the people on the endangered species list. So I guess it wasn't too surprising that I would be having bad dreams. But looking back at it, especially in the light of the second event that was about to unfold, the first one hardly seems to rise to the level of a footnote. But in that brief space of time between the first calamity and the second one, it seemed momentous enough to me. After all, my life as an entrepreneur, and a recently minted CEO, was about to come crashing down. It wasn't a happy time. But, like I said, that was before.

So much has changed since then. Little things, like my response to the formerly pleasant sight of a blue September sky, or the sound of a low-flying plane, both of which now cause my stomach to reflexively ball in a knot. Or the sensation of my racing heart in the moments just prior to turning on the television or pulling-up a news page on the Internet, in anticipation of another unthinkable headline.

And then there's the big things, mostly in the form of people and places that have been forever altered, or have disappeared altogether. I can still remember a time when I actually looked forward to the future. I had grown accustomed to running towards it, eyes wide open, arms carelessly outstretched, like a child running for his stocking on Christmas morning. The sooner we got to the new millennium, I thought, the sooner we'd catch up with the shiny new future. But as Yogi Berra once said, the future ain't what it used to be and, ironically, the bright light that lit the path to that happy place was extinguished on a beautiful sunny day. And, like a lot of people I know, I've been lost in the dark ever since.

In case you were wondering, the third thing to greet me on that morning, somewhat incongruously, was a beautiful smile.

"Tony?"

The sound of my name was accompanied by a gentle touch on my foot.

"Good morning, Tony," the voice repeated. "It's 7:30, sleepy head, time to wake up."

"Howie?" I replied.

"No, it's me, Marcella. Who's Howie?"

I opened my eyes. "Marcella?"

I could make out a blurry smile that came into better view when I squinted. The smile belonged to my office assistant, Marcella Pavone, and besides having great teeth, she was a woman who was exceptionally competent at every assignment she was given. She also happened to be gorgeous. It was an accident. Really. I knew she was the right person for the job the moment I read her résumé and her stellar reference letters. And, for what it's worth, I'm generally not easily impressed by much of anything, including a woman's looks. Given these facts, I'm pretty sure I would have hired her even if she looked like Groucho Marx. Ok, maybe not.

So there she was, staring down at me with that broad, blindingly white smile, and I could feel my heart begin to race—the good kind, in this case. For an instant, I had the passing, pleasant fantasy that she was waking up beside me, her long, wavy, black hair falling over her lithe, nude body, which was still exhausted from a pulsating night of horizontal gymnastics.

Then she gently placed my eyeglasses on my face, and when I looked again, the fantasy vanished. Same gorgeous smile, but her face was freshly painted, her hair was very much in order and she was fully dressed. I looked around, confused and disorientated, to say nothing of being disappointed, as I began to make sense of the dimly lit decor around me. It was my office.

"Are you awake, Tony? Don't make me come in here and wake you again, mister," she said with a little laugh.

By around 9:00 p.m. the night before, I had resigned myself to another night of sleeping on the sofa, second one in a row. So I sent Marcella an email asking her to come in a little early to get me stoked up for another day of fun and excitement at the office. Apparently, she got it.

"The coffee is on, and I put fresh clothes and a towel in the bathroom for you," Marcella said as she carefully adjusted the position of my eyeglasses. "I'll be in the conference room setting up for the meeting."

I smiled and nodded, but said nothing in an effort to spare her a blast of morning breath.

My name is Tony Mascelle, and once upon a time I was the CEO of one of those fabled, and now deceased, dotcom-boom-to-bust companies that everyone once loved back then, but eventually learned to hate. Frankly, I don't blame them, especially since the big bubble burst. But don't panic: this isn't another one of those terminally boring, post-mortem essays on that subject. As far as I'm concerned, there's already been enough written about that topic to last us at least until the next financial meltdown.

Besides, who really cares about the ravings of a bunch of twenty-something, former paper millionaires, who ended up unemployed and pretty much broke? In any case, I think my memory of the details have gotten a little foggy. As far as I can still recall, you can probably sum it all up as a temporary bout of mass financial insanity. Anything I had to say on the subject beyond that would be useless and probably self-serving bullshit. Do I sound bitter?

"Howie?" I frowned at the sound of the name as it rolled off my tongue, and I rolled off the hard, faux-leather coach and headed for the shower located in the back of my office. Howie was an old college roommate. But why the hell would I be having a dream about him?

By the way, an office with a private shower may sound a little over the top—and I'm sure many offices that have one are—but not this one. My office was just your basic, poorly lit, Lower Manhattan, entrepreneur slave quarters that happened to be equipped with a utility closet–sized bathroom, complete with worn vinyl tile, a tiny fiberglass shower, and cheap, plastic plumbing fixtures that frequently came off in my hands. I'm not sure, but I think this building may have been a hotel in a previous life, and my office was a room that rented out by the hour.

I stretched and let the hot water begin to work its magic. The haze cleared, the stiffness in my back eased, and I momentarily erased the anxiety building in my gut at the thought of the coming day's activities, which included a make-or-break meeting with my current investors and potentially some new ones, or at least I hoped so.

What I didn't know then was that it would be the last time that I would wake up in my old life. Tomorrow, I would wake up in my new one. And what I once thought was an event of epic importance, like that meeting that I was so worried about, would in retrospect seem mundane to the point of absurdity. My old life was over, and nothing would ever be the same. Nothing. Ever.

Chapter 14

Howie intruded in my brain again as I turned off the water. I could almost hear his voice. The weird thing is that, for reasons I don't understand, I never remember my dreams. I have no idea why. I'm sure that there've been some great ones: fast cars, big yachts, private jets, beautiful women—and I never seem to recall any of that stuff. But have one about dopey Howie and it sticks in my brain like a splinter. Well, whatever the reason, I was sure it wasn't a good omen. Don't take that to mean that I'm a superstitious guy or anything, because I'm not. Except when I fly.

I exited the shower and, as I reached for the towel, I noticed a small, yellow piece of paper stuck to the wall above the rack. It was a sticky note from Marcella; she does this. It read, "I reviewed the materials for the meeting this morning. Nice job!" At the bottom of the note was a little smiley face.

I expectantly sank my face into the fluffy, dry cotton surface of the towel. Oh, yes, there it was, I could smell her. She has this perfume that actually smelled a little bit like my mom's, which should make me feel creepy, but it also had this unique Marcella smell. I was wondering if maybe she and Mom, by some cosmic coincidence, wore the same perfume. That would be strange.

Yeah, strange, which brings me back to the Howie dream. It was actually more of a memory, I think, about the first day we met in my college dorm. One minute I'm offering him a tentative greeting and the next he's rambling on about the evils of sleeping in on weekends. As I would soon discover, Howie was true to his word. He was up and out every morning before dawn.

Personally, I've never found that hour of the day to be sufficiently interesting to bother waking up just to see it. And even when matters require an early rise, like now, my brain takes a little extra time to reboot, but only after I swat the snooze button six or seven times—or I'm roused by a beautiful woman.

By the way, for you morning people out there: people like me, who aren't, tend to find you generally annoying. It's not that I would care, except for that air of superiority you all seem to have. It really bugs the rest of us normal people. Just thought you should know.

Anyway, Howie's impromptu lecture that first day covered an amazing range of topics besides sleeping hours, including, of all things, the Pilgrims. The Pilgrims? The way I remember him explaining it was that the vast North American wilderness was loaded with all kinds of dangerous animals—bears, lions, vultures, turkeys—well, dangerous or ugly—and then there were those sometimes unpleasant folks with the bows and arrows, who were no picnic, either. Turns out, all of this could make life a rather tentative business, and if you overslept, you might just miss some of the horror.

Okay, maybe that wasn't his point. But we did eventually get to the genealogy lesson which, I think, *was* the point and—surprise, surprise! —he informed me that his ancestors arrived in the New World on the *Mayflower*. At first, to be honest, I was kinda enjoying the story and the whole WASP thing. He was really working it: high-pitched, nasal voice, clenched teeth, nose in the air, prep-school accent, the whole package. After about thirty minutes, my thoughts started to turn towards throwing the idiot out of the third-floor window of the dorm.

Looking back at it, I guess it could have been true that for Howard's ancestors, getting up earlier might be the difference between eating or starving, living or dying. I mean, these people risked their lives, traveling for months on a rat-infested, leaking wooden tub, and, by some miracle, managed to cross a big ocean, only to find themselves on an untamed frontier: neck deep in bugs, mud, disease, starvation and frequently, some very pissed-off natives. That's to say nothing of having to crap in a ditch in the middle of the woods during New England winters. So, maybe, some of that anxiety programming was still running in the pineal brain of one Howard Lawrence Tucker. On the other hand, maybe Howie was just programmed to put on airs. Who knows?

My ancestors, all of whom hail from Italy, played the New World emigration game a little differently. First, they found the place, then they explored it, and finally they named it. When they eventually got tired of the whole "New World thing", they went home to where life and the weather were significantly more civilized. Then, between pleasant strolls on warm Mediterranean beaches and shots of grappa, they sketched some maps of the place—as best as they could remember—and made a small fortune selling these rather primitive charts to Howie's people. What a racket, huh? As anyone who has imbibed grappa on a warm sunny day will tell you, the accuracy of those things was probably more than a little shaky. But at least they gave the New World some names and showed Howie's folks how to get here... more or less.

Then Howard's crazy forebears, crappy maps in hand, loaded their luggage on the leaky wooden tubs, one of which was called the *Mayflower*, and floated off into near-certain oblivion. After a few centuries passed and Howard's folks, or what was left of them, paved the roads, established a reliable supply of food, and finished building housing with central heating and indoor plumbing, my people figured it was the right time to make the move. They then proceeded to book passage on real ships, ones made of steel and equipped with steam engines, reliable navigation equipment, lifeboats, and maybe even a radio or two. They may have traveled in steerage on these big vessels, but compared to the Pilgrims, they were living large.

By the time they arrived in America, most of the bugs, mud and disease were under control, but like Howie's people, my ancestors were also met by pissed-off natives. Fortunately, these natives were descendants from the passengers on the *Mayflower*. Other than being sleep-deprived and humor-challenged, they really weren't so bad, and definitely less intimidating and dangerous than the original natives... though not nearly as well dressed.

I wiped the shower down with the washcloth. I wasn't very comfortable with the idea of Marcella taking care of this personal stuff, like waking me up in the office and the shower prep and all. She had volunteered for the job one day, and I just went with the flow. But it still made me feel guilty, so I tried to help out a little bit. My mother once told me how important it was to wipe down the shower when you're finished. I never really understood why. I figured it would dry all by itself, eventually. It must be one of those mother things.

I heard a gentle knock on the bathroom door.

"How's it going in there?" Marcella said from the other side.

"Good, you want to see?"

"Are you decent?"

"Well, that depends. How do you feel about hairy chests?"

"Very funny. Everything is all set in the conference room and you've got about forty minutes before the meeting gets started, so hurry up, okay?"

Maybe that's why I had the Howie dream: I was worried about being surrounded by vultures and turkeys—A.K.A. venture capitalists —at this morning's fight for survival—A.K.A. an investor meeting—in this wilderness known as Manhattan.

"Okay, thanks. I'll be out in a minute."

"I've got to run out and get some donuts and stuff. I'll be right back," she said.

Oooh, donuts. "Don't forget the chocolate ones with the white icing."

"Tony, do I ever forget the chocolate ones with the white icing?"

"No, but you know how forgetful you are when you're under pressure."

"You're the one that's forgetful when you're under pressure, not me."

"Oh, right. I forgot."

She laughed. "I'll be right back, hurry up in there."

Oh, Marcella... God I wanted her. Despite her melodious Italian name, her sculpted, aquiline face and her full, lithe body, her accent demonstrated that she was actually from jolly-ole England. In one respect, at least, I looked forward to these mornings. A person can do worse than to wake up to such a beautiful vision. I mean, let's face it: At the time I was a single, twenty-seven-year-old guy who worked ridiculous hours and had no time for a personal life. In other words, I couldn't remember the last time the one-eyed dragon saw any action outside of a wet dream—which I couldn't remember anyway. As for Marcella: did I mention she was beautiful? I mean *really* beautiful, the kind that causes men and women to stop talking and turn to look when she entered a room. I sensed she knew I was interested in her on a personal level, and she seemed to communicate a mutual interest in me. But we had never taken it beyond a working relationship.

Why? Well, for starters, I'm a bit of a Boy Scout, which means I try to obey the Byzantine, P.C. rules and maxims required of a man in my position, and of my generation. These rules, in addition to generating a sterile office environment, tend to make life pretty boring. But if I were twenty-five years older and, say, the President of the United States, Marcella and I would have long since engaged in some memorable sex in this very bathroom.

Of course, another possible reason for my good behavior may have had something to do with the feelings I had for her. We'd been working closely together since I hired her about seven months ago. Within a few weeks, she got to know me so well that she could usually anticipate my needs or questions before I knew what they were. It was actually a little weird at first; she seemed like an old friend, even though I barely knew her. Since that time, I've grown to like her. A lot. Maybe, if and when some of my paper millions were magically transformed into hard currency, I thought, I would have the time and resources to have a personal life and give her the attention she deserved.

On the other hand, since she worked for me, this would qualify as sexual harassment. So first, I would have to fire her. Rules are rules.

Chapter 15

This morning's meeting would likely determine if we, meaning my company, survived or not. By the end of the day we would either have a new infusion of working capital to keep us alive for another six months, or we'd be history. I'd spent most of the previous seventy-two hours preparing for it, and I was ready. I hoped my audience was as well.

It had been a year since the infamous blood bath of April 2000 when the NASDAQ, led by the plummet in technology stocks, began its historic downhill run. I read somewhere that six or seven trillion dollars' worth of wealth was wiped out in a matter of weeks. And it wasn't over yet. As the Chinese would say, I was living in interesting times. God help me.

Most people in the business who had enough brains to draw a breath knew that this ending was inevitable. But few people knew, or at least admitted, that it was going to be this bad. Now, a year later, many were beginning to compare it with the infamous Japanese stock market collapse in the late 80s. Some were even making comparisons to the crash in 1929. In this strange new world, the bulls were nowhere to be seen, and even some of the bears were getting nervous.

Our lead investor, a venture capital firm called The Alley Group, headed by Pat Clemens, had spent the early years telling us to take as much money from investors as we could get our hands on and spend it as fast as we could. The theoretical purpose of this theoretical strategy was to outgrow the other seven companies who were competing in our space. When people, like me, tried to introduce mundane concepts like revenues and earnings, Pat dismissed them as nonessential remnants of an ancient civilization. And, since Pat was the principal of the firm that had become our lead investor—and also the chairman of the company's board—we pretty much followed his lead, like it or not.

Now, three rounds of layoffs later, we were staring down the barrel of the gun of economic reality, and it was a really big gun. The rules of the ancients were back in control of the economy, and to use a biblical metaphor, our god of liquidity had forsaken us and we were refugees in the desert of the Internet economy, cursed to wander here and there in search of the promised land of the initial public offering. In the meantime, Pat Clemens had made a concerted effort to place the blame for this debacle on everything and everyone else. That's why I was confident that he, along with the other VCs and investment-banker assholes that started this whole mess, will have long and prosperous careers. But, if there really is a God, when these idiots die, they'll be assigned a corner office in one of the hotter places in hell. There I go again: fester, fester, fester...

Marcella, who was still out, had things under control in the conference room. The folders, pens and coffee mugs were all neatly distributed to the empty seats around the large, oval table. She also left me another note on the door, saying the coffee was done. It included a smiley face with a little arm, hand, and a finger pointing me in the right direction. Such a comedian. I walked over to the coffee machine, poured a cup, and then walked back to one of the big windows overlooking the street.

Ah, New York: the city that never sleeps, at least when there is a buck to be made. I don't get this town, never have. I'm a Long Island kid, born and raised about sixty miles east of where I was standing. Not very far on the map, but it might as well be on Jupiter if you compare the mentality. Where I grew up, people actually worked for a living, and they made things they could hold in their hands.

But in this town, they seem to make nothing except words on paper, or in my case on a computer screen. It seems to me that almost everyone who works here is paid to protect one half of the city from the other half. And I'm not just talking about the cops and firemen, either. The bankers protect their depositors from the borrowers, the brokers protect the investors from the issuers, and let's not forget the lawyers who protect their clients from other lawyers. The accountants, agents, consultants, public relations people, regulators, inspectors, courts, newspaper and television reporters, doctors, dentists, insurers, and politicians are all trying to stop someone or something from hurting someone or something else—or they're just protecting people from themselves. At least that's what they tell you they're doing. So, this whole town is basically one huge protection racket. If everyone woke up one day and suddenly, by some miracle, became intelligent, honest, and trustworthy, every person here would be on the longest unemployment line in history. Well, almost; the people who make the donuts would still be working. You got-ta eat. *What is taking Marcella so long with my chocolate donut?*

As I mentioned, my building was located in Lower Manhattan. According to the realtor, the neighborhood is called Kips Bay, although she didn't seem too sure. As she explained it, the exact borders are a little fuzzy. Despite the name, there's no bay in the neighborhood. I discovered this when I asked the realtor why there wasn't a water view from my office. She gave me a strange look and told me that Kips Bay, which was used by the British to invade Manhattan during the Revolutionary War, was filled in by the locals following the Brit's eviction. I love history. When I suggested to the realtor that I thought that the locals should have forgiven the old bay for that sin rather than erasing it, she looked at me as if I was a retarded child and asked for an extra month's security deposit. Not everyone gets my humor.

Anyway, it's an okay neighborhood. I mean it's definitely not comparable to one of those posh, uptown havens and it doesn't ooze much in the way of downtown chic, either—and that's fine by me. In fact, just five years ago, only an idiot would have risked walking around here during the night, and most times of the day. But in the intervening years, this neighborhood, like Manhattan in general, became a lot more livable and rents, driven by the technology boom and a competent mayor, exploded. Now things were changing again. During the single year following the bursting of the internet bubble, office rents around here have plunged.

From the conference room window, there was a view of a building across the street, which, like mine was old: built perhaps seventy-five years ago, in the neoclassical-something-or-other style. A coating of soot concealed what was once probably an attractive brick façade.

I think it was the open window that caught my attention, probably because it was a cold April day and it seemed odd that someone would leave it wide open. On the other hand, this is New York, the capital of odd, so I'm not really sure why I noticed it, but I did.

As I stood there sipping my coffee and watching the featureless black opening, I saw some movement, and then a small flash. A moment later, someone walked over to the window and slid it down. I could not see the face, which was covered by the dirty windowpane above, but I thought, by the clothing, it might have been a woman.

Kyle Orr arrived a moment later and greeted me with a leaden "good morning." I returned the greeting with a bit more cheer.

"Where's Jan?" he asked.

"Haven't you seen her?"

Kyle shook his head.

Kyle, Jan Toomey and I, the founders of the company, met while I was at my last gig - a second-tier investment-banking firm downtown. Kyle worked in the Mergers and Acquisitions department and I was the firm's head technology geek. My job was to make sure that everyone's computer, operating system, and applications were up and working with a minimum of fuss and nonsense, and I was pretty good at it.

I joined the firm right out of college as a programming manager. The pitch the campus recruiter gave me was that the job was a challenging position that would stretch my abilities and provide opportunities for personal and professional development. He also said that the salary and benefits were great. But four months into it, the only thing that was getting stretched was my arms over my head, usually accompanied by a yawn. He was right about the salary and benefits though; they were great. So great, in fact, that they made me fat and lazy. In less than a year I was running the department and was still bored.

Then one day I woke up to discover that this thing called the Internet, a technology that I had been playing with since my freshman year, had been "discovered" by Wall Street. On that happy day, some brilliant investment banking analyst unilaterally declared that it was the hottest thing since bikini underwear. The amazing thing was that neither I nor anyone I knew in the technology business got it—at least not at first. The Internet, while definitely useful, was by that time twenty-five years old. The only new thing about it was a facelift, in the form of a new piece of software called a browser. But the browser used programming ideas that were almost twenty years old. So, apparently on Wall Street, basic math looked like this: twenty-five plus twenty equals new. Go figure.

Well, as everyone now knows, the bucks were soon being shoveled at anyone and anything with an "E" prefix or a ".com" suffix. And the greedy clowns on Wall Street were right out front and directing one of the greatest wealth transfers in history: from the sixty-something year-old investors, who were completely clueless, to the twenty-something techno-geek hordes, who were mostly clueless. The last time anything on this scale happened, Hannibal had sacked an AARP convention in Rome.

Naturally, our friends in the venture capital and investment banking business were the self-assigned head barbarians, and grabbing the lion's share of the spoils. And they were aided and abetted by various hangers-on: lawyers, accountants, analysts, finders, and virtually every other type of consultant and overnight expert you can imagine, and frankly, some that you couldn't—or at least I couldn't, until I started meeting them.

So one day Kyle, a guy about my age, hunts me down and buys me lunch at an expensive restaurant on the premise of company business and, no doubt, on the company dime. During said lunch, Kyle starts talking about all of the Internet action on the Street and then tells me that people like me are the new golden children. When I responded with a blank stare, he explained that programmers with Internet experience could write their own ticket.

The most interesting part of this meeting is that, with the exception of an occasional glimpse of him on the elevator, I never met Kyle before the day he introduced himself to me, so I didn't know what he knew about my experience or how he got the information in the first place. At some point, I made a smart-ass comment suggesting that he should bring that observation to the attention of my boss, expecting that he would drop the subject. But no, he went right on with the pitch, and then advised me that I should forget about the boss and what he thought, adding that the guy was an old fart from the pre-Internet dark ages and that he would never get it. Well, he was right about that part, at least.

When he asked me to tell him about my Internet experience I shrugged and told him that I wrote my senior thesis on what was then a rather obscure area called data mining on multi-tier computer networks. He looked at me as if I was speaking Swahili, so I explained that it was a way to search through huge amounts of data on very large networks, like the Internet, efficiently and quickly. "Holy shit", was all he could say. I guess he liked my answer.

A few weeks later, I find myself sitting with Kyle and Jan in Pat Clemens's office. Jan and Pat were principals at a small mid-town venture capital firm that no one ever heard of before, called the Alley Group. Next thing I know, they invest five million dollars. And just like that, I became a paper millionaire. I suddenly owned a big chunk of a company with a post-money valuation of fifteen million dollars. That was November 1998. I promptly quit my boring, well-paying job with the great benefits—Kyle quit his on the same day—and Jan got Pat's blessing to join our company. Presto: instant Internet start-up.

I have to tell you that all of this seemed completely bizarre to me. Especially since the new company was based on nothing more than Kyle's thirty-page business plan and my senior thesis, plus a few thousand lines of code that I had written about two years before. The code was on a single floppy disk that had been gathering dust in a box in my closet. What a country, huh?

I tried to raise this curious subject once or twice with my new-found partners and received some really dirty looks in return. So I shut up and went with the flow, just like the rest of the barbarian hordes that I was reading about every day.

Marcella walked back into the conference room just as the rest of the group started filtering in. She seemed preoccupied, and I noticed that she was twirling a strand of her hair into a tight curl around her index finger. I guess it was her version of a nervous fidget. Hey, it was better than an eye-tic.

She walked over to me and, as was her habit, gave me a quick scan. If I had been wearing a tie she would have straightened it, but I wasn't, so she didn't. I figured she was just checking the basic stuff: belt in all the loops, matching socks, shoes on the right feet, and so on. Some men might have been insulted by this, but not me. I'm not exactly sure what this says about me—or her, for that matter.

"My, we're looking much more awake, even a little happy," she said.

"Awake, maybe, but not happy. Where's my donut?"

She made a pouty face. "Poor baby. Say 'Ahhh.'"

I did, and she placed a piece of chocolaty goodness in my mouth.

"What's today?" I asked her.

"Friday."

"Perfect. A Howie dream, and it's Friday the thirteenth."

She gave me a puzzled look and asked again, "Who's Howie?"

"I'll tell you later."

She handed me a napkin and said. "Friday the thirteenth is just another day. You're not superstitious, are you?"

"No, except when I fly."

"Well, you're not flying, so don't worry about it. Besides, it's Friday the sixth, not the thirteenth, that's next Friday. Did you get my note?"

"It's the sixth?"

"Yes Tony. What made you think it was the thirteenth?"

I shrugged. "I don't know, maybe it was my dream."

"So, did you get my note?"

"Which one?"

"The one in the bathroom."

I smiled and nodded.

"So, cheer up. You're going to kick butt today."

"Hope so."

"There does seem to be one small glitch." Marcella advised me.

"What?"

"Jan still hasn't shown up, and I don't have any messages from her."

This was not happening. One of the company's founders, and a key executive, was going to be late for a life-or-death investor meeting? And if that's not bad enough, one of the investors was her former boss.

"I checked every number we have. Nothing."

"Well, check them again; just get her ass in here! Please."

Marcella nodded and walked away.

The meeting started out okay, but as expected, it didn't take long for it to turn into a real shit storm. I gave my part of the presentation, and then Kyle gave his. Since Jan never showed up, I had to give her part as well to round things out. About halfway through, our small audience began interrupting me with short, curt questions interspersed with occasional snickers of incredulity. Not a good sign.

It's not that the presentation wasn't good, and it wasn't that it lacked accuracy. Frankly, it didn't matter what we presented, because the sharks in the room smelled blood, and the sharp-tooth pricks just couldn't contain themselves. Next was the really fun part, when we turned to the topic of valuation and terms. It started warm and the temperature quickly increased from there. It went back and forth, getting louder and more animated as we went. One moment we were confidently making projections into the future, and the next we were reliving our brief and turbulent past. It wasn't long before our strong and positive sales pitch began resembling the ramblings of the condemned begging for mercy.

As I said, I was there with Kyle, no Jan, in front of these three charming fellows representing existing or prospective investors, two from the Alley Group and another newly minted venture capital investor who said his name was Richard. He did most of the talking for their side. He told us to call him Dick, which turned out to be appropriate, and accurate.

So this meeting goes on for a couple of hours. Kyle just zones out and starts staring out of the window. For most of the time it was just me and the Dick going at it for what seemed like days. By the end I was able to negotiate half of the funding we were looking for, and we had to make it last twice as long as we originally planned. This meant, of course, that we had to make more people cuts. More painful still were the terms of the financing. Without getting into the awful details, Kyle, Jan, and I had most of our remaining founders' stake in the company wiped out.

Most of the bad-news terms were unmercifully delivered by the Dick, and just when he had us reeling, he proposed that all executive managers take a 30 percent cut in salaries. When I explained that we just did that two months ago, he stared at me stone-faced, as if I were being ungrateful.

It was a very painful outcome. However, on the bright side, we bought another twelve months to turn this thing around. The fact that we got any new money at all was a small miracle, considering the state of the financial markets. Most dot-coms were dropping like flies. Of our seven original competitors, there was only one left. The other six had died painful, public deaths over the past few months. So, the good news was that we would live to fight another day. The bad news was that we would be making someone else rich if we succeeded. But the three of us had decided months ago that failure was not an option. We were all young and, hopefully, had long careers ahead of us. If nothing else, we wanted to salvage our reputations. Whatever else we could save was a bonus. Besides, the prospect of being former dotcom executives and looking for a job in this market scared the hell out of us.

So the meeting ended and we all got up, except Kyle, who just sat there, now staring at the wall. Dick, now fully satiated on his recent meal of raw meat and blood, was a new man. He came over with a big smile on his face, shook my hand and said something like, "You're a tough negotiator and I look forward to our success in the future". I said, "Go screw yourself, you vulture prick". Okay, I didn't say that. I can't remember what I said, but it was probably something pathetic like, "Yes, great doing business with you too, Dickey".

He and the other two guys from the Alley Group said their goodbyes and left, leaving me standing with my back to the window and half-sitting on the window ledge. The door closed and I took a deep breath and tried to get my brain unwound.

Kyle stood up and walked over.

"So what's up with you?" I asked Kyle, who was now staring blankly out of the window again, like some duck that had been whacked on the head.

"Nothing."

"Nothing? I'm mixing it up with these assholes for two hours and you didn't say a word."

"I thought you were handling it just fine."

"Well, thanks a lot, but I could have used a little support there a couple of times."

"Anyway", he said, "it's over. We have the funding and now we can try to pull this thing out."

"We don't have the funding yet, Kyle. They still have to complete the due diligence and we have to rewrite the business plan to reflect the new financing before we get dollar one. So let's get to work on the details so we don't screw this thing up. And where the hell is Jan?"

Kyle didn't answer.

I turned and looked out of the window, trying to figure out what the hell was so interesting. It was the same scene as earlier, except now there were three cop cars and a coroner's van parked in front of the building across the street. "I wonder what's going on down there."

Kyle, who could not see down to the street from where he standing, cautiously approached the window and looked down at the scene. Two men emerged from the front of the building rolling a stretcher carrying a black plastic bag, apparently filled with a body. The men quickly rolled the thing over to the coroner's van, opened the back doors, and expertly slid it in.

"What the hell?" Kyle mumbled to himself.

"What do you think happened?" I asked.

Again, no reply.

"Well, there goes the neighborhood. Again."

Chapter 16

A hand tore the blindfold from his head and the gag from his mouth. David Henkel squinted into the bright lights. It was like staring into the sun. It felt like the sun too. The hot, heavy air caused the moisture to pour from his skin, something he was accustomed to by now, but the lights seemed to turn his sweat into steam.

His swollen face was caked with blood around his eyes, nose and mouth from the daily beatings. But he could handle that. It was the electric shocks that were unbearable, especially when they drove the ends of the copper battery cables into his groin.

He craned his neck to look around the tent. He was kneeling on a dirt floor, hands bound behind his back. His ankles were tied so tightly that he could not feel his toes anymore, which was probably just as well. The parts of his body that he could feel were searing with pain.

He looked up and found one of his hosts examining him like he was a trapped animal, like one of the rabbits he use to snare back home with his dad, in Kentucky. He remembered the look of fear in the rabbits' eyes as they awaited their fate, and he recalled his strong urge to set them free.

Home. He could hardly remember the place anymore. Just occasional, misty, glimpses, like a fleeting mirage in this goddamned desert. How long had it been? Two years? Three? His last leave home was during Bosnia. He was in charge of a black-ops mission to smuggle weapons to the Bosnian-Muslim forces via Croatia using C-130 transports. He like Bosnia. It was so green, just like home. And the sea in Dubrovnik was the bluest he'd ever seen. And he liked the Bosnians. They deserved the help, and he was happy to be a part of it.

Then they shipped him here, to this hell-hole, this fucking waste land, where nothing grows, except the body count. He thought he had done a good job in Bosnia, and they told him he had. They promised him a rotation back home. Then, they changed their minds and told him that he was needed here.

Langley had ignored Ahmad Shah Massoud for years, in favor of a Pakistani puppet called Gulbuddin Hekmatya. The fucking Paks and their Taliban friends were turning out to be worse than the Soviets ever were. When Langley finally woke up and figured out that Massoud might be one of the good guys, they sent Henkel in to make contact. The dossier on Massoud indicated that he was someone who could be trusted, and who also deserved their help. When he finally met the man, he was not disappointed.

They called Massoud the *Lion of Panjshir*. What Henkel saw was more than just another desert warrior. This man was a natural born leader. But the question was, could he really be trusted. More specifically, could the incredible information that Massoud gave him be trusted. The man once said to Henkel, that the CIA brass thought they knew everything, but they didn't. He was right about that. He also said that their former allies against the Soviets, the Taliban and their Al Qaeda collaborators, were planning on striking Americans where they lived. Henkel didn't fully understand what that meant at first, but by the end of the conversation, he did.

Massoud explained, slowly and clearly, that he was not talking about another foreign base or outpost. They were going to hit America at home. It was incredible. Unbelievable. But he trusted this man. He couldn't even explain why, but he did. His biggest problem, he thought at the time, was what to tell Langley. If he relayed Massoud's message unfiltered, they might conclude that he was just another warlord trying to provoke America into eliminating his political enemies. But if he didn't tell them, and it was the truth. . . *my God*.

But it turned out not to be his biggest problem, after-all. Because he never made it back to tell anyone. He was captured, by Massoud's enemies, on a desolate desert road about two weeks ago. No, it had to be nearly three now.

He suddenly came to the realization that no one was coming for him. He had been abandoned, left behind like a pile of camel shit to dry in the burning desert sun, and would never get a chance to deliver Massoud's warning to anyone.

Henkel closed his eyes. At that moment all he could think about was home, and the feeling of the cool summer rain on his skin, the dappled sunlight filtering through the green leaves, and the sensation of stomping through the street puddles, when he was a boy.

"Water." Henkel croaked out between parched, cracked lips. It wasn't a question, or a request, simply a statement of fact, of need.

A man in a white thawb waved his hand and a moment later, the blinding lights faded. He walked over to Henkel holding a small, plastic cup. He touched it to Henkel's lips. The water was piss-warm and had a strong metallic taste, but it was the best water he ever drank. When the man removed the cup, Henkel tried to grab it with his teeth, but it was gone too fast.

The man held up an object in his other hand. It was Henkel's bible. "You are a religious man, I see." The man said examining the book with intense, deeply set, brown eyes.

Henkel could not help nodding slightly.

The man smiled, causing the scar on his left jaw to flush red. "We are both religious men. We both worship the same god, the god of Abraham." His English, Henkel noted, was good and his accent indicated an expensive education.

Henkel looked down at the dirt. "Yes, same god, different prophet."

"Oh, no, that is not correct. The Christian prophet, Jesus, is our prophet as well, peace be unto him. But, you do not believe in our prophet, Muhammad. Do you?"

Henkel continued staring at the floor, wishing he had said nothing, and determined to say nothing more. He knew that this conversation would not lead to anything good.

"It does not seem right to me Colonel that we believe in your prophet, but you do not even acknowledge ours." The man stopped speaking; apparently waiting for a reply from his captive, but there was none. He placed the bible down on a steel folding table and then knelt down in front of Henkel.

"Do you know what else is not right, Colonel? That men, like you, men who fear God, come here to kill men like me, who also fear God. You and I both hate the same things. For your entire life, you have watched your culture slowly dissolve away, like steel in a bath of acid. Immorality of every kind; drugs and alcohol consumed like food and water; pornography, sexual licentiousness, children born without fathers, or even mothers, to care for them – and even this level of depravity does not satisfy the evil ones. They justify these sins by claiming that they favor nature's law over God's Law, as if they were some ignorant tribe of pagans living lost in a forest."

The man shook in head in disgust. "Then, we all bore witness as they defiled the laws of both God and nature, as your so-called civilization entered the realm of the unthinkable; children being ripped from their mother's wombs, and newborn babies being left in garbage bins to die, or drowned like rats in bathtubs, or strapped into the back seat of a car driven into a lake. Then, in another adventure into depravity, men who become women, and women who have become men. And what is next? Will we see men marrying men and women marrying women? Will you begin to sacrifice your children on the fires of pagan gods, or in your sterile laboratories, perhaps consuming their flesh to satisfy your demand for eternal youth, like it was all part of your nature-god's plan? You dare call us savages?" The man laughed. It was not a friendly laugh.

"Well, perhaps it is part of someone's plan, someone's law." The man continued. "We call him Satan."

Henkel looked up and stared angrily into his antagonist's eyes. "There is evil everywhere. In America, in this country, in this tent."

The man in the white thawb stood abruptly and clenched his jaws so tightly that it made his scar turn white, like the flesh on a dead man's face. He took a deep breath and regained his composure. "Yes, there is." He responded calmly. "But in this country, in this tent, we fight it, we do not embrace it. It is this evil that will reign everywhere if the people you work for succeed."

"It is the biggest irony of all, don't you think? The very people we are fighting, people like you, are not these unclean savages whose way of life repulses us both. They are cowards and hide themselves in their dark towers, behind their words, thousands of miles away. Your press and your media, which are a tool of truth-hiding and misinformation; they carry out the plan of the enemy, of an idolizing cult of personalities, and spread scandals among the believers to repel the people away from their religion, away from their God."

"But they are too cowardly to pick up a weapon and defend their indefensible words and deeds, themselves. So it is left to people like you – the very ones who have tried to stop Satan's ascendancy in your own country, who have tried to stop this same enemy that worships him, you come here and kill us, like we are the enemy. You have lost your war at home. Now your children's minds are polluted with their words. While you take them to hear the words of God, for a single hour, on a single day of the week, every other day they are fed the words of Satan; on your televisions, in their classrooms, every waking moment they are bathed in his filth. So, now, having lost the war to Satan at home, you come here to our lands and help Him conquer us? You and I should be allies against him, and yet you come here and kill us, as if you were Satan's blind and ignorant slaves. But you are not blind, and you are not ignorant, so in a way you are worse than the savages that you work for. Now it is time for you to meet God. Explain it to Him. Perhaps he will understand. I do not."

Henkel was about to respond, but the man brought the back of his hand across Henkel's mouth, silencing him, and causing the wounds on his mouth and nose to begin seeping blood again. The bright lights came back on as the man with the scar turned abruptly and walked towards the tent's exit. Henkel thought he was going to leave, but he stopped and nodded in the direction of the lights.

Three bearded men approached Henkel. The glare from the lights veiled the details of their faces until he was within their reach. Two of them grabbed him on either side. One hand grabbed his hair and twisted his head up as the third looked down at him with a lifeless, white eye. It was surrounded by hairless, scarred flesh - from a fire or an explosion, Henkel thought analytically. He'd seen similar scars before. But it was the man's other eye, the left one, which made his stomach cringe - a ferocious black void, filled with a hatred so deep it seemed bottomless. Henkel knew, the instant he saw this man's tortured face, that it would be the last one he would ever see. He considered the irony of being killed at the hands of people who claimed to be the saviors of the very people he came here to help, the same people he had helped in Bosnia

Massoud's message. Henkel thought quickly.

The one-eyed man held a piece of wrinkled notepaper in his left hand and a long serrated butcher's knife in his right. He spat on Henkel, disappeared behind his back and began to speak in a hesitant, heavily accented English, struggling to read the words clearly.

"From Our Great Sheik, Osama Bin Laden, we send this reply to the Crusading Americans who have said that the explosions at Riyadh and Al-Khobar had taught them one lesson: that is not to withdraw when attacked by coward terrorists."

Henkel began a recitation of his own. Strong words, but also hesitant and broken. "Our Father who art in heaven hallowed be thy name..."

"We say to them that this talk can induce a grieving mother to laughter, and shows the fears that have enshrined you all. Where was this false courage of yours when the explosion in Beirut took place in 1983? You were turned into scattered bits and pieces at that time; 241 mainly marines soldiers were killed. And where was this courage of yours when two explosions made you to leave Aden in less than twenty four hours!"

"...thy... kingdom come thy will be done on earth as it is..."

"But your most disgraceful case was in Somalia; where, after vigorous propaganda about the power of the USA and its post-cold war leadership of the new world order, you moved tens of thousands of international forces, including twenty eight thousand American soldiers into Somalia. However, when tens of your solders were killed in minor battles and one American Pilot was dragged in the streets of Mogadishu, you left the area carrying disappointment, humiliation, defeat and your dead with you."

"...in heaven forgive us this day as we forgive those who trespass against us and..."

"Then Clinton appeared in front of the whole world threatening and promising revenge, but these threats were merely a preparation for withdrawal. You had been disgraced by Allah and you withdrew; the extent of your impotence and weaknesses became very clear. It was a pleasure for the hearts of every Muslim and a remedy to the chests of believing nations to see you defeated in the three Islamic cities of Beirut, Aden and Mogadishu."

"... lead... us not into temptation but deliver us Lord from..."

"I say to you: The sons of the land of the Holy Places had come out to fight against the Russian in Afghanistan, the Serb in

Bosnia-Herzegovina and today they are fighting in Chechnya and, by the Permission of Allah, they have been made victorious over your partner, the Russians. By the command of Allah, they are also fighting in Tajikistan."

"... evil for thine is the kingdom and the power and the glory Lord for ever and ever amen..."

"I say to you that: These youths love death as you love life."

"...forgive me Lord..."

"Those youths know that their rewards in fighting you, the USA, is double than their rewards in fighting someone else not from the people of the book. They have no intention except to enter paradise by killing you. An infidel, and enemy of God like you, cannot be in the same hell with his righteous executioner."

"... for my sins."

"The youths also reciting the All Mighty words of: 'so when you meet in battle those who disbelieve, then smite their necks'. Those youths will not ask you for explanations, they will tell you singing there is nothing between us need to be explained, there is only killing and neck smiting."

The man raised the butcher's knife before the camera, and then brought it down on the side of Henkel's neck. Henkel instantly pulled away and fell to the ground, but the three men fell upon him, and as two held his body and his head, the third began to saw through the skin, into flesh and quickly to the bone. Blood sprayed everywhere, Henkel's screams filled the tent, then gurgling and finally all was silent except the teeth of the blade finishing its work. The blood-spattered butcher then stood and held Henkel's head up in front of the camera.

"There is nothing between us need to be explained, there is only killing and neck smiting."

Chapter 17

I was strapped to my desk for the rest of the day, revising the latest versions of the business plan and the financials. I made a mental note to speak with Jan about some of her assumptions regarding product development schedules—when she finally decided to show up, of course. Then there were some strange vendor transactions, which I did not recognize, and that Kyle had approved. Not good.

Marcella poked her head in and said, "Hey, it's getting late; just wanted to check to see if you needed anything else before I leave."

I stretched and glanced at the clock on the corner of my desk. "Wow, almost seven already?"

Marcella walked over to the credenza, picked up the half-eaten sandwich that she brought at lunchtime, and threw it into the wastebasket.

"I guess you're getting tired of ham and Swiss," she said, smiling.

"No, it's fine. I just wasn't very hungry after this morning's meeting."

"Yes, I know, you didn't even finish your donut."

I smiled and shrugged.

"I was going to ask you how it went, but based on your mood, I think I know."

"Well," I said, "it could have been worse."

"How much worse?"

"We managed to get some new money, but not as much as we had hoped. Unfortunately, the price was pretty high."

"That bad?"

"Let me put it this way: we'll have to put the wedding off a few years until I save enough to afford it."

That comment took her off-guard. Her face blushed and took on an odd combination of expressions. I was immediately sorry I said it. I can be a real smart-ass sometimes. She knew that, but I usually did not make those sorts of jokes, especially not with her. There was, as I mentioned earlier, a part of me that wasn't joking, but I also knew that this was no time to make her life, or mine, any more complicated than they were already going to be over the next few months.

"Where's Kyle and Jan?" I asked, clumsily changing the subject.

She regained her professional demeanor and said, "Kyle left for lunch around one and never came back, and I haven't seen Jan all day."

I rubbed my temples with the palms of my hands and let that sink in. "Okay, thanks for all of your help today. You went above and beyond, as usual." I took a deep breath and let it out slowly. "I'll see you in the morning."

"Tony, tomorrow is Saturday."

"Oh, right. Have a great weekend, then. See you on Monday."

She about to leave, then stopped and turned back towards me. "I wanted to . . .," She said as she bit the lower right side of her lip and smiled. "I wanted to ask you if. . .," She hesitated again, this time turning her head to the side before continuing. "Do you think there will be more people let go?"

"Unfortunately, it looks like that's going to be necessary," I said softly.

"Am I going to be one of them?"

I laughed. "Not a chance, unless I leave with you."

She continued smiling, but I could see that her eyes were wet. She nodded her head in silence.

"Okay?" I asked.

"Okay," She replied.

"Is there anything else that you're wondering about?"

She crossed her arms on her chest, rolled her eyes towards the ceiling and theatrically tapped her right foot on the floor. "Not right now, but ask me again sometime, Okay?"

"Okay, I will."

Chapter 18

By the time I left the building, it was dark and the air was heavy with impending rain, or maybe snow. I was too tired to go home and cook, but I was also too hungry to skip it. Besides, there didn't seem to be much of a point in my spending another Friday night alone in my apartment with my thoughts. I was in the mood to seek refuge in a crowd of strangers. If you have ever worked or lived in New York, or another big town I suppose, you'll probably understand what I mean.

I walked the few blocks downtown to the *Bull and Bear* on Second Avenue, just north of Eighteenth Street. I passed this place at least once every day, going either to or from my office, but I've only stopped here a few times. Actually, now that I think about it, the first time was with Kyle and Jan.

We were just starting out with our new enterprise and hadn't started blowing perfectly good money on completely useless parties or expensive dinning yet, which somehow became SOP six months later. Instead, we would spend Friday nights at dives like this one. It was a long time ago, or at least it seemed that way, and given my current financial circumstances, it looked like a good call tonight.

The first thing that grabs you about these places is the smell: that odd combination of stale beer, cigarette smoke, burnt chop meat and over-used fryer oil. I took a seat at the far end of the bar. I love dark, loud places like these, and I'm even fond of that disgusting smell, which reminded me of those cheap bars I hung out in on Long Island when I was going to college, and in Manhattan in the early years before I knew anything about being a CEO, or cared. I thought my next business venture could be to figure out how to bottle and sell that smell. I even had a name: "Eau de Rat Hole."

Well, there you go. I was already looking forward to the next chapter in my life. Okay, so I was not planning to become the next fragrance magnate, but as each day past, it became increasingly clear that things were winding down with my present company, this morning's new funding opportunity notwithstanding. Because, despite what I thought about saving the company, I wasn't going to be able to pull it off without Kyle and Jan. I originally thought that they were as desperate to save it as I was but, based on their performance today, or lack thereof, they clearly were not. Therefore, absent a major change in their demeanor, or a minor miracle, it was just a matter of time.

I suddenly felt lost and disorientated. I'd spent way too much time over the past two years with people I either didn't know, or didn't like; sipping wine at cocktail parties, eating sushi at business luncheons, partaking of fusion cuisine at investor meetings and a seemingly never-ending feast of bizarrely expensive champagne, bottled water, hummus, and couscous—whatever the hell that is. Now, suddenly, I was staring down the jaws of thirty, and eating alone in a shitty old Manhattan bar on a Friday night. What the hell happened?

I ordered a double cheeseburger with extra fries and a pint of house ale. So there I was, feeling like an old fart, watching my dreams slip between my fingers, reminiscing about my misspent youth, thinking about Marcella, and trying to eat myself to death - or at least into a coma. Boy, I hadn't had this much fun on a Friday night in a long time.

It must have been a slow sports night because the TV over the bar was tuned to the news channel. It also must have been the night off for the bubble-headed bleach-blonde who was the regular anchor for this particular station. The woman on the tube was young and pretty, but there was nothing blond about her. Still, she did seem to have that same empty-eyed stare. So, I watched the boob tube with one eye and spied my fellow bar patrons with the other. No one was even remotely familiar, which was good—except maybe for this one guy sitting at the end of the bar's dog leg next to the wall.

He seemed a little familiar, like someone you meet for the first time who looks like someone you think you once knew... but you aren't sure. Well, anyway, he was sitting in the shadows, in a bar that was one big shadow, so I really couldn't make him out very clearly. He turned, we made eye contact, and then he began to act a little uneasy; slumping down in his seat and moving further into the corner. Whoever he was, he didn't seem real interested in talking to me. *Hey pal, relax; I don't give a shit, promise.*

I turned both eyes back on the tube and tuned into world events. The anchor's expression was full of sadness - or was it remorse? The image of a somber, brown, granite monolith appeared on the screen. The news anchor informed us, "A memorial to the victims of the USS *Cole* attack is under construction at the Norfolk Naval Station in Virginia. A terrorist organization known as Al Qaida claimed responsibility for the bombing, which took place last year on October 12 while the *Cole* was in the Yemeni port of Aden. The attack against the United States Navy destroyer killed seventeen American sailors and injured thirty-nine. It was the deadliest attack against a United States Naval vessel since 1987 when the USS *Stark* was attacked by an Iraqi jet fighter, killing 37 US sailors. The dedication for the *Cole* memorial is scheduled to take place this fall on the one-year anniversary of the attack."

A moment later, the woman's expression changed, as if someone had thrown a switch. The frown was replaced with a smile and she reported; "the twenty-one man and three-woman crew of a US spy plane who were being held in China for eleven days landed safely at their home base." The image on the screen switched to a happy scene of smiling and cheering families and well-wishers.

Then, just as magically as it had appeared, the anchor's ebullient mood became somber once again, as she reported, "Exactly one year ago today the US stock market plunged. The Dow was down more than 600 points to 10305, and the NASDAQ fell 355 points to 3321 from its peak in March of over 5000, capping one of the worst weeks ever for US stocks. But of course, as we all now know, that was just the beginning of the end for the NASDAQ, which recently dipped below 2000, wiping out trillions of dollars of wealth, and some say we're not finished with the bad news yet."

I was not sure, but I could have sworn I saw a little smile break through on the anchor's face with that last sentence. I wondered if maybe she was thinking about a cheating ex-boyfriend; some sleazy stockbroker who had gotten his comeuppance by being canned after the crash. Or perhaps her crappy former boss lost his shirt in the market. On the other hand, maybe she was just anticipating the next happy story, and her expression-circuits blew a fuse.

I waved down the bartender. "Hey, isn't there a game on or something?"

The bartender responded with an empty stare. "You think I would be watching this shit if there was?"

Good point. I ordered another pint. I tuned out again, finished my burger, and scarfed down the remaining fries. Aaah, I could feel my gut expanding and my arteries hardening already. I was thinking about asking the bartender for an ice cream soda when the guy near the wall, the one slouched down in the shadows trying to avoid me, walked over.

"Hey, Tony, right?" He said with an accent I didn't recognize.

Even though he was closer, and in better light now, I still could not place the face. "Yup. Do I know you?"

He rolled his head and shrugged his shoulders. "Yeah, we went to college together. You remember, at Stony Brook?"

I looked at him and tried to remember. I really hate these embarrassing little meetings. Why can't people just tell you who the hell they are rather than turning a reunion into a quiz show? "Okay, you got me, I can't remember. What's your name?"

"Oh, come on, you don't remember me from chemistry class?" He said as he held out his arms, as if my getting a better look at his torso would help my memory.

His long, black, wavy hair, matched the unkempt appearance of his walrus mustache and large, bushy eyebrows that waved at me over his wire rimmed glasses. But I couldn't see his eyes through the dark lenses.

So I sat there, pretending I was thinking, and wondering what kind of asshole wears dark glasses in a dark bar, at night. I was just about to tell him that I had no recollection of him whatsoever, but for some reason, I decided to play along. "Oh yeah, chemistry class. Yeah, I remember now, organic chemistry in our junior year, right?"

"Noooo, not organic chemistry!"

God, I hate this. The bartender brought me a fresh pint and I took a long, thoughtful swig. "Not organic chemistry?"

"Nooo, inorganic chemistry in our freshman year."

Go away, dummy. "Freshman chemistry?"

"Come on, you remember that guy who taught da class in da bomb shelter?"

"The bomb shelter?" It was actually starting to come back.

"Yeah, da bomb shelter. He gets up in front of a class of 400 freshmen who are scared shitless about the midterm, and he tells us we're a bunch of losers and he's only there because they make him teach, but he would rather be in the lab doing something important?"

I did remember that, and I remembered the bomb shelter, but I did not remember this guy.

"Oh, yeah. The bomb shelter," I said.

"What was that guy's name?" he asked himself.

"Hmmm, Wilson, maybe?" I suggested as I took another swig.

"Wilson? Yeah? Well, whatever his name was... what an asshole, right?"

"Right!" *But who the hell are you?*

The "bomb shelter", if you're curious, was the unofficial name for the Javits Lecture Center; a mangled pile of windowless concrete that contained—you guessed it—dark, cavernous lecture halls that resembled Hitler's Berlin bunker, or at least that's what they looked like to us. The building was probably the brainchild of some demented, 1970s lunatic of an architect, who was strung out on something at the time. Either that or he thought he was supposed to be designing the ventilation shaft for the subterranean warehouse that stored the remains of the Roswell aliens. Then, to make it a little bit more of a horror show, it looked like they gave the building project to some jack-off of a state contractor who hit the lowest bid. Did I mention that I did not find the building very warm and inviting?

"Yeah, the bomb shelter. What a nightmare." I replied.

"Do you remember the story about that poor, dead kid?" he asked.

I did, indeed. There was a story circulating at the time—probably bullshit —that a few years before I got there some poor, stressed-out physics student had committed suicide in Lecture Hall 100 during an exam, and no one noticed until the body started to stink a few days later. As unbelievable as it was when I first heard it, it actually began to sound plausible by the end of my first semester.

So, I went with it. "Oh yeah, I remember now."

Then he gracefully bowed and, with one smooth motion, swept the glasses off his face with his left hand and held out his right. "How da hell are you, Tony? Man, it's been what, nine years maybe, right?"

"Eight, I think."

"Eight? Holy shit, the time really flies, right?"

"Right." *This is just what I needed tonight.* "Sure does, yup, eight years!"

"You was just a baby den. I remember you like it was yesterday."

"Great." *Who is this guy*?

"Yeah, dis little college kid walk-in' around dis big campus."

"I wasn't little. I was six-one."

"You seemed like you was kind-a little, on that big campus, maybe."

I don't think so.

"But hey, you was really smart."

"Thanks."

"I remember when I first met you. I said, 'dis is one smart little guy.'"

"I don't remember that."

"Yes you do, Tony, wassa madda wit you? It was right around that time when you father... You remember that thing you told me about?"

Suddenly, I did remember. His mustache and the long hair threw me, but just then it came back. "Nunzio?"

"See, you do remember."

I nodded.

"That was a terrible thing. How are your parents now, anyhow?"

"Fine, living in Florida."

"Really? Florida? Dats nice."

The guy looked at me like I was lying to him, which I was. Only one of my parents was living in Florida.

"Yes, Florida," I repeated.

"Florida is a nice place, but it's a little too hot for me," he said.

"Me too."

"Well, it's great see-in' you again, Tony."

"Same here."

"Hey, you okay, pal?" he asked.

"I'm fine. Why?"

"You look a little stressed out, that's all."

"Long day." I said.

"Yeah, it sucks, work-in' for a livin'."

I was tempted to ask him what he did for a *livin'*, but I decided to let it pass. I replied, "Yes it does."

He informed me, "Hey, it's the weekend, get some sleep and you'll feel betta. Okay?"

Yeah, sleep, good idea.

"Well, I gotta go. See you around."

"Yeah, see you around," I replied with some relief.

He shook my hand again, put his glasses back on his face with the same graceful movement and walked quickly towards the door, disappearing into the dark, the smoky haze and the people. I returned to my beer.

Wow, how's that for a major flashback? I thought about that year: 1993, my dad, and Crazy Nunzio. Then it occurred to me—maybe that is what the Howie dream was all about?

What a messed-up time that was. I was in the computer science program at Stony Brook, one of the most competitive, cut-throat programs in the country, and I was really struggling. You figure graduating from high school in the top one percent of my class of 800 kids would have prepared me for it. However, keeping up with the Chinese kids, who were some of the best and brightest from a class of about one billion or so, was definitely a challenge I was unprepared for. And of course, being the hellishly Darwinian place that Stony Brook was, everybody was graded on a steep curve. I remember a couple of times busting my ass getting a 90 on a test, but because of the average, I ended up getting a B as a grade.

So there I was, in the middle of this unbelievable stress and my dad almost gets killed on the job. I remember that it was right around my birthday, in September. My dad, a Suffolk County detective at the time, was one of the many cops on both sides of my family. All the others were NYPD. But dad decided he didn't want to raise his kids in one of the Five Boroughs of New York City, and the thought of commuting two or three hours a day from Long Island was not very appealing either. In any event, there was no way my mom, who lost an uncle on the job, was going to allow her husband to become fodder for those dangerous New York streets. So, he joined the force in Suffolk and, as a result, took a lot of flak from my uncles, who, as I said, were all NYPD.

I remember that they were always bugging him about being overpaid and underworked. I remember my uncle Joe once said that it was more dangerous being a security guard in a hospital nursery than being on the job at SCPD. I think some of it took a toll, because Dad was always volunteering for the toughest, most dangerous duty he could find. Well, as they say, be careful what you wish for.

Over the years, my dad had earned a reputation as a guy who was always upfront and out-front, and someone with pristine integrity. So, when Internal Affairs discovers that the mob, which had been making moves for years in the Long Island trash-hauling business, narcotics, gambling, and God knows what else, had one or more dirty SCPD cops in their pocket, they came to my dad and asked him if he wanted to volunteer for some cloak-and-dagger duty to smoke the creeps out. He eagerly jumped right in. I remember that for six months, he worked all kinds of strange hours, and I hardly ever saw him in the daylight during that summer before I left for college.

So, about three weeks into the fall semester I get a call from Uncle Joe, telling me that Dad was evacuated by helicopter to the Nassau County Medical Center, with two gunshot wounds in his chest. I remember that day like a sort of slow-motion nightmare. By the time I got to the hospital he was just getting out of surgery. My mom, a witness to the whole thing, was an incoherent wreck. My Uncle Joe and my Uncle Mike were there along with some of Dad's SCPD friends, keeping an eye out for him and my mom. When I asked my uncles about what happened, Uncle Joe walked me up the hall, away from mom, and told me the story.

Apparently, during his investigation, my dad succeeded in identifying one of the dirty cops. Unfortunately, this prick got to my dad before he could do anything about it. Late the previous night, he and Mom had been on the way home from a rare night out and Dad, who always kept his piece and a police radio with him, stopped to help a patrol car that had just radioed in with some engine trouble. Turns out it was a setup. When he got out of the car to help, the two guys in the car, dressed like cops, got out and opened fire on him. Dad said he thought he remembered getting off some rounds before being taken down in a hail of fire, but he really wasn't sure.

My uncle stopped talking at that point, looked at the ceiling for a few seconds, and ran his fingers through his hair before he could continue. He told me that if it wasn't for a passing motorist, who happened to be an EMT, Dad wouldn't have made it to the hospital alive. When the police got there, they found mom standing over him. He was on the ground, unconscious, having already been patched up by this unknown EMT guy who went to get more help. By the time the ambulance showed up they thought dad was dead. But my mom screamed at them and told them he was still alive and not to stop trying to resuscitate him, which they eventually did. The guys dressed as cops, the ones who shot him, were dead. Each had a single gunshot wound to the head. And the EMT guy had disappeared, and was never heard from again.

Dad was listed in critical condition for a week. But two weeks later he was sitting up in bed and talking up a storm. Nine months later, after receiving several commendations for bravery, good police work, and being a pretty good shot, he was back on the job. My uncles never again made a comment about the easy SCPD duty, and my mom never let my dad volunteer for anything more dangerous than security duty in a hospital nursery.

Before dad left the hospital, I told him that I was going to drop out for a semester to help him and Mom out around the house. But he told me no, and made me promise to stay in school, to hang in there, which I did, and I managed to squeak out a B for that semester. Later, during the Christmas recess, while he was still out on disability, he and I had the chance to talk about what had happened. He said that it was hard to remember anything that he could make much sense of. He was pretty sure the fake cops were still standing and shooting at him when he went down, so he never understood how he could have shot either of them. Everything had happened so fast.

When he told his supervisor about this, he was told to let it alone. "The bad guys are dead, the good guy is alive, happy ending, end of story."

But it wasn't the end of the story, because his supervisor, along with the rest of the brass, were trying to deal with a small war raging on the inside of the SCPD, and a bigger one outside of it. Thanks to dad's undercover work, Internal Affairs found two cops who were on the take, and they were sent away for a long time. Six other people, who either knew, or should have known about it, got demoted, fired, or retired. In the meantime, the other, larger, war was raging on the streets of Long Island.

It was triggered by the same event, my dad's shooting, but in this case wise-guys were turning up dead all over the place, or disappearing entirely. It was widely suspected that the local SCPD, along with maybe some NYPD cops, were behind at least some of this unofficial justice. But no one was ever busted, and no one, naturally, ever admitted to it.

After a while, things settled down and went back to normal. The Long Island mob, what was left of them, retreated back under their rock. Dad spent two more quiet years on the force, all the time trying to find that EMT that saved his life, but he never did. After he retired, he and Mom moved to sunny Fort Lauderdale and mom still lives there. Dad passed away less than two years after the move. He never saw me graduate. The official cause of death was a massive stroke. No one ever said anything, but we all knew in our hearts that the cause of death was probably the wounds he received four years earlier. It just took a little more time for the bullets to find their mark.

Anyway, I remember walking around campus the rest of that first semester like a zombie, still in shock and perpetually tired. For a while, I was driving back and forth between school and home almost every day to help Mom around the house, and I was studying almost every remaining waking hour.

Then, out of nowhere, this guy Nunzio suddenly shows up in my life. When I first laid eyes on him I thought he was in the ROTC, or had just come out of the military or something, because he definitely had that military look: lean, muscular build, close-cropped hair, neatly tucked shirt-tails, ramrod-straight back, and he acted like he was in perpetual preparation to kick someone's ass. His English back then was almost unrecognizable and he spoke in clipped, but polite sentences, when he talked at all. One minute I never saw this guy before, and the next minute he's in every one of my classes. In fact, for most of the rest of that semester, it seemed like this strange character was never more than ten feet away from me, and my friends were beginning to ask questions. I guess most of them were afraid of him. His accent sounded like it was Italian, sort of, and so we dubbed him Nunzio. This soon became Crazy Nunzio, for reasons I think I've made clear already.

Now that I think of it, we never actually learned his real name. He simply started answering to the one we gave him, as if he was some sort of stray dog. I also don't recall telling him about what happened to my dad.

Oddly enough, my dorm-mate Howie was one of the few guys who didn't seem spooked by Nunzio. He actually hung in there and watched my back. I remember thinking about how out of character that seemed for a preppy-twit like Howie.

Then one day Nunzio disappeared. A little while later Howie told me that he had come into a seven-figure trust fund on his recent birthday, so he thought it was time to see the world. "And besides," he explained, "Stony Brook really sucked." But before he left he looked me straight in the eye and told me that, should I see Nunzio again, I should stay away from him. He also informed me that every instinct in his body told him that this guy was serious trouble. "Maybe the trouble won't come today or tomorrow, but sooner or later this guy was going to be a big problem."

At that point, I asked Howie if he needed a traveling companion. He just laughed, so I guess the answer was no. Then we shook hands and said goodbye. By the end of the week, he was gone. About a month later, the semester was over and I left for Christmas break. I remember thinking about what a strange pair of characters they were. I never heard from, or of, either of them again—until today: one in a dream, and the other in a crappy New York watering hole.

I emptied my glass, paid the tab and tipped the bartender. Before I left, I made a pass at the small, dingy men's room and re-deposited some of the beer I drank. While standing there, staring at the moldy tiles above the urinal, I tried to reassemble the time-ordered sequence of that bizarre year's events. Something was out of sequence, but I could not put my finger on it at first. Then it started to congeal in my beer-soaked brain: Did Howie and I meet on the first day of school, or did he show up later during that semester? Was it before or *after* Nunzio's appearance? I shook my head—actually, I shook both of them—zipped my fly, and steered for the exit.

I walked out into the cold night air, now filled with icy rain, and started jogging the few blocks home to my apartment. On the way, I thought about the meeting that morning in the office, about Marcella, and I thought about the Howie dream.

I guess I was right; it was a bad omen. Or, maybe, sometime over the previous couple of days I saw, felt, or sensed something that brought that time back into my mind, and the dream was just my brain's way of processing this new information - or sending out a warning ping to get my attention. The mind, as they say, works in mysterious ways. I thought again about the open window in the building across the street this morning: the flash, the police, and the coroners carrying the body out.

I was not sure about what I had seen, but I was sure about two things: I knew that I would be finding out more about the events across the street in the not-too-distant future; and I was also very sure that the reappearance of Crazy Nunzio was not a coincidence.

As Howie said, sooner or later this guy was going to be a big problem, and now he was back. The two events, the Nunzio sighting tonight and the body bag across the street this morning, were somehow connected: like clouds and rain, like guns and flashes, like killers and corpses.

Chapter 19

She was sixteen, perhaps seventeen: a Russian, or maybe a Ukrainian. He liked them younger, but she would do.

The drugs he gave her made it very difficult to stand, or to focus one's eyes, so he was amused when she tried to run. He watched her stumble across the room, almost making it to the door. Laughing, he grabbed a handful of her long, blond hair and pulled back hard, throwing her to the floor at his feet. As the girl struggled to stand again, he grabbed her blouse with both hands and with a single, practiced motion, ripped it away. Again, she turned to run to the door, but before she completed her first step he bought the back of his hand down, hard across her face. She slumped to the floor, this time laying there motionless. He grabbed her by one ankle and began dragging her to the bed. Just as he was beginning to really enjoy himself, he was interrupted by a timid knocking on the door.

"Who is it?" He screamed at the unseen intruder.

"It is Adib, sir. There is an urgent message for you."

"Not now, you worm."

"It is the one from America, sir, the one you've been waiting for."

Uday Hussein dropped the girl's leg and reached for his shirt on the bed.

When the door suddenly opened, Adib Shabaan reflexively took a step backwards.

"Where is it?" Uday barked as he buttoned his shirt over a black forest of chest hair.

"There", Adib said, pointing to a computer screen across the room. As he spoke, Adib's eyes slowly drifted toward the hairless, white scar on Uday's chest. He tried to look away but he could not help himself. The scar, along with a bullet lodged in Uday's spine; one of the eight that stuck him, were the sole remnants of a 1996 assassination attempt. Most people never knew of it. Those that did were never sure if it was true or a rumor, and in any event, no one dared speak of it. The gruesome fate of the failed assassin was all that was needed to keep similar attempts at bay. But just for good measure, Uday turned his wrath on the failed assassin's family, friends, and a good portion of the man's former village. Even some of Uday's bodyguards could not escape his deadly retribution. They, along with a few innocent witnesses, were also removed from the ranks of the living. With the exception of the scar, and the bullet in his spine, the entire event, and everyone even remotely connected to it, had been erased.

"What are you looking at?" Uday shouted.

Adib immediately looked away and shook his head. "Nothing, sir."

"Make sure my little pigeon doesn't get away," Uday said motioning to the girl on the floor. Adib obediently closed the door and stood beside it. Uday, limping on his left leg, walked across the room as he finished buttoning his shirt.

It had been more than seven years since his search began and now, finally, he had his first real lead. A small flashing icon announced the presence of the new email. He clicked the icon and entered his password, and before the system had a chance to request it, he placed his right thumb on the biometric scanner. There was a momentary hum as the program scanned and verified his identity, and then it began decrypting the message.

Eleven thumbnail-sized pages appeared on the screen. He clicked on the first one. It was a copy of the police report: photographs, coroner's report... it was all here. Uday checked the date and time of the documents and discovered that they were only minutes old. He smiled at the thought that he probably had the information before the investigating detectives in America did. He also had names, addresses, phone records, locations: everything he needed to implement the plan. His spy was expensive, but every now and then, he proved to be worth every penny.

Uday picked up the phone and dialed. "It is confirmed," he said into the receiver. "The body found in New Jersey has the same identifying characteristics that we've been looking for. I have just forwarded the information to you. I want a man on this now, and I want a team of *Fedayeen* in place within twenty-four hours! Do you understand?"

He gave a few additional curt instructions to the man on the other end, and then hung up. Then he redialed. When he heard someone pick up the line, he immediately began his report, quickly summarizing the events of the past twenty-four hours, including the latest information from his spy in America. No questions were asked and only a few, short grunts came in response. To an untrained ear, the one-sided conversation would have given the impression of disinterest. But, after years of learning how to interpret his father's sounds, Uday knew otherwise. He knew how to read Saddam, and his father was very interested in the news, very interested indeed.

Uday remembered the day when it all began. It was 1990, and the world seemed to lie at his father's feet. When Saddam spoke the world listened, and much of it trembled as well. He was the new Suleiman, destined to unite the Middle East and Asia under the sword of Islam, or more correctly, under his own sword. Then the Dark Times came and swept it all away.

Uday flinched at the memory of the ceaseless bombing that hammered Baghdad's seemingly impenetrable defenses into dust.

For years following that disgraceful defeat, his father thought of little else besides revenge: revenge against the Great Satan, America, and against Bush; the Devil incarnate. Then the day came when the world witnessed a seemingly impossible event:

the daring attack on the World Trade Center in February 1993.

The success of Saddam's little investment had finally, and surprisingly, paid off. It was the first time anyone had succeeded in bringing the war directly to his enemy, on their own soil. And who were these conspirators, and how did they accomplish this great deed? They were nothing more than a band of ignorant, religious fanatics with no training, no command structure and virtually no resources. Nonetheless, they succeeded where others had failed, and it was this success that inspired Saddam to action.

When a foreign intermediary requesting financial support for this plan first approached him, he turned them away. But over time, as he became more assured that the attack could never be traced back to him, he relented. In the end, his thirst for revenge outweighed even his highly tuned instinct for survival. So, he finally agreed to sponsor it, and then watched in amazement as this ragged band of amateurs simply walked into the country, through America's wide-open doors, and its non-existent border security, right into the belly of the beast. Incredibly, they planned and implemented their attack, without detection, within sight of their target. These American idiots were so busy welcoming immigrants, and showing them off to the rest of the World as proof of their superior compassion, to even consider that some of them might actually present a mortal danger to their very existence. How these American bastards could have survived as long as they did was a complete mystery to him.

After that first success, there were no limits, Saddam explained to his sons. Using similar tactics, combined with the vast resources at his disposal, he would bring America to its knees. His next strike was scheduled to be executed just two months later, in Kuwait. Bush and most of his family, along with many of his White House co-conspirators, would be blown from the face of the earth. It would be an especially sweet vindication since the attack would come during the anniversary visit intended to mark their victory over him.

But just at the supreme moment of vengeance, something

went terribly wrong, and the entire plan had to be abandoned. Who had defeated it? He demanded to know.

First, Saddam turned his wrath on the incompetent cowards in Baghdad who had failed their Great Leader. Uday was happy to help his father with that assignment. However, it was that weakling American President, Clinton, who was his most effective, albeit unwitting, accomplice in this task. Clinton, in revenge for the failed assassination attempt on Bush, made targets of Saddam's security forces with his missiles. But all Clinton accomplished was to help Saddam with the work he had already planned. Saddam made sure that those who survived did not live long after the dust settled.

Then there were the Others. It would require months of patient investigation before he even detected a hint of their existence, and months more before he finally realized that it was this mysterious enemy that was directly responsible for thwarting his plan.

This organization was so secretive that even those they protected did not know they existed. He soon concluded that the only way to avoid a recurrence of his failure was to find these ghosts, whoever they were, and wipe them out. Initially they evaded every attempt. But Saddam never gave up once he had the scent of blood in his nostrils. And Saddam chose Uday, his oldest and most loyal son, to help satisfy this blood lust.

Uday smiled at the thought of his proposal, one of stealth and cunning, one he knew his father would approve of, as he ultimately did. They would fight fire with fire, allying themselves with the same type of people who had succeeded where Iraqi intelligence had failed - the ever-present community of religious fanatics, who had for centuries served the needs of those who wanted an enemy dead.

For nearly a thousand years, a ruthless tribe, known as the Assassins, terrorized both Christian and Muslim rulers. Any who refused to subscribe to their ascetic Islamic beliefs were subjected to a reign of mayhem and death. And, of course, they were always available as killers for hire, if the price was right.

Their original base of operations was an impregnable mountain fortress in what is now northwestern Iran. This once-extinct cult of highly trained killers was recently resurrected with a new name: Al Qaeda. They operated from a natural fortress of rugged mountains, valleys and caves, and used the identical tactics of terror.

With the long-awaited information from America now in his hands, Uday would unleash them, along with a few of his own highly trained killers, and finally destroy the mysterious Christian interlopers, once and for all. He would provide his team of killers with all the resources they needed for success and then let them take the war to the enemy. It was this strategy that had worked in New York before, and it would be the same one that he would use successfully again.

Uday's meek younger brother, Qusay, was unconvinced, however. He thought that this solution could be a cure worse than the disease. "How could we align ourselves with these eleventh-century madmen?" He asked. "They wanted to destroy Saddam as much as they wanted to destroy anyone." Saddam put Qusay's concerns at ease when he recounted the subterfuge of his great hero, Stalin. When the circumstances required a confrontation with the British and the Americans, Stalin allied himself with the Nazis. Then, just months later, he joined his former foes to defeat the Nazis, and he did so without hesitation. Saddam knew, as did Stalin, that there were no permanent allies and no permanent enemies. You used whom you needed to use, when you needed to use them. Or, as the great Arab saying succinctly explained, "The enemy of my enemy is my friend."

"When the mysterious Christian ghosts are gone, and the systematic destruction of America is at last underway," his father promised, "we will also destroy Al Qaeda, before they turn their wrath on us." Or more correctly, when the time came, he would let his old enemy, the Americans, do it for him. Saddam laughed at the thought of the punishment that the fanatics would receive from the wounded and flailing animal that America would soon become.

Now that great day had finally arrived; the beginning of a long, bloody war with the bastard Americans that would leave their so-called civilization in smoking ruins. But, first things first. Before they could begin the destruction of America, those who were protecting them must be reduced to ashes.

Uday hoped that Saddam was satisfied with his eldest son's brilliance, at least for the moment. He hung up the phone and logged off the computer. "Get my car," Uday barked at Adib as he opened the bedroom door. "I'll be done with this bird in ten minutes, and then you can clean up the mess."

Uday stopped suddenly, turned, looked directly into Adib's eyes and growled. "And the next time you want to look at my scar, you will be watching it from the *falaqa*."

Uday slammed the door in Adib's face. Adib closed his eyes as the image of the *falaqa* appeared in his mind. It was Uday's favorite punishment: a simple medieval torture device consisting of a rod with clamps that held the victim's ankles and feet in the air. The torturer would then beat the victim's bare soles with a stick. Adib remembered one occasion where he witnessed one of Uday's butlers receiving 160 *falaqa* for the sin of serving Uday's food on the wrong type of plate. The man never walked normally again. Adib erased the image from his mind, opened his eyes and reached for the phone.

As he picked up the receiver, the girl behind the door began to scream. Uday's driver picked up the phone on the other end as the screams became pealing shrieks of pain and horror. Adib yelled over the sound and into the phone. "Bring his car up, now." As Adib was placing the phone back in its cradle, the screaming behind the door stopped abruptly.

Chapter 20

By the time I woke up on Saturday morning, the previous night's storm had passed, and the sky over New York was pale blue and cloudless. A gusty wind blew from the northwest, trailing the path of the previous night's storm out to sea. But the pattern of streets and buildings made a direct northwest-to-southeast trek impossible, so the wind, just like any other New York pedestrian, was forced to navigate the grid.

I lay in my bed listening to its plaintive moan as it ran to the east, snaked around the northeast corner of my building, and then rattled my windows as it raced south over the wet pavement, passing by my apartment and then repeating the pattern at the next corner, and the next, until reaching the open space of the East River, then down to New York Harbor and finally out past the Verrazano-Narrows Bridge to the freedom of the open waters of the North Atlantic. New York is a tough town; not even the breeze gets a break.

By the afternoon the wind had abated somewhat and the sun had warmed things up sufficiently for me to open a window and let the fresh spring air into my small kitchen, which doubled as my home office. I was supposed to be working, but I guess the spell of spring had gotten the best of me, because all I was actually thinking about was Marcella. I just could not get her out of my head, and the thought of her was distracting me to the point of making me restlessly pace the floor. I kept replaying the conversation between us in the office the night before, over and over in my head.

There are times when a decision or action—one way or the other, embraced or rejected, spoken or silenced—changes your life for better or worse. Life is filled with these moments. At the time of their occurrence, they are so easy to miss. They seem no different from any other mundane moment and are often not recognized for what they are. Nevertheless, for whatever reason, I seem strangely attuned to them. I may be clueless about what the outcome may be, but I can usually see these moments pass right in front of me. One such moment came last night. It had arrived just before Marcella left the office, and it was gone the moment the door closed behind her. And I just sat there, like an idiot, and let her go. Now, I was wondering if I would ever get a second chance.

I walked over to my computer and pulled up the company's contact list. You would think that after months of working together, that I would have her home number in my head, or at least close at hand. But I could only remember calling her once at home, and that was due to a snow storm. It was pretty bad, at least by New York standards, so I decided to close the office. But in Marcella's case it turned out to be in vain because she left home early that morning and had trudged through the storm and was almost at the office by the time I called. Typical Marcella.

Anyway, I decided that I wasn't going to wait to see if I would get a second chance; I was going to make one. In so doing I guess I also decided that it was time to make my life, and hers, a little bit more complicated. I picked up the phone and, after a moment of hesitation, dialed.

"Hey, Marcella?"

"Tony, is that you?"

"Yeah it's me. Do you play softball?"

Silence.

"Marcella?"

"Softball?"

"Yeah, do you play?"

"Sure… why?"

"Well, it's supposed to be a nice day, and some of my family belongs to a league, and tomorrow's the first practice game." I blurted out in a single breath, which must have sounded a little bizarre. "It's pretty informal, just a friendly family game. I thought maybe you could meet me there."

There was silence on the other end for what seemed like an hour, so I was about to say something to let her off the hook, but just then she said, "I would really like that."

"You sure?"

"Yes, of course. Where and what time"

"Prospect Park. That's in Brooklyn. You know it?"

"I'll find it."

I gave her the rest of the details and said goodbye, followed by a hopeful, "See you tomorrow."

After my brief but satisfying conversation with Marcella, my focus had miraculously returned. The game was scheduled for 2:00 p.m., which gave me plenty of time to finish the modifications to the business plan. Unfortunately, I had to waste that miracle on the incredibly depressing results on the spreadsheet.

We would need to lay off thirty more people, which would leave only twenty-four. This was compared to the one hundred-ten people employed at our peak. I scanned through the names of the unfortunate for the fifth time. All of them, having escaped past cuts, were good people. Making any cut is painful, but making the third one is a bitch.

Anyone who's done this will tell you that it's one of the worst things they've ever had to do in their working life. Easy to say, I know, but it's true, especially in this case. After all, we were all founding brothers and sisters of this Internet Revolution that was supposed to change the world, changes that we were supposed to make together. But as everyone now knows, the fortress of economics is not so quick to fall to twenty-something revolutionaries. The wizard behind the curtain, as it turned out, was a fraud, the Land of Oz was a myth, and now we were back in Kansas, Dorothy. But I'm mixing metaphors. Again.

The point is, is that not only did I have to cut good people loose; I had to do it at the worst possible time for them. The same skills, which were so highly prized two years ago that they caused many companies, like mine, to get into salary bidding wars, were now virtually worthless. These same people, who had salaries that were once well into six figures, probably wouldn't be able to find any job at any salary. What a world, what a world.

A few days ago, I had lunch with an old friend. He was a recent addition to the growing list of displaced *Dot-Goners*, as they now euphemistically called themselves. At one point, we just sat there in utter amazement at the whole thing. The closest comparison we could think of was one of those amazingly wild college parties. You know the kind: where you're doing and saying things that are so outlandish that, should you remember saying them the next day, you'd wish you were dead. That is the only way to explain all of the screwed-up things that were said and done during the dot-com years; it was just a huge, out-of-control party. And I'll tell you something else. At every wild party there are always a few people who can't seem to get enough and hang out way too long. Everyone else goes home, the host goes to bed, and in the morning, when he wakes up, he finds this asshole with a lamp shade on his head, stripped to his underwear, and puking in the kitchen sink. The night before this guy was the life of the party. The next morning you're calling the cops to arrest the poor bastard for vandalism. It hadn't started yet, but it would soon enough. A lot of people were going to get really screwed, all with the help and approval of the other people who were also having the same great time at the same great party. The only difference is how long they stayed.

I finished the spreadsheet stuff, and my depressing reminiscing, the next morning. Then I left to meet Marcella for a softball game in Brooklyn. I had a really big smile on my face.

Chapter 21

Pat Clemens sat at his desk behind a copy of the *New York Times,* reading the business section and digesting the latest dot-com news. There was no end in sight for the collapsing Bubble economy that continued to take its toll, from Wall Street to Silicon Valley, including the huge losses being borne by his own firm, the Alley Group. He smiled to himself. At least it wasn't his money.

His secretary knocked on the open door and said, "I have someone on the phone who wants to speak to you."

"Who is it?"

"He wouldn't give his name, but he said it was urgent."

"Okay, I'll take it on line two. Please close the door on your way out."

He waited for the door to close, and then picked up the phone. "Clemens, the Alley Group."

The voice on the other end asked, "Is this a secure line?"

"Yes."

"Looks like they took the bait."

"And?"

"And, we missed them."

"We missed them? How is that possible?" Clemens asked, trying to keep his voice calm.

"They're good. We knew that."

Clemens hesitated before he asked the next question, because he was sure he already knew the answer. "Is she okay?"

Hesitation. Then the voice said, "I'm afraid not."

"Oh, fuck! What happened?"

"I don't have the time to cover this now, and it won't change anything anyway. The bottom line is that the people assigned to her screwed up, and she's dead."

"What about him?"

"We've doubled his detail. If they try again we'll be there."

"I've heard that before," Clemens replied. "Maybe it's time we take him into custody and shut this thing down."

"No. We've put too much into this to bail out now."

"Have you discussed this with Langley?" Pat Clemens asked.

"No, and we will not be having that conversation until this is resolved, one way or the other."

"I'm not sure they're going to be too happy about losing one, possibly two, to this operation. Are you?"

"It depends on the outcome, doesn't it? Besides, it's not like these are innocent bystanders. If you play with fire, you can get burned."

"Yeah, that's great, except we gave them the matches and the gasoline," Clemens said in disgust. "Make sure you don't screw up the next one, or we may not see them again for another seven years. Right around the time we get out of prison."

"I'll keep you informed."

Clemens heard a click. "Asshole," he said, hanging up.

Chapter 22

By the time I arrived at the softball field Marcella was surrounded by my aunts, uncles, and cousins, and they were examining her like she was some sort of circus animal. As I approached the action, I could hear the questions flying: "What's your name, sweetie?" "How long have you known Tony, honey?" "Where do you live, darling?" Blah, blah, blah. Through the barrage she smiled politely, nodded and answered quickly and succinctly. What a trouper.

While all this was happening my uncle Joe stood by, wearing a really evil-looking grin on his face that, no doubt, previewed the types of questions he wanted to ask. My other uncles, Mike, Frank and Larry, where warming up on the field, all business as usual, and probably wondering if the newbie could play ball.

I considered my uncles as I approached. Even now, through my adult eyes, they were impressive men. Uncle Frank, and Uncle Mike, like my Uncle Joe, are cops in New York City. Uncle Joe is uptown at the 19th precinct, Uncle Frank is Downtown at the First, near Wall Street, and Uncle Mike works in Brooklyn. Larry works right around the corner from Frank, but he's the black sheep of the family; a New York City fireman.

My memories of growing up around these guys are filled with an odd mix of awe and fear. They are all big men, but my Uncle Larry was the most awesome of them all: a huge, silent, cinder block of a man. I remember once as a kid, while I was playing with my cousins, at some party held at his house, and probably raising holy hell, my Aunt Anne, Uncle Larry's wife, tried to get us under control. It wasn't working, so she warned us that she was going to send in the grizzly bear if we didn't calm down. Apparently, we still hadn't complied, because I remember, not long after, the doorway being filled with this huge shadow. It was Uncle Larry, of course. I think he had to interrupt his card game, or something else important, because he was not very happy. So, in a deep, monotone voice, he explained to us that he was sent by Aunt Anne. He also informed us, in his not-so-subtle way, that male grizzly bears had the unfortunate habit of killing and eating noisy bear cubs.

Point made. Things stayed calm after that.

Don't get me wrong: I always felt loved and safe around my dad and uncles, but there was always that little sense of anxiety when these guys were around. It wasn't just me, either; all of my cousins had the same mix of emotions when it came to the Mascelle men; even my friends were mysteriously well behaved in the presence of these guys. They seemed safe enough... but why risk it?

Years later, I can recall overhearing a conversation between my mother and my Aunt Mary on the subject. They were talking about a mutual friend who was getting married to a man that neither of them liked very much, but they just couldn't quite put their finger on why. He was nice enough, he was good-looking, and he treated their friend very well. Then my mom commented that he was like a dog on a leash. She said that her friend liked her men that way. My Aunt Mary responded with a wry smile, saying, "Yeah, there are dog women, and there are cat women, and then there are women like us." When mom asked her what she meant she said, "We prefer large, barely trainable wildlife" *Lions and tigers and bears, oh, no.*

Her point, I guess, was that my uncles were trainable but not tame, dependable but not predictable. In short, they were a little dangerous, and my mother and my aunts wouldn't want them any other way.

Marcella peered through the crowed, caught sight of me, and gave me a tactical little wave. Immediately the entire tribe turned and began walking towards me, leaving Marcella standing alone, relieved and, apparently, amused. I made the rounds: kissing, hugging, shaking hands, and dodging most of the questions with silence or a shrug. My Aunt Nina shot a look in my direction indicating that she was not going to be dodged. I gave her a smile and said, "Hey, we just work together," which really didn't make her very happy, but I just left it there for the moment.

I started towards Marcella and the crowd parted like a stage curtain, all of them watching intensely as I approached her. I suddenly realized that greeting her with a handshake could turn them into an ugly mob. The look on Marcella's face indicated that she also appreciated the gravity of the moment, but she seemed to be really enjoying this situation for some odd reason. I walked up, smiled at her, and gave her a light peck on the cheek.

I could feel the pressure from the mob subside a little, and there was a half-hearted round of applause. But my Aunt Nina, who obviously thought less of the greeting than everyone else, gave me a Bronx cheer.

Marcella and I sat down on a blanket. The damp grass smelled good and felt good under my hands. She handed me a beer and a sandwich and said. "You're a little late."

"Sorry, did I miss anything interesting?"

"Oh, maybe."

I looked at her and she could see I was concerned. "Don't worry," she said, "I told them the wedding was postponed due to economic circumstances." Then she laughed: head back, mouth open—a really good laugh. Touché.

"That's very funny... really," I said.

We finished lunch and then proceeded to pick teams, and as one might have predicted, Marcella and I found ourselves on opposite sides. The game started and things were quiet for the first two innings, as the mostly middle-aged bodies warmed up and the supply of beer began to dwindle.

A word about beer may be in order here. My family is very serious about drinking beer, but they don't drink serious beer. If it's imported, fashionable, brown, or from some yuppie microbrewery, you're not likely to find it at a Mascelle family outing. We like the simple, straight suds, and that basically means Bud, Piels, and Schaeffer. Also, we have been known to drink rather large volumes of the stuff. At one time, I understand, there was a standing family provisioning rule that stated that the proper amount of beer for any family outing was equivalent to one case per man per day. This, of course, has changed due to contemporary sensibilities about weight, alcoholism, and of course DWI. Now it's more like three six-packs per man per day. It makes me proud to know that the family is growing, evolving to a higher plateau of social awareness.

Anyway, by the third inning I was feeling fine, relaxed, warm all over, and ready to show Marcella that I had the right stuff to father her children. I was up at bat and my Uncle Joe was pitching. He's a spotty pitcher on his best days, but he was really throwing some wild ones by this time.

It was a full count, but you could see his confidence in the way he was swilling his beer. So he throws a low, fast one and I connect with one of those satisfying, solid slams. Marcella, in the meantime, is watching from deep in left field, where she was deposited by Uncle Joe to keep her out of trouble and from under foot. And—you guessed it—the ball is heading for deep left field in a very high arc. So I start running for first, but all the time I'm watching the ball and Marcella, and she's just standing there, looking up at it. My uncle Joe is screaming, along with the rest of the family, for her to catch it, except for my Aunt Rose who, in stunned silence, is praying that she doesn't get creamed by it.

I'm taking this all in as I round first base. At that point I stopped to watch the ball arc down as Marcella starts to move backwards and to her left, her glove still motionless at her side as the ball flies right for her head. Suddenly everyone was very quiet, and we were probably all thinking the same thing: bing! A ball right between her eyes.

At the very last second, Marcella sweeps the glove up and gracefully makes the catch. A thundering round of applause replaced the hush that had gripped the field a moment ago. Marcella smiled at her audience, shrugged her shoulders and then burned one to Uncle Joe that made him wince in pain when it hit his glove.

That was it; it was out of my hands. There was no way the tribe was going to let her quit the family team. Either I was going to marry her or, failing threats and intimidation, they would arrange a marriage for her with one of my loser cousins. Uncle Larry, who probably made a crack about the low likelihood of Marcella making the catch, got a shot in the arm from Aunt Mary. Uncle Frank got excited and shot me a look of surprised satisfaction, even though he was on my team and my date just robbed me of a home run. Uncle Joe got another beer.

I was wondering what to expect when Marcella got up to bat, and I found out soon enough. Up until that point in the game, she seemed mysteriously anchored to the bottom of the lineup; but in the next inning, after a brief but intense team conference between Aunt Rose and Uncle Joe, she magically popped to the top of the batting order. As if to solidify her position as a superior member of the team, and to eliminate any doubt about our pending matrimony, Marcella whacked a line drive past Uncle Frank who, by the way, fed her a sweet pitch. I could swear that he was setting me up, because he practically stepped aside and let the ball pass him as it went in my direction. I picked it up on a bad bounce in center field — expertly I might add—and threw it to my cousin Steve, who was covering second base. Marcella beat the throw to second by sliding in on her butt. Then she got up and proceeded to dust off her fanny in my direction and, just for good measure, gave it a little wiggle as she smiled over her shoulder at me in a way that made my cheeks flush—and moved me in other ways as well. My cousin Steve put his arm around her shoulders and said something into her ear.

"Hey, second baseman," I yelled, "pay attention to the batter up." My cousin Steve and I have always been very close, more like brothers than cousins, so when he turned towards me I naturally gave him a look that conveyed his imminent death if he did not take his hands off my woman. Is testosterone great, or what?

It went on like this for the entire game—two games really: the one between the two softball teams that everyone was playing and the one between Marcella and me that everyone was watching. Marcella and I both demonstrated our prowess to each other on the field, and at bat. Maybe our kids would go pro. In the end, her team won 7–5. I think Uncle Frank sold us out.

Chapter 23

A lone pedestrian perused a travel guide as he walked through the busy streets of Brooklyn. He looked up occasionally to note a street sign or a building address, and then quickly returned his attention to the booklet.

To a local observer he would have appeared to be nothing more than a hapless tourist, or perhaps a visitor looking for a friend's home; that's assuming he was noticed at all. But on closer examination, his intense, deeply set brown eyes, and the scar that ran along his left jawline, might cause them to reassess their original assumptions about who and what this man was.

The *who* was Ahmed Shakir, and the *what* was subterfuge and assassination. He was, in fact, practicing part of his craft at this very moment. It was one of the first lessons his trainers taught him, and he was a very good student.

He stopped at a newspaper-dispensing machine, slipped a few coins into the slot and, as he removed the paper, casually glanced back in the direction from which he came, confirming that he was not being followed. If he discovered someone tailing him, he was fully prepared to practice one of his other skills. This one involved driving the tip of an ice pick, currently located in his jacket pocket, into the ear, and then the brain, of his curious victim.

He resumed walking with long and powerful steps: in a fluid, almost cat-like movement.

Despite his feigned ignorance of his surroundings, this was not his first visit to this neighborhood. As a senior officer in the special branch of the Iraqi military intelligence establishment known as Unit 999, he was often required to travel the streets of this infernal country. But this time his visit had special significance, and this fact made him uncharacteristically happy, so much so that he had to consciously stifle a reflexive grin.

He turned right at the corner, walked about two hundred feet and stopped. He looked across the street at what appeared to be an ordinary building, entirely at home in this rather ordinary Brooklyn neighborhood. The only details that set the five-story building apart from its neighbors was some ornamental trim on the higher stories and a sign over the door in Arabic. But Ahmed Shakir knew that this building was anything but ordinary.

The sign identified the building as the Jubail Mosque, but more relevantly, it was the de facto US headquarters of a front organization that concealed a poisoned, Islamic dagger aimed at the heart of the Great Satan itself. Now that dagger was being prepared for a strike that the infidels could not even begin to comprehend.

To Ahmed Shakir, and his brothers in arms, it was a holy shrine to their craft and mission and a spiritual home to some of the greatest leaders and agents of the Jihad. These were the warriors who succeeded in assassinating their enemies, and very nearly in destroying the infidel's idol to the thing they worshipped above all else, their god of money. But the men who Ahmed Shakir admired most of all were the brilliant double agents that for nearly twenty years, painted a masterpiece of deceit and destruction that undermined and defeated his two most hated opponents, the FBI and the CIA.

He again casually glanced in all directions, then crossed the street and entered the front door of the mosque. After walking a few paces into the building, he stopped and placed his right hand on the wall nearest to him and took a deep breath, as though he was trying to draw inspiration from the very substance of the place. He whispered, "We will finish what you started. This time, they will come down."

He resumed walking towards the back of the building and down the stairway to the basement, entering a long, narrow corridor. He walked through the door at the end. There were seven men in the room and they stood and saluted as he entered.

The last time he saw them they were dressed in black coveralls and were navigating the live-fire course, through a staccato of Kalashnikov rifles, at an installation discreetly located twenty miles southeast of Baghdad. The facility was part of the army base at Salman Pak and was the training ground for the ferociously loyal military organization known as the Saddam Fedayeen, which reported directly to Uday Hussein.

Ahmed Shakir studied the seven men. Their faces were young and hungry, and their bodies were lean and ready for combat. Four of them were the cream of the crop, recruited to work for Unit 999 for deep penetration operations like this one. The remaining three came from another training facility, one located in the mountains of Afghanistan. They were not Fedayeen, not even Iraqis, but according to his sources, they were also the best that their particular organization had to offer. Moreover, based on their performance to date, including what he had witnessed them do to a certain American Colonel named Henkel, he was satisfied that this assessment was accurate.

Ahmed noticed with satisfaction that all of the men were now dressed in a different uniform. Someone had done a masterful job of clothing them in the proper American garb: blue jeans, polo shirts and jogging shoes. Their facial hair was gone and their haircuts were exceptionally ordinary. He also noticed the bulging black duffel bag beside each man's seat containing their black coveralls, along with the rest of the equipment that they would be using very soon.

Ahmed Shakir made a motion with his hand and the men immediately returned to their seats. "Today," he said, "marks the beginning of the new Islamic empire and the end of the Christian world. As you all know, we've been escalating our covert operations against the Great Satan since our fearless Mujahedin leader, Saddam Hussein, launched our campaign of vengeance against those who have defiled our holy Islamic lands. With the help and alliance of our Muslim brothers from Sudan, Yemen, Afghanistan, Egypt, Saudi Arabia, Chechnya and Iran, all of whom you've trained with at Salman Pak, we will strike a mortal blow to the heart of this empire of infidels."

Ahmed Shakir began to slowly pace before his attentive audience. "During the first eight centuries, after the great prophet Mohammad gave us the true word of Allah, blessings be unto him, Islam defeated every enemy in its path. Our armies enjoyed victory after victory throughout Arabia, North Africa, Palestine, and Turkey. These regions, which are now synonymous with Islam, were all once the lands of the infidel Christians and Jews. Islam conquered them all. We turned their churches and synagogues into our mosques. We made the surviving Christians and Jews into believers or slaves. And when the Christian Crusaders attempted to retake our newly acquired territories, they were defeated and turned back. Our armies brought the holy words of the Qur'an and the holy sword of Islam to every corner of the world and every infidel kingdom. Then, we had only one single enemy territory left to conquer: Europe. And there our victorious armies continued their Fatah in the heart of the infidel's last remaining refuges. We were on the verge of wiping out the Christians everywhere and forever."

Ahmed Shakir stopped, took a deep breath and then continued. "And then darkness began to fall on our Empire. It began with our first defeat on the island of Sicily, at the hands of the bastard Normans. Then, after hundreds of years of ceaseless conflict, there was another defining battle on the Island of Malta, just fifty miles from the first ones. Between those two battles there were countless others, large and small, throughout the empire. But the battle of Malta marked the beginning of the end for our dream of a global caliphate. And our defeat on Malta came at the hands of one descended from those same Norman bastards. Now, more than four-hundred years later, the dream of our global Islamist Empire lives again, and the Holy Qur'an and the Holy Sword of Islam are on the march once more."

Ahmed Shakir turned and smiled as he looked at the eager faces before him. "Now, as then, we are confronted by this same intractable enemy. Their seed threatens our ultimate victory once again, on a new island, in a new world. But this time, we have the advantage. This time it will be Islam that will succeed in conquering the island. We will move against them from the sky, the sea, and the land. Your victories will mark the first of many to come. You are the edge of that great sword, the elite, handpicked and trained for this mission to prepare the field of battle for the Islamic armies to come. You represent the beginning of the end for the Christian world and their masters, the Jews."

Ahmed Shakir raised his arms over his head and shouted, "Allahu Akbar!" The seven men came to their feet, raised their hands, and they all repeated the words in a loud, zealous chant.

Chapter 24

There was no denying it, the day was perfect. At the end of the softball game, Marcella and I sat on the blanket and watched as the family said their goodbyes. My Aunt Anne made a point of coming over to us before she left to deliver the family verdict.

She gave Marcella a kiss on the head. "Nice to see that my nephew has some brains", she said to Marcella as she gave me a cold stare. *Jeez, what did I do to deserve that*?

I made a face at my aunt and mimicked her comment back to her, which got me a slap on the head.

She continued, "If this bum gives you any trouble, sweetie, you just let me know."

Marcella laughed and said, "Okay, Aunt Anne."

Oh great, the sweetie and the bum. I wondered who was on whose side. "So much for blood loyalty," I commented.

Aunt Anne smiled and gently grabbed my cheek between her thumb and finger and shook it the way she used to when I was young. "Don't get on my bad side, mister, or the only blood we'll be talking about will be yours." Then she kissed me on the head and walked away.

For some reason Marcella thought that this exchange with my aunt was very amusing.

I shrugged. "So, I guess they like you better than me," I commented.

"You think so?"

I nodded and smiled. "Can't say I blame them."

She kissed me on the cheek.

"So, now what?" I asked.

"Now what... what?"

"Now what-what? What-what, do you think?"

She started laughing again. "Oh, that what".

I thought about that for a moment and said, "Are we talking about the same what, here?"

"I don't know; what-what are you talking about?" Her cheeks flushed.

I tried to get serious. "You know what-what — oh, shit! Can we stop talking in code?"

She covered her face with her hands. I reached over, moved her hands away, and looked into that beautiful face, the same one that had greeted me from my sleep on so many mornings when all I had of her were fantasies. Now here she was, not as an employee, and not for business, but here for me, and for real. I have to admit it was all a little confusing, a little sudden and very unnerving. Nevertheless, here we were.

She moved her face toward mine until it was so close I could feel her breath on my lips. "We had a good day today, didn't we, Mr. Mascelle?"

"Yes we did Ms. Pavone, a very good day."

She kissed me gently on the lips. Then she stood up and reached down for my hand. I got up and she put her arm around my back, I put mine around her, and we started walking.

The fact that she hadn't answered my question wasn't lost on me. So, while I was thinking about how to rephrase it, I thought I should try to first figure out what I was trying to ask her. Actually, I was asking multiple questions without actually committing to anything. I was asking her to have dinner with me, to be with me, and yes, to sleep with me... all at the same time, but without really asking anything. As I said, all of this had me rattled. To make things more complicated, she probably knew all of this before I did, and in her way she was having a little fun at my expense. But I think she was also giving me a chance to get off the hook, if I wanted to get off, but I didn't. Not this time. A cool breeze began to blow, she shivered, and I held her closer.

She said, "how about if we get some dinner, then go home and think about this a little?"

"Your place or mine?"

"Your place for you, and my place for me," she replied.

I said, "I know that this may not the best time to start a relationship, and that it's probably going to be a little complicated."

She stopped walking, turned, and looked at me, but seemed to be focused on a spot behind my head. The smile left her face. "Yes, it will be complicated," she said.

I waited until she looked back into my eyes, and when she did her smiled returned. I kissed her this time and said, "Hey, we'll figure it out as we go."

"Sounds like a plan." She said returning the kiss.

When we got to the parking lot I asked her. "Where did you park?"

"I took the subway from SoHo."

"I have an idea. I drove here, so how about if we find someplace around here for dinner, and then I'll drive you back home?"

She nodded and asked, "What are you hungry for?"

I looked at her and smiled.

She punched me in the arm. "Pig. I mean what kind of food?"

"Oh. How about Italian?"

"Me too."

We found my gray Taurus in the empty parking lot and drove to a nondescript local Italian restaurant and pizzeria. I ordered the lasagna and she ordered the house salad.

A lady friend of mine once told me that women who order salad on their first date want to project the image of slender good health. I found this revelation odd. I always thought that women were too smart to think that guys were that stupid. In any event, since I'd known Marcella for over six months, I figured we should be past that point in our relationship, so I just assumed that she really just wanted the salad. On the other hand, if she ordered the 64-ounce T-bone with the baked potato and the all-you-can-eat salad bar on our next date, I'd have to reassess some of my assumptions about women.

The conversation over dinner was light and one-sided, mostly covering topics about me and my family. I tried, without much success, to prod Marcella into telling me more about her and her family, but when I did, the conversation kept falling into awkward silences.

After dinner, we drove back to Manhattan.

"How was the lasagna?" Marcella asked.

"Huh?"

"Your dinner?"

"Oh, it was okay, but not as good as Grandma's. How was your salad?"

"Not bad. I'm usually not much of a salad eater, but I wasn't in the mood for a big meal. But don't worry, I'll make up for it next time. I can eat like a pig."

Good reply. I think. I turned north onto Flatbush Avenue. I said, "Next time we'll make a stop in Little Italy. I know a place that serves you family style. They keep feeding you until you fall off your chair and beg for mercy."

"That would be nice. I've never been there."

"You live in SoHo and you haven't been to Little Italy?"

"Hey, what can I say? I'm new in town and my boss is a slave driver."

"What a jerk he must be."

She laughed, maybe a little too hard, I thought.

Up until that point in the conversation we both avoided the subject of work, but then she asked me, "Who is Howie?"

The question confused me at first, but then I remembered.

"Oh, you mean this morning?"

"Yes."

I thought for a moment, then said, "To tell you the truth, I'm not sure."

Just then, something caught my eye in the rearview mirror, but when I looked again, it was gone.

"Everything okay?" Marcella asked.

"Yeah."

I returned my eyes back to the road in front of me and Marcella returned to the conversation.

"You're not sure who he is?"

"Oh, yes, he was a college roommate."

"So you were friends, then."

"Not really, and I haven't seen him for years, haven't even thought about him."

"That seems strange."

I smiled. "Yes, it does. In fact, very strange."

I stopped talking again. This time I could see it; on the roof of a car behind me. I could make out the characteristic shape of a police cruiser's flashers. He was matching my speed as other vehicles cautiously passed in the other lane. I glanced at my speedometer.

Marcella looked back and spotted it also. "Are you speeding?"

"Not even close."

"He seems interested in you."

"Yeah."

"A relative?" She asked.

"I doubt it. I would be holding a summons by now."

We both laughed uncomfortably.

Marcella lifted her handbag from her lap and placed it on the floor between her legs.

"Do you have something in that bag I should know about?"

"No, just putting it where I can find it. Just in case he stops us and I need my ID."

Suddenly the cruiser picked up speed and seemed to be bearing down. He was coming on so fast that, for a moment, I thought he was going to rear-end us. I put my arm out in front of Marcella and braced myself anticipating a collision, but at the last possible moment, he veered into the other lane and passed us. As he flashed by I could see was looking at us, but I couldn't make out his face.

"Jesus-Christ. What the hell was that about?" I said.

I looked over at Marcella; her shoulders were tense and she was fidgeting with her hair, curling it into a loop around her right index finger again. "You okay?"

"I'm fine. Continue."

"Continue with what?"

"With what you were talking about? You said something was very strange." She commented, as if the near collision with the police cruiser was of no interest to her. It took me a moment to refocus my thoughts.

"Oh, that. It was something that happened later that same day, that night, actually. I ran into this other guy. I knew him from college too, and I also hadn't seen him since around last time I saw Howie. About eight years ago. Talk about strange."

"Coincidence?"

"Probably." I lied.

"You look worried, Tony. Was this other guy a friend?"

"I actually don't know what he was. I'm not even sure I know what his real name is. We called him Crazy Nunzio, but it was a name we made up for him. He never told us his real name."

Marcella ran her fingers through her hair and seemed uncomfortable again.

"What?" I asked.

"Nothing." She smiled.

"Well, anyway", I continued, "It doesn't matter. I probably won't see Crazy Nunzio or Howie again for another eight years."

She shrugged. "Probably not."

I thought I should lighten things up a little so I turned to Marcella and asked. "So what did he whisper in your ear?"

"What? Who?"

"You know who. My cousin Steve, when you were on second base."

"Why? Are you jealous?"

"Of him? Are you kidding? I was just wondering."

"He said you were a very good guy."

"Oh bull! You're just saying that to make me feel guilty about being jealous."

She rested her head on my shoulder and said, "See? I knew you were jealous."

Marcella wrapped her arm around mine and we drove on in silence for a while. At some point, she must have dozed off, because I noticed the rhythm of her breathing had changed, and I felt an occasional muscle twitch. Considering the circumstances, a nap seemed justifiable, I guess.

First-time meetings with my family, and a long day of softball, will do that. Also, being naturally optimistic, and a little horny, I hoped that her resting might also be a precursor to a long night of some other sporting activities. On the other hand, maybe I just bored her to sleep. I'll find out soon enough.

I turned onto the Manhattan Bridge entrance and drove west over the East River. The skyline of Manhattan was beautifully lit up and, as usual, the Twin Towers dominated the scene with the sheer power of their enormous and seemingly immovable mass. I considered waking up Marcella so she could enjoy the view with me, but she seemed too content to disturb. Besides, I really liked the way she felt on my shoulder and the smell of her hair.

I started thinking about the Howie dream again, and began wondering about his strange family baggage. Stuff that was deposited so long ago that he had no idea who those people from the *Mayflower* even were. They were gone, even their names were lost in time, but the baggage remained; causing poor Howie extremely early, anxiety laden, wake-up calls - every morning.

I didn't know it yet, but I was in for a wake-up call by some family baggage myself. Like Howie's, mine was also about life and death, and some of that baggage had just passed by a few moments ago inside a speeding police cruiser. It was also sitting in the car seat next to me, sleeping like an angel on my shoulder.

Actually, now that I think about it, it turns out that my baggage was mostly about death.

Chapter 25

Ibrahim al-Kondoz was waiting at the corner of Flatbush Avenue, and slid the gearshift into drive just as their car passed. He was expecting the female to be alone. His orders were simple: execute the woman on sight. But that would have to wait now, because he was also given strict instructions not to harm the American who was now driving the car. There were other plans for him. Only later would the American die, and Ibrahim would be there to carry out that order as well.

No, tonight would be just another boring night of surveillance. So many nights like this had past, and still he had not drawn first blood. Fortunately, he had long ago developed the patience appropriate for a man in his trade. Ibrahim al-Kondoz was a Sayyad; a word in Arabic that contained multiple meanings: a skillful searcher, a tracker, a hunter of knowledge and a hunter of men; or in this case, a woman. He had traveled so far and waited so long. Now, he would have to be patient a little while longer.

His journey started with a series of trials that would lead up to this very moment. His first trial was by fire—literally. He was just a teenage boy then, made to endure weeks of weapons training and live-fire drills on a special operations base. It was famous for producing only two products; highly motivated and disciplined graduates prepared for the next steps in their training, and failures who were dead.

The whizzing sound of the bullets terrified many of the other boys. He remembered being surprised to discover this. Often they would freeze like stone statues in the middle of the course; some even wet themselves. If they remained so, the bullets eventually found them. As with all of the program's failures, an unmarked grave in the desert was their reward for being a coward. No one would ever find their bodies, even if there were someone who cared enough to search for them. The remote, featureless terrain guaranteed that these dead would remain lost and forgotten, forever.

Ibrahim, for his part, had reacted to the gunfire very differently. Yes, his heart would race, like theirs, and he would sweat like an animal, like them. But it was excitement, not fear, that filled his heart. Sometimes the sound of the bullets, the ones that came very close to his head, would even make him laugh.

There were times when he missed that excitement and that place in the desert that was once his home. He was never sure of its exact location. He spent most of the first day blindfolded as he was shuttled from a ground vehicle to an aircraft and back again. When he was at last relieved of his temporary blindness he found himself surrounded by the other boys, none of whom he had ever met before. Even though they were strangers to him, they were all somehow familiar. They all possessed that same hungry look in their eyes, and despite the warm greetings and smiles during their introductions, he would soon discover that they also all possessed the same intense hatred, one with a singular focus: to make the infidels pay with their screams, their tears, and most of all, their blood.

When he completed his training in the desert, he assumed he had received all of the training that he required. Nevertheless, his commander told him that more would come, and it did. For four years, he learned everything from penetrating foreign intelligence services, to building explosives with household materials. But he never expected that his American enemies would provide his final training. What could the Americans possible teach him that he had not already learned? Certainly, nothing that was important to his mission. Again, he was wrong.

What he learned from the Americans was, in many ways, more important than what he had learned during all of the previous years of his training. Because the Americans taught him how to be one of them, to think like one of them, and most importantly, how to access the vast quantities of information that was never more than a few keystrokes, or mouse-clicks, away. The thought of that irony brought a smile to his face.

Soon after arriving in America, he dissolved into his new

identity, becoming as inconspicuous as his new father and mother. His new parents were complete strangers to him, of course. Before he arrived in America, he learned to speak and read the infidel's language and then, after three years of public school in America, and four years of college, only the slightest accent remained.

As for his new parents, the very first sight of him frightened them. It was an appropriate reaction under the circumstances, but they could hardly imagine how appropriate.

They were from the Pashtun region on the border between Afghanistan and Pakistan, just like his real parents. They even shared some of his memories of the place. Their dialect and customs were also the same, and if he permitted himself the luxury, he could sometimes see his parents' faces in theirs: not surprising, considering that he had not set eyes on his real parents' faces since he was a child of just ten years of age. His fake parents came to America as refugees at around the same time his real ones were being murdered in Afghanistan. A part of him was saddened by the thought that these happy, living versions of his parents, would end up meeting a similarly violent end. It was even more troubling that their deaths would have to come by his own hands. But his teacher at the madrassa told him that the real cause of their deaths would be the infidels. His teacher also explained that this man and woman would die martyrs for the glory of Allah and live together in paradise for all eternity. When the day finally came, seven years later, he did everything he could to make it as painless as possible.

The last time he saw his real parents, along with his two brothers and his sister, they lay in neat rows among the dead of his village. His entire life, as he once knew it, was erased in a few hours of unrelenting horror.

The merciless Russians, in their massive helicopter gunships, killed everything that moved. He could still hear the sound of the rotors mixed with the screams of his people. Then there were the tanks and their steel treads, dripping with the blood and flesh of his neighbors. His young mind could not comprehend how a human being could slaughter people so mercilessly. But he understood now. Eventually his fear and sadness turned to rage, and he longed to seek revenge on the Russians. Not long after, the Russians were defeated and left his country in disgrace. This made him sad, and even more angry. By leaving, the evil cowards had denied him his right of vengeance.

Then the Americans came. He had once been told that the Americans, who hated the Russians as much as he did, helped his people to defeat them. He was told that they were his people's friends. However, as his teacher would later explain, this was a lie. The Russians and the Americans were one and the same enemy, and he told Ibrahim that he should visit his revenge on one just as he would on the other. His teacher was a wise man.

His real parents' faces, their voices, and the feel of their touch had almost entirely faded by now. Today they seemed like fragments from another life, or even someone else's memories. But one thing had not dimmed, and it never would: his thirst for vengeance against the ones who took them from him. Russian or American, it did not matter. He would never forget, never rest, until that day came. Now, it was so very near.

These thoughts made his heart beat faster, and he felt his hands tighten on the steering wheel. He consciously loosened his grip and glanced down at his uniform, reflexively brushing the NYPD badge with his right hand. He enjoyed his time at the police academy; almost as much as his stay in the desert. He knew that, someday, he would miss being a police officer in New York. This false life of his was destined to be left behind, one way or the other.

He returned his mind to the present and his attention to his prey. He pressed the accelerator of the police cruiser in order to close the gap, and then he began wondering if he could resist the temptation to draw blood tonight. His foot pressed down harder, as if it had a mind of its own.

Chapter 26

"A little cold tonight, for April." The man said as he reached down and took a copy of the *New York Times* from a stack on the sidewalk.

He looked over the rim of his sunglasses and scanned the headlines. Then, half annoyed, half amused, he responded to the silent stare from the newsstand proprietor by reaching into his pocket and throwing a crumpled dollar bill on the counter.

There was no news about the incident yet, at least not in this edition. He made a mental note to check the late night television reports, and then glanced impatiently at his watch. It was after nine, and they should be here by now.

He walked a few feet, and entering the shadows of a nearby building, lifted the newspaper close to his face. A gentle touch of his index finger on the bridge of his sunglasses brought a three-dimensional image to life, which filled his visual field and seemed to float over the surface of the newspaper.

It occurred to him that the sight of a man reading a newspaper, at night and on a dark street, might attract unwanted attention, especially since he was wearing sunglasses. He made another mental note to tell the geniuses back at the lab that they needed to get out into the real world more often.

A few moments after his eyes began scanning the image he found what he was looking for. A small blinking light was converging on his position. *Almost here.* With a second press, the image disappeared.

He crossed Mulberry Street, walked in the direction of the old Saint Patrick's Cathedral and caught sight of the gray sedan driving down the street towards him. He again touched his index finger to his eyeglasses, this time to the top right side of the frame, and engaged the zoom-locking feature, just as the Ford Taurus passed by. The system's software identified and locked onto the car's license plate, highlighting it within a small illuminated frame. Then the numbers on the plate seemed to magically zoom in and come into sharp focus. He smiled. *Impressive*!

The car stopped at the front of a brick building about a block away, and a young man and woman exited the car. They walked towards the entrance, stopped in the middle of the sidewalk and faced each other. He noticed with some surprise that they were standing very close, their bodies touching. They spoke for a few moments and then, to his additional surprise, they wrapped their arms around each other and kissed. It was a very long kiss. Then the women said something, turned, and walked into the building. Her man friend, now smiling broadly, returned to his car and drove away.

A few moments later, the women reemerged from the building and walked down the street towards his position near the cathedral. He ducked further into the shadows of the doorway located at the front of the church. As he waited for her to approach, he noticed something in her walk that he hadn't before. Her steps were lighter somehow, and as she got closer, he could see a smile on her face. But he was not wondering about what was making her so happy. He was thinking about how to stop it. He moved towards her suddenly.

The sound startled her, but she quickly regained her composure as she watched his approach. "Do you always have to sneak up on me like that?" she complained.

He smiled and wagged his bushy eyebrows over the sunglasses, which he then gracefully removed. "Good evening, Marcella. My, my, we're out awfully late tonight, aren't we?"

She ignored his comment, reached out, and took the sunglasses from his hand. She examined them for a moment, placed them on her own face, and then pressed the bridge of the frame. "Interesting. When did you get these?"

"They issued them a few days ago. Takes a little while to get used to, they make me dizzy sometimes." He smiled. "But they might be better than the handheld units: more discreet. Maybe."

Marcella removed the sunglasses and handed them back to him. "I don't think so; you look weird walking around with sunglasses in the middle of the night."

"I think Tony thought so too."

Marcella looked at him in silence, then said, "You mean in the bar on Friday night, Crazy Nunzio?"

He smiled and said, "He looked like he recognized me, so I said hello."

"How could you be so careless?"

"It doesn't matter. He just knows me as a strange friend from his college days. In fact, he barely remembered me, and I did the whole Nunzio act too, but it still took him a while to remember."

"What were you thinking?"

"Actually, I was a little hurt when he didn't remember me," he said, feigning a pout.

Marcella looked at him closely. "I think you need a vacation, Mario. Either that, or you're losing your mind?"

"Maybe both. Look, you know where this is going." He reminded her. "In a little while it's not going to matter if he knows who we are, or not."

"What does that mean?"

"You know what it means. And speaking of carelessness, what was all that kissing and hugging about?"

"What are you talking about? You know it's part of my cover," Marcella replied curtly.

"Wow. That was some very impressive acting."

She brushed off the comment and changed the subject. "So what do you have for me?"

Mario took a deep breath and then said, "You look like you could use something to read." He pointed with his chin at the newspaper stand across the street. He smiled at Marcella's puzzled look and said, "Come, there is someone I want you to meet."

They crossed the street to the newsstand and Mario picked up a sports magazine from one of the racks.

The man in the booth gave Mario a stern look and said, "Finished reading the paper already?"

Mario said to Marcella. "This wise guy is Gunter. Say hello, Gunter."

Gunter's frown turned immediately to a broad grin. "Hello, Marcella."

He was tall and very powerfully built. She studied his sharply dimpled chin, blond hair, and blue eyes.

"It's very nice to meet you at last," he said.

"Same here."

Marcella processed his accent, which was German-sounding. Then she said, "You must be the new guy from Castelrotto that I've been hearing about."

Gunter offered a polite correction. "You mean Kastelruth?"

Marcella recalled the details of his dossier. He was twenty-five and a former resident of Castelrotto, or Kastelruth, as the German-speaking residents called it, a town in Trentino-Alto Adige, a northern Alpine region that was annexed by Italy following World War I. Formerly a part of Austria, its residents were still mostly German-speaking and maintained their Austrian traditions. His Italian and German were supposed to be perfect, and his English, Spanish, and French were not bad either. Coupled with his excellent physical abilities, he would make a very formidable addition to the team, assuming he could learn to manage some of his other natural gifts. His dossier had particularly focused on his tendency towards highly aggressive tactics. He would have to learn to control that.

Marcella smiled and shrugged. "Right, Kastelruth."

Gunter asked, "So, you've heard about me?"

"Yes, of course. Is it true that you know how to yodel?" Marcella inquired with genuine interest.

Mario rolled his eyes. "Okay, that's enough. You two can discuss yodeling another time, maybe over a nice dish of wurst and sauerkraut. Gunter, I would like you to update us on the latest intelligence."

Gunter replied, "We're still working on it. What we know now is that the gentleman on Friday morning, the one across the street from the office, was a trained mercenary, very different from that first amateur in New Jersey a few days ago."

"It doesn't make sense," Marcella said. "They were supposed to make it look like an accident. Shooting him with a high-powered rifle just doesn't fit."

Gunter agreed. "Yes, that much is obvious. Perhaps they have something else motivating them now. Maybe they think that he's on to them, and are now more concerned now about covering their tracks."

"Possible, but not likely." Mario said.

"If not," Gunter replied, "there are only two other possibilities. Either someone else wants him dead, or the target was someone else in the room. Both of those seem even less probable than the first."

Marcella turned to Mario. "So, now what?"

"I'm leaving town for a day or two," Mario said. "I want you eyes-on Tony, twenty-four-seven. Gunter will fill in for me as your backup while I'm gone."

Marcella's eye's widened. "Excuse us, Gunter," Marcella said abruptly.

Marcella led Mario away from the newsstand and out of earshot of Gunter. She said, "This is definitely not a good time for you to leave, especially since Gunter doesn't have much in the way of field experience."

Mario shrugged. "I know that, and they know that, but I was ordered to go anyway."

Marcella asked. "And what happens if...?"

"Don't ask questions when you already have the answers for them." Mario advised her.

Marcella didn't reply; she looked away.

Mario said, "I need you to tell me that what I just saw between you and him was just acting, on your part."

"Don't worry, Nun-zio,"she said, accenting the syllables of the name mockingly. "When the time comes, it won't affect me. If anything, my reaction time and my aim will be even better than usual. You know I'm ready for this assignment. If there was any doubt in your mind, the job I did Friday morning should have put it to rest."

He continued looking at her, but she refused to make eye contact. "You know the rules, Marcella, and you know why we're here."

"Yes, I know. Are we finished?"

He nodded. She turned abruptly and started walking back to the apartment building. He watched her until she disappeared into the entrance.

"Part of your cover, my ass," Mario said to himself.

He turned towards Gunter, waved goodbye and started to walk towards the corner. Suddenly an instinct tugged at his sleeve. He slowed his walk, almost stopping, and glanced into the darkness behind him. Nothing. He shrugged off the feeling and resumed walking. He was overreacting, he decided. Things had been so quiet for so long. It took time to get one's internal radar recalibrated. This was a good thing, he thought. Quiet assignments are not only boring, but they could also be dangerously so. His instincts needed exercise, just like his body and mind. Now, however, boredom was not the problem, over-stimulation was. He needed to center himself and not allow his instincts to take things too far in the other direction. He also needed to remember his training. Mario knew he would need it in the days and weeks ahead.

A block away, there was a police cruiser, carefully tucked into the shadows between two old brick buildings. The occupant watched Mario walked to the corner, hail a cab, and get in.

Chapter 27

I had all of Sunday night to think about Marcella, the softball game, dinner, the drive home, and our goodnight kiss—especially the kiss. I must have been grinning like an idiot all the way home. But, by Monday morning it all seemed like a distant memory. I had to focus on the business at hand: specifically, saving my company from extinction. It would require all of my attention if I was going to succeed.

The morning was clear and felt surprisingly warm for this time of year, so I decided to forgo the cab ride and walk. As I approached the entrance of my office building, I noticed a large, black, nondescript sedan parked out in front. At first, I thought it might be from our car service, but as I got closer, I could tell by the dirty windows and scuffed bumpers that it wasn't a limo. A blue dome light perched on the dashboard confirmed this impression.

I took the stairs, three at a time, and opened the door to the office, anticipating seeing Marcella at her usual position behind her desk, but she was missing. I noticed that the conference room door down the hall was open and I walked closer until I heard her voice, and then others I did not recognize.

"Good morning", I said to Marcella as I examined the two men standing at the other end of the room, both of whom were looking out of the window.

"Good morning, Tony," she said in a low voice as she cautiously rolled her eyes towards the strangers and shrugged her shoulders.

The two gentlemen turned towards me simultaneously. Their eyes made a quick scan from my head to my shoes before their mouths assumed official smiles. The one to my right said in a deep, monotone voice, "Good morning Mr. Mascelle." He appeared the senior of the two by at least twenty years.

"Good morning. Can I help you, gentlemen?"

The younger of the two responded first. "My name is Detective Sean McKeown. I'm with NYPD homicide, and this is Federal Agent Paul Barella."

I felt my right eyebrow rise involuntarily. *Federal agent*?

Detective McKeown had a large, round face, round green eyes, and a belly to match both. He stood straight, shoulders back, which had the effect of making his belly press forward against a single, courageous button that held his navy blue polyester sports jacket closed. He was about my height—six feet, plus or minus—and in his early-to-mid forties. Despite his ominous title, Detective McKeown seemed like your average NYPD Irish cop that I had seen at many family gatherings during my entire life. The prominent gut was no doubt the product of many determined years of consuming large quantities of basic beer with his fellow NYPD cops, people just like my uncles. His presence seemed no more intimidating or alien than that.

Agent Barella, the Fed guy, was another matter, however. I examined him as he examined me. His wrinkled, sagging jowls seemed to maintain their position as he rotated his head, giving him the almost comic appearance of an old bloodhound taking on a new scent in preparation for yet another hunt. Curved pedestals of puffy flesh underlined his brown eyes. But, despite his apparent age and his loose, fleshy face, his body appeared to be lean and hard. He was dressed in what could only have been a custom-made suit, charcoal gray, which fit perfectly to the remnants of a body that once, no doubt, impressed both friend and foe alike, to say nothing of the ladies. There was something else about him though, something even more unnerving. I think it was the look in his eye, a sort of familiar twinkle that seemed to say, 'Hello, Mr. Mascelle, good to meet you again.' Did I say bloodhound? Maybe wolf would be a more apt description.

"Mr. Mascelle?"

I turned towards McKeown, who I suddenly noticed was speaking. “We’re investigating a homicide that occurred Friday morning, across the street in a vacant office, in that building, there,” he gestured with his thumb.

I asked, “Which office?” As if I didn’t already know.

The detective turned and pointed towards the window I was watching Friday, when I saw the flash and then someone, perhaps a woman, close it. “That one, the one directly across the street from this room,” McKeown informed me.

I looked out towards the window across the street. “I see. And you were wondering if we saw anything?”

Agent Barella looked directly into my eyes. He moved closer, no more than two feet away, and replied, “Yes.”

“Yes, Mr. Mascelle,” Detective McKeown repeated, glancing sideways at his strange partner. “We were wondering if you saw anything unusual yesterday morning between, say, eight and nine-thirty.”

I cleared my throat. “You guys can call me Tony. And no, nothing unusual, not really.”

“Not really?” Agent Barella said again, still staring at me.

“No.” I stared back at him. This guy was really starting to grate on me. “We were in a very intense meeting and weren’t paying attention to anything outside of this room. We saw the police cars and, later, the coroner's van, I think, show up after the meeting, around ten-thirty or eleven.”

“Intense?” Agent Barella asked.

I was immediately sorry I used that word. “Well, let’s just say that we were totally involved with the matters at hand... in this room, that is. So we weren’t paying any attention to what was going on across the street.” *Or anywhere else, for that matter.*

"Who else was at the meeting?" McKeown asked.

I told him who was there and who wasn't and gave him a brief description of the subjects discussed.

"And where can we find Mr. Orr and Ms. Toomey?" McKeown inquired.

I looked towards Marcella.

"I haven't seen either of them this morning yet," she informed us.

"I guess they haven't come in yet," I said as I continued to look at Marcella, avoiding looking back at McKeown. I didn't want him or Barella to see the surprise in my eyes. Barella noticed anyway.

"Strange?" Agent Barella commented.

Can't you form complete sentences of more than two words, you homely bastard? "Yes, it is a little unusual," I replied.

Kyle left early on Friday and I hadn't seen Jan since Thursday, and now they were both missing again on Monday morning. This was actually very weird behavior for both of them. It was especially bizarre when we had everything riding on completing the new business plan and reviewing the legal documents for the new financing.

I turned and looked towards Detective McKeown. "They might have run into a problem commuting in this morning. Everything is flooded after that storm over the weekend." It was a pretty weak excuse, but frankly, I didn't know what else to say.

After a few moments of awkward silence, Detective McKeown handed his card to me and said, "Okay, Tony, I would appreciate it if you would have them contact me as soon as they get in."

"Sure, as soon as I see them."

Both McKeown and Barella turned and walked towards the door of the conference room, but before they left, Agent Barella turned those eyes on me again. He paused for what seemed like minutes and then asked me, "Do you know of any reason why someone would want to harm Mr. Orr or Ms. Toomey?"

The question took me completely off-guard, and I think that was Barella's purpose in asking it the way he did. "I have no idea. What do you mean, 'harm them'?"

"It's a pretty simple question, Mr. Mascelle, and I think you know what I mean."

Apparently, Barella was clearly capable of forming multi-worded sentences, and I had a 'be careful what you wish for' moment. "You mean like, kill?"

"Yes, something like that."

"No, Agent Barella, I don't know of anyone who would want to hurt, or kill, either of them."

I looked at McKeown and it was clear that agent Barella's question had taken him by surprise also.

McKeown looked at Barella and then at me. "What about you, Tony? Can you think of any reason why someone would want to hurt you or, maybe, Ms. Pavone?" He motioned toward, Marcella, who was now standing right next to me.

I looked at Marcella, who gave me an apprehensive shrug, and then back at him. "No, Detective, we can't. There is obviously something more here that you're not telling us." I let the comment hang in the air, but neither of them responded.

"That's all we can say right now," Detective McKeown informed me. "I'll be back in contact with you soon. Please remember to have Mr. Orr and Ms. Toomey contact me as soon as they get in. We will see ourselves out. Thank you for your cooperation, and have a nice day."

Marcella and I remained motionless as they left. We listened to their steps fade, then heard the entrance door of the office suite open, and then close.

"Someone may be trying to kill you; have a nice day?" I said aloud.

After a moment Marcella asked, "So, what was that about, Tony?"

"I have no idea."

"Do you think we're in some kind of danger?"

"No. I think these jerks were just trying to mess with our heads."

"Why?" Marcella asked.

"I don't know, but I have family and friends in the NYPD and I intend to find out. I'll make a few calls; in the meantime, try to get hold of Kyle and Jan."

She looked at me for some additional reassurance, but I could offer nothing more than an arm around her shoulder and a gentle squeeze.

"Don't worry," I said. I felt powerless to offer anything more reassuring.

She smiled at me. "Okay, boss."

Chapter 28

I picked up the phone, and dialed my Uncle Joe at the 19th Precinct. He was out so I left a message.

Marcella spent the next half hour calling and recalling all of the contact numbers we had for Kyle and Jan. She couldn't find them so she left urgent, but appropriately cryptic, messages for each of them.

Around noon, Uncle Joe called back. I closed my office door and picked up the phone.

"Hey buddy, everything okay?" he asked immediately.

I guess when you have twenty-two years on the job in New York and you get an unexpected call from your nephew at work on a Monday morning, you tend to assume the worst. I turned my chair around, towards the window, and looked across the street.

"Hi Uncle Joe. I'm fine, but I might have a little problem."

I told him about the visit from McKeown and Barella. He informed me that he knew McKeown, and that he was surprised that his colleague didn't make the connection that I was from the same family that was so well represented on the NYPD.

"Never heard of this Barella guy," he said. "But that's not especially surprising if he's a Fed."

"What do you think this is about, Uncle Joe?"

"I have no way of knowing, Tony. Obviously, someone got whacked across the street. If the *federales* are involved, it probably was not your everyday murder. In fact, if they're involved it's probably some pretty serious shit. Did anyone say anything about why they seemed concerned about your safety?"

"No, but McKeown said I should have a nice day on his way

out."

My uncle laughed. "Hey buddy, that's SOP. We get graded on how friendly we are to the good citizens. If he knew you had family on the job he would have told you to watch your back, which is what I'm telling you to do, at least until I talk to McKeown and find out what's cooking. Have your friends showed up yet?"

"No, not yet."

"Have they done this sort of thing before? I mean, not coming in without letting someone know?"

"Never."

After a pause Uncle Joe said, "That's not a good sign, buddy."

"Yeah, I know."

"Did you tell the detective everything you remembered?"

I hesitated.

"Hey, Tony, don't mess around here, pal. Did you tell them everything, or not?"

"Not everything. I saw something, or thought I did," I said.

I told him about the flash and the closing of the window.

"Why didn't you tell McKeown about that?"

"I don't know, I just thought it was pretty meaningless."

"Meaningless? Shit, Tony, you probably saw the murder and maybe the murderer. What the hell were you thinking?"

"I don't know, Uncle Joe. I guess I was a little shook up. Hey, no excuses."

The truth was I knew exactly why I didn't say anything. It had something to do with my unexpected meeting with my friend

Crazy Nunzio, and it also had something to do with what happened to my dad. I did not want to get involved in this thing if it had anything to do with that nightmare.

Uncle Joe interrupted my thoughts. "Okay, don't worry about it. I'll get hold of McKeown and have him get another statement from you. This time you tell him everything. Is that clear? I mean everything."

"Yes sir."

"And when you're done with that, I want you to think about taking some time off: just a few days until we find your friends and this thing gets sorted out. You can go out to my place on Fire Island for some R&R. The key is in a flower pot, under the deck, near the front entrance."

"I can't go to Watch Hill, Uncle Joe. I can't just disappear from here, not now. There's a lot of major shit going on here right now."

"I don't really give a damn, Tony. You can talk to your people and get your messages over your cell phone, or whatever. It's just for a few days."

"What do I do about Marcella? I can't just run and hide and leave her here alone. She might be in danger, too."

"Well, you can take her out to Fire Island with you. It's practically a ghost town this time of year. And it's kind-a romantic... you know."

I didn't say anything for a moment and then asked, "What do you mean?"

"Hey, if I have to paint a picture, pal, then maybe you were adopted," he said with a chuckle.

"She's a nice girl Uncle Joe; I don't think she'll just agree to spend a few days on a deserted beach with her boss."

"Is this thing with her serious, or not?"

"I like her. A lot."

"That sounds pretty serious. It's about time; you ain't getting any younger, buddy."

"Thanks, I needed that."

"By the time I was your age I had a wife, a house, and two kids. Besides, she's a knockout, and not a bad ballplayer, either."

"Okay, Uncle Joe, you made your point."

"Then it's settled. You take your future missus out to Fire Island and cool your heels while the cops figure this out. Hey, maybe you'll get lucky and she'll let you sample the goods."

"Sample the goods?"

Uncle Joe chuckled again and then asked, "By the way, does your mom know?"

"Know what?"

"That you're engaged?"

"We're not engaged."

"That you're serious."

"No."

There was a silence. "Does Marcella know?"

I didn't say anything.

"You always were a complicated kid, Tony. Well, then this should be a very interesting little vacation, and probably long overdue. So, are we clear on the plan?"

"Yes, sir."

"Bye Tony."

"Bye Uncle Joe."

I hung up the phone and then considered what I had just agreed to. "Shit." I turned my chair around and found Marcella standing not eight feet from my desk.

"Would you stop that?" I said.

"Stop what?"

"Sneaking up on me."

"Sorry. Never been to Watch Hill; when do we go?"

"I don't know, Marcella. I can't just leave, not now. The financing will evaporate, and the company with it."

"I think you should listen to your uncle and get away for a little while."

"I need to think."

"Did he say anything about me?" Marcella asked.

He sure did. "Yes." I said smiling.

"What?"

"He said you're a great ballplayer."

"That's it?"

"Hey, it doesn't get any better than that from Uncle Joe."

Chapter 29

Kyle Orr sat at a table in the back of the restaurant, impatiently watching the front door. Jan was supposed to meet him here over two hours ago, but there was no sign of her—no calls, no messages and no emails—nothing! He shifted in his seat and checked his wristwatch for the fifth time in as many minutes.

"Would you like another Perrier, sir?" the waiter sniffed.

The sound of the waiter's voice startled Orr. "No!" he barked, after regaining his composure.

Orr reviewed the plan in his head again. He was sure he had not forgotten any of the details, and the last time he saw Jan everything was on track. Then she suddenly disappeared. He had been in a near panic since, trying to relocate her. This rendezvous had been preplanned, just in case something went wrong, and apparently, it had. But what?

Neither of them had been back to the office since they lost contact with each other, and the plan under these circumstances was to never go back. Kyle had considered all of the possible scenarios, and he kept coming up with the same answer. There was only one logical explanation: Tony had found out about the plan and had acted first. A chill went down his spine just thinking about it.

The plan was supposed to be neat and easy. An envelope of money delivered to a stranger, the deed gets done, and the company's and, more importantly, his and Jan's financial problems go away. Then on Friday, everything seemed to unravel. The whole thing seemed like a bad dream now, one that he could not wake up from.

At first he had a difficult time convincing himself that Tony could be either that sharp or that ruthless, but then he recalled the story Tony had once told him about the attempt on his father's life, seven or eight years ago. Orr also recalled some of the other details, especially the conclusion: lots of dead or missing enemies, all apparently killed in revenge. Half of Tony's family were cops. Sicilian cops. Why had he not factored that into the plan? If he had, he and Jan would have gone immediately to Plan B. But it was too late for that now.

If Tony had discovered their plan, or if one of his relatives had figured it out, then it was definitely time for Kyle Orr and Jan Toomey to disappear to a place as far away as possible, as soon as possible.

"What a stupid fucking move," he said aloud.

"I'm sorry, sir, I didn't get that."

Orr looked to his right and saw the waiter still standing there. He looked at his watch again, and then turned back to the waiter. "Get me the check!"

"Yes sir."

As Kyle Orr left the restaurant, he reached for his cell phone and dialed Jan's mobile number one more time. No answer. Then he dialed her home number. She didn't answer there either. When her home answering machine picked up the call he said, "Hey, it's me. You missed our meeting. We need to move. Now. Call me immediately."

What Kyle Orr did not know, and would never know, was that Jan Toomey was there, but it was impossible for her to answer the phone, because she was lying on the living room floor in a pool of her own blood.

Chapter 30

Detective Sean McKeown rubbed his temples with the tips of his fingers. He felt another headache coming on. From the moment he set eyes on the crime scene he knew that this case would be trouble.

In reality, all of his cases were trouble for someone, the victim being first and foremost. Then there was the perp or perps, who would also have their share of trouble as soon as McKeown was on their trail and moving them inexorably closer to a nice, cozy cell for the remainder of their miserable lives. However, that was not the kind of trouble he was worried about. This was different, very different, and somewhere in his aching head, he had the unsettling feeling that the outcome would be one he would never forget, the same way you never forget a bad nightmare, or one of those horror movies with chainsaws and axes. And it was only Monday.

The window behind him admitted a few fading rays of late afternoon sun, which illuminated the dog-eared desk calendar lying on his scarred mahogany desk. On the surface of the calendar sat twelve photographs, neatly arranged from wide-angle to close-ups. McKeown's worn leather chair produced a plaintive groan as he leaned forward to rest his elbows on the desktop. The phone interrupted his ruminations. Without looking away from the photos, he picked up the receiver.

McKeown said, "Oh, yes, hello, Joe. I've been meaning to call you. I guess your nephew beat me to it."

The two men went through the customary greetings, chatting briefly about their mutual acquaintances and their respective careers as fellow NYPD detectives. They also shared recollections of having met once or twice. Having gone through the formalities of properly establishing the foundation of professional brotherhood, Joe came right to the point.

"Tony told me about the visit with you and this Fed guy

today."

"Yeah, the Fed's name is Barella. I would have given you a heads-up before we visited your nephew, but this guy is by-the-book and he was dogging me the whole time."

"Sean, I know under the circumstances you can't disclose information about the investigation to me, but Tony said you asked him some questions that seemed to suggest that he might be in danger."

"Yeah, I guess I did."

"So you think my nephew has a problem with his safety?"

"I think he might. Him, or possibly one of his coworkers."

"Well, can you give me something here so I can size up the risk for myself?" Joe said, getting a little frustrated with McKeown's evasiveness.

McKeown thought a while, looked down at the photographs and then said, "As you probably know from your nephew, we found a body across the street."

"Yeah, he told me that."

"Right. What he does not know is that we also found a rifle with the body. It was a professional rig, Joe." McKeown let the words sink in.

"He was a shooter?"

"Looks that way."

"And he was found directly across from my nephew's office?"

"Right."

"Okay, but there are probably dozens of potential targets that could be hit from that window. Right?"

"Right."

"So maybe it has nothing to do with my nephew."

"Maybe."

"Hey, Sean, give me a break here."

"Look, Joe, I can't give you any more details than that."

"Come on, Sean! I went through this shit once already with Tony's dad. Damn near lost him. So, maybe I'm being a little overprotective, but if there is any reason to believe that someone is after my nephew, I need to know."

"I remember some of that... that incident with your brother."

Joe listened to the words and heard the message in McKeown's tone.

"What are you saying, Sean?"

"What I'm saying is that I started to do a little discreet background check on my new Fed friend Barella. It took all of five minutes to discover that he was also involved with the investigation of that incident with your brother."

"Are you saying this may be connected?"

"I'm not saying anything, at least not until I learn more about him, which I'm still working on." McKeown smiled to himself, thinking that this process of discovery would be nearly impossible without the help of some of his old friends at Fed Plaza.

Joe Mascelle interrupted his thoughts. "If you were me, Sean, what would you do?"

"That's an easy question to answer. I'd have my nephew go on vacation for a while: someplace remote, until we can figure out what's going on."

"Right."

"I'm sorry I can't be more helpful right now."

"I understand. Look, I also called for another reason. When I spoke with Tony he said there was something else he remembered about that Friday morning, something he didn't tell you." Joe told McKeown about what his nephew said he had witnessed; the flash and then someone closing the window.

"Why didn't Tony tell us that this morning?"

"I guess you had him off-guard; he said he didn't think it was important."

"Not important?"

"Yeah, I know."

"Have his two friends shown up yet?" McKeown asked.

"No, and he said they never do this sort of thing."

"That's not a good sign."

"Nope."

"Joe, I'm going to pay your nephew another call. I hope you made a clear impression on him regarding the consequences of withholding information during a murder investigation."

"Yeah, I did."

"I hope so. Shit like that gets people moved from the witness list to the suspect list, real fast."

"Understand."

"Give me your stuff so I can stay in touch."

Joe rattled off his contact information as McKeown scribbled it on an unused corner of his mangled desk calendar.

"Stay tuned."

"Thanks, Sean."

McKeown hung up the phone and turned back to the photographs. He studied the face of the dead man again and walked his mind through the probable series of events of that Friday morning, moving his eyes from one photograph to the next.

The victim, Hispanic or maybe Middle Eastern, twenty-five to thirty, short, cropped hair, with an athletic—no, a military build. McKeown was sure he was probably former military or paramilitary, based on the weapon type. The body was found lying on its right side. The rifle was under his body, and his hand loosely arranged around the grip. McKeown could imagine how his body was arranged a moment before the bullet entered his skull: in a kneeling, ready-to-fire position, except he was now lying ninety degrees off the vertical.

The body was found in the center of the room. *Standard sniper tactics,* McKeown thought, reflecting on his own training in the 82nd Airborne. The shooter positioned himself several feet back, away from the opening of the window, so that he and his rifle would be nearly invisible to someone looking into the unlit room from across the street. He thought about his conversation with Joe Mascelle, the part where Joe commented that there could be dozens of potential targets from that window. But if this is where the victim was originally positioned for his shot, there could be only one target: someone in the room directly across the street—the conference room where Tony Mascelle and his people were meeting.

There were no indications that the body had been moved, so McKeown was sure it lay where it had fallen. The shooter's target, or targets, were in that conference room. Or at least the dead shooter thought they were.

Cause of death? McKeown flipped through the folder looking

for the coroner's conclusion, even though he already knew the answer - a single, close-range shot to the back of his head. The report described a small entrance wound about the size of a finger, but noted that there was no exit wound. It went on to describe how the bullet fragmented into countless tiny pieces and in so doing instantly turned the victim's brain into something with the consistency of wet scrambled eggs. Well, it did not say that exactly, but that is what it meant. The end result, besides a dead guy with a head full of soup where his brain should have been, was that there was no ballistic evidence. Just like Barella described.

So, apparently, one professional shooter was setting up for a shot, and another comes up from behind and pops him with a single, close-range head shot using a specially designed bullet: ice cold, and very professional. All of this was pretty interesting by itself. After all, ninety-nine percent of homicide cases are just the standard amateur stuff: gang-banger does a drive-by, or husband whacks boyfriend, or wife whacks husband, or pimp whacks hooker. But it wasn't every day you saw a case of a professional assassin whacking another professional assassin. In fact, in his nineteen years on the force, with twelve of them in homicide, McKeown had never seen or heard of anything like this before.

He had seen cases of wise-guys getting whacked by their fellow wise- guys, but he wouldn't put them in the same category as this one. Those cases were more like pimp whacking hooker: noisy, messy, and usually with lots of tracks left behind to follow. No, this was unique, but it was even more than that. One detail that he found on the body pushed it into the realm of the bizarre. He hadn't believed it when he first saw it with his own eyes, but somehow rereading the report made it real, but at the same time even more bizarre.

He skimmed the coroner's report again, looking for the specific detail. When he found it he read it aloud, as if doing so might provide some clue as to what it meant. But the words simply stated the objective facts with no emotion or surprise, as if it was just another detail listed along with dozens of others. His mind tried to absorb the words "non-human blood."

He knew the coroner who wrote the report. He seemed just like any other, ordinary guy when he was off duty, but the man's job was anything but ordinary. On a daily basis, he worked waist-deep in a world that bordered on the ragged edge of reality. Even a veteran homicide detective, like McKeown, had a difficult time understanding how people like him did what they did. Like everyone in the business, McKeown spent a lot of time close to the never-never land of murder and death. However, a homicide detective, in reality, usually spends only minutes with a corpse. Then someone tags 'em and bags 'em. After that, most of a detective's time is spent talking to witnesses, friends, family, suspects, and other detectives: the living. Most of his relationship with the dead is limited to looking at photographs, as he was doing now. But his coroner friend lived in the land of the dead and spoke, almost exclusively, with them. If that wasn't a unique enough skill, McKeown was especially impressed by a coroner's ability to objectively describe their observations, no matter how gut-wrenching, awful, or—in this case—bizarre the observation might be. Remarkable feat, McKeown thought, but while admiring these skills, he never envied the job.

McKeown read the sentence once more and then picked up and examined the close-up of the victim's face. Between the man's lifeless eyes and above the bridge of his nose was a wet, red cross of blood, mixed with oil. He said the words aloud. "Nonhuman blood."

He was sure that it was this photograph that flipped the switch, which turned on the machine in Washington. That machine showed up in his bedroom two days ago, Saturday morning, at around 7:00 a.m. It was supposed to be his day off.

Chapter 31

McKeown's arm flailed around, reaching for the beeper on the nightstand by the bed. He quickly silenced the thing before it woke his wife. He squinted at the green numbers on the tiny LCD screen. He did not recognize the phone number, but he did recognize the Washington, DC area code: 202.

He put on his robe and, while wondering what the hell could be so important to justify a page at 7:00 a.m. on a Saturday morning, walked to the phone in the kitchen to return the call.

A deep voice replied from the other end, "Agent Barella."

"Yes, Agent Barella, this is Detective McKeown," he replied in a low voice. "How can I help you?"

"I read your report. It was flagged by our computers." Barella replied.

McKeown stretched and wiped the sleep from his eyes. "What report?"

"The preliminary homicide report, from yesterday."

"The one on East 25th Street: the one with the dead shooter?"

"That's the one."

McKeown tried to process all of this. *How the hell did Washington get that report, and so soon...?* Then he remembered something that answered his question.

It was a project implemented after the 1993 Trade Center bombing. All NYPD computers were linked directly to the FBI network. The idea was to enable the fabled, but seemingly never realized, goal of data sharing between local and federal law enforcement with the hope of heading off another such terrorist disaster.

In the seven years since its completion, he never once gave it any further thought. This was largely because, following the announcement that the system was live and in use, he never heard another word about it. Not a peep. No one else in his department had either. They all had naturally assumed that it was just another expensive pork-barrel project that, once completed, would serve no other purpose than fattening the ego of the politician who had sponsored it, and the bottom line of the company that built it. Apparently, they were all mistaken.

"Detective?"

"Right, okay. So, again, how may I help you?"

"I've been working on a case for some time. There are certain similarities between my case and the one you reported."

"What sort of similarities?"

"I'd rather discuss them with you in person."

"No problem, as long as you're going to make the trip up here." *Because there is no way in hell I'd ever get the expenses approved to go to DC to see you.*

"Yes, of course."

"Fine, what day next week would. . ."

"Actually, I would like to see you this morning."

"This morning?" McKeown laughed.

"Yes, Detective, if it's not a problem."

Well, actually, it is a problem. It's Saturday, and I'm off duty. "I'm not sure if that's possible, Agent Barella."

There was a moment of silence on the other end. Then Barella said, "It is very important, Detective."

"I'm sure it is, but I'm also sure that it can wait until Monday. The body is in the morgue and I can guarantee it will still be there on Monday."

"I'd rather not wait."

"Well, I'll see if I can get ahold of my supervisor and get him to authorize it. Can I reach you at this number for the next hour?"

"Yes."

"Okay, talk to you later." McKeown hung up the phone and then chuckled at the prospect of Jack Sachel, his supervisor, authorizing overtime at the request of some dummy from DC.

It took all of five seconds for McKeown to track down Sachel on his cell phone. He was on his way to an early round of Saturday morning golf, as usual. McKeown told him about Barella's call and his interest in the recent homicide case. As expected, Sachel thought that the request was some sort of prank.

"Hey Sean," he said. "You're a little late for an April Fool's joke, aren't you?"

"I'm not joking, Jack; this guy wants to hear back from me ASAP."

"Okay, let me call the commish's office; maybe I can find someone, but I doubt it. I'll call back in an hour, or two... maybe three."

McKeown hung up the phone, made some coffee, and skimmed the previous day's *Daily News* as he waited. Then he heard a movement in the hallway, followed by a small, sleepy voice.

"Hi Daddy, what are you doing up so early?"

"Good morning, baby," he said to his twelve-year-old daughter, Mary. "Everything is fine. I just got a call from the office; I may have to go into work today."

Mary shuffled across the kitchen, grabbed a bowl, a box of

corn flakes from the cupboard and some milk from the refrigerator and sat down across from her father. He placed a spoon and napkin next to her bowl as she poured the milk. Then he watched her eat her corn flakes as he sipped his coffee.

The phone rang. McKeown picked it up on the first ring and said, "That was quick." Then he listened for a few moments and hung up.

Well, whatever it was, it hadn't taken very long to clear it with the brass. McKeown looked at his watch: about sixteen minutes. He got up, gave his daughter a hug and a peck on the head, then headed for the bathroom.

"So, you have to go in, Daddy?"

"Yes, baby, I'm afraid so. Let's be quiet so we don't wake Mommy and your sister."

****

McKeown was in his office by 9:15 a.m. and, sitting there waiting for him, was Agent Paul Barella.

"Good morning, Detective McKeown", Barella said as McKeown entered his office.

"Agent Barella?"

"Yes," Barella said as he extended his hand. McKeown took it. "I must have misunderstood. I thought you were in DC when you called this morning. I didn't expect to see you until this afternoon."

"Did I say DC?" Barella shrugged.

McKeown was about to ask, but just sat down and tried not to react. Still, he couldn't help letting a little of his surprise leak out in his expression. Amazing, he thought. It would have taken days for McKeown to get authorization for a trip like that. Then it would have been an all-day affair, involving vehicles with wheels. This guy must have his own private jet... or maybe he had a red cape and blue tights on under his suit.

"Okay, Agent Barella, now that we're both here, face to face on a Saturday morning, which happens to be my day off, perhaps you can tell me what's so important that it couldn't wait until Monday."

Agent Barella replied in a polite but firm monotone voice.

"I can tell you that it is a matter of national security."

"Yes, of course, but you could have told me that over the phone."

"That is true, Detective. I am not here to tell you that. I am here to see the body and the crime scene, and to speak with the witnesses. But I think it's important for you to understand up front that this is a national security matter of the utmost importance."

McKeown could already feel his blood pressure rising. "Yes, Agent Barella, you just said that it was a national security matter. And if there was any doubt in my mind, the fact that you had a chartered jet fly you to New York on ten minutes' notice appears to confirm that this is a very, very important case to you and the people you work for. It still doesn't tell me anything useful as to why you're here and why this is so important."

"Has an autopsy been completed on the body?"

"No, but it is scheduled." McKeown looked down at his watch a moment. "Let's see, oh yes, it's scheduled for Monday, just like I indicated on the phone this morning." He looked at Barella and smiled tightly.

Barella ignored the sarcasm and said, "Your preliminary report indicated a single shot in the back of the head, no exit wound. Correct?"

"Correct."

"You also indicated in your report a red oily substance in the form of an X on his forehead."

"That's true." *McKeown knew that was coming.*

"Anything else noteworthy not mentioned in your initial report?" Barella asked patiently.

"Let's see, a bullet to the brain with no exit wound, a red oily X on his forehead, and... oh yes: a military-grade assassin's rig. I think that covers all the high points."

"Look, Detective, I realize that this is an inconvenience to you and your family..."

"No, Agent Barella", McKeown interrupted, "not an inconvenience, an annoyance. I would be happy to cooperate with you or anyone else from our federal government, any-time, any-place, but as usual the federal MO is what causes the friction. You people think you can just jump on a jet, yell 'national security,' and everyone comes to attention. Well, it doesn't work that way, Agent Barella. If you want obedience, you just got it. On the other hand, if you want cooperation, as in *partnership,* that's another matter. Do I make myself clear?"

"Yes, Detective, crystal clear." Barella took a deep breath and sat back in his chair. "There are a lot of details."

"I like details." McKeown informed him.

"Okay, if you insist." It was then that Barella described the unusual type of exploding bullet that he correctly suspected would be found during the autopsy.

"It is not your standard metal fragments left by a conventional munition, but a power-like substance made of an inert ceramic material." Barella then he added, "This type of material is currently being used to develop state-of-the-art munitions by multiple government contractors."

McKeown sat back in his chair and smiled. "I'm almost afraid to ask why someone in the federal government would be funding the development of an untraceable exploding bullet."

"It's really not that mysterious, Detective. If you design a bullet that disintegrates on impact, it greatly minimizes the possibility of collateral damage caused by a bullet leaving the target and hitting someone or something else, or ricocheting after a miss and having a similar negative effect. These characteristics make these munitions perfect for certain applications, such as use on aircraft by air marshals, where loose bullets flying around a pressurized cabin can have potentially serious side-effects. Since these bullets are all but untraceable, they are being designed with a chemical marker that's impregnated into the material so that a crime lab, like yours, can trace the powder back to its origins."

"Okay, so assuming that you're correct, I guess we can presume that at least one of these new bullets was liberated from some mysterious government laboratory and found itself in this guy's head. So, when the coroner completes the autopsy and finds such a substance in the victim's brain, you will then be able to help us trace it. Right?"

"No, I'm afraid we won't."

"No?" McKeown responded in mock astonishment. "Let me guess; it's a national security issue, right?"

"No, Detective, I'm not going to tell you that."

"Oh, good, I feel better already."

"Can we dispense with the sarcasm, please? It's not very productive."

"Sorry, please continue." McKeown said.

"The work on this new type of bullet is still in the early stages, which is to say that none of them have, or could have been stolen from the lab, because they don't exist in a form that you or I could load into a standard weapon yet."

"I'm confused. I thought you said that your contractors developed these things."

"No detective, they are developing something like them."

"So someone beat you fed guys to the finish line? That's very interesting."

Barella continued. "What's even more interesting is that the bullet that you will likely find in your victim's head will, if I'm right, match samples that date back for nearly forty years."

"Forty years?"

"That's correct. We actually got the idea for the one that we're developing from whoever this shooter is. As I mentioned, there has been a relatively new push by federal and local law enforcement authorities to develop a bullet that won't hurt bystanders or damage pressurized airplanes. Three years ago we were asked, by a civilian commission exploring new ideas in this area, what characteristics could achieve these ends. We suggested developing a bullet that turned into powder on impact. The committee thought we were brilliant, but in fact, we were simply relying on what we've seen in this case. So we had some old information declassified and passed it on."

"So you have a perp, that is sophisticated enough to develop and manufacture special munitions that even the United States government doesn't have access to, and they've had this technology for forty years?"

"Correct."

"Another country?"

"Maybe", Barella replied, "but in the years since they first appeared we've only seen them in very specific circumstances."

"All close-range shots?"

"Most, but not all. The MO is usually to get a close shot to the head. These things were probably designed for this very specific purpose. The shape and structure of the human skull provides a relatively hard containment vessel, so the forces and the fragments are more easily contained. Moreover, with a close-in shot you can use a fairly ordinary size projectile and charge. But, there have been some instances when they have been used for long-distance work. Under those circumstances the projectile and the charge are larger, so the behavior is less predictable."

"I'm not sure what any of that means, Agent Barella."

Barella shifted uncomfortably in his chair as he considered his reply.

"Well, a long-range shot requires a larger charge, which means you need a more robust projectile to withstand the resulting forces. If it was not made more robust, it could break up on the way to the target, or even disintegrate before it leaves the barrel. Plus, at a distance, a head shot is obviously harder to make. Therefore, if you made a perfectly square head shot from a distance, say a hundred yards, you would probably have the same or a similar effect – and with no exit wound. But, if it hit off to one side of the head the effect could be very different."

"How different?"

"For one, it would probably make a significant exit wound."

"How significant?" McKeown inquired.

"Very. It could be as large as what you would expect from a standard high-powered rifle bullet, possibly even larger."

"Why?" McKeown asked.

"Because this type of bullet might only partially fragment, let's say into some powder and then two or three large pieces, rather than entirely into powder like it was designed to do. So, effectively, you would then have multiple, relatively large, spinning splinters leaving the skull, rather than a large streamlined one. The effect would be similar to an exit would from a shotgun blast, for instance. Get the picture?"

McKeown nodded. "And, in that case, you would also lose the advantage of avoiding collateral damage to other people around the target, right?"

"Yes, correct. The larger fragments could hit other targets, at least those in close range. However, the range and damage could be significantly magnified in cases were the first impact is with a less bony part of the body, say a neck wound. In that case the fragments could still have enough momentum and mass to cause quite a bit of damage to the people and things surrounding the target."

McKeown digested what Barella had just described and commented. "You seem to have a lot of experience with this."

"I'm afraid I do." Barella responded coolly.

McKeown noticed that Barella's professional demeanor was momentarily replaced by something else. He could swear it was sadness or remorse, but it was there for just a moment and then it was gone.

Barella continued, "There are also other similarities besides the ballistics."

"Let me guess", McKeown said, "the red X on the forehead."

"Correct."

"Any idea what the hell that's about?"

"I can tell you that when you analyze it, you will find that it is comprised mostly of oil, the type of oil routinely used by Catholic priests to administer the last rites. The red stuff is blood mixed with the oil, but it is not the victim's blood; in fact it's not human. It's from a lamb. Oh, and by the way, that X is actually a cross, as in Christian."

"Lamb's blood? Are you kidding me?"

"Do I look like the kind of man that likes to make jokes, Detective?"

"A cross? Last rites? What, some crazy that thinks he's a priest or something?"

Barella gave McKeown's rhetorical question a half-smile. "Oh, and one other little bit of information. I didn't just arrive in your office from DC this morning." Barella said holding up his cell phone for McKeown to see. "I called you from Newark, New Jersey. I was there talking to another perplexed detective about another mysterious murder victim. Same wound, same exploding bullet, same cross on the forehead. But this one, unlike the one you found, was not a pro, just some loser with a rap sheet as long as the Macy's parade. They found the body yesterday. The estimated time of death was approximately three days ago."

McKeown sat in silence trying to digest what he had just heard.

Barella broke the silence. "So how am I doing, Detective? Am I cooperating enough yet?"

Chapter 32

McKeown sighed as he remembered that initial discussion with Barella on Saturday morning. It had been a long day, but not as long as today. He was looking forward to going home and getting some dinner, when he noticed movement out of the corner of his eye. He looked up and said, "Come in, Agent Barella."

Barella walked in, stood in front of McKeown's desk, and looked down at the photos and files scattered over its surface.

"Coroner's report?" Barella inquired.

"Yes".

"I guess it must be Monday."

"Yup, have a seat."

Barella sat. "And?"

"You were right. The coroner confirmed that there is nothing but some ceramic powder scattered in the victim's brain. He said he has never seen anything like it. He also confirmed that the cross thing on the forehead is comprised of oil and non-human blood. But he doesn't know it's lamb's blood yet."

"Don't tell him," Barella replied.

McKeown sat back in his chair and eyed Barella with suspicion. "Why not?"

Barella smiled. "Why ruin the surprise?"

McKeown was not amused.

Barella reached into his jacket pocket and pulled out a large brown envelope. "Here, with my compliments, and those of the Tenafly Police Department." Barella dropped the envelope on the desk in front of McKeown.

"What's this?" McKeown asked.

"Another murder. I just came from New Jersey. Same MO. They think that the time of death was Wednesday night or Thursday morning. Oh, and it just happens to be Mr. Mascelle's friend and coworker, Jan Toomey."

McKeown sat up straight and said, "Okay, Sherlock, everything you predicted on Saturday was right on the money, so now maybe you can tell me what this case is about, or at least what you think it's about."

"I wish I could, I really do, but I'm afraid I'm not at liberty to say."

"You're not at liberty to say? Look, Agent Barella, we've had our little chat about cooperation. I've done my part. You were allowed to inspect the body, just as you requested, and I went with you this morning to speak with the witnesses, just as we agreed. Now it's your turn. Besides, I think it would be in everyone's interest if we continue to cooperate on this case. Don't you? You know that young man we spoke with today, Tony Mascelle? Half his family are either cops or firemen in this town, and they have a lot of friends. A few years ago his father was almost killed by the mob, so they are likely to become a little nervous as some of these rather odd facts begin to emerge. I can help you with that, but you need to help me."

"I'm sorry, Detective; it's been deemed a national security matter. As of now this is a federal investigation." Barella waited for that to sink in. "As such, there is nothing I can tell you that you don't already know."

McKeown looked at Barella with a half-smile, as if this much bullshit didn't deserve the effort required for a full one. But he got nothing back but more of Barella's monotone drag. "So if there is nothing else, Detective, I'll be on my way."

McKeown's half-smile disappeared as he stood up and walked to the window behind his desk. He looked out at the view of a grimy brick wall less than five feet away and pinched his right eyebrow between his index finger and thumb, something he habitually did when he was getting pissed off. "You didn't come up here to speak to me about this case, did you? You came up here to shut this investigation down and move the jurisdiction to DC, right?"

Barella stood, but said nothing in response.

McKeown continued. "Look, I'm all fine and good with national security matters, Agent Barella. Really, I am. But what we have here is a murder of a guy who was, by all indications, in the act of committing a murder. Now, that's a little unusual, to say the least. But there is also a detail or two—crosses, lamb's blood, and apparently two other murders with the same MO in the next state—that pushes the case into territory that is... what's the French saying? Oh, yes: 'pretty fucking weird.' So, unless your name is Rod Serling and this office is a movie set, I have a major problem with a wacko murderer who is very probably a serial killer who's been at it for a very long time."

Barella looked completely calm, almost distracted. "Yes, Detective, as we've discussed, it is not your everyday murder and it happened in your backyard. So I understand your concern. But it also happened across state lines in New Jersey, which makes it a federal investigation."

"Really? Thank you for that little lesson in interstate jurisdiction. Now maybe you can throw me a bone and answer a question or two that I have."

"I'm sorry, I can't. I wish it were different."

"You're telling me that I have a serial murderer on my hands and you want me to go to my supervisor and tell him, 'Sorry, it's a national security matter, don't worry, be happy'?"

"I'm not telling you what to tell him, Detective. That's not my concern. Furthermore, I've already discussed this with your supervisor, and for that matter, we have discussed it with the entire chain of command, right up to the mayor—you know, that guy in Gracie Mansion who happened to be a very busy federal prosecutor in his previous career? They know about this situation, and have agreed to let us handle it. Also, you and Chief Sachel will be informed in writing that this case is now, officially, within the jurisdiction of the New York City regional office of the FBI, and that you are to take no action on this case without my permission. Do you understand?"

McKeown bit his lower lip and nodded stiffly without saying a word. Barella abruptly turned and left, closing the office door on his way out. McKeown muttered, "Asshole." He looked down at the envelope that Barella had deposited on his desk, opened it, and flipped through the photographs until he came to the close-up of the victim.

The young woman's face was resting on its right side against a tile floor, in a pool of blood. Both of her lifeless eyes stared into the camera. Above the eyes, painted in the middle of her forehead, was what appeared to be a cross of dried blood. McKeown picked up the phone and dialed.

"Hello, Joe? This is Sean again... yeah, but a change in plans. I need to meet with you and your nephew. As soon as possible."

Chapter 33

It was about 7:00 p.m. when I called Kyle Orr's apartment, but there was no answer. Then I tried his cell phone, and to my surprise, he picked it up on the first ring.

"Where are you?" He asked.

"I'm at work, where the hell are you?"

He didn't reply at first and then stammered, "I had some things to take care of, got to go."

"Wait, Kyle, we need to talk about what happened across the street, you know, on Friday with the..."

We were cutoff in mid-sentence. I put the receiver down.

Uncle Joe was sitting across from me in my office and listening. He asked, "Well, what did he say?"

"Not much, and then the call was disconnected. I think he hung up on me."

"That's interesting."

"He sounded scared."

"And no answer at Ms. Toomey's?"

"No. I left another message."

My uncle was interrupted mid-thought by a knock on the door. It was McKeown, and without bothering to waste time on formalities, he began filling us in on his recent meeting with Agent Paul Barella, including details about the murder that occurred across the street from my office the previous Friday.

I found some of those details a little unsettling, which is to say he was really scaring the shit out of me. According to McKeown, the guy, whom he referred to as the "shooter", was probably trying to kill someone in the conference room before someone else interrupted the plan by firing a bullet into the back of his head. He also took us through some other very odd details—at least they seemed odd to me. Something about a red cross of lamb's blood on the victim's forehead and a disintegrating bullet in the victim's brain. I frankly didn't know what to make of this information, but a glance at my Uncle Joe's facial expression was all I needed to confirm that this was definitely not your average NYPD murder case. In fact, Uncle Joe asked McKeown to repeat what he said about the cross and the exploding munition. By the third round, my uncle just sat there staring at McKeown in stunned silence and, as I might have explained before, we don't do a lot of silence in this family, stunned or otherwise.

McKeown then broke my uncle's spell by describing how the mysterious Agent Barella changed the jurisdiction of the case from the NYPD to the FBI. This had the effect of causing my uncle's jaw muscles to flex with anger and his brow to furrow.

"Bullshit!" Uncle Joe spat out.

McKeown shrugged. "My sentiments exactly." Then he asked us. "Anything new here?"

Uncle Joe informed him, "Tony finally reached Kyle Orr just before you arrived."

"And?" McKeown asked as he turned towards me.

"He hung up on me," I said. "And I still haven't been able to reach Jan."

Detective McKeown slowly paced the living room floor, as he pinched his eyebrow and murmured to himself.

Uncle Joe said to McKeown, "What the hell is going on here, Sean?"

"Be goddamned if I know. But I can tell you this, I'm not going to be much more help here at the moment, Joe. Technically, I'm not supposed to be having this conversation with either of you. But I couldn't leave a fellow cop in a spot like this, not without at least giving him some of the facts. And the facts are the problem: they just don't fit, at least not yet. The only advice I can give you is the same I gave you before, and that is to get your nephew out of town until we can sort this out."

"Until *we* sort it out? As in, you and me?"

"That's what I'm suggesting," McKeown replied.

I said to McKeown, "I thought you said that you were taken off the case."

Detectives Sean McKeown and Joe Mascelle both smiled at each other, turned to me, and said simultaneously, "Fuck 'em."

McKeown said to me, "Hey, give your friend Kyle another try. I'll talk to him this time."

I dialed and listened to the phone ring. "No answer."

"Okay, if he wants to play hard-to-get, let's go get him. We'll start by visiting Mr. Orr's premises. Maybe we'll find him there, maybe not. But it's the only logical place to start looking."

"Sounds like a plan," my uncle replied. Then he turned to me and said, "In the meantime, you get packed, Tony. It's time for you and Marcella to get the hell outta Dodge."

Chapter 34

Kyle Orr snapped the lid of his cell phone closed. "Shit! Mascelle knows. He already fucking knows!"

He slipped the phone into his shirt pocket and walked quickly into the bedroom. On the bed was a large, bulging duffel bag. Next to it was a matching suitcase. The rest of the bed was covered with clothes and personal items.

"No time to screw around with this," Orr said to himself as he began haphazardly throwing the items on his bed into the open suitcase, filling it with all it could hold, and then some. He mashed down the suitcase cover and closed the zipper.

He was packing everything he would need for the rest of his life, because this was plan B, which meant he was never coming back to this city, or this country, again. He and Jan had already skimmed enough money from the companies' accounts to set them up in Costa Rica for a while. There they would find a nice, comfortable cottage on a beach somewhere, let the dust settle, and then figure out what their next move would be.

The only problem was that he still could not find Jan. Maybe she panicked and went directly to the airport. Then another thought entered his mind, which made him break out in a sweat. Maybe she took the money and left without him. "You bitch," he muttered to himself. "I will find you and kill you myself if you left me high and dry."

The sound of the doorbell startled him. He froze. It rang again. A bead of sweat rolled down the side of his face. He wiped it away and then carefully and quietly moved towards the apartment's front door. As he did, the doorbell rang a third time. He could see movement on the other side of the door through the space near the floor, so he froze and waited. Then he heard the sound of something being dropped, followed by footsteps walking away.

He remained motionless until the sound of the footsteps disappeared. He carefully unlocked and opened the door a crack, and looked around. No one was there. On the floor, he saw a large, brown envelope. He opened the door just wide enough to retrieve it, and then he closed and locked it again. The package was addressed to him, but it had no other markings, not even a return address.

As he was examining it, the phone rang. He walked over to it and was about to pick it up but hesitated. He slammed the brown package down on the table next to the ringing phone.

It could be Jan, he thought, but it's probably Mascelle again, and he's probably already found Jan.

"To hell with it, I'm outta here."

He walked to the bedroom, grabbed his bags, and left the apartment.

When he entered the elevator he hit the button for the parking garage. The elevator stopped and Kyle exited out into the dim light of the cool, damp basement, and then walked quickly towards his car. As he walked he reconsidered the facts. *Mascelle couldn't have found Jan already, and there's no way she left me. She has to be at the airport, probably hiding in the bathroom, waiting for me to get there and board the flight.*

The sound of approaching footsteps intruded on his thoughts. "Relax, it's just a neighbor," he whispered to himself.

As the steps came closer, he began to prepare himself for a meeting with one of his fellow tenants. He only knew a few of them. Most of them were just nameless faces or faceless names, but he would have to say something intelligent if he happened to recognize this particular one. He already had a prepared statement: he was going on a business trip to Europe. *See you in a couple of weeks,* he rehearsed in his mind. He looked around but could not see anyone yet.

He approached his car, hit the unlock button on the key fob, but nothing happened. He hit it again, still nothing. The footsteps were approaching, more quickly now. He fumbled for the door key and tried to put it into the lock. The steps were now running towards him. The keys slipped from his grasp and dropped to the floor. The sound echoed off the concrete walls. "Oh, shit!" he said as he knelt down to retrieve them. As he did, he could see movement in his peripheral vision approaching from his right. He left the keys where they fell and began to stand.

"Mr. Orr?"

Orr looked up to see Bill Gacy, the building's security manager, standing over him.

"Oh, hi, Bill."

"Hi, I just wanted to ask if you got the package I left for you."

"Package?"

"Yes, a large brown envelope? I was just up at your apartment a little while ago. I rang but no one answered, so I left it next to your door."

"Oh, Okay, I'll look for it when I get back."

Bill Gacy looked at Orr's two large bags then back at Orr with a puzzled expression. "Looks like you're going to be gone a while."

"Yeah, I'm going on a business trip to Europe, see you in a couple of weeks."

"Well, do you want me to retrieve that package and put it in a safe place till you come back?"

"Yeah, that would be great, Bill, would you do that for me please?"

"Sure, no problem, but the thing is, the guy who delivered it said it was from someone really important, so I brought it up when I saw you come in a little while ago."

"Who did he say it was from?"

"Well, I have her name up at the desk, I think it was Jan... yeah, Jan, and the last name was something that started with a T."

"Toomey, Jan Toomey?" Orr asked.

"Yeah, that's it."

"When did he leave it?"

"Well, according to Sam's note, Friday morning. Sam fills in for me when I'm out," Bill explained. "My wife, she had this problem... well, it's a personal thing. Anyway, I had to take some time off to get her to the doc and stuff. So, Sam filled in for me. He said he hadn't seen you for days, so he left the package for me to give to you."

"Friday morning?"

"Yes. Were you expecting it?"

Orr ignored the question and said, "Oh, okay, great. I'll go up and get the package before I leave. Thanks, Bill."

"Hey, not a problem. Sorry for the delay in getting it to you. Well, you have a safe trip, Mr. Orr, see you in a couple."

"Right, see you in a couple, Bill."

Bill Gacy smiled and left. Orr found his keys, loaded his bags into the trunk, locked the car, and hurried back up to his apartment.

He went to unlock the front door, but it wasn't locked. *I forgot to lock the door*? He shook his head. *Well, that won't matter anymore, will it*? He walked over to the phone table where he remembered dropping the package, but it wasn't there.

That's strange. He could have sworn he left it near the phone. He retraced his steps in his mind, and walked into the bedroom to see if he left it there. He found it sitting on the bed.

As he reached down to pick it up he felt a presence in the room, but before he could turn, an arm closed around the front of his neck. His heart immediately began pounding as he struggled to get away, but the arm was like a mechanical vise and it continued to close around him.

The last thing that Kyle Orr would ever hear was the dull sound of his own vertebrae being snapped. His body went limp. The arm released its grip, allowing Orr's body to slump to the floor. His killer picked up the package and left the apartment.

Chapter 35

Sean McKeown and Joe Mascelle stood at the reception desk in Kyle Orr's apartment building watching the attendant as he spoke on the phone.

Mascelle asked McKeown, "So, it was Barella who gave you the information about Jan Toomey's murder?"

"Yeah. I would have told you earlier, but I didn't think it was a good idea to bring it up in front of your nephew."

Mascelle turned and looked at McKeown. "Why? I think the more he knows the better."

"Not necessarily, Joe. I know this is not going to make you happy, but Tony and his girlfriend are still potential suspects."

Joe shook his head. "I know my nephew; he would never do anything like this."

"Come on, Joe, think. How many times have we both heard those words? And how many times are those words followed by the arrest of the very same person that we were told couldn't possibly have done it? I know this is hard for you. It's probably why I shouldn't have involved you in this case in the first place. But here we are, and I need you to tell me that you're going to keep all possibilities on the table, including the unthinkable ones. If you can't Joe, I think you need to walk away from this now."

Joe Mascelle sighed and nodded his head. "You're right, Sean." Then he caught a movement out of the corner of his eye and when he turned back towards the reception desk he discovered the attendant, who was no longer on the phone, standing right in front of him, and with an interested expression on his face. "Did you get all of that, pal?" Mascelle asked impatiently.

"May I help you gentlemen?" The attendant inquired.

"Yes, we're here to see Kyle Orr," Joe Mascelle informed him.

"May I ask who is calling on him?"

McKeown flashed his badge at the man. "This is police business, Bill," McKeown said as he glanced at the attendant's nametag. "Please call Mr. Orr's apartment and inform him that he has visitors of an official nature."

"I will be happy to sir, but I believe he's on an extended business trip."

"Well, that's nice. Call him anyway."

Bill Gacy dialed, listened a few moments, then said, "Sorry, no answer."

Joe Mascelle asked, "When was the last time you saw Mr. Orr?"

"Earlier today, in the garage loading his bags into his car. That's when he told me about his trip."

"What time did he leave?"

"I didn't see him leave."

"Don't you monitor traffic in and out of the garage with security cameras?"

"Of course we do. But the car never left; it's still there."

Bill Gacy then replied to the puzzled look on the men's faces by adding, "I assumed he decided to take a taxi to the airport... you know, last minute change of plans."

"Wouldn't you also know about that?"

"Not necessarily."

"Get the key to the apartment and let's go, now." McKeown said as he gestured toward the bank of elevators.

As McKeown and Mascelle followed Bill Gacy to the elevator, they examined the lavishly decorated lobby of the Upper East Side apartment building, which was located directly across the street from Central Park.

"Nice place." Mascelle commented.

"Yeah, real nice. I thought your nephew said something about his company having financial problems and salary cutbacks?"

Joe smiled and nodded. "My nephew's apartment looks like a rat's nest, compared to this place. Apparently, Mr. Orr didn't get the memo."

The three men exited on the third floor and walked the few paces to Kyle Orr's door. Bill Gacy rang the bell, but there was no response. He tried again, this time calling out, "Mr. Orr?"

Detective McKeown took over and pounded on the door. Nothing.

Joe Mascelle said, "I think I see signs of a forced entry."

Sean McKeown looked at Mascelle. "Yeah, I think so too."

Bill Gacy was confused. "I don't see anything."

"Looks like probable cause to me," Joe Mascelle said, ignoring Gacy.

"Yeah, me too; open it," he said to Bill Gacy.

The three men walked into the dimly lit apartment. Bill Gacy stopped cold, deciding he would rather wait by the door. It did not take long for Mascelle and McKeown to find the body. It was in the bedroom, eyes wide open and the head was twisted to the right side and up at an unnatural angle.

"This is starting to get annoying," Mascelle commented.

McKeown touched Orr's cheek. "Still warm. Must have just happened."

Bill Gacy finally followed them in, took one look at the body, ran to the bathroom sink and threw up.

"I might as well get this over with," McKeown commented as he dialed Jack Sachel's number on his cell phone.

Mascelle walked over to where Bill Gacy was bent over the sink and said, "Hey pal, when you're done, go downstairs and wait for the cops and direct them up here." Gacy wiped his mouth on his sleeve, nodded and left.

"Hey, Jack, it's Sean," McKeown said into the phone. "We have another one. No, same case. You know, the shooter on the Lower East Side. The one that the feds took over."

Joe Mascelle could not hear the words but he could tell that the guy on the other end was not very happy.

"Yesterday", McKeown said into the phone. "Barella produced the paper work from Central that said that the NYPD was off the case and that Fed Plaza was taking over. He said that you were notified."

McKeown listened for a while and then said. "Okay, will do." He hung up, placed the phone in his pocket and looked at Mascelle. McKeown's face was turning flush with anger.

"What's going on, Sean?"

"That was my boss. Well Joe, the good news is that I am apparently still officially on the case. The bad news is that Barella has been lying his ass off. You just can't trust those damn feds to be straight with you."

"So what do you think the story is with this Barella guy?" Joe asked.

"Who knows? FBI, CIA, NSA? Pick an acronym."

"So what's the next move?"

"Well, I've got to get down to HQ to give Sachel a full report, and probably a sedative."

"Jack Sachel?"

"Yeah, you know that pain in my ass?" McKeown asked.

Joe smiled. "Black-Jack Sachel? Yeah, I know him alright. Shit, we were partners for five years. I got his booty out of the dooty on more than one occasion. If you don't mind, I'd like to tag along to say hi."

"What the hell. This case just gets better by the minute. Hey, do me a favor; keep that comment I made about Jack between us, okay?"

"No problem. Besides, he knows he's a pain in the ass. It's part of his shtick."

Joe Mascelle suddenly stopped talking and held up his hand towards Sean. Then he whispered, "You hear that?"

"Window?"

Mascelle nodded.

Mascelle and McKeown both reached for their guns and quickly moved towards the bedroom door and the living room beyond, with Joe Mascelle in the lead. McKeown was right behind Mascelle, but before he reached the doorway, he heard Mascelle yell, "Freeze! Police!" He simultaneously moved to his left, taking a kneeling firing position.

McKeown stepped into the opening to his right and aimed his gun in the same direction as Mascelle's. There was nothing in front of him except an open window.

"You see anything?" McKeown asked.

By the time the words left his mouth, Joe Mascelle was running for the open window yelling back, "White male, twenty to thirty, six feet, 175 to 185, blond hair, black T-shirt and jeans, sunglasses, big chin with a dimple." By the time he was finished with his description he was already on the fire escape and back in a firing position. McKeown joined him, and the two of them looked down scanning left and right. There was no sign of him.

Then McKeown pointed. "There. Jesus, he's going up? What kind of escape plan is that?"

Mascelle replied, "At the rate that monkey is climbing, I'd say a pretty damn good one. Look at him go!" He snapped his pistol back into his shoulder holster and started up the escape ladder. "Sean, I'll flush this guy. You get down to the street; he's gotta come down sooner or later."

McKeown, eying the height of the building, said. "You up for this, Joe? I mean, we're getting a little too old for this shit, aren't we?"

Joe, still climbing, thought about a newspaper headline in tomorrow's morning edition: *Fifty-something-year-old, Out-of-shape Detective Falls to His Death in Pursuit of George of the Jungle.* He yelled down to McKeown. "Yeah, but do I have a choice? This may be the only break we get in this case, and my nephew's neck is on the line."

"I hear you. Good luck. Don't do anything stupid."

"Too late!"

Chapter 36

Fifteen stories of fire escape stairs later, Joe Mascelle reached the roof. His heart was pounding, his face was drenched with sweat, and his legs felt like overcooked spaghetti. He carefully peeked over the roof's ledge, but he didn't see any movement. Then he began to move cautiously over the ledge and onto the roof, low and slow with his gun in hand, trying not to give away his position with the sound of his gasping breaths.

He moved past a bank of large, gray air conditioning evaporators that were, thankfully, making more noise than his lungs were. He peeked around the corner and saw the roof access door. It was wide open. "Shit."

He stood up and ran for the entrance and then down the first two flights of metal stairs. He stopped suddenly and listened. Nothing. "You tricky bastard," he said to himself as he began running back up the stairs towards the roof, which he reached just in time to see the perp jump back onto the fire escape. "Here we go again," he said as he ran in pursuit, gun still drawn.

Joe Mascelle stood at the roof's edge and looked for *George*. Suddenly the prospect of taking the trip back down by way of the fire escape seemed even more intimidating than the trip up. "Holy shit. This guy must really be a monkey," he said as he watched the perp moving down three rungs at a time. He debated giving up the chase, for just a moment, but then decided that the stakes were too high. He also decided not to holster his gun, thinking that maybe he'd get lucky and have a clear shot at some point; in fact, luck was the only way he was going to catch this guy. But this last decision turned out to be a very bad one. He stepped over the roof's ledge onto the fire escape, lost his balance and could not recover with only one free hand.

The fall knocked the wind out of him. However, that was the least of his problems. His momentum carried him across the platform and under the lower rung of the safety rail. As soon as he realized that he was going over the edge, he instinctively released his grip on the gun and reached out for something, anything, that could stop his motion and prevent the two-hundred-foot plunge beyond. He managed to grab the edge of the platform at the last moment. He looked down and watched his pistol fall as he hung there with his feet dangling in the clear air.

It was not long before his fingers, gripping the steel grating, started to go numb. *Oh shit, Mascelle, what the hell were you thinking*? He looked around, trying to find a foothold. There was none he could reach. Then he tried to lift himself up with his arms. He lifted himself maybe six inches, which wasn't even close to what he needed to get his leg up onto the platform. Suddenly, the thought crossed his mind that this might be it, that the imaginary headline he conjured up a few minutes ago as a source of self-deprecating humor might actually be tomorrow's lead story.

"What a way to go, Mascelle, you fat old man. What were you thinking?" he said to himself again.

Then he felt a strong grip on his wrist. "Sean?" He looked up. It wasn't McKeown. It was the perp, who a moment ago was several stories below him and well on his way to freedom.

"I have you," the man said with what seemed to Mascelle to be a German accent. "Give me your other hand."

Mascelle looked at him suspiciously. "How do I know you won't let go?"

Mascelle was surprised to see that his question brought a warm smile to the young man's face.

"Trust me, I won't let go."

Mascelle gave him his other hand and then *George* gave him a heave onto the landing.

The perp asked, "Are you okay?"

Mascelle got up stiffly and said, "Yeah, never felt better. So, now what?"

"Well," the man said, "I did just save your life, so you could let me go. But you won't, will you?"

Mascelle shook his head. "I'm afraid not. I wouldn't be doing my job if I did."

"No, you wouldn't."

The man lifted his sunglasses from his face and revealed two bright blue eyes, which seemed to be smiling also. Then he dropped the glasses to the grating and crushed them under his foot. Mascelle's eyes followed the glasses and when he looked back up he noticed that the man had his hands out and crossed in front of him. Mascelle took the cuffs out of his belt pouch and placed them on the man's wrists.

"What a shame. They looked like expensive sunglasses," Mascelle commented.

"No, just cheap imitations," the perp informed him.

Mascelle reached down, picked up the crushed glasses and noticed small electrical wires poking out from the broken frame. He tucked them into his shirt pocket.

"My name is Detective Joe Mascelle. Thanks for the help. What's your name?"

"Gunter."

"Well, Gunter, we have a problem. It involves a number of murders, including that of Kyle Orr. I hope you can be as helpful with providing information that leads to the arrest of the murderer, or murderers, as you were just saving me from my first and last flying lesson."

"Who is Kyle Orr?"

"He's the dead guy in the apartment, where you were a few minutes ago."

Gunter shrugged and said, "I do not know this man."

"Gee, how did I know you were going to say that?"

Gunter just smiled in response.

Mascelle asked, "Stairs or fire escape?"

"Stairs. They are safer."

Chapter 37

Jack Sachel looked up from the files on his desk as Sean McKeown and Joe Mascelle walked into his office. He frowned at McKeown, who led the way, but then his expression lightened when Joe walked in.

"Hey, Joseph. I thought I might be seeing you soon." Sachel said as he stood and extended a big, brown hand.

"Hey buddy, it's been a while," Mascelle said, shaking Sachel's hand. "How's Thelma and little Jack?"

"Thelma is doing fine and Little Jack graduates from the Naval Academy in about four weeks. How's your gang?"

"Everybody is do-in' great. At least, we were until this shit started happening."

"Yeah, and it's a strange one, Joe. In fact, the last time I saw something this strange it was that thing with your brother Paul out on the Island. How's his missus doing these days?"

"Still in Florida, at that nice quiet condo with the other senior inmates. We've tried to convince her to come back up since Paul died, but she refuses."

"Does she know?"

"Not yet. I didn't want to get Marie all worked up until I knew more about what's going on. Hope you don't mind if I tag along on this one?"

"Well, I could tell you that, by the book, the answer is no way. Then you would remind me of a few chits that you hold and make me feel real guilty. And, in any event, you would just tell me to screw myself and tag along anyway. So my answer is, you're not here and I haven't seen you. You're Sean's problem. So why don't you two take a seat so the three of us can go over the details on this one?"

"You always were a practical man, Jack." Joe said as the three of them sat.

A few minutes into Sean McKeown's briefing, Sachel interrupted and asked, "Why would Tony lie about what he saw?"

McKeown looked at Mascelle, prompting him to answer the question. "Scared... stupid... both. I think he had a flashback to what happened to his dad. We all went through hell, but Tony really had a bad time. I think he's afraid to relive that nightmare."

"Why? Does he think they're connected?"

"I don't know, Jack," Mascelle said.

"What does your gut tell you, Joe?"

"My head's telling me no. But my gut tells me yes."

The three of them said nothing as the words hung in the air.

Sachel said to Mascelle, "When we worked together, I remember you had some of the best instincts of any cop I worked with before — or since, for that matter." Sachel turned to McKeown. "No offense, Sean."

"None taken."

Sachel turned back to Mascelle. "If your gut is telling you that this is somehow related, then I think we need to work on the assumption that it is. Is your gut telling you anything else, like how it may be related?"

"Not yet."

Sachel said, "Well, you should make some plans for Tony to go on vacation for a little while."

"Yeah, we've done that, him and his secretary."

"His secretary?" Sachel asked.

"Yeah, she was also in the conference room on the day in question."

McKeown said, "You know, it may have nothing to do with Tony. The targets may have been the two victims that are already dead, Jan Toomey and Kyle Orr. Or, the target or targets could have been someone else in that room."

Mascelle said, "We'll track down everyone — everyone who's not already dead, that is — and try to get some answers."

Sachel said, "So tell me about the perp you nabbed today."

Mascelle replied, "Not much to tell, yet. Says his name is Gunter. He won't tell us anything else. No last name and no ID. We ran his prints and also got nothing. But he was wearing these." Mascelle pulled the broken sunglasses out of his pocket and handed them to Sachel.

Sachel asked, "What happened to them?"

"He dropped them on the floor and then crushed them with his foot."

Sachel examined the wires poking out from the frame. "Any idea what these are for?"

"Looks like spook stuff. Maybe CIA," Mascelle commented.

Sachel said, "A tall, blond, blue-eyed spy named Gunter? Sure, that works. Maybe he's a Nazi."

"A Nazi?" Mascelle asked with a smile.

"Yeah, sure, like in the movies. It's always the Nazis. Tall, blond, bad-ass, überman, with high-tech stuff like this... either that or South African white supremacists."

Mascelle and McKeown joined Jack in a laugh. "Yeah, nice theory, Jack. I think you've been polishing that seat with your ass too long," Mascelle said. "Besides, this particular überman saved my bacon. I was in pursuit when I suddenly found myself hanging by my fingertips two hundred feet in the air. This guy, who was home free by that time, came back and gave me a hand. I was toast, Jack. My wife would be making funeral arrangements around now, if this guy hadn't turned around and help me."

Jack Sachel sat forward in his chair. He placed his fingertips together and looked over them at Mascelle. "What happened then?"

"He asked me to let him go. I said no, so he let me arrest him. I didn't even have my piece at the time. He just put out his hands and I cuffed him."

After another moment of thought, Sachel said, "So this guy must be a government agent of some kind. Ours, or someone else's. You think he's the killer?"

"Maybe. But if he is, his motivations and his MO are definitely not the standard ones."

Jack Sachel replied, "So, the bad news is that Gunter isn't going to tell us anything. The good news is that sooner or later we're going to have a visitor from whatever agency or government he works for." He reached over and handed the broken sunglasses to McKeown. "Get these to the lab right away. Maybe they can tell us which, if any, of our friends in Fed-land uses stuff like this."

"Will do." McKeown said, taking the sunglasses.

Sachel said to McKeown, "Speaking of feds, what's the story with this Barella guy?"

McKeown responded, "I don't know, but I have some contacts at Federal Plaza and I'm calling in a few chits to find out. Whoever this guy is, he obviously knows a lot more about what's going on than he's telling us. In fact, he seems intent on keeping us in the dark. If we can find out who he is, it might shed some light on what this is all about."

Jack Sachel said, "Good. Do that. In the meantime, I'll check with an old army buddy of mine. He's a mucky-muck in DC with top-secret clearance. He won't be able to provide us with any classified information, but there's usually lots of unclassified stuff lying around that can help, if you know where to look for it, and he does."

McKeown said to Sachel, "I'd also like to get some special help on this."

"Special? You mean Sandy? I thought she drove you crazy."

"She does. But she's really good with the weird cases."

"I'll talk with her supervisor. In the meantime, why don't you talk to her to get her take on this?"

"Okay."

The three men got up. Sachel reached over shook Joe's hand and said, "Good seeing you again, pal. We've been out of touch too long."

"Yeah, how did we let that happen?"

"Hey... wife, kids, bills, the job... it happens. How about we get together again, soon?"

"That would be great, Jack."

"Thelma and I are having a big graduation party for Jack Junior on May 29th. Can you and Anne make it?"

"I don't know what's on the schedule that day, but we'll be there."

"Great, see you both then. Be careful on this one, Joseph, okay?"

"Hey, you know how careful I am," Mascelle smiled.

Joe and Sean turned and headed for the door.

"Hey Sean, can I speak with you a minute?" Sachel asked.

Joe nodded and walked out, leaving Sachel and McKeown alone.

"This is obviously going to be a really interesting case, Sean," Sachel said. "But you got the right guy with you on this. You can trust him with your life. I know, because I did, and he paid up big-time. Take very good care of my man there. He's like family. I want him to be at my son's party, and with a smile on his face. You understand?"

"I got it, Jack."

"And take care of yourself too, okay?"

"Right."

McKeown turned to leave.

"One other thing, Sean," Sachel said.

McKeown turned back.

"We discussed how there might be another potential victim that was sitting in that conference room. What we didn't discuss is the possibility that one, or maybe more, of the perps may also have been in that room, and this includes Tony."

"Yeah, I got that and I discussed it with Joe, but I'm still wondering what happens if things begin to point to his nephew. He really should not be anywhere near this case. You know that, right?"

"If it was anybody else, I would agree. But if things go down that way, Joe will be the first man to raise the flag and bow out."

McKeown nodded. "Okay, Jack, we'll play it by ear."

Chapter 38

"Penn Station," I said to the driver as I closed the door of the cab.

It was an April weekday morning in New York: sunny, reasonably warm, and with a light southwest breeze. It was not exactly beach weather, but I've stayed at my uncle's Fire Island cottage during this time of year before, and the off-season solitude usually nicely compensated for whatever April weather might lack in warmth and predictability.

The cab stopped at the Seventh Avenue entrance to Pennsylvania Station. Marcella was waiting near the taxi stand with a single, small suitcase in her hand and a very large pocketbook over her shoulder, which was almost as big as the suitcase. She wore blue jeans, a white turtleneck sweater, open-toed sandals and a big, toothy smile. She waved her right arm in broad strokes above her head and began bouncing on her toes as soon as she caught site of me.

Seeing her there like that, as excited as a schoolgirl, almost made me grateful to whomever was trying to kill me—or whomever they were trying to kill. Okay, maybe grateful was not the right term, but I was at least a little ambivalent. At that moment, all of my fears about lurking murderers, and anxieties about a failing business, were erased and replaced by the thought of Marcella and I sharing a small cottage on a remote and deserted beach. Alone. It may have been a Tuesday morning in April, but it felt like a Friday night just before Christmas.

I exited the cab and walked over to her. She gave me a proper little hug with one arm. Despite the platonic nature of the contact, I should have felt a little guilty about the propriety of taking my employee to a remote place for an undetermined period of time, under circumstances which would likely result in at least one encounter of carnal knowledge. On the other hand, I might be dead in a week, so screw political correctness.

I held my bag in my right hand and lifted Marcella's with my left. It was surprisingly heavy and I commented, "What do you have in here, a cannon?"

"Just lots of girl stuff, silly, all packed tightly in a very small bag."

We took the escalator down into the concrete and tile-lined bowels of the train station that was located under Madison Square Garden. The corridor at the bottom was once part of an imposing Gilded Age Greek revival structure built of travertine marble and designed by the legendary architectural giants McKim, Mead, and White. Its Doric columns and soaring, glass-enclosed spaces once stood twenty stories high.

However, in a spasm of incredibly bad taste, or a monumental act of cultural vandalism - depending on your point of view - the building was demolished in the 1960s. To add insult to injury, it was replaced by a round, lifeless, monolithic eyesore, the current Madison Square Garden, which was designed by the former CEO of a toothpaste company, and a wannabe architect, who was apparently from the same demented architectural school as the person, or persons, responsible for the Bomb Shelter at Stony Brook. Maybe someone should convince these people to stick to their day jobs.

Marcella and I walked through the dungeon-like remnants of the original station, which as I said was the only surviving part of the original building except for some bits and pieces that were replanted or grafted onto other structures in and around the city. What was left in the basement was not very inspiring architecturally, but it was a hell of an improvement over what it used to look like a few years ago: a world resembling something out of Dante's inferno. It now even had its very own K-Mart. What progress, huh?

Anyway, we took a second escalator down two more flights to the Long Island Railroad platform and boarded the shiny, new 11:16 Montauk train for the hour-and-forty-five-minute ride out to Patchogue Village.

Just a few years ago we would have been treated to an agonizing ride on a dilapidated, 1950s-vintage wreck of a passenger car. Somewhere in the demented logic machine, known as the MTA, it was determined that it was essential to destroy Penn Station, a building designed to last centuries, after only a few decades, but to keep for centuries railroad cars that were designed to last only a few decades. Fortunately, in the last few years, most of these museum pieces were being replaced with new cars that made the trip almost pleasant. The only alternative was a two or three hour drive on some of the most congested highways east of Los Angeles.

After a short trip through a dark tunnel, that took us under the East River, the train emerged into the sunlight on the Long Island side. We changed trains at Jamaica Station for the one to Montauk Point, which would make a stop in Patchogue.

The off-peak train was virtually empty, so Marcella and I had the car almost to ourselves. I placed my bag in the overhead and took the window seat. Marcella placed her bag and pocketbook on the seat next to the aisle, which had the effect of causing us to squeeze together in the remaining space available near the window. I found that interesting and, after mentally smacking myself in the head for not thinking of it first, I reached over and held her hand as we both watched Long Island pass by the window.

Long Island is home. I was born here, and with the exception of the last few years in the city, I lived here all of my life. Despite its distinct and discernible island geography, Long Island's exact boundaries are, believe it or not, somewhat controversial. Sort-of like Kips Bay: where it begins and ends depends upon whom you ask.

For a mapmaker or a mariner, Long Island is the fish-shaped land mass, surrounded by water, with its nose at the river east of Manhattan and the tip of its tail flukes at Orient and Montauk Points, the north and south forks, respectively. However, the head of the fish, comprised of Brooklyn and Queens, was long ago consumed, both politically and culturally, by New York City. So, even though many of the residents living there would not necessarily identify themselves as citizens of the City, you would be hard pressed to find any of them who considered themselves Islanders, and no one out on the east end of Long Island would, either. So, according to most people, the two remaining eastern counties, Nassau and Suffolk, are all that remains of Long Island proper.

However, for some, Nassau County, for all of its past Gold Coast, countrified glory, now belongs more to the city than to the Island, and these folks consider the westernmost terminus of Long Island to be Suffolk County's western border, with all points east belonging to the Island.

And then there is the view of some of the old-timers, out east where I'm from, who consider the farthest western terminus of Long Island to be a north-to-south line drawn between Port Jefferson on the north shore and Patchogue to the south. As for the folks who live on the rest of the fish to the west, as far as the old-timers are concerned, they can call themselves anything they want... but they are not Islanders.

I knew one of these guys when I was a boy. He was a newspaper route customer of mine; a mean, cantankerous old fart by the name of McDonald. His first name was Mister. My mother, always the diplomat, politely described him as colorful.

One of Mr. McDonald's colorful little habits was completing virtually every sentence with the word "goddammit,"as in, "Stop missing the stoop with the newspaper, Tony, goddammit"; or, "the Mets lost another game last night, goddammit"; or, "have a nice day. . ." Well, you get the idea.

He must have been at least eighty back then, but he still mowed his lawn with a manual, engine-less push mower. To the neighborhood kids he was the resident ogre, but for some odd reason, he seemed to tolerate me.

Mister McDonald was also a proud veteran of the "Great War," by which he was referring to World War One, and he proved it once by showing me the army helmet that he kept polished and hanging on a nail in his shed next to a small, folding army shovel. He once confided to me that The War put an end to civilized warfare, because it resulted in the widespread use of what he thought were the four worst inventions in the history of mankind: the machine gun, the tank, poison gas, and the airplane. Now, to most people, especially a Long Island kid delivering newspapers, this would all seem a bit confusing. But, when you heard Mister McDonald explain it, it seemed perfectly rational.

This subject, by the way, came up when I asked him if he had ever shot anyone during the war, and he told me that he had never fired a shot in anger. However, before I could complete a sigh of relief, he told me that the only proper way to kill a man was when you were close enough to look him in the eyes. He knew this, he explained, because he had killed seven men and he was looking in the eyes of every one of them when he did it. A bayonet or knife was his preferred method, but the pointy end of a shovel, under the chin, would do in a pinch. Gulp.

I was actually never clear on whether his victims were the enemy, or perhaps fellow soldiers. For that matter, he never said anything about where and when these encounters took place. I just assumed he was talking about The War, but who knew, really. I tried to stay away from the shed, and the folding shovel, after that.

One of Mister McDonald's other proud claims to fame was that he was the last in a long line of Long Island McDonalds that stretched back to before the Revolutionary War. This claim was often the subject of some heated debate among the kids in the neighborhood. It was the part about being the last of the line that was most controversial. One kid said he heard a rumor that Mister McDonald had a wife and children, but when he fell on hard times he decided to "cook 'em 'n eat 'em," as the old man might say. Other kids theorized that his family was still alive and well, but he kept them locked up in the shed, sharpening his shovel and polishing his helmet.

In any event, I can clearly recall Mister McDonald obsessing for years over the systematic eastward march of the "city scum," as he liked to call the invaders from points west. He once told me that, "One day they will swarm over the entire island, marching all the way to the very end at Orient Point, building ugly tract housing and strip malls all along the way."

I guess he turned out to right, because while there are still some open, undeveloped areas remaining in western Suffolk and Nassau, the last of them are disappearing rapidly under the never-ending onslaught of eastward migration from the Five Boroughs of New York City. Most of the remaining open areas can be found in Brookhaven, a town in Suffolk County, and points east, in the form of large tracts of forest called the Pine Barrens, where tough little pine trees manage to grow and thrive in soil that's not fit to grow much of anything else... except tract housing and strip malls.

Mister McDonald explained to me that, one day, the last remaining true Long Islanders like him would sail over to Plum Island and make a final stand. Looking back at it, I think he may have been trying to recruit me for the siege.

Plum Island, in case you do not know, is a tiny mound of sand and rock a few thousand yards east of Orient Point. Mister McDonald said that the federal government had a lab there where they conducted secret biological warfare experiments on animals. He also informed me that, when the final day of reckoning came, he would implement his master plan to defend Plum Island from the city scum, a plan that included using wooden catapults to launch infected livestock from the lab at the invaders: chickens, sheep, goats, pigs - maybe cows... whatever it took. He also told me that the government's animal experiments and his plan were top secret, and that if I ever told anyone he would shave my head – with his lawn mower. Mister

McDonald's plan eventually became a heated topic of discussion among the neighborhood kids. Okay, so maybe I told a couple of my friends.

Since that time, a book of the same name was written about Plum Island, and now everyone knows about the secret animal experiments, including the city scum. So, I don't think Mister McDonald's plan would still work, the element of surprise now being lost and all. Another Long Island kid wrote the book, but he's not from my neighborhood. Good thing, too; Mister McDonald is about a hundred years old now, but he still owns and operates a push lawn mower and keeps his shiny helmet on the nail next to the army shovel in the shed. I hope the two of them never meet.

Marcella asked me, "What's so funny?"

"Huh?"

"You have a big grin on your face. What are you thinking about?"

"Oh, just doing a little reminiscing about the good-ole days, when I was a kid, growing up around here."

I have this theory that every neighborhood has its own version of a Mister McDonald. And no matter how beautiful, or God-awful-shitty, a neighborhood is, there's always a like-minded character trying to keep someone else out. If it's not the country folks trying to keep out the city scum, it's some inner-city equivalent trying to keep out the suburban yuppie scum. Around and around it goes.

Chapter 39

Marcella reached into her bag and pulled out a book. She needed both her hands to do it, so she placed my hand, the one that she was holding, over her shoulder. Then she curled up next to me and started reading.

"What are you reading?"

"Something by Patterson, it's called *First to Die.*"

"Sounds depressing."

She smiled. "It's a suspense novel about people who are searching for a killer who is stalking newlywed couples."

"Geez, isn't that plot a little too close to our present situation for comfort?"

"Well, now that you mention it, yes. But I bought it two weeks ago, before I found myself running for my life with a man. . ." She hesitated, touched my leg with her now-free hand, and said, "... with a man that I like a lot."

I pulled her a little closer and said, "Try to get some tips on how to stay alive for the next few days. Okay?"

She laughed and returned to her reading.

We passed over the gridlocked Long Island Expressway as we traveled east. In about an hour, the densely populated areas of Queens and Nassau counties gave way to the more open terrain of Suffolk County. After computer science, my favorite subject in school was history, and according to my favorite history teacher, Suffolk was the first region of the Island to be settled by the English in the mid-seventeenth century, and is one of the oldest counties in the country.

It is, and always has been, more a part of New England than of New York. In fact, I remember reading somewhere that the

Dutch settlers of New York, then called New Amsterdam, and the English settlers of New England divided Long Island at a point approximately where the Nassau and Suffolk County border is today. The Dutch took everything to the west, and the English from Massachusetts and Connecticut took the rest. Ultimately, the English got it all and then they proceeded to write the Dutch right out of the history books. All that remains of their existence are a few odd-sounding names like Bronx, Yonkers, Brooklyn, Vanderbilt, and Roosevelt.

Since we're on the subject of history, we should probably cover a little local folklore and terminology for the benefit of the uninitiated. To the natives, Long Island is not *an* island. It is *The* Island. Yes, there are other islands around here, including Manhattan Island, but who cares? If Manhattan was so great, people from there wouldn't be spending so much time out here, would they? Also, the proper terminology is "I live *on* Long Island," not "*in* Long Island." I realize that this might seem like a minor grammatical point, but not for the locals. If you want to immediately identify yourself as city scum, just tell one of the local crazies, like Mr. McDonald, that you have a summer house *in* Long Island. It will be a short conversation. Tell them you have a summer house *in Laungk* Island and you may well be injured, because people who can't pronounce the word *long* are not really from here, and the locals don't find this pronunciation a source of much amusement, in any event. Never, ever, tell a loco-local that you have a summer house *in Laungk* Island and you wish they would stop clogging up *your* roads and beaches with their pickup trucks full of brats, because you may end up missing. Try to remember that you are the clueless, summer, city scum and that it is, after all, their fucking island. Hey, don't shoot the messenger. I'm just offering a few friendly safety tips here... goddammit. But I digress.

Marcella looked up from her book. "How much longer?"

"Not long now, maybe ten or fifteen minutes."

She looked around for the first time, taking in the sights

outside the window. "Wow, it's almost like the country out here. So how long did you live in Long Island?"

I corrected her. "You mean, how long did I live *on* Long Island?"

She smiled and said, "Yes, that's what I just asked."

The train left Sayville, the next stop was Patchogue, and we were just about on time.

I said to Marcella, "Almost my entire life."

Although most of my family, like me, has long since moved on, our connection to the place hasn't changed much. Patchogue, in my head and, I guess, in my heart, is still home. My roots there go back two generations, beginning with my grandparents who first arrived as teenagers in the 1920s, along with hundreds of other Italian immigrants. They worked long hours in the local mills, restaurants, shops, and boat yards, contributing their labor and skills to the local economy.

Both of my grandparents worked and, I'm told, fell in love while employed at a local factory called the Lace Mill. During ordinary times the factory produced, as you may have already guessed, lace, as well as other fine textiles for consumption in some of America's finest homes, especially those in New York City. The factory furnished considerably less fine textiles to soldiers during the War to End All Wars, a.k.a. The Great War. Twenty years later, to its considerable chagrin, the world discovered that that war didn't end much of anything except millions of young lives in the trenches of Europe. So they renamed it *World War I.*

After the war ended, the Lace Mill returned to civilian production during the rather brief intermission between World War I and World War II, or as my history teacher liked to call it, "World War, The Sequel." I love history. From 1940 through 1945, war production swelled the ranks at the Mill to well over a thousand.

My grandfather, the youngest of eight children, told me once about those days, or at least some of them. He said he hated working in the Mill, but there were very few other options around during the Great Depression. So, when America finally got into the Second World War, following the "Day of Infamy" on December 7, 1941, he didn't walk, but ran, to the nearest recruiter on Main Street to join the US Marine Corps.

It never occurred to me at the time, but I later realized that he was not exactly a young man when he enlisted. He was, in fact, in his mid-twenties. He didn't have to go, and I have often since wondered what would have possessed him to leave his home and his sweetheart to fight the Japanese on some bug and disease infested island in the middle of the Pacific.

I once read that about 1.2 million men in World War II were of Italian lineage: an incredible figure, when you think about it. I don't believe that the working conditions in the country's mills can readily account for this. I think Grandpa and the others of his generation and situation joined mostly because they were really pissed-off about Pearl Harbor. But Grandpa did once admit that there were times, when the bullets and shells were flying, that he would have given his right arm to be back in Patchogue, and back at his job at the Lace Mill.

Grandpa kept both of his arms, but lost part of his left foot to shrapnel on an island called Tarawa. After spending months in a series of hospitals, they sent him home, back to Patchogue and the Lace Mill. After that, and until the day he died, he thought he got the best of that bargain.

The Lace Mill closed within ten years after the end of World War II. Turns out it could not compete with the cheap imports coming from, among other places, Japan. The very same people who blew my grandfather's foot off, and killed or maimed many of his friends, later took his job away. But that was long before my time. I only vaguely remember the place as a burnt-out hulk that eventually succumbed to the wrecking ball.

On the bright side, however, they made the site into a nice department store that looks like an old lace mill, sort of, and now it sells products made in China and Mexico. Apparently, the Japanese couldn't compete in the export business with these new guys. All's well that ends well, I always say.

The train stopped and a disembodied, automated train-voice said, "This is the train to Montauk. This station is Patchogue... *bing*."

Marcella and I got off the train and took the short walk to the Watch Hill ferry terminal, which consisted of a small, brown cedar building located at the head of Patchogue River. The building was closed and locked, as you would expect it to be this time of the year, but the departure schedule was posted outside, in a glass-enclosed case. A quick scan informed us that the next boat to Watch Hill would be departing in about an hour. I suggested to Marcella that we leave our bags at the terminal and take another short walk to a local grocery store for some provisions.

"Do you think our bags will be safe here?" she asked, frowning.

"Sure, I don't think anyone will be interested in stealing our underwear."

"Well, just the same, I'll stay here and watch the bags while you go, okay?"

I smiled. "Okay, city girl, I'll be right back."

Our final destination was a tiny Fire Island community called Watch Hill. It had very few amenities, and only a handful of places to buy food and supplies, and I doubted that any of them would be open this early in the season. So, I stocked up on an assortment of bread, canned soup, dried pasta, tomato sauce, cold cuts, and other such provisions that I thought would hold us over for a few days in relative comfort. I also knew my uncle usually kept the place well stocked with the other essentials of life: bottled water, various non-perishable liquids containing copious amounts of ethanol, and Sinatra CDs. What else could we possibly need? Well, to be honest I did hesitate for a moment when I saw a display of condoms behind the register, but it was only for a second.

By the time I got back to the ferry terminal, neither Marcella nor our bags were where I left them. I looked to my left across the large expanse of lawn that ran south along the river walk and spotted Marcella about fifty yards away. *Oh my God.* I felt my heart start to thump in my head as I began running towards her. She was sprawled out, face-down, on the lawn next to the luggage.

The groceries began to tumble out of the bags in my arms and I finally dropped them entirely as I picked up speed. When I got within fifty feet of her, her head popped up and she gave me a puzzled smile as she repositioned the top of her bathing suit.

"No peeking, you!" she said.

By then, feeling like an ass, I slowed to a walk, and tried to look as casual and calm as possible, despite the trail of groceries on the lawn behind me.

"Tony, your face is white. Are you okay?"

"I'm fine," I said as I started to breathe again.

She stood up, saw the scattered groceries and then looked back at me.

"Were you worried about me—that I was hurt?"

I shrugged and smiled as I stood there wordless. Marcella had removed her jeans, her sweater, and her shoes. She was wearing a blue, one-piece, backless swimsuit, the kind worn by people who are serious about their swimming. She pouted at me and threw her long hair over one shoulder.

Her bathing suit clung to every detail of her perfect body,

outlining the shape of her breasts and her firm abdomen. She also had these amazingly long, slender legs. It was a body that revealed a dedication to swimming, jogging or weight training; something pretty strenuous. She was, as they say, cut.

She blushed when she noticed my stare. Then she walked over, put her arms around my neck and gave me a peck on the cheek. I noticed that she was wearing my favorite perfume.

"You're very cute when you're being protective." She said into my ear.

"Maybe I was just trying to jump your bones," I said as I looked into her eyes. Then I got serious and said, "I'm sorry if I startled you."

"Me too." She released her arms. "What a great day it's turning out to be," she said, changing the subject. "Can you believe how warm it is for this time of year? I thought I'd get a jump-start on my tan. Look how white I am."

I looked, and she was right: things were certainly beginning to warm up. "Yeah, white. Well, don't let me stop you," I said, recovering my composure and turning to gather up the groceries.

"No, the tan can wait." She slipped her sweater and pants back over her swimsuit and helped me gather things up.

"Why haven't we done this before?" she said.

"What?"

"Gone to the beach together."

"I don't know, maybe because no one was trying to kill us before?" I replied.

"Not very funny."

"Right. It's probably all in McKeown's imagination, and we should be back at the office trying to resuscitate our dying company rather than running away from some fictitious assassin."

I looked at her and could see that my last, thoughtless comment had struck a nerve.

She said, "I know this sounds stupid under the circumstances, but I've really been looking forward to this."

"No, I'm the one who's being stupid," I said, trying to remove my foot from my mouth.

She admitted. "No, you're right, I'm acting like a teenager. Sorry." She ran her fingers through her hair, pulling long strands over her head until her face was nearly concealed.

I reminded myself that, if and when we started to have a good time again, I would keep my big mouth shut and go with the flow for once in my life. I walked over to her and took her hand away from her hair and gently placed some of the strands behind her ear. I said to her, "I say stupid things when I'm scared or nervous."

"Which one? I mean, are you scared or nervous?" she inquired with a little smile.

"Both."

Then she gave me one of those big, toothy, smiles. God, she had great teeth. "Don't be nervous," she said.

Wow! I wasn't sure what that meant, but the way she said it made me want to immediately start swimming to Fire Island.

Chapter 40

The ferry was the same vessels that had been making this run for as long as I could remember. It was about eighty feet in length with a red bottom, blue topsides and a cabin painted in white. On the transom, written in large, blue capital lettering was the name *QUAIAPEN*. I remember being told, during a grade school field trip on this same old boat, that it was the name of a local Indian queen or sachem. According to my history teacher she died horribly, in a battle with some of the early English settlers – probably some of Howie's relatives.

When the ferry arrived it was empty, and it left essentially in the same condition, plus three; Marcella, me, and this one other guy dressed in a uniform. Marcella and I sat in the last row. The other passenger sat forward, next to the door of the pilothouse. He was wearing one of those brown, Smokey-the-Bear hats, so I surmised that he was probably a Fire Island National Park ranger, but the distance, the rows of benches between us, and the hat, concealed everything but the back of his neck.

The twin diesel engines started and a black plume of smoke rose from the stern of the vessel.

The company that owned and operated the ferry was one among several that ran these services up and down the length of Fire Island. A local family that had been in the business for the past seventy-five years operated this particular one. I used to be friends with one of them; she was my age and we dated on and off in high school. But, I hadn't seen or heard of her since. The boat had two decks: a main, enclosed deck below, and a second, open one above where Marcella and I were sitting. At the very front of the boat was the aforementioned pilothouse, occupied by a young man, the captain, who appeared to be not much more than eighteen years old.

Marcella eyed the guy and said, "That's not the captain, is it?"

"I hope so. Why?"

"He looks a little young."

I shrugged. "Don't worry, it's a family business and he's probably been making this trip since before he could walk."

Marcella smiled politely, but she didn't seem too convinced.

So, being a smart-ass who hates to miss an opportunity to make a wise-crack, I said, "By the way, the life preservers are in the overhead racks down below, just in case Junior up there has a little accident."

That comment got me a punch in the arm, which I enjoyed.

After a slow cruise down the Patchogue River, past the empty marinas, and the uninhabited dockside restaurants, we passed the rock jetty and then the entrance lights that stood at the mouth of the river.

It occurred to me that in less than six weeks, Memorial Day would transform this sleepy scene into the bustling, noisy center of a popular summer destination. In the meantime, Marcella and I had the place virtually to ourselves. My uncle's comment came back to me: "It's kinda romantic this time of year."

It also occurred to me that I should have been thinking about what was going on back in New York with the company, Kyle, Jan, and the murder investigation. But for whatever reason, I wasn't. I felt like I was playing hooky, like when I was a kid, spending the day in front of the tube in my pajamas watching reruns of *Batman* and *Flipper*. Bottom-line? Uncle Joe's idea was looking better every minute.

As we entered the Great South Bay, the boy-captain throttled up the engines from a quiet idle to a thunderous growl. The boat's speed increased, and with it the strength of the wind increased accordingly. Coupled with a fresh breeze blowing from the south, conditions on deck went from refreshing to uncomfortable rather quickly.

"It's getting pretty cold up here. Do you want to go below?" I asked Marcella, who was obviously beginning to feel the effects of the cool spring air.

"No, I'm fine. I will if you want, though."

"No, I'm fine if you're fine."

She smiled and moved closer, and I put my arm tightly around her shoulders.

The ferry made a straight track from the mouth of the river through the channel marked by green and red buoys. As it sped away from the shore towards the center of the bay, the size and frequency of the waves increased, as did the sea spray from the pounding bow of the boat.

Very few other boats were out on the bay today, and those that I could see were scattered in the distance. A couple of sailboats were out, taking advantage of the pleasant weather and the fresh spring breeze blowing off the Atlantic. There were also two other boats milling around in the distance as well, but they were not there for pleasure. They had the distinctive, flat-decked profile of a workboat—a clam boat, to be precise.

I looked toward the wheelhouse and noticed that the captain had been joined inside by the ranger who, I could now see, was dressed in full park ranger regalia: gray shirt, green pants and, of course, the aforementioned brown, wide-brimmed hat. He looked back at me and gave a friendly wave and I waved back. A few moments later, the ranger left the wheelhouse and walked towards us.

"Tony, is that you?"

I almost immediately recognized the bright blue eyes and sharp facial features. "Billy? Hey, how are you?"

"I'm doing fine, just fine. Wow, what's it been... ten, twelve years?"

"Yeah, something like that," I said. *Why does this keep happening to me?*

Billy and I did a quick exchange of verbal notes. You know: how's the family, what have you been up to, whatever happened to so-and-so, etc., etc.

Billy said, "I heard that you were some kind of big-shot entrepreneur in New York."

I gave him the story in a highly compressed form, because frankly, I was not prepared to have a two-man class reunion in the middle of the Great South Bay. Besides, what was I going to tell him? My company was going down the toilet, and someone might be trying to kill me?

Then I said to Bill, "I heard from some high school friends, a while back, that you had a job in Washington. I thought they said it was with the FBI or something like that."

Bill shrugged the question off and turned his attention towards Marcella, "So, who's your friend?"

"Oh, sorry, Marcella this is an old high school friend of mine, Billy Hoffenburg. Billy, this is Marcella, a ... my friend from work."

I explained to Marcella that Bill and I grew up a few doors away from each other and, obviously, attended high school together. I further informed her that Bill was a jock and had jock friends, while I hung out with the computer geeks. But, despite our different interests, we spent a lot of time together outside of school, because it turned out that Bill was interested in playing computer games and I liked playing softball, so we actually did have some things in common.

Bill and I also liked to use my father's Boston Whaler during the summer months, and took part in the annual Fire Island teenage mating rituals. These consisted of the standard activities involving young men making fools of themselves while chasing after young, bikini-clad hotties. It was the most fun I ever had in a public place, with or without my clothes on. But I decided not to bring up any of those details with Marcella in earshot.

Marcella appeared to be genuinely pleased to meet one of my old pals, and Bill seemed to share the feeling. That's when I remembered that hanging out with Billy presented both risks and benefits. He was, in the jargon of the time, a babe magnet. Something about that big chin and his blue eyes, combined with a ten-year-old's non-threatening charm, made him the immediate focus of any female within a two-hundred-yard radius.

The fact that he was usually the tallest guy in the room, and had the body of a Greek god, probably helped a little, too. So, the benefits worked like this: wherever Billy went, the girls would soon follow. If you wanted to find him at the beach, all you had to do was look for the swarming bikinis. So, naturally, when we went to the beach I stayed as close to Billy as possible. Trust me, it paid off.

Marcella and Billy exchanged further pleasantries and then he pierced Marcella with his blue eyes... yeah, same old Billy. This is where the risky part came in. Fortunately, Bill was no longer a Greek god. In fact he had developed quite a paunch. I remember he loved to drink this especially vile, pitch-black stout beer. A lead weight would probably float in this stuff. You didn't drink it as much as chew it. It had to be at least a thousand calories a pint, which didn't matter if you were a teenage jock, but it did if you weren't. He used to call me a wimp for drinking Bud. He called it piss in a can. I told him that the stout was going to make him fat and stupid someday. It looked to me like the sludge had finally caught up with old Billy. Frankly, under the circumstances, I was relieved to see that I had won at least one-half of that argument, hopefully both halves.

He explained to Marcella that he joined the Park Service a year after he graduated from college. "I just made a run back to the mainland to pick up some gear," he said through his toothy smile. "I was too lazy to take the skiff, so I hitched a ride with

Pete." He waved his thumb towards the captain in the wheelhouse.

The skiff? Is that the same thing as a rowboat? Apparently, Billy thought the word skiff sounded more ranger-like. Personally, I haven't heard the term used since Ranger Rick and Flipper rescued Sandy and Bud from one of their many misadventures in Coral Keys, those crazy kids. I guess Billy played hooky and watched some 60s reruns, himself.

Ranger Bill then commented with concerned authority, "Great day for the beach, but you're getting a late start today. You don't have too many hours before the last ferry returns to the mainland."

"Actually," I said, "we'll be staying at my uncle's place a few days." *Not that it's any of your business, you idiot.* I smiled politely.

Bill looked at Marcella and then grinned at me while nodding his approval. I mean, what a pig, right? Marcella smiled, turned a little red, and then looked out at the bay.

While we were all smiling, or grinning and apparently in an effort to change the subject, she inquired, "What are they doing?" She said pointing to one of the clam boats in the distance.

I said, "They're clamming. Those big, scissor-like things are called tongs. They dig the teeth into the bottom and pull the clams up a few at a time."

Marcella said, "It must be a tough way to make a living."

Ranger Bill jumped in. "It certainly is, now. My father told me that when he was in college, he dug clams part-time to cover tuition. He said he could make more in two days than most of his friends made in a week working at land-side jobs."

I guess most of his dad's friends were park rangers. "Is that so?" I replied.

He continued. "My father said there were so many of these boats out here back then that you could practically walk across the bay on them."

Old Bill was on a roll now.

"Really? Wow!" Marcella said.

My turn. "When I was a kid and we had summer parties, I would come home with a bushel of them, and serve them on the half-shell."

"Yeah, he had some great parties," Billy interrupted. "Hey, whatever happened to Laura? Weren't you two engaged or something?"

I shrugged that comment off and continued, "Now these guys are a dying breed, and a dozen clams is a high-priced delicacy."

"I've eaten them a few times," Marcella said. "I prefer them baked. Sometimes I'll eat them fried. But I'll never eat them raw."

"It's an acquired taste," I replied. "Sort of like stout beer, right Bill?"

Bill saw me looking at his gut and gave me an unpleasant smile.

"Right."

Marcella said, "What happened?"

"To Laura?" Bill inquired with a grin. "I don't know. What happened to Laura, Tony?"

"I think she meant, what happened to all of the clam boats, Bill." *You schmuck.*

"Oh, the same old story," Bill said, with official-sounding disgust. "People came in droves and the bay couldn't handle the load. So the clams went the way of the oysters and scallops. In fact, an entire way of life on the Great South Bay—the life of the baymen, the oystermen, and the clammers—had begun a long decline before we were born. Only a few sad remnants remain. It's difficult to imagine now, but the oyster industry in this little bay was a multimillion-dollar international industry that provided a good living for thousands of men who dredged the bays and others who worked in the factories. Or, at least, that's what they told me in class when they taught me about the local history." He grinned

Old Billy was just a cornucopia of information. The know-it-all continued.

"At one point in time, the oysters from this bay were so highly valued that a law was passed defining them as *superior oysters*, and they were given the official name of *Blue Points*. The industry grew until the turn of the century—the last one, of course. There were oyster processing factories scattered all along the shore, and hundreds of thousands of barrels of oysters were shucked, packed in wooden barrels, and shipped from the bay to cities all over the country, even to Europe."

I covered my mouth and yawned. He ignored me.

"But eventually overfishing and pollution sank the industry. Mother Nature contributed a new inlet in 1931 that opened the bay to the ocean, and finally a hurricane of historic magnitude, in 1938, wiped out what was left. Hey, they don't call her *a mother* for nothing."

Marcella looked confused. I gave him a polite smile.

Bill continued, "Today you're almost as likely to find a humpback whale in the bay as a wild oyster. The only oyster industry left exists in the form of a small company a few miles west called, appropriately enough, the Blue Point Oyster Company. The oysters are bred and grown under controlled conditions inside of hatcheries. The clamming industry also still exists today, but it's only a shadow of what it was when my father was a boy. And with the uncontrolled flood of people still moving out from the city, it's just a matter of time before that disappears, too."

I was tempted to ask Ranger Bill if he and Mister McDonald were exchanging notes. Just then, the ferry began to make a slow turn to the southeast towards the distant opening of the long, narrow channel that would terminate at the Watch Hill ferry landing.

Chapter 41

Fire Island, which was a featureless gray line low on the horizon thirty minutes ago, began revealing more details as we approached the entrance to the Watch Hill channel. A series of low hills, which were actually large sand dunes separated by blowouts, became visible, and we could also see the watchtower at Davis Park, another small beach community just west of Watch Hill, consisting of a somewhat larger marina, a grocery store, and a favorite local hangout called the Casino.

Bill's monotone spiel was starting to grate on my nerves. It was somewhat odd actually, almost as if he was reading it from crib-notes written on his forearms, or that he had recently memorized an entire guidebook. It didn't sound natural somehow, and if you knew Bill back when he was the macho jock, it definitely didn't sound normal coming from him.

Bill shifted to a different subject.

"We're now entering the Watch Hill channel," he said, "which, while clearly visible on a navigation chart, is indiscernible from the surrounding waters except for a line of small buoys marking its north and south boundaries. It's a clear day, so the captain will use the range markers at the eastern end of the channel to line up the ferry in the center. In poor visibility, however, navigating it can be a delicate operation, even for an experienced captain. The center of the channel is barely six feet deep, and about forty feet from the center on either side of the channel there are sand bars that reduce the depth to a few inches in some places. During the summer you can often witness the strange sight of people standing in ankle-deep water a half-mile from the beach and not fifty feet from where the ferries are cruising in the channel."

Marcella looked in the direction that Bill was pointing. I guess she was trying to envision people standing on the water. I didn't have to imagine it, because Billy and I used to be two of those people. The sand bars were once loaded with clams, and if you knew what you were doing, you could dig half a bushel with your toes in a couple of hours. I also remember Billy occasionally flipping the bird to the gawking tourists coming in on the ferry. *Welcome to Fire Island*!

"Over the years", Billy droned on, "This part of the bay has become infamous for destroying propellers, grounding boats and occasionally causing serious injuries or worse. Mostly the victims were, and are, people unfamiliar with these waters. But some of the locals who know these waters well can get into trouble too, especially if they're returning from a beach party or bar." He smiled and shrugged at his little inside joke.

"Yeah Bill, remember that time I let you drive my dad's Whaler after that party at the Casino? I think I still have that bump on my head where I smashed into the console when you ran us aground."

Billy rolled his eyes as if I was making it up, but I wasn't. The ferry engines throttled down as we passed the two buoys that marked the entrance of the long channel.

Billy returned his attention to Marcella, who seemed to be working very hard not to smile at my wisecracks. "The Watch Hill Marina serves as the main marine base for the National Park Service, which is responsible for overseeing the five-mile-long Fire Island National Seashore," Billy said. "If you like miles of unspoiled white sand beaches, which most people do, it is probably the best national park in the Northeast, and one of the best anywhere in the country, as far as beaches go. I was very lucky to get posted here."

"Hey, is that a dolphin?" I said, looking in no particular direction.

Billy tried to follow my gaze. "Where?"

"Are there dolphins in the bay?" Marcella asked Ranger Bill.

Bill, regaining his composure, and his senses, shook his head at me and said, "Not anymore."

Not anymore? I smiled and said, "Never mind, it was nothing."

At that point, Marcella looked at me and gave me another punch in the arm. I'm sure at this point Bill would have loved to take a shot at me too, but he was demonstrating remarkable restraint. Was I having fun, or what?

Bill asked where he left off.

"Nice beaches," I replied.

"Right. So geologically speaking, Fire Island is little more than a single, long, sandbar. With the exception of an occasion inlet, it runs parallel to, and almost the entire length of, Long Island. Like Long Island, its geological identity is distinct from its cultural one. Geologically this sandbar begins in the east, in Southampton, and proceeds to Jamaica Bay just a few miles from Manhattan. But, as with much of the extreme western portion of Long Island, like Brooklyn and Queens, the western reaches of Fire Island have become densely developed urban areas. They are more part of New York City than Long Island."

"Maybe it was a shark." I said.

"Oh, stop," Marcella scolded.

Billy, knowing an opportunity when he saw one, said, "Maybe. Could have been a mako."

"What's that?" Marcella asked. "Like a baby shark?"

Billy said, "No, the mako shark can grow to well over a thousand pounds, and they are deadly."

Ooh, good one, Bill.

"What would a fish like that eat in a little bay like this?" Marcella asked.

"You mean besides humans?" I inquired.

Marcella rolled her eyes at me. I was actually starting to enjoy Ranger Bill's tour.

Bill continued, "They love to feed on bluefish, which sometimes come into the bay in large schools. They're nasty little bastards themselves, by the way. Bluefish are the only species of fish known to kill other fish for fun."

"Oh, come on, how do you know when a fish is having fun?" Marcella asked.

"Must be their toothy grin," I chimed in. I thought that was pretty funny, but that comment got me a look from both of them indicating that I might be acting stupid and childish, which of course, I was. Oh, well.

Bill continued. "We know because they have been observed maiming and killing hundreds of their prey without eating them. And boy, can they maim and kill. They can churn the water like a washing machine. We call it a 'feeding frenzy' or a 'bluefish blitz'. They're really fond of bunker, at type of bait fish, which will willingly run themselves high and dry on the sand, where they will suffocate, rather than be shredded by the marauding bluefish schools. Bluefish will eat almost anything in the water, even each other. But not sharks, of course, but only because the sharks eat the bluefish first."

Marcella's eyes were getting pretty wide now. "Well, at least I don't have to worry about being eaten by the bluefish," she commented with some hesitant relief.

Bill said, "That's true. As long as you don't wear anything shiny, like jewelry, when you're in the water." Bill hesitated with an expectant smile, and then said. "There was that one case a few years ago in New Jersey. A woman went into the water wearing shinny earrings. Some bluefish came by and thought the earrings looked tasty. They ate the earrings, and both her ears off in the process."

Marcella sat there in silence, a hand over her open mouth. It occurred to me that Marcella was not enjoying the tour anymore, so neither was I. At this rate, she'd end up spending the next few days hiding under the bed in a fetal position. I interrupted. "Good thing the water is too cold to swim in this time of year. So what were you saying about New York City, Bill?" I asked trying to change the subject to something less nightmarish.

"Oh, right, I was about to say that about seventy years ago, a man by the name of Robert Moses had the vision and good sense to halt the uncontrollable eastern spread of development along the tenuous and fragile stretch of barrier beach. He did it by building a chain of low-density state parks in Nassau and Western Suffolk Counties, ending, appropriately enough, at a lighthouse that's been around since George Washington. This lighthouse, known as the Fire Island Lighthouse, was recently restored and is now operating again." He pointed westward. "If you look, you might just barely make it out on the horizon from here. That lighthouse is the beacon that marks the entrance to this entire sanctuary."

Marcella and I looked in the direction Bill was pointing, but we couldn't see anything but blue sky. The ferry began its approach to the marina entrance and the captain lowered the throttles back to a near idle.

Bill said, "There are no roads to speak of east of the lighthouse, and the only wheeled vehicles beyond that point consists of an occasional four-wheel-drive truck rigged with fishing poles, a fishing permit, and a beer cooler. And, with the exception of a few small communities consisting of modest summer cottages and the occasional marina or campground facility, there's nothing but wide-open beaches and dunes from the lighthouse eastward. Also, some narrow boardwalks snake through the salt marsh and between the dunes, connecting these communities and providing an occasional elevated walkway that crosses over the dunes to the ocean."

I noticed, with relief, that the ferry had begun its docking maneuvers, which meant we would be disembarking in a few moments and, I hoped, leaving Ranger Bill behind.

"The point is that all of these miles of underdeveloped beach property east and west of the lighthouse would have long ago become part of the sprawling, congested mess now commonly found in and around New York City, and down the coast of New Jersey, were it not for the firewall of state parks constructed by Robert Moses, which are themselves considered to be the crown jewels of the New York State park system."

Despite his flat, uninspired delivery, I must say that I was impressed with Bill's transformation from a formerly mindless sports-jock to a fountain of useful historical information. I think I might have to reassess my opinions about Park Ranger School, or wherever they trained these people.

As for Bill's spiel about Robert Moses, to most people not from around here, he is either unknown or, if they know anything about him, they don't seem to have anything nice to say. But, if you're from the Island, he's a salient, omnipresent character. The best places on Long Island—the ones where you want to swim or picnic or hike on a bright summer's day, or drive with the windows down and the sunroof open, or play a round of golf — were all designed and built by this man. It's actually not possible to go anywhere really pleasant on Long Island without encountering at least one of his many creations. The strange thing is that, until you're old enough to travel to other places, you can't really fully appreciate his work. Growing up here, you just assume that everyone has a large number of beautiful public beaches, parks, pools, boardwalk, and all connected by tree-lined parkways. After you start traveling, you realize that virtually no one else does. The few that do, likely have them because they had some local landscape architect or city planner who visited Long Island at some point and fell in love with one or more of Moses's creations. Even Walt Disney was inspired by this guy. If this sounds like platitudes, consider this: Moses designed and built parkways that not only get you to your destination, but are destinations in themselves. The man had the ability to transform purely utilitarian strips of concrete highways into tree-lined nature trails that you can drive sixty miles per hour on. How cool is that?

So Ranger Bill, like me and most other Long Islanders I guess, considers Robert Moses to be an okay guy, or at least they think the stuff he built was pretty cool, even if they don't know another thing about him. After all, if a man can be judged by his works, what else do you need to know about Moses that you can't discover at Jones Beach?

However, for all of his vision, foresight, hard work, and dedication, Robert Moses was ultimately rewarded by first being attacked, then sacked, and finally forgotten. As his final reward, during the waning days of his long life, he was treated to a public excoriation as a corrupt, power-hungry bureaucrat, a wrecker of New York City neighborhoods, and similar such unhappy bullshit. Some morons went so far as to compare him with Stalin. The old man died not long after, so he was spared the public trial and execution. Lucky him, and God bless America.

Marcella and I gathered our things and prepared to leave the ferry. Billy cheerfully volunteered to help us carry our bags. Actually, to be more accurate, he volunteered to carry Marcella's bag. She politely declined, but good ol' Billy would not take no for an answer and practically tried to wrestle Marcella's bag away from her. I was amused to see that Marcella was winning the contest, when suddenly she decided to take mercy on Bill and released it. At that point, he nearly fell down the stairs.

He caught his balance just before he went down in a heap, regained his composure and commented that he thought Marcella's bag was remarkably heavy for its size. I smiled and nodded.

Chapter 42

We left the ferry and Billy behind, and began the long walk to the cottage. I pulled out my cell phone to check the signal, but there was not a single bar registering. So, we stopped at a payphone next to the small ferry terminal and I called Uncle Joe to tell him that we made it safely to Fire Island, and that everything was fine. He wasn't in, so I left a message.

The Watch Hill marina was empty, with the exception of a single green and white motorboat that was tied up on the southern side of the docking area. The colors and the large emblem on its cabin sides indicated that it belonged to the National Park Service.

"That must be Ranger Bill's skiff," I commented. There must have been something in my tone.

Marcella smiled and said, "I thought you two were friends?"

I was pretty sure I knew where this line of questioning was leading. This was where I was scolded for being a jealous jerk. I said, "We were, a long time ago. You know what they call some old friends?"

"No, what?"

"Familiar strangers," I replied. "There's very little that Bill and I have in common anymore, except for a few memories."

"How about the same interest in women?"

There it was. I shrugged. "Bill will take an interest in any woman. I like to think I'm a little more selective."

Marcella took my hand and squeezed it. "I think I like it when you're jealous."

What? Me? Jealous? "I'm just giving you the scoop on the lover-boy with the funny hat."

Marcella stopped walking and pulled me towards her. I turned and she caught me by surprise with a kiss: not your ordinary, friendly peck on the cheek this time, but a long, wet one on the lips. I guess it had the desired impact, because when she pulled back, my lips were just hanging out there in space. She then verified that she had my undivided attention by asking, "Are you listening?"

I pulled in my lips and grunted in affirmation.

"I'm not interested in anyone else besides you. I haven't been since the moment I set my eyes on you. Nod your head if you understand what I just said."

I nodded.

"Okay, it's settled then, right?"

"Right. Can we close the deal with another kiss?"

"Later." Marcella then pulled a pair of expensive-looking sunglasses out of her bag, placed them on her face, then took my hand and gave it a tug. "Lead on," she said.

We walked around the perimeter of the harbor and took a right turn at the first intersection, then walked south towards the ocean side of the island. The boardwalk ended at a concrete walk that ran east and west between the dunes, down the center of the Island. We took another right and followed it. After a short distance the concrete walk came to another boardwalk, this one narrow and elevated, which snaked through the small trees and brush between the dunes.

We walked single file, with Marcella hesitantly taking the lead. Our feet were about six feet above the ground in places and there were no handrails, so she took her time. At one point, she stumbled and I grabbed onto her arm to help her recover her balance.

"Are you okay?" I asked.

"Yes, just a little unsteady." She took off her sunglasses and put them back in her handbag.

"We're almost there. You want me to carry your suitcase?"

"No, I'm fine now, thanks!"

We arrived at my Uncle Joe's place a few minutes later: a small, white clapboard cottage typical of the homes out here.

"Wow, this really is beautiful, Tony." Marcella said as she admired the compact, two-story structure.

In truth, I was impressed with the sight of the place, myself. It had been years since my last visit. I remembered a pretty basic beach shack, but Uncle Joe had obviously invested a good deal of time and money since then. It was still the same simple cottage I remembered, but he had added a new deck and little details here and there, like green storm shutters and flowerpots, that really spruced the place up.

I found the key where Uncle Joe said it would be, and unlocked the door. The interior was dark, and it took a moment for our eyes to adjust as we placed our bags on the floor. "I'll get some light in here." I said walking across the living room and over to the window blinds, which I opened. The room was immediately flooded with light from the large windows that stretched almost the entire length of the living room wall.

"How beautiful," Marcella said. I followed her gaze through the salt-stained panes of glass and was struck by the beauty of the pounding surf. The memories of past summers came back, slowly at first and then faster, with more detail, until I could picture a raucous seen of volleyball with my cousins, my aunts and uncles gathered around the barbecue pit, and my parents walking down the beach, arm in arm.

I recalled the hot summer days and the cool evenings with the breeze blowing in from the ocean; dinner with my family; the sunsets and moonrises; but most of all the sensation of waking up in the morning with the sound of the ocean surf, the smell of the sea, and the first rays of the morning sun, all streaming in through the bedroom window at the same time, with me lying there in anticipation of another day at the beach.

I said, "It's been a while. I forgot how fantastic the view was." I took her hand. "Let me give you the nickel tour."

Chapter 43

I led her through the place, showing her each of the rooms on the first floor, and then took her upstairs to the bedrooms.

"This was my room when I was a kid. Well, actually I shared it with two or three of my cousins, but it felt like mine."

"You must have had a wonderful time growing up here during the summers; you were a very lucky little boy."

"Yeah, I guess I was. It's funny how you grow up in a place like this and you really don't appreciate how special it is, and how special that time was, until you grow older and look back on it."

So there I was, alone with Marcella, a woman whom I'd known for seven months, but really didn't know at all. And we were standing in my old bedroom: the very place where I had countless teenage fantasies—to say nothing of a few wet dreams—about being alone with just such a beautiful woman. So, I looked into her eyes and she looked into mine, and I said in a soft voice, "Hey, you must be hungry. Come on, I'll make us something to eat."

Okay, so I was a little nervous. She was too, I think, and I could see some relief behind her bright smile when she heard the words. What would Uncle Joe say if he saw me now?

We returned to the living room and I said to Marcella, "We're pretty limited with amenities here. Uncle Joe doesn't allow a TV, radio, or telephone, and cell phone coverage is between poor and non-existent."

Marcella asked, "Okay, so what are our choices?"

"Basically, we have a CD player."

"Great! What kind of music do you have?"

I flipped through a shoebox full of dusty CDs. "Well, we have Frank Sinatra, Tony Bennett, Frank Sinatra, the Lettermen, Frank Sinatra, someone called Andrea Bocelli—I have no idea—and did I mention Frank Sinatra?"

"The Lettermen?"

"Don't ask; you don't want to know, trust me."

Marcella said, "How about some Bocelli?"

"Yeah? Who is she?"

Marcella laughed. "It's a he, silly!"

"But Andrea is a girl's name."

"It's An-DRE-a," she said with an Italian accent, adding hand gestures for emphasis.

"Yeah, that's what I said, Andrea."

"Trust me, he is a he," she replied.

I pulled out the CD case and looked at the cover. "I guess that explains the beard."

She walked over and took the CD from me. "Oooh, this is the *Romanza* CD," she said.

"Is that good?"

"Yes, it's very good. Your uncle has great taste."

"Hey, it runs in the family."

She smiled and looked at me, cocking her head. "Yes," she said. "Things tend to work like that."

I was still trying to process that somewhat mysterious comment, when I said, "Okay, I'll handle dinner, you handle the entertainment."

I walked towards the adjoining kitchen and Marcella put the CD in the player. A moment later, the room filled with some very Italian-sounding music. I turned and watched as she closed her eyes, gracefully moved her long, beautiful neck from side to side. Then the singing began. *He was definitely a he.*

Marcella opened her eyes, slipped off her shoes, placed her hands on her hips and smiled at me. Then she began dancing, gracefully gliding towards me in rhythm with the music. She danced like she was on a stage, or on a cloud in a dream. A good dream. A really good one.

My heart began to thump in my chest. I guess it was trying to tell me something, probably something I already knew. Like, I was in way over my head with this woman – or maybe it was just trying to remind to start breathing again, before I fell over from lack of oxygen.

A few magic moments later, Marcella was standing right in front of me and looking up into my eyes. She gently lifted my hands with hers and twirled beneath them, then leaned back against my chest and placed my left hand on her hip and held my right hand over our heads, moving her hips to the music. *Whew, I'm a goner!*

"Well, what do you think?" She asked.

"Huh? Oh, I can get used to it… I think."

"Good."

"Where did you learn to dance like that?"

"Lessons. When I was a girl."

"It was… is… beautiful."

"Thank you."

"I'm not a big dancer." I confessed.

"That's okay, I'm a good teacher."

Gulp.

She stopped, turned, took my arm and said playfully. "I'm hungry. Let's see what's for dinner."

We found a box of pasta and a jar of tomato sauce in the pantry, and Marcella and I prepared a fast meal. Then I uncorked a decent bottle of Valpolicella from my uncle's booze closet. Like I said, we're beer people, but sometimes the occasion calls for something special and, being a cop, my uncle always likes to be prepared. God bless him.

Marcella put on a thick cotton sweater and socks, and I put on a windbreaker, and we took the food and wine out onto the deck and sat in two wooden Adirondack chairs facing the ocean. The air was still, and we watched the tide come in, and the sun go down.

By the time the stars came out, the plates and the bottle were long emptied, and we were enjoying mugs of hot cocoa.

The thought of how we came to be here was a distant memory. I was very relaxed, and she looked so too. I moved my chair as close to her's as possible, took her hand in mine and said, "This was a great day. Thanks for coming."

She looked at me, squeezed my hand and said, "Thanks for the invitation."

The air was cool and clear now, which seemed to amplify the sound of the waves breaking on the beach; the deep rumble was followed by a fizzing sound as the waves' remnants splashed a retreat back into the Atlantic. I looked to the east where the sky was an inky black, but I could just discern a small patch of sky on the horizon that was beginning to glow.

"Look." I said staring at the point in the distance.

Marcella followed my gaze to the area of slightly illuminated sky.

"Do you see it?" I asked

"I think so. What is it?"

"You'll see."

In a few moments, the brightness of the sky began to increase rapidly until a small, bright sliver of light appeared on the horizon. Then, bit by bit, the rest of the yellow-orange disk appeared and cast a path of light towards us over the calm surface of the ocean.

She placed her hand over her mouth. "Oh, it's beautiful. And look how big it is! I've never seen such an enormous moon before," Marcella beamed.

I turned and looked at her face, which was now evenly lit by the golden light. She was so beautiful, but it was the wonder in her eyes that I will never forget: like a child seeing a rising moon for the first time.

She caught me staring at her, gently ran her fingers through my hair and then pointed to the horizon. "Not at me, at the moon. You're missing it."

No, I'm not. I turned back and felt her wrap her arm around mine. I said, "This brings back some great memories. My parents would sit out here together, just like we're doing now, and watch the sunsets, then the stars and the moon rise. I remember barging in on them and sitting on my dad's lap on a number of occasions. I guess that was one of the advantages of being an only child; I had my parents all to myself, whether they liked it or not." I laughed.

"Did they spoil you?"

"I guess they did, a little. I remember on this one night; a hot, humid breeze was coming off the ocean, and I started complaining about how uncomfortable I was. So, my dad told me to close my eyes, which I did, and then he told me to concentrate, which I tried, at least for a while, but I didn't know what I was concentrating on, so I asked him. He said, 'Shush. Do you feel that?' I told him the only thing I felt was the warm air. But then he blew gently on my cheek. 'How about that?' I told him that I felt him breathing on me. Then he explained that the warm ocean breeze was the breath of God, and that if I listened very carefully I could hear him whispering my name. Then I heard it: God whispering my name. It was probably just my mom playing along, but I was sure it was God at the time."

"Oh, how beautiful that is," Marcella beamed. "Your father sounds like a poet."

"He was a cop. He passed away a few years ago."

Marcella said. "Oh, I'm sorry."

I shrugged. "He was actually a pretty tough guy, most of the time anyway: a man's man and all that. But sometimes he could surprise you, like that time. I guess he was sort of a poet, in his own way. In a different age I think, maybe, they would have called him a warrior-poet."

Marcella asked, "You were an only child, in a big Italian family like yours? Why no siblings?"

"I don't know," I replied. "Maybe my parents figured that once you get it perfect, why take a chance. I mean, if their first kid was like my cousin Steve, I think they would have definitely had more kids."

Marcella laughed. "And modest, too."

"Well, maybe not perfect, or even especially bright for that matter. After that first night, I tried to listen for my name being whispered every night. For a week. And it always turned out the same way. I would doze off, and the next thing I would remember is my dad tucking me into my bed. I guess they got some time alone, after all. I think he set me up."

Marcella squeezed my hand and said, "Good for him."

After we listened to Andy—Andre—whatever—for a while, I put on a Sinatra CD. Old Blue Eyes began belting out the number about witchcraft. Very appropriate choice, if I do say so myself.

Marcella asked. "Where's your mom?"

"She lives in Florida."

Marcella lifted my arm and put it around her shoulder, and we sat there a while in silence, as Frank began telling us about his love life, starting from when he was twenty-five.

"Maybe someday I'll get to meet her."

"Oh, I definitely think so. My aunts and uncles have probably already reported to her on your softball skills, and they are probably preparing a dossier on you as we speak. What about your folks?"

"They both died when I was young. Car accident. I was raised by nuns in a convent." She looked at me and smiled. "I know that sounds like some sort of joke, but it's true. I think I remember my parents," Marcella said, her voice now beginning to tremble a little. "But sometimes, I'm not sure if it's really them or just my imagination."

We both stopped talking. It was right around the time that Frank began explaining how he was doing it his way.

I'd be lying if I didn't admit that I was hoping that the verbal foreplay would lead to the real thing. On the other hand, I was just enjoying the sound of her voice, and the way she listened with genuine interest to every word I said. I could not remember the last time I'd talked so much about my life, or a time when anyone seemed to care as much as she seemed to.

Before we knew it, it was late and we were both pretty tired. I walked her to her room and we stopped outside of the bedroom door and kissed. She said, "Don't take this the wrong way, Tony, but I can't."

I smiled and said, "Hey, no problem, I understand."

"I don't think you do, but you're a gentleman, and I thank you for trying to understand, anyway."

We kissed again and she disappeared into her room, and I went to mine. I half-opened the window that faced the ocean, stripped to my briefs, and jumped in between the cool sheets. It felt like summer vacation again. And for a few moments, before I fell into a deep sleep, I experienced that childlike state of mind where my only concern was planning the next day's activities at the beach.

Chapter 44

It was early, maybe six o'clock, and I lay there for a while watching the dim morning light begin to illuminate the room, and wondered why I was awake so early. Then I remembered my dream, or at least part of it. There was a white horse, it was galloping on a beach, I think. It was weird remembering my dreams. I never had before.

From outside the open window, I heard some birds squawking. Maybe they woke me. It must have been mating season or something, because they were making quite a racket. I looked over and saw two of the stupid things on the windowsill. They looked like they were staring each other down between squawks, sort of like Bill and I on the ferry yesterday: same looks on our faces, but absent the beaks and feathers. Ah, spring.

A moment later, I heard a whoosh of wings and the bird chatter was replaced by the distant rumbling of the surf. I love that sound. A gentle breeze rustled the curtains and the smell of the ocean wafted into the room. Then I smelled fresh coffee and something else cooking: pancakes, maybe, and eggs, I think. I lay there a while and just enjoyed it. I guessed Marcella is an early riser. Maybe I could get used to that.

I got out of bed and took care of the morning bathroom stuff, threw on a pair of shorts and a T-shirt, and went down to see what was for breakfast. I found Marcella sitting at the kitchen table, bright-eyed and dressed in a neat little outfit that included white pants and an aqua blouse. Her long hair was tucked up inside a white, wide-brimmed canvas hat. She was sitting at the table, which was set for two, and sipping from her coffee mug. She smiled when I walked in.

"Good morning, sleepyhead."

I could definitely get used to this. "Good morning. Are those pancakes I smell?"

"Yes, right over there," she said, pointing to the other side of the table. "I hope you don't mind. I took some liberties with your kitchen."

"Not at all." I checked out the spread. "Hey, this looks great. Thanks!"

And it was great. Pancakes, with some of the eggs that survived being dropped at the ferry terminal yesterday, and some of the ham as well. She watched me as I ate, her mug in one hand and her head in the other.

Despite the fact that I slept alone, it was the best morning-after breakfast I'd ever had. "So what would you like to do today?" I asked her.

"I don't know. It's supposed to be another warm day. We could just sit on the deck and watch the surf, or maybe take a walk on the beach." She stretched her arms over her head.

"That sounds like a plan. Hey, my uncle has a sailing dinghy around here somewhere; maybe I'll take you for a sail after the walk."

"Sailing?"

"Yeah, ever been?"

"No," she replied.

"I think you'll like it."

"Won't the water be a little too cold?"

"Not if we stay in the boat."

We cleared the dishes; she washed, I dried. Then we left for our walk. Marcella carried her large handbag over her shoulder, which she had declined to leave at the house. What is it with women and large handbags? She straightened her hat and asked me if I brought one. "You might get a burn today." She warned.

I shrugged. "Never use one, never burn. Italian skin, you know." Well, that wasn't entirely true. I remember getting a bad sunburn once. It was late spring and a friend and I decided we should get our teenage bods tuned-up for the season, and of course the beach-babes, with a little workout. His older brother happened to belong to a health club and he lent us his pass. We spent the day in the gym pumping iron. Actually, we spent most of the time talking about all the girls we wanted to plug and watching other people pumping iron. Anyway, on our way to the showers, we noticed a little closet-sized room with a sign on the door indicating is was a tanning room. The sign also explained that first-timers should not use it for more than five minutes. Being responsible young men, we followed the instructions to the letter. Being clueless, teenaged idiots, we continued to follow the instructions five or six more times. I never knew that skin could turn that color. We could walk again pretty well by July; we were peeling like a couple of snakes, but we could walk.

Just as predicted, it turned out to be a sunny, warm day. The temperature, according to the thermometer on the wall of the visitor's center, reached 82 degrees by 1:00 p.m., and the air was pretty still. I flexed my muscles, sucked in my gut, and then stripped off my shirt.

It's not that unusual to have an occasional great day like this in late April or early May, around here. But usually I find myself somewhere else, like my office in Manhattan, imagining how great it would be to be at the beach, on Fire Island. I was here this time, and tonight Marcella and I would still be here, and alone again, staring at the stars through the clear spring sky, listening to Frank, or that Andy guy, and toasting to another perfect day.

Speaking of toasting, my Mediterranean complexion, as I said, usually makes me impervious to sunburn, except in extreme circumstances such as the aforementioned tanning room. Apparently, spending several hours in the sun, on the first warm day in spring, also qualifies as an extreme circumstance.

"Ooh, you're getting pretty red, Tony," Marcella said as she looked at the back of my shoulders.

"Yeah?"

I was toasting, all right. I grunted my shirt back on and we headed back to the cottage. When we got there, Marcella introduced me to a sunburn remedy that she learned from the nuns. The recipe called for milk and honey. *A sunburn remedy invented by nuns that contained milk and honey*?

Fortunately, I brought some milk with us the previous day, and my uncle had some honey in one of the cupboards. The best part was that Marcella volunteered to rub it on me. Perfect. I could not have planned it better. I lay down on a large towel on the living room floor and she started very gently on my neck, then my shoulders, then back and down to my legs. She told me to turn over, which was a little tricky, since I was sticking to the towel on contact, like a bug on flypaper. I finally got over and she resumed her careful application of the gunk on my chest. As she moved down towards my abdomen, she noticed that my shorts were moving in an unusual way. Seems that my friend, the one with the single eye, decided to come up for a look, just to see what was going on. She smiled, blushed and then handed me the cup containing the concoction.

"I think you should do the rest," she said, being careful to focus on the part of my body with two eyes.

"Oh, don't worry about him," I said. "He's just curious about the milk and honey."

"I think you should do the rest," she repeated.

I did as I was told.

Over the next few days, Marcella and I settled into a daily routine, but it didn't seem routine at all. Even washing the dishes and taking out the garbage was exciting. Okay, so maybe not exciting, but I couldn't remember a moment when I wasn't enjoying her company, and I think she felt the same way. We ate breakfast, lunch, and dinner together, walked on the beach, watched the sunrises and the sunsets, and at night we would talk. Sometimes I would tell her one of the local pirate or ghost stories. Sometimes we would read and hold hands, or just watch the stars in silence. The only time we didn't spend together was when we slept. Did I mention that I was a Boy Scout? By the way, you should know, in case you don't already, that what they say about cold showers is a lie.

Before we knew it, it was Friday morning and our supplies were starting to run low, so we decided to take the long walk down to the lone grocery store at Davis Park. Since it was early in the season, it was a long shot that it would even be open. If not, we would have to jump on the ferry and head back to the mainland for provisions.

When we began our walk after breakfast, I noticed that the wind had shifted to the southeast, which is usually an indication that a storm is brewing. However, the clear skies and unseasonably warm weather stayed with us. Looking back on it, I wish I'd known just how dark and stormy the next twenty-four hours were going to be. If I had, we would have been on the next ferry, and gotten the hell out of there.

Chapter 45

It was *ocho y media*, eight thirty, and the large square and lamp lit cobblestone streets were packed with spectators. Most of them were proud citizens of this ancient city of Toledo, but many were also from the surrounding countryside of Castilla-La Mancha. Others were tourists, some having travelled hundreds, or thousands, of miles to be here. They were all gathered to witness a unique spectacle that occurred only once each year, on this very special day.

Castilla-La Mancha was the peculiar southern province of Spain that was well known as the former stomping grounds of conquering Romans, pillaging Visigoths, invading Arabs, avenging Christian crusaders, and more recently, the mercilessly successful conquistadors who explored, sacked and ultimately settled the New World on the heels of Christopher Columbus's four voyages. It was also famous, somewhat incongruously, as the home of Cervantes and the imaginary fiefdom of his harmless and legendarily witless warrior, Don Quixote.

This country, this province, and this city, were so thick with history that it almost seemed to seep from its ancient walls. The great Catholic cathedral that stood in the center of the crowded square had been built upon the remnants of a former mosque. The mosque had been built upon the foundations of an even more ancient Christian cathedral, which in turn, was built upon the ruins of a pagan Roman temple that had stood, well-worn and weathered, before Christ was even born. The same history was also written on the faces of the people gathered in the square: dark Arab hair, curved Roman noses, and blue Visigoth eyes, were all well represented, as was the straight-backed determination and passion of the crusaders and conquistadors who once stood where they stood now.

It was the season of *Semana Santa*, and today was the Friday before Easter, Good Friday, the solemn day of Christ's crucifixion. Throughout the Christian world, the faithful gathered to commemorate this holy event, but nowhere was the ceremony more solemn, or more spectacular, than in Toledo.

In the distance, the rhythmic sounds of the procession could be heard approaching the square. When the first float appeared a cheer went up from the crowd. It was a massive platform, blanketed with red carnations, and in its center was a scene depicting a moment from the last hours of Christ's life. On this first float, Christ was depicted praying in the Garden of Gethsemane, surrounded by his sleeping apostles.

The enormous structure, which weighed hundreds of pounds, was borne on the shoulders of twenty of the stoutest townsmen, and they were themselves festooned in the traditional garments of the Spanish clergy: tall, pointed hats, long flowing robes and veils that covered their faces entirely, with the exception of two small openings for their eyes. To a Spaniard these costumes evoked the solemn and holy tone of the event, but to an American's eyes, the scene would have immediately prompted a moment of shocked disbelief as the crimes of the Klu Klux Klan came to mind. The style of the garments was nearly identical to those of that cruel and uniquely American institution, right down to the emblems on their chests depicting a shield and cross. The only noticeable difference in appearance was the color. These elaborate Spanish robes were not white, but black, purple, blue and red.

As the float approached, the rhythmic clacking of long wooden staffs filled the night air. At the top of each staff was a horseshoe-shaped holder designed to bear the weight of the heavy wooden rail that supported the platform above. As each of the bearers took a step the huge platform swayed from side to side, and upon each of these swaying movements, the canes were brought down simultaneously upon the cobblestones of the street. *Clack ... clack ... clack* ... one hypnotic beat after the next. A priest, who walked unencumbered in front of the float, then shouted a single, terse command that brought the float to a halt. Another command and the poles were simultaneously placed under the rail of the float, and then a few more commands followed until the float rested in the horseshoes, thereby momentarily relieving the bearers of the platform's burden.

As the bearers rested, a woman dressed in black and standing in the crowd began to recite a prayer. Then more commands followed as the float was lifted upon their shoulders again and the procession through the square resumed. A brass band behind them played a solemn dirge in time with the *clack-clack-clack* of the canes. The first float was followed by another, this one depicting the betrayal of Jesus by Judas. Over the coming hours of the procession, there would be fourteen floats in all, with the final one revealing Christ's body wrapped in clean linen, and being laid to rest in a tomb.

A solemn-looking figure in his late twenties stood above the crowd on a balcony located across the street, and he watched the activities in the square with sad brown eyes. He brushed his fingers through hair that matched the color of his eyes, as he puffed on a cigarette that dangled from his lips. He wore gray slacks and a gray sports jacket over a black silk shirt, which seemed to contrast sharply with the otherwise cheerful visage of the red brick building behind him that was festooned with baroque flourishes around its windows and roof-line, and adorned with flowery pots, all lit dramatically by hidden spotlights on each of its seven stories. In many other European cities, and in every American one, this two-hundred-year-old building would have been considered an historic treasure. But compared to many of the other ancient buildings in Toledo, it was little more than a pretentious newcomer.

A second figure walked onto the balcony and stood beside the first. Both of them watched the procession below. The newcomer was older, had long black unkempt hair, and a walrus mustache. He was a full head taller than the younger man and wore a pair of worn blue jeans, dark sunglasses, a red polo shirt, and a black leather jacket with a Harley Davidson decal on the back.

The second man commented, "The band sounds good this

year." As he spoke, his bushy eyebrows waved over his glasses in the direction of his younger companion.

"Yes? When was the last time you heard this band?" The younger man inquired with a thick French accent.

"Never," the second responded with a smile.

The Frenchman, who did not find this in the least amusing, shook his head and returned his attention to the street below. After a brief interlude of silence the Frenchman asked, "What is that you're eating?"

"This?" The second replied, holding up the object in his hand. He tilted his head towards the building across the square displaying the yellow arches. "It's a *McNifico*. It's very good—not as good as a Whopper, but I can't find a Burger King in this crappy little town. Want a bite?" He said holding up the burger.

"Disgusting. You've been in America too long,"

"Ahhh, America, I've only been gone a short while, but already I miss her." The second said in a faux Italian accent.

"It is such an ugly country. How could anyone miss it?"

"Ugly? What would you know, you provincial little man?"

"I know because I've been there. It is an ugly country with ugly people." The Frenchman returned his attention to the procession in the street below.

Then the second man smiled as a thought, really a taunt, came to mind. "And then there is the Statue of Liberty."

The Frenchman turned slightly and looked back at him.

"Oh, she is so beautiful. She is the most famous symbol of America, you know, and she has the face of an Italian woman."

"She does not! She was made by a Frenchman and the face was modeled after his mother."

"No, no, I'm afraid you're mistaken. Bartholdi was an Italian living in France with his Italian mother. You know... like Napoleon."

"Napoleon? What the hell are you taking about?"

"No, it's true. Napoleon was Italian; it is the language the man spoke. He could barely speak any French. You know why I am certain of these things? Because if Bartholdi had been French, the Statue of Liberty would have a sour puss. And if Napoleon was French, he would never have won a battle."

"You are an ass!"

"You sure you don't want a bite?" The second man said, offering the remnants of the burger to the Frenchman again. "What, you don't like hamburgers? What's the matta wit you?"

"Disgusting, just like you," the Frenchman sneered.

"Well, I'd offer you some French food, but I haven't seen any places here that serve frog legs or those slimy little snails. But maybe you could ask one of da nice people down there if you could forage around in their garden for some dinner. I'm sure they'd be happy to get rid of the little pests." He said, imitating his antagonist's sneering face.

"What's that they call you in America? Crazy Nunzio, right? I can see why."

"I understand they call you 'The Little Turd'", the second man said as he finished his burger and threw the crumpled wrapper at the Frenchman.

"You're an arrogant bastard, just like an American. I cannot believe the bishop wastes resources—even resources like you—on them. You can't make defenders of the faith out of people who are ignorant of history and who can barely find Europe on a map."

"What they lack in history and geography they more than

make up for in faith and in balls," the older man said as he lit a cigarette.

"Oh, really? Our mission is all about history and geography."

"No, it's all about faith and balls. If it were not for their faith, kings and dictators would still rule Europe. And if weren't for their balls, you would be speaking German, listening to Wagner, and walking like this." He said as he made goose-step motions with his arms and legs. "But since you're French, I wouldn't expect you to understand anything about either faith or balls."

"If it wasn't for us they would never have won their independence in the first place."

"Oh, yes, you saved them from those monsters, the British. My God, if it were not for you they might be speaking English, or perhaps drinking tea. Maybe they would be forced to recite Shakespeare and watch debates in Parliament. Ooooh, what a nightmare you saved them from!"

"I think you, like everyone else, overrate them. You can never count on the Americans when you need them."

The second man threw up his hands in exasperation. "You can never count on them? You mean like people counted on the French to end the slaughter in the Balkans, or the starvation in Somalia, or stop that maniac in Iraq, or hold back the godless Communists? Every time the shit hits the fan, someone expects them to stand in the breeze. And when they do, they get criticized for taking too long to get there, or staying too long, or not staying long enough, or doing too much, or doing too little. When was the last time someone asked the French for help? No one ever does, and do you know why? Because no one is that stupid."

The older man discarded his cigarette and the two antagonists began squaring off like two fighters in a boxing ring or, more accurately, two knife fighters in an alley. They simultaneously moved their right hands behind their backs and fingered the small daggers tucked under their belts.

Suddenly a deep voice boomed out from the darkness inside of the room behind them. "That's enough, both of you!"

Both men on the balcony froze and automatically came to attention.

"Every time I leave you two alone you act like six-year-olds."

The Frenchman said, "He started it."

"I did not, you started it!"

"You said I didn't have any balls."

"I offered you something to eat and you were rude."

"Mario! Andre! Enough, enough, enough! I should have left you two little beasts in the orphanage. When will you two ever grow up?"

The men hung their heads and mumbled an apology as the old man walked out onto the balcony. He placed a hand on each of their heads, grabbed a handful of hair and then shook both of their heads in mock exasperation. Then he stopped, patted them, and affectionately kissed them each on the top of the head. He said in English that was thickly accented with Spanish, "Why can't you two learn to get along? You are like my very own children, and I wish you would love each other as if you were blood brothers. Now, come in and speak with me."

Chapter 46

We passed Billy Hoffenburg on our way to the grocery store in Davis Park. He was walking toward us from the opposite direction and carrying a couple of grocery bags. His appearance triggered mixed emotions. On the one hand, I could see that the store in Davis Park was open. That was the good news. The bad news was that he found us again.

"Good morning," Bill said as he approached and greeted us with a lift of his big chin.

"Good morning, Bill," Marcella said.

I grunted a hello. Actually, I was feeling more secure with Marcella, so the thought of Bill hanging around us was a little less intimidating today than the other day. On the other hand, I didn't see any point in pushing my luck.

"Where are you two headed this morning?" Bill asked.

I replied, "We're running a little low on groceries, so we thought we would pick some up at the Davis Park store, if they're open."

Bill held up his grocery bags to give us a better look. "Well, you're in luck. And the ferry just brought over a load of fresh produce."

"Oh, that's perfect," Marcella said.

"Hey, do you two have any activities planned for today? I mean, outdoor activities?" Bill said with a grin.

I ignored his comment and quickly compiled a list of activities in my head that would fill today and tomorrow's daylight hours. But, before I could open my mouth and share them with Bill, Marcella replied, "No, we were just going shopping; nothing else planned."

Well, that was that. I just smiled and nodded. "Nope, no plans today."

Bill said, "How would you two like to take a tour of Fire Island?"

"That sounds fantastic!" Marcella beamed.

I said. "That sounds great Bill, but we wouldn't want to impose on you."

"Hey, it's no problem, really. I make my rounds on horseback at least twice a week. It takes two or three hours, and I would appreciate the company."

"Horses!" Marcella said nearly leaping into the air. "I love horses!"

Oh God, not horses. "Yeah, horses... sounds like fun."

"Okay, little lady. Meet you two outlaws at the corral at high noon." Bill replied in his best John Wayne impression.

I asked, "Where's the corral, there, Duke?"

Billy pointed his chin over his shoulder and said, "Can't miss it, pardner. It's over yonder. See the roof of the big barn?"

I looked and saw a roof to the east. Actually, I didn't need to see it; all I had to do was follow my nose.

"Okay. We'll think about it," I said to him tentatively. "Maybe we'll swing by around noon." *Unless I can talk Marcella out of it.*

About two hours later Marcella and I returned from Davis Park with our groceries. While I was there I tried to call Uncle Joe's office, again. I thought the cell coverage might be better in Davis, but I still could not get a signal. I found another pay phone and left another message, informing him that all was well with Marcella and me.

In the meantime, the skies become overcast and the

temperature began to drop, but Marcella kept chatting me up the entire time about riding horses on the beach. I suggested that the weather wasn't very good for riding, but she brushed that off and told me that she'd ridden in the rain many times before. So, I tried a different tack, suggesting that riding horses on the beach was dangerous.

"Hundreds of people die every year," I said. "They fall off their horses and the stupid animals kick them in the head. Next thing they know, they're fish food."

She looked at me like I had feathers growing out of my ears. "I've never heard of anyone dying like that."

Me neither, but it sounded good. "No? I read it somewhere. Newsday, I think."

She obviously was not buying it, so I resigned myself to the inevitable. We put away the groceries, changed into jeans and sweaters, and then followed the smell to the horses.

We found Billy in the barn. By this time the smell was making my eyes water, but Marcella seemed unfazed. She knocked on the partially opened barn door and then walked in. The structure must have been a relatively recent addition to Watch Hill, because it wasn't here the last time I visited, and it appeared to be relatively new. I remembered that there were a couple of nice cottages here once, but that was some time ago. They fell victim to the US government's powers of eminent domain soon after the national park was established here. The feds were good enough to let the existing owners die before they tore down the cottages, but their children and grandchildren obviously weren't so lucky. The brown barn that replaced the cottages was a plain wooden structure that looked more like a suburban garage than a barn. After my eyes adjusted to the dim light inside I noticed someone brushing a dark gray horse.

"Hello? Bill?" I called into the interior.

"Hey, come on in," he replied.

"How long ago did they build this?" I asked.

"Oh, four, maybe five years ago."

I looked around the inside of the barn and walked over to one of the walls. It was adorned with all sorts of tools and leathery horse stuff that I couldn't identify. I pointed to a serious-looking machete with a three-foot blade. I asked Bill, "Hey, what's this for, unruly tourists?"

He smiled. *That's for you, asshole, if you give me any more lip*. He didn't say that, but I bet he was thinking it. Billy then asked, "So, how have you two been enjoying your stay?"

"Great, thanks," I said.

Billy walked over to us and he looked at my neck. "Wow, that's a pretty nasty sunburn." He pulled my collar back to get a better look.

I said to him, "No big deal," as I tried not to wince at the pain. *Prick.*

Marcella said, "We thought we would take you up on that offer of a tour."

"Hey, great timing. I was just preparing to take a ride around the park on my buddy Shadow this morning. I can set you two up with Trancer and Willy over there, and we can all go together. That is, if you are okay with riding a horse," he said, smiling in my direction.

"That would be great!" Marcella said effusively. "I haven't ridden in years, but I used to be pretty good at it."

Billy kept his eyes on me. "How about you, Tony? You like horses?"

"I love horses." *I'll take mine medium rare with onions and mushrooms*. I smiled back at him. "Let's ride, pardner."

Actually, my cousin Steve talked me into a trail ride once. But it wasn't a lot of fun. My ass would go up and the saddle would go down, and then the saddle would go up and my ass would go down. Somewhere in the middle the two smashed together. It was one hour of unmitigated misery followed by a week of walking around with a red ass and blue balls. Yeah, horses... no problem. "Saddle up!"

Billy and Marcella got what's-their-names ready to ride. While they did, they shared horse-riding tales and exchanged riding tips. Most of it was lost on me, especially when they started talking about something called dressage. Based on how they swooned when discussing it, I initially thought it was some sort of sexual position from the *Kama Sutra*.

I made a mental note to look it up. I was sure about one thing, though: my horse-riding skills were going to be severely tested with these two. I was also having second thoughts about the wisdom of bringing Marcella and Billy in such close proximity again.

In order to compensate for my horse riding inadequacies I selected Willy as my mount. He was a huge white mountain of horseflesh with a long mane and tail. I remember reading somewhere that, when confronted by a gang of hoodlums, pick the biggest one and kick the shit out of him; that will teach the rest of the smaller guys not to screw with you. This was not exactly the same thing, but I hoped the analogy would apply.

Billy said, "I think Marcella or I should ride Willy."

I said to him, "Why? He looks friendly enough."

"Actually he's a retired cavalry horse from West Point."

"Cavalry? Those crazy guys are still fighting on horses?"

Bill said, "They use them for the parade grounds, ceremonies and such. Anyway, Willy is a handful. He is very smart, very strong, and will give you a hard time if he senses that you're an inexperienced rider."

"Thanks, but I'll give it a try, just the same," I replied.

"Okay, tough guy, it's your butt in the saddle," Billy said.

Chapter 47

We led the horses out of the barn. Marcella and Billy mounted up and waited for me to do the same. I approached Willy-the-beast cautiously from the side and patted him on the neck.

"You must be an idiot if they named you Willy," I whispered to the horse. I could swear he gave me a dirty look. I said to Bill, "What kind of name is Willy for such a... great horse?"

"Actually, his name is William, as in William the Conqueror."

"Now that's a proper name for a horse like you. William." *You white mountain of horse steaks.* He continued to stare at me with his left eye. I think he was sizing me up, and probably thinking evil horse thoughts. I made a mental note to keep him away from the water; I did not want to become another tragic statistic.

Several embarrassing moments later, I managed to climb on top of him. Holy shit, it was like sitting on the roof of a bus. I tried to look nonchalant as I tightened my grip, one hand on the reins and the other on the saddle horn, until my knuckles turned white. Billy watched with a big smile, but Marcella looked on silently with an odd expression on her face. It wasn't amusement, for sure, and it wasn't fear. Maybe she was just impressed by my pigheadedness. She brought her horse around and came close to us, and then said quietly to William, "You mind your master's will." Then she turned towards me and said something strange in a voice that hardly seemed to belong to her.

"Be patient," she said. "Your body will remember, and when it does, your mount will obey you."

I smiled as I began considering the possibility of using that line on her later, when the two of us were alone again... assuming this saddle didn't make me a eunuch in the meantime. But she was completely serious. And I could swear I briefly heard a different accent in her voice. Strange, very strange.

So off we went: Billy up front, Marcella in the middle, and me bringing up the rear with William. It didn't require an expert's eye to see that William was a magnificent animal. His massive hooves pounded the sand, almost in a marching tempo, as he moved forward. The ride was a little rough for a while, but I eventually got used to his rhythm and settled into the saddle surprisingly well—at least I was surprised. Marcella looked back at me on occasion to see how I was doing.

"See?" she said. "I told you your body would remember. You two would be the envy of Stupor Mundi."

"Who? Stupid Monday?" I asked.

She laughed. "No, not Stupid Monday, Stupor Mundi. It's Latin. It means 'Wonder of the World.' It was the name given to a great Norman ruler. And it's also the name of a very great horse."

"I'm confused."

"Don't worry about it." She said reassuringly. "It's a long story."

"Tell me about it sometime."

She smiled and shrugged. "Maybe."

So, there I was, riding Stupid Monday, or whatever, feeling pretty good about myself, and I was even impressing Marcella. I think.

We reached the beach, and I had to admit that it was an amazing sensation riding along the seemingly endless stretch of sand. The sky was still that angry, steel-gray color. Nevertheless, the view, the surf, and the ocean stretching to the horizon was incredible. We turned the horses to the east, and Billy started the tour.

"The National Park Service was established in 1916 to preserve outstanding examples of America's natural, cultural, and recreational resources for the enjoyment, education, and inspiration of this and future generations..."

Jesus, Billy, tell me we are not starting the tour in 1916.

"The National Park System consists of 378 parks located in nearly every state and territory of the nation. The Service's mission is to preserve these treasures and makes them available to millions of visitors from throughout the country and the world every year."

I said to Marcella, "Are you taking notes? I forgot my pencil."

Marcella laughed and Bill ignored me, again. I think he was making this a habit.

"Fire Island National Seashore contains the only federally designated wilderness area in New York State..." *blah-blah...*"established by an Act of Congress in 1964. It contains 19,500 acres and stretches for thirty-two miles..." *blah-blah-blah...* "some of the remote areas of the park provide the four million annual visitors with a sense of what Fire Island looked like before European colonization..." *blah.*

I interrupted Bill's monologue. "That's got to be a little tricky with four million half naked, snow-white people running around with sunglasses and beach chairs."

That comment got me a visual reprimand from both of them. I might enjoy this tour after all. Okay, so maybe I was being a little juvenile. But, you have to understand a little history to fully appreciate the irony. Billy, as I said, was once a jock, and he, along with his jock friends, could not have cared less about any of this history stuff when we were growing up around here. Once, in an epic moment of stupidity, I let my then-girlfriend talk me into taking a similar park tour. I didn't have any interest in Fire Island wildlife beyond her, of course. She was really hot. What was her name again? Kim something. Anyway, when Bill later found about it, he and his asshole friends were merciless. They christened me with a new pet name, "Poindexter", among others, which I had to live with for months afterwards. The worst part is that after all of this pain, the little hottie blew me off for one of Bill's friends. So here he is giving the same tour—poorly I might add—all to impress Marcella. So naturally, I figured it was time for a little friendly payback. Hey, what can I say, I'm Sicilian, and we never forget a slight.

I tuned back into the tour. "The Seashore has three visitor centers, one campground, twenty-one miles of beaches, seventeen miles of hiking trails, maintenance facilities, headquarters buildings, employee housing units, a ferry terminal, and a parking lot on the mainland..." *blah-blah-blah-blah...* "backpackers, camping, canoeing, lots of wildlife..." *Including, undoubtedly, a partridge in a pear tree.*

As on the ferry trip over, Billy's presentation was sounding pretty canned. I was half expecting him to roll up his sleeves to check the notes scribbled on his forearms at any moment, and I was also tempted to say so, but I felt I had already filled my current quota of dirty looks, so I decided against it.

"How many people work for the park?" Marcella asked.

"There are about fifteen full-time rangers, plus another thirty-five or so people including part-time rangers, maintenance people, staff, et cetera. When you consider the size of the park and the mainland stations, we are always spread thin. This time of year, the wilderness area out here is pretty much empty, except for me and one or two other rangers who shuttle between Fire Island and the mainland office in Patchogue."

Ranger Bill then informed us that we were riding through the Otis Pike Wilderness Area, where we could "experience the most unparalleled sense of remoteness in the New York metropolitan region."

Oooohhh.

Marcella asked, "Who was Otis Pike?"

Ranger Bill was speechless for a moment and then said, "I

think he was some sort of politician." He gave it some more thought. "He must have been a pretty important guy to have an entire park named after him."

I wasn't going to let him off the hook that easy. I said, "That's not a very satisfying answer, Bill. Shouldn't you know stuff like that?"

Bill shrugged.

I continued, "I would really like to know."

Bill said, "I'll find out and get back to you."

"Can you? Great."

"By the way Tony," Bill said, "this is going to be a long ride and the sun's rays can be very damaging to unprotected skin." He smiled. "Remember to use sunscreen."

"Thanks for the safety tip." *Asshole.*

We rode along the beach until we reached a break in the dune line. We could see the shrubs and trees in the low-lying area towards the bay side of the island.

Marcella said, "I'm surprised there are so many trees this close to the beach."

"Many people are," Billy reported. "There is a very special area west of here near Sailors Haven called the Sunken Forest that also surprises many visitors, who don't expect to find such a well-developed forest just a few hundred yards from the surf."

Marcella asked, "What kind of trees can survive here?"

"Mostly sassafras, holly, black oak, red cedar, swamp maple and an occasional pitch pine."

I said, "Wow, Billy, I'm impressed."

"Yeah? Thanks."

"By the trees, I mean."

"Sassafras?" Marcella asked.

"Yup, very twisty, reddish-brown trees with leaves that look like mittens," Billy replied. "People used to make tea and root beer from the roots. Sometimes you'll spot little birds that peck holes in the bark and appear to drink the sap. They're called, appropriately enough, yellow-bellied sapsuckers."

"Actually, they are more interested in eating the bugs that get stuck to the sap after it runs out of the tree," I added.

Bill looked at me. "Very good; that's correct. How did you know that?"

"Some guy named Poindexter told me."

Bill shrugged and continued. "Some of these small trees, believe it or not, are 200 or 300 years old. And the entire area is filled with many animal species not normally associated with a beach habitat: red fox, gray squirrel, eastern cottontail rabbit, long-tailed weasel, and the black racer."

"The black what?" Marcella asked.

"The black racer," Bill responded. "It's a snake."

"Are they poisonous?" Marcella asked.

Bill replied, "No and they're not aggressive, unless you bother them."

"What about bears?" I asked.

Bill looked at me like my ear feathers were back. "What about them?"

"Bears?" Marcella responded.

"No bears," Bill said, shaking his head at me.

"You sure? I thought I saw some tracks."

Bill said to me, "Did I mention that some of the mushrooms around here are hallucinogenic? I think you should stop eating the mushrooms, Tony."

We rode north away from the beach and through the break in the dunes. The vegetation became increasingly dense and Bill led us through a narrow path in the thick foliage. Meanwhile, I kept an eye on the ground, watching for snakes.

Marcella asked me, "What are you looking at?"

I didn't look up. "Bear tracks."

Bill stopped and pointed to a small tree. "This is *Prunus serotina,* the black cherry tree."

Marcella asked Bill, "Can the cherries be eaten?"

"The birds love them. And some people find them tasty. They make jellies and pies with them after they ripen in the late summer or early fall. But they're a little too sour for my taste. Plus, you have to be careful."

"Careful? Why?" I asked.

Bill replied, "Because the leaves, pits, and branches contain cyanide."

"Cyanide? People risk cyanide poisoning to make jelly out of this stuff?"

Bill nodded. "Yeah, it seems a little risky to me, too."

This comment made me think about that incident in Jonestown where hundreds of otherwise sensible people committed mass suicide by drinking cyanide-laced Kool-Aid. The incongruous image of Bill, in full ranger regalia and sitting around a campfire with his jock friends, passing around a glass of black cherry juice, came to mind.

"Tony? Hello, Tony?"

"What?" I replied.

"What's so funny?" Bill asked.

I shrugged.

Marcella, in the meantime, was gazing intently at the thicket of trees ahead, and said, "Did you see that?"

"See what?" I asked.

"I thought I saw something move in the trees over there."

"A snake?"

"No. Something big."

Bill and I looked in the direction that she was indicating. I didn't see anything, but I thought I heard some movement.

Bill said, "It's probably a white-tailed deer. It's the largest animal on the island. Some of the bucks can weigh in at over 150 pounds."

Ranger Bill's comment caught my attention. "I've never seen a deer out here," I said.

"They were relatively rare when we hung out here as kids," Bill informed me. "But their numbers on Fire Island have increased dramatically over the past decade. We estimate there are probably somewhere between 500 and a thousand of them scattered along the length of Fire Island."

I asked Marcella, "Did it look like Bambi?"

"I didn't get a very good look at it, but, maybe."

Bill rode ahead and we followed close behind. After a couple of hundred feet, he stopped suddenly and began staring at something to the right of the path, where there was a break in the foliage. Marcella and I caught up with him.

I heard Bill mumbling something to himself as we approached. I tried to follow his gaze and said to him, "What's up, Bill?"

Bill moved his horse through the opening. Then he said something that I could make out loud and clear: "What the hell?"

Marcella and I followed him into a large, round, clearing, maybe two hundred feet in diameter. There was nothing standing taller than a blade of grass a few inches from the ground. All of the trees and bushes were completely gone.

Chapter 48

The expression on Bill's face was an odd combination of confusion, anger, and maybe a little fear.

From my perspective, it looked like a large group of overzealous campers did a nice job of clearing a campsite for about a hundred tents.

"Campers?" I asked Billy.

He thought about that, and then shook his head. "Can't be. We have well publicized campgrounds to the west of here with all of the facilities any camper could want: showers, boardwalks, barbeque pits, the works. Besides, no one would be able to miss a camping party of that size this time of year, and I haven't seen a single camper this season, yet."

"Aliens?"

I expected Bill to ignore me, or tell me to shut up, but instead he said, "Not unless they decided to use axes, rather than ray guns, to clear the trees." He pointed to a large pile of brush towards the northern end of the circle. Even from a distance, I could see the telltale marks made by an ax at the base of some of the tree trunks.

I looked over toward Marcella. Her horse was right where I expected it to be, but she was gone. Then I saw a movement out of the corner of my eye. She was crouching in the center of the clearing, looking down at the ground. For a moment, she reminded me of one of those Indian scouts from an old western. *He go this way, Kemo-Sabe.*

She stood up and walked back towards Bill and me. She didn't look very happy, but I couldn't get an exact read on her emotions because she was wearing her sunglasses again, which seemed to have materialized from thin air, or more likely from her carry-on luggage bag that doubled as a purse.

I asked her, "Find anything interesting?"

She shook her head. "Nope." Then she looked up at the sky and said, "We should probably start heading back. Looks like a storm is heading this way."

The sky looked the same way it did earlier, when I tried to convince her to abort the tour in the first place. That must be some special pair of sunglasses. But I'm smart enough to know when to go with the flow, or at least I was learning.

"Yeah," I said to Bill. "We should probably start heading back. Besides, you'll probably want to report this to headquarters, or whatever."

Bill looked at Marcella and me and said, "Yes, we should get back. I need to find out what's going on here. Maybe one of the other rangers knows. If not, I'm going to need to get some help to hunt these assholes down and get them out of the park. Forever."

Chapter 49

By the time we got back to the barn, I was exhausted. My legs ached, my back was in a knot and my ass felt like it had been used as a punching bag. Marcella must have been tired too, because she didn't say a word during the entire ride. In fact, she could barely manage a believable smile, when I managed to get her attention at all. The tension on her face also suggested that there might be something else bothering her. I was going to ask her what the problem was, but thought it would be more appropriate to wait until we were alone.

After parting will Bill, on the walk back to the cottage, there was more of the same silent distraction. To make matters worse, she stumbled while trying to negotiate the narrow boardwalk and sprained her ankle.

She recovered her balance and just avoided falling off the elevated portion of the walk. In the process, she dropped her sunglasses. When I reached to pick them up for her, she beat me to it.

"You okay?" I asked.

"I'm fine, just a little sprain."

She slung her bag over her shoulder and examined her sunglasses. She must have accidentally stepped on them during her near fall, because they appeared to be broken. She examined them and then, making a grunting sound through her clenched teeth, threw them into her bag. She limped towards me with a defeated look on her face.

I inflated my chest, held my arms up, and while flexing them I said. "Would you like your brave knight to carry you, my lady?"

Marcella apparently thought this was amusing, because she seemed to relax a little, and then gave me a warm smile. She also surprised me by playing along. "So tell me, my brave lord, to which order of knights do you belong?"

That was not exactly the response I was expecting, and my obvious hesitation made her laugh.

"Uh, let's see?" I said. "I want ye to guess. If ye are right I will be at ye service for the rest of my life."

Marcella stopped laughing and her smile vanished. She moved closer to me and that strange look reappeared, the Stupid-Monday one. She brought her face very close to mine and looked into my eyes. Then she examined my upraised arms and my inflated chest.

"Hurry up and complete ye inspection my lady, I can't hold this pose forever."

A smiled flashed across her face momentarily, and then she was serious again. Upon completing her inspection, she moved within a few inches of my face and again stared into my eyes. "You belong to the greatest order of knights that has ever defended Christendom. The order that was the most ferocious in battle, and the most compassionate in peace: the Order of Saint John."

"Wow!" I said. "Ye are a good guesser. How could ye tell? Can I put my arms down now?"

My quip did nothing to relax her intensity this time.

"I can tell by your eyes," she said. "They tell me that you are the direct descendant of the greatest warrior of the Order. You have his eyes: that strange combination of gray, blue, and green, like the color of the sky just before a terrible storm."

Hoping to break her spell I said, "Okay then, you win: slave for life." She kept staring as I picked her up in my arms. She didn't even protest, which, I thought, couldn't be a bad sign. So I was hoping for the best as I carried her into the house.

The house was dark and Marcella reached over to turn on the

switch for the lights, but nothing happened.

I said, "that's strange, ye castle must have blown a fuse, my lady." I looked at her with some seriousness now and asked, "Do we need the lights at the moment?"

She kissed me on the cheek and said, "Yes, we do. Put me down, my brave knight and fix the castle's fuse."

"As you wish, my lady." *Damn*!

Marcella followed me, as I walked towards the closet to inspect the fuse box. She said, "It's really pretty dark in here. Will you be able to see anything in that closet?"

I kept up the knight thing. "Be not afraid of the dark. My eyes, in addition to being a little stormy, are like those of the cat. I am a knight who can see his prey in the dark, pretty much." Hey, that was not bad: a knight who can see in the dark. Maybe she wasn't appreciating this stuff, but I was.

Of course, I would have taken a flashlight, but I happened to know that there was a small window in the utility closet that provided plenty of light, even this late in the day. Whoever built this place put it in there for occasions just like this one.

I decided to make a little more of a show of it, so I turned to Marcella, who was now standing about twenty feet away, and opened the closet door. "Behold the light, my lady."

I was standing to one side as the door opened, and as it did, I noticed that her smile suddenly disappeared and her face was transformed, once again. But, it was not the face of knightly adoration. This one was different, very different: it looked like the face of a predator, and she was staring directly at me.

As I tried to decipher her odd expression, I noticed her right hand reaching into her ever-present shoulder bag. It was a smooth, but lightning-fast motion, and when her hand reemerged it was holding a very large gun. Then everything began to move in slow motion.

Her eyes were wide now, and intensely focused, and she began shouting at me as her face contorted, but I couldn't understand what she was yelling about. Another moment flashed by. She fell to one knee and got into what I immediately recognized as a firing position. Instinctively I moved to the side, trying to get myself out of her aim. Then I heard the deafening report of the gun, and could swear I felt the breeze from the bullet as it passed by me, on its way into the closet.

While the ringing in my ears was still subsiding, and before I fully understood what had happened, Marcella began walking towards me. The air was full of the smell of cordite, and I could see a wisp of smoke in the beams of light shining into the room from the window in the closet. I stood motionless, my eyes following this stranger as she passed within inches of where I was standing. I did not recognize her as the woman that I knew, neither the one that I had known as my office assistant, or the woman whom I had lived with for the past few days. I raised my hands slightly in a defensive gesture, as she passed, but she did not seem to even notice I was standing there.

My eyes continued to follow her as she walked by me, and into the closet, her body silhouetted against the light and smoke. She knelt down next to a motionless form on the floor. It took me a little while to process the image, until I realized that there was a man slumped against the rear wall of the closet. She removed a weapon from his hand, placing it on the floor beside her. She then pressed two fingers to the side of his neck as she simultaneously removed a set of odd-looking goggles covering his face.

The bullet had hit the goggles dead center, in the middle of a small box between the two eyepieces, and broken wires and shattered electrical components were hanging out of it. She stood up, inspected the goggles briefly and then threw them on the floor. The man's forehead and face, which were formerly concealed by the goggles, were covered with small, light-gray fragments along with a powdery substance of the same color. There were also several, small, pellet-sized wounds in his forehead that were seeping blood and mixing with the dusty debris. Blood was also running from his nose and ears and I noticed that his body was twitching.

Marcella aimed her gun and, without hesitation, fired another bullet into the man's skull. I jumped at the sound of the gun's second report and started stepping away, as I watched blood begin to drain from a new entry wound in his forehead. She placed her gun back into her bag, pulled out a small glass vial, opened it, and touched the tip of her thumb to the opening. Flipping the vial upside down, she started mumbling words that sounded like a prayer, then she reached down and made a cross with her thumb on the man's forehead, just above the second wound.

The dead guy in the closet was clothed in a black jumpsuit, and he stopped twitching by the time Marcella placed the vial back in her bag.

She picked up the man's weapon. I backtracked down the hall and felt my stomach tighten, and a cold sweat forming on my brow, as the reality of what had just transpired precipitated in my brain. I said to her, "What the hell just happened Marcella? Who is... was that guy?"

She walked toward me inspecting the dead man's gun. It appeared to be some kind of compact assault weapon, like the ones the bad guys carry in spy films. It was equipped with a shoulder strap that she placed her arm through and then over her head, slinging it behind her back. She looked up at me, and her face, the one that I knew and recognized, reappeared. "You're in danger, Tony", was all she said as she took my hand and led me out of the house.

"Where did you get that gun in your bag? Why did you kill him?"

She replied calmly, almost as if she was distracted by something else.

"No time to explain now; let's move."

Chapter 50

Mario and Andre followed the bishop into the dimly lit room and sat in the two chairs before his desk. The bishop closed the door to the balcony that overlooked the square where the Good Friday procession was taking place, and then said, "I overheard your discussion about the Americans. In a way, you are both right. They are ignorant of history, which can be a curse. As it has so often been said, those who forget history are doomed to repeat it. However, it can also be a blessing, I think. They are spared having to wear it around their necks like a millstone, as is often done here in Europe and the rest of the world."

The older man smiled and shot a sideways glance at Andre. "I remember a story told by one of our Irish brothers, after he returned from a visit to America. It was a story about two Irish families who had a long, well known, and ignominious history in Ireland, one of them Catholic and the other Protestant. Each family could recite every slight, every injustice, and every murder committed one against the other, going back for two centuries. Then one day, about eighty years ago, one young son from each of these families left for America. They left about the same time, but on different ships, and each unknown to the other. These men both eventually prospered in America and then had families of their own. One day, a son from each of these men met, became friends and started a business together. They, in turn, prospered and had families. Then one of these men introduced his son to his business partner's daughter, and in due time these children married and had a child themselves. So, while the two old men from Ireland were together celebrating the birth of their great-grandchild in America, their two clans were back in Ireland continuing a centuries-old blood feud, based on centuries-old recollections of the past."

The bishop shook his head and smiled. "Neither of the old men in America could clearly remember what the feud was about, and in any event, they avoided discussing it, because it would only cause their children or grandchildren to laugh, or worse, to offer them a condescending pat on the head. There are many stories like this in America, our Irish brother claims. Protestants and Catholics, Christians and Jews, even Muslims and Jews, as well as others of other religions and other races. He said that there are so many different people in America, but that there were no tribes: at least, not ones based upon the blood and loyalties of the past."

The bishop stared at a point on the other side of the room. "What a luxury it would be, to be free of one's past. To shrug the heavy burden off your shoulders, and leave it in the dust at the side of the road. One can almost imagine the relief. But it is not a luxury some men are afforded." The old man sighed, looked at his two younger companions and then smiled again.

"It makes one wonder, sometimes, about the true value of being well versed in the things of the past. Stories like the one our Irish brother told give me an abiding sense of hope for the future."

The Bishop bowed his head, whispered a few words in prayer, and then made the sign of the cross. Both of the younger men mimicked his gestures.

The bishop then looked at Mario. "I also agree with your assessment of their... " He frowned looking for an appropriate word. "Shall we say, intestinal fortitude?"

"Yes, sir."

The bishop turned his attention to the Frenchman. "So tell me, Andre, what news do you bring to me from beautiful France?"

"The family is well and happy. There are no threats against any of them," Andre said, then hesitated. "And Julian is to marry in October."

The bishop clapped his hands in delight. "Ah, Julian, the shopkeeper in Burgundy. How wonderful! Tell me about him and his future bride."

"He is a very clever man, and very active in his community, a natural leader. He is also quite content with his village life." Andre fell silent.

The bishop waited a moment, and then broke the silence by asking, "And his bride?"

"His bride, Nichol Doyet, is a lovely woman from the same village. Her family has lived there for nearly five centuries."

The bishop looked suspiciously at Andre. "I don't recall that name."

Andre confessed, "She is not on the list, sir."

"Not on the list? How did this happen?"

"He met her in school."

"And what is your assessment of her family's contribution to the protection of the faith?" The bishop inquired.

"Well, they are mostly farmers and shopkeepers, like Julian's family," Andre continued, stammering slightly. "And they have a family tradition of being pacifists."

"I see," the bishop said, eying Andre. "Well, what about during the two great wars?"

"Her great-grandfather, who was the only family member suitable for service, took an extended tour in Spain during the Great War, so he did not serve." Andre quickly added. "But her grandfather was a member of the Vichy party during the second war."

This seemed to lighten the Bishop's mood, at least momentarily.

Andre continued, "But, he fled France for Algeria, after six weeks."

The Bishop's brow furrowed. "I see. And you believe that

Julian is intent on marrying into this family?"

"It would seem so, sir."

"Well, my son, this does not sound like an encouraging match. I would like you to consider actions that might be taken to... promote a more appropriate match for Julian." The bishop then said forcefully. "With someone on the list. This is why there is a list. Is it not?"

"But, sir, the wedding arrangements are already being made.... "

The bishop cut him off, his voice becoming harsh. "We are supposed to be protecting defenders of the faith, not defenders of self-interests. This sounds like a bad match for our man. Do you not agree?"

The Frenchman could see by the expression on the bishop's face that there was only one possible response. He shrugged. "Yes sir, of course."

"Is there any other news from France?"

"No sir."

"Very well. Then, if you would go for a moment into the next room, while I speak with Brother Mario, I will call you back in a few moments to discuss the details."

With that, the Frenchman bowed and abruptly left the room.

"Sounds like a very exciting assignment," Mario said with a smirk.

The bishop gave him a stern look. "You know, Mario, you were one of my best students, but I wonder about whether I should have taken the cane to you more often when you were a child. I can still make up for it now, you know."

"Yes, sir; sorry sir."

"And you do seem to be adapting to American life very well," The Bishop said while looking Mario over. "What is with the hair and these clothes? You look like Marlon Brando."

Mario smiled. "You think so?"

"It was not intended as a compliment. I think you are getting a little carried away with your legend. Get your hair cut, trim that thing above your lip, and buy some clothes that don't have holes in them!"

Mario nodded at the command. "Yes, sir."

The bishop walked around the desk and gently touched a hand on Mario's shoulder, and then led him back out onto the balcony. The old man watched the procession in silence as another elaborately decorated float went by, this one with the depiction of Christ on the cross. The bishop crossed himself and Mario aped the gesture.

"Look at them," the bishop said. "Tourists, looking for something interesting to do on a Friday night. This ritual is centuries old and commemorates the most solemn event of our faith. But to most of them, it is little more than entertainment. The faith is dying here in Europe, the pews are empty. In the past we had to defend the faith against invaders. Now it is dying from simple neglect."

Mario shrugged but remained silent as he watched the people below.

"So tell me about young Anthony," the bishop inquired.

"Tony."

"Who?"

"He prefers to be called Tony."

"Tony?" the bishop huffed. "Very well, tell me about young Tony."

"He has developed into quite a strong man. You can see his ancestors in his determination and his leadership skills."

"And this recent unsavory incident?"

"The usual motivation: money. As the CEO of a small company, he was required by his investors to take out an insurance policy on his life, with the company as the beneficiary. It is called a key man life insurance policy, commonly required by investors in start-up companies. If he dies, the insurance benefit is paid to the company. It is supposed to compensate the shareholders for losing someone who is important to their investment, and it is meant to provide extra resources to find someone new to replace him."

The bishop frowned. "So such a policy is paid not to a family member, a wife or child who loves him, but to strangers, who care for him only as an investment?"

"Yes sir."

"And how big is such a payment, if he should die?"

"In this case, it was ten million dollars."

The bishop looked at Mario in stunned silence. "Who would be so foolish as to dare the devil in this way?"

Mario replied, "It is very common in America. Of course, in this case, when the company started to run out of money, his two business companions hatched a plan to finance the company with the proceeds from the insurance. They simply needed to arrange Tony's death in a way that appeared not to be connected to them or the company. We found out about it through a contact who uncovered the plan to kill him, and we took it from there. We found the first assassin with no problem; he was an amateur. With the second, it was a little more difficult, but we also found him as well."

The old man said, "I understand that you found him just

before he pulled the trigger."

"No, sir. That is not true. He was still setting up."

"Still, it was a little close for comfort, do you not think?"

"They have a saying in America: 'An inch is as good as a mile'."

"What does that mean? That we did a good job?"

Mario shrugged his shoulders, "It means that it was good enough."

"How would you characterize him?"

"The second assassin?"

"Yes."

"He was very professional. He had military-grade equipment and very good evasion capabilities, which is why we almost missed him."

Mario watched as the old man processed this information.

The bishop then asked. "How would you characterize the first assassin?"

"The one in New Jersey? The opposite: very unprofessional. He was your basic incompetent thug."

"And this incompetent one, it was he who met with the female plotter, correct?"

"Yes, sir. A few days before, we observed their meeting at a restaurant." Mario smiled. "It could not have been any easier than if they had invited us to join them for dinner."

"And the second man, the professional one, when did you first observe him and the plotters?"

"We didn't; we missed it. We discovered him the same

morning we stopped him."

"Does this not seem strange to you? Does it make sense that these plotters would find one so capable, and one so incompetent? And why were there two of them in the first place?"

Mario leaned his head to one side and looked at the bishop, and the bishop looked back into Mario's eyes. After a moment of thought Mario said, "To tell you the truth, sir, it did seem a little strange. There were also inconsistencies in the details, the ones about how they were planning to kill Tony. The first man was planning to make it appear to be a traffic accident. But the second... well, it certainly wasn't going to appear accidental. And that could have very well led the police to the motives and then the plotters themselves. In any event, it seems doubtful that the insurance company would have paid the benefit under such a circumstance, at least not without further lengthy, private investigations."

"And what is the status of the two plotters?"

"The woman is no longer a threat, and the last report we have about her male accomplice is that he is planning to leave the country, but we have his apartment under surveillance, just in case he returns."

"Under whose surveillance?"

"Brother Gunter's."

The old man pinched his chin between his thumb and forefinger and considered what Mario had just reported. He led Mario back into his office and sat down in a large red chair next to a floor lamp. The light illuminated the bishop's face in a way that made its fleshy folds and creases more pronounced. "And how is the additional arrangement you've made for Tony's protection working out?"

Mario smiled. "Sister Marcella? She's been acting as his

personal assistant for months now, and they get along very well. She is with him most of the day, and knows where he is at all times."

The bishop raised his right eyebrow. "Was she there in the room, the day the second assassin attempted to kill Tony?"

"There?" Mario smiled. "She was there, alright. She resolved the matter across the street personally. Then she returned to the meeting room."

"Where are they now?"

"They are on their way to a remote hiding place until things settle down." Mario said.

"That may not be a good thing."

"Oh, no sir, their relationship is perfectly under control and, of course, she's very well acquainted with what happened to Tony's father and mother. No, don't worry about that. She knows that personal interactions with him are forbidden."

"No, you do not understand; it may compromise Tony's safety," the old man said raising his voice for the first time.

"No, the danger is gone. And besides, what better protection could you have than from someone who is with you all of the time? Do not worry, she is very good and very professional. The incident with the second assassin proves that beyond any doubt."

"You still don't understand, Mario."

Mario smiled and raised his hands in an attempt at calming the bishop. "It will work out, trust me."

"No, you don't see the other problem, the larger picture… think!" The old man chided, sitting back in his chair and looking up towards the ceiling.

"What other problem?"

"The other problem that caused me to summon you here in the first place. Think! Think about the second assassin."

Mario shook his head slowly. "He's not a problem anymore."

"But the people that hired him are. It was obviously not one of Tony's associates that hired the second man. It was someone else, someone with lots of resources, someone with access to highly trained mercenaries, and someone who had no interest in collecting the insurance money."

"Who?"

"I'm not sure who, but I have a suspicion. There is a man; his name is Barella. He is an agent with the American Secret Service and, for a very long time, has been investigating some of our activities and trying to find us. At least that is what we believe he is doing. We have not seen much of him lately, but recent reports indicate a sudden renewed interest on his part. This matter with the second assassin may now shed more light on his intentions."

"You believe that this man, Barella, hired the second assassin? Why?"

"Yes. Why?" The old man repeated as he let out a long sigh.

Mario had never seen such a look of consternation on the bishop's face before.

"What is the problem, sir?"

"What I am about to tell you now, you can tell no one. No one! I don't even want you to repeat it back to me. Do you understand?"

"Yes sir, no one; of course."

"A long time ago," the old man began, "before you were born and when I was still a young knight, I took part in a mission. It was the type of mission that tested my faith, that tested the faith of us all. Until recently we thought it was finally and forever behind us. But we think now that this is no longer true." The bishop took another long breath. "Agent Barella seems determined to keep it alive and in the present."

"I do not understand," Mario said with growing confusion.

"Agent Barella has spent nearly forty years investigating a murder. For the first thirty he was able to gather only a few hints, but never enough pieces to put the entire picture together. Then, about seven years ago, another one of our missions may have given him the additional information he needed, and may have finally led him directly to us."

"This man must be crazy," Mario said, laughing. "Who would spend forty years investigating a murder?"

The bishop said in a low voice, "He may be obsessed, but he is not crazy. We think he intends to seek revenge against us. He may even be plotting the destruction of the entire Brotherhood. And this man has the resources to do it."

The bishop then fell silent as Mario tried to process this strange information. Mario considered the facts systematically, as he was trained to do. Barella was an agent of the US government, a man who had spent forty years trying to solve a murder that, apparently, the Brotherhood had something to do with. Now Barella, because of this murder, had the will and the means to destroy a four-hundred-year-old global organization. But why?

Mario at first found it difficult to imagine how someone could find the will to pursue a forty-year-old vendetta. It was possible; it certainly had been done before. But by what means? Where could he get those resources? His government? Why would he and his government want to do such a thing? Then he considered the irony of his own question. He worked for an organization that had existed for four hundred years, for one purpose: to keep a four-hundred-year-old promise. So why not a forty-year-old vendetta? And that left the central and most important questions. Who? Who had been murdered forty years ago? Who could be that important?

Then a thought crept into his mind. It was a memory, actually, although he did not realize it at first. Then it all came back to him. The memory was of a crazy rumor he once heard, as a very young man, not long after he joined the Brotherhood. All of the parts seem to fit. His eyes grew wide with understanding as he looked at the silent old man sitting in front of him, and then Mario said, "Not forty years ago, thirty-eight years ago."

The bishop nodded. "The assassin, the one that you found at the last moment across the street from Tony's office, was not trying to kill Tony. He was trying to kill Marcella. She is in grave danger. And because of her proximity to Tony, he is also."

Mario reached for his cell phone and quickly typed a text message, a warning for Marcella. But he was afraid that it wasn't going to reach her in time. She would only get it after turning on her communication device, but she would not attempt that with Tony around. Given their current circumstances, and their constant close proximity, Mario could not be sure when she would get it. There was another possibility, however, the new communication device, the one configured to look like a pair of sunglasses. But Mario wasn't even sure that she had received one yet, and if so, he could not be sure she had them with her.

He dialed his phone, listened for a while, then hung up and began dialing a second time.

"What are you doing?" The bishop asked.

"I sent a warning to Marcella, but I'm not sure my message will get to her in time. So I tried calling Brother Gunter, to tell him to find her and get them to another safe location."

"And?"

"He didn't answer."

Mario held the phone to his ear and listened to the ringing as he was explaining to the bishop. Then someone picked up on the other side and he redirected his attention to the call. "Hello," Mario said. "Yes it's me. Tony needs your help."

After a short, cryptic conversation, Mario hung up the phone.

The bishop asked with suspicion, "Who was that?"

"You know who; the only person immediately available who can help both Tony and Marcella."

"You can't be serious."

"It's our only option until I find Brother Gunter, or I get back there and figure out what's going on myself."

"You get back there. Be on the next plane," the bishop said firmly.

"Yes sir."

Chapter 51

Marcella and I reached the main boardwalk in the front of the beach house, and she began scanning its length in both directions. "Do you know what time the next ferry leaves?"

I did not reply.

"Tony? Are you listening to me? What time is the next ferry?"

I tried to concentrate on what she was saying, but my head was dazed. I shook it off and looked at my watch. "The last ferry left Watch Hill over two hours ago, and the last one from Davis Park leaves in five minutes, and I doubt if we will make it, especially with your injured ankle."

"We have to get out of here; we have to get off this island. We have to try to make that ferry, Tony."

Marcella began to walk in the direction of Davis Park as fast as her limp would allow, and I followed closely behind. "Marcella, what is going on? Since when does my administrative assistant carry a gun?"

She replied curtly, "We both knew we were in possible danger, so I took one to be safe."

I laughed. "You took one to be safe? So, you just happened to have one lying around in your kitchen drawer? Stop lying to me, Marcella. Tell me what this is about."

"I was scared, so I bought the gun a couple of days after the murder across the street, and brought it with me on this trip for protection."

I grabbed her arm, stopped her and then looked into her eyes. She wouldn't make eye contact. "I see, you got a gun permit for a concealed weapon in New York City in three days, over a weekend? I'm supposed to believe that? Oh, and let's not forget the part where you took some shooting lessons yesterday and became an instant, expert marksman."

"It was a lucky shot."

"Lucky shot, my ass! You were more than twenty feet away from that guy and you put a bullet right between his eyes! My dad was a cop, remember? I know enough about guns to know that it was no lucky shot. I also know that people don't normally carry around little vials of oil so they can administer the last rites to people they happen to shoot in the head, twice, unless they happen to be a very disturbed priest."

"Tony, please, we have no time for this! We have to get to that ferry." With one quick, expert movement of her arm, she freed it from my grip and began walking away.

I caught up to her and again grabbed her arm. When she turned and looked at me, the predator was back.

"Which Marcella am I talking to now? The one I've known for seven months, or some killer that just showed up with a gun?"

Her face softened. She placed her free hand gently on the side of my face and she looked as though she was about to cry. "I didn't want this to happen. I didn't want you to see this." She withdrew her hand from my face and started to curl a strand of her hair around her index finger. "I will explain everything Tony, but please, we have to get to the ferry and off this island before nightfall. Our lives—your life, depends on it."

"We should go to the ranger station and tell Bill about this," I replied.

"Did you see those goggles on the man's face in the closet? They were military-grade night vision goggles. He was a professional, probably a mercenary, and he is almost certainly not alone. They can see in the dark, we can't. Soon it will be dark. Bill can't help us now, and we can't help him anymore, either."

"What does that mean?"

"That clearing in the woods we saw earlier today, it's a staging area, probably a landing zone for a helicopter. There are more of these people coming, assuming that they are not already here. Billy probably already knows this. Or knew it."

"Meaning what?"

"Meaning that he was either one of them, or if he wasn't, he's already dead."

With that ominous note, she took my hand and led me down the walk towards Davis Park.

Her head kept darting back and forth, machinelike, the entire time, apparently assessing the terrain and scanning the environment for threats. We reached a clearing on the walk, near the crest of a large dune, which afforded a view to the ferry terminal that was about a half-mile away. We were just in time to hear the ferry horn blow, signaling its departure. Marcella and I waved our arms and shouted in hopes that someone would see or hear us, but it was no use. A few moments later, the ferry left the dock and started out towards the channel.

"Are you sure that was the last ferry, Tony?"

"Yes. This time of year, they run a light schedule. The next one arrives tomorrow morning at eight-thirty."

Marcella ran her left hand through her hair. "Is there any other way off? There must be a bridge or something somewhere."

"There is. One is over there," I said, pointing to the east, and then pointing to the west, "and there is another one over there. All we have to do is figure out how to get past several miles of road-less beach, at night, while we're being hunted by people with night vision goggles and helicopters."

"There must be another way."

"What makes you so sure there are more of these guys?" I asked.

"I told you, that was probably a landing zone back there. And professionals like that never work alone. They usually work in teams of two, probably three or more on a remote job like this. And there may be more than one team, so there could be two, four, or more of them out there somewhere."

I took her arm gently and turned her so she faced me. "Who are *they*, Marcella... and who are *you*?"

"They are people who want very badly to kill you. Your partners, Kyle Orr and Jan Toomey, hired professional killers."

"What are you talking about? Why would they want me dead?"

"You have a ten-million-dollar key man life insurance policy, remember?"

"So what? If I die, the money goes to finance the company, not Kyle and Jan."

"Exactly. They are trying to finance your company with your key man life insurance policy. You are found dead, the company suddenly has ten million dollars in the bank, and they tell the new investors to go away."

My stomach winced, hard, and I started to feel flush. "What the hell are you talking about? You think Jan and Kyle are trying to kill me to finance the company's operations?"

"That, plus their own lifestyles. They've been siphoning off money from the company for more than a year. They knew that the due-diligence process with the new investors would turn up that fact. So they decided to collect the insurance money now and eventually siphon off enough of that to live happily ever after on a beach, just like this one, somewhere."

"When did this supposed murder plot get hatched?"

"Just before I came on the scene. I took the job as your assistant to protect you when we became suspicious that you might be in danger."

"Who is *we*?"

"I can't tell you who we are. I've already told you more than I should have."

"This is the most screwed-up thing I've ever heard!"

"It may sound that way, but it's true, Tony."

I said, almost shouting now, "I don't believe it!"

Marcella said to me, "Every week you hear about some guy putting a bullet in a cab driver, or a tourist, for fifty or a hundred bucks. Why can't you believe that someone would kill you for ten *million* dollars? Orr and Toomey were desperate. They were also greedy. Greedy and desperate people will kill someone, anyone, for ten million dollars, and they didn't even have to do it themselves. For a hundred thousand dollars they could hire the best assassin in the world. We're talking ex-special forces. So, for about five percent of the money that they would have collected on the insurance policy, they could easily have hired five of the best killers on the planet."

I noticed that she was speaking of Kyle and Jan in the past tense. But I ignored that for a moment and asked, "How could you possibly know it's them?"

"We know that keeping the insurance policy current was Orr's idea, even after you told him to cancel it, and that increasing the amount from five to ten million was Toomey's. Plus, we had them under surveillance when they met with one of the killers."

I thought about that. In fact, I remembered that meeting I had with Kyle. We were doing a top-to-bottom budget review. The goal was to eliminate any and all unnecessary expenses in order to slow our burn rate. I specifically remember telling him to cut the key man policy when it came up for renewal. I also remember his rather odd response. He said he thought it was selfish for me to get rid of the policy. "Suppose you die? The whole company will go down with you. Is that fair?"

I was momentarily speechless with astonishment when he said that. I guess it was because the last thing I imagined happening was someone collecting on that policy. It was even more astonishing in light of the fact that I had recently discovered that Kyle was making maneuvers with the board to have me replaced as CEO—by himself of course. I nipped that coup attempt in the bud, but it did not take a rocket scientist to see the rather odd contradiction: someone cannot claim you're indispensable one minute, and try to get you fired the next. Thinking back on it, my first instinct was to force the asshole to quit. But, we were already neck-deep in the refinancing process, and I just couldn't risk the negative impression a senior-level management defection would have had on potential investors at that moment.

"Tony! Hello? Are you with me, Tony?" Marcella grabbed my hand and started towards the ferry terminal again.

"Where are we going, Marcella?"

"We need to get out of here."

"No, I want to talk about Jan and Kyle."

"We don't have time for that now."

"There's no ferry coming for us tonight. We have plenty of time."

"No, we don't! That is what I keep telling you. We need to move, now! There's a marina down there, right?"

"Yes."

"So we'll find a boat and make our own way home."

"Marcella, the marina is empty this time of year."

"Let's hope not. Let's get down there and find a boat."

I said, "I know where there's a boat, at Watch Hill. Bill's boat is probably sitting right where left it, when we came in on Tuesday."

"No, it's too dangerous to go back there. It's in the direction of the landing zone. And suppose Bill is still alive, and he's working with these guys? We could be walking right into a trap."

She began pulling me west towards Davis Park again and I said, "So, assuming we get back to the mainland, we tell the police about Jan and Kyle, right?"

"Yes," she replied.

"Don't you think they're more likely to arrest us than them? The only evidence of a crime is that body in my uncle's closet, and there is no connection between it and them at all."

"Jan and Kyle are not the problem. The problem is the other assassin, or assassins, they hired to kill you."

"Alright, so we call the police, and then we tell Jan and Kyle that we're on to their plan, and they can call them off."

"That won't work either. Come on, Tony, let's move a little faster."

"Why won't that work?"

Marcella changed the subject. "Do you know how to use one of these?" she asked, waving the gun in my face.

"I don't like guns. Answer my question; why can't we just get them to call it off?" The knot in my stomach became a ball. "Why won't it work, Marcella?" I repeated loudly.

She said, "It won't work because they're dead. Okay?"

"What do you mean, they're dead?"

"There's not a lot of room for interpretation in that statement, Tony. They're dead, just like the one they hired to shoot you from across the street, and the one we just left in the closet."

"Jesus Christ, Marcella. Did you kill them?"

"I had help. Happy now?"

I grabbed her and stopped suddenly, which made her stumble. "Answer my other question."

"Which one? I lost track."

"Bullshit. I want to know who you are."

"It's a long, long, story, Tony."

"I have time."

"No, you don't. One of the other shooters out there may have you in his cross-hairs right now."

"Marcella, I'm not taking one more step until you answer that question."

"Tony, please! We have to keep moving."

"Tell me who you are. Now!"

"Okay, I'll tell you this: my job is to protect you. That is why I took the job as your assistant, and that is why I'm here. My job is to keep you alive."

"Who do you work for?"

"I work for you."

"You know what I'm asking. Who hired you to protect me? Who trained you? Who pays you?"

"People who value your life more than their own. I can't tell you any more than that. Besides, you wouldn't believe me if I did. Now let's get down to the marina and find a boat."

She started dragging me by the arm again, and I decided to drop it and go along, for two reasons. First, I figured I had succeeded in getting something out of her, and I was pretty confident that I would eventually get the rest of the story when the time was right, assuming I wasn't going to die in the next fifteen seconds. The other reason? Well, that *was* the other reason: I didn't want to get shot by one of those assholes in the black pajamas.

As we walked I tried to digest what she had just told me. Without thinking, I blurted out. "So, all of this time we spent together, you were just doing your job? Everything you said, the kissing, the hand-holding, the hugging; that was just an act, it was all bullshit. Wasn't it?"

Marcella stopped walking and turned. She looked at me with a shocked and angry expression on her face, and then down and away. Her fists clenched as she started pacing back and forth. In a moment her lips began to quiver and tears began running down her cheeks. Then she looked up at me again, and through clenched teeth spat out, "An act? You think I was acting? No! How could you even think that? I have killed for you, and I will die protecting you. This is not an act!" She turned abruptly and began limping in the direction of Davis Park.

It occurred to me that we just had our first fight. I also realized that, since one of us was heavily armed, it could have been our last, or at least my last.

"Marcella! Stop!"

She kept walking. I caught up with her and said, "I'm sorry. That wasn't fair. I didn't mean that."

She grunted, and wipe her nose on her sleeve, but didn't say anything. We kept walking.

The marina was empty, just as I thought it would be. But there was one small sailboat anchored to the east side of the channel, about two hundred yards offshore.

Marcella pointed to it and said, "There, we'll use that one."

"How do you plan on getting out there?"

"It's not that far, we can swim."

"Forget it, Marcella."

She looked at me. "Why? Don't tell me you can't swim."

"Oh, I can swim alright. But since the water is about thirty-five degrees, we'll probably die of hypothermia before anyone gets a chance to shoot us."

"That's a chance we'll have to take."

"Marcella, it's no chance at all. Have you ever tried to swim in water that cold? I have, but I wasn't stupid enough to try it on purpose. We'd be lucky to get halfway there before we drown. And even if by some miracle we manage to survive long enough to get there, how do you propose to lift your body, weighted down with wet clothes, two or three feet out of the water and onto the deck using hands that are completely numb and useless?"

"We have no choice."

"Wait a minute," I said, "Let me think." There had to be another option.

I looked around the marina trying to think of a plan B. I said, "Whoever owns that boat must have gotten ashore somehow. There must be a dinghy around here somewhere."

I noticed that one of the houses fronting the bay had its shutters open and curtains drawn. The owner had probably sailed over early in the season to open up the house for Memorial Day, and then took a ferry back to the mainland, leaving the sailboat behind. "Come on, I think I know where we can find one."

We walked over to the house and checked out the property, but we found nothing that would float. Just as we were about to give up I noticed a storage shed built under the second-story deck on the bay side of the property. I checked the door. "I guess you wouldn't happen to have the key for this padlock in that bag of yours, would you?" I inquired.

Without hesitation, she grabbed a large log from a nearby woodpile and charged the door. I barely had time to get out of the way as she slammed through it with what sounded like a war cry.

"Hey, I thought you were trying to save my life?"

Marcella grabbed my arm and pulled me into the darkness of the shed. Then, clenching the front of my shirt with both of her hands, she slammed me into the wall. She glared at me with eyes that were still teary. Then she relaxed her hands, reached up and put them on each side on my head and kissed me, long and hard. She pulled away, looked into my eyes, and asked with a firm voice. "Does that feel like I'm acting?"

"No. I said I was sorry. Really, I am. Well, I'm not sorry about getting the kiss . . ."

"Shut up." She kissed me again. I stopped talking. She said. "Someday, you will understand how I feel about you, but not now. You need to trust me."

"I do."

"Really?"

"Yes. Now let's find the damn dingy and get the hell out of here."

We nearly walked into the small fiberglass boat leaning on the wall next to the door. We set it down on its keel and threw in the oars, along with Marcella's newly acquired machine gun.

I looked around the interior of the shed in the dim light.

"What are you looking for?" Marcella asked.

"A shiny helmet and a folding shovel."

"What?"

"Never mind."

We each grabbed an end, and began dragging the boat towards the beach.

When we got to the bay, we took off our shoes, threw them in the dinghy, and began wading into the water as we pushed and floated it. Marcella cringed when she felt the cold water on her feet.

I smiled at her.

"Don't say it," she growled. So I didn't.

She got into the dinghy and I pushed it off, jumped in, set the oars in the locks and started to row toward the anchored sailboat. There was a stiff breeze blowing from the northeast at about fifteen knots and gusting to maybe twenty. The force of the wind was nearly directly against our efforts and, combined with the swells, made our progress very slow. To make matters worse, my glasses were being covered with salt spray, so it was hard to even see where I was going.

By the time we made it to the sailboat, the swells had built to the point of making the dinghy unstable. I grabbed the rail of the larger boat amidships, where I knew the rocking would be the least extreme, and told Marcella to carefully get on, which she did. Then it was my turn. Just as I stood up a sudden swell caught the larger boat and slammed it into the dinghy, and it nearly capsized. I struggled to maintain my balance, recovering it just in time to avoid an ice-water bath. Not wanting to press my luck, I decided to jump onto the larger boat before the next swell hit, and in my haste, banged my knee on the rail on the way over.

"Where's the other gun?" Marcella asked as I clutched my

knee and went down inside the cockpit in pain. I didn't say anything for a few moments, and then finally said, "I'm okay, thanks."

"Tony, we need that other gun."

"I'm not getting back into that thing to find it, and neither are you. Besides, there's about a foot of water in the bottom of it by now, so unless it's designed to be submersible, it's not going to be very helpful to us."

She rolled her eyes at me. "I'll get it."

"Forget the gun, Marcella; let's just get the motor started and leave."

I limped to the stern of the boat, looking for the small outboard motor that was typically mounted on the transom of a sailboat of this size. It wasn't there, but I found it under the aft hatch of the lazarette. The lower unit of the motor went through a small opening in the hull bottom that was enclosed by a watertight box. The box was open at the top where the upper unit of the motor was mounted with screw clamps. I'd been around boats like this most of my life and felt immediately at home. I was also relieved to discover that the motor was a late model 9.9-horsepower outboard. I went to work setting the throttle and the choke in the starting position, squeezed the primer bulb on the gas line a few times, and then began pulling the starter cord. After about a dozen pulls, the motor gave no signs of starting.

"What's the matter with it?" Marcella asked.

"I don't know." I kept pulling on the cord until my arm began to go numb.

"Can't we just sail out of here without the motor?" She asked.

"No, the wind is blowing in the direction we need to go, and the channel is much too narrow to tack out of here without running aground."

The look on Marcella's face indicated that she had no idea what I was taking about, so I said, "Unless we get this motor started we're not going anywhere."

I decided to remove the engine cover and check the motor. I knew enough about outboards to find an obvious problem, which is exactly what I found.

"Shit!"

Marcella asked, "What's the problem, Tony?"

"They cut the spark plug wires."

Just as I finished saying that, Marcella grabbed me by the collar and pulled me down into the cockpit. An instant later, I heard a high-pitched whizzing sound, passing by my ear.

Chapter 52

Marcella was lying on top of me, with her body protectively stretched out over mine.

"Marcella, get down here besides me."

"No. Did you see where the shot came from?"

"I'm not sure. I think, maybe, I saw a flash at the top of the dune over by the restaurant. Now get off of me and get down here; I don't need you to protect me."

"Protecting you is why I'm here."

I grabbed her with both arms and rolled over until she was under me. "There, that's better. I don't give a damn who hired you to protect me. I'm a big boy and I can take care of myself, thank you very much."

"Tony, please, get off of me. He'll see you." She struggled, but I didn't let her move.

"Who hired you?"

"Someone who thinks you're very, very important: so important that my life and others are expendable."

"Who and why?"

"Someone who made a promise a long time ago."

"Does this have something to do with the people that tried to kill my father?"

"No, but the failed attempt on your father's life has something to do with us."

"I don't understand."

She let out a grunt and, with one surprisingly strong movement, rolled me over and beside her. The cockpit of the boat was barely large enough for us to fit, and we ended up facing each other with our arms and legs tightly entwined.

"Okay", I said, "this will work. I've been trying to get you in this position since we got here." Then I gave her a kiss on the lips.

Marcella let out a gasp and started to yell at me in Italian. I didn't understand what she was saying, because I never learned the language from my grandparents, but I did recognize the word "stupido", so I got the gist of the monologue.

"Hey", I said, "I thought you were from England."

"Get serious Tony! I don't think you appreciate what's going on here."

Marcella's face was full of fear and I thought she was going to start crying again. Oddly, I didn't feel fear so much as, well, exhilaration. I know this may sound a little bizarre, but the whole thing had pushed me so far beyond the bounds of my normal life that it was hard to take any of it seriously. Here I was, wrapped around this beautiful woman in the cockpit of a sailboat, and she turns out not to be the woman I thought I knew, but instead was a complete fabrication. She wasn't even an administrative assistant; she was a bodyguard who was really good with a gun.

If that was not sufficiently bizarre, she was also on a secret mission to protect me from some strange people wearing black pajamas who were trying to kill me. They were also pretty good with guns, and, it turns out, were doing a pretty good job on that score, as well. She wasn't even from Jolly-Olde England; she was from Grandpa and Grandma's old country which, so far, might have been the only good news. So, basically, I felt like I was living inside of a James Bond flick, and I figured if I was going to die anyway, I might as well start enjoying it.

"Okay, Marcella, calm down. Let's think about the situation here. We are on a rocking boat, it's very windy and it's almost dark. So, we are not going to be an easy target."

She gave this some thought and said, "True, it's too dark to get a good view of us, but too light to use the night-vision scope. And the sun is on the horizon, and probably right in his eyes."

"See? We'll be okay."

She abruptly shook her head and looked at me like I was a retarded child. I hate that look. She continued with her professional analysis of our tactical situation. "But as we lie here, he is moving closer, and around to the west for a better shot. It will be dark soon and eventually he will be close enough so we will be an easy target through his starlight scope. We have to do something besides lie here, and do it now."

"Okay. The motor is history; the wind and narrow channel make it impossible to sail out; and soon we won't be able to move out of this cockpit without getting shot. I'm open for suggestions."

Marcella thought again, then said, "The only way is to jump into the water and swim ashore. We'll be harder to hit when we're swimming, so we may have a chance."

"Marcella, we covered this, didn't we? The water is too cold. We'll drown before we even get close to shore."

"Well, Tony, then I'm open for suggestions."

It was my turn to come up with a plan. I looked up at the masthead and checked the wind vane. Then I got up and peeked over at the shore, but got back down quickly. "Okay, how about this? We cut the anchor line and let the boat drift in the wind until it runs aground. This boat draws maybe three feet of water, and in these conditions, the wind and the waves will probably drive us up onto the beach even further. That should get us most of the way to shore and into shallow water, so we can move more quickly, and at least keep some parts of our bodies dry."

Marcella nodded. "Sounds like a plan."

"Okay, good, so all we need is a knife."

Marcella reached into her bag and pulled one out: but not some dainty pocket knife with a bottle opener and nail file, mind you, but one of those Rambo, army-surplus-looking things with a long, curved, serrated, double-edged blade.

I looked at this beast and said, "Hey, nice pocket knife. Does it have a compass in the handle?"

She ignored the stupid question and said, "I'll be right back."

"No, I'll do it, Marcella."

She barked at me, "You stay here under cover."

"No," I said calmly, "give me that thing and I'll do it. I know my way around boats, and besides, I can move faster, because I don't have a sprained ankle."

"What about your knee?"

"It's fine." I lied.

She reluctantly conceded the argument and handed me the knife. I was surprised by its weight and nearly dropped it.

"Tony, please let me do this."

"No, I can do it, really."

I was tempted to put the thing between my teeth, pirate-like, but thought better of that and slipped it, gingerly, though my belt behind my back.

I said to her, "I'll be right back," suppressing the impulse to follow that comment up with, "aargggh, matey."

"Stay low," she admonished as I exited the cockpit on the port side. I did just that, using the cabin top for cover.

I took my time crawling to the anchor line and managed

to get there unseen, apparently, because the asshole with the rifle didn't take any shots at my head. As I began cutting the line, it occurred to me that I might be better off staying on the bow and using the cabin, between me and the shore, for cover as the boat drifted towards the beach.

The serrated edge of the knife made quick work of the line, but as soon as it parted, the bow of the boat suddenly began swinging away from the wind and towards the beach, making me a great target from the shore. As the bow started to come around, I concluded that crawling back to the cockpit would be too slow and therefore a really bad idea, so I got up and made a run for it.

I didn't get past my second step when I felt a sharp sting in my right shoulder. I didn't hear the report of the rifle, but I knew what had happened. The pain seemed to shoot through my body like an electric charge and my head became light. But I kept myself focused on Marcella and the cockpit, and made a dive for it. I landed in an awkward position that knocked the wind out of me and I started to fade out, but then I heard Marcella's voice yelling in my ear, her mouth only inches away.

"Tony, your shoulder is bleeding; you've been hit!"

I shook off the haze and looked around to get reoriented.

Marcella slipped my jacket off. I heard the sound of a ripping shirt and felt a searing pain. She inspected the wound closely in the dim light and expertly felt around it as she tried to trace the bullet's path. I winced and jerked away.

"That hurts! Just leave it!"

"It looks like a superficial wound. Move your shoulder for me."

I followed her instructions.

Marcella looked into my eyes and said through clenched teeth,

"You were lucky. Let me do it next time."

I said, "I'm fine."

"You won't be fine if he gets another shot at you!"

"Give me the gun," I said.

"You said you don't know how to use one."

"Give me the gun, Marcella."

She reached into her bag, fished out the weapon and handed it to me. I took it, ejected the magazine, checked the load, reinserted the magazine, loaded a round in the chamber and made sure that the safety was off.

I said, "I don't like guns; I didn't say I didn't know how to use one. Half my family is on the job, and all the boys get mandatory firearms training right after their first communion."

The James Bond movie thing had disappeared; I was scared, but mostly I felt an uncontrollable sense of rage. I had a very clear image in my mind of finding that son-of-a-bitch with the rifle and putting a bullet in his heart. I'd never felt anything like it before, but then, of course, no one had ever shot me before, either. I moved up towards the cockpit coaming trying to position myself to get a bead on this guy.

"Where are you going?" Marcella asked incredulously.

"I think it's time that we started firing back, don't you?"

She grabbed me by the arm and started pulling me back down. "Are you insane? You'll never hit him with a handgun at this range! All you'll succeed in doing is making yourself a target."

The words had barely left her mouth when we heard four more shots hit the boat. They thudded loudly as they struck the fiberglass hull. This was followed by the sound of shattering fiberglass as the bullets flew around the inside of the boat, punching even more holes in the hull. At first I thought the shooter was losing his patience and firing in frustration.

I said, "Kinda gives a whole new meaning to the name Fire Island. Get it? Gunfire, Fire Island?"

Marcella didn't think that was funny for some reason, but I did, right up to the point when I heard the sound of rushing water. Then it occurred to me, that he wasn't taking wild shots; he was aiming at the waterline.

"He's trying to sink the boat," I said.

"I know. How long do you think we have?"

"It depends on the bilge pump. If it's a high-capacity pump, we could be afloat for hours."

On the other hand, I didn't hear the distinctive, high-pitched whine of a bilge pump, and so assumed the shooter had disabled the pump when he cut the wires on the outboard. This guy had anticipated our attempt to leave using this boat and had turned an escape route into a trap, one which Marcella and I had walked right into. I figured we'd be swimming a lot sooner than we expected, but I didn't see any need to tell this to Marcella. She had probably figured it out already, anyway.

"I'm sorry, Tony," Marcella said as tears welled up in her eyes.

I put my good arm around her shoulder and held her close. "There is nothing to be sorry about."

"I failed you. I was supposed to protect you."

"Hey, we're not dead yet," I said, gently wiping her wet cheeks with my fingers. Maybe it was my turn to protect her, for a change.

As the boat settled lower, it began to list to one side.

Fortunately, it was away from the direction of the shooter, so we remained concealed from his fire. But the sun was down now, and soon any move we made would make us an easy target for a night-vision equipped scope.

I listened to the sound of the dinghy pounding against the hull at the stern of the boat. It was on the listing side, and away from the shore, so we could get into it without the sniper seeing us. But then what? If we drifted away from the larger boat we'd be sitting ducks. If we just sat there in the dinghy we'd end up with the same result when the larger boat sank and exposed us to his rifle fire.

I asked Marcella, "What happens to night-vision goggles if there is a sudden bright light?"

"The light causes them to flare; it essentially makes them useless."

"Take this," I said, handing her the gun.

"Now where are you going?"

"I have an idea. I need to find something in the cabin."

"Be careful!"

Yes dear.

I struggled up to a position to inspect the three weatherboards positioned in the companionway. "It's not locked." I said with some relief, and began removing and tossing them over the side. The cabin was dark. "Do you have any matches, or a lighter in that handbag of yours?"

Marcella pulled out a small flashlight and handed it to me. "Keep the beam pointed down, and turn it off as soon as possible."

No wonder why that thing weighed a ton. I was tempted to ask her if she had a spare outboard motor in there somewhere. I turned the flashlight on and began searching for the only other thing that might get us out of here alive. I immediately saw that the cabin was already filled with a foot of water. Cushions, sail bags, life preservers, and other smaller floating objects were sloshing around. We didn't have much time.

What I was looking for should be close by, and suddenly, there it was: the emergency kit, stuffed in a small shelf over the galley sink. I turned off the flashlight and pulled it out. Then I grabbed two of the sail bags floating around inside the cabin. I dragged them out and placed them in the cockpit seats.

"The flares," Marcella exclaimed as she noticed what I was carrying.

"Yeah, they should be bright enough to blind his night vision."

The wet sail bags, which were now in the seats above us, were draining into the cockpit, soaking us both in icy water. I felt Marcella's body begin to tremble. I reached up, grabbed one of the bags, and tossed it over the side of the boat where the dingy was tied. I repeated this with the other sail bag and then returned to Marcella and the flares.

"Now what?" Marcella asked.

"Now we wait until the boat's keel hits bottom. When the boat comes to rest, we'll be as close to shore as we're going to get. Then we light the flares, toss them in the dinghy, and push it off. Hopefully, it will disable his night vision long enough for us to slip off the side of the boat, and swim like hell to the beach. Before he gets another shot, or we freeze and drown."

Marcella nodded her understanding. We waited. The boat drifted for what seemed like a long time, and we held each other as close as possible to conserve body heat. I wrapped my arms and legs around her. She looked up at me and gave me a smile through her shivering lips.

We finally felt the boat bump on the bottom a few times, and the waves began to drive it up on the beach. I opened the emergency kit. There was only one remaining flare and I held my breath, praying as I struck it with the igniter. On the third strike the night was filled with an intense red, incandescent light. I carefully threw the flare on top of the wet sail bags in the dinghy. Then I reached over and untied the dinghy's line from the cleat and pushed it off. Then we waited.

Initially the dinghy was concealed from the shooter by the hull of the sailboat that was heeling at a severe angle, its rail now just inches above the water. We were moments from sinking completely. Then the wind caught the dinghy and pushed it away from the floundering hull and into the clear sight of the beach.

We heard a blast of gunfire from a weapon on full automatic, this time aimed at the dinghy. I looked up and identified the asshole's position. In the mean time, I couldn't help but smile at the strange sight of the dinghy bobbing wildly in the surf, with most of the rounds missing their mark. The ones that did hit sent bits of fiberglass and sailcloth flying. A few moments later the dinghy was swamped and nearly out of sight. It didn't sink completely, however, probably because of floatation material built into the hull. The dinghy remained afloat, topped with a pile of sail bags, and a bright red flare sitting on top of them, like a combustible cherry sitting on a lemon meringue pie. Soon the whole pile began burning, glowing even brighter and further taunting the jerk with the gun, who was still firing wildly at it. It occurred to me that I would not be enjoying the moment so much if Marcella and I were in that dinghy.

The icy water finally filled the entire cockpit and Marcella gasped at the stabbing sensation.

I said to her through my chattering teeth, "I told you it was cold."

"Shut up and let's get moving."

Geez, what a grumpy-pants.

Our plan was to distract and blind the shooter with the decoy dinghy and the flare; get into the water and swim ashore; get a good fix on his location from the muzzle flashes and then, as they say, bring the battle to the enemy. The dinghy and flare part of the plan seemed to be working just fine. The rest of the plan, especially the part where we took the ice water bath, wouldn't be quite so easy.

"I think we should split up now," Marcella said. "You come up to him from the west, and I will come from the east. Here, take the gun."

"No, you keep it. I've grown attached to this knife."

We got into the water, which was too deep to wade in. I guess the boat drew more than I thought. As quietly as we could, we began to swim separately towards the shore. The pain in my shoulder prevented me from using my injured arm, so I side-stroked using my good one. I soon lost sight of Marcella in the darkness, which was good. If I couldn't see her, the shooter probably couldn't either, at least as long as the flare kept burning and making it impossible for him to use the night-vision scope.

After about thirty yards the cold water made the pain in my wounded shoulder subside to the point where I could start to use it again to swim. I knew that this was, at best, a mixed blessing. Ten yards later I began to lose all sensation in both arms and legs and the shore still appeared to be very far away.

I was beginning to wonder if either Marcella or I were going to make it, when I felt my feet touch the sandy bottom. I started to use my legs to push myself forward, but I kept low in the water to conceal my approach.

By the time I reached the shore, my body was trembling intensely. But I considered this a good sign, since I remembered from a boating safety class that the onset of severe hypothermia is indicated by the cessation of this response. I crawled onto the beach, found an area where the marsh grass grew right to the water's edge, and crawled up into it. The shooter was silent at the moment, presumably waiting for the flare to burn out, or maybe he was standing over me, about to put a bullet in my head.

I guesstimated that the muzzle flashes had been coming from a small dune about fifty yards east of me. If Marcella made it ashore, she should be somewhere on the other side of him, moving towards him from the east. I removed the knife from my belt and began to make my way; slow, low and quiet, towards his position.

I had covered about half the distance when the flare on the dinghy went out. There was a lapse of about a minute, and then all hell broke loose. A long staccato of automatic fire and bright muzzle flashes, followed by the whizzing sounds of bullets, came in my direction. He had apparently figured out what our attack plan was. He also knew, or was guessing, the direction from which I was approaching and was sweeping arcs of fire toward my position.

My only cover was a thin veil of reeds and marsh grass, which is to say that there wasn't any cover to speak of. It was just a matter of time before a bullet was fired in my direction, and found its target. *Great plan, Tony.*

A long burst of fire narrowly missed my head and I tried to will my body into the sand and mud. Then the firing stopped. I figured the guy had to reload at some point. I looked around in the dark and tried to find a path of escape, when the silence was broken by a single shot. I noticed that it sounded different from that of the rifle.

I stayed motionless for a few moments more, preparing for a resumption of the firing. When it didn't, I decided the only way out was to make a run directly at him. I got up in a crouching position and was about to charge when I heard Marcella's voice. It was weak, barely audible. "Tony?"

"Marcella, are you all right?"

She replied. "Thank God, you're okay. I'm here; stay low and follow my voice."

I found her kneeling over the man's body. His eyes were staring at the night sky and I could see a growing puddle of blood on the ground under the back of his head. Marcella was still dripping with water and she was shivering badly as she made a cross of red oil on the shooter's forehead. The first thought that came to mind was that it was good to be alive. The second, admittedly strange thought, was that having a wife who knew how to use a gun could really come in handy. I was in complete awe of the enigmatic woman before me. Whoever she was.

I helped her to her feet, wrapped my good arm around her, and headed towards the nearest cottage.

She said, "You did a great job drawing his fire."

"Thanks." We both laughed.

Her shivering was getting worse and then she stumbled on her injured ankle and fell to one knee. I lifted her, into my arms this time.

"You can't carry me with your wounded shoulder," she protested. I ignored her, and the pain, which had returned, and kept walking towards the door of the cottage. She buried her face in my neck, and I could feel her trembling lips and warm breath.

When we got to the door Marcella reached out with a weak hand and tried the knob. It was locked, of course. I wasn't in a very patient mood, for some odd reason, so I didn't bother to search for a key under the mat. I stepped back and gave the door a swift, hard kick. It slammed open with a loud bang, accompanied by the sound of breaking window glass.

I said to her, "We need to get out of these clothes before

hypothermia sets in." She didn't say anything, but I could hear the sound of her teeth chattering. I took her to the nearest bedroom and put her down.

She stood there shivering, as helpless as a child, watching me in the dim light, and cooperating as I removed her wet clothes. I threw them in a pile on the floor. She got under the covers, and I found some blankets in a nearby closet and piled them on her. Then I took off my own cloths and lay down next to her. We wrapped our naked bodies together and rubbed each other's backs with our hands. Eventually, the shivering stopped.

Another nearly full moon had risen, and the light fell on us as we lay there, motionlessly wrapped in each other's arms. For a while we just looked at each other, listening to the others breathing. Then our hands began to explore: cautiously at first, and then more freely, and finally desperately. The sensation of cold was gone, along with any pain from my shoulder, or inhibition from my body. I rolled her over and lay on top of her. She closed her eyes and whispered something in my ear that I could not make out. Then she slid her knees up and lifted her hips, repeating the phrase a little louder, almost like a chant, now in time with the rocking rhythm of our bodies. It sounded like, "It's forbidden," and she repeated the words over and over again. She opened her eyes and looked into mine and I kissed away her words. A moment later the only sounds in the room was our rapid breathing, a rhythmic panting from the old brass bed, and a plaintive grunting from the wooden planks on the floor.

Chapter 53

When I woke, the room was dimly lit by the predawn sky. Marcella's head lay upon my chest, surrounded by a pillow of her long black hair. I brushed some of her hair away from her face, placed it gently behind her ear, and watched her sleep. After a time, I tried carefully moving from beneath her, hoping not to wake her.

"Tony?"

"Yes, Marcella, I'm here. Go back to sleep."

"Where are you going?"

"I'm going to find us both some dry clothes, and maybe some coffee."

She stretched and sat up, struggling to wrap a blanket around herself. I helped and then gave her a kiss. "Are you okay?"

She smiled, nodded her head, and returned the kiss.

I hesitated for a moment and then said, "You know, I think I've been in love with you for some time. But I never let it fully sink in. This past week has been the best week of my life."

"You love me?" she asked.

"I mean, I didn't like getting shot."

She moved her head over, and gently kissed my wounded shoulder. "But it was just a flesh wound. So, you love me?"

I continued. "And taking a ride on that U-boat with sails, to say nothing of the ice-water bath, wasn't fun either. So let's not do that again."

She glanced at the pile of wet clothes on the floor and then back at me, running her hand against my bare chest. "That seemed to work out okay. You really love me?"

I observed with a smile, "Good point, that did turn out pretty well, didn't it?"

"Tony?"

I looked in her eyes and stopped smiling. "Yes, I love you."

"Even if I carry a gun?"

"Well, I'm not that happy about the gun thing."

She formed her beautiful lips into a pout and said, "It's a dangerous world. You... we need protection."

"True. But maybe we can get you a nice lead pipe, or one of those electrical stun things, something a little less noisy."

"But you still love me, even with the gun?"

"Yes, Marcella. I still love you."

She put her arms around my neck and kissed me on the lips, and then on both of my eyes. Then she whispered into my ear, "I've loved you most of my life, Anthony Mascelle."

"Most of your life?" I whispered back.

"Yes, since I was a little girl."

"You mean, when you were at the convent with the nuns?"

She nodded. "From the moment they showed me your picture."

"You're not from England, are you?" I continued in a whisper.

"No. I never said I was. I'm from Italy. The convent is in Piedmonte." Her English accent was transformed as she pronounced the name in perfect Italian.

I asked her. "Where did the English accent come from?"

"The convent was in Italy, but the nuns who taught me

English were from London."

"Where is Piedmonte?" I asked.

"It's a region in northern Italy. I'm from a small town there called Pavone."

"Ah, Pavone. That's where you got the last name?"

"Sì, il mio nome di famiglia. It is my family name"

"Well things are starting to get a little clearer."

"Why is it so important that you know so much about me?" she asked with a curious smile.

"Hmmm. Well, first off, I'm just trying to catch up. Second, because someday I want to visit there."

"You and me?"

"You, me, our kids... grandpa always told me to marry a girl from the old country. Can you make lasagna?"

Tears came to her eyes, but then she laughed them away. "Boy, the nuns will really be surprised to see us," she said, as she got lost in a thought.

I kissed her again, bringing her back from wherever she went. It was a long kiss, and the thought of getting back under the covers came to mind, but I pushed the impulse away. I was pretty sure we were in no immediate danger, because if there were more of the black-pajama guys out there we would have heard from them by now. Nonetheless, we needed to get out of here and onto the first ferry back to the mainland, especially if Marcella was right about the clearing being a staging area, and a landing zone for a helicopter. If there were more of these people coming, they'd probably be coming soon.

I sat up and swung my feet out of bed. The floor was ice cold and the room air was not much warmer. "I'll be right back with some fresh clothes. Can I borrow one of those blankets?" I asked her.

"No. But I promise to close my eyes," she said.

"You promise?"

"Sure, I'll give you one minute before I look."

I stood up and checked the closet in the room, but it was empty.

Marcella said, "Fifty-nine, sixty," and then she whistled at me.

"That wasn't a minute," I protested.

"No? Sorry, my watch doesn't seem to be working. Must be the salt water." She grinned.

"You're not wearing a watch." I said.

She laughed.

I found a storage closet down the hall. It contained shelves stacked with clear plastic bags full of linens, towels and clothing. I found two decent pair of jeans and some undershirts and sweaters that would fit each of us. I also found some underwear. Boy, was I feeling guilty about this. The sunk boat, the smashed door, and now stealing someone's underwear. Someday I'd have to apologize to the owners... as soon as I figured out who they were.

I dressed quickly and brought the other clothes into Marcella.

"Here, these should fit," I said, holding up a pair of men's boxer shorts.

She took them and hesitated, then shrugged her shoulders and moved to the edge of the bed. She said. "I guess it would be fruitless to ask you to close your eyes."

I just smiled, walked across the room, and sat in the chair

opposite the bed, facing her. Then I informed her, "Ready when you are."

She blushed at first, then she made the best of it. She slowly and sensually stood up and let the blankets slide to the floor. The sight of her perfect body in the morning light took my breath away. She slid her feet into the boxer shorts and lifted them to her waist as she looked into my eyes. Then she turned her rear end in my direction and slowly slipped the jeans up. I got up and began to retreat to the kitchen.

"Where are you going? Tony?"

I turned towards her and said, "I'm going to find some coffee—before we end up back in bed."

She stood up, buttoned the jeans, placed her hands over her bare breasts, and made a pouting face. "Ciao, Tony."

"Ciao, Marcella," I replied in my best faux Italian, and left the room.

I found instant coffee, some crackers and strawberry preserves in the cupboard. I put a pot of water on the stove and went out on the porch to wait for it to come to a boil.

From the porch I could see the sun just beginning to rise over the salt marsh to the east. The morning air was cold but refreshing, and there was a light mist covering the ground. It was too early to determine if the sky was going to be gray or blue, but I thought I could detect some blue above the horizon to the northeast.

I continued watching as the sun began to light up the bay. In a few moments, the mainland came into view. Then my eyes followed the horizon to the place where Marcella and I came ashore. I could make out the mast of the sailboat, which was sticking out of the water at an extreme angle, pointing northwest. The dinghy, however, was nowhere in sight. I hesitantly moved my eyes over to the dune where we left the shooter's body, and thought about what a strange mix of heaven and hell the previous night was.

I was just about to return to the kitchen when I noticed that the tall grass had been disturbed in the area near the shooter. Then I noticed something else, a line of trampled grass moving to the southeast of it. The first thought that came to my mind was that we left Marcella's handgun and the assassin's rifle by the body, which meant that, except for a knife, we were completely unarmed. *Stupid*!

I started moving quickly, but cautiously, towards the clearing, hoping that I still had time to correct a potentially fatal oversight. When I got there, both guns were gone, and so was the body. The grass and the sand indicated that the body had been dragged, back to the east towards Watch Hill. My stomach fell as I considered the possibilities. I turned and ran back to the house.

I was still about thirty yards away when I heard the sound of a man screaming in pain, and then I heard shots. A man in black exited the house. His hair and upper body were wet and steaming. He began running towards Watch Hill, with one hand covering his face.

My heart was pounding as I entered the kitchen, and I began thinking the unthinkable. The first thing I noticed was the pot lying in a puddle, near the kitchen door. Then I found Marcella.

She was laying with her back against the stove. The burner, where I had left the pot, was still lit. She sat slumped over, motionless, blood oozing through her sweater from a wound in her chest. I knelt down next to her, lifted her, held her in my arms, and rocked her gently. Her skin was already turning gray, and her body was limp. I could hear my own sobbing, but the sound seemed to belong to someone else. "Marcella, open your eyes, please don't die, please Marcella, please."

Then I stopped rocking her. I kissed her lips, and I placed her gently down on the floor. Her arms dropped beside her body and a small black object fell out of one of her hands, and rolled away, out of sight.

In an instant, my life had changed. Again. She was gone. Thoughts of her flooded into my mind. There were thoughts of us together over the past days and months, and there were imagined thoughts of times that had not, and would never, become reality. Then all of the images disappeared, as if someone turned a light off in my head.

It would be accurate to say that the next thought I had wasn't really a thought at all. I could only describe it as a feeling of intense rage, which is correct, but wholly inadequate as a description. I wanted to find the guy in the black pajamas, and anyone else with him. Then I wanted to end them all. Completely, irrevocably, without hesitation, without mercy, and without a shred of concern for my continued existence on this earth.

I found Marcella's knife in the pile of wet clothing in the bedroom and placed it in my belt. By the time I left the house, my body was trembling with rage.

I ran, in full stride, in the same direction as the man in black, who was heading east and, I presumed, to the helicopter-landing zone that we found yesterday. I felt the rough splintered surface of the boardwalk against the bottom of my bare feet and somewhere in my brain the pain of cuts and splinters were registering as numb sensations. I did not start to close the distance on him until after I passed my uncle's cabin. Then I lost sight of him around a bend in the walk. As I rounded the bend, I felt the whoosh and heard the now-familiar crack of a bullet passing very close to my ear, and felt a slight tug on the left side of my collar. I kept running without missing a stride until he appeared from behind a bush about one hundred feet in front of me on the boardwalk, where he stood in a firing position. The left side of his face was red and blistered and his eye was swollen closed. As I ran, I lifted the knife out of my belt.

The sensation of the throw was smooth, and it seemed to be as natural and familiar as throwing a softball. I had no intention or goal, to the extent that I thought about the action at all. It was entirely reactive, like flinching, or raising a hand to block a fist. After its release, I lost sight of the knife for a moment, and when it reappeared, the only part I could discern was the grip protruding from the man's throat.

It didn't seem at all strange to me, at the time, that I managed to hit him with a knife, at a full run, with that degree of accuracy and from that distance. Looking back on it, I assumed that the knife was probably specifically designed and balanced for precisely such a task. But, it still seems to me now, to have been an almost miraculous feat; if putting an eight-inch blade into another human being's body qualifies as a miracle. I also realize now that I'm probably only still alive today because of his poorly aimed shot at me. I'm very sure he wouldn't have missed if he had had two functioning eyes. The fact that he didn't was due to Marcella's use of the boiling pot of water as a weapon in the kitchen. She was still protecting me, even after she was already dead.

The man dropped the gun and reached for the knife in his throat with both hands as he folded to the ground in slow motion before my eyes. He was mumbling something as his chest heaved and blood gurgled from his mouth and from the wound in his neck. I picked up the pistol by his side and checked the clip and chamber. I remember asking him who he was and why he had killed Marcella. But before he could reply, and in fact before I even completed my sentence, his breathing stopped.

I removed a spare ammunition clip from his body and placed it in my back pocket. A moment later I heard, and then saw, a small helicopter hovering in the distance. I assumed that it was taking off from the clearing behind the dunes. I also assumed that they were wondering what was taking their murderous friend so long to return to the staging area.

Apparently, the pilot caught sight of me because he turned

and began his approach. There were two men in the helicopter, the pilot and a man next to him with a rifle. They were both dressed in the same black pajamas, and the one with the rifle made hand signals to the pilot and pointed in my direction. *Come and get me, you fuckers.*

The helicopter descended and moved in low, rotating so that the man with the rifle could get a clear shot at me. I heard gunfire, not from the helicopter, but from my right, or behind me; it was hard to tell. It never occurred to me to duck or run. All of my attention was singularly focused on the guys in the sky as the world around me began to move in slow motion. I took a deep breath, brought the gun up, aimed, and squeezed the trigger.

They never had a chance. Before the helicopter had the opportunity to fully swing around, and the rifleman had a clean shot at me, I put five rounds through the windshield, into the pilot's face. Then I emptied the remaining rounds into the chest of the man with the rifle as he came around. I swiveled to my right, ejecting the spent magazine as I moved. The empty clip landed on the boardwalk close to my bare left foot, and just as that sensation registered in my brain, I saw a yellow-orange flash in my left peripheral vision and simultaneously felt the warmth of the fireball that erupted like a volcano from where the helicopter slammed into the ground.

A booming sound, accompanied by a whoosh of air, and a rain of sand and small fragments of plastic and metal, reached me by the time I pushed home the new magazine, finishing the reload.

Two men with automatic weapons were running over the dune from the ocean side of the island to my right and in the direction of the smoldering black pyre that was, until very recently, a perfectly good helicopter. I jumped off the boardwalk, crouched down in the nearby brush, and watched them approach. I guess the prospect of taking the next ferry, or swimming back to the mainland, did not appeal to them very much because they looked very unhappy. *Tough shit, assholes.*

They scanned the scene around the wreckage and then began walking in my direction. As they got closer I could hear them speaking to each other but couldn't make out the words. I steadied the gun against the rail on the boardwalk, held my breath, aimed at the man closest to me, and then squeezed the trigger three times in rapid succession. An instant later there was a crimson cloud where his head used to be. The other man behind him was also hit. He was thrown back by the bullet's impact and then fell to all fours on the boardwalk. He stood up and pressed his left hand to his right shoulder and began to run in the opposite direction. I jumped up onto the boardwalk and emptied the entire clip at him, but he made it to the top of the dune and headed down the other side and out of sight. *Damn it*!

I looked to the right and saw the roof of the horse barn above the tops of the trees, threw the empty gun away and began running the fifty yards to the barn. I found William in his stable with a bridle but no saddle. I grabbed the machete that was hanging from its nail on the wall, and jumped onto William's back. He seemed to read my mind and headed for the door in full stride; I just hung on and pointed him over the top of the dune, and he did the rest.

By the time William and I made it to the beach, I couldn't find the guy anywhere. But William did. He reared and wheeled, nearly throwing me off. When he came down on all fours, his head was pointed at the asshole in black, about a hundred yards down the beach.

The killer was on his knees in front of an open duffel bag. He appeared to be reaching for something with his remaining good hand and I had no doubt about what it was: a gun of some sort. I instinctively pulled back hard on William's reins. As I hesitated, I felt my mind retreat from its state of rage and I made momentary contact with rational thought. There was no way I was going to survive this. It didn't really matter what kind of gun the prick had, because William and I were a big target. Even if he had an eighteenth-century musket he was more than a match for me, the horse, and this oversized steak knife from the barn.

Then William reared again. This time the motion was smooth, and I felt in complete control of my body, and his. Upon William's return to earth, he began pumping his legs in powerful rhythmic thrusts, in time with the blasts of breath coming from his bellows-like chest, and the beating of his massive heart, which I could feel through the sides of my legs. Our breathing and our hearts began to synchronize, as though we somehow merged into a single animal.

What happened next is hard to forget, but it's even harder to explain. The rational part of my brain seemed to abandon me, receding away into a tiny, insignificant point of light in the distance. It was replaced by something else, something primitive, irrational and vicious: like a wild, tormented animal trapped in a cage. I brought the machete up from my side and pointed it at my target. Then I loosed William's reins and, at the same time, freed this raging beast inside of me, as well. We charged the enemy at full gallop. The man in black stood up, pulled out an automatic weapon and began firing. I saw the muzzle flashes and thought I could feel the bullets whizzing by my head, but William and I just kept bearing down.

The machete was raised high above my head now, and I actually don't remember hearing the gunfire, William's hooves striking the ground, the sound of the ocean, or anything else for that matter, except for an odd, faraway sound that seemed to be coming from inside of my head. I could not identify it at first, but it sounded like an animal screaming in rage. Then I realized that the sound was coming from me, from deep inside my chest, erupting out of my mouth and hurtling at the assassin.

The guy emptied his clip, threw the gun into the sand, and drew a long serrated blade from behind his back. Everything was still moving in slow motion, but was more vivid and sharp than before. I was close enough to see his face. One eye was a lifeless white marble surrounded by scarred flesh. I guess that explained why all of his shots missed, and why I wasn't already dead. His other eye, the left one, was as black as the ass-end of an eight-ball and was ferociously staring back at me with defiant hatred. I clenched and bared my teeth in anticipation of the kill. I must have looked like some kind of smiling lunatic, because at the last moment the defiance drained from his face, and was replaced by fear. He turned to run, which turned out to be a bad move. After a few strides, William and I caught up with him.

The machete split the man's head down the middle, like a watermelon, opening it to his neck. His body dropped to the ground, but not before blood gushed from his head, spraying like a fountain into my face. I felt it in my eyes and on my teeth, and could taste it on my tongue. Thinking back on it, I should have been repulsed, but all I remember was a whooping sound and the sensation of my hand waving the machete over my head.

I looked down at William, who was circling and looking for another target to charge. The world around me, still silenced, seemed to regress. I looked towards the ocean and watched the mute surf for a few moments as my vision became blurred, and then faded to black.

Chapter 54

A sudden gust of wind caught the lapel of Sean McKeown's overcoat. It blew the collar up and around his neck as he stood stiffly on the Watch Hill dock waiting for the next ferry to arrive. He pressed his cell phone close to his ear, wondered where the beautiful spring weather had gone, and kicked himself for wearing his thin black overcoat that was obviously no match for the late-season blast of frigid Canadian air blowing over the flat profile of the wetlands along the bay side of Fire Island.

"Okay, Joe", he said into the phone. "Good to hear that your nephew is stable. Thanks for the call, and let me know when he comes to. Okay, as soon as we finish up here, I'll get back to you and give you a briefing on what we found. Okay, bye." McKeown ended the call, stuffed his hands and the phone deep into his coat pockets and turned his back to another gust of wind as the ferry approached the dock.

He noticed a blonde head pop out of one of the vessel's windows. The woman smiled and waved as soon as she made eye contact with him. A few moments later, the deckhands finished tying the ferry up and a gangplank extended from its side with a noisy, mechanical clang.

The blonde woman's schoolgirl-like walk across the gangplank and onto the boardwalk brought a smile to McKeown's face.

Detective Samantha Taylor, a.k.a. Sandy Taylor, was a thirty-something-year-old enigma. Despite the fact that she shunned makeup, nail polish, blow dryers or, apparently, any fixtures or accoutrements of a contemporary American female, most men found Sandy extraordinarily attractive. However, by all indications, she could not care less. Sean was among the few members of the department that she trusted, and he was among the very few colleagues that both respected and tolerated her rather extraordinary foibles.

The friction between her and the other members of the NYPD was not the type that normally strained relationships between the members of the new and evolving ranks of an increasingly integrated New York City Police department. In fact, she seemed almost oblivious to most of the standard categories, causes and issues, including those derived from the hard-edged, foul-mouthed, testosterone-driven culture that generated a seemingly limitless supply of sexist jabs, racial epithets, ethnic stereotypes and homophobic remarks that passed as humor among her male colleagues. Except for an occasional eye-roll or head-shake she usually didn't react, or care about that either. On the very rare occasion when she heard a remark that she actually considered funny, she might even respond with a passing smile. Which is not to say that she wasn't friendly, or personable. She was. And someone who hadn't seen her other, darker, side might even describe her as bubbly.

"Hi, Sean," Sandy said with a high falsetto voice. "Long time, no see."

Sandy's face had already turned a bright red from exposure to the cold wind. She pushed her eyeglasses up on her nose with a flick of her index finger, and then tucked her platinum-blonde hair inside her fur-lined hood, before zipping her snow parka up to her chin.

"Hi, Sandy," McKeown replied. "Thanks for coming."

"Yeah right, Sean. Like I'm going to say no to you and Chief Jack. I may be crazy, but I'm not stupid."

She offered her cheek and he gave her a peck. She was the only detective he had ever greeted with a kiss, and probably the only one he ever would.

The first time they met, about five years ago, they were both newly minted detectives, and he had worked with her, on and off, on a number of cases since then. Except for an occasional rough spot, they generally worked well together. There was never any issue of professional rivalry between them, because Sean had long ago buried any interest in climbing the promotion ladder within the department, principally because he could not think of a job that he would rather do than the one he was currently doing. As for Sandy, she didn't seem to have an ambitious bone in her body. Their relationship also developed sans any romantic attraction between them. McKeown was a happily married man, and since Sandy apparent had no romantic interest in any man, the relationship had quickly evolved into one more akin to that of an older brother and a younger sister. But, she could be a very challenging sibling.

Sandy looked around at her surroundings. "So this is Fire Island? What's all the fuss about? Looks kind-a primitive to me."

McKeown inquired. "You've never been here? I thought you grew up on the Island?"

"I did," she said, "but I never liked the beach. I burn too easy, and the sand and water mess up my books. I went to the beach a couple of times with my folks, when I was young, but I've never been here."

Sean laughed and asked rhetorically, "So a girl named Sandy that doesn't like the beach?"

This, of course, was vintage Sandy. McKeown not only wasn't surprised by such odd revelations, he expected them. But, the bottom line for McKeown, always the practical man, was results. At the end of the day, their professional relationship worked and they got those results. As far as he was concerned, based on that standard, Sandy Taylor was probably the best partner he had ever had. The means to those results, however, could take their toll.

He remembered the first time they met. She looked like she was straight out of the police academy. Sean could not imagine how she had managed to earn a detective's shield at so young an age. He, probably like many of his colleagues, concluded that she had earned the shield, not on the job, but in the bedroom. Now, when he thought about that first impression of her, he winced at the stupidity of that conclusion.

Their first case together involved the murder of a prostitute, and it provided all of the information that anyone would need to conclude that Sandy was a true prodigy, if ever there was one. The murdered woman's body was found in her apartment on the lower east side of Manhattan. Beaten to death with what would turn out to be a baseball bat. Sandy arrived on the crime scene and spent all of ten minutes hovering over the corpse, pacing back and forth, and sometimes circling it. Occasionally, she picked up an item of clothing, or some other bit or piece of evidence at the scene, but at all times, she continued to stare at the corpse with a glazed look on her face, as though she were somehow communicating with the recently deceased.

Sean could clearly recall the faces of the other people at that crime scene, watching Sandy as if she were some sort of psychotic. However, as Sean, and the others, would find out this was just part of her mysterious process: the subtle part, as it turned out. The less subtle part began when she suddenly left the apartment, jumped into a patrol car and drove away with the tires screeching and smoking. Apparently, something the deceased women said to Sandy Taylor really pissed her off. It wasn't even Sandy's car. Sean managed to catch up and dive into the cruiser's passenger seat just as she pulled away.

She drove the car through Manhattan traffic as if she was a demon-possessed, not uttering a single word the entire time. McKeown tried at first to calm her down, but when she repeatedly ignored him, he just sat in the passenger seat, gritted his teeth and held on for his life.

She slammed on the brakes in front of a ratty-looking apartment building in Hell's Kitchen. The sudden stop nearly caused Sean's head to hit the windshield. "Goddamn it, Sandy, calm down before you kill one of us."

Before the words finished leaving his mouth, she jumped out of the car and ran towards the building. He followed her inside and up two flights of stairs. By the time he caught up with her, she had already kicked down an apartment door. She did not bother taking the time to check the building's address, or the apartment number; she didn't even stop for a moment of reflection or caution to consider that there might be someone on the other side of that door with a shotgun aimed at her face.

When Sean finally found her, she was in the bedroom of the apartment, and she was standing over a huge black guy, holding a baseball bat over his head. Sean would later find out that the bat was the murder weapon used to kill the prostitute, and the man was the victim's pimp and murderer.

However, the *really* bizarre part, the part that still gave Sean the chills when he thought about it, was what Sandy was doing when he arrived on the scene. She was speaking to the man in a sad, angry, scolding voice, but it was not a voice Sean recognized. Apparently, however, the big black guy did, because he was curled up on the bed, sobbing like a child and repeating the same thing over and over again: "I'm sorry baby, I didn't mean it, I didn't mean to kill you, please forgive me baby, I'm sorry… "

All Sean could do was to watch all of this, almost as if he were not there. In a few minutes, Sandy's spell passed, and she transformed back into her normal, personable self. On her way out, she simply shrugged her shoulders at Pat and led the handcuffed and blubbering suspect back to the patrol car.

Over the years Sean and Sandy had worked together on about a dozen cases, some more bizarre and some less. He noticed a pattern: the more unsolvable the case was, the more unearthly Sandy's abilities appeared to be. Sean never complained about it. Sandy was Sandy and results were results. Nevertheless, McKeown also knew that someday, one of them would pay a heavy price. It came as some relief to him, when she took a transfer out of his precinct.

Months later, he heard rumors that she was being investigated by Internal Affairs. Then he heard that she was on suspension pending a psychological review. At that point, Jack Sachel stepped in and rescued her. She was reassigned back to his precinct and Sachel buried her behind a desk stacked with open case files in the missing persons section. Sachel only pulled her out on special assignments, like this one.

McKeown found Jack Sachel's protectiveness of Sandy odd, at least at first. Sachel had never seemed like a very sympathetic person to Sean, so he once asked Jack why he rescued Sandy. Jack's answer was short, sweet and to the point. He told Sean that he once overheard his boss, an old-fashioned Irish cop, say something in response to a similar question once raised by someone who did not like Jack Sachel because he considered Jack an uppity black man. "My former boss said, 'Never shoot your mavericks, because someday they may save your ass.'" Sachel told Sean that later on, his boss repeated this admonition to him in private and told him never to forget it, and he never did.

Sandy smiled at Sean and then asked abruptly. "Okay, Sean, so why am I here?"

McKeown took a moment to change gears into his official mode. "Well, we've got a pretty interesting case here. It is somehow connected with a multiple-murder case I've been working on. We're coordinating with the NYPD, Suffolk County PD, and two New Jersey police departments."

"Wow, must be some body count."

"At least nine and counting."

"So it's a weird one, huh?"

"Yeah, it's pretty weird," McKeown said with a smile. "I thought it was right up your alley."

"Is this your average, run-of-the-mill weird, like the one with the voodoo guy and the fighting chickens in Harlem?"

"You mean the fighting cocks?"

"Yeah, whatever, is it like that?"

"No, I'm afraid this one is a lot weirder than that."

"Wow, it does sound like my kind of case."

McKeown and Taylor began walking along the boardwalk, away from the ferry terminal and towards the ocean side of the island. As they walked, McKeown filled her in about the dead shooter, with the cross on his forehead, who was found last Friday in New York City, and the murders of Jan Toomey and Kyle Orr.

None of this information seemed to affect Sandy in any way. She just listened, absorbed and stored it. Sean then told her about Tony Mascelle and the possible, but unlikely, link between this case and the one with his father's, eight years ago. That seemed to pique her interest, but it was hard to tell with Sandy, sometimes. Finally, he told her what he knew so far about the most recent episode that had just occurred on Fire Island yesterday, including the apparent death and subsequent disappearance of Marcella Pavone.

"So, what's your gut tell you, Sean?" Sandy asked.

"Well, with the number of shooters involved, the body count, the type and number of weapons used, and the helicopter, I'm thinking drug syndicate. Who else would have those kinds of resources or, for that matter, the balls to start a war on this scale?"

"And the connection with Mr. Mascelle and his employees?" She asked.

"I don't know, but if I were to guess, they're using his company, with or without his knowledge, as a means of laundering drug money, concealing drug distribution operations or both."

"So, who else besides you and me are assigned to this from the NYPD?" she asked.

"Well, officially we're not on this case. We think it may be under federal jurisdiction."

Sandy Taylor looked at him. Sean shrugged. "And unofficially?" she asked.

"You and me, and whoever we can convince Jack to loan us. Plus we have Detective Joe Mascelle, Tony Mascelle's uncle."

"Uncle Joe? That doesn't sound too kosher, Sean."

"Joe Mascelle is a former partner and a long-time friend of the chief."

"Ah, a friend of Chief Jack... that's different."

"He's also the guy that made a few calls to the Suffolk County PD to get their cooperation on our visit out here today. Of course, they're also not officially on the case." McKeown continued, "Joe is a good guy and a good detective."

"When do I get to meet him?"

"Right now; he's with his nephew at the hospital. Given the circumstances, he decided his first, best efforts should be to stay close to Tony and be there when the kid wakes up."

"So, how's Tony doing?"

"The docs expect him to be fine, but an inch to one side and I would be attending a funeral."

Sandy said, "Two states, four jurisdictions... so where are the feds?"

"Oh they're here; you just can't see them at the moment."

"What does that mean?"

"It means they've decided to play it alone and mysterious, as usual. Some guy called Barella showed up in my office one day and the next day he's telling me some bullshit about the case being entirely in the fed's jurisdiction."

"Let me guess: a matter of national security, right?"

"Right. So this guy is here one minute and gone the next, but he's not gone-gone, he's just not visible. And at some point he'll show up again, maybe say something profound, or nothing at all, and then disappear again."

"So what, if anything, did Barella tell you so far?"

"According to him, they've been tracking this killer, or killers, for a very long time."

"How long?"

"For decades. Whoever they are, they have access to technology that no one else has."

"Like?"

"Like munitions that explode following entry, leaving no exit wounds and virtually no forensic evidence."

Sandy said, "Yeah, I read the coroner's report on the way out here. So what's with the cross-on-the-forehead thing?"

"Well, just your standard stuff: oil mixed with lamb's blood."

"Right."

"All the victims have the same MO?"

"No. Now there are at least two. The other thing we're seeing are broken necks: the kind of stuff that a Special Forces guy might do."

"You think this is the same perp with the strange bullets?"

"Maybe, but I don't think so."

"So all of the bodies have either a single bullet to the head or a neck that was twisted like a chicken's, right?" Sandy asked.

"Well, not everybody." McKeown said as they walked to the top of the dune. He nodded his head in the direction of the scene between the two dune lines. Sandy turned, looked and gasped.

"Oh my God, it looks like a war zone!" she said as she stared at the still smoldering wreckage of the helicopter and the line of body bags that lay in the sand on either side of the walkway bisecting the area.

"And this isn't all of it; we're still finding bodies. We won't have a complete picture until Tony wakes up and gives his side of the story. But based on what we know now, a lot of this is Tony Mascelle's handiwork."

"Huh? Jack gave me the impression that Tony was a nerdy computer guy." Sandy Taylor said

"Yeah, I had the same impression. But apparently he has another side that no one has met before, maybe not even him. A park ranger found him yesterday. He was lying semi-conscious on the back of a big horse, with a bloody machete in one hand and the reins in the other. I'll show you later whose blood is probably on the machete. Anyway, let me give you the tour and then we can go back to the mainland and speak to Mr. Mascelle this afternoon."

"Lead on, Sean," Sandy said.

Chapter 55

"Wow, there's something you don't see every day," Sandy said as she examined the man's split head. "He did this with that?" she said as she pointed to the bloody machete inside a large, transparent evidence bag.

"Looks like the murder weapon to me," A Suffolk County police detective replied as he zipped up the bag containing the body.

"The coroner will tell us for sure, but what else could do that?" The detective shook his head as he stood up. "Mascelle's kid must have some set. The dead guy emptied a full clip at him on full automatic as the kid charged him on a horse, like he was some sort of medieval knight."

"Or a postal worker having a really bad day," Sandy replied.

The detective laughed and held out his hand. "Bob Crowley, SCPD homicide, and the detective in charge of this case, unless you're with the federal government, in which case I'm here looking for sea shells."

"This is Sandy Taylor, NYPD, she's on special assignment," Sean McKeown said.

"Nice to meet you," Sandy said as she shook Crowley's hand.

"Okay, now that the greetings and introductions are done, how can I be of help to you two?" Crowley asked.

"Well, I would like to have a look at the rest of the crime scene without having it disturbed any further by your men," Sandy said.

Sean McKeown shifted nervously on his feet at the sound of Sandy's undiplomatic response. Bob Crowley gave McKeown a look of surprise and then responded to Sandy. "Well, this is SCPD jurisdiction, Detective Taylor, and we've already collected all the evidence that's important to the case."

"Wanna-bet?" Sandy replied.

Sean McKeown cut in. "Can I talk to you alone for a minute, Bob?"

"Yeah."

"Excuse us for a minute or two, okay, Sandy?" McKeown said as he walked Crowley down the boardwalk several yards.

"No problem, Sean," Sandy replied with a smile.

"What's the deal with her?" Crowley asked.

McKeown took a deep breath. "Yeah, I know, Bob."

"When I agreed that we would cooperate on this, I did it out of courtesy to Tony Mascelle's dad, who is former SCPD. But I don't need some character in here trying to make the next grade by giving me shit about how I'm handling my crime scene."

"Look, Bob, she's not what she seems. I brought her in on this case because she's good. She can be a little abrupt at times, but she doesn't have a mean bone in her body, or a politically correct one, either. And, once this case is solved, she'll be as sweet as a lamb again and won't give a shit about who takes the credit for solving it. In fact, I've worked with her on a lot of tough cases. She gives 200 percent and then, when it's solved, habitually refuses credit for some of the most brilliant detective work I've ever seen. It's the only thing about her that really caused friction between us."

Bob Crowley looked back at Sandy, who was pacing up and down the boardwalk like a Labrador retriever and scanning the crime scene around her. He shook his head. "She's acting a little, well... a little nuts, Sean."

Sean smiled as he watched Crowley watching Sandy. "What she lacks in social graces she more that makes up for in results.

Trust me on this."

"Okay. But, to be straight with you, I've already seen enough strange shit today to give me a really bad feeling about this case: so bad that I'm even considering just letting the boys from Washington have it, which is about as bad as it gets. You promise to keep your pretty savant there on a leash, and I'll give you my department's full cooperation on this one. The way I figure it, she can't be as bad as working with the feds. Can she?"

"She's a really good detective; you won't be sorry."

"Okay, give me a minute, and I'll call my guys. Then I'll give you the tour."

"Thanks, Bob."

McKeown walked back toward Sandy while Crowley radioed his people with new instructions. Sandy was still engaged in her retriever-like pacing when McKeown placed his hand on her shoulder. She stopped and smiled at him. "Everything okay with Bob?" she asked innocently.

"Yeah, everything is fine. He said we have his complete cooperation, and he's asking his men to stop and wait for us to complete our scene investigation."

"Oh, great! What a nice guy he is," she said with genuine sincerity.

"Yes, he is."

"I'm getting some great stuff here Sean. Signal-to-noise is excellent."

Crowley rejoined them. "Signal to noise?" Crowley inquired.

Sean smiled and shrugged his shoulders.

Crowley looked Sandy up and down and said, "Okay, so let's get started."

"I already did," Sandy replied, getting immediately back to the subject at hand. "Look!" she said. "The kid, Tony right?"

"Yeah, Tony," Detective Crowley said.

"He ran this way, then stopped here and began popping off rounds."

"Yeah, we found some casings on the walk over here."

"No, they came later," Sandy said as she stepped off the boardwalk and searched around the bushes. She picked up three shell casings.

"How do you know it was Tony doing the shooting?" Crowley asked.

Sandy hesitated and then said, "I just do."

She walked west and found a dried puddle of blood on the walk. "Wow, nice throw. Boy, this guy was really pissed."

Crowley asked. "What do you mean, nice throw?"

Sandy was distracted and continued her search without responding at first. Then she turned around and faced the two men. She made a movement with her right arm, like she was throwing a ball. "He made the throw from here, at a full run, while the guy was shooting at him. Right in the throat. This was the guy who shot his girlfriend, I think. Mr. Mascelle is not your average computer geek, that's for sure."

She ran back to the men and nearly knocked them both off the boardwalk as she passed, then she suddenly stopped. "He emptied an entire magazine here." She bent down, picked up a spent magazine that had fallen beneath the boardwalk, and stood again. "He was shooting at this angle." She held her arms out and up at a forty-five degree angle over her head. "Then he turned this way, to his right, jumps down and waits for their approach. Two more of them."

"Then what?" McKeown asked.

"There. He ran to the horse-house-thingy. See his foot prints?"

Both men looked and saw some blotches in the dry sand, which may or may not have been footprints that went in the direction of what appeared to be a barn surrounded by a corral.

"Okay, so Tony shoots down the helicopter, then he runs to the barn?" McKeown asked.

"No, first he shoots down the helicopter, then he fires at the guys over there." She went silent and stared. "Yes, there were two more of them. He gets one with a head shot after he gets the first one with the knife. Wounds the third guy, and then goes after him."

"Whoa," Crowley said, "how the hell do you know all of this?"

Sandy just smiled and shrugged her shoulders. "Am I wrong?"

"Did you talk with one of my guys already?" Crowley asked.

Sandy said, "No I just got here, Bob, and I haven't talked with anyone except Sean and you."

"Well then how the hell could you know that we found a guy that had most of his head shot off right there, and the other guy with the knife in his throat over there?"

Sandy ignored the question and moved in the direction of the dune. She held her arms out like a bird and skipped along a path near the footprints in the sand.

Crowley watched Sandy's bizarre behavior for a moment and then turned back to McKeown. "Okay, Sean, so what the hell is this?" Crowley asked.

"Like I said Bob; she's gifted."

"Gifted, my ass. She's either lying about not having information from my guys, was here when it happened or she's the Amazing Kreskin in drag."

"Well, I can tell you I've never seen her lie, and she definitely wasn't here when it happened. You can draw your own conclusions about the third option."

Crowley looked at Sean. "So you've seen her do this before?"

"Many times, and she's just getting warmed up. You really haven't seen anything yet."

They walked towards her and listened as she began to talk in a whisper to herself. "The other one ran over the dune this way." She said as she walked to the top of the dune and pointed to the east along the beach. "Oh my, he was really scared. Big horse with crazy man coming at-ya, better run faster. Oops, you missed, but Tony didn't." She ran down to the beach and then headed east about two hundred yards. McKeown and Crowley followed. Sandy stopped where the sand was soaked with blood.

She suddenly yelled back to Crowley. "Hey, how many bodies did you find so far?"

Crowley counted in his head and then yelled back, "Seven males."

"There's one you missed, over there." She pointed to what looked like a tool shed by the barn. "Better bag it before it gets really stinky."

McKeown called back to her, "Is it Marcella?"

"No. It's a guy in some kind-a uniform, I think."

Crowley and McKeown began walking over to the shed as Sandy continued her dance-like movements back toward the stable.

Crowley hit the button on his radio. "Hey Dan, I need you

over here; we've located another body."

McKeown smiled and said, "Aren't you going to at least check first?"

"Do I need to?"

"No, but it usually takes a while for people to, well, get used to her."

"Yeah, I can imagine that it does. But I'm a pretty fast learner." As they approached the shed, Crowley added, "Besides, the wind is blowing from that direction, and I think he's already getting a little stinky."

Crowley opened the shed door and found a body crumpled on the floor. The man, dressed in what appeared to be a park ranger's uniform, had his neck twisted unnaturally to one side.

"There's something I don't get," Crowley said.

"What?"

"Why was she so upset about my guys disturbing the crime scene? It's not like she actually needs one."

McKeown laughed. "I asked her the same question once. She told me that there were three reasons. First, it's by the book; second, it's sometimes helpful; and third, it's polite."

Three uniformed officers arrived huffing, one of them carrying a body bag.

"Wait a minute," Crowley said to the others as he turned to McKeown. "Do you want to ask her if she wants to see this one before we bag him? I just want to be polite."

McKeown and Crowley looked over at the stable. Sandy was in the corral standing next to one of the horses with her face only a few inches away from the animal's nose. She was waving her arms like a bird and lifting and dropping her feet like she was marching. All the while, she was talking in a loud voice directly to the animal, and it seemed to be paying attention. A moment later, she stopped the bizarre movements and started wagging her finger at the horse's nose as if she was scolding a naughty child.

Crowley turned and looked at the faces of his three officers, and then said to McKeown, "You think you can get her to tone it down a notch or two? She's scaring my men."

McKeown nodded and began walking quickly towards the stable. "Sandy!"

Chapter 56

"Hello? Sandy?"

"Hi, Sean!"

"You okay?"

She gave him a puzzled look, then looked over at Crowley and his men in the distance. She covered her mouth.

"Oh, that. Yeah, I'm fine. Did I make a scene?"

"Well, yes, a little."

"Sorry, poor old horse is a little hard of hearing."

"You done with the horse? Bob wants to know if you want to check out the body in the shed before his men tag and bag it."

"Oh, that was nice of Bob. Yeah, let's have a look."

The two of them walked back over to the other men where Sandy introduced herself to Crowley's officers by giving a little wave to each of them. "Hi, I'm Sandy Taylor."

The three officers waved back but said nothing. Sandy walked into the shed and examined the body. She came out a few moments later and said, "Okay, I'm done. You can take him whenever you're ready."

Bob Crowley said. "There's only one small problem. I spoke with someone at the ranger station this morning and they seemed to indicate that all of their people are accounted for."

Sandy shrugged, and looked back at the uniform on the body. "Well, dressed like that, he looks a little too old to be a Boy Scout." She walked back to the body, went silent for a moment, and then said. "Not a park ranger. But, he knew Tony. And he knew a friend of Tony's also." Sandy placed a hand under her chin as if she was trying to hold her head up. "Try giving our federal friends a call and see if they can ID him."

Crowley said, "I'll call the FBI later and see when they're planning on getting their prima-donna asses out here."

Sandy said, "I didn't mean the people in the Hoover Building, I meant the ones at Langley."

Before Crowley could reply, Sandy said, "Okay, we know what happened here and on the beach over the dunes. Now let's figure out what made Tony so mad. Let's retrace the way he came."

Sandy started to walk and then stopped abruptly. "Oh, I found this little gem on the beach," she said, holding up an object that appeared to be a medallion of some sort. "It looks like some sort of religious medal. Came off the dead guy with the split head, probably." She held it up closer to them. The gold medallion glinted as it twisted slowly on the end of the heavy chain, which also appeared to be made of gold. On one side was the image of some sort of building, a citadel or castle. On the other side was the image of a bearded man on a horse. "See the blood and the clean cut in the chain?" She made a cutting sound and a slashing movement with her hand. "Okay if I hang onto this for a little while, Bob?"

"No problem, just let my guys book it first."

"Okay," she said as she dropped it in a plastic bag and then handed it to one of the officers. Then she abruptly turned and walked towards the boardwalk as McKeown and Crowley followed her in the direction of Davis Park.

Both of the men were having a difficult time keeping up, and the distance between them and Sandy increased to about a hundred feet. Then she stopped, looked down, jumped off the boardwalk and disappeared. They were standing about where they were earlier, when she found the shell casings and the empty magazine. By the time the men arrived at the spot where she had jumped, she was already walking back toward them from a large dune on the ocean side of the island. She hopped back on the walk and said, "Tony was standing right here."

"You already said that before, but what's up there?" Crowley asked, pointing to the dune.

"I'm not sure," Sandy said. "Strange . . ." She went silent as she stared back at the dune. "A tiger ... no, a lioness. Wow, I can smell her, but I can't see her. How cool is that?"

McKeown asked, "You smell a lion?"

"No, silly, I said lioness. A sweet smell, perfume maybe."

Crowley looked at McKeown and he rolled his eyes. "A lion wearing perfume? This is really getting weird!"

McKeown's attention remained focused on Sandy. "What else, Sandy?"

"I can't see her face, Sean. It's like she won't allow herself to be seen. I can smell her and feel her, but not see her. Proud, afraid, sad, she's trying to protect him. But she won't let me see her."

"Is what you're seeing a woman?" McKeown asked. "Like maybe Tony's girlfriend?"

"No, not her, another. Older." Sandy's eyes were staring into the distance, at the dune, as she spoke. "Loves him. Very strange... very strange. It's almost like she knows I'm here."

Then she abruptly stopped talking, came out of her trance and smiled at both of the men. "This way, guys."

"You know what she's talking about, Sean?" Crowley asked.

"I think so. There was someone or something else here helping Tony."

"A lion?"

"No Bob, not a lion, a lioness. Try to keep up," McKeown said as he gave Crowley a sideways smile.

"Yeah, right, a lioness. I knew that."

The three of them walked for about ten minutes through the brush-covered area between two lines of dunes that ran parallel to the walk. Sandy stopped several times, looked around, and then without a word continued walking.

"There," she said, pointing to the bay on her right.

McKeown and Crowley, who had fallen behind again, caught up with her and looked in the direction she was pointing.

"There... what?" Crowley asked.

"In the water, the sailboat mast, you see it about half a mile away?"

"I don't see anything," Crowley replied.

"Sean, do you see it?" Sandy asked.

McKeown squinted in the direction. "I don't see it either, Sandy."

"Well, it's there. About ten feet of the mast is sticking out of the water, at an extreme angle. They were on that boat."

"Who's they?" McKeown asked.

"Tony and his girlfriend."

"They were also in one of these little places here," she said, pointing at a group of cottages towards the ocean side of the island. She went silent again. "That one."

Crowley shook his head in amazement and then said, "That's Joe Mascelle's place. It's the first place we looked for them. We found blood in the closet."

"Right between the eyes. She's quite a shot." Sandy Taylor

informed them.

"Who?" McKeown asked.

"His girlfriend."

"Tony's secretary, Marcella?"

"That's the one."

Crowley said, "Two of the guys we found on the beach were already dead and in body bags. One guy had a hole between the eyes and the other in the back of the head. Strange, too. No exit wound in either case and. . . "

"They had a red X on their foreheads," McKeown said, finishing Crowley's sentence.

"Yeah, what's that about?" Crowley asked.

"When we figure that out we'll probably know what the hell is going on here." McKeown turned to Sandy. "You think Marcella shot both of them?"

"That's no X, it's a cross. Yup, she gave the guys the last rites, and she's definitely no secretary."

"Are you sure?"

Sandy smiled. "Come on, Sean, you know better than to ask a question like that."

Sandy continued. "They left the house in a hurry, headed that way. They tried to catch the last boat out. When they missed it they tried to sail off the island using the sailboat. It gets shot up and sinks, and they swim ashore. One lands over here and one over there." Sandy stood facing the bay and pointing east and west with each hand. She stopped and closed her eyes.

"What then?" McKeown asked.

"They, no... she got the guy with a shot to the back of the

head, right over there." She pointed to an area in the marsh grass that was disturbed.

Sandy suddenly gasped and began to run down the boardwalk, leaving the men behind her. They followed but she kept well ahead of them. They saw her jump off the boardwalk and then run behind one of the bayside cottages.

When they found her, she was sitting on the kitchen floor next to a large blood stain. She had her face in her hands and was weeping. "Here, she's shot, dying, Tony is holding her. So sad... so sad," she said as she rocked slowly back and forth.

Crowley stood back, surveying this bizarre scene in silence.

McKeown walked over to where Sandy sat and crouched down, putting his hands on her shoulders. Sandy's weeping suddenly stopped and she looked up with a face filled with rage. She jumped up, knocking McKeown over and ran towards the door.

McKeown yelled at Crowley. "Stop her!"

Crowley was momentarily stunned by what he was seeing, and McKeown yelled again as he got to his feet, "Grab her Bob!"

Sandy was just passing Crowley when he reached out and grabbed the collar of her coat to slow her down. With surprising strength, she began dragging him out of the doorway behind her. He reached for her with his other hand and they both fell in a heap on the grass in front of the cottage steps. Crowley was on his back with Sandy lying with her back on top of his chest. He held her tight, with his arms around her waist. She could not get up, but she kept flailing her arms and legs in the air, and she began growling.

McKeown ran over, grabbed her arms and began to speak to her in a soft tone. "Sandy, it's okay, calm down." He repeated it again until she stopped flailing and started to relax. It all passed in a few moments, but it seemed like an hour to Crowley.

McKeown said to him, "Okay Bob, you can let her up."

"You sure?"

"Yeah, she's alright now."

Crowley slowly released his grip. Sandy stood up and brushed herself off. Then she looked down and saw Crowley lying on the ground. "Jesus, Bob, what are you doing down there?" She reached down a hand to help him up, but he held his hands up and away from her.

"I'm okay, thanks." Crowley said.

Crowley got up and put some distance between himself and Sandy, who was now looking around her surroundings with a puzzled look on her face. "What the hell?" she said. Then she looked over at Sean. "Oh my God! Did I just have one of those things?"

McKeown smiled and nodded at her.

"What things?" Crowley asked. "A seizure?"

"Not exactly." McKeown informed him. "We just saw what Tony Mascelle felt like yesterday when he went to find the men who shot his girlfriend."

"I told you he was really pissed," Sandy said with a girlish smile. "Oooh, wait!" She said turning to go back into the cottage.

"I don't think that's a good idea, Sandy," Sean said as she passed him.

She ignored his protest and went back inside.

McKeown followed her into the small bedroom. She scanned the room, looked over at the unmade bed, and then walked over to a pile of clothing on the floor next to the bed. Crouching, she touched it with her hand.

"Find something?" McKeown asked from the other side of the

room.

She sat on the bed and closed her eyes. "It's forbidden."

"What's forbidden?"

She smiled and crossed her arms over her body covering her breasts with her hands.

"Sandy?"

"Yes," Sandy replied as she reached down and lifted a sample of clothing from the pile.

"You think its Marcella's?"

Sandy brought it close to her nose and sniffed it. "Definitely, and Tony's too."

Then she stood and left the room, passing McKeown as she walked toward the kitchen. McKeown watched as she made a dance-like series of movements in the kitchen, which he presumed were reenactments of Marcella's movements that morning. Then she suddenly slumped to the floor.

"Aha," she said as she lifted a plastic bag out of her pocket. Then, carefully reaching down with her gloved hand, she picked up a small black capsule that had rolled under one of the kitchen cabinets.

"Looks like a big vitamin pill," Crowley said from behind a watchful McKeown.

Sandy gave the object a slight squeeze and a very small needle popped out of its end. A tiny drop of liquid appeared on the tip of the needle. "Nope, definitely not a vitamin pill." Sandy sniffed it and smiled. "This is very interesting."

Chapter 57

When I opened my eyes, Uncle Joe was looking down at me and calling my name. I was also surrounded by other people, none of whom I recognized. There was a severe pounding in my head and I felt a sticky substance in my left eye. My brain registered a sensation of floating, and eventually enough of it began functioning again to conclude that I was being carried on a stretcher.

"Can you hear me Tony?" My uncle said yelling over a loud throbbing sound.

"Marcella." I said, laboring to talk over the noise.

My uncle was still trying to say something when his voice was muted and the throbbing noise subsided, as if a door had been closed. The surface I was lying upon began to spin, and I lost consciousness again.

I woke up in a hospital room and I heard talking; I looked over towards the sound and saw a doctor and a nurse at the foot of my bed. They looked back at me. The doctor had a friendly, round, bearded face with dark brown eyes, and spoke to me with an accent I did not recognize.

"Hello, Tony. My name is Dr. Dulaimy. How do you feel?"

I tried to answer, but no sound came out, so I nodded my head.

"Tony, you are at the University Hospital at Stony Brook. You have been asleep for about thirty hours. They brought you in yesterday from Fire Island by helicopter. Do you understand what I'm saying to you Tony?"

I nodded and did my best to reply in the affirmative with a weak grunt.

"Okay, that's good. You are going to be fine, so do not worry.

You were shot twice: once though your shoulder and another bullet grazed your head. You are a very lucky man. However, like I said, don't worry; neither of the wounds are life threatening. You do have a concussion, so we are going to keep you here under observation for the next day or two. You should be back on your feet and ready for another adventure in no time." He smiled. "They tell me you were found slumped over on the back of a horse." He paused. I guess he was expecting me to make a comment, but I just stared at the wall and didn't reply. He regained his doctor-like composure and said. "Your family and some police officers are here and they would like to speak with you. Do you feel up to it?"

I nodded.

"Are you sure?" The nurse added.

"Yes," I said in a faint, dry voice.

Dr. Dulaimy nodded to the nurse and she left the room. A few moments later my mother, Uncle Joe, and Agent Barella walked in. Mom kissed me gently on my forehead and she took my hand and held it. "Thank God you're okay," she said, and then kissed me again.

I turned to Uncle Joe. "Marcella?" I said, as my throat tightened with emotion. I could feel tears begin to run down my cheeks.

"Where is she?" Uncle Joe asked me.

"What do you mean where is she? I left her in the cabin at Davis Park. She was on the kitchen floor. You didn't find her? Oh, my God."

"The police have been all over that island, Tony. We found blood on the kitchen floor in a bayside cabin that was broken into. We also found what we assumed was yours and Marcella's clothing in a wet pile in the bedroom. But we did not find Marcella."

"She's there," I said. "I left her body in the kitchen."

"Her body?" Uncle Joe said with a puzzled face.

"Tony, can you tell us what happened?" Mom asked in a calm voice.

I informed her. "We went to the Island to hide. But they found us and then they hunted us. We tried to get away, but the motor and the wind..." I shook my head and closed my eyes as the scrambled images came back. I explained, in short, non-sequential sentences, how we tried to escape on the sailboat and how the sniper sank it by shooting holes in it.

"What happened then?" Uncle Joe asked.

My head began to pound, but I continued to fill in the details, as best as I could remember them. At first I saw them as an observer watching the events unfold like flashing pictures, then my perspective changed and I found myself in the middle, as a participant, and as the source of the death and destruction. My body began to tremble. About half an hour later, I finally concluded the story. "I was out of ammunition so I went after that last son-of-a bitch with a machete."

"We found a lot of bodies at Watch Hill," Uncle Joe said. "But we didn't find Marcella."

"Why would someone take her body, Uncle Joe?"

Apparently, Barella got what he came for, because he turned and quietly left the room at that point.

I went over the story several times more, each version with greater detail as it became clearer in my head. I also told them what Marcella said about Kyle and Jan and the plot to kill me. But, each time we returned to the part where Marcella died in my arms on the kitchen floor, my brain would seize.

Uncle Joe told me that they searched for her everywhere, thinking that she may still have been alive and perhaps crawled away from the cabin. However, they did not find her. In fact, there was no sign of her moving, or being moved. With the exception of her blood on the floor, and her wet clothes in the bedroom, she had vanished.

At some point, I began having trouble keeping my mind focused and my eyes open and I started dozing-off mid-sentence.

Then the nurse came into the room and chased everyone out.

Chapter 58

"Tony?"

"Yes, Marcella, I'm here. Go back to sleep."

"Where are you going?"

I didn't answer.

"Ciao, Tony."

I opened my eyes to see my mother looking down at me. There were tears in her eyes. "Hi honey, how are you feeling?"

I rubbed my face and tried to make sense of my surroundings.

"Hi Mom… I'm doing alright."

She leaned over, gave me a kiss on my cheek, and said, "There are some people here with your Uncle Joe. They want to speak with you. Do you feel up to it?"

I nodded and looked over to see Sean McKeown, standing next to my Uncle Joe, and there was also a blonde woman who I assumed was a detective as well.

McKeown was his usual pensive and rumpled self. He was wearing a frown and a baggy overcoat that looked like it came from the wardrobe room of a film noir movie set. The woman, who McKeown introduced as Detective Sandy Taylor, was younger—about my age I think—and very pretty, for a cop. However, by the expression on her face, she didn't seem to have fully assimilated her surroundings. She was in the intensive care unit of a hospital, and in the presence of a wounded victim, me, as well as two NYPD officers investigating what was probably one of the worst incidents of murder and, perhaps, terrorism in New York's history. But to look at her, you would think she was standing in line at an amusement park, anxiously awaiting her turn to enter the fun-house.

She was actually smiling at my mother and me as if she had a secret to tell us and couldn't hold it in any longer.

McKeown said to me. "Good to see that... "

The he hesitated for an instant as he considered his next words. *You're alive? You killed all those bad guys for us? You're finally under house arrest*?

He finally completed his sentence. "...You're doing better." He gestured to the blonde woman again and said, "Detective Taylor has been assigned to help your uncle and I out on this case."

I nodded a greeting toward her and she startled me by shooting a hand in the air and then giving me a really friendly wave. I concluded, then and there, that whoever this woman was, she must be completely bats.

McKeown informed me, "We've just come back from Fire Island, and things appear to check out with the story that you told your uncle. But we have a few questions that we wanted to ask in order to fill in some of the missing pieces, okay?"

I nodded.

"Well, I'll start by asking one of my previous questions again. Do you have any idea who would want to hurt you or Marcella, or why?"

"No."

"How about Kyle Orr or Jan Toomey?"

I wasn't sure I understood that question, so I asked, "Are you asking me if I think that Kyle or Jan wanted to hurt Marcella and me? Or are you asking if I think someone wanted to hurt them?"

McKeown's expression indicated he thought that was an interesting response. "Either?"

I thought about that and concluded that I was not prepared to answer either question. I said, "My head is really starting to pound." It really was. "Can we continue this later?"

McKeown looked at my uncle and then back at me.

Uncle Joe said, "Try to answer the question, Tony." His tone was an odd combination of caring uncle and impatient cop.

I said, "No. Did you ask them?"

McKeown responded, "I thought someone would have told you by now. Both of them have been murdered."

Well detective, someone actually did tell me. I placed my fingers to my temples and tried to stop the pounding. I didn't seriously think it would help the headache, but maybe it would convince my visitors to leave, or the nurse to rescue me again.

"Take a look at these photographs," McKeown said, handing over a manila folder.

I began studying them. "There's the one who shot Marcella."

"How do you know which one shot her?" McKeown asked.

I retold the story. "... I heard a man's voice screaming, like he was in pain, then the gunshots, and I see him running out of the house. I was close enough later to see his face. Marcella must have tried to defend herself with a pot of boiling water. His face was red, singed, and one eye looked like it was swollen shut." I told them about how he kept missing while he was trying to shoot me as I ran toward him with the knife. "His injured eye is probably the only reason why I'm here talking to you now." I thought about Marcella again. "She saved my life four times, once after she was already dead, and I didn't save her a single time." I bit my lip and tears rolled down my cheeks.

"Okay," Uncle Joe interrupted. "Keep looking through the photos, Tony, and tell us if you recognize anyone else."

I flipped through a few more and came to one that stopped me cold. It was a man in a park ranger's uniform, sans the hat. By the look of his neck, his gray skin and his lifeless eyes, I was sure the man was dead. I remembered what Marcella said that night: *"Bill can't help us now, and we can't help him anymore."*

I said, "This is Billy Hoffenburg."

"That name sounds familiar," Uncle Joe commented.

"It should be; I grew up with him. We spent several summers hanging out at the beach house together when we were in high school. Marcella and I ran into him on the ferry, on the trip over."

"When was the last time you saw him before that?" McKeown asked.

I said, "High school, I think."

Then I told McKeown and Uncle Joe about the tour on horseback, and about the clearing, the one we found east of Watch Hill. I also described how surprised Bill seemed by its discovery. "Marcella said it was a landing zone for a helicopter, and she was right, because that's where the helicopter was coming from when I shot it down."

McKeown nodded.

I asked, "Does his family know he's dead?"

My uncle responded, "No, we didn't know who he was until now."

"You mean, none of the other park rangers could identify him? How is that possible?" I asked.

McKeown said, "It's possible because he wasn't a park ranger."

I was puzzling over that statement when I noticed Detective Sandy Taylor moving around to the opposite side of my bed. I watched her with one eye as I responded to McKeown. "What do you mean? What was he?"

Taylor stepped closer and touched my arm in what seemed like an act of consolation, until her grip became firm and her hand began to tremble. When I looked up, I noticed that her eyes were closed, and that her eyes darting around beneath her eyelids. *What the hell is this?*

McKeown asked me, "Did Marcella take any drugs?"

That question took me by surprise. "What kind of drugs?"

"Any kind."

"You mean like medication, or are you talking about illegal drugs?"

"Either," he said to me.

"She took no drugs of any kind that I know of." I responded angrily.

"And what about you, Tony? Do you take any sort of drugs?"

"No. Why are you asking me these questions?"

Detective Taylor dangled a plastic bag in front of my face. It contained a small, shinny, black capsule. "Ever see this before?" she asked.

"No, what is it?"

"It's a miniature hypodermic syringe." She said to me. "It's really cool. When you squeeze it, a little needle pops out and injects this stuff. See?" She said as she pressed it between her thumb and forefinger.

"What stuff?" I asked.

"Well, that's what we want to know," McKeown said. "We've never seen anything like this device before, and no one we've talked to so far has, either. What we do know is that the dead guys on Fire Island, and the one in New York, had no ID but they look like their country of origin could be South or Central America."

At this point Detective Taylor looked at McKeown with a strange smile, as if she were amused, or maybe nervous, about what McKeown had just said, but McKeown did not seem to notice and continued.

"And we know that whoever is behind this has a huge amount of resources, and apparently no restraint or hesitation in using those resources to kill a lot of people. We also know that your company has been in dire financial straits for the past year and that two of your employees are now dead—murdered. So when you put all of those pieces together, you tend to come up with two words: drug cartel."

Chapter 59

Sandy Taylor drove out of the Stony Brook University Medical Center parking lot and onto County Road 97, headed south.

"So, you think it's a Middle Eastern drug cartel?" McKeown asked from the passenger seat with a touch of incredulity in his voice.

"Nope. What I said is that I don't think these guys are from Central or South America."

"Why do you say that?" McKeown responded abruptly. "All the pieces seem to fit."

"Yes, the pieces seem to fit, Sean," Sandy said with as sympathetic a voice as she was capable of. "But they're not Hispanic. They don't feel like that; they feel Middle Eastern."

"They *feel* Middle Eastern?"

"Yeah Sean, you know exactly what I'm talking about. And if you don't trust me and these *feelings* that I have, you shouldn't have brought me in on this case in the first place." Sandy bit her lower lip. "You already know how this *thing* of mine works. You remember how I explained it to you once? It's sort of like a cell phone call; sometimes the information is crystal clear, like on the beach yesterday, but most of the time there's static, often lots of it, and sometimes the call gets dropped all together. Remember? So, I can say with near certainty that they are not from Latin America, and I'm pretty sure they're origin is the Middle East. But that's all I can say right now."

McKeown sighed and started pinching his right eyebrow. "Okay, let's assume for a moment that these guys are from the Middle East. What's the drug connection?"

Sandy turned onto the entrance ramp to the Long Island Expressway. "I don't know yet. I'm not even convinced that there is a drug connection. There are other explanations for that little injector-capsule-thing that may have nothing to do with the illegal drug trade or drug cartels."

"Like what?"

"I'm not sure. It could be a weapon, for all I know. Look Sean, I just got here, but one thing seems very clear to me, we shouldn't spend a lot of time trying to fit this investigation into one of the usual pigeonholes; at least not until we've had more time to take a closer look at some of the evidence. The good news is that we collected some good stuff on Fire Island. We just need some time to digest it."

She thought about the two plastic evidence bags: one with the strange, pill-like injector and the other with the bloodied medallion from the dead man on the beach. Sandy repeated, "We need time to digest it... I need time to digest it."

"I know Sandy, but time is not on our side, here. This morning the stories about the murders in Manhattan and New Jersey became high profile in the press, and tomorrow Fire Island is going to make the front page of every local newspaper, and most national ones, and we still can't even give the chief a clue about what it's all about."

"I know it sucks, Sean, but that's where we are right now. You deal with Jack; buy us some time to work it, do some research, and it will lead to somewhere, eventually."

Sean nodded. "So where next?"

"Well, I guess you need to visit Chief Jack and fill him in. But before you do that, you need to drop me at the library."

McKeown grinned. "How about if you drop me at the library and you visit Sachel?"

Sandy returned the smile. "You hate libraries: no comic books."

"Hey, that's not true. They have comic books."

"Not the part I'm going to."

Sandy picked her way through the growing highway congestion until she found the entrance to the HOV lane, and they drove in silence for a while. After a few minutes, Sean noticed that the car was drifting towards the concrete median. He looked over at Sandy and noticed that her eyelids were sagging.

"Sandy!"

She started to attention and swerved to the right, re-centering the car in the lane.

"Sorry Sean."

"You okay?"

"I didn't sleep well last night."

"Insomnia, or the other thing?"

"The other thing, only worse than usual."

"How much worse?" McKeown Asked.

"Like nothing before."

"Tell me."

The disjointed images replayed in her mind - smoke and fire rising in a blue sky, people flying in airplanes and fuzzy snapshots of others flying through the clear air without them. The scenes were as vivid in her mind's eye as they had been the night before. But it was the sound that she couldn't bear. Voices of hundreds, perhaps thousands, screaming in horror.

She shook her head. "There's no point, none of it makes any sense."

Sandy fell silent again and stared blankly out of the windshield. McKeown recognized the look on her face. She'd flipped off the switch in her head, shutting down the projector so she wouldn't have to watch the movie again.

After a while, McKeown said gently, "Last time you told me about something like this, it was related to the case we were working on. Remember?"

Sandy nodded.

"And now?"

"I'm not sure, but I think so."

Eighty long, silent minutes later Sandy pulled up to the Fifth Avenue entrance of the massive marble edifice that was the central block of the New York Public Library. She opened the car door and gave McKeown a tired smile. "Good luck with Jack."

McKeown responded, "Good luck with your research, and please hurry up."

Sandy pointed towards the library and said, "You see that lion?"

McKeown looked in the direction she was pointing. He saw one of the big lion sculptures that guarded the entrance to the library. He nodded.

Sandy said, "His name is Patience, and that other one is called Fortitude. We're going to need both to crack this one, Sean."

Sean gave her a puzzled look. "That's funny, I thought *that* one was Fortitude."

She rolled her eyes and said, "See-ya, Sean."

Sandy ascended the steps, past the lions, and into the large foyer, crossing towards the elevator. A few moments later, she was on the third floor, standing in the massive, football-field-sized main reading room and looking out over a seemingly endless line of reading desks. The sight of this room never failed to impress her. The massive arched windows, the low-slung chandeliers, all crowned by an ornate, fifty-foot-high, cathedral ceiling. The collective effect gave the impression of a house of worship more than that of a library. The walls were lined for their entire length with tightly packed bookshelves two stories high. However, this was just a sample of the riches that were contained in this massive building, to say nothing of the eighty-five other libraries that constituted the whole of the New York Public Library System, distributed among Manhattan, Staten Island, and the Bronx. With over forty million items, it was one of the leading research libraries in the world.

That was why she was here: if the information she needed existed anywhere, it was probably here. The problem, of course, was in trying to find a tiny speck of information in this massive sea of materials. To accomplish that, she would need help, and she knew exactly where to find that.

She turned to the right, walked to the end of the Great Room, and entered the Astor Rare Books and Manuscripts Room. She was greeted by a warm smile coming from a small, narrow-faced man with a bald, slightly pointed head - and then by a big, breath-robbing bear hug, which was remarkable given the man's seemingly slight physique. His name was Tom Lancaster.

"Heeellooo, darling girl!" he said with a faint English accent that had significantly diminished over the past ten years that she had known him. Sandy noticed that some of the patrons in the room began to stare at them. While she was always happy to see Tommy, she never failed to be a little embarrassed by his effusive greetings. More so because he seemed not to care at all about the inappropriate volume of his voice in the otherwise tomb-like quiet of his environs.

"Hello Tommy," she whispered, giving him a peck on his cheek.

He took her by the hand and guided her to a seat as he suddenly returned to the whisper-like volume appropriate for the setting. "I was so excited when you called. Is this about what

I think it is: the Fire Island thing?" he asked with barely contained excitement.

She looked at him. "Yes, I've been asked to help. How did you know already?"

"I have my sources, young lady." Then with a pinched face and clenched fists he said, "It must be a weird one, huh?"

Sandy put a hand to her mouth to stifle a giggle. "Yeah, I'm afraid so, Tommy. It's also connected with the recent murders in Manhattan and New Jersey."

He pushed his wire-framed glasses up onto the bridge of his narrow nose and peered at her with wide, astonished eyes. "My God, Sandy, I heard about that on the news this morning while I was ironing my clothes. When you called earlier, I said to myself, 'I bet these guys are completely stumped, and I bet they've called in my dear, sweet girl Sandy to save the day.'"

Sandy responded to his comment by raising an eyebrow and turning her head slightly as she stared at him. "You were ironing your clothes?" She didn't think anyone did that any more, and then she self-consciously straightened and smoothed the arms and lapel of her blazer.

He stopped a moment, watched her with some puzzlement, and then continued. "So what do we have to work with, my dear?"

Sandy reached into her pocket and pulled out the two plastic bags and held them out for him to see. "We've come across some very interesting stuff, Tommy: stuff I've never seen before. I know you can help me, though."

Lancaster brought his face close to the bags and peered into them. "Hmmm... very interesting."

Then Sandy noticed that his face suddenly became pale. He sat back in his chair. "You okay, Tommy?" Sandy asked.

Thomas Lancaster raised the back of his right hand to his forehead. "Is that what I think it is?"

Sandy turned her attention to the bag that had him transfixed. It was the one with the medallion. She noticed that he was staring at the blood and gore that coated parts of the chain. "Yes, Tommy, I'm afraid so."

Lancaster moved his hand to his chest and said, "Oh, my."

"Tommy?"

He cleared his throat and looked at Sandy. "Yes, well, enough of that; let's get on with it, shall we?"

Sandy touched him on his arm. "Are you sure?"

"Why, yes, of course, honey. Okay, so what can you tell me about the former owner of this little gem?"

"We have very few facts at this point, Tommy."

"Sandy! Come, my dear, you and I both know what we're talking about here. I'm much more interested in what you've divined with that very special ability of yours, than in police facts. So tell me Sandy, what's this guy about?"

Sandy smiled and nodded. "I'm pretty sure that he and his collaborators are from the Middle East. But they are more than collaborators; they're more like brothers, but not blood brothers."

"Ah! So... some sort of tribal relationship?"

"Yes, like that, but it's religious in nature: a very intense religious belief. Extreme is probably the best word I can use to describe it."

"Interesting," Lancaster said. "Okay, so what were they doing here?"

Sandy said, "That's what we're trying to figure out, Tommy."

"No, Sandy, I don't think you understand my question. I'm not asking you what their specific mission was. I'm asking you to tell me what their common purpose was, their collective occupation. What does that feel like to you? How many were here: two, ten, a hundred? Were they here for a religious convention, to visit a religious shrine, for a shopping spree on Fifth Avenue? And how were they dressed? What was their collective psyche?"

"Oh, that. Well, they are killers, professional killers. We don't know who exactly their target or targets were, but they are—actually, were—most definitely professional assassins."

"Assassins!" Lancaster said with a snap of his fingers. "By God, I think that's it; that's exactly it!"

He stood suddenly and walked past her, disappearing into an adjoining, smaller room filled with ten-foot high bookshelves. She listened to the sound of his footsteps fade into the distance and then heard a mechanical sound, which she guessed to be a rolling ladder of some sort. Ten minutes later, Lancaster emerged with a large volume in his hands. He placed it on a cleared area of his desk and blew on the cover, producing a cloud of fine dust. Then he opened it and began paging through it, slowly and methodically.

Sandy, standing behind him, waved her hands in the air trying to deflect the dust cloud, and then placed a hand on his shoulder and peered over it at the book.

After a long period of silent page flipping, Lancaster whispered, "Here it is, Sandy." His face pressed close to the page of the massive catalog of medieval prints and he pointed to an image. He moved over to his left, permitting Sandy to join him in a close comparison of the citadel-like image on the medallion with the picture in the book. "I thought it looked familiar. It's Alamut!" He said.

Sandy nodded, "Looks like a match to me, Tommy. Oh, and

look here," she said, running her fingers down to the bottom of the facing page. She turned the medallion over and placed it next to the second image. The equestrian on the reverse side of the medallion now had a name: Hassan E-Sabbah. Lancaster's face was glowing. "This is amazing!" he said, loud enough to again attract annoyed stares from the other patrons. "Did I ever tell you that I wrote my thesis on the holy wars, during the Middle Ages? This stuff is where I live, honey."

Sandy looked around, and his eyes followed hers. "Oops," he said, covering his mouth. They both lowered their voices and returned their attention to the book.

Chapter 60

Except for an occasional passing nurse, I was alone again. The room was dark, except for the fading, dappled orange light filtering through the treetops and into the large window of my room. The view of the sun, disappearing beneath the surface of the Long Island Sound, made me think about the sunsets on Fire Island—and about Marcella. A movement caught out of the corner of my eye interrupted my melancholy. When I turned to look, I thought I saw someone moving near the door.

"Who's there?" I asked. No reply. A few minutes later, a shadowy figure emerged and the lights came on. Through squinting eyes, I recognized the face of the man standing by the door.

"Hello, Mr. Mascelle," he said in a low but cordial voice.

"Hello, Agent Barella. Were you just here?"

He looked puzzled. "No, but I'm here now." He walked over to the bed and pulled up a chair. He placed a folder on the bedside serving table and rolled it within reach.

"I know you've been through a tough time and need to recover, but it's important for me to speak with you while your memories are still fresh."

"I've already described everything I can remember," I advised him.

"Have you?"

"Yes, I have. Everything."

He nodded. "Okay, but I want you to do something else for me. I want you to look at these pictures and tell me if you recognize any of the people in them." He opened the folder and pushed it toward me.

"Again?"

"Yes, again."

"Is there anyone in particular I'm looking for this time, Agent Barella?"

"If I told you, it wouldn't be any fun. Would it?"

I began flipping through the stack. Each page consisted of a collage of photographs. All were of very severe-looking men, just like the surveillance camera shots you see on detective shows. However, there were other images as well, computer processed ones, showing each of the subjects with various haircuts and different amounts of facial hair, at different ages, and with varying amounts of body fat. The image processing was very sophisticated indicating the kind of imaging technology, I thought, that only a federal agency could afford.

"This one," I said. "He looks like the one who shot Marcella."

"Good, keep looking."

I obediently did so. Then I found another familiar face.

"This one looks like the guy in the closet at my uncle's place. Before he had the bullet hole between his eyes."

"Anyone else?"

I continued flipping through the pictures and was almost finished, when I saw another face.

"Someone else you recognize, Mr. Mascelle?"

I stared at the image and let it sink in. McKeown's photos did not include this one, which I thought was interesting.

"Well? Do you recognize him?" Barella asked again.

"Yes."

"Do you know who he is?"

"Is he connected with those other men on Fire Island?" I inquired.

"Yes."

I turned through the pages containing the man's image, and then back and forth several times. It was the shot of him with the mustache that was most familiar.

"I think he's someone I knew, a long time ago."

"How long ago?" Barella asked.

"I met him in school."

"What school, where?"

"Not far from here actually: my freshman year at the campus, across the road. He was a student also, or at least that's what I thought at the time."

"Why did you think he was a student?" Barella asked.

"Well, he attended classes for a while."

"Was he a friend?"

I thought about that question before I answered. "Not exactly a friend. But he used to be around me a lot."

"Do you remember his name?"

"Well, not really."

Agent Barella was starting to get impatient with me. "What do you mean not really? Do you remember his name or not?"

"I remember the name my friends and I gave him, but I doubt it was his real name. We called him Nunzio, Crazy Nunzio, and he never seemed to mind; he just accepted the name, so that's what we called him."

Barella did not seem to think that this was strange at all. "So he followed you around campus? When did this start and for how long did it last?"

I corrected Barella. "I said he hung around with us."

"Okay, when did he start hanging around you?"

"It was right after that thing with my dad, when he was shot. It was during my first semester, and he left towards the end of the same semester and never came back."

Barella pointed to the picture I was looking at. "He looks a little old to be a college student. Is this what he looked like then?"

"No, he looked more like this," I said, pointing to a picture of him with a clean face and crew cut. "But this is what he looks like now." I said pointing back to the photo with him wearing the big mustache.

"So you've seen him recently. Do you remember where?"

"Yes, at a bar in Manhattan, that night."

"Which night?"

"You know, that Friday, when this all started, with the murder across the street from my office, just before I met you and McKeown."

I took Barella through my meeting with Crazy Nunzio at The Bull and Bear on Second Avenue. He listened carefully, but it seemed to me that none of this was really surprising or even interesting, to him. It was as if I was telling him things he already knew. When I finished my story, I asked him if he wanted me to continue looking through the picture book.

"No, Mr. Mascelle, I think I have what I need. Thank you for your cooperation."

"So, in other words, you got what you came for, Agent

Barella. You wanted to know if I was telling the truth, and I am. So, do you still think I have something to do with this insanity?"

Barella walked towards the door, and then he stopped, turned and asked, "Are you making any plans to travel?"

"Travel?"

"Yes, Mr. Mascelle, you know: trains, planes, automobiles?"

"No. Why?"

"You have no plans to leave the country?"

"No, why would I?"

"No reason I can think of. I just wanted to know."

"Well, now you do. I have no plans to leave or go anywhere."

"Good," Barella said as he turned to leave again.

"You didn't answer my question." I said.

"What question?"

"The one about me being involved with all of this."

Barella informed me. "Mr. Mascelle, you have everything to do with this. You may not have any idea about why or how, but I can assure you that you do."

I opened my mouth and was just about to get the first word out, when he disappeared from the room. "Prick!"

A nurse came in just then. She smiled and informed me that her name was Jenean. Without a further word, she began to check my vitals. I just laid there and let her do her thing.

She finished, and began to exit the room. "Did he find you?"

"Yes, Agent Barella just left."

"No, not the prick, the first one."

"Who?"

"The tall one with the funny accent and big mustache. Did he find you?"

I didn't reply.

"Are you okay? You look a little pale," she said.

"I'm fine." Then I nodded. "Yes, he found me. Thanks."

Chapter 61

Sean McKeown and Joe Mascelle climbed the steps of the New York Public Library and entered the building.

Joe Mascelle said, "Something's really starting to bother me about this case, Sean. It seems we're always playing catch up with the perps. I mean, how the hell did they find my nephew at my Fire Island beach house so quickly? Besides you and me, who else knew about it?"

"To tell you the truth, Joe, I was going to ask you the same question. The only person I told was Jack Sachel, and I didn't even give him the details, because I didn't know them."

Joe Mascelle shrugged and said, "So, what's this guy's name again, the one we're meeting today, and why is he important?"

Sean replied, "Thomas Lancaster. He's a Brit. He graduated from Oxford in the late seventies, then received a doctorate from Harvard in some obscure field in history. He's currently a professor at Columbia University, but also does some freelance work on occasion. Sandy uses him as a consultant, now and then, and I've also been told some federal-types have too. To tell you the truth Joe, I've only met this guy once before, so I don't know what he knows that can help us and why Sandy thinks he can. But I know Sandy, and if she thinks we need to meet him, I think it's worth the time."

Joe Mascelle replied with a puzzled look. "Yeah, I've been meaning to speak to you about her. I spoke with Bob Crowley at SCPD."

"Yeah, what did he say?"

Joe replied. "Well, he mentioned she likes to dance... with horses."

"She wasn't dancing with the horse, exactly. She was gathering information."

"Gathering information?"

"I'll be the first to admit that her methods are a little unorthodox." McKeown said, patiently.

"Unorthodox? Sean, she talks to animals, for Christ-sake. Don't you think that you're understating things a little bit?"

"Joe, I've worked with Sandy for years, and if you want to get somewhere on this, and get there quickly, you want her on the case."

"I definitely want to get somewhere with this, Sean; my nephew's life is on the line. But if it starts turning really strange, like pentagrams and shit, I'm outta here. I have an immortal soul I need to worry about."

McKeown laughed. "Yeah, me too, at least the last time I checked."

Mascelle said, "Maybe it's just me, but I've never had any luck using egghead-researchers - or psychics, for that matter. It's your investigation, but we seem to have a full-scale war on our hands here, and the brass in several jurisdictions are about to have a collective stroke unless we start giving them some answers. So, I hope this history professor isn't wasting our time - or our careers will be the only history we're going to be worried about."

"Yeah Joe, I know that. I was the guy that had to meet with Jack Sachel to give him the bad news today, remember? So I got a preview of what the brass looks like when they're having a collective stroke."

"I heard. But don't worry about Jack. He's one of the good guys. He'll have our backs. Unless we really screw up. The ones you have to worry about are the snakes at City Hall. They're the assholes who'll cut your balls off and serve them up as an appetizer at their next cocktail party."

McKeown said, "On that subject, you may find that Lancaster

is a bit eccentric. He may give you a little shit, but just try to ignore it. He's about five feet tall, weighs ninety pounds soaking wet, and he's gay. He's loud, but pretty much harmless."

"Is *eccentric* your polite way of saying *asshole*?" Mascelle asked.

"Pretty much."

"Great. A pretty, blonde colleague with an affinity for large, talking animals - and a small, gay asshole. Do I need this shit right now?"

****

"Gentlemen, this is Professor Thomas Lancaster," Sandy said to Sean and Joe as they entered the room. She turned to Lancaster and said, "I think you've met Sean, and this is Detective Joe Mascelle."

Lancaster placed his hands on his hips and scanned both men. Then he said, "Why Sean, so good to see you again! What's it been, three, maybe four years?"

Sean McKeown returned a tight, insincere grin. "Something like that."

Lancaster moved closer to McKeown and examined him. "I think I've also met this suit before. Still shopping at Kmart?" Then, lightly tapping his fingers on McKeown's prominent gut he continued, "And at Dunkin' Donuts, too, I see."

Sean McKeown rolled his eyes, then shot back, "Yeah, that's right, Lancaster, and both of those establishments have signs on the door indicating that no Englishmen need apply."

Lancaster stepped back, clapped his hands together and let out a big laugh. "Ah, and you still have that wonderful Irish sense of humor. I love it!"

"Yeah," Joe Mascelle's baritone voice rumbled. "He's just a

regular, jolly-ol', fucking leprechaun," addressing no one in particular. "So now that we covered all of the niceties, and the ethnic slurs, can someone explain to me who this English queen is, and why it was so important for us to be here?"

Sandy Taylor gave Joe Mascelle an impatient stare and said deliberately, "Dr. Lancaster is a professor of history and applied linguistics."

Joe Mascelle replied, "Yeah? Linguistics? Why didn't you say so? I like mine *al dente*."

Lancaster gave Sandy a nod of thanks and then turned his attention to Joe Mascelle. "Ooh, you must be Tony's uncle. My goodness, you're so... large. You know, Detective, sarcasm is often the last refuge of a small intellect."

"You should know."

McKeown raised an eyebrow. He didn't know Joe Mascelle well enough yet, so he couldn't tell where this exchange might lead. What he did know is that if Professor Lancaster had an even passing acquaintance with sanity, he wouldn't want to discover what kind of damage a six-two, two-hundred-seventy-pound, NYPD detective of Italian decent could inflict.

"Okay, gentlemen, let's turn it down a notch," Sandy said with her hands outstretched.

Lancaster continued in a more sedate tone. "To answer your question, Detective Mascelle, I'm sort of an historian of history. The vast majority of our history, you see, is not in the history books. The most interesting part of it, is what's omitted from the written record. If one knows what's missing, and can gain an understanding as to why, this information can sometimes tell us as much about the past as what's in the books themselves—sometimes it tells us more."

Sandy chimed in, "Dr. Lancaster is in many ways a detective, like us. And like us, he's as interested in what's missing from the crime scene, as what's found there."

"That's precisely right, Sandy, thank you," Lancaster beamed.

Sean McKeown gave a slight nod to Sandy. Joe Mascelle yawned.

Lancaster said, "One of my detective tools is symbology. As the name implies, symbology is the study of symbols of all types: objects, pictures, the written word, sounds, or a particular mark that represents something by association, resemblance, or convention. A simple example would be a red octagon as a symbol that means 'stop.' Another familiar one would be the symbols that you might find on maps, like crossed sabers indicating the location of a battlefield. History is filled with such symbols. In my specific field, language also consists of symbols. For example, names are symbols representing individuals. Etymology is the study of words and onomatology is a sub-specialty which focuses on the study of names, and their origins. Much of our hidden history can be divined in the names of people and places. You see, almost always, the names and symbols, as well as the historical omissions, are there for some purpose. In short, my job is to use symbols, words, and names to help uncover the history that was left out of the history books."

Mascelle said, "I have no idea what you're talking about."

Lancaster responded, "Why don't I find that terribly surprising, Detective? Let's use a person's name as a simple example, shall we? A name, in many ancient cultures, use to be something very much akin to what a business card, or even a very brief biography, is today. It told you something about the person's tribal origins, geographical origins, occupation, and sometimes even about some specific, important, historical event that the person, or an ancestor, was involved with."

Mascelle said, "Is there a point in my future, Doctor? This history stuff is all nice and good if you like that sort of thing. But in case you haven't been told, the body bags are stacking up at the morgue, and we have every reason to believe that whoever is behind this mayhem is out there right now planning some more. So, can we cut to the chase, Doc? Can you tell me why I'm here?"

"Well, if you step this way, Detective Mascelle, I'll show you why you're here. But please, try not to drag your knuckles on the new carpet." Lancaster smiled, placed his hands on his hips, turned and led the way. "This way, all."

Mascelle responded to that last comment with a very unfriendly stare. Then he said to McKeown, "This guy better have something good for us, or I swear I'm going to personally add him to the body count."

McKeown and Mascelle followed Sandy Taylor and Thomas Lancaster into a small, paneled room. Lancaster took a seat behind what appeared to be a laboratory table and held a black capsule in a large pair of tweezers. He examined it under the bright beam of the desk lamp through a large magnifying glass mounted to a flexible arm. He then adjusted the glass to get a closer look and proceeded to gently squeeze the object. A tiny, sharp needle emerged from the top of the one-inch-long, capsule-shaped container and then, at the tip of the needle, a drop of clear liquid appeared.

"This is one of the objects that Sandy discovered." Lancaster said. "I've never seen anything quite like it before. However, it has many of the characteristics of modern injectors that are used by certain members of contemporary intelligence agencies such as the CIA, MI6, and the former KGB. They use such devices for covert, clandestine and otherwise generally unpleasant operations. Nevertheless, from what I can see so far, the materials used on this particular object are extremely unusual. So, I would rule out all of those organizations as the source."

"What about the materials?" Sean McKeown asked.

"Well," Lancaster replied, trying to be patient with the interruptions. "It appears to be made of bone, or perhaps ivory, of all things. Chemical analysis is a little outside of my field, so I suggest that you have both the capsule and the contents analyzed by your lab people. Or, if you prefer, I can recommend a good one. But until I have that information, I can only make wild guesses about what this thing is, and that's not going to help anyone."

McKeown said, "Look, professor, we're here because Sandy said you could help us make some sense of these objects." McKeown turned his attention to Sandy Taylor. "Sandy?"

Sandy said, "Tommy, tell them about the medallion."

Lancaster held up the plastic bag containing the medallion and smiled at Sandy. "This, my dear, was a truly remarkable find!" The professor said with excitement.

"Yeah?" Mascelle responded. "If you think that's exciting you should see your girlfriend dance. With horses."

Lancaster looked at Mascelle and smiled. "I gather you've been witness to Sandy's considerable natural gifts."

Mascelle said, "No, not personally, but based on the descriptions I've heard so far, I don't know if the word *gift* applies."

Lancaster sighed. "Mr. Mascelle, in ancient times, someone like Sandy was so highly valued that she would have been an object of veneration—you know, as in oracle and Greece."

"Maybe." Mascelle replied. "But in somewhat less ancient times they would have taken a very different kind of interest in her talents. She would have been an object of ignition, as in witch and Salem."

Sandy's chin fell to her chest.

Mascelle changed the subject. "Never mind that; let's get on with it, professor."

Lancaster gave Joe an icy stare and pointed to an open volume on his desk, "Sandy and I found an historical reference to the medallion."

Mascelle and McKeown approached and then looked down at the book. Tom Lancaster had placed the medallion on one of the pages. And there, in painted replica, was an exact match. There was also handwritten text on the page, but in a language neither man could read.

"Latin?" Mascelle asked.

"Yes. This volume is a copy form an original housed in the Vatican archives. The Vatican original is about four hundred years old. But it is, itself, a copy of what we think is the original manuscript, now lost. We estimate the original to be in excess of eight hundred years old."

"So, how old does that make the medallion?" McKeown asked.

"Again, for us to know how old the medallion is, we would need to do extensive testing. It could be old, but given its condition, I doubt it. Actually, in the context of what it represents, and what it says about its late owner, it would be far more interesting if it were recently made."

"I don't understand," McKeown said.

Lancaster replied, "This book describes dangerous and unpleasant individuals, groups, and cults of the day. What we would call today a rogue's gallery, or perhaps an enemies list, if you will."

"So these people who wore the medallion back then were the enemies of the Vatican?" McKeown inquired.

"Yes, at least in some cases. However, the original document was not of Vatican, or even Western, origin. This is a translation of a text that was originally written in Arabic, probably from the region we now call Syria — or perhaps Iraq; it's difficult to be certain."

McKeown looked at Sandy and said, "I guess that knocks out the Central American drug cartel theory."

Sandy nodded. "I'm afraid so."

Joe Mascelle commented, "Well, don't be too upset. I mean, I really would prefer this to be almost anything else besides some kind of Colombian drug war."

"I wouldn't be too sure about that, Detective," Sandy replied. "Tommy, tell them about the inscription."

"What inscription?" McKeown asked.

"This one, Sean," Lancaster said, pointing to the bottom of the medallion.

McKeown and Mascelle moved in for a closer look and saw a decorative script where Lancaster indicated.

"Let me guess; it's Arabic." Mascelle said.

"Correct, Detective."

"So, what does it say?"

"Translated directly, it says 'hashashiyyin', which literally means hashish."

McKeown asked, "Hashish, as in the drug?"

"Yes."

McKeown looked again at Sandy. "So this is about a Middle Eastern drug war?"

"No Sean, it's really not about drugs at all," Sandy said. "Continue, Tommy."

"Yes, hashish is a drug, and it's of Middle Eastern origin. But look here," Lancaster said, flipping the medallion over.

McKeown asked, "The guy on the horse?"

"Yes, his name, according to the inscription, is Hassan E-Sabbah."

"Right," Joe Mascelle said. "Hassan E... whatever. So, why isn't he riding a camel?"

Lancaster gave Mascelle a disgusted look. "The Arabs, Detective, practically invented our contemporary equestrian traditions."

"Yeah, right, whatever. So who's the guy on the horse?"

"It's more important to describe *what* he is. Hassan E-Sabbah was an Assassin, and I believe that the man that was wearing this medallion was also."

Joe Mascelle looked at Tom Lancaster for a long time. Then he shook his head and said, "Wow, that's truly an amazing deduction, professor. This guy was an assassin! Really? Are you kidding me? My pet rabbit could have figured out he was an assassin. What was your first clue? The pile of dead bodies?" Mascelle looked at Sean and said, "Look, Sean, with all due respect, we've got a bunch of bad guys out there who may be hunting my nephew. I think my first impression of this visit was correct; it's a total waste of time. We need to get the hell out of this book bullshit and back to basic, street-side detective work."

"Wait a minute!" Sandy screamed.

The volume and intensity of her response took Mascelle by surprise.

"You're not going anywhere until you open that melon on your shoulders that you call a head, and listen to the rest of what Dr. Lancaster is trying to tell you."

Mascelle was stunned into silence. Sean McKeown, who was

very familiar with this side of Sandy Taylor's personality, wasn't. In fact, he was wondering what took her so long to lose it.

McKeown said to Mascelle, "Look, Joe, let's give the man a few more minutes. If by that time you want to leave, we'll leave."

Mascelle nodded.

Sandy then said, in an inappropriately loud and angry voice, "Continue, Tommy."

Lancaster, a little disorientated by this exchange, moved his gaze from Sandy back to the other two men in the room. He cleared his throat. "Detective Mascelle, I didn't mean to imply that the man who wore this medallion was just any assassin. What I was trying to explain is that he is a member of *the Assassins*, with a capital 'A.'"

McKeown and Mascelle stared back in silence.

Lancaster continued. "You see, the word 'assassin' that we use today has a history, which, as you now know, is my field of study. The Hashshashins were a Muslim cult comprised of a sect known as Ismailis, from the Nizari sub-sect. They were active in Persia, a region that today encompasses Iran, Iraq, and Syria. They were known to be active from about 1090 to 1270, or so. It was a small sect, but it inspired terror out of all proportion to their scant numbers and territory. The members were organized into rigid classes, based upon their initiation into the secrets of the order, and sought martyrdom and followed orders with unquestioned devotion. Their primary tactic was fearlessly executed suicide assassinations. Some of their victims were crusaders, which is how we in the West obtained the word *assassin* that we use today. They were that infamous."

Lancaster stopped, scanned his audience's faces and then continued. "However, most of their targets were key personnel of Muslim kingdoms in nearby lands, such as Sultans and viziers who were following a lifestyle that was unacceptable to the Assassins, which is why there's a record of them in this book.

Their fellow Muslims hated and feared them more than the Christians did. Their terror tactics were so effective, and their home base of Alamut such a strong fortress, that nobody could stop them. As a result, they could force their political will onto any nearby Islamic kingdom. It was from this mountain home that their leader obtained his evil celebrity as 'the old man of the mountains,' by spreading terror throughout the Muslim world, and later, the Christian world. As for their name, Hashashi, it comes from the usage of hashish by the movement's leaders. We believe that hashish first originated in western Asia, as this region was among the first to cultivate the cannabis plant. More reliably, it may have originated in northern India, which also has very ancient social and ceremonial traditions in the production and use of hashish, locally known as *charas*."

"Tommy, I don't think they need all of those details," Sandy said.

"Quite right: cut to the chase, and all of that. In any event, as I said, the cult's name, Hashashi, morphed over time into our word, assassin. The personal goal of an Assassin was to achieve martyrdom by dying in the act of killing the enemies of Islam. In an account given by Marco Polo, the cult's leaders would drug young men with a very powerful version of the substance that cast them into a deep sleep. Then they were carried into a beautiful secret garden, and when they came to, they were surrounded by beautiful, naked virgins and were told that they were in Paradise. After a few hours of bliss, they were drugged again and returned to the harsh reality of their former, poverty-stricken, miserable lives. Their new leader then told them that he had given them a glimpse of Paradise and that they could go back if they entered his service and followed his instructions, or died while doing so. Thus, he recruited an army of assassins who were the first, and to date, the worst, terrorist gang the world has ever seen. There's even an account that describes just how zealous these people were. One of the leaders of the sect wanted to demonstrate his followers' absolute obedience to an observer. So, he lined several of them up on the highest wall of their citadel. He then picked one at random and ordered him to jump to his death, and he did."

"Drugs and naked women," Mascelle said. "That's enough to get any clueless, teenage imbecile motivated to do something really insane. The only thing they were missing was an electric guitar and a drummer. So, what's this got to do with this case, the one in the here and now, doctor?"

"It is believed, by some of the government people that I consult for, that the same, or very similar, methods are currently being employed by a contemporary cult called El-Kaide, or Al-Queda, or something similar to that. Did I tell you how confusing Arab spelling can be? Anyway, as with their predecessor, they have several strong, nearly impregnable fortresses in the mountains of Afghanistan, and for years, they've been indoctrinating their chosen assassins with the same promise of Paradise in exchange for the assassination of their enemies, both Christian and Muslim. That is the connection to the here and now, Detective."

Sandy sat down in a chair next to Lancaster and looked admiringly at him. Tom smiled back at her and then looked at his watch and said, "Well, not bad: it only took a couple of hours to figure this out... not bad at all."

"Not bad, my butt, Tommy. If it were anyone else but you, it would have taken days to track this down. We owe you big time, pal."

Lancaster blushed slightly and waved his hand as if swatting a fly. "Hey, girl, just doing my job."

"Yeah, high-five," Mascelle commented dryly, as he gave Sean an impatient look.

McKeown said, "Tom, all of this is interesting—fascinating, really—but what does it have to do with this case?"

"Well, Detective, for starters, we may assume that Mr.

Mascelle's nephew is being hunted by a group of assassins. And not just any old assassins, mind you, but the original thing. The bad-dest, meanest motherfuckers you can possibly imagine." Tom Lancaster put his hand over his mouth. "Oh my, did I really say that?"

Sandy ignored Tom and stared silently into space. McKeown turned to her. "Sandy?"

She looked at him and smiled. "I've got a million thoughts, Sean, but none of them makes any sense. What in God's name is a group of Muslim fanatics, inspired by a thirteenth-century murder cult, doing in New York in the twenty-first century, trying to kill a young, nerdy, American guy who probably couldn't find the Middle East on a map?"

Lancaster said, "Well, you just said it then, didn't you, Sandy? Whatever the reason is, they think they are doing it in the name of God. That may not sound too helpful, but it at least tells us something about what it isn't. It's not about a business or a drug deal gone bad, for instance."

Joe Mascelle said, "I don't think we can conclude much of anything from this except that they're after Tony."

"How do we know that, Joe?" Sandy asked.

Mascelle replied, "Tony said that Marcella told him that she was there to protect him from someone. I don't exactly understand what that means, but it does obviously indicate that someone was out to get him."

McKeown chimed in. "But if that's true, why would they go to such extreme ends to hunt Tony down and then leave after killing only Marcella? Remember the order of events: Tony was out checking the dead guy in the brush. The assassin goes into the cabin, kills Marcella, and then flees the scene. If they wanted Tony dead, that would have been the best time to do it. Right?"

Joe Mascelle nodded. "You got a point there, Sean. On the

other hand, the man just had his face scalded. Maybe he was running to get some help from the others. I don't know, none of this makes any fucking sense to me."

Tom Lancaster's eyes pinched, "Tell me again about what Tony said. That part about Marcella protecting him."

"That's it, that's all he said."

Lancaster asked, "Do you know what he meant?"

"No, and I don't think he knows either."

Lancaster put his head in his hands. "I'm missing something here. It's right there, in my brain, but I can't quite grasp it." A moment after those words left his mouth; Thomas Lancaster's eyes went wide. He reached over and picked up the second bag containing the small, black vial. He opened the bag and removed the capsule with a pair of tweezers. Then he took a second pair of tweezers and held the very end of the capsule with them.

Sandy said. "Tommy, be careful; we're going to need that thing as evidence."

Tom Lancaster ignored the protest and gave the end of the capsule a quick twist. There was a tiny popping sound as the capsule parted in the middle, resulting in two halves. A miniscule pool of liquid formed on the table beneath the capsule. Tom Lancaster took the half with the needle and set it aside. He placed the other half under the magnifying glass and examined the inside of it under the bright light. And there it was: a symbol etched into the side of the capsule's wall.

"You shall know his love when you see the sign," Lancaster whispered. He looked up and stared at Joe Mascelle for a long, silent moment. "Detective, how do you spell your last name?"

Joe Mascelle gave Lancaster an impatient look. "What?"

"Your name, Detective; you do know how to spell it, don't you?"

"M-A-S-C-E-L-L-E. Are you going to write me up in a complaint to my boss, or something?"

Lancaster continued to stare at Joe and then began shaking his head. "Can't be."

Lancaster stood up and approached Mascelle. "Do you know where your paternal ancestors came from?"

"Sicily. Why?"

"Where in Sicily?"

"I don't know. Some place in the south, I think. I can't remember the damn name. Starts with an 'S.' Why?"

McKeown was getting impatient now, too. "Hey Tom, can we cut the crap? What's on your mind?"

Lancaster asked Mascelle, "Your ancestral home... is it called Sciacca?"

"Yeah, that sounds right. Who gives a shit?"

"Who gives a shit?" Lancaster repeated in a passable imitation of Mascelle's baritone voice. "Oh, I can guarantee you're going to give a shit, Detective."

"Tommy, you got to tell us what you're talking about," Sandy Taylor implored.

Lancaster said, "Do you remember what I said about how good the Hashashi were? They had some of the best military organization and tactics in the world. They also invented, or stole, some of the best technology to use for their evil ends. These guys were always outnumbered: five, ten, a hundred to one. Nevertheless, they still won virtually every engagement, every battle. Today the military calls this asymmetrical warfare. These people practically invented it. Their tactics were hated by those who had big armies and lots of resources. However, they were also admired, or at least imitated, by others who didn't. Many smaller military organizations, with much fewer resources, adopted the same military organizational structure, the same tactics, and even the same technology. Technology, like this," he said pointing to the capsule.

"When I was a graduate student in Boston, one of my professors told me about a story, a legend, that he was researching. At least he thought it was a legend. It was an epic on the scale of a Greek myth, spanning centuries and generations. He spent years trying to uncover its origins. The more he searched, the less convinced he was that the story was just a simple myth. So, one night we're having a beer in a pub, and he starts telling me about it."

"It began with this rather ordinary young man from Sciacca who becomes a hero during the siege of Rhodes, and then again on the island of Malta. He was an old warrior by that time. And in order to win the battle, he had to kill his own son. I remember thinking that the man must have been a real prick to kill his son, just to win a battle. Then my friend told me the rest of the story. It was nearly dawn when he finished."

Lancaster held up the broken section of the capsule with the tweezers and reexamined it. "The answer to our mystery is this symbol, inside this little capsule. And it's there," Lancaster said, gesturing towards Joe Mascelle. "In his name, appropriately enough."

Lancaster's eyes refocused on the wall behind Sandy and she could see that he was processing something. A tear came to Lancaster's eye as he whispered to himself. "If only you lived to see this, Victor."

Then he laughed, shook his head, and said. "Okay, I'll tell you, but I warn you, you're never going believe a word of it."

"Why don't you try us?" Mascelle barked.

"Okay, detective. But before I do, is there any chance that you were adopted?"

Mascelle was about to tell Lancaster to go screw himself when his reply was interrupted by the sound of his pager, which was immediately followed by the same sound emanating from Sean and Sandy.

Mascelle said, "It's from Jack."

"This can't be good news," Sandy commented.

McKeown looked at both of them. "Do either of you want to volunteer to return this?" When he received no reply, he said to Lancaster, "I need to use your phone, Doctor."

Lancaster handed him one from his desk.

"Yeah Jack, this is Sean. What's up?"

After a few moments of silence, McKeown said into the phone, "Both of them? How is that possible? Okay, Jack, we're on the way."

McKeown placed the handset onto the receiver. He looked at Joe and said, "You're not going to believe this, either. Our CIA friend, Gunter, has disappeared. And the guy from Fire Island—the one who was masquerading as a park ranger—he's gone, too."

Joe Mascelle and Sandy stared at Sean in stunned silence.

Lancaster took the opportunity to comment. "A CIA agent called Gunter? Oh, I love that name." When he noticed that all three of his visitors were staring at him, he regained his composure and said, "What self-respecting CIA agent would pretend to be a park ranger?"

Sandy said, "We're actually not sure either of them is with the CIA."

"Yes, of course." Lancaster said. "Always so mysterious, those fellows. And you know how antsy they get when you take away their guns and put handcuffs on them. They probably teamed up and made their escape together. Very resourceful chaps, don't you think?"

Sandy hesitated and then said, "Nice theory, Tommy, but I don't think so. They were in two different buildings across town from each other, and the guy dressed up as the park ranger was stone-cold dead."

"My, my, those CIA fellows *are* resourceful, aren't they? I guess they don't call them spooks for nothing." Lancaster laughed, but no one else in the room thought it was very funny.

Joe Mascelle closed his eyes and shook his head. Then he turned toward the exit with Sean close on his heels. "We've got to get back there before Jack has an embolism."

"But detective," Lancaster protested. "Don't you want to hear my theory about your last name?"

Mascelle said over his shoulder, "Frankly, Doctor, I think we've heard enough about your theories. Why don't you let us play detective and you can play... whatever it is that you play."

McKeown said, "You know Joe, it was getting kind of interesting. You sure you don't want to hear the rest of it?"

"I'll tell you what, Sean. You call Jack and tell him we've been delayed so some fruitcake can tell us a crazy story about some medieval legend from Malta, or Rhodes, or wherever the hell he's from, and I'll stay and listen to it as long as you like."

McKeown mumbled, "Well, if you put it that way."

Sandy Taylor called after the men as they left. "I'm going to stay and hear him out. I'll meet you guys later."

"Yeah, you do that," Mascelle shot back.

Chapter 62

Five days had passed since I initially woke up in the hospital. Doctor Dulaimy, a regular visitor, said my head wound had begun to heal nicely, but the scar might be a little ugly for a while. He also explained that my shoulder wouldn't be fully operational for some time. As a result, he decided that I should stay a while longer, advising me to be patient in order to give things time to properly heal. I nodded in agreement, but felt anything but patient. I wanted to get out of this place.

Then what would I do? Go back to the office and pack up my things? Try to find Marcella's body? It was a very frustrating time. My mother's visits were my only consolation. She spent almost all day with me, sitting by my bed and reading to me, or we would watch television together. It was almost like being a boy again, and having her all to myself. But, even this made me feel unsettled. It was hard not to admit that I wasn't serving any useful purpose at precisely the time when there were so many things to do, even if I didn't precisely know what they were. Little Tony just couldn't hide out in the hospital with his mommy forever.

I kept in daily contact with Uncle Joe, but the investigation seemed to have come to a dead end. Or at least, that was my impression. He couldn't tell me why someone was trying to kill me, and they never found Marcella's body.

I kept pressing him and McKeown for new information. But again, I was told to be patient. What Uncle Joe did say, is that he was confident that I was no longer in danger, but that didn't exactly square with the presence of the cop who was stationed outside of my room twenty-four hours a day. I considered telling Uncle Joe about the hospital visit by Barella, and what he said, or about the possible sighting of Crazy Nunzio, who was suspect number one, as far as I was concerned. But I didn't. I don't know why exactly, but I didn't.

I spoke about Marcella with my mother several times during the long hours we spent together. Whenever I did, I couldn't prevent tears from coming to either my eyes or her's. It felt odd speaking with her about someone she'd never met. But in some strange way, mom almost seemed to know her. I guess my aunts had kept her fully apprised of what they knew about Marcella, but it seemed deeper than that. By the time the tears came to my eyes, hers were usually already flowing.

At one point she said something to me that really took me by surprise. It wasn't just what she said, it was how she said it, like there was something she knew that I didn't.

She asked me if I remembered the day that my father was shot. I told her that I did, of course. Then she explained that by the time the ambulance had arrived, my father's skin was cold and gray. The EMTs were sure he was dead, but she insisted that he wasn't. It was only after they found a very faint pulse that they changed their minds and began rushing him to the hospital. The point of the story, she said, was that Marcella may well have been still alive when I held her in my arms, and she may be still alive today.

I was silent as she spoke—stunned, really. Then she asked me, "If she were alive, what would you do?"

"I would find her," I said. "I would marry her, if she would have me."

"And if she wouldn't have you?"

I said, "I would keep bugging her until she gave up and agreed. Besides, she told me that she loved me. She said that she loved me for most of her life. I don't know what that means, exactly, but it sounds like a yes to me." Then I shook my head, turned away, and began to sob again. I held up my hand and said. "Please, Mom, stop, I can't do this. It's too painful. She's gone. I'll never see her again... at least, not alive."

"Don't you do that!" My mother replied with an almost angry

voice. "Don't you give up on her! If you want her—I mean, really want her, don't give up. Be a man, be your father's son, and find her. And then you can ask her yourself. And, as long as she wants you, you refuse to take no for an answer. No matter what anyone else says, no matter how they try to stop you, if you love her, you find her, and you bring her home."

My mother, now also sobbing, got up, gave me kiss on the head, and whispered in my ear. "You get out of here, Tony, and go find Marcella." She turned and left before I had a chance to reply.

Well, I did not intend to just lie there for another week anyway. People had tried to kill me, goddamn it, and despite Uncle Joe's assurances, they could still be trying to kill me. And they killed Marcella, a woman I loved, I think. I mean, I think they killed her. I was sure she was dead when I held her in my arms that day, but by this time, I wasn't so sure. My mom's surprising confidence in Marcella's survival was certainly a factor in my motivation. On the other hand, I had no reason to believe that mom's pep-talk was based on anything other than emotion and blind hope. On the other, other hand, Marcella's body didn't just walk away, unless she was alive. Right?

A few hours later I was standing in my office.

Chapter 63

The doctors and nurses weren't too happy about my sudden departure, and neither was the cop stationed outside of my hospital room. I presumed that since I was no longer in danger, he was there to just catch up on his reading. Alternatively, maybe someone wanted me watched, because they still thought I was a drug cartel kingpin.

In any event, I was now standing in my office, and I still had no idea what to do next. Since my company had cratered in the meantime, I sure had plenty of time to do it. The Dick had decided to pull the funding as soon as he caught wind of the shooting and dying and stuff. All this blood and death was bad for business, you know. Well, I guess I can't blame him, under the circumstances. Actually, I could. That shit should have stuck with his commitment, but since he's just above pond scum on the evolutionary tree, such behavior is to be expected.

The rent for the office was paid up through September. So, being a creature of habit, and also having no other place to work, I decided to use the office as the base for my investigation. Besides, it's not like people were lined up around the block to rent it. Hell, I wasn't even sure who my current landlord was, given the bankruptcies and turnover in the real estate business.

All of my people were already gone, fired by a small group of professional grim reapers hired by our friendly neighborhood investors at the Alley Group. I sat by the phone on my desk and listened to the first seven or eight phone messages, all from my former employees. Some were sad, some angry, some just wanted to say goodbye. I turned off the machine with dozens left unplayed.

Next, I went through Marcella's desk, her computer, and paper files, looking for something—a clue, a connection with her past, a relative's phone number or address, information about her childhood home... something, anything. I found nothing. But it was a really interesting kind of nothing. What I mean is that I found absolutely nothing: zero. No emails from friends or families, no photos, no birthday or Christmas cards, no credit card receipts, nothing indicating that she even existed.

I gave up on her office and went back to mine. Maybe I already had what I needed. Somewhere. I searched all of the information on my computer again, and again I found nothing. I also considered that I might have a paper form or file that might provide something meaningful. I just needed to figure out where I put it. Unfortunately, while I'm really good at finding information on computers, I was really bad at finding things in the real world. Whenever I needed to find something like that, Marcella would find it for me, usually right under my nose.

I was startled by the sound of a knock coming from the front of the office. I froze and listened. A knock again. Then a voice calling my name.

"Tony?"

It was a female voice, but not one I recognized. I picked up the softball bat that was leaning on the wall next to the coat rack in my office, and began walking in the direction of my unexpected and unwelcome visitor.

I found a woman standing by Marcella's desk, examining the mess I had made of its contents, which were now scattered all over its surface. She had her back to me so I could not see the woman's face and she couldn't see me approaching.

"Hello Tony. You're not going to hit me with that bat, are you?"

She turned and smiled at me. It was that odd, female detective I met at the hospital.

"What do you want?" I asked as I lowered the bat.

"Do you remember me?"

"Yes, Sandy... something, right?"

"Sandy Taylor. I'm working with detective McKeown."

"Where is he?"

"He's not here. I'm alone." She said.

"So, what do you want?"

"There's something we need to talk about."

"I'm listening."

Detective Taylor looked like she wasn't sleeping well. I noticed that her eyes were puffy and her face looked a little pale. She looked away from my gaze and then, by the look on her face, began contemplating something she wanted to say to me.

"Why don't you have a seat?" I said, pointing to the chair by the desk.

She slumped into the chair. I remained standing.

"I don't know where to begin," she said. "And I'm afraid if I'm not careful I will frighten you, or worse, you'll think I'm crazy."

Too late. "Don't worry about it. Say what you came to say."

"First, it's very important for you to understand that you are very important. You're special, and you are needed. Here."

I ignored the part about being important and special and asked. "Needed where?"

"Here, in New York."

"Well, I'm not sure what you're talking about, but I have no plans to leave."

"Yes Tony, you do. You just don't know it yet. What I'm trying to tell you is that you can't leave, you mustn't leave. I know it will be hard not to, but if you do, I guarantee, you will be very sorry that you did."

"Are you threatening me?" I asked with anger in my voice.

"No, you see, you don't understand. What I'm trying to explain is that something is going to happen here, soon, weeks, maybe months, I'm not exactly sure, there's too much static, and too much information, I can't feel it clearly, but it's coming soon."

"What are you talking about? What's going to happen?"

"Something terrible. Unimaginable."

"What?" I asked.

"I don't know, not exactly, but I know it's probably going to happen. I also know that if you're not here it will happen, and if you are here, it might not."

"Detective, you're speaking gibberish. Frankly, you do sound a little nuts."

"Yes I know. Some people think that." She laughed. "A lot do, actually. You see, I have this gift. Well, it's more of a curse, sometimes. Most people can't understand what I'm talking about, and never will. But, I think you can, because you have it too. I felt it when I touched you in the hospital."

"You felt what?"

"Those dreams that you've been having, the ones that began recently. They're not really dreams. You know that, don't you?"

I didn't say anything. I just stared at her and wondered how she knew.

She continued, "Those dreams are actually windows on events that haven't happened yet. It's not just a coincidence when the things you see in your dreams come true. It's a rare gift, especially for a man. I have that gift, had it most of my life. The older I get, the worse it gets, meaning they get clearer, and they happen more often, and at any time; even during the day when I'm wide awake. My grandmother had them as well. She told me they can start appearing at any time during a person's life, usually when you're under stress. Mine first appeared when I was entering puberty. Yours, I suspect, resulted from the stress you're under at work. So, you have some insight into what I'm talking about based on your own experience. But it's still too new, too early, for you to fully understand."

She stopped talking. I guess she was waiting for me to reply, but I had no idea what to say.

"Look, Tony, I know this is all very confusing, and it sounds crazy, but in your heart, you know that what I'm saying rings true. So, all you need to do is to understand this. Soon, something will cause you to want to leave here. It will be very hard to resist doing that. If you choose to go, you will gain one thing and lose another. If you choose to stay, you will gain the other thing, and lose the first. You must decide which path you will take. All I can do is to try to convince you to stay, here, with me. We need each other. If we're going to stop this thing from happening we need to work together. If you leave I will be alone, and I won't be able to do it by myself."

I noticed tears in her eyes. She lifted a hand and wiped them away. Then she stood up, walked towards me and repeated herself. "We need each other, but you must choose." She handed me her business card and then surprised me by giving me a hug. When she did, she touched my shoulder wound and I flinched. She released me, and avoiding my eyes, turned and left.

What a strange woman!

I locked the front entrance to the office, just in case someone else was planning an unexpected visit, checked the bandage on my shoulder and then went back to my desk. I sat there for a while, thought about what Detective Taylor had just told me, and considered my options. Then my thoughts turned back to my mysterious Marcella, trying to determine what my next gumshoe-investigator move was going to be to find her.

Without help from someone who knew what they were doing, my investigation was at a dead end. Notwithstanding detective Taylor's strange behavior, and the bizarre claims concerning the paranormal crap, she had offered to help me. At least that's what it sounded like. I looked at her business card and considered calling her. Then I thought better of it, and dropped the card in the wastebasket.

Before I knew it, it was late and, as was my habit, I fell asleep in my clothes on the sofa in the office. I had a dream, or whatever these things are.

I was in a dark place, a cave I think, and I was lying face up on some sort of cold, hard platform. Someone, a woman, was standing above me waving what appeared to be a heavy stone object. I couldn't make out her face in the dark, but then she looked down at me. In the dim light, I recognized the face of Sandy Taylor, but she was very old, white as a ghost, her face was covered in moles and blemishes, and her eyes were black and lifeless. She started mumbling something that I couldn't understand at first. Then I heard her say something very clearly. "Sleeper now awaken, lest your people and your kingdom be forsaken."

I felt a hand on my foot and I sat upright.

It was morning and no one else was there. I got up, walked into the bathroom and got into the shower. The memory of the dream seemed to drain away with the water beneath my feet.

I let myself air dry for a few minutes while I replaced the bandage on my shoulder and substituted the one on my head with a less ugly, over-sized, Band-Aid. Then I reached for the towel and slowly brought it up to my face. I was avoiding this moment, and looking forward to it at the same time: I could still smell Marcella. Then images of her lifeless body filled my head. I pushed the towel away. A small piece of yellow paper fluttered to the floor. I wasn't sure where it came from, but I reached down, picked it up, and read it.

A few hours later, I was at a boarding gate, at JFK International Airport. Destination: Pavone, Italy.

Chapter 64

"Barella?" Sandy said into the phone. "The mysterious Fed guy?"

"Yeah, none other. Said he wants to meet and get everyone updated."

"Does that mean we're going to update each other, or we're just going to update him?"

"No idea, I'm only doing this because Jack insists."

"Okay, Sean, I'll be there in twenty. By the way, I can't wait to tell you about Tom Lancaster's theory on Mascelle's last name."

"Yeah? Interesting?"

"Very interesting. I think I can finally start making heads and tails out of this thing we're dealing with."

"Good job, Sandy; I knew you would find something."

"I had a lot of help. Tell you about it when I see you." She hung up her cell phone as the taxi sped south towards the 13th Precinct.

Sandy met Sean outside of Jack Sachel's office and was about to give him a briefing when Sean asked her, "Can you do it in two minutes?"

"No way," she replied. "The short version will take at least ten."

"Then tell me after the meeting with Jack. That numb-nuts Barella is already in there, so we have no time."

Sandy followed McKeown down the corridor towards Jack Sachel's office. "By the way," Sean said, "I just got the report from the lab. The perps on Fire Island are confirmed as Middle-Eastern in origin. Specifically, four are ethnically Arab, the other three are Persian, and that includes the one with the medallion.

The shooter in Manhattan is also Arab."

"Excellent," she replied with a smile.

"Yes, you were right; now stop gloating."

"I'm not gloating. I'm too tired to gloat. I'm just relieved that they weren't something else, like something weird that no one thought of yet, Albanians or something."

"Yeah, this case is confusing enough. So now, let's hear what our friend from Washington has to add, if anything. By the way, let's keep that stuff about Lancaster's theory to ourselves for now, at least until I have a chance to hear it first. We're probably already going to be facing some serious credibility issues just trying to explain the part about the Assassin nut-job with the medallion." Sean knocked on Jack Sachel's door.

Jack called them in and pointed to a couple of chairs by his desk. Barella was standing near the wall at the other end of the office. McKeown looked around, expecting to see Joe Mascelle, but he was absent. It occurred to him that Jack might have excluded Joe from the meeting to avoid having to answer embarrassing questions: like why Joe was involved in an investigation when his nephew was a possible suspect.

Barella walked over to them and extended his hand. "Hi, Detective McKeown, good to see you again," he said as they shook hands. "And you must be Detective Taylor," he said, reaching his hand out to Sandy. She took it, looked closely into his eyes, and gave him a little smile. "Yes, I am. Hi."

All of them sat and Jack Sachel began the meeting. "Agent Barella and I have had an opportunity to exchange our views on issues pertaining to jurisdiction and cooperation on this case." Jack paused and smiled at Barella. "It's clear that we don't agree on all of the cogent points, but we do both agree that, given the special gravity of this particular case, every effort should be made to bring this matter to a successful outcome at the earliest possible time."

McKeown listened with some interest, not so much in what Jack said, but how he said it. It seemed to be a prepared statement that was being read for the record, and McKeown wondered if this meeting was being recorded.

"Furthermore, just so everyone comes to this in the right spirit, we've been instructed by our superiors that this matter must be given the very highest priority, regardless of real or perceived jurisdictional issues. To put it succinctly, New York City, Albany, and Washington want this dealt with, and dealt with now, or heads are going to roll."

He turned to Sean and caught him in mid-thought. "Sean, can you start by providing Agent Barella with a briefing of your findings to date?"

McKeown reviewed the latest information from the investigation, beginning with an analysis of the evidence collected to date. "We've collected a large number of items into evidence including shell casings, spent magazines, weapons, helicopter wreckage and a total of twelve bodies; the shooter in Manhattan that started this investigation, Kyle Orr and Jan Toomey, the ex-con in New Jersey who we suspect is a hired killer, and the eight on Fire Island, which includes William Hoffenberg. This count excludes Marcella Pavone, who is missing and presumed dead. We've questioned the only known surviving witness, Tony Mascelle and his account of the events appears to fit with the evidence at the scenes, or at least at those where he was present. Tony also identified Hoffenberg as a former high school friend, and provided us with the information that leads us to believe that Marcella, his former employee, is dead. The only other potential suspect is a man who identified himself as Gunter, no last name. He was apprehended at Orr's apartment building, but he is now missing, and we have reason to believe that his employers may be a domestic or foreign intelligence service. At one point we were beginning to formulate the hypothesis that this might all be related to a South or Central American drug cartel war; however, recent information appears to make that a very unlikely scenario."

"What information is that?" Sachel asked.

"I just heard from the lab before I walked into the room, and they said that the people in the black pajamas, the seven on Fire Island and the Shooter in Manhattan, were not Hispanics; five are Arabs, and three are Persians."

McKeown stopped to catch his breath, and then asked Sandy, "Am I missing anything?"

"Yes, the body stolen from the morgue," Sandy said.

"Right." McKeown continued, "The body of the man Tony Mascelle identified as his former high school friend, Hoffenberg, was stolen around the same time that Gunter disappeared. We have no idea how someone managed to smuggle the body out of the coroner's office. However, we do know that the man was not a Park Ranger."

"Any idea who he was working for, yet?" Jack Sachel asked McKeown, then glancing at Barella.

"We're not sure, but we believe he was probably also a member of a domestic or foreign intelligence service."

Barella sat quietly, taking all of this in. Then he looked at Sandy, who seemed to want to add something. Barella turned his attention back to McKeown and said, "So, up until very recently, you thought that this was a probable drug cartel war, or something of that sort?"

"Yes, all of the evidence appeared to point in that direction," McKeown said.

"So what's your best theory now?" Barella asked.

"Based on what we have, as of now, we don't have a new theory on what the big picture looks like, I'm sorry to say. But we're starting to get at least some of the pieces to fit together."

Sean McKeown then said, "Sandy, why don't you brief us on the medallion?"

Sandy smiled, reached into her pocket, and pulled out the plastic bag containing the gold medallion. "We found this on the beach. It belonged to one of the perpetrators: one of the Persians, or more accurately, an Iranian. The markings on it belong to a Muslim cult that supposedly went extinct in the thirteenth century. They were called the Assassins. They were actually the original assassins, the ones from whom the name is derived."

"The Assassins?" Jack Sachel asked. "Are you telling me that we have a gang of medieval killers running around New York, murdering high-tech executives and their employees? This sounds a little implausible to me, Sandy. What's their motive?"

Sandy shrugged her shoulders. "This is fresh off the presses, Jack; we're still trying to figure that part out."

"Can I see that?" Barella asked Sandy. She handed it over and he examined it. "Yes, the Alamut fortress." He turned it over. "And Sabbah on the flip side." He looked at Chief Sachel and said, "The ruler of the Ismaili, the most terrifying organization the world has ever known. This man was so evil that he had both of his sons killed: one for carrying out an unauthorized murder, and the other for drinking wine. Not a very nice person." He looked at McKeown. "And you found this at the scene on Fire Island?"

McKeown nodded.

"Interesting. And you had its origin's identified in, what, less than ninety-six hours?" Barella continued. "Pretty impressive. My compliments. It took us considerably longer to accomplish that."

Sandy was beaming, but McKeown just nodded, saying, "So, you have obviously seen this before."

"Yes, several times. Our sources indicate that one or more

terrorist organization has formed over recent years using the Assassins as both an operational and a political, or ideological, model."

Jack Sachel, who had been sitting quietly, listening to the exchange, asked, "Operational and political model? What does that mean?"

Sandy looked at Barella, who gave her a nod. She said to Jack, "They used assassination, and the threat of it, as a weapon of terror to influence their neighbors, or more accurately, impose their political will on them."

"And it worked," Barella added, "for about two hundred years, until a Mongol warlord finally wiped them out. Or at least, that's what everyone thought. Actually, they were just dispersed throughout Asia. One sect, called the Thugs, became quite powerful in India."

"They were called the Thugs?" Jack asked with some amazement.

"Yes," Barella continued, "they were the original Thugs, just as in the case of the Assassins. These words that we use in our everyday vocabulary have historical origins, and these people are it. For most of the last thousand years, throughout the Middle East and the Far East, these cults have existed. There are official British accounts, given as late as the nineteenth century, that the Ismaili were still active in Syria, in one form or another. And now, we have very recent information that indicates that they are still in existence today." Barella handed the medallion to Jack Sachel. "They're small groups to be sure, but we believe they have operated continuously, along with other similar cults in Iraq, East Africa, Malaysia and, of course, Iran, where they are thought to have originated."

"Iran, as in our Fire Island Persian." Sandy commented.

"Yes, precisely," Barella said. "We've also identified the fingerprints of one of the other bodies as an Iraqi agent."

"As in Saddam Hussein?" Jack asked.

"None other," Barella replied.

"I don't understand," McKeown said. "Why would Arabs and Persians cooperate, or for that matter, Iraq and Iran? I'm no Middle East expert, but I thought they were sworn enemies. No?"

"Yes, Detective McKeown, you're correct. At least on one level. When we Westerners look at a map of the Middle East, we see neat borders drawn between countries with different names, languages, flags and religions. We see the usual alliances, conflicts and wars. However, many of these things can be misinterpreted. Those lines on the map that constitute borders, for instance, are largely the artificial remnants of European colonial lords who drew them up to meet their own purposes. And what we perceive as mortal enemies, like Iraq and Iran, are only the result of recent, short-term situations. What is easy to forget is that this region has an historical memory that goes back thousands of years, and there are political, social, religious, and even blood ties that go back as far as that, or longer. But most importantly, what drives these cults is an idea, and ideas have no borders, nationality, or language."

"But why would a religious cult from Iran, and an Iraqi secular dictator like Saddam Hussein, join forces? What could be so threatening to cause them to put aside their enmity?" Sandy asked.

Barella replied, "There is an age-old Arab adage: 'The enemy of my enemy is my friend.' There is a well-documented history of the Assassins forming temporary alliances of convenience, even with Christian Crusaders, in order to destroy Muslim enemies of more immediate concern. As for Saddam, the same applies. He is known to be a student of Joseph Stalin, who formed an alliance with Germany against Britain one moment and then formed an alliance with the Allies against Germany the next. Saddam is desperate for a win, and he's also insane. A desperate and insane tyrant is capable of anything. Consider the attempt to kill former president Bush and his family while they visited Kuwait in 1993. Only a very insane, and very desperate, man would have attempted that."

Jack Sachel took a deep breath and sat back in his chair. "Agent Barella, this history lesson is fascinating, really, but I don't see how this has anything to do with a bunch of murderers running around in twenty-first-century New York, killing our citizens."

Barella looked at Jack with an almost amused stare and then said, "Chief, there is another saying that I think you should really get comfortable with: 'What's past is prologue.' Like it or not, New York, in fact the entire New World, is now in the middle of this ancient game of deadly chess, and if we're going to keep our people safe and alive, or for that matter survive at all, we'd better learn the rules of the game and learn those rules very fast."

The look on Jack Sachel's face indicated that he was not satisfied with that answer. "Agent Barella," he said through clenched teeth, "my interest in Middle Eastern history is limited to that which improves my people's ability to solve the case at hand and prevent other citizens from joining the list of victims. We obviously recognize that there is a much bigger picture here than what we knew about a few days ago. But frankly, I'm only concerned now with that part of the picture that helps me solve this case. It's also clear that there is a lot here that we need to know about, and that you're not telling us. Like, for instance, what is the connection between Tony Mascelle and these madmen from the desert?" Jack's volume had increased to a roar during this last sentence and was accented by his clenched fist slamming onto the top of his desk.

Barella took a deep breath and then sat up in his chair. "Chief Sachel, you well know that I am limited in what I can tell you because of national security matters. What I can say, with some confidence, is that as far as we know, the primary target of those Assassins was not Tony Mascelle, but Marcella Pavone and her associates. Mascelle was used to ferret out the real targets. The rest of the victims, as well as Mr. Mascelle, are either incidental to the case or peripheral to it. We believe these people got what they came for, and at least for the present, there should be no more of these incidents."

"How sure are you of that?" McKeown asked.

"Based on our analysis of what happened, our knowledge of who's involved, and our intel on what their motives are, we are confident in this conclusion."

"So if I were to ask you to say that you were 100 percent confident that these Assassins, or Thugs, or whatever the hell they are, are not still trying to kill Tony Mascelle, or some other citizen of New York, you would say what?"

"Detective, if you're asking me to give you a guarantee, I can't. Our intelligence is limited. All I can say is that we are confident in our assessment of the status of this case."

Sean McKeown looked at Chief Sachel. A shrug of his shoulders was all he needed to communicate to Jack that he thought Barella was probably telling the truth. There was a long silence. Then Sandy reached into her pocket, pulled out the other plastic bag, and handed it to Barella.

She said, "We also found this. We haven't had the chance to fully analyze it yet, but maybe you've seen it before?"

Barella took the bag and, without opening it, examined the small capsule that Tom Lancaster had reassembled from its two halves. Through the plastic, Barella placed his fingers gently on the sides of the black capsule and pressed his fingers together. The tiny needle emerged from the end. "Yes, we've seen this before, also," he said, stone-faced.

Chapter 65

Jack Sachel and Sean McKeown sat at Sachel's desk drinking coffee from brown paper cups, when Joe Mascelle walked in.

"Hi Joseph, have a seat," Sachel said.

Mascelle sat, turned to Sean, and said, "I passed Detective Taylor in the hall on the way in. She doesn't seem too happy with me. Did she get up on the wrong side of the bed this morning, or did she just leap straight up and grab the ceiling with her claws?"

McKeown said, "I don't think she likes you very much, but I can't imagine why."

Mascelle changed the subject. "So, did the Fed give you anything useful?"

Sean McKeown looked at Sachel and then said, "Not really. He did verify Lancaster's theory about the medallion and the Assassins. Seemed pretty surprised with how quickly we came up with it."

"Yeah, he's a Fed. They're always surprised when they meet anybody that they think is half as clever as they think they are themselves."

Sachel smiled and said, "Come on, Joe, give Sandy Taylor her due. I admit she's a little out there sometimes, but she's good. Admit it."

"Yeah, yeah," Mascelle replied. "So, where is she now, at a séance?"

Sachel sighed and said, "I asked her to wait outside a few minutes while we had a chat. I guess that was a good call. You really don't like her, do you?"

Mascelle shrugged. "It doesn't matter if I like her. What matters is whether she's a good detective or not. I'm a simple man Jack, you know that. I've never trusted anything but good, solid detective work. I've got no time or interest in this paranormal crap."

"Yeah, I get it. It makes me a little uncomfortable too. But we need her on this one. I think you might agree, when you hear what I'm about to tell you."

"Shoot."

"Let me start by asking you both a question that's been bothering me since this case dropped out of an otherwise beautiful blue weekend sky onto to my already cluttered desk: can either of you explain how the perps, whoever and whatever they are, seem to always be three steps ahead of us?"

McKeown and Mascelle both nodded their heads. Mascelle said, "Sean and I were wondering about that too. How did they know where my nephew was holed-up on Fire Island, for example? It must have taken them days to assemble that team and the equipment; they even had time to clear a landing zone out there. So, they must have known about it almost as soon as I thought of it."

Sachel inquired, "So, do either of you know how?"

Both men responded with a look of anticipation, because it was clear that Jack knew something that they didn't. Their suspicion was confirmed when he pushed a small piece of paper across the desk. They both looked at it. There were fifteen numbers handwritten on the paper: 137957187565030.

"What's this?" McKeown asked.

Joe Mascelle looked at the paper and said, "Too long to be a phone or social security number. What is it?"

"Sandy Taylor gave it to me this morning," Jack Sachel said as he shifted uncomfortably in his chair. "She told me that she had a dream last night."

McKeown said, "A dream? She didn't tell me anything about it."

"What? She's dreaming secret passwords now, Jack? Jesus!" Mascelle said. "Maybe I should use it to buy a lottery ticket."

"Yeah, well, here's the thing," Sachel said to Mascelle. "She gave this to me because she said you made her feel like a freak. She was too embarrassed to mention it, even to Sean, when you were around. That's a problem, Joe. Whatever it is that she does, and however she does it, doesn't really matter to me. She's already shown herself to be valuable on this case—very valuable. I'm not asking you to like it, but you need to respect it, or at least keep an open mind."

Joe Mascelle shrugged in reply.

McKeown said, "I have a feeling that there's something else you want to tell us, Jack."

"Yeah, and that's the other thing. When she gave it to me, I asked her what it meant. She said she didn't know, but she knew it was important to this case. Look at the numbers again. See anything interesting?"

Both of the men looked and shook their heads. Then Sachel said, "I didn't either, at first." He picked up a pencil and placed a line between the numbers 5 and 7. "How about now?"

"Yeah, the second half looks like a phone number, Brooklyn probably," McKeown said.

"Yeah, that's what I thought. So I checked it out. It's the home number of an NYPD cop who lives in Flatbush. Anybody want to take a guess at what the first five numbers are?"

"Badge number?" Joe Mascelle asked.

"Very good, Joe. It's the same guy's badge number. His name is Ibrahim al-Kondoz."

"That's interesting," Mascelle replied.

"Yeah. It is interesting, isn't it? Here's another thing that's interesting: he's not a native. He was born in Afghanistan, in the mountainous region near the Pakistani border."

"So what, Jack? Not all NYPD cops have good Irish names anymore," McKeown said.

"Look at me, Sean. Don't pull that PC crap on a guy with this face."

There was a moment of silence. Then Jack Sachel said, "I had one of my people check this guy out. Everything seemed pretty normal until we looked at his computer access activities. He's been looking at the police reports on this case since day one."

Silence again.

"Is there any legit reason why he'd be looking at them?" McKeown asked.

"None that we can determine," Sachel replied.

"Holy shit!" Mascelle said. "We've got a leak inside?"

"Don't know, but it's starting to look that way."

"So what's next, Internal Affairs?" Mascelle asked.

"Nope, not yet, anyway." Sachel replied. "It's still too thin. The guy could say he was curious about the case and was being nosey. Wouldn't be the first time that's happened. And then, as Sean was so kind to point out, there's the potential political fallout. As you know, since the Trade Center bombing, the NYPD has stepped up efforts to recruit Muslims onto the force to improve the lines of communication with that community. If someone starts making accusations based on some very thin evidence, we'll not only undermine our ability to find out what's going on, we could set back the department's relations with the Muslim community for years."

"Yeah, not to mention what they would say if they found out the source was a dream," Joe Mascelle said with a smile.

Jack did not return the smile. "Not very funny, partner. Your nephew's ass is literally on the line here, and the brass is up all of our asses about our apparent lack of progress on this case. Then there is the third thing, which is something you don't know about yet. Recently, there's been a lot communication going back and forth between NYPD and various federal agencies. We're talking memos, meetings, visits, et cetera. At first, I thought it was the usual, periodic Fed-land shit. But this time, it's more than that. What they're telling us is that the so-called Muslim street-chatter, here and abroad, is up, big-time. They don't know what or where the activity is focused, but the last time it was at this level they tried to blow up the Towers. The point, is that we have this very unhappy confluence of events that's making everyone, including me, very edgy."

Joe Mascelle's pager went off. He checked the number on the screen. "It's a message from Tony. Let me get this, Jack."

Sachel and McKeown watched Mascelle's expression as he listened to the message. They knew it was bad news before Mascelle hung up.

Joe Mascelle reported, "Tony said he was boarding a flight to Malpensa, Italy. He's going to look for Marcella. He said something about a note from her. The note said to meet her in some place called Pavone."

Sachel said, "Joe, I thought Tony said she was dead."

"He did."

Sean McKeown pinched his eyebrow between his fingers. "Doesn't make sense. If she's alive, why would she be luring him to another continent where she knows he will be more exposed to danger? I doubt the letter is from her. It must be a trick." McKeown was tempted to add that it also could be a lie. But why would Tony lie about that? For an excuse to leave the country?

Sachel said, "Barella told Tony not to leave the country. When he finds out, he's probably going to send an Interpol request to have Tony arrested. Even if the letter is from Marcella, Tony is going to end up in jail."

"I got to get on the next plane, Jack," Joe Mascelle said as he stood.

"No, Joe. Sit down. Here's what we're going to do about this. I want you to work with Sandy and see if we can get anything more concrete on this Ibrahim guy. I don't have to tell you that this is unofficial and needs to be kept very quiet. Assuming this isn't just a nosy cop, we'll take it to Internal Affairs, but not before we sweat this guy. Once it's in the IA's hands, the union reps and lawyers come in, and we're not getting shit out of this guy, at that point."

Joe Mascelle rolled his eyes. "You want me to work with Taylor. What's this, my penance?"

"Partially. But mostly it's because I need someone I can trust with my life, or in this case, my career. I need you to run point on this. And I also need someone very motivated. If this guy is trying to help get your nephew wacked, I'd say that makes you perfectly qualified."

"What about me, Jack?" McKeown asked.

Mascelle added. "Yeah, what about Sean? And what about my nephew?"

"Sean, I need you on the next plane to Milan. You're going to find the kid and get his ass back here, pronto. If he gives you any trouble, you arrest him. It's for his own good and his safety, and it's better than having him booked under some European jurisdiction, or by the feds. If they get him first, we can't help him anymore."

"Why don't you let me go and find my nephew and let Sean stay here and work with Sandy?"

"That won't work, Joe. I let you tag along on this case because of who you are. But you know damn well it was against every regulation in the book. There's no way to hide a foreign excursion, even if you paid for the trip yourself. No: Sean goes, you stay here and work with Sandy."

Joe Mascelle nodded his head. "I guess you're right." He looked at Sean. "You find my nephew and bring him home in once piece Sean, so I can smack the shit out of him the next time I see him."

"Will do."

Jack Sachel stood up. "Okay, guys, let's get to it. Sean, get with Marcie outside. She'll arrange to have your tickets and itinerary waiting for you by the time you get to the airport." Sachel handed McKeown a thick brown envelope.

"What's this?" McKeown asked.

"Some reading material about Barella, for the flight. It's from my friend in DC."

"Good?"

"I just had time to skim it, but I'd say so. On the other hand, it may provide more questions than answers. We're definitely through the looking glass on this one."

Sachel turned to Joe. "Sandy is waiting for you in the coffee room. Good luck and good hunting, gentlemen."

Mascelle and McKeown turned and began walking towards the door. Joe stopped and turned back towards Sachel. "So who figured out the numbers thing?"

"What? You mean splitting the badge and the phone number?"

"Yeah."

"That was me," Sachel replied.

"Impressive. And I thought this office was turning your detective's mind to mush."

"Yeah, I impressed myself on that one, too. I guess my brain isn't mush yet. But the real work was done by your friend in the coffee room. You want to hear what her dream was about?"

"I'm almost afraid to ask."

Sachel smiled. "She said she had a dream about a man-sized rat. He was standing on two feet and wearing a blue turban on his head. The numbers were on a sign on the turban."

"Weird."

"Give her a chance, Joe."

Chapter 66

The Milan-bound Alitalia flight was somewhere off the coast of Long Island and, according to the voice from the cockpit, climbing to thirty-six thousand feet. I was sitting in the aisle seat, row number twenty-three, on flight number thirty-two, and was trying to decide if this number combination was a bad omen. Did I mention that I'm a little superstitious when I fly?

The pilot's accent sounded like he worked at a rodeo on the weekends, so I was pretty sure that he wasn't a *paisano,* which was confirmed when he informed us that the flight was operated by Delta Airlines. Maybe no one from Italy likes to fly, including their pilots.

The stewardess brought me a drink, Dewars and water, and she asked me with a pleasant, Southwestern accent if I would like a newspaper. I was tempted to ask her if she'd been to any rodeos lately, but instead I asked, "Do you have the *Wall Street Journal*?"

"Of course," she said, lifting a thin paper from the stack on her cart and handing it to me. The front page informed me that it was the European edition of the *Wall Street Journal.*

"Where's the rest of it?"

She smiled. "That's all there is, I'm afraid."

I examined the page. Besides the day's business headlines, it informed me that the price of the paper was two pounds sterling. What kind of idiot would pay four bucks for this pathetic little newspaper?

I read for a few minutes, which was about all I needed, and then sat back in my seat and scanned the passengers around me. The plane was mostly empty, and the center row that I was sitting in was entirely empty, so I was looking forward to stretching out across the seats and getting some sleep as soon as this thing leveled off and my heart stopped pounding in my chest.

That was the good news. The bad news was that there was a cranky little three-year-old named Jonathan sitting across the aisle immediately to my right. He had a toy gun and was shooting at all of the nice passengers around him. I knew he was a three-year-old, because he was acting like one. I knew his name was Jonathan because his mother, a pretty, but very tired-looking blonde, kept saying it over and over in a variety of curt sentences: Jonathan, sit down. Jonathan, stop screaming. Jonathan, stop turning the stewardess light on and off. Jonathan, stop shooting the nice passengers, and so on.

She didn't look like she enjoyed flying, either. But I think it was for a different reason than mine. I don't like flying because I'm afraid the damn plane might crash. I think she didn't like it because it wouldn't crash soon enough. I tried giving Jonathan a mean look, but it didn't work. He just grinned, aimed at my head, and pulled the trigger. I sat there wondering why there wasn't a regulation against toy guns and three-year-olds aboard commercial flights, and I also tried to figure out a way of discreetly slipping Jonathan a sip or two of my drink.

I took the letter out of my pocket and read it again, for about the twentieth time. The message contained two simple sentences, but at the same time it was filled with infinite complexity. It said, "I'm alive, and I love you. Meet me in Pavone, at the Castle." And, of course, it was written in what appeared to be Marcella's handwriting.

Was she alive, or was this some sort of trick? How was it possible that she was alive? I felt her die in my arms. And if she wasn't dead, how did she disappear from Fire Island and end up in Pavone, wherever the hell that is?

My mind compiled a list of questions to ask her, if and when I found her still among the living, starting with three: who are you, where did you come from, and what the fuck is going on? Okay, so maybe there would be a fourth question in there somewhere, like: would you marry me?

I didn't know it at the moment, but I was about to get the answers to the first three questions, and a lot of others I hadn't even thought to ask yet, and get them before the plane landed in Milan. The fourth would have to wait until I found her, if I found her. I mean, considering all of the weird shit I've seen over the past couple of weeks, is it really so hard to believe that someone could have forged her handwriting? If that were the case, the question would be why. To get me away from the protection of my uncles and the NYPD? Or maybe, just to eliminate my home-field advantage. I guess I would discover the answer to that question eventually, too. In fact, the answer to that question just might be the last thing I heard before someone put a bullet in my head, or some other part of my body. I considered this outcome before I left New York. But all I could hear was my Mother's voice: "If you love her, you find her, and you bring her home."

I caught a movement out of the corner of my eye. Some jerk was moving into the aisle seat on the other side of my row. So much for me spreading out and getting some sleep. I reclined the seat-back and tried getting comfortable in the upright position.

After a while, the plane reached cruising altitude and leveled off and, with the exception of the din from the engines, it almost felt as if we were standing still. It wasn't long before I fell asleep.

****

My brain conjured up an image of Marcella sitting in a brightly lit field covered with tiny, multi-colored flowers that were dancing in a gentle breeze. She was sitting on a white bed, just as she was that morning on Fire Island: her breasts covered by her hands, a smile on her face, and love for me in her eyes. I could smell the sea air mixed with the sweet smell of her skin and the flowers in the field. She began to beckon to me with her right hand and I tried to go to her, but I could not move my legs.

Then, suddenly, she disappeared, the flowers wilted away, and the light was replaced by a gray scene depicting a dead man in black on a beach with his head split open. I looked down and noticed that I was sitting on a horse, a white one, which looked just like William. Then the horse's bare back and neck became encased in shiny steel armor.

An instant later, my nose was filled with a stench that I had never smelled before, but somehow I knew exactly what it was. When I looked up, the single corpse on the beach was replaced by a field covered with thousands of corpses, the slaughter extending for as far as I could see in any direction.

I heard a strange, rhythmic sound to my right and turned to see a citadel's walls framed by two very tall stone towers on each side. The sound was coming from men standing on the walls who were chanting something over and over again, but I could not understand the words. Then I saw several other men standing on each of the towers to the right and left.

Arrows appeared in the sky. I couldn't tell where they were coming from, but I watched as two of them struck each of the towers. Both towers burst into flames on impact and more arrows followed in a steady stream, until both towers were completely ablaze. The smoke from the fires billowed into a clear blue sky and formed two long, gray plumes that stretched to the horizon.

One of the men on the tower to the right suddenly leaped off. I watched him fall, and saw him hit the ground with a loud thump. Then another followed from the left tower in the same way. Another and another from each tower leaped to their deaths until the thumping sound of the bodies hitting the ground became a nearly unbroken rumble. I wanted to turn away from the sight, but I could not move either my head or my eyes from the scene. It was then that the stone towers were transformed into towers of steel and glass, as the bodies continued to rain down.

Chapter 67

By the time Detectives Joe Mascelle and Sandy Taylor began their stakeout in Brooklyn the streets were dark, but Taylor's mood was even darker. Mascelle sat in the driver's seat of the Ford sedan with one eye on the entrance of Officer Ibrahim al-Kondoz's Flatbush apartment across the street, and the other eye on the stony-faced woman sitting next to him.

He handed her a white paper bag. "Donut?"

"I don't eat junk food."

Mascelle pulled the bag back and mumbled. "Donuts, junk food? What kind of cop are you?"

"I'm a freak, remember?"

"Hey, I never said that."

"That's right. You said I was a witch."

"I never said that either." Then, with a feigned British accent, Mascelle said, "I was merely making an historical reference. We were, after all, having an intellectual exchange about the nuances of historical interpretation at the time, and I didn't want that little twit Lancaster to think he was the only smart guy in the room." Mascelle smiled.

Taylor glared at him. "Oh, that really worked out well. We were all very impressed with you, really."

Mascelle said, "Okay, I admit it. I was a little outta-line. I'm not the sharpest pin in the box, and I'm not the most open-minded, either. I'll even admit that you're a better cop than I originally thought."

"Gee, thanks. Does that qualify as an apology where you come from?"

"I guess. Besides, there were extenuating circumstances that explain my anti-social behavior."

"Like what?"

"I was in pain."

"What kind of pain?"

"My knuckles were killing me. Must have been that new carpet in Lancaster's office."

Sandy Taylor smiled, in spite of herself.

Mascelle continued, "Look, I've got nothing against you personally. I'm just very suspicious of shortcuts. The way I came up, it's all about doing the work. I was taught to work the case hard, keep your eyes open, and in the end you usually get to the solution. This stuff that you do just doesn't feel right. It feels like cheating."

"Cheating? How the hell is it cheating? And believe me, what I do is no shortcut. You're not the first person to be freaked out by it, and you won't be the last. But what am I supposed to do? It's not like I can help it. It's just something that happens. And when it does, all I can do is either choose to use it, maybe to save a life, or I can pretend it's not there and let the chips fall where they may. But I can't do that. For whatever reason, God gave me this ability, and I think he wants me to use it to do something good. That's why I became a cop in the first place."

"So, you're religious?" Mascelle asked.

"Yes."

"Like the Bible and Jesus, or like Stonehenge and the Earth Mother?"

"I'm Catholic, wise guy."

"I feel better already. So, how does your priest feel about this special gift of yours?"

"What do you mean?"

"I mean, is he okay with it, or does he hold up a cross and begin mumbling something in Latin whenever you enter the room?"

"Oh, stop it. Where did you get the idea that being psychic, or whatever this is, was somehow anti-Christian? The Bible is filled with stories about prophets predicting the future, and faith-healing, and people performing miracles of all sorts. The only difference is that, in the Bible, most of these people are men. But in pre-Christian times, female prophets, priestesses, and oracles were common. That's why they burned the witches in Salem: because men, like you, were threatened by powerful women."

Mascelle adjusted his position in the car seat. "This isn't going to turn into a women's lib convention, is it?"

"No, but you have to admit that we live in a male-dominated world."

"Really?" Mascelle commented, rolling his eyes.

"Yes, really. Men get all the breaks. Everything is designed around them, and for them."

"Well, I'm not going to argue that point. . ."

"Good, you must be smarter than I thought."

"May I finish my sentence, Detective Taylor?"

"Sorry, go ahead."

"The world does seem to be centered on men's needs. But a good detective looks at a situation like that and always asks the next question: why?"

Mascelle looked at Sandy Taylor and waited in silence. She looked back at him and said, "You want an answer to that?"

"Yes. Haven't you ever considered the question?"

"Well, not really, because the answer is obvious. Men control everything, that's why."

"Oh, please! Is that the best you can do?"

"Okay smart guy, why?"

"Where do you live?" Mascelle asked.

"On the Upper West Side. Why?"

"Why not in the South Bronx?"

Taylor squinted her eyes and shook her head. "Because I don't want to wear a bullet-proof vest just to walk to the corner grocery. Where are you going with this?"

"It's dangerous, right? But why?"

"Because gang-bangers are all over the place shooting innocent people."

"Why?"

"Because they're poor and live in old tenements with bad plumbing and rats."

"Yeah, I knew you'd say something like that. There are lots of poor people, and the vast majority of them are honest, decent, law-abiding folks. It's not that."

"Are you going to sit there and tell me that someone's living conditions don't contribute to the local crime level?" Taylor asked.

"Well, let's see. Maybe you're right. I know these people that live in Pennsylvania, and they live in conditions that would make inner city people cringe. I mean, real nineteenth-century stuff, like no indoor plumbing, no electricity, and no refrigeration. And nobody has a car. These people ride horses to work. They're called Amish. Yeah, real bad-asses, those people. Don't want to be caught wandering around their neighborhood at night. One of those crazies might show up wearing coveralls, and a straw hat, and force you to drink a glass of apple cider."

"Okay, smart guy, so why are there gang-bangers, then?"

"Are these gang-bangers men or women?" Mascelle asked.

"They're men, of course."

"Yes, of course, they're men. But why?"

Sandy said, "Because men have testosterone... because men are dangerous."

"All men have testosterone, but not all men are dangerous. You're sitting alone in a car, at night, in Flatbush, with one right now and he has a gun. You don't look afraid."

"I have a gun too."

"Be serious."

"I don't know, Joe. You're not dangerous because your parents loved you, because you went to Sunday school, because you were a Boy Scout or played in Little League or something. I don't know. Why?"

"All of the above."

"So what's your point?"

"That *is* the point. I'm not dangerous because a lot of people invested a lot of time and resources teaching me not to be dangerous. Look, it's simple: we don't live in a world based on guys' rules. If we did, everything would look like the South Bronx. I mean, you're Catholic, you went to Sunday school, right? Have you ever really thought about all those stories you heard there? For example, where does the Bible say Jesus came from?"

"From Bethlehem. I'm not following you."

Mascelle said, "He came from a virgin birth, right? In other words Jesus, and everything he ever said, or did, or symbolized, was entirely the product of his mother: a woman, last time I checked. No man was involved. Just Mary, with some help from God."

"So?"

"What do you mean, so? Think about it. He was born in the Roman world. Those people were artists of death and destruction. And when they weren't conquering, raping, and pillaging, they were slaughtering people in the Coliseum just to entertain themselves. Romans, Mongols, Mayans, Aztecs... even the ancient Hebrews—none of them were any picnic. If a woman in Jesus' time messed up, she was stoned to death. Anytime you have a civilization that involves the ritual killing or sacrifice of people or animals, you can be pretty sure the guys wrote the rules. When Jesus was born, the whole world was the inner city. Brute force, law of the jungle, eat or be eaten. That's what a male-dominated society looks like. That's not the world we live in. We live in a turn-the-other cheek, love-thy-neighbor, and hug-your-children-everyday world. This ain't guy stuff; it's gal stuff. Jesus took Judaism, and the rest of the screwed-up, pagan world, and showed it another way. The female way. Get it?"

Taylor shrugged. "Interesting theory."

"You don't look convinced."

"Nope."

Mascelle continued. "Think about our friends in Sand-land. They don't do the turn-the-other-cheek thing there. Over there, it's still an eye for an eye, a tooth for a tooth. You're sitting with a strange man, wearing pants, carrying a gun, and talking back. You think this happens over there? No way. Over there you'd be sitting at home with a bag over your head, waiting for hubby to come home along with twelve children and two other wives. That's the kind of society a guy would design. Our society was designed by women."

"Well, if you want more wives, move to Saudi Arabia; no one's stopping you."

"You're missing the point. I'm not complaining. I like this world. But I like it because I was taught to value it. I'll tell you something: the only difference between me and those gang-bangers in the Bronx is my training. I could have been just like them, and anyone of them could have been sitting right here with you, and you wouldn't be any more afraid of them than you are of me. It's all about the testosterone versus the training. Ever notice that you don't seem to read about inner-city female gangs wandering Central Park on wildings? They don't get training either, but they also don't have massive amounts of testosterone coursing through their bodies. Ever notice that the people in Somalia, Rwanda, Bosnia, or the Middle East causing all the havoc and death, all seem to be guys?"

"Of course." Taylor replied.

Mascelle said. "Right, of course. It's because the most dangerous animal on Earth is not a human; it's a human male between the ages of fifteen and twenty-five. The only difference between where you live and a neighborhood in the South Bronx, or between Somalia and the USA, is that the safe places developed rules, rituals, and institutions that control and direct young men's passions long enough for them to grow older, wiser, and more mellow. Like me." He concluded with a smile.

"You sure are old. But I don't know about the wiser and mellower part."

"And I'm the wise-guy, right? Look, if you want to know why neighborhoods fail, or cities fail, or countries or entire civilizations fail, it's as simple as that. The ones that know how to control and direct the testosterone-driven passions of their young men survive and thrive. The ones that can't, or won't, are toast. When that happens, the ritual human sacrifices return, but in a different, more contemporary form, like the ritual of gang initiations involving drive-by shootings, or by the suicide bombers in the Middle-East blowing themselves up. Successful societies give young men more attention, not because they like them better, but because they need it more. And if you do it right, you not only avoid this danger, you turn a potential liability into an asset. I won't use my gun to hurt you, because I've been trained my entire life to protect you with it. That same testosterone-driven passion can also be harnessed to discover new drugs, write poems, build a skyscraper, or launch a man to the moon. It's like in school. The naturally smart kids do great because school is intuitive; the rules and the environment are natural to them. The dumb kids, on the other hand, need extra help and have to study harder because they don't get the rules. It's not intuitive, not at first anyway. The school doesn't spend all of that extra time and attention on them because they like them more. They do it because they need it more. Out here, in the world, or at least in the part that's still civilized, a society gives young men the extra help, the extra training, because the rules in our society are not intuitive to them. We're the dumb kids. Women are the smart ones. Men need the extra help. And if we don't get it, nobody's going to be very happy for very long."

Taylor looked at Mascelle for a long time and then said, "So, that's the world according to Joe Mascelle?"

"Some of it. I have other theories, too." He smiled.

"Well, there seems to be more in that big, thick head of yours than I thought."

"Pretty good, huh? It's kinda amazing how much a guy can figure out while he's sitting in the john."

"Now, there's a mental image I could have gone all day without."

Mascelle laughed.

Taylor was silent for a few moments. She started grinning and said, "I can see how a guy could be attracted to the prospect of having more than one wife."

"Oh really?" Mascelle replied. "I can't. I love my wife, but she's a full-time job. Anyone who thinks he can handle more than one is a little off in the head, in my opinion. And anyone who thinks he can handle five or more should be locked up in a padded cell, because he's definitely a danger to himself, to say nothing of the people around him. That's why the people in Sand-land are still living in the dark ages. They're too tired and too angry to figure out how to build a space ship, because they're dealing with all of these women and children yelling and screaming all day."

"I'm not sure, but I think that may have been the most sexist comment I've ever heard in my life," Sandy said, staring at him.

"Yeah? Which part?"

Sandy shook her head. "Well, I'm not saying I necessarily agree with you on any of this, but for a guy who drags his knuckles on the ground, you're pretty insightful sometimes. I think. I'm glad we had this talk."

"Me too. It's good to get in touch with my inner child, or inner female, or whatever the hell women tell guys they need to be touching these days."

Sandy said. "Getting in touch with your inner child? You? I'd like to see that."

"Hey, I resent that. I tried it once. I did. But the little bastard bit me, so I smacked him around and put him in a homeless shelter."

"I think that's a lyric from a Don Henley song."

"He must have stole it from me."

"You're nuts. You know that?"

"I guess that makes two of us." Mascelle picked up the donut bag and noticed Taylor's eyes following it. "You sure you don't want one?"

"What kind do you have?"

"Well, I didn't know what you liked, so I told them to mix them up." Joe reached into the bag. "Here, how about a chocolate one with white icing."

Sandy made a face. "Who eats chocolate donuts?"

Mascelle smiled. "Yeah, right? But my nephew Tony loves 'em. What can I say? He's always been a complicated kid." Mascelle's smile faded.

"What?" Sandy asked.

Mascelle replied, "The last time I said that to him we were talking about Marcella. What a sin. She was a beautiful girl." Mascelle's eyes stared off into the distance as his ham hock-sized fists closed around the bag. "When I find the people who are responsible for all of this, I'm going to show them what an eye for an eye really means."

Sandy interrupted his thoughts. "Hey, you got any jellies?"

"Huh?"

"Jelly donuts? You got any?"

Joe looked at Sandy and his smile returned. "Are you kidding? They're the best." He handed her the bag.

As she fished around in the bag, he said, "So I guess that comment about not eating junk food was a big, fat lie."

"Not really. It depends on how you define junk food. I think fresh fish, vegetables, and yogurt are junk food. I can eat steak and jelly donuts all day long."

Joe Mascelle raised an eyebrow. "Wow."

Sandy took a big bite of a donut and the jelly started to run down her chin. She mumbled. "You want to hear that story?"

He passed her a napkin. "Huh?"

Mascelle watched her as she finished chewing and swallowing.

"The story, you know—the one that Lancaster told me about after you left, all huffy?"

"Nah, I'm not interested in fairy tales. Pun intended."

"You're so rude. It's a really good story. I promise, you'll like it."

"If I listen, are you gonna tell me I was adopted?"

"Not anymore."

"I guess that's a good sign. Right?"

"It's a very good sign."

"Okay, shoot."

Chapter 68

I sat upright, hitting the seat tray with my knee and spilling the remaining contents of the glass. As I wiped up the spill with a napkin, I heard the pilot say something about beginning the plane's descent into Malpensa. Suddenly I remembered what Detective Sandy Taylor told me about my dreams, and also about my leaving the country. How could she possibly know, when even I didn't at the time?

I saw movement out of the corner of my eye, again. I assumed it was the same guy who had moved into the opposite aisle seat earlier in the flight. He was still there, apparently, and I think he turned to look at me. Then he started to move over, to the seat closer to me. He sat back, glanced over again, and then moved over another seat. *Oh, great, what's this guy going to do, put his head on my lap and go night-night*? I turned to tell him to back off, but when I saw his face, my throat tightened and no words came out.

"Hey, Tony, you get some rest?"

I stayed silent. I could feel the plane starting to descend, along with my stomach. My eyes started darting around the cabin, looking for a cop, the captain, a stewardess, anybody with a uniform or a gun, but all I could find was Jonathan, who was now sleeping with his head on the arm rest and drooling. His mother was gone, probably in the lavatory taking a sedative, so there wasn't even a witness.

I checked my watch. It was around five o'clock in the morning, New York time. The cabin was still dimly lit, but the prick next to me had his sunglasses on. He must have been sick the day they taught the lesson on being inconspicuous, in assassins' school, or spy class, or wherever the hell he came from.

Just then, the stewardess passed and left a breakfast box on my tray. Crazy Nunzio waved her off with a smile. It occurred to me that he was now within easy reach, so I looked down at my tray: plastic cup, plastic folk, plastic knife. *How the hell can anyone defend themselves with this shit*? I picked up the mostly green banana and tested the weight in my hand. Nunzio smiled as he studied me, made a pouting face, and then, as if reading my mind, said in his best news anchor voice, "Man attacks fellow passenger with green banana, details at six."

He was silent for a moment and then said, "Come on, Tony, drop the banana and say hello to an old friend." I noticed his former Italian accent was now almost indiscernible.

"Hello. Now go away."

"Go away? Where can I go?"

I pointed to the emergency exit door over the wing. "See where that leads."

"Tony, are you mad at me? What did I do to make you so mad, my friend? This is such a nice surprise, meeting like this, right?" he asked as he waved his eyebrows over the sunglasses and wiggled his big mustache.

"Surprise my ass," I said in a whisper.

"Okay, so it's not a surprise for me, but you looked surprised," he retorted with a big stupid grin.

"What do you want?"

"Nothing, really. Just wanted to talk a little."

"About what?"

"Stuff, you know... some of the things that have been going on lately."

I said to him, "You left the note from Marcella, didn't you?"

"Note?"

"Why did you leave it?" I asked.

"What note?"

Liar. "So what are you doing here, Nunzio, or whatever your name is?"

"It's Mario."

"Okay, so what the hell do you want from me, Mario?"

"Well, when I found out that you were taking this little trip, I thought we could talk, alone, over the Atlantic, where no one could hear us. You know, there are a lot of pissed-off people running around, and they all seem to have guns."

I heard a little snort and looked over at Jonathan. He was twitching in his sleep. "Yeah, I noticed. So go ahead and talk," I said.

He moved over to the seat next to mine, took off the sunglasses, and looked into my eyes. He was very close. I could feel his breath on my face. It smelled like cigarettes. My hand tightened around the banana.

"Well, go ahead and start talking," I repeated.

"Hmmm, where do I start?"

"You can start by telling me why you're trying to kill me, and why you killed Marcella, and then stole her body, you son-of-a-bitch, and then maybe I'll just cut your throat so you'll die quickly like a pig, rather than gut you and watch you die slowly, like... a pig."

"Wow, that must be some banana. Where did all this hostility come from?"

Frankly, I didn't know where it came from; it was probably a line from a Clint Eastwood movie, or something, buried in a deep, dark place inside my brain. I was normally a pretty constrained kind of guy, but ever since that thing on the beach at Fire Island, I'd been exploring unknown territories of extreme behavior. All I knew then was that I really wanted to kill this son of a bitch.

"Tony, you've got your facts all wrong. Believe me, if the people I worked for wanted you dead, you would have been dead a long, long time ago. In fact you would never have been born."

"What the hell does that mean?"

"It means that my job is not to kill you. My job is to keep you alive."

"You're doing a great job."

"What do you mean? You're not dead, are you?"

"No, but Marcella is."

He smiled in a way that made me hesitate. "Marcella's job was also to keep you alive."

I'd heard similar words before, from Marcella in fact, but I still had no idea what they meant. So, naturally, my next question was, "What do you mean?"

"I mean that Marcella worked for me. Her job was to stay close to you and keep you safe."

"What are you talking about?"

"I'm talking about a promise made a long, long time ago."

"That's what she said."

He gave me a curious look. "Then you know? She told you?"

"She said that she was there to keep a promise. But she never explained what that meant."

"Well, it's a very long story."

I looked at my watch again. "We have about fifteen minutes

before we land, and neither of us seems to be going anywhere."

"You mean you don't want me to leave anymore?" he said, pointing to the emergency exit.

"Just shut up and talk."

"Well, let's see. Once upon a time, long ago, and in a faraway land, there was this cool guy named Sebastiano. Sebastiano was one of the Knights of Saint John, later called the Knights of Malta."

So the story started. Before long he was telling me how this guy, Sebastiano, was responsible for saving Europe from enslavement by the Muslims, by turning them back from places like Rhodes and Malta, four hundred years ago.

He continued, "Most people don't know, or don't want to remember, that all of those places that are now occupied by Muslims were once Christian. The Muslims came in, usually slaughtered most of the inhabitants and enslaved the rest, unless of course you converted to Islam. Most people also don't know that all of Europe almost fell to the same fate, and would have if it were not for a handful of incredibly brave men, Sebastiano being one of them—in fact, one of the greatest of them."

"Malta? Muslims? What are you talking about?"

"Hey, I said it was a long story."

"We only have ten minutes left, so can we fast-forward to the goddamn present?"

"You know, Marcella said you curse too much. It's not very becoming."

I gave him an angry look.

"Okay, so I will try to quicken it up. Bottom line, Sebastiano and the Knights of Malta save Christendom."

"Great, you said that. So what?"

"Are you going to listen?"

"Yes."

"In order to save Christendom he was required to engage in mortal combat with a representative sent by Suleiman the Magnificent. The winner of the contest wins Malta. Win Malta and you win Europe. Unfortunately, the Sultan's representative is also Sebastiano's son by the Sultan's own daughter." He stopped, thought, and then said. "Sebastiano met her during the campaign on Rhodes after he, Sebastiano, nearly destroyed the Sultan's army during a great battle. Then they fell in love, and... you know."

"Yeah, I get it; he was screwing the Sultan's daughter while he was fucking the Sultan's army."

He ignored me and continued. "So, when Sebastiano finds this out, he naturally refuses the challenge, the one on Malta, and he tries to get someone else do it. You know, like a designated hitter." He smiled. "Good metaphor, yes?"

I ignored him this time.

"Okay, so he tries to get out of it, but he can't, because his son, who is the commander of the army that is attacking Malta, wants to kill him and he won't allow a substitute."

"Sounds like one of my mother's soap operas."

"Well, actually, that may be more accurate than you might imagine."

I looked at him, expecting an explanation, but he just continued with the original story.

"The forces defending Malta, the Knights, were in pretty bad shape after months of this siege, and they were outnumbered by, like, ten-to-one. The Knights were also sick, starving, and not very optimistic, so it was pretty much over for them and, therefore, for the rest of Europe too. So, Sebastiano finally agrees to the contest. Besides, if he doesn't, the Pope excommunicates him, and his family. If he goes through with it, and wins, the Pope promises to protect all of Sebastiano's sons, and all of his son's sons, and so on and so forth, from their enemies, forever."

"What if he—this Sebastiano guy—goes through with it and loses? Does the Pope still keep up his end of the bargain?"

Mario smiled. "Like I said, if the Muslims win Malta, they eventually win Europe. So, there is no Pope, and Saint Peter's Basilica becomes a mosque, like Sophia in Constantinople. You get the idea?"

"Yes, but I still don't have the slightest idea what this has to do with me!" Some of the people in the cabin started to look in our direction.

"Tony, you're raising your voice."

"Continue."

"Oh come on, don't you get it?" Mario said with some exasperation.

"No." Then, as they say, a light went on in my head.

Chapter 69

Joe Mascelle looked over at Sandy Taylor and smiled. "You mean this guy Sebastiano knocked-up the Sultan's daughter? I'm starting to like this story."

She gave him an exasperated look. "Stop interrupting, and stop drooling all over the donuts."

Mascelle picked up the bag, crushed it and threw it into the back seat. "All gone."

"You ate all of them?"

"Hey, I had some help here."

Mascelle noticed that Taylor's attention had suddenly turned to the apartment building across the street.

"What?" Joe Mascelle asked.

"Shhh," She replied with a barely audible sound.

A man carrying a briefcase exited the building. "Is that him?" she asked.

"Yeah, that looks like our guy. Officer Ibrahim al-Kondoz."

The man turned right at the next corner and began walking east down State Street. Sandy waited for Joe to start the car, but he didn't. She looked over and found him staring at her. "What?" She asked.

"That's amazing. How did you know he was going to come out of that door just then?"

Taylor gave him a puzzled look. "Didn't we just have a long conversation about this special ability of mine?"

"Yeah," Mascelle said. "But up until now all I knew was what other people told me. I never actually witnessed it myself."

"Don't be too impressed. The light in the foyer came on."

"Oh."

"Start the car, Joe."

"Relax, he's a cop. You don't want to be too early or we'll tip him off." Joe Mascelle waited another thirty seconds and then turned the key.

They followed their target to the corner of Bond Street. "I knew he was going to do that," Mascelle said as he watched the man disappear down a block with one-way traffic moving against them. He pulled the car over.

"I need to hoof this or we're gonna lose him, if we haven't already. You stay with the car. If I need you, I'll call."

"We should stick together," Taylor said.

He handed her a closed-frequency handheld radio and put the matching headset around his ear. "You want both of us to follow him on foot? And what, pretend we're on a date?"

"We don't have to hold hands," she said.

Mascelle smiled. "Just stay with the car and be alert. Talk if you have to, otherwise double squelch to acknowledge."

"Don't be a hero, Joe."

"Not my style."

Mascelle walked quickly towards the corner and disappeared from Taylor's sight.

A few minutes later she heard his voice. "Got him. He's heading east, and still against traffic. Obviously worried about being followed. Wait for me at Fourth and Atlantic."

She keyed the radio twice as she put the car into drive.

Minutes later Mascelle's voice came over the radio. "I'm near Third. He's making a left into a parking lot."

Taylor replied in a whisper, "Hey, Joe, isn't that where that mosque is? The one where they planned the Trade Center bombing?"

"Yes it is. Coincidence?"

"Yeah, right. Be careful."

Mascelle made the left into the parking lot and took cover between two panel trucks sitting at the loading dock. He heard movement behind him, but before he could turn to see where it was coming from, everything went black.

Sandy was sitting in the car at Fourth and Atlantic, and was starting to get nervous. It had been more than five minutes since Joe's last contact. She keyed the radio again to get his attention. Nothing. "Joe, give me some feedback, partner," she whispered into the radio. Still nothing.

Oh, no! She left the car and started jogging. Just as she rounded the corner, she heard the gunshot. She drew her pistol and ran flat out. Her head began racing with images as she approached the scene. She saw three people. Joe was on the ground to her left and he wasn't moving. The other two were to her right, one lying and one kneeling. She ran up, aimed her gun and yelled. "Freeze, police!"

The person lying on the ground looked like Officer al-Kondoz. But she couldn't be sure, because a part of his skull was missing and his right eye had popped out of its socket. The person kneeling over him was a woman in her late fifties or early sixties. Sandy said, "Place the gun on the ground, put your hands behind your head, and stand up slowly."

The women complied. Sandy grabbed the woman's arms, moving them down and behind her back, snapping the cuffs on. She felt something in the woman's hand; something hard and oily. Sandy took it and held it up to the light. It was a small glass vial. She turned the women around and looked into her eyes. Sandy sniffed the air. She recognized the smell.

What happened next made Sandy's muscles stiffen. She caught herself and relaxed, the way her grandmother had taught her. The images were sepia-toned and began flashing in her mind's eye as if they were old photos mounted in an album and someone was flipping quickly through the pages. She saw Joe crouched behind a panel truck and a briefcase coming down hard on his head from behind. Then the image zoomed out just enough so she could see Officer al-Kondoz standing over Joe's body and pointing a gun at his head. He was squeezing the trigger, and at that moment the image turned deep red, which she knew was the color of rage or hatred. Then she heard the shot, the same one that she had heard before, as she was rounding the corner. Al-Kondoz fell to the ground, gun in hand, and then the older woman appeared with a gun that was still smoking.

As this woman entered the scene, the color of the image in Sandy's mind turned from red to light blue: the color of devotion and love. Then the images suddenly changed again and Sandy's mind was transported to another place and time. She was back at the beach, and could see Tony Mascelle in the distance. He was firing at a helicopter. Sandy had seen some of these images before, that day on Fire Island with Sean McKeown and Bob Crowley. Now she knew who they came from.

Sandy came back to the present and gestured toward Joe Mascelle. "Is my partner okay?"

The woman replied, "He's going to have a nasty headache when he wakes up, maybe a concussion, but he'll live. First the gymnastics on the fire escape the other day, and now this. He's getting careless in his old age. Let this guy sneak right up behind him. Could have been much, much worse."

Sandy said, "You've been a very busy lady - since you left

Miami. First Fire Island, and now this."

The woman gave Sandy a puzzled look. "How did you know?"

"Long story." Sandy said. "Turn around."

The woman did as she was told. Sandy unlocked and removed the cuffs. "I need you out there. I can't keep an eye on all of these guys by myself."

Sandy handed the glass vial back to her. "Here, you may need this."

The woman responded with a surprised look and then a genuine, "Thank you."

Sandy shrugged, turned, and knelt down next to Joe. She used her penlight to check his pupils, and then she checked his pulse. She finished and placed her hand gently on Joe's hand.

"No, thank you," Sandy said. "I never would have forgiven myself if anything had happened to him."

"Me neither," The woman said as she watched Sandy looking at Joe. The woman hesitated for a moment and then said, "He's happily married, honey; you understand that, right?"

"Yes," Sandy said nodding. "I know."

Chapter 70

The plane was descending on its approach to Milan's international airport. Mario smiled and said to me. "See? You do get it! You are the great-great-great-great, etcetera, etcetera, grandson of Sebastiano, the Great Knight of Malta who saved Europe from slavery over four hundred years ago. Your last name, Mascelle, is derived from his name of legend, Mascelle Del Leone—which means Jaws of the Lion, which is another long story about that first battle on Rhodes that I just mentioned. But let's discuss that some other time. So, my job, and Marcella's job until recently, was to keep that promise made to him over four hundred years ago."

I sat there for a while trying to digest it. This couldn't possibly be true. *I mean... how the hell*?

"Pretty unbelievable, isn't it?" he said.

I nodded. "Why would you, Marcella, or anybody, risk your lives to save mine, because of some four-hundred-year-old promise made thousands of miles away?"

"It's my job. I was taken out of an orphanage, like many of us are, and I swore an oath to do this job, to protect you. I was trained from the time I was twelve to do it."

"Who trained you, and who pays for all of this?"

"Well, ultimately, the Vatican does."

"You mean you work for the Pope, and he sends you around killing people to keep me alive?"

"Well, no, actually. I said the Vatican. The Pope has no idea that we even exist. You see, the Vatican is thousands of years old. It's like a really big, really old house, and it has this huge attic, sort-of, that contains all kinds of old junk that a pope, who is only around for a few years, never really sees or hears about. But we're up there, with all of the other old junk, and just continue to do what we do. Nice to know that some of the money you put in the collection plate on Sundays does you some good, doesn't it?"

"I don't go to church."

"Yeah, I know; maybe we need to talk about that."

"Not now. Continue."

"Right. So I guess you want to know what's going on with all these weirdoes who are trying to kill you. Right?"

"Right, let's talk about the weirdoes." *Starting with you.*

"Okay, so here it gets a little complicated, and maybe a little confusing."

"Try me."

"Alright, here we go. So we have this order, sub-order really, called the Brotherhood of the Knights of Malta, and, as I said, our job is to protect you guys from being killed."

"Right. Your job is to keep me from dying. I got it."

"No, no, everyone dies. Heart attacks, cancer, car accidents... that's not in our job description. Our job is to keep you from being killed by someone, from being murdered. Hey, that can be hard enough, believe me."

"Okay, so you are supposed to keep me and my family from being killed, right?"

"No, we don't protect sisters, moms, or aunts: just you, your dad, uncles, grandpa, etcetera. The deal was to keep only his sons safe. You know, back in the old days, it was all about sons, sons, sons. Daughters didn't matter too much."

"Yeah, right, the good old days. So you're supposed to protect me from whom? Who would want to kill me?"

"Whoever, it doesn't matter. We just keep you from dying—I

mean, being killed - by anyone who wants you dead. Understand?"

"Oh, yeah, of course."

"Sounds hard to believe, I know. There is a saying: 'Fact is stranger than fiction'... or something like that."

"Yeah, I've heard of it. So let's get back to where we started. Why is someone trying to kill me?"

"Well, that all started simply enough. Pretty mundane, actually. You are, or were, the CEO of that little company that went bankrupt recently. A few months ago, when things were really starting to look bad, your friends Mr. CFO Kyle and Ms. COO Jan, get an idea about how to solve the company's money problems." He went on to tell me the same story about the hit men that Marcella did, but in more detail. He concluded, "Then Kyle and Jan take a nice, long, expensive vacation, and when they come back, they give themselves a big raise, and then save the company, and everyone is happy—except you, because you're dead."

I shook my head, partially in disbelief and partially in disgust.

He continued. "Someone who works with us caught the change on the insurance documents and thought it was a little strange, especially when Jan forged your signature on them. Hey, did you know that it only cost five thousand dollars more per year in premiums to go from a one million dollar insurance policy to ten million?"

"I had no idea."

"Well, anyway, when we looked into it, we found out that they hired this guy to kill you. He was an idiot, so tracking him down was easy. Then they hired this other guy, or so we thought, and he was a real pro. Tracking him was harder, but we did, and we stopped him too."

"You mean that dead guy across the street from my office, the one that started all of this?"

"Right. We stopped him just as he was going to put a bullet through some part of your body—maybe your head, probably your heart—head is usually better, but sometimes it can be a hard shot to make, you know."

"Yeah, I can see how that might be a problem. So you killed this guy that morning?"

"No, not me. Marcella."

"Marcella killed him?"

He nodded. "When she went out that morning."

I thought about that. "You mean when she was going to get the donuts?"

"Yeah, but she was actually making a donut—in the back of this guy's head." He let out a little chuckle. "Sorry, that was not a good thing to say." Then he made the sign of the cross three times.

"What did you just do there?"

"What?"

"The crossing thing?"

"It's a sin to kill."

"Really?"

"Except, not in the service of the Vatican, well, not really. It is, but then they give you a dispensation, a pass, but you have to follow certain rules. If you don't, you go to hell."

"They give you a get-out-of-hell pass?"

"Yeah, like that, but they really get mad if you start to enjoy it."

"Yes, that would be bad."

"It would be a sin," he replied with complete seriousness.

"I guess you've got to have principles, if you work for the Vatican."

He gave me a strange look. "So, as I was saying, this guy got close, but Marcella got him first. She was very good, you know."

"Yes, I know. I saw her in action on Fire Island. So, what happened to Kyle and Jan?"

"Well, they were a verifiable threat to you, so, you know."

"You mean Marcella killed them too?"

"No, no, that was my job. She was too busy with you on Fire Island."

"Right, she was busy." I stopped and thought about this. So, I was sitting three inches away from a guy who killed two of my business associates. I thought I should feel guilty, or angry, or something. But this whole story was either part of the bad dream I just had—and if so, I would wake up and finish that drink sitting on the tray in front of me—or this story was just insane enough to be the truth. I reached over and picked up the empty cup. No, it was definitively not a dream. In that case, screw them both. I had a suspicion they were up to something, although I didn't think either of them had the balls, or whatever, to kill me for insurance money.

I said. "Okay, so the—what do you call him, hit-man?"

"That's so passé. Shooter is good: simple and to the point."

"Okay, so Marcella kills the shooter across the street, and you kill Kyle and Jan."

"No."

"I thought you said you killed them."

"No, I said it was my job, but someone got to Kyle first."

My head was starting to hurt again. I looked at him, waiting for an explanation, but he just smiled.

"So who killed him?" I asked.

"You know, those guys, the ones you... met on the beach?"

"If those cretins were trying to kill me, why did they kill Kyle and Marcella, and then leave me breathing?"

"Well, that's the reason I needed to talk to you. You see, sometimes these things take on a life of their own. They just get out of control, and when they do they can get pretty messy. Like that thing with your dad a few years ago."

"You were involved with that?"

"Of course. You remember me from Stony Brook, don't you?"

"Were you the guy who saved his life?"

"No, that was someone else." He smiled again.

"I hope the Vatican gave whoever it was a promotion, or an extra ration of red meat, or something."

Mario laughed. "Red meat! You're a funny guy. Actually, they were very unhappy. You see, your dad almost died, and the Brotherhood really doesn't like it when one of you guys gets holes in you. But, on the other hand, they did keep your dad alive long enough for him to make it to the hospital."

I thought about this and said, "And then, while he was recovering, you were told to watch me at school, right?"

"Yes."

"Was I in any danger?"

"No, not that we knew of, but better safe than sorry. So they gave me the job to watch you while the rest of the team cleaned up the mess."

"You mean all of the killings that took place in the following months, the ones that everyone thought were reprisals from cops, were actually your people?"

"Some, not all. There were some reprisals from your dad's and uncle's friends, and some of the bad guys got panicky and started killing each other. That's sort of how we work. We get the ball rolling, spread some rumors, and the rest usually takes care of itself."

"Except in my case now, right?"

"Right. Unfortunately, we opened, as you would say, a very big can of worms: two big cans, actually. The first one is with a nasty little group from the Middle East. They were sent by Mr. Saddam Hussein. Those are the guys you and Marcella met on the beach, and the same guys that killed your business associate, Kyle. Also, the shooter across the street from your office was one of them too. The one we thought was hired by your business associates. We found out later that he was one of the Saddam guys too."

"Wait a minute. Saddam Hussein, as in Iraq?"

"The very same one."

"Why would he want to kill me?"

"He didn't want you; he wanted Marcella and me and the rest of the Brotherhood. You were just the bait. You see, they've been looking for us for a while, to settle an old score. When this thing with Kyle and Jan came up and we moved in and did our thing, they were able to track you and then, eventually, us."

"How?"

"We leave certain signs—calling cards, sort of—that are a little unusual."

"What kind of calling cards?"

"Well, we are very religious people, so we are required to administer the last rites to the people we... stop from killing you. It's part of the rules. So, they keep finding these bodies that have oil crosses on their heads, which is a pretty unique thing to find on someone, sometimes. So this comes up in an FBI or police report, and the bad guys get it somehow, and they hang around you until we show up. Then they start shooting."

"You administer the last rites to the people you kill? Hey, great idea."

"What can I say? We work for the Vatican. It's part of the rules."

"Yeah, I got that. So tell me: why does Saddam want to kill you?"

"Well, you remember that thing with President Bush in 1993? After he left office, someone tried to kill him when he was in Kuwait?"

I remembered a little about the incident. I remember they eventually tracked it back to Saddam. He wanted to kill Bush out of revenge for the Gulf War. When they found out, Clinton tried to send a few guided missiles up Saddam's ass. "Yes I remember."

"Well, we stopped him from doing that."

"You stopped who from doing what?"

"We stopped Saddam from killing Bush."

"Why? Is Bush a relative of mine?"

"No, but one of the guys in his secret service detail was: a distant relative you never heard of. He was part of the close protection team for the president and we were, in turn, part of his close protection team. Saddam's guys are not very subtle, so the job involved something very big and very loud. So, chances are, our guy, your relative, would be one of the people who ended up dead along with the president, assuming Saddam's guys succeeded in pulling it off."

"So you saved the president's bodyguard and accidentally saved the president too?"

"Yeah, basically, but we had another reason; we really wanted to save the president as well."

"Why?"

"Well, let's just say we thought that saving the president's life would be a good thing. Evening up an old score, you might say."

"I don't understand."

"That's okay. You don't want to know. Even if I told you, you wouldn't believe me."

"Oh right, you're going to tell me something more unbelievable than the bullshit you just told me?"

"Trust me, this would really blow your mind. Anyway, back to the main event here. So these guys are using you to smoke us out and kill us, and so your investigation into Marcella's death and disappearance is not a good thing right now. Besides, you now know who shot her and why, and I can also tell you who took her away from that little beach house."

"You did?"

"No, not me personally. Someone that was part of the team sent to protect you, when we finally figured out what we had on our hands. We came a little late for Marcella, unfortunately, but she kept you alive long enough for us to figure it out. And then, by the time we showed up, you and that big horse finished off the rest of them." He smiled. "That was a beautiful thing, with the machete. I'm really sorry I missed that. You know, Sebastiano would be very proud of you. You definitely have his warrior side in your blood."

"Great, thanks. So, now what?"

"We lay low for a little while until we sort things out."

"What about the other, second can of worms you mentioned?"

"Oh, yes, that. Well, you've met Mr. Barella?"

"Yeah," I said with a face and tone indicating how I felt about Agent Barella.

"Well, we don't like him too much either. He is a federal agent on special assignment. He's been after us for a very long time. He doesn't know exactly who we are, but he's collected enough clues over the years to have a pretty good picture. So he's after us, and he's also using you to smoke us out."

"Why?"

"Basically for the same reason Saddam and company are. He has an old score to settle with us and he wants us out of business. But that, as they say, is another story."

We spent the rest of the flight talking about my ancestors and my guardian killer-angels, the Brotherhood. Mario—no last name, just Mario—also gave me a quick education about Sebastiano and Basilah, the Sultan's daughter and Sebastiano's lover. He told me about Sebastiano's family in Sciacca, my ancestors, and Ghazawan 'the great and terrible', his son by Basilah. Ghazawan was apparently in severe need of some professional counseling, because he definitely had some daddy issues, to say nothing of some anger management problems. But, instead, Sebastiano had to kill him to save Malta and Europe. I guess that's what passed as anger management therapy back then.

He also told me about the group that Saddam had hired to

wipe out the Brotherhood. They're called the Assassins. These guys were the real thing, too: in fact, the original thing, when it came to killing for hire.

Mario concluded this story by saying. "It's a miracle you survived on Fire Island."

"It would have been a better miracle if Marcella survived also," I replied.

Mario stared into empty space. It was the first time that he wasn't wearing a silly looking smirk. Then he turned, looked at me and nodded, his smile reappearing. This one was warm, even kind of normal, for a professional killer. "Did you love her?" He asked.

"Yes," I said without hesitation. "I think I loved her for a while, but the conditions were not right. I should have..." My words trailed off with my thoughts.

"You still do? Even though you know who she is, and what she did?"

"Yes." In fact, I realized that in some strange way I loved her more when I discovered what she was. I didn't know the whole story then, and probably still don't, but I knew she would lay down her life for me, and I was more than willing to do the same for her. "I wish she were here talking to you, instead of me," I said.

"She would not have liked that outcome. She did her job, and you're safe."

"Is that all it was? Just doing her job?"

"I'll tell you a little secret. It started out that way. It is, in fact, forbidden for members of the Brotherhood to become personally involved with those we protect. But, she did love you and she told me so: not in so many words, but I knew. We were working on reassigning her when all of this stuff started to happen. By that time, we thought moving her would be too risky for you."

"I wish you had reassigned her. She would still be alive."

"You would be happy, even if you never saw her again?"

"Yes. But you know what? I would have found her."

Mario replied. "Perhaps."

The pilot came on the speaker, announcing our final approach into Malpensa International Airport. Seat backs and tray tables went up. Mario and I stopped talking and stared at the seats and heads in front of us.

The plane touched down and, as we came to a stop, I asked Mario, "So what do I do now?"

"Like I said, we need to lay low for a while, you do the same, either at home or here in Italy."

"I've never been to Italy before. I wouldn't know where or how to lay low."

"Well, I just happen to know some people that could provide you with a tour guide. Someone who could take you around, show you the sights: places and things the tourists never get to see. They could even show you where your family came from in Sicily, and where your great ancestor made history on Rhodes and Malta."

"I thought you wanted to avoid me, and the two cans of worms following me."

"That's true, but no matter what, we still have to protect you. And it would probably be easier to do that here, on our home turf. Besides, it would not be me. We would find someone unsuspected by Barella, or Saddam's guys."

I said, "I'll think about it."

We left the plane and walked towards the customs area. I got in the line with the sign that said "non-EU members" and Mario went to the EU member's line and stood next to me. I asked him, "Suppose I decide to stay and take you up on your offer for a tour guide; how do I get in touch with you, or whoever?"

Mario laughed. "Tony, we have been in touch with you since the day you were born. Don't worry, if you stick around, someone will show up."

We both arrived at a yellow line painted on the floor and waited for our turn to approach the customs officers. The woman in the booth waved Mario over, but before he left he held out his hand towards me. "Well, it's been a pleasure speaking with you, old friend."

I took his hand and shook it. "Yes, and thank you, for saving my life, and my father's life, and all the way back to—whenever."

At that point his posture changed instantly and alarmingly from the casual, slumped-over Euro-trash mode to something very different. He snapped upright and to attention. The smile disappeared, and even his voice changed. He said, "It has been my honor and privilege to protect your life with my life." Then he bowed gracefully, turned, and walked to the customs agent's window. After finishing his document check-in he started walking away. I watched him fade into the distance as I continued to stand at the yellow line waiting for the large group in front of me to finish being processed. Then Mario suddenly turned and called back to me.

"Tony, I didn't write that note."

"What?"

"And I never said she was dead."

I started to walk towards him. "You mean Marcella?"

Suddenly there was shouting, and three armed customs officers approached me and stood in my path. I stopped and watched Mario. He smiled and gave me a little wave.

Then he was gone.

Chapter 71

I picked up my luggage at the baggage carousel and followed the pictograph-laden signs towards what I hoped was the ground transportation area. My appearance on the sidewalk, in front of the terminal, drew the immediate interest of a half-dozen men, who suddenly began converging on my position. A man with salt-and-pepper hair and small, blue, piercing eyes, led the pack.

"Hello, mister. You need taxi?"

"Yes."

"Where you go? Milano?"

"Yes." I reached into my computer case, pulled out my itinerary and showed the man the name and address of my hotel. "You know it?"

"Yes, sure."

"How much?"

"Oh, long drive, but I give you good price."

I shrugged. "Okay, let's go." The rest of the drivers retreated and began pursuing other disorientated travelers, or disappointed, returned to their cars, newspapers and coffees.

He grabbed my bags and lifted them with two large hands, which were attached to shoulders that would have qualified him to be a lineman for the Green Bay Packers.

"They have wheels," I said as I rushed to follow him out to an old, black, banged-up Mercedes. He threw my bags into the filthy trunk and then unlocked and opened my door.

"You say something?" He asked me with a polite smile.

I shrugged. "Never mind."

"Good car, yes?"

"Oh, yes. Great car."

We exited the airport and entered the lane that led to the Autostrada. He drove cautiously, and slowly. I noticed the cars in the other lanes swerving to avoid us, as apoplectic drivers delivered creative hand gestures, as they passed by.

I said, "I heard that people drive very fast in Italy."

"Me drive good, no?"

"Oh, yes, you're exceptional."

"You mind if me smoke?" He asked just as he was lighting up.

I guess not.

"You American?"

"Yes." I cracked the window open.

It was obvious, even to me, that this guy did not have an Italian accent. But, just to be polite, I asked him if he was Italian.

"No, me Polish."

I usually like to talk to cab drivers back home, but I wasn't really in the mood to get chatty with this one, not after that surreal conversation on the plane, and that move that Mario pulled at customs.

"How long have you been in Italy?" I asked.

"Come from Poland, one month."

"Is that so?"

He volunteered the fact that he was a mechanic, and that he came from some town near Krakow called Rib-nick, or Rub-neck, or something.

"You come Italy before?"

"No, it's my first time."

"You come business or pleasure?"

"Both."

"You speak Italian?" he asked.

Geez, this was going to be a long cab ride. "No. How's your Italian?"

"No speak Italian, but English okay, yes?"

"Yes, your English is very good." I lied.

Well, I was feeling right at home. New York cab drivers come from everywhere, except New York, so it was kind of comforting to hear the foreign accent coming from the front seat. In fact, I can't remember ever riding in a cab in New York, or anywhere else, that was driven by an American-sounding guy. Wouldn't that be weird?

I sat back and watched the countryside roll by, as Mario's words kept replaying in my mind: *I never said she was dead.* But did that mean she was alive? Or, was he just screwing with me?

"Where in America you come from?"

"Huh? Oh, from New York."

"Wow, New York. Great city."

Well, I had Marcella's note. It was in her handwriting. It said she loved me and that I was to meet her at a castle called Pavone. I did some research, and sure enough, there was a castle by that name about an hour and a half west of Milan. But was that an invitation from her, from Mario, from the Brotherhood, from all of the above—or maybe from someone else?

The driver was still talking.

"Great, biggest, best in world. The city that never sleep."

"You've been there?" I asked.

"No, no, I see in movie. But maybe someday. Hard to get visa to America. I ask many time, but America say no."

Well, that was his first mistake: asking. I thought about telling him that he should just sneak in without a visa, and then everything would be okay.

"You know, many Polish people in America," he said.

"Yes?"

"Oh, yes, many, many."

"I think I know some Polish people in America," I said.

So, I have this meeting on an airplane, get a family history lesson and a second invitation to hang around in Italy—this one from my new old friend Mario.

The driver was still talking. "Yes. Many in America, and Germany, Italy, England—we Polish people everywhere."

"That's nice."

Apparently, Mario and Company wanted me to stick around, but why? He said I was being used as bait to lure the Brotherhood out by both Barella and the Saddam guys—the Assassins—and that would be bad. So why would they want me to hang around?

"That's why Europe people don't like us."

"What?"

"Europe people don't like us. You know, Bulgarians, Romanians, Czechs, Hungarians, French... "

Maybe the Brotherhood, if there is such a thing, wanted to use me for bait also. *Now there's a twist.*

"What?" I asked. "Why don't they like Polish people?"

"Because we Polish people everywhere."

"They don't like you because you're everywhere?"

"Yes, don't like."

"I don't understand."

"We are many. Work hard. Work cheap." He smiled.

I felt as if I were being played, like a rook in someone's game of chess. I didn't like being used, and I didn't like being bait for Barella, the Brotherhood, or anyone else, for that matter. But if there was a chance that Marcella was alive...

"Fuck 'em," I said aloud.

The driver laughed. "Yes, fuck them if they no can take joke. They just mad they not Polish people too. My name Stanislav, nice meet you."

"My name is Tony. It's nice to meet you too, Stanislav."

For the rest of the trip we spoke about European politics, the weather, Italian politics, his favorite restaurants, Polish politics, car repair techniques and American movies. Boy, could this guy talk. By the time he dropped me at my hotel, the cab fare was about a billion lira, which, after lopping off a few dozen zeros, translated into about fifty bucks. He said it was usually about seventy. So I gave Stanislav a big tip. I think. He thanked me and handed me a receipt and his business card.

"Hey Tony, you need car, you call me, okay?"

I took the card and looked at it. The only thing I could read was the number at the bottom. I nodded. "Okay, if I need you, I'll call you."

Chapter 72

The Hotel Milano was small, and everything else seemed to match: small lobby, small reception desk, and small people. There was marble everywhere: floors, walls, and tabletops. Along the walls were glass enclosed displays of Roman artifacts and busts of various Caesars, some of whom I could identify - and statues of naked women - most of whom I couldn't. The combined effect made me feel like I was in one of my aunts' bathrooms.

The man behind the desk wore a black suit and a white shirt that was open at the collar. His name tag read "Luciano". He looked at me, stole a glance at the Band-Aid on my head, and raised an eyebrow. Then with a smirk, he said, "Buon giorno, signore."

"Hello. My name is Tony Mascelle."

Luciano asked me if I was checking in and I told him I was. Then he asked me how my flight from America was. I said it was fine and then asked him how he knew where I was from.

His smirk became a smile. "Lucky guess."

Funny guy.

He made a few keystrokes on an ancient-looking computer and asked me for my passport, which I gave him.

"I will keep this; you may pick it up later. Yes?"

"Okay."

He handed me a key with a solid brass, bell-shaped object attached to it that had a worn number 37 stamped on it. I held it in my hand; it must have weighed five pounds. I was trying to figure out how I was going to fit this thing into my pocket and walk around town without my pants falling to my knees, when Luciano, anticipating my next question, interrupted my thoughts.

"You leave the key at the desk when you leave the room."

I looked at him and nodded, but did not say anything.

"Not like in America," he said, making a motion with his hand as if he was sliding a card in a slot. "Here we do this." He motioned as though he was turning a key in a lock.

I smiled and nodded again. He pointed to the elevator.

The linen closet–sized elevator rattled up two floors. I made a mental note to speak with my travel agent. I remembered telling her that I wanted a four-star hotel, and if this place qualified, they must be working on a ten-star system.

The room was, well, small, and with a small bed, naturally. I began wondering how I was going to fit into it without hurting something and suddenly started to miss that shitty old couch in my office. On the upside, the room was nicely furnished with lots of marble on the floor, walls and pretty much everywhere in the bathroom. The tub was equipped with a showerhead oddly positioned in the middle of the back wall, rather than at one end, and there was no shower door - or even a curtain - for that matter. I guess that explained the shower drain located in the middle of the bathroom floor. At one end of the tub, a thin line that went from the rim to a lever on the wall, suspended a large red tab.

I was examining this odd fixture, and wondering what it was, when the phone rang. I picked it up.

"Hello?"

"Hello Mr. Mascelle."

There was static on the line, so I did not recognize the voice at first. I did after the next sentence, however.

"I thought you had no plans to leave the country? Mr. Mascelle." the voice said.

"How did you find me, Agent Barella?"

"We have our ways."

"That sounds like a line from a B-movie."

"Doesn't matter what it sounds like, Mr. Mascelle; why did you leave the country when you said you weren't going to?"

"That was some time ago, and I didn't have any plans then."

"You still should have told me that you were leaving; why did you leave?" He repeated.

"I thought someone should try to investigate this case, given the fact that no one else seems to be."

"It is not safe or appropriate for you to be playing detective, or secret agent, Mr. Mascelle. You should return home, at once."

"Why? Do you have some authority over me that I should know about?"

"Mr. Mascelle, this whole situation will be a lot easier on you if you give me your full cooperation, and at the moment you don't sound very cooperative."

"Exactly what situation are you talking about? Everyone seems to have fallen asleep on this case, at least the last time I checked. No one even bothered to return my calls."

"You didn't call me."

"Okay, so now that I have you on the phone, what have you discovered about the death and disappearance of my... employee, Marcella Pavone?"

"We've made substantial progress in the case, but I can't share the details with you at this time."

"Sounds like bullshit to me. I think I know more about this case than you and Detective McKeown combined." I was immediately sorry I said that. For some reason, I keep doing that with this guy.

"Oh really, Mr. Mascelle? Tell me what you know and how you know it."

"I'm a private citizen, Agent Barella; I don't answer to the NYPD, the FBI, the CIA, or whatever fucking agency you work for. If you want information, I suggest you get off your ass and start getting it, and stop calling me Mr. Mascelle; it's Tony. Or better yet, just stop calling me."

He started to say something, but I hung up the phone. After a few moments, the phone rang again. I ignored it and went into the bathroom to take a shower.

The lack of sleep and the jet lag were starting to catch up with me. I was still struggling to process all of the new information from Mario, and now Barella was on my case—literally. The jerk had found me almost as soon as I arrived at my hotel. I'm sure he intended to make the impression on me that he was the all-knowing and all-seeing government agent and that he wasn't to be screwed with. I should have told him that Mario had found me first, just to piss him off.

In fact, I now had to assume that everyone probably knew I was here, and that they all wanted to talk to me, follow me, or kill me, depending on whose side they were on. I wasn't sure how they found me so fast, but I had a hunch.

After the shower, I got dressed and went down to the front desk, heaved my room key onto it, and then rang the bell for the attendant. Luciano appeared, smiled and said, "Buon giorno. There is a message for you; it's urgent."

He handed me an envelope along with my passport and I put them both in my bag.

"So why did you need my passport?" I asked.

"Interpol."

"Who?"

"Interpol is the police in Europe, like the FBI. We take everyone's passport, and we enter the numbers so Interpol knows where you are."

Well, there was the answer to the question about how Barella found me. He probably found out that I had left, and where I was going, as soon as I showed my passport for check-in at the airport in New York. Then he simply waited for me to check into my hotel, and his friends at Interpol did the rest.

"I see. All hotels do this?" I asked.

"Almost. Some no, like youth hostels and private rooming, but almost all."

"I need a cell phone. Can you tell me where I can find a store that will sell me one?"

"Of course. Go out, make right, and go three blocks. Across the street you will see a T-Mobile store."

"Thank you."

Thanks to Barella's thoughtful call, I already knew what the urgent message was, so I left the envelope unopened in my bag. I walked across the street and bought the phone with cash. The guy behind the counter was happy to take my greenbacks, although I think he screwed me on the exchange rate. I had credit cards, and I even had my own cell phone with me, and it was the type of phone that would work in Europe as well as at home. But I thought it might save me a few bucks on phone calls if I purchased a local one—or at least that's what I would tell anyone who asked. Actually, I was more interested in making it a little more challenging for my new friends at Interpol, my old friend Mr. Barella, and whoever he worked for, to track my whereabouts. They obviously had already zeroed in on my hotel, were probably working on a tap for the phone in my room, and were possibly also trying to track the cell phone that I brought with me from New York. But since I wasn't ready to enjoy an extended, possibly handcuffed, visit with either Barella or an Interpol cop, I turned off and removed the battery from my old phone, and stashed it in my jacket pocket.

In addition to a new cell phone, I needed a new location, and I needed to stay off the grid as much as possible. Maybe I was being paranoid, but I doubted it. I found an ATM machine across the street from my hotel and withdrew enough cash to hold me over for a few days. *Damn, I knew that guy screwed me on the exchange rate*!

Interpol would see that transaction, but since they already knew where I was, it didn't matter very much. Besides, I wasn't planning on sticking around much longer, anyway. I pulled Stanislav's card out and dialed the number.

Someone answered with a grunt.

"Hello, Stanislav?"

"Yes, I Stanislav."

"Hi, this is Tony, the guy you drove from the airport this morning. You gave me your card."

"Oh, yes, from New York."

"Yes. Look, I need to drive around a couple of days and I thought you could help."

"Yes, I help."

"How much?"

"Oh, for you, two hundred, American, for day."

I hesitated.

He continued, "Including tip, but you pay fuel. Okay?"

"Yes, okay, I'll pay for fuel and two hundred for you at the end of each day. Agreed?"

He agreed. I told him to meet me at the corner near the T-Mobile shop. He arrived in less than five minutes with a big smile and a cigarette hanging between his lips. I got into the back seat.

"Where we go?" he asked.

"About seventy miles west of here, there is an old castle called Pavone. It's near a town called Ivrea. Ever hear of it?"

"Ivrea, no. But I have map."

"Its north of Turin," I said.

He studied his map. "Ah, here, Ivrea. Okay, we go."

"Okay."

"Now?" he asked.

"Yes, let's go."

"You no go hotel to get?" He made a hand gesture as if holding something.

"My luggage? No, we can stop somewhere on the way and I'll pick up some clothes and stuff."

He looked at me in the rear view mirror for a moment. "Okay, we go now Pavone."

I watched the city go by as we snaked through the streets of Milan towards the A4 autostrada, the main highway that runs west towards Turin. Milan was a mix of beautiful old buildings with intricately carved stone, but everything was covered with soot and endless tracks of graffiti, and the streets and sidewalks were strewn with garbage. The graffiti was everywhere a person could reach with a marker or a can of spray paint, and some places where they couldn't. It was in the same style and scale of the stuff I remember seeing as a kid in the worst parts of Harlem or the Bronx. Fortunately, most of this crap was gone from cities in the States by now. Not so here. I felt a little embarrassed by the thought that here was an example of our cultural gift to the World. Italy gives us Da Vinci, Michelangelo, and the Sistine Chapel, and we give them graffiti, grunge, and rap music in return. What a deal.

"You like city?" Stanislav asked.

"No, not really." Okay, maybe I was a little cranky. But I was still on New York time, which meant that as far as my brain was concerned, it was about seven in the morning. And, as I might have mentioned, I'm not a big morning person. Besides, I was running on only about four hours of restless sleep and had a long, and no doubt exciting, day ahead of me.

"No? Milano famous city. Biggest in Italy. Good clothes buy here."

"Terrific. Look, I need to get some sleep, so wake me up when we get close to Ivrea, okay?"

"Okay, me shut up, you sleep."

"Thanks."

I put my head back and that was the last thing I remembered until I heard Stanislav's voice again.

"Hey, Tony, you wake up now."

I sat up and looked around. We were out of the city and in the country somewhere. "Yes, I'm awake, are we there yet?"

"No, about fifty minute to Ivrea."

"So, we're halfway there?"

"Yes, halfway."

"Why are you waking me up?"

"There, see." Stanislav made a gesture toward the rear window.

I turned and looked. The road was empty, except for a gray car, about three hundred yards back. "So?"

"I think he follows us," Stanislav said.

"Why do you think that?"

He shrugged. "I think so."

It occurred to me, that maybe, Stanislav was watching too many American spy movies.

He asked, "Hey, you want for me to lose him?"

He was definitely watching too many spy movies. "Lose him?"

"Yes, you know, like in spy movie," he said as he made hand gestures indicating a car racing away at high speed and motor sounds with his lips.

"No!"

"You sure."

"Yes, I'm sure."

"Hey, you in some trouble or something?"

"No. Why do you say that?"

"You no get luggage at hotel, and you check in morning but not stay at hotel at night. Little strange."

"I'm not in trouble; I just have an urgent meeting."

"Okay, you say so."

I did not think that Stanislav believed my explanation, but he kept driving. He also kept looking back at the gray car. When I check again, ten minutes had passed, and it was still back there at the same distance.

Stanislav said, "Car still there."

"Maybe he's just going to Ivrea like we are."

"Maybe."

"Okay, if you're so nervous about it, get off at the next exit and see what he does."

"And if me right and he follows?"

"Then you lose him," I said, making the same hand gestures and the motor sound with my lips that he did. I actually considered the idea of Stanislav losing the car ridiculous. Assuming we were being followed in the first place, the only thing grandpa could possibly lose was a moped, and I wasn't even sure about that.

Stanislav smiled and said, "Okay, deal."

He drove another few miles on the Autostrada and then exited onto a two-lane country road surrounded by farmland. We were heading southwest and, according to the road signs, towards a town called Santhia. I looked back, and the gray car was gone.

"See, he's not there," I said.

"Okay, maybe me wrong, we see."

He kept driving on the road, which took us through town and then back onto a second rural road heading toward a town called Cigliano. There was little else around except for an occasional farmhouse and some strange-looking Italian cows grazing along the highway. There wasn't another car in sight.

After twenty minutes of this, I started dozing off again.

"Hey, Tony, you look," Stanislav said.

Startled, I turned around and saw what appeared to be the same gray car about a half-mile away and closing fast. "You think that's the same car?" I asked.

"Yes, me think so." Just as he said this, I felt the car lurch forward and watched his face, through the rear view mirror, as it was transformed from a placid expression into that of a man on a mission—a spy mission. *God help me.*

"What are you doing?" I yelled over the whine of the car's engine and Stanislav slammed the shift into fifth gear.

"You know; me lose him."

"We don't even know if that's the same car."

"Do now," he said.

I looked back at the gray car and, even at this speed, it was clearly still closing on us.

"Oh, shit."

Chapter 73

Stanislav had the gas pedal on the floor. I don't know how fast we were going, but even the stupid-looking Italian cows, grazing along the highway, were in full retreat. Well, most of them were.

"Hey! Watch out for that cow!" I yelled at Stanislav, as I dug my hands into the seat cushion, searching for the seat belt that I prayed was in there somewhere.

"No cow. Buffalo. They use, make Italian cheese."

The reassuring sound of the click, and the feeling of the belt pressing against my chest, allowed me to start breathing again.

"What?"

"You know, mozzarella, ricotta... Italian cheese."

Oh great! I was worried about being creamed, and this idiot was giving me a culinary lesson on Italian dairy products. "Just watch out for the things with the hooves, whatever the hell they are."

The highway passed in a blur of green and gray until it merged into a city road. When he reached the intersection, Stanislav slammed on the brakes, took a hard right turn, and then an immediate, screeching left. We drove another mile or so until we discovered that the road was a dead end. I turned to look for the gray car, at about the same time Stanislav put the car into a spin.

At first, I thought he had lost control, and that we were soon to become a twisted steel pretzel with a mushy red filling. But as I watched him make small rapid corrections to the wheel, brake, and gas pedal, it became clear that he was in complete control. He expertly swung the rear of the car around so that for a moment, we were going in reverse, and then he slammed on the gas pedal again and we lurched forward, moving head-on for the gray sedan. Stanislav drove directly into its path and, just as we were about to collide, both cars swerved out of each other's way. As we passed, the driver of the gray car lost control. He fishtailed, and then plowed into the window of a small shop.

Stanislav did not look back, but he did smile when he heard the crash. Then he sped off in the direction of the Autostrada.

"I thought you said you were an auto mechanic."

"Yes, me mechanic."

"You learned to drive like that in a Polish repair shop?"

I didn't need a little voice in my head to figure out that Stanislav was full of shit.

"Me drive cars better than me fix cars."

"Remind me not to let you fix my car."

He laughed and shrugged his shoulders. "Me good driver, no? Not like that guy," he said, waving his thumb backwards.

We got back onto the A4, headed north towards Ivrea, and then exited at Pavone Canavese.

"Okay, where we go now?" Stanislav asked.

"Head towards the center of town and you'll see it." Actually, I had no idea if we would see anything. My research indicated that the Castle Pavone, like most castles, I guess, sat on top of a big hill in the middle of the town. The area around the town looked mostly like flat farmland. So, chances are, we should be able to see this thing as we got closer.

Sure enough, about five minutes later, off in the distance, the castle came into view. It was perched on top of a very steep, rocky promontory, and it looked like the real thing, towers and all. The problem was trying to find the road to get to it. We snaked around the streets of the town until we finally discovered a small sign that directed us toward the castle. A very narrow road led to a long, steep driveway and then to a gravel parking lot. Stanislav parked the car close to what appeared to be the castle's entrance.

"We park here in case we need to leave fast. I stay in car. You go, and if you hear horn, you come back fast. Okay?"

"Okay." I nodded.

I left the car and walked across the parking lot towards the brooding citadel. There was a long, wooden ramp running along the front of the castle wall that appeared to lead toward an entrance of some kind. Weeds were growing through the boards of the walkway and high along it on each side, so I could not actually see where the thing was leading me.

At the end, I found a massive wooden door that was badly weathered to a dark gray color. It was inset into a stone passage about three feet wide and barely over six feet high. The passage opening was framed with brick mixed with a reddish-brown stone. A large, rusty padlock on the door's heavy deadbolt indicated that they were apparently not expecting visitors. In fact, it looked like the place had been abandoned a long time ago.

I banged on the door. I wasn't expecting someone to answer but, having come all this way, I thought I should at least make the effort so I wouldn't feel stupid on the flight back home. There was no response. I banged again. This time, I heard a loud, metallic click and the door began to open slowly. The interesting thing was that the padlock and dead bolt never moved. They were apparently just props placed there for visual effect.

After my eyes adjusted to the dim light inside, I noticed that the low passage was empty and continued about fifteen or twenty feet to a second door. This one, like the last, was also massive and made of wood, but it was recently stained and set in a frame of stone that was painted white.

"Hello?" I said into the void as I approached. I received a reply in the form of crackling static that echoed in the chamber.

Then a thickly accented voice, which came from no apparent source said, "Hello, how may I help you?"

I walked closer and could see a small speaker and a surveillance camera mounted in the space above and to the right of the second door. I looked into the lens of the camera and said, "My name is Tony Mascelle, and I'm here to meet a friend."

There was no reply, except for the sound of the first door, now behind me, closing. I turned and was about to run for it, but I hesitated for just a moment too long. The chamber became much darker and would have been completely black were it not for the single, small bulb mounted on the wall to my left. A surge of primeval panic caused my heart to beat faster, at the thought of being trapped in this masonry tomb. However, no sooner did the door behind me close, than the door in front begin to open with a clang and plaintive moan.

On the other side of the open portal was a courtyard that was surrounded by high stone walls and towers, and was transected by a brick path. In front of me, a section of the wall was only waist-high, revealing a beautiful vista of the valley below. I followed the brick path, which curved to the right as it proceeded downhill and around a bend to an alcove with tall glass windows. As I approached for a closer look, the center glass panel slid open. I walked through the entrance into a large room.

There was a long desk, the type you find at expensive, old hotels. Behind it stood a man dressed in black. He smiled as I approached, but it did not seem like a very friendly smile.

His slicked-back, widow's-peaked hair was as black as his clothing, and I noticed a long, narrow scar along his left jaw-line that appeared to be faded with age. He focused on me with deeply set brown eyes. Then, with a deep, monotone voice said, "Good afternoon, sir." His voice was thickly accented, and if I didn't know better, this guy could have just come off the set of a Bela Lugosi film. *Creepy.*

I could not tell the origin of the accent, but I knew it wasn't Italian, and I hoped it wasn't from Transylvania.

I looked for a name tag, but found none. So, I said to Vlad, "I'm here to meet a woman. Her name is Marcella Pavone."

He smiled, bowed his head slightly, and directed me towards a room to my left.

The windowless room was illuminated by a few naked bulbs hanging from the ceiling, providing just enough light to accent its cavern-like shape, structure and size. The room was comprised entirely of rough red brick: floors, walls and even the ceiling were made of the same stuff, which undulated off into the distance in a series of arches. About fifty feet from the entrance, I noticed a single, small desk positioned under one of the light bulbs. A man sat at the desk reading a newspaper, and across from him was an empty chair. I could not make out his features in the dim light. I started to walk towards him.

"Hello," I said. "My name is Tony Mascelle, and I'm looking for Marcella Pavone."

I listened to my voice echo off the walls and ceilings as the figure just sat there motionless, and in silence.

"Hello?" I repeated. Still no answer.

As I came closer his features became recognizable, and I finally received a response.

"I thought you said she was dead, Tony."

The New York accent was as unmistakable as the plump, red, Irish face.

"Oh, shit," I said to myself, unfortunately a little too loudly. I flinched at the sound of my words echoing in the chamber.

McKeown glared at me. "That's no way to greet an old friend," he purred, almost to himself, as he kneaded his right eyebrow between two fingers. Then he said, a little louder, "You're not sorry to see me again, are you, Tony?"

"No, that's... I mean, I was just surprised. This seems to be happening to me a lot today."

"What does that mean?"

"It means that I'm surprised to see you, Detective," I said, trying to be pleasant. "Who expects to see an Irish cop from the Lower East Side sitting alone and reading a newspaper in an Italian tomb, inside a castle, outside of Turin... How did you find me?"

"You left that message with your uncle."

"But I was boarding the airplane when I left it. How did you get here before I did?"

"I don't know. I was wondering what took you so long. I was on the next flight out and I came here directly from the airport." McKeown yawned. "God, I'm beat. Can't sleep on airplanes, and I can't even find a decent cup of coffee around here. Look at this."

He picked up a saucer and held it under the light for me to see. On the saucer sat an empty espresso cup along with two very small cookies.

"There wasn't enough coffee in there for a New York–sized mouse." He complained pointing to the miniature cup. "And what are these? Tic Tacs?" He asked rhetorically gesturing to the tiny cookies. Then he picked up the newspaper in front of him and waved it at me. "And you see this? It was the only thing in English. It cost me four bucks." He was holding the European version of the *Wall Street Journal*. "There's about six pages in it, no sports section, no comics, no obituaries. How do people live here?"

I smiled and shrugged.

McKeown stopped his ranting, put the newspaper down and leaned back in his chair. He pointed with his chin to the chair on the other side of the desk, and then folded his arms across his chest as I sat down. He said, "So, Tony, you didn't answer my question."

"Which one?"

"The one about Marcella being dead. Is she, or isn't she?"

Changing the subject, I asked "What kind of place is this?"

"It's some kind of exclusive hotel, or retreat, for businessmen, I think. Based on what they charged me for the mini-coffee with the Tic-Tacs, it's *very* exclusive. I can't wait until the chief sees my expense report. He's going to go ballistic. Again." McKeown caught himself and then looked sternly at me. "Stop trying to change the subject and answer the question."

I thought for a moment and answered honestly, "I don't know. I thought she was dead, but now I'm not sure."

"I don't understand."

"I'm not sure I do, either. It's a very complex story."

McKeown smiled. "That's okay, I like complex stories. So tell me about it."

"Why? I'm a private citizen. I don't have an obligation to report to you or anyone else at the NYPD, the FBI, or any other badge, for that matter."

Was I really having this same conversation again, or was it déjà vu? What I really needed was some sleep, and to make matters worse the wound in my shoulder was starting to ache, and the one on my head was throbbing for the first time since I left the hospital.

"Tony? Are you still with me?"

"Yeah."

"As I was saying, that may be technically true. But you're still a suspect, so the exchange of information could be helpful to both of us."

"Oh, bullshit, Detective! Don't try to pull that crap with me. I'm no more a suspect in this mess than you are."

"Well, actually, that's not quite true." McKeown said sympathetically, ignoring my terse response. "According to the facts, to say nothing of Agent Barella, you are most definitely a suspect, my friend."

"On what basis?"

"Tony, are you kidding me? Two of your employees, Jan Toomey and Kyle Orr, are dead: murdered. Another one, Marcella Pavone, is missing and presumed dead. We know you were the last one to see the last two, and possibly all three, alive. This is not to mention the pile of bodies left lying around on Fire Island, and the shooter across the street from your office that started this whole mess. And then, if all that is not sufficient to raise suspicion, you leave the country very suddenly after a federal agent specifically tells you not to. So, yes, you are very much a suspect."

"Barella is full of shit. He never told me not to leave. He asked me if I had plans to leave and, at the time, I didn't. So I told him the truth."

"It didn't occur to you to notify someone about your plans before you left, especially since you knew that this investigation was still underway?"

"I left that message with my uncle. Besides, I had no indication that there was an investigation still underway. I tried calling you several times, and your office kept giving me some lame excuse about you not being available, and you never returned my calls. So, I naturally concluded that you had moved on to something else and didn't want to be bothered."

McKeown shifted uncomfortably in his chair. "Moved on? This case has been a full-time job for me, and then some. When did you try to reach me?"

"Several times while I was in the hospital, and then again after I left. Why?"

"Do you remember who you spoke with?" McKeown asked.

"No, and I didn't ask. I assumed he worked for you."

McKeown kneaded his eyebrow and thought about this. "Interesting."

"Why is that interesting?" I asked.

"Never mind that. I need to know what you know and I need to know it now."

I told him about the letter and how I found it. But, I decided not to tell him about Mario, a.k.a. Crazy Nunzio. I just assumed that would make me more of a suspect than I apparently already was.

He said, "We need to get back to New York before Barella tracks you down. If he arrests you here, there's nothing your uncle or I can do about it."

"He called me, you know."

"Who, Barella?"

I nodded.

"When?"

"He called my hotel this morning. I wasn't there more than five minutes before the phone rang."

"He must have gotten the information from Interpol,"

McKeown said. “He knew your location as soon as you registered at the front desk with your passport.”

“Yeah, I figured that out. That’s pretty Orwellian, don't you think?”

“Hey, you’re one of those techno guys, right?”

I nodded.

“Ain’t technology great?” McKeown said in a sarcastic tone. “So what else do you know about this case, Tony?”

I turned the question around on him. “How about if you tell me what you and Barella know. You said you were working on it; what have you learned, Detective?”

“You’re changing the subject again, Tony.”

“Yes I am. If you want to get, you need to give. I gave you some information, now it’s your turn.”

I think I heard that line in a detective movie once and I was wondering if it was going to work, when McKeown smiled and said to me, “You haven’t given me anything yet.” Then he sat up. “Okay, I’ll go first, but it’s kind of a complex story.”

I said, “That’s okay, I like complex stories.”

“Are you going to listen, or what, wise guy?”

Chapter 74

McKeown said to me, "For starters, let's get something straight about me and Agent Barella. We are not, and never have been, working together. That first day we spoke with you in your office was the second time I met the man. The first time was two days prior. And what I'm going to tell you is as much about my investigation into Mr. Barella, as it is about this entire case."

"Wait, I don't understand. You're not working with Barella on this? You're investigating him? When did he become a suspect?"

"He's not... not exactly."

McKeown explained the mysterious and sudden appearance of Barella the Saturday before they both came to see me. He also told me about Barella's mysterious powers with the mayor's office and how he managed to get himself assigned as the primary investigator.

"From the moment this guy became lead investigator, I, along with everyone in my precinct, was shut out." McKeown said. "I complained about it to my boss, but when he tried to push it up the chain, he was told to go away. So he told me officially to lay-off, but unofficially he told me to crawl up this guy's ass with a magnifying glass and a blowtorch."

I did not even attempt to process that image. I said, "Sounds like the usual inter-agency rivalry that you read about in the papers. Why are you telling me about this?"

"Believe me Tony, there's nothing usual about this guy or this case. Local cops and feds don't get along; that's true and it has always been true. But I'm talking about something very different here. This guy has an agenda, and it's personal as much as professional. Despite his cold, objective, Fed-like exterior, inside this guy is a raging bull. If I can figure who the target of his rage is and why, I'll probably figure out what this case is about." McKeown stared at me during an unnaturally long pause.

"You mean, me?" I asked.

"Not exactly. He's not after you, but he thinks he can find what he's looking for through you, or more correctly, through your family."

"How do you know that?"

"I'll tell you how. Do you remember that thing with your father, that shooting a few years ago? Well, I had a hunch and we checked some of the records. Turns out that Barella requested and received copies of all the files. Almost as soon as your father arrived at the hospital, Barella was all over that case. He probably never set foot in New York, but secretly he started investigating the case from his perch in DC. And another thing: this guy is not with the FBI, like he led me to believe."

"So what are you going to tell me next, Detective? He's with the CIA?"

McKeown responded to my little taunt with a smile that made me feel uncomfortable. "Nope, but we'll get to them next. Barella is with the Secret Service, and the Service is interested in only three things: counterfeiting, fraud, and executive security. Guess which division Barella belongs to? I'll give you a hint: it's not the counterfeiting or the fraud divisions."

I was tempted to inquire about the CIA thing, but instead I asked, "Why would a guy who is supposed to be protecting the president get involved with this?"

"Exactly. But that, as they say, is just the tip of the iceberg. The more I dig, the stranger it gets, and I'm digging up stuff that I know is somehow related, but I can't put the pieces together, not yet anyway."

"How strange?"

"For example, your friend Billy Hoffenburg. As you already know, he's not a park ranger. Well, it turns out that *he* worked for the CIA."

"Billy worked for the CIA? This is some sort of joke, right?"

"Nope. He was originally with the ATF, and stationed in Dallas, up until about six months ago when the CIA recruited him."

I was getting lost in Fed acronym hell, and I guess McKeown could tell by the look on my face, so he said. "ATF stands for Alcohol, Tobacco, and Firearms."

"Sounds like a Texas frat party."

McKeown ignored me and continued. "According to your company's employment records, you hired Marcella Pavone about seven months ago. Is that correct, Tony?"

How did they get my employment records? "Yes."

"Well, just so happens that's right around the same time the CIA hired your friend Bill."

"So?"

McKeown said, "So, let's look at the big picture now. We have a friend of yours who's trying to pass himself off as a park ranger, but he happens to be a spook from Langley. And he just happens to be hired by the CIA around the same time you hired Marcella, who's trying to pass herself off as your personal assistant. But she happens to be—what? A bodyguard? Another spook? And where is she from? Then the two of them just happen to show up on your ferry ride to Fire Island. Coincidence? I don't think so."

I said, "So where are you going with this, Detective? Do you think Marcella and Bill were working together? You think she was working for the CIA, too?"

"I'm not saying yes, and I'm not saying no. But as you well know, she sure could handle a gun like someone who was."

I commented, "The more facts you give me, the less clear the picture becomes."

McKeown pinched his eyebrow again, "Yeah, ain't it great? And I'm just warming up. Now we come to the fun part, the part with Barella pretending to be an FBI agent. According to the official government records, he is no longer employed by any government agency, including the Secret Service."

By this time, I was getting really confused, but McKeown was on a roll, so I held my questions. Actually, I couldn't think of an intelligent one to ask.

"But wait," he said, "it gets stranger still, because Barella's last official assignment with the Secret Service was a very long time ago when he worked for a secret division within the Secret Service that is specifically assigned the task of what they refer to as fault analysis."

"Sounds like the name of a quality control department in a tech company." I said, half-jokingly.

"Well, that pretty much describes it. He was, and as I just recently found out, still is part of quality control. His job is to figure out what works and what doesn't, and how to fix things when they break."

"I don't get it. Why would this department and his employment there be a secret?"

"I asked myself the same question. At first I thought that it might have something to do with the Washington mindset. You know, if you don't make mistakes, how can you officially recognize an entity designed to fix them? Then we managed to get hold of some information that I think answers that question. This guy's last official case, before he supposedly left the Service, began in 1963."

He looked at me as if this information somehow clarified the subject. I guess it was obvious, again, that I had no idea what he was talking about.

"The Kennedy assassination, Tony."

"This guy is still investigating that? You must be kidding. Talk about milking an assignment."

McKeown laughed. "Yeah, it would seem so. Especially for a case that was supposed to have been solved and officially closed a very long time ago. But it explains why he's off the official record. As long as the investigation was being conducted by an entity that really doesn't exist, and by someone who really doesn't work there, no one starts to ask embarrassing questions like why is the Secret Service is still officially investigating a case that was closed more than thirty years ago."

McKeown stopped talking as we both listened to the glass entrance door slide open and then close. We looked in the direction of the sound. A figure, approaching us from the entrance, stared back at us.

"Barella's job," McKeown continued, "was, and is, to review and analyze the Service's performance, focusing on the successes and failures—especially the failures—and then write reports about how to improve the Service. Isn't that right, Agent Barella?"

"Specifically, my job is to improve the Service's ability to protect the president," Barella said. "I'm impressed with your detective work, Detective."

McKeown gave a deadpan response. "Thanks."

Barella turned to me. "Why, Mr. Mascelle, you look surprised to see me."

"Not at all." I replied. "The way my day is going, I expect my mother to walk through that door any minute now."

Barella processed that for a moment, smiled momentarily, and then informed us. "The most infamous and most studied failure in Secret Service history was the 1963 assassination of President John Fitzgerald Kennedy. I spent most of my career studying that case. The few insiders who know of my work have, on occasion, claimed that I also became a little too, well, obsessed with it."

"Is that the same thing as being called a crackpot?" McKeown inquired.

I laughed. Barella didn't.

"Maybe." Barella replied. "Nobody really wanted to hear what I had to say, and calling someone a crackpot is a quick and easy way to silence them."

"So what were you saying that nobody wanted to hear?"

"What everyone said they wanted to know—who didn't kill JFK."

"You mean, like Oswald?" McKeown asked.

Barella nodded.

I said. "My uncle's Labrador Retriever could have figured that out. Nobody believes Oswald killed Kennedy."

Barella gave me a stern look. "Some people do: the people who need to believe it. And the ones who don't, believe the other story—the one *they're* supposed to believe—that the Mafia and the CIA killed him. From Washington's perspective, it didn't matter which lie you believed, so long as you never got hold of the truth. They sold the Oswald story to the public and then, when people started to shoot enough holes in it, they built a new story inside the old one. We were the ones who floated the story about the CIA and the Mafia conspiracy."

"How did the CIA feel about that?" McKeown inquired.

"They were okay with it. In fact, it was their idea."

"Why would the CIA want to be blamed for a presidential

assassination?" I asked.

"They didn't, really. They simply wanted to obfuscate the truth, like everyone else did. Because the truth, or what we thought was the truth at the time, would have had some very unfortunate consequences."

"Obfuscate the truth?" McKeown said wryly. "Like you've been doing for the past two weeks? Like you're doing with this fantastic story you're telling us now?"

"I did that for your own safety, Detective. And Mr. Mascelle's safety, as well."

"What does that mean?" I asked.

Barella took a deep breath. "We'll get to that next. Where was I?"

I said. "Something about the CIA taking the blame for Kennedy's assassination. What in hell would motivate them to do that?"

Barella asked, "Did you ever hear of Operation Mongoose?"

I said nothing, but McKeown jumped to attention. "Yeah, isn't that the secret plan that the Kennedys hatched to use Mafia hit men to kill Castro?"

"That's the one, and they almost pulled it off. Operation Mongoose became public knowledge in the mid-seventies, but at the time of the earliest investigations, immediately following the assassination, it was top secret. When the CIA finally told us about it, we concluded, as they did, that Castro killed JFK in retribution. In addition, there was lots of other evidence that pointed to Cuba."

"So why the bullshit cover stories?" I asked.

"Well, young man, you have to understand the world at that time: you know, before you were born."

"Okay, so educate me, old guy."

"The short story goes something like this. It's April 1961, less than three months after Kennedy was sworn in, and he gives the green light for the Bay of Pigs invasion. Do you know anything about the Bay of Pigs, Mr. Mascelle?"

"Yes, Agent Barella, it's the one where the exiled Cubans tried to topple Castro, right?"

"Correct," Barella replied. "Unfortunately, in the middle of the operation, Kennedy loses his nerve and bails out on the Cuban exiles, who were still trying to get a foothold on the beach. The invasion was a complete disaster. Score: Castro one, Kennedy zero."

McKeown suddenly looked over Barella's shoulder. I followed his gaze and saw Vlad, the desk attendant, standing directly behind Barella. He was holding something large in his hands, but it was difficult to see what it was in the dim light, and with Barella's body in the way.

The Count said, "Would you care for a chair?"

Barella appeared to be a little startled, but he regained his composure, nodded, and took the folding chair from the man. Then he waited for the guy to leave. After an uncomfortably long pause, Vlad made a slow and solemn bow, turned, and walked back into the shadows from which he came.

"Creepy," Barella said.

I said, "Seems like a nice guy to me."

McKeown said, "Bay of Pigs."

"Right. So, as a result of that disaster, Khrushchev naturally concludes that Kennedy didn't have any balls, which he declared to the world by building the Berlin Wall four months later. Of course, Kennedy figures this out pretty fast, actually commenting to a New York Times reporter, after meeting Khrushchev in

Vienna, that he might have a credibility problem with the Soviets. No shit, Sherlock. He also told the same reporter that he had a plan to regain it - by sticking one in Khrushchev's face. The plan? Triple the number of American troops in the Soviets' backyard—a place called Vietnam—and he triples them again a few months later. This buildup continues until, by the end of Kennedy's presidency; our military engagement in Vietnam was completely transformed. We went from about 100 military advisers to 16,000 combat troops, we began the Agent Orange program of defoliation, the American public was treated to their first shocking look at Buddhist Monks immolating themselves, and we began a program of American-supported political overthrows and assassinations that would eventually mutate into the Phoenix Program that claimed more than 24,000 victims. Kennedy started with South Vietnam's President Diem, and his brother, who were assassinated just weeks before Kennedy."

Barella unfolded the chair and set it down on the floor. "Well, boys will be boys, so this little game goes on, tit-for-tat, for the next year or so. In the meantime, Operation Mongoose, under the direct supervision of Bobby Kennedy, goes into overdrive. You would think that killing a dictator trapped on a Caribbean island a mere 90 miles from Miami would have been a relatively easy task for a joint CIA and Mafia operation. In fact, it should have been a turkey-shoot. But no, it turns into a real-life parody of *The Gang That Couldn't Shoot Straight.* These idiots tried everything from poisoned fish to exploding cigars, and they missed him every time. As a result of all of this, Castro, somewhat understandably, becomes a little paranoid. So he invites the Soviets in and, for good measure, encourages them to bring in troops and place nuclear missiles in Cuba as a deterrent to a second American-sponsored, or led, invasion. Khrushchev figures that if Kennedy can put American combat forces in his backyard, in Vietnam, then why not return the favor - in Cuba? So Khrushchev happily obliges."

Barella slipped off his suit jacket and hung it on the back of the chair, treating us to the sight of a large, shiny handgun in his shoulder holster.

"Unfortunately, as a result of a collection of miscalculations, this friendly little game of nuclear chicken nearly spirals out of control, which brings us to the Cuban Missile Crisis in October 1962, the event that very nearly ended everything and everyone. Fortunately, through another series of mistakes and miscalculations, Kennedy manages, by sheer, dumb luck, to avoid this confrontation with the Soviets, which we now all know, brought us within minutes of a full-blown nuclear exchange and World War III."

Barella loosened his tie, and sat down. "After that crisis is over, the Kennedy PR machine goes into overdrive, and he is hailed as a modern day Solomon, domestically and internationally, for avoiding nuclear Armageddon. No one in the media, of course, mentions that the original cause of the missile crisis, to say nothing of the looming disaster of the decade-long Vietnam War, was due to Kennedy's screw-up at the Bay of Pigs. However, Castro and the Soviets remembered. So, as a result of the negotiations with the Soviets to end the missile crisis, and to avoid a future nuclear Armageddon, we, the United States of America, promise never, ever, to mess around with Cuba again. Score? Castro two, Kennedy zero."

McKeown said, "Sounds like a pretty lopsided game. Can't wait to hear what happens next."

"Well, that should have been the end of it," Barella said, "but, as everyone knows, the Kennedy brothers hated to lose. So, that arrogant bastard, along with his vicious-prick of a brother, Bobby, continue with their private little game of whack-the-dictator. This new operation is called AMWORLD."

"Never heard of that." McKeown commented.

"No, you wouldn't have. But you will. Someday. AMWORLD turned out to be not so little, or so private. Millions were spent on everything from retraining and equipping another invasion force of exiles, to stepping up the assassination or overthrow of Castro. The scale of this operation made Mongoose look like a pilot study. There are still four or five million pages of classified documents that have been withheld from at least five Congressional investigations into the Kennedy assassination."

I commented, "Five million pages? I hope you're planning to summarize."

"You know, Mr. Mascelle," Barella sneered, "you may think you're a comedian, but I don't find you very funny."

"Not everyone does."

McKeown chuckled. "Shut-up Tony, and let the man speak. This is pretty interesting stuff."

Barella continued. "So this new plan, AMWORLD, is the same as the old plan, but on steroids. The project kicks-off in June of 63, about seven months after JFK promised Khrushchev that he would not do this stuff anymore, and was supposed to go into operation on December 1st of the same year. But, JFK is killed less than two weeks before, and Bobby finds himself suddenly unemployed. Score? Castro three, Kennedy, a big fat zero."

The three of us sat in silence for a moment, contemplating the death of a president.

"By the time we figured all of this out, we were struck with two immediate emotions. First, was the unspoken satisfaction that Kennedy, that son of a bitch, got what he had coming."

I blurted out, "What! Are you kidding me? You're a member of the Secret Service, and you were happy with a president getting assassinated?"

"I didn't say happy, Mr. Mascelle! But the bottom line is that the idiot made a promise as the President of the United States to leave Cuba alone, and then broke it because of a personal vendetta, as if he was some sort of Mafia don. And in so doing, he risked putting the whole country, in fact the entire planet, in mortal danger of nuclear annihilation—a second time. The other emotion was the sheer horror at the thought of what would happen if this information were ever released to the public. Kennedy became almost a god in the months after his death. The Solomon simile was replaced with the King Arthur and Camelot myth. So we knew that if we told the American public what we believed at the time—that Castro was behind the assassination—they would have demanded an invasion of Cuba. Then we would be right back to where we were in the Cuban Missile Crisis: the US and the Soviets, face-to-face, over a nuclear chasm."

McKeown nodded.

"So, the CIA, along with the rest of us, concluded that this would be bad, and that there was no way we were going to let that happen. Again. We constructed the story within a story: the one where the CIA and the Mafia were responsible. In the final analysis, we didn't care who got the blame, so long as it wasn't who we actually thought it was: Castro. We hoped that by the time the truth came out, if ever, nobody would care, because Castro would be an old man or dead, and Cuba would have already been invaded by millions of American tourists armed with sunglasses, sandals, and tons of American greenbacks."

McKeown commented, "Are you telling me that with all of the Kennedy worshipers, in all of the branches of government, nobody in their various circles had access to this information, or were able to figure out that Castro was the perp? That doesn't seem too plausible to me."

"I didn't say that, did I, Detective? In fact, we are quite certain that at least some of the fine, upstanding members of that clan, and their friends in the media, came to the exact same conclusion that we did, and probably even had some of the same hard evidence that we had to prove it. Nonetheless, they have been very helpful in keeping the Castro story secret all of these years."

"But after all of this time, with the Soviet Union gone, why would they still keep it a secret?" I asked.

"Simple, really. Ask yourself this question: if you're a close relative or friend of a former President of the United States who was assassinated, and you and other members of your clan were terminally ambitious politicians who liked to use that badge of honor for your personal, social, and political gain, would you want history to remember JFK as a King Arthur who was cut down in his prime by a single, crazy assassin, or would you prefer, instead, a lengthy investigation that would make information available that portrayed JFK as an incompetent, vindictive prick who nearly brought nuclear disaster to his country and the world—twice?"

"Good point," McKeown said.

"Oh, please!" I responded. "The entire country seems to be under the impression that Kennedy was one of the greatest presidents in American history, and you want me to believe your portrait of him and his administration as some sort of Willy Wonka and the shit-head factory? Why? Who's your favorite president? Calvin Coolidge, or was it Eisenhower?"

I think I must have struck a nerve, because Barella's nostrils flared and his jaw muscles tensed, then he looked at me in a very unpleasant way. I wasn't sure if I should duck or take a shower.

He said, "Eisenhower was the president in fact that the Kennedy-worshippers claim JFK was in fiction. It would almost be funny if it wasn't so goddamn tragic. The American people replaced Eisenhower, a man who had more domestic and international experience as a soldier, and a leader, and a statesman, in his pinky, than the entire Kennedy clan had in the sum of all of their bodies. Eisenhower was a West Point–trained leader, and a disciplined soldier who had honor and courage. He was the victorious supreme allied commander in the worst war in human history, and he won it by holding together the most delicate and complex alliance ever conceived. As president, he built the most sophisticated and technologically advanced ground, air, and intelligence defense capabilities in the history of the world, and at the same time maintained the most prosperous economy America has ever known. And if that's not enough, he drove more advances in civil rights than any president since Lincoln."

To tell you the truth, I knew less about Eisenhower then I did about Barella thirty minutes ago, which is to say almost nothing. I was simply trying to find one of Agent Barella's buttons to push, and I guess I succeeded. Now, I was beginning to think that it may not have been a very good idea.

He continued. "Because Eisenhower was too busy doing the job and not bragging about it, like those idiots from Harvard Yard, people thought he was just coasting along like some clueless old man. But it was the American public that was clueless, especially when they replaced him with a man who wasn't fit to shine his shoes, to say nothing of wearing them. And we live with the legacy of that electoral disaster to this day."

Boy, I thought I was bitter.

Barella informed us. "Before JFK, a presidential election was tantamount to a public executive interview. Only serious people with serious resumés would even consider applying for the job. Then Kennedy comes along and turns it into a Hollywood beauty contest. It's not about the resumé anymore, it's about the bullshit. And you know what, the American public still doesn't get it, because they've been doing the same thing ever since. The clown that just left the Oval Office was hailed as the next Kennedy. And they were right! They replaced a war hero: the former head of the CIA, a former vice president, and the same man that led us to victory in Iraq in less than a week – in the greatest victory since Henry the Fifth at Agincourt."

I interrupted him. "You mean the guy who, after 100 hours of kicking Saddam's ass, told everyone to take a nap, and then pack their bags for home? That's what you call competence and balls? So, now, someday, someone may have to go back and finish the job he left undone, right?" I was also tempted to raise the subject of the current White House occupant, Bush's spawn, who just stole a national election - but Barella's face was already turning a dangerous color of red, and I didn't want to be responsible for him having a heart attack – or committing manslaughter, especially if I was the victim. But, despite my comment and his crimson complexion, he barely skipped a beat.

"And what did they elect then, Mr. Mascelle? That clueless bumpkin from Arkansas, a national embarrassment who, like Kennedy, couldn't keep his pecker in his pocket. And when he wasn't getting a blow job from one of his interns, he was losing the launch codes for our nuclear arsenal."

McKeown and I both perked up when we heard that last comment. McKeown asked, "What was that about losing nuclear launch codes?"

Barella replied, "You've heard of the nuclear football?"

McKeown nodded. "Yes, that's the briefcase carried by a military officer who accompanies the president at all times. In the event of a nuclear war, the president uses it to order a nuclear counterstrike. Right?"

"Correct," Barella replied. "And there is also something called the biscuit, a small plastic card that contains the launch codes. The president is supposed to have it on his person at all times. Without it, no one, not even the President of the United States, can launch our missiles. No ticky, no shirty."

There was a long silence while Barella admired our teeth through our gaping jaws. Finally, I asked, "How long did he lose it for? I mean we're talking a few minutes; not hours or days, right?"

Barella replied, stoned-faced, "The idiot didn't even know the thing was missing until a military officer requested it so he could replace it with an updated one, containing the new codes. This is done every few months as a security measure. So, to answer your question, it was missing not for minutes, or hours, or days, but for weeks or months. The idiot could not even tell them, because he didn't have any idea. Think about that, the next time you lay your head down on a pillow, Mr. Mascelle. The launch codes for our entire nuclear arsenal were missing for weeks, or months. Not only couldn't the president use them, but someone else could have."

It occurred to me that Barella, or someone like him, was trained to protect the president with his life, even jumping in front of a gun and taking a bullet, if necessary. I wondered if Barella would have done that for Clinton. Frankly, I was wondering if anyone would have done it, if what he just told me was true.

Barella continued. "On Clinton's watch, the nut jobs in the Middle East came to the dangerous—but, based on this moron's performance - entirely rational conclusion that our country was ball-less. And it was on his watch that they started planning and implementing what we're seeing today. Bit by bit, year by year, they would hit us. Nothing like a gunshot wound to the heart, just death by a thousand cuts. In 1993 there was the bombing of the Twin Towers, and then Somalia in the same year; in 1995 there was the car bombing in Saudi Arabia; that was followed in 1996 by the Khobar Towers bombing; then our African embassies in 1998; and then the USS *Cole* in 2000. They were testing us, and we failed. They were building their nerve and sharpening their skills, and now we're just sitting here bleeding, too weak and confused to do anything about it, and waiting for the big one. The entire government has been bleeding talent for the past eight years. You can't see it yet, because it's internal bleeding. But you wait: one punch and we'll be coughing-up blood. Even the occasional rare, remaining example of competence and balls was rejected by these assholes, but you'll never hear about them until it's already over. Guys like the FBI's John O'Neill in New York, for example, who is the only person who seems to actually understand what the hell these madmen in Sand-land are up to—but he's been put on a shelf. Why? Because he's politically incorrect. Because he likes expensive suits; because, unlike his masters in Washington, he has balls."

I was about to ask Barella who the hell John O'Neill was, but the man was on a roll—or having a psychotic incident—so I felt it would be impolite to interrupt.

"You've heard about men with balls, right, Mr. Mascelle? You may have even read about them in the history books. You know who the heroes were when I was your age? Edmund Hillary, Charles Lindbergh, Chuck Yeager, and Neil Armstrong. These men literally risked their lives, exploring new frontiers and taking us to other planets. Who do you and this current pathetic generation have as heroes? Self-important geeks like Bill Gates, Steve Jobs, Mark Andresen, and Jeff Bezos? Little men, like you, with their little keyboards writing their little programs for their little computers so they can send each other a limitless number of useless little email messages while they listen to Boy George on their Walkman and sip on a Mocha Frappuccino. It's no wonder the assholes in the desert think they can wipe us out with a few well-placed explosive charges. They think this whole goddamn country has become a pathetic, empty shell, just waiting to implode on its own."

Boy George and Mocha Frappuccino? Actually, I was more of a café latte and Goo Goo Dolls man, but I didn't think Barella really cared, and if he did, I didn't think he would be very impressed. In any event, this guy was making my head hurt, and I was going to suggest that he go fuck himself. Then I remembered the loaded weapon he was carrying, so I tried a different tack.

"You're a Republican, aren't you?"

For some reason Agent Barella didn't seem to think that was very funny, but I did get a little chuckle out of McKeown. I continued, "So, politics and inane speeches aside, what the hell does this bullshit have to do with me? You're suggesting that all of this crap is somehow related to Castro killing Kennedy? Even if I believed that, which I don't, what's the connection with me and all the shit that's been happening over the past two weeks?"

McKeown commented, "I think we're about to hear the story-within-the-story-within-the-story that pulls this all together. Right, Agent Barella?"

"Right," Barella replied. "Where was I again?"

"Kennedy is dead, God is in his heaven, and all is right with the world," McKeown said.

"Correct. So, nothing bad happened, and for a long time things went very quiet. The conspiracy nuts turned the Kennedy assassination into a multi-billion dollar industry employing thousands of hard-working, tax-paying Americans. Kennedy continued to be remembered as one of the greatest men ever to walk the Earth, and we didn't invade Cuba, thereby avoiding World War III and nuclear Armageddon. And, naturally, my research and my crackpot theories, continued to be ignored. So everything was great, and we all almost forgot about the whole, goddamn, sorry mess. And then came April 1993 . . ."

Chapter 75

I looked at McKeown. *April 1993?*

McKeown just smiled and shrugged his shoulders. I think he was enjoying this.

Barella continued. "Do you remember the assassination attempt on former President George Bush in Kuwait?"

I sure did; heard all about it on the plane this morning. I gave Barella a blank stare. McKeown gave him an enthusiastic nod. *Teacher's pet.*

"Okay, so Bush is visiting Kuwait between April 14 and April 16, 1993, to commemorate the Allied victory in the Persian Gulf War. Accompanying Bush were his wife, two of his sons, the former Secretary of State James Baker, former Chief of Staff John Sununu, and Bush's former Treasury Secretary, Nicholas Brady. They complete the trip and everyone gets home safely. However, a week or two later we learn from our friends in Kuwait that they have arrested seventeen people suspected in a plot to kill Bush and his entire entourage. The plan involved using explosives hidden in a Toyota Land Cruiser, which contained about two hundred pounds of plastic explosives connected to a remote detonator."

McKeown asked. "How did they figure out it was Saddam?"

"I was part of the team that examined the components." Barella said. "When we compared them with other examples of Saddam's handiwork, it checked out: same methods and same materials. Then a group of FBI and CIA agents went over to Kuwait and spoke with the suspects. They got confessions from two of them. The plan was to locate the Land Cruiser on the route of the motorcade and detonate it remotely, as the president and his entourage passed. Simple and effective, but not too clean, creative, or specific. Then, on June 26, after representatives of the Secret Service, the FBI, the CIA, and others in the Department of

Justice discussed the results of the investigation with Clinton's people, he ordered the launch of twenty-three Tomahawk cruise missiles at a building in downtown Baghdad that housed the Iraqi Intelligence Service. Unfortunately, since the missiles were timed to strike at around 2:00 a.m., the only people we probably killed were a few janitors. That was our retaliation for the attempted assassination of the former President of the United States, most of his immediate family, and members of his former administration. Quick, easy, and ball-less. Vintage Clinton."

I informed Barella. "I guess if Bush took out Saddam when he had a chance, it wouldn't have been an issue. Would it?"

Barella responded to my insightful analysis with an angry stare.

He continued. "After that, as far as everyone in the White House was concerned, the matter was closed. But this is when my job really began. I had to figure out how close they got to succeeding in killing the former president, and a lot of other very important people with him. Most importantly, I needed to understand what went wrong—or right—to prevent it from happening in the first place. The most disturbing thing was that the Service, and everyone else involved in planning the visit and protecting the president, were completely clueless. We never would have even known about any of this were it not for the call from the Kuwaitis, and that came only long after the fact. This, as you can imagine, is not a good scenario, and as you can also imagine, there were a lot of red faces around the table. If they had pulled it off, it would have been a nightmare. And if that wasn't bad enough, it would have happened at the hands of an enemy, in a foreign land."

McKeown added, "Yeah, the whole Middle East would have been dancing in the streets and singing praises to Saddam."

"Exactly," Barella replied. "The blow to American prestige would have been incalculable. Saddam would have been transformed from a world-class loser, into a hero, on the Arab street overnight, and it would have opened the door to every nut-job and malcontent on the planet to follow suit. As far as we knew then, we escaped what would have been the worst attack on an American presidential delegation, and on American prestige, in history, but only by sheer, dumb luck."

As I listened to Barella tell the story, some of the pieces began to fall into place. "But it wasn't just luck, was it?" I asked.

"No it wasn't. It's taken me thirty-eight years to put all of the pieces together, and now I've finally got the last piece, and you're it, Mr. Mascelle. And I can tell by the look on your face you know exactly where I'm going with this, don't you?"

I didn't say anything. My mind was still trying to process this whole bizarre story. My dad, me, Marcella, Mario, the Brotherhood, and now, Bush and Kennedy. My head was starting to throb again, just trying to keep this puzzle together.

Barella continued. "When we started to look more closely into what almost happened in Kuwait, we started to find some very interesting links with 1963. For example, the Kuwaitis gave us access to two other conspirators—or rather, their remains. Both died of close-range shots to the head. Neither had any signs of normal ballistics, and they both had oily, red crosses on their heads. The poor Kuwaitis were really confused by that, since both of these guys were known to be Muslims."

"The disappearing bullets you told me about?" McKeown asked.

"Correct. We found only the ceramic powder that matched the chemical signature of the stuff we found in Kennedy's brain, or what was left of it."

"Didn't Kennedy's brain get lost, or something?" McKeown asked.

"Yeah, and as far as you know, it's lost, and it will never be found." Barella replied.

McKeown began to thoughtfully pinch his eyebrow between his fingers. "The magic bullet," he said to himself. Then he looked at Barella. "That description you gave me the other day, the one in my office about the long-range version of these things, how they can fragment, leave the first target and hit others nearby—you weren't speaking hypothetically, were you?"

"I'm afraid not."

"You were describing how that guy, governor what's-his-name, sitting in the front seat of Kennedy's limo, managed to get hit three times by the same bullet that hit JFK in the back."

"Yes, Texas Governor Connally and the magic bullet. It was magic all right, but it wasn't the one they found on the gurney. The real one hit Kennedy in the back, and fragmented into multiple pieces as it left his neck. Three of maybe six fragments hit the Governor: in his chest, his wrist and his thigh. The remaining fragments, including the three that hit him, then simply disappeared as seemingly innocuous dust. But we found microscopic remnants in all of the wounds, in the vehicle, even some on the street."

"So the bullet they recovered on Connally's hospital gurney *was* planted there."

"Yes, of course."

"Holy shit," McKeown whispered.

Barella nodded. "So, now we have these completely separate events, thirty years apart, involving the assassination or attempted assassination of a president, and they are linked by a very unique piece of evidence. Well, needless to say, we were scratching our heads, trying to figure out what the two had in common. Then, about five months after the Kuwait incident, that thing with your dad occurred, and it all became a little clearer," he said to me.

I sat up involuntarily as the final piece came together with an almost audible click in my head.

Barella nodded at me. "The guys that tried to kill your dad were killed with the same munitions. In addition, they had red, oily crosses painted on their foreheads that matched the ones on the two bodies in Kuwait. And there was one other connection, as it turns out." Barella pulled a small plastic box out of his pocket. He opened it, lifted a capsule-sized black object and held it up for us to see. "Remember I told you that there were several close attempts on Castro's life? Well, one of them was very close; in fact, we thought he was dead from a gunshot wound to the abdomen in '62. Somehow, he managed to survive long enough to make it to a hospital, after being driven fifty miles over dirt roads. We were at a loss to explain how he survived, until one of our people at the hospital discovered something that looked just like this. It was found in Castro's thigh. By the time we got it, we found just traces of its contents, but enough was left to analyze. It's derived from hydrogen sulfide and cobra venom."

I interrupted. "They shot him and then tried to poison him?"

"No, this is what saved his life—and your father's, by the way. It's a chemical that is designed to slow down a person's metabolism. It puts them into a sort of coma; buys an extra few hours of time to take someone who is critically wounded and get them help. It has a very unique chemical signature that matched a chemical signature that we found in your dad's blood."

McKeown interrupted my thoughts. "Maybe I'm stupid, but I still can't put this puzzle together." McKeown looked at me and asked. "Do you understand what he's talking about?"

I turned to McKeown and was about to explain to him that, apparently, I have a famous relative who lives in Cuba; the same man who's been running the place for the last forty years. But, at that moment, the chamber was filled with a deafening bang and I watched as McKeown fell backwards out of his chair.

Chapter 76

McKeown fell in what seemed like slow motion, his face contorted with pain, with a cloud of blood and tissue appearing on the wall behind him.

I broke my stare, ignored the ringing in my ears and searched for the source of the bullet's report. The masonry construction of the room seemed to form a perfect echo chamber causing the sound to come from everywhere, and nowhere.

Barella, who was in front of the desk a moment before, had disappeared. I started to look down to see if he was also hit, but just then, a hard tug on my collar dropped me to the floor behind the desk.

"Get down, Mr. Mascelle," Barella said as I hit the floor hard next to him. Apparently, at some point, Barella had managed to leap over the desk and found cover behind it. He released my collar and rolled over to check the pulse in McKeown's neck. Then he tore off McKeown's tie and shirt and began feeling his chest and abdomen. I watched Barella, thinking about what an amazing leap over the desk that must have been, especially for an old guy, when my thoughts were interrupted by Barella's bark. "Did you see the direction it came from? Hey, wake up, Mr. Mascelle! Did you see the shooter?"

I shook my head. Barella looked up from McKeown, who began moaning with each breath, and said, "He's alive, but if we don't get him some medical attention soon, we're going to lose him." He grabbed the gun from McKeown's waist holster and handed it to me. "If you're really the guy who took out the black pajamas on Fire Island, I don't need to tell you how to use this. Right?"

I nodded and took the gun. Barella then reached into his shirt pocket and pulled out a white, cylindrical capsule, about the size of a small thimble and, while squeezing it between his fingers, plunged it into McKeown's thigh.

"What's that?" I asked.

Barella said, "It's our version of their black capsule."

Just then, I heard a voice calling my name. "Hey Tony," the voice said. "Are you okay?"

"Stanislav, is that you?"

"Yes, I'm here."

I looked to see where the voice was coming from. I spotted Stanislav's head peeking out over a wall about fifty feet away. Barella got up and grabbed me. "Stay down," Barella said, just as I hear another loud bang. Barella fell back, taking me with him.

A pool of blood formed on Barella's white shirt, below his right shoulder.

"A friend of yours?" Barella asked with a wince.

"You're hit."

"Really? You must be a detective. Who is that guy?"

"He's my driver."

"Oh, your driver. Great. Where did you find him?"

"He found me, at the airport."

"Was that the one who was driving when we were following you?"

"That was you, in the gray car?" I asked.

Another shot, followed by a crack as the bullet passed just over my head, and then an explosion of dust and brick fragments as the round hit the wall a few feet behind me.

"Stay down," Barella croaked out. "Yes, that was me—us—in the gray car."

"Who's us?" I asked.

"Me and Agent Jackson."

I felt a momentary sense of relief. "So, we should be expecting the cavalry any second now, right?"

"We should," Barella said, trying to look at his watch. "I can't focus my eyes. What time is it?"

I looked at his watch and said, "About three-twenty."

"Well, I left Jackson watching the entrance. If he's not here in two minutes, it means he's not coming. Understand?"

"Yes. Then what?"

"Then we have a serious problem with your driver. He has us trapped like rats in here. Did you remember to tip him?" Barella inquired, letting out a weak laugh.

"Very funny." I said.

"Didn't it seem a little strange to you that a cab driver could handle a car like that?"

I noticed a wheezing sound in his voice now, and his eyes became glassy.

I replied "He said he was a mechanic."

Barella looked confused by my answer. On the other hand, he may have been going into shock.

I peeked over the desk to try to get a look at where Stanislav was and saw a movement near the wall where I had spotted him before. I looked down, Barella was unconscious and McKeown wasn't moaning any more, but his chest was moving slightly. I checked Barella's neck for a pulse. I didn't feel one, but since I had no idea what I was feeling for, it was not necessarily a problem. I placed my finger under his nose and felt for a breath. He was still breathing, but he was losing blood fast. There was a pool of it now, on the floor next to him.

I had to do something, but what? I looked over the top of the desk again, searching for an escape path. Just then, a bullet ricocheted off of the top of the desk, sending wood splinters into my face. "Shit!"

I put McKeown's pistol in my right hand and reached down with my left to grab Barella's. I aimed with one, in the direction of the last shot. I kept firing, in an arching pattern across the entire length of the wall until I emptied the clip. The brick and mortar on the wall erupted into a cloud of dust and fragments. As soon as the gun was empty, I threw it away and began to run toward the entrance while I fired with the second one. I reached a large square column about forty feet from the desk, about twenty feet from the exit, and took cover behind it. I was not sure how many rounds were left in the gun, probably two, three at most.

I waited and watched for movement until I finally saw a head pop up, Stanislav's head. He was behind the wall where I last saw him. This time, however, I was behind him. He was still looking at the desk where I was a moment ago. I took aim at the back of his head.

"Hey, Tony, stop shooting at me, and stay down." When he received no answer he asked, "Hey, you okay?"

I'm just great, you bastard, but you're not going to be, I said to myself, as I slowly squeezed the trigger. Just before the round went off I heard another shot coming from the distance. I saw the muzzle flash this time. It came from a dark corner in front of me and slightly to my left. The bullet hit the wall behind the desk where McKeown and Barella lay dying. Then Stanislav, who also saw the flash, aimed at the same corner with what appeared to be a military-style assault weapon. His gun roared to life in a near-continuous, deafening staccato. The corner exploded as Stanislav raked it with fire. Bricks shattered and pieces were flying out from the wall, with some dropping nearly whole from the ceiling.

Jesus!

Stanislav did not stop firing until his magazine was empty. A moment later, a figure dressed in black coveralls, staggered out from the shadows and dropped face-first onto the debris-covered floor.

Stanislav reloaded and then began to move quickly toward the fallen figure, but stayed low as he moved, keeping his aim on the body. He rolled the man onto his back, and checked for a pulse.

Then he yelled again towards my previous position behind the desk. "Hey, Tony, you okay?"

I replied this time. "I'm fine; how are you, Stanislav?"

I didn't need to say it very loudly, because by that time I was standing right behind him with my gun at the back of his head.

"Oh, there you are," he said calmly. "Hey, don't shoot me yet."

"So, besides being a car mechanic and a liar, who are you?" I asked.

"I never say me car mechanic. Me mechanic that fix other stuff, with that," he said as he pointed to the assault rifle on the floor next to him.

He reached into his pocket and I pressed the muzzle of the gun into the back of his head. "I would stop moving if I were you," I said, "unless you want to sample some of *my* mechanical skills. What's in your pocket?"

He froze. "They tell me you got good moves. They tell truth; I never see you get across room."

I repeated, "What's in the pocket?"

"I show you."

"Remove it very slowly unless you want to feel a draft in the middle of your brain."

He removed a small vial. I recognized what it was the moment I saw it, but I asked anyway. "What is that?"

"It is oil, for last rites. Okay? If you have to shoot, let me do this first; I don't want to go to hell." He slowly unscrewed the cap, placed his thumb over the open top, and tilted it. He then took his thumb and made a cross on the head of the man, who was by now leaking all over the floor from several wounds. Then Stanislav whispered a prayer and made the sign of the cross in the air over the body.

"You're with the Brotherhood?"

"Yes. Brother Mario asked me to keep eye on you."

"But, you're Polish."

He turned and looked at me like he was insulted. "Yeah? So is Pope. Like I say, we Polish people everywhere."

"That prayer didn't sound like it was Polish; it sounded Italian. You said you didn't speak Italian."

"I say prayer in Latin. What is matter with you, you not go to church or something? You should know stuff like this."

I knew it was Latin, but I was so relieved that I was not dead, at least at the moment, that I was getting a little giddy. Apparently, Stanislav was not getting the joke.

"My friends need help, or they're not going to make it," I said pointing towards the desk.

Stanislav got up and we walked to where Barella and McKeown were laying. He checked their vitals. "They both bad." He took a satchel out of his back pocket.

"What is that?" I asked. Just as I did I saw a small, black, pill-shaped cylinders roll out of the satchel into Stanislav's hand.

He said, "This special medicine, stop bleeding and make slow down body, how do you say? Like coma, so do not die so fast. Give more time to get help."

I heard a small, mechanical click as the needle sprung from the cylinder and delivered its contents directly into Barella's blood stream. "Same stuff saved you tata," Stanislav said.

"Saved my what?"

Stanislav thought a moment. "Poppa, father, da-da... you know, when he shot long time ago, you understand?"

I nodded with interest, because this was indeed interesting. Not so much the part about the strange medicine in the little black capsules, I already knew about that. But that Stanislav was giving me this information so freely. One minute I'm being treated like the proverbial mushroom; kept in the dark and fed a lot of shit, and the next minute I'm getting double doses of the bright, sunny truth—from completely independent sources, no less—and I had no idea why.

"This very old. Make from snake... what is word?" He made a face with teeth showing.

"It's made from snake venom?"

"Yes, some say so. Some say made from strange flower too. I do not know, it secret. But we carry at all time, mostly for us, if we get shot, we use." He said, making a gesture as if he were injecting himself with a needle into his neck. "We trained to do, then we go to deep sleep, then Brotherhood come get us and make us live again, maybe."

You inject yourself if you're wounded. Also interesting. I thought about Marcella lying on the floor in the kitchen that morning. *Was that what I saw falling out of her hand and rolling across the floor?*

"Or sometimes we use on other people, like now."

He went to place the end of a second cylinder against

McKeown's neck but I stopped him. I lifted the spent white capsule that lay on the floor next to Barella and held it in front of him. He gave me a puzzled look.

I said, "He doesn't need it, we already gave it to him."

I looked down, and Barella was already turning a gray color, the same color as McKeown and Marcella. "They look like they're dead," I said.

"Yes, it normal, but they dead only little while. We get help now or both dead forever." He got up, pulled out a cell phone, and I followed him outside.

Chapter 77

The police showed up first, followed by an ambulance a few minutes later. Stanislav walked over to the person who appeared to be in charge and showed him his credentials. I don't know what kind of credentials they were, but the cop's face had a strange combination of emotions – surprise, awe - but mostly confusion. *Hey pal, join the club.* Whatever they were, they worked, because after a few words with the cop and the EMTs, Stanislav turned and simply walked away.

He stared at me as he passed, apparently wondering why I was just standing there, and then gestured with a wag of his finger. I followed.

"I can't leave them," I said, motioning to where Barella and McKeown were being loaded into the ambulance.

"No reason you stay. They live or die, nothing you can do. In God's hands, not yours. Now you need to go somewhere safe or maybe you end up same as them. We think this place here safe for you. But we wrong. Something very bad is happening."

"What is this place? It's not really a hotel, is it?" I asked.

"No, no hotel, training place. Marcella, she trains here. Was very safe. But not safe now."

"How did you know I needed help in there?"

"Me not know. Me needed to go pee," He said, pointing between his legs.

"Really? Do you always bring an assault rifle to the men's room?"

"No. Me go to bush outside near parking lot, then me find dead guy in bush, so I think maybe me need gun and you need help. So I come."

"Dead guy?"

"Yes, he wear suit."

Barella was right, Agent Jackson wasn't coming. "Did you come in through the main entrance?"

"Yes."

"What happened to Vlad?"

"Who?"

"The guy at the front desk?"

"I no see nobody there."

I knew that creep was up to something. I said, "Stanislav, I came here to find Marcella. I need to know if she's alive, and if so, where she is."

He stopped walking suddenly and looked at me. "Wait here, very important you stay here."

I was wondering what that meant, when Stanislav walked over to a bush and took a leak. When he returned, he said, "Whew, me feel better now. Could not go before. Dead guy in bush stare at me. Okay, we go now, quickly."

"Wait," I said. "What about Marcella?"

He put a cigarette in his mouth, lit it and took a long drag. "I don't know these things."

"Bullshit! You know, Stanislav. Swear to God that you don't know. She's alive, isn't she? That day in the cabin when I held her, I thought she was dead, but she wasn't dead. She injected herself with that stuff you gave Barella. Then Mario, or someone else, got her out of there and saved her. Didn't they?"

"Tony, I can't tell you these things. Believe me, if I could, I would. I can only tell you this: if she live, she will be someplace very safe, the same place I need take you now."

"This sounds like more bullshit, Stanislav!"

"Tony, I swear to you that if she live and wish to see you again, you will find her at this place."

"Okay, let's go." I added, "By the way, you left your gun back in the building."

"What gun? Me have no gun. Me work for Vatican." He pulled out the credentials that he showed the Italian cop. It was a Vatican passport. "You still have gun?" He asked me.

"Yes." I pointed to the hard lump at the back of my waist.

He started to walk towards the car again. "Good, we may need. But leave it there now, unless you want to answer many questions of Carabinieri," he said, gesturing with his thumb toward the police behind us.

"So, where are we going, exactly?"

"Like I say, we go place very safe."

"Where?"

Stanislav looked at me and smiled. "Same place this all start, four centuries ago: Saint Angelo."

I guess he was expecting some sign of recognition at the sound of the name, but he found none. Why does everyone keep doing that? I'm not a God-damn encyclopedia.

With a look of exasperation Stanislav repeated it, "Saint Angelo!" saying it louder, as if the volume might help, but it didn't. He continued, "You know, Valetta, Malta—near Italy?" I shrugged.

"Hey, what they teach you in school in America?"

"I must have been sick."

"Italy, you know, country shape like boot. Pope live there."

"Why don't you cut the quiz-show crap and just tell me where we're going?"

"Malta, small island south of Sicily; you know where Sicily is, yes?"

"Yes, I know where Sicily is."

"Good. This island, Malta, about ninety kilometers south of there. It is where the Knights of Malta defended Europe from the Muslim invaders. It is where your ancestor, Sebastiano, lead the Knights in their defeat of the Muslims. It is where he made deal with Vatican so Knights promise to defend all of his sons, and their sons, and their sons." He rotated his hand in the air.

Yeah, I get it.

"Which is why me here, and why you here. You get this?" he asked.

I nodded. It was finally starting to sink in.

"Okay, so we go, you be safe, and maybe you get answers, too."

"What about Marcella?"

"If she is alive and wants to see you," he repeated.

I guessed, for the time being, I would have to settle for that cryptic answer.

When we reached the car he relieved me of the gun in my waistband. He put it on the floor of the front passenger seat next to a short-barreled, pump-action shotgun.

"How do you know I'll be any safer there then I am here?"

"When you see Saint Angelo, you will know."

Chapter 78

Stanislav drove like a rocket, south to Genoa. At some point, I asked him if there was a speed limit. He explained that there was, but since this was Italy, nobody apparently cared.

About ten minutes into the ride, he instructed me to retrieve an old leather brief case that was under his seat.

"What's this?" I asked.

"You open, but be very careful."

Oh great, what's next, high explosives? I found a brown paper bag inside the case. "Okay, now what?"

"Remove items from bag and place in brief case. Be careful!"

I reached into the bag and very carefully felt around the insides. The first object I touched was round and hard, with a smooth surface. It felt like an egg, because that is exactly what it was. I looked up and saw Stanislav smiling at me through the rear-view mirror.

"What the hell is this?" I asked.

"Breakfast. Me no had time to eat."

I handed the egg to him, over the seat. "Smart ass."

He thought that was pretty funny, to the point where he almost choked on his cigarette. "What? You think I have bomb in there? There more egg and cheese for you, if you want."

"No thanks, but I'm thirsty."

"There two bottles in bag under other seat. Only drink from one with gas."

I nodded, even though I has no idea what he was talking about, and would have ignored him, in any event, after the crap he just pulled with the eggs. I retrieved the second bag, found two bottles of Pellegrino, opened one at random and drank. My mouth and throat were immediately on fire. I choked and spit the fluid out on the floor.

"You no listen, you drink one with *no gas*." Stanislav said.

"What the hell was that?"

"Special vodka. I make myself. Very strong. Me drink, or me use for petrol, sometimes." He laughed. "Good, no? You like?"

Ha, ha. I open the second bottle and carefully sipped. This one was water, carbonated water, the kind with *gas*.

"Give me other bottle." Stanislav said.

I passed up the vodka and he took two big gulps. "Good, yes?"

"Oh, yeah, breakfast of champions."

He laughed again.

I said, "Between the cigarettes and the petrol for breakfast, you're not going to live very long."

"No one in this job live long."

"Well, I'm not in your job and would like to, so please slow down the car and the vodka consumption."

"I only go 170 kilometers. Like German autobahn, yes?"

Since I had never been to Germany, I had no idea. I double-checked my seat belt.

About five minutes later, there were blue flashing lights in the distance behind us.

"See, I told you."

Stanislav ignored my comment and stepped harder on the

accelerator.

The vehicle with the flashing lights continued to close on us, and even faster than before.

"That strange." Stanislav said. "Carabinieri never do this before."

"Do what?"

"Drive like that. They go over 200 kilometers. Not normal."

Stanislav did not have to explain any further for me to figure out that someone other than the Italian police was probably following us. "So now what?"

"You listen careful. Take this." He handed the shotgun to me.

"You know how to use?"

I nodded. "Yes."

"The seat, you pull hard, it come down. Get in trunk, then pull seat up. No matter what happen, you stay in trunk. Understand?"

I nodded again. "What happens if you're right? Suppose they start shooting at the car, aren't the bullets going to start bouncing around inside the trunk?"

"No worry, back of car armor. Bullet no get in. No matter what, you stay. If someone open trunk, and not me, you blow head off with gun, then you run. No matter what happen to me, you run." He repeated forcefully.

With those reassuring words, I checked the safety on the shotgun, making sure it was on, then squirmed my way into the dark, smelly, hot trunk. The rim of the spare tire was jammed into the small of my back, and something else, probably the car jack, was pressed up against my side. I rested the shotgun on my chest making sure the barrel was pointed away from my head and the stock away from my balls.

If the shooting outside didn't start soon, I thought, I would begin myself, and my first target would be Stanislav. With that thought, I heard a loud thump on the trunk. It was immediately followed by a gun report in the distance behind us. I wouldn't exactly say that I was relieved to hear it, but at least I didn't feel like an idiot for agreeing to climb into this coffin in the first place.

Several more bullets hit the trunk and then I heard the sound of shattering glass. The car began slowing and then stopped. The driver's door opened and I thought I heard, or felt, Stanislav get out. Then the sound of tires coming to a screeching halt was followed by more gunfire. Stanislav must have left the car, because none of the bullet were hitting steel or glass anymore.

So I lay there, in the dark, contemplating my next move with Stanislav's admonition playing in my head. "No matter what, you stay." *Fuck that.*

I reached up to push the back of the seat forward to see if I could get a look around, but just then I heard one of the car doors open. Then someone, or something, landed heavily in the back seat. More doors opened and then slammed shut, and the car started to move again. Two, maybe three, men were talking in what sounded like Arabic. So, I decided to take Stanislav's advice and stay put. At least for the moment.

Chapter 79

We drove for about thirty minutes before they switched to a country road, and the ride got bumpy. Five minutes later, the country road became no road and I started bouncing around in the trunk like a large kernel of popcorn. I tried to steady myself so I wouldn't attract the attention of the people in the passenger compartment. I was also trying to prevent the rim of the spare tire from breaking my spine and praying that the safety on the shotgun hadn't accidentally moved to the firing position.

The car finally stopped, doors opened, shut, and then there was silence. After ten minutes, I decided it was time to try poking my head out from behind the seat again. I knew it was dangerous, but I'd rather be shot than spend another minute in the damn trunk.

I gently eased the seat open. I did not see or hear anyone so I rolled out of the trunk, and then crawled out of the driver's side rear door, shotgun in tow. Stanislav's car was parked in some high brush, I'm assuming for the purpose of concealing it from whoever might be searching for us.

I continued crawling until I reached the edge of a dirt road. Two other vehicles were parked near a small, stone cottage. The first was the police car that had been following us. The second was a large van. With the exception of one nervous-looking guy sitting behind the van's wheel, there was no one else in sight.

At this point, I had another important decision to make. Since none of these assholes apparently knew I was in the trunk, I could simply crawl away in the thick brush and, hopefully, find some help. I knew that was exactly what Stanislav's plan must have been: distract these guys long enough for me to run for it. On the other hand, I had no idea where I was or where the nearest help could be found. So, by the time I got help, Stanislav might be dead, assuming he wasn't already. I didn't think he was. If they wanted him dead, I would have found his body in the car already. Which meant only one thing: that he was alive in that cottage, and probably being treated to some very creative interrogation techniques.

So, the plan shaped up like this: I would check out the building to see if Stanislav was there, and whether he was alive or dead. If I found him dead I would leave, and if not... well, I'd figure that out later. If Stanislav was alive and I managed to get us both out of this mess, he'd probably shoot me himself for not listening to him. But, that's a risk I'd just have to take.

I started belly-crawling towards the cottage, being careful to stay concealed from the guy sitting in the van. I was several minutes into my approach when I heard the sound of a man's voice. He was shouting in what sounded like Arabic, and then I heard another man scream. Now I had the answer to my question about whether Stanislav was alive or dead, and I also knew exactly where he was. I kept crawling, but moved faster.

I found a small window on the side of the cottage nearest me and I looked through the filthy pane of glass into the poorly lit room. I could make out six men, five in what appeared to be police uniforms, sitting or standing in a circle around the sixth. The sixth guy, who was naked and hanging from his wrists on a hook embedded in the ceiling, was being screamed at by one of the five men standing nearest him. As I watched, the interrogator brought up the two ends of what appeared to be battery jumper-cables. In the jaws of the cables were a pair of wet sponges. He jammed the two sponges into the hanging man's groin. The man's body stiffened, and when the cables were withdrawn, he screamed. Although I couldn't see his face, I knew that Stanislav was the guy getting his balls fried, which really pissed me off. Then, the five spectators began to laugh at the sound of his screaming, and a couple even clapped their hands.

It was then that the switch went off in my head, for the second time. The first time was on Fire Island when I found Marcella dying in the kitchen of another small cottage. I took a deep breath, in an attempt to contain the little beast that was clawing to get out of that cage in my head. If I was going to get Stanislav and I out of here alive, I needed to use at least a little of my rational brain before I unleashed that scary little bastard again. At that moment, I had what I though was a pretty rational idea, and then I had a plan.

I began moving back to Stanislav's car. I kept low, but I did not have the time or patience for crawling.

It took a couple of seconds to find what I was looking for under the passenger's seat. I took both bottles out and unscrewed their caps. I smelled the contents of each and placed the one with Stanislav's homemade vodka-jet-fuel down and took a long gulp from the other. I was really thirsty. Then I emptied the remaining water from the bottle and divided the vodka between the two bottles. I tore one of Stanislav's cloth napkins into two halves, and stuffed one into the neck of each bottle. Then I carefully turned the bottles upside-down and let the vodka soak the cloth.

I'm not sure what my parents would think of their son's newly evolving destructive skills, but I thought Mr. Molotov would be pretty impressed. I grabbed Stanislav's lighter from the car's ashtray, slung the strap of the shotgun over my back, picked up my two beverage containers with the wet rags sticking out of their tops, and started to move towards the vehicles parked in front of the cottage.

It didn't take long for the guy in the van to spot me, which is understandable since I wasn't making any attempt to conceal myself at this point, and there wasn't any cover between me and my targets in any event; so I decided to move in as fast as possible before he had a chance to shoot me.

What surprised me was the look on the van driver's face when he saw the flaming bottles in my hands. I expected the guy to get mad, or at least highly motivated, and start firing from the van's window. However, that's not what happened. This guy looked like he was shitting himself. I launched the first bottle at the nearest target, the car. It landed just short, but as it hit the ground and broke, the content sprayed-out beneath the car and then ignited with a satisfyingly large flash and loud *wooomf.*

By that time, the guy in the van had started the ignition and began moving, so I didn't even have time to appreciate my handiwork on the first target before I had to launch the second bottle at the van. This one hit the top of the cargo area with a thump, followed by a very interesting blue and yellow fireball that climbed into the sky.

The van's occupant continued his attempt at an escape, while driving in reverse. The dirt road was narrow, and I guess he decided he did not have enough time to turn the thing around. I took the shotgun off my back and brought it up. The man was looking right at me when I pulled the trigger. The recoil pounded my shoulder back, and the windshield in front of the diver's face exploded in a cloud of glass and blood. *Wow, this cannon could really do some damage.*

Then I took a knee, and aimed towards the front door of the cottage and waited for the occupants to leave the roach motel. It did not take long for them to come streaming out.

I recognized the first guy as the one having all the fun with the jumper-cables. He didn't see me at first because he was staring at the car, now fully engulfed in flames, and was holding up his hand in front of his face, trying to shield it from the intense heat. He looked at me just as I squeezed the trigger. His hand and head disappeared in a cloud of blood and flesh that splattered over the stone wall behind him.

The four other guys hesitated just a moment too long. One was carrying an automatic weapon, but I put a round in his chest before he could get a shot at me. The impact nearly broke him in half.

Then something really strange happened. The other three just started running down the dirt road towards the burning van that was still slowly moving in reverse. As they did, they kept firing wildly over their shoulders at me. If it wasn't for the blood and the fire all over the place, it would have resembled a scene from the Keystone Kops.

I aimed at the guy closest to me and missed. I re-aimed and fired again. The next shot hit low, severing his leg mid-thigh, and he dropped to the ground in a heap. The remaining two threw down their weapons and kept running, reaching the van just as it backed into a deep drainage ditch at the side of the road. The passenger compartment was now fully ablaze and the nose of the van was pointed high enough into the sky so that I could see the undercarriage.

I decided that the remaining bad-guys were too busy running for their lives, to be a threat, at least for now, so I ran into the cottage to retrieve Stanislav. I untied him and laid him on the floor. He wasn't moving, but he was still alive. I found a blanket in the nearby bedroom and covered him with it. Then I went back to the front door to check on the burning van.

The van was by now a pyre of flames and black smoke, and the surviving Keystone Kops were nowhere to be seen. I walked back over to Stanislav and knelt down next to him.

The last thing I remember was an immense flash of light.

Chapter 80

By the time I regained consciousness it was nighttime. I knew this because I could see stars and a half-moon shining above me. The fact that I was looking at the night sky from inside the cottage didn't seem the least bit strange to me, at least not at first, so I just lay there on my back and admired the pretty moon and looked for familiar constellations. My brain completed its reboot right around the time I found the Big Dipper. Then I began to wonder what happened to the roof. It was there the last time I checked.

I sat up, straitened my eyeglasses and looked around in the dim light. With the exception of the stone walls, most of the cottage was gone. Well, it wasn't gone: just moved to different, widely dispersed locations. Something had blown the place to pieces, and it did not take long to surmise what it probably was. The jumpy looking driver of the van was nervous for a reason; he was sitting in a vehicle packed with high explosives. And his two comrades weren't running away from me, they were running to put out the fire before the thing blew everyone, and everything, to hell.

I tried standing. It was slow and painful. My shirt and pants were covered with dust, and torn in numerous places where small pieces of shrapnel were embedded in the skin of my arms, legs and torso. Some of the wounds were seeping blood.

I removed my glasses, straightened the bent frames and tried to blow some of the dust and debris off the lenses. Then I remembered that I left Stanislav on the floor somewhere, and I began to carefully comb through the debris until I found him.

I heard a grunt.

"Stanislav, can you hear me?" I repeated it several times until he finally replied.

"Ta-ta?"

"No, it's Tony. Are you able to move?"

Stanislav opened his eyes and looked up at me. He was confused, and obviously in a lot of pain: not surprising, considering what he had just gone through, including the party that the shit-heads were having with him before the blast.

I carefully removed the wreckage lying on and around him and then retrieved the blanket, which had been blown across the room, and covered him again. I found most of his clothes, and helped him dress himself.

"Tony, you okay?" he said, finally regaining his senses.

"We're both a little banged up, but we're alive," I said, smiling down at him.

"What happened to bad guys?"

He looked around and seemed to be getting confused again.

"What happen to house?"

"Vodka."

"Vodka?"

"Yeah, I told you that stuff was bad for your health."

As he finished dressing, I filled him in on some of the details that he missed while he was just hanging around.

As expected, he scolded me for not running when I had a chance. "Next time you run, and not look back!"

"Next time? You mean I might have to save you with a vodka-bomb, again?"

He smiled and shook his head. "You crazy, you know?"

I located the shotgun, slung it over my shoulder, and then helped Stanislav to his feet.

We emerged from the cottage at the location where the front door formerly stood and found a smoldering pile of metal wreckage that was formerly a police car. The charred remains of bad guys were scattered around a field of debris, burning wreckage, and vegetation. It was another war zone, just like the one on Fire Island. However, all things considered, I'd rather be at the beach.

Down the road, I could just make out what was left of the van, which had mostly vaporized. The only recognizable part was the twisted remains of the undercarriage, which was still in the ditch and pointing nose-up in the air.

Stanislav and I stared at it for a moment. It occurred to me that the peculiar position of the van's chassis and its steel mass had probably deflected at least some of the blast up and away from the cottage. It wasn't necessary to speculate about what would have happened if the van was sitting level, or perhaps a little closer to us, when it blew up; we'd both be crispy critters, just like our former captors were now.

Stanislav looked at me and said, "You really good at this. You know? I think maybe I no need protect you. Maybe I need protect bad guys."

I shrugged. "I can't help it. They keep pissing me off."

We walked over to his car. The brush that was around it had been blown or burnt away, the paint was singed, and the windows were all blown out.

I said, "I think the Brotherhood owes you a new car."

"It look like me feel," Stanislav said weakly.

He hobbled over to the driver's door, opened it, and carefully brushed the glass fragments and other debris off the driver's seat. He slid in behind the wheel, found the key still in the ignition and turned it before I could laugh at him for trying. The damn thing coughed to life.

He looked at my stunned face through the missing sunroof and smiled. “Good car, yes?”

I nodded. “You want to sell it?”

I opened the passenger door, got in, and buckled my seat belt.

“No,” he said. “Only have two hundred thousand kilometers. A little paint, a little glass, and it good as new.”

It was my turn. “You're crazy, you know?”

He shrugged, smiled, and began to drive.

Miraculously one of the headlights was still working, and with the windshield blown away, we had a surprisingly clear view of the road, and not a bad breeze, either. “Do you know where we're going?” I asked.

“Back to highway, me hope.”

Turns out he was right; we were heading towards the highway. But we didn't get that far.

Chapter 81

Cars blocked the road, and there was a small army of uniformed men behind the vehicles taking aim at us with automatic weapons. About a half-dozen more were standing in the road, all of them were also dressed in uniforms, and aiming automatic weapons in our direction - except for this one guy who was wearing civilian clothing and, as near as I could tell, wasn't aiming or carrying anything that was capable of making a loud noise. Unfortunately for him, his facial features made him look a lot like one of the bad guys we just escaped from. He also looked like he was in charge. So naturally, I rested the barrel of the shotgun on the dashboard and I aimed at him. Then I waited for the fun to begin. Again.

Stanislav said. "No fire. Real Carabinieri, they here to help."

"How can you tell?"

"I know one you aim at."

"That guy? He looks like a terrorist to me."

"No terrorist, trust me, you definitely no want to shoot that one."

"You sure? I can just wing him."

"Put gun down. Please."

It occurred to me that there was a risk that Stanislav's vision, or his judgment, might well have been affected by his recent ordeal, but I put the weapon down anyway. Besides, if they were the bad guys, there was no way we were going to survive more than five seconds, once they opened fire.

Stanislav stopped the car and, without hesitation, got out and staggered toward the civilian. He put out his hand, and the two of them shook. At that point, Stanislav's knees buckled and the other guy caught him in a bear hug just before he hit the ground.

A moment later, several EMTs showed up, laid Stanislav out on a stretcher, and took him away.

While all of this was happening, the man in civilian clothing walked over, stood in front of the car, and stared at me through the missing windshield. "Mr. Mascelle, I presume."

He said it in a monotone voice that immediately reminded me of Barella.

"None other."

He walked to the open driver's door and sat down in the seat next to me. I pulled the shotgun towards me and cradled it in my arms. My mother once told me that you can never be too careful with strangers.

"I've been looking for you," he said.

"And now you found me."

"Looks like you've had another rough day."

"Do I know you?"

"I'm agent Castro. I work—worked—with Agent Barella. I was supposed to be at that meeting, at the castle earlier today, but I was delayed."

Castro? Interesting. He was thirty-something and had thick, black, wavy hair, a sharp, curved nose, and a strong jaw line. I said, "Too bad you missed it, we could have used a little extra help."

"Yeah, I know."

"Did they make it?"

"McKeown did, but he's going to be out of action for a while. Barella didn't."

"Sorry to hear that. I was just getting to know him." The tone in my voice, or the look on my face, must have indicated to agent Castro that I was not telling the entire truth.

Castro said. "He was a good man; you may not believe it, but he was. He'll be missed."

"How did you find me?"

"Well, it didn't exactly require a lot of detective work. I just followed the trail of bodies and smoldering wreckage."

"What can I say? I'm having a bad month. You'd never know it, but just two weeks ago, I'd get stressed-out over an investor meeting."

Castro surprised me with a broad grin. "Yeah, shit happens."

"Yes it does." I yawned.

Castro looked me over. "You should probably spend some time with one of our medics and take care of those wounds before they get infected. Then I'll have someone take you back to your hotel in Milan for food, a hot shower, and some sleep. One of my guys will take you to the airport in the morning."

As Castro was speaking, I felt something brush the side of my head. I reached up to find the remnants of the Band-Aid that was, until recently, covering the wound on my head. It was dangling at the side of my face. I ripped it off, tossed it out of the windshield in front of me, and said to Castro, "I appreciate the offer, but you must know by now that I didn't come here for a vacation. I came here to find someone, and I'm not leaving until I do."

"I knew you were going to say that. Okay, plan B. After the medics clean you up a little, I'll have someone put you up in a place around here, find you some food and new clothing, and you can spend the night, and sleep on it. Then we'll discuss the matter in the morning. Okay?"

I was too tired to argue. "Fair enough."

He held out his hand. "I'm glad we had a chance to meet."

I took his hand. "I'm glad I didn't shoot you."

Chapter 82

I had another one of those dreams. It was like the one on the plane. Except it was different, clearer somehow. The arrows striking the glass towers had sprouted wings, like birds, or maybe airplanes. However, the worst part was still the sound, the thumping of the bodies as they hit the ground. This time I could also see their faces, and I recognized them. I couldn't tell you their names, but I knew who they were. It's hard to explain.

Someone began calling my name. I opened my eyes and saw Stanislav looking down at me.

"Time to wake up, Tony."

I sat up and looked around the room. "What time is it?"

"Four o-clock."

It seemed a little light for that hour of the morning. I asked, "Why are you waking me up so early?"

"Four o-clock in evening," Stanislav said.

Stanislav then responded to my confused look. "You sleep all day. Okay, you need. Dress now, and meet me in lobby."

"Are you okay?" I asked him.

"Better than yesterday. I sleep some too. I see you downstairs. Castro want to talk to us."

Moving as fast as my stiff, aching body would allow, I dressed in the new clothing, left on the chair next to the bed, and went downstairs.

I found Stanislav and Agent Castro in the lobby near the entrance, surrounded by six very serious looking men. They were dressed in Italian police uniforms. These guys were lean and mean and looked like they probably killed people for a living. The attempt to conceal their obviously deadly dispositions behind the Carabinieri guise seemed almost comical. Castro smiled and waved me over.

"Sleep well?" he asked.

"I guess I did."

"Walk with me."

He led me out of the building to where two cars waited with their engines running. He pointed to one and said. "This car will take you to the airport, for that flight home."

I said. "I thought we talked about this already. I'm not leaving until I find Marcella."

He nodded. "This other car will take you to where you want to go, or at least where you think you want to go. Which car you get into is entirely your choice."

"Right. So, what's the catch?"

"If you get into that second car you may not live long enough to reach your destination."

I motioned towards the six men who were now standing around us. "And them?"

"They'll be going with you, and so will Stanislav."

"I guess it's safe to assume that these are not members of the Italian police force."

"No, they definitely are not. But, they are good guys,"

"Funny, they don't look like good guys?"

He smiled. "They're more than good, they're the best."

I waited for more information, but none was offered.

Finally I said, "So, what are we waiting for? Let's go."

Castro said, "Tony, listen to me carefully. You've been through a lot. And all things considered, it's a miracle that you're still alive. If you get into that car, there is a very real possibility that you might end up dead. Do you understand?"

Why does everyone keep thinking it's a miracle? Maybe I'm just a pretty good shot - for a computer geek, anyway. "Yes, I understand."

I looked at the six men and asked. "Do you guys have names?" They nodded, but said nothing.

Okay… "Great, let's go."

Agent Castro pulled out a pair of handcuffs and placed them on Stanislav, who didn't resist as they were locked on his wrists. Stanislav looked at me and shrugged. Another pair appeared in Castro's hands as he approached me.

"What's this about?" I asked.

Castro sighed. "Those men that you met yesterday were on a mission. Part of it was to deliver two packages. The first package was that bomb that you so cleverly disabled."

"You mean the one I blew up?"

"Yeah, same thing."

"What was the second package?"

"You."

"I see. So, these six gorillas here are going to pretend to be them and deliver me to wherever I was supposed to be delivered?"

"Correct."

"And the bomb?"

"That was delivered earlier today. It wasn't a real one of course, but they don't know that yet."

"So, what happens after the two packages are delivered?"

"Don't worry about that. You just need to go along for the ride, and be you. These guys will take care of the rest."

"Do I get a gun at some point?"

"No."

By the look on Castro's face, I concluded that the questions, and the negotiations, were at an end.

"You can still get in the other car and go home. I very strongly recommend that option," Castro said patiently.

I put my wrists out. Castro shook his head and put the cuffs on.

The six men divided into two teams. Three of them came with me and Stanislav in one of the cars, and the other three followed in the second. I said to the guys sitting on each side of me in the back seat. "Castro lied." They both looked at me. "He said that the other car was going to the airport." Nothing. Not even a smile. Did I mention that not everyone gets my humor?

According to the signs on the highway, we were driving south to Genoa, apparently on the same road, and in the same direction, that Stanislav and I were driving yesterday. By the time we arrived at the outskirts of the city the sun was low in the sky and its light bathed the buildings in a way I never recall seeing before, except maybe in one of those Italian Renaissance paintings that you see in museums. The sky in those pictures always struck me as beautiful, but somehow oddly cartoon-like, especially compared with the meticulously created realism of the city scene beneath. As it turns out, they were pretty realistic depictions after all.

We drove around a traffic circle as we entered the main square of the town. In the center of it, was a large monument dedicated to *Cristoforo Colombo La Patria*. Stanislav gave a little salute to it and said to me, "This man and your ancestor alive together, same time in history, understand?"

"Yes, they were contemporaries."

"Yes. Your ancestor stopped the Muslims at Rhodes and Malta. And this man find America near same time. He give Christians the wealth and power to push Muslims back to where they come from. If we no had men these like, we would not be Christians. We would be Muslims, both here and America. Understand?"

I nodded. That was an interesting theory, I thought. The Christian world had been on the run for centuries, continually contracting in the face of Muslim expansion. But old Sebastiano and his comrades in arms bought some time. Not a lot, but just enough for Columbus and Christian Europe to discover and begin exploiting the wealth of the New World. Once the gold and silver began pouring in, Europe could afford to build the navies and equip armies in a way that neither they, nor their Muslim foes, could have previously imagined. The wealth and trade also enabled the arts and sciences to flourish under the patronage of newly enriched traders and merchants. Then, if my Western History serves, the endless wars and naval engagements between the Spanish, English, French, and Dutch over the New World's resources, real estate, and trade routes, rapidly advanced the art and science of warfare in Western Europe and the Americas. When added to the other new ideas and inventions, emerging on both sides of the Atlantic, the Christian world soon left the Muslim, and much of the rest of the world, centuries behind in terms of technological advances.

"Yes." I said. "I understand."

We turned onto a concrete pier and drove past several large terminal buildings. As we passed the buildings, I could hear the beating sound of a helicopter rotor. We pulled up to where the thing was sitting, at the end of the pier. The six gorillas jumped out and unceremoniously manhandled us towards the helicopter's door. They were pretty good actors - at least I hoped so. Stanislav, oblivious to the rough treatment, said, "We take private flight to Malta, first class."

I found the childlike excitement in his voice to be a little bizarre under the circumstances. I was about to tell him about my little problem with flying, when our little tour group was greeted at the door by two severe-looking pilots.

It was a nice helicopter. The exterior was painted white with a blue stripe that ran along the side towards the tail. Except for its color, it reminded me of one of those massive Coast Guard rescue helicopters. However, unlike those utilitarian rescue machines, the interior of this bird was very plush. I was surprised by the opulence until I noticed the emblem on the back of the light gray, leather seats, which consisted of two crossed keys with a crown in the middle. On top of the crown was a crucifix. It did not require the eye of a Catholic scholar to recognize it as the papal insignia.

I looked at Stanislav, who was taking a seat across the row next to me. He said, "Nice, yes? We go first class," he repeated.

"Yeah, not bad." *So long as we don't end up dead.*

The eight of us took our seats in the passenger cabin, and both pilots returned to the cockpit. I heard the engines whine as they began to power up, and then the thumping of the rotors.

"Long flight, about four hour. You buckle and relax," Stanislav said to me, gesturing to the seat belt. I enthusiastically complied.

The beating sound of the rotor grew to a massive rumbling, and then with a roar from the blades, we were airborne over the Ligurian Sea. The view of Genoa and the coast of the Italian Riviera were spectacular, and for a moment, I forgot that I didn't like to fly, and also how I got here.

I leaned my head back in my seat and tried to replay the

events of the last few days. The images and the information came in confusing flashes; it was hard to process it all. The idea that a promise made to someone in the distant past, could somehow result in such a cataclysmic series of events in the present, was hard to digest. So much death. I wondered how much of the story still lay outside my view. I assumed I would find out soon enough.

The last thought I had before falling asleep was the image of Marcella in bed on that morning on Fire Island, waving for me to come back to her, and I wondered what would have happened if I had.

I felt a hand tapping my shoulder. When I opened my eyes, Stanislav was looking down at me again. "You wake up now. Pilot say we land for fuel."

I looked out of the window. The sun had set, but there was still enough light coming from the horizon to see that there was nothing but water in every direction. Then I saw a small speck in the distance. "We're going to land on that?" I asked Stanislav.

His usual jovial expression looked tense, or perhaps confused. Maybe he was a bad flier too.

"Everything okay?" I asked him.

"Me not sure. Distance to Malta about one thousand kilometers. This machine has more than enough petrol to make. Don't know why we land. You be alert."

The speck grew until I could make out what appeared to be an oil tanker–sized ship. We landed on a green circle painted on the foredeck.

The pilots cut the power to the engines, and as the sound of the spinning rotors began to disappear, our six beefy companions started exiting the aircraft. On their way out one of them handed Stanislav the key to the handcuffs and gestured for us to stay in our seats. Stanislav and I watched through the window as they began walking casually towards the back of the ship. They climbed the stairs up to the bridge deck and disappeared behind a steel door.

I whispered to Stanislav, "Didn't Agent Castro tell you what the plan was?"

"No, I get same answer, like you."

It occurred to me that I really had no idea who Castro was, and since, like an idiot, I never asked him for his credentials, I wasn't even sure *he* was one of the good guys. But, how could he not be? I mean, if he wasn't one of them, we'd be dead already. Right?

The rotors had come to a full stop and everything became eerily quiet. The only sound was that of the sea, as the ship continued to plow through the waves. As I was mulling over this latest bizarre turn of events, two men wearing crew coveralls seemed to appear out of thin air on the ship's deck, and they began walking towards the helicopter. The pilot and the co-pilot, who were still at the controls, must have spotted them too because they got up and exited the aircraft. With an outstretched arm, one of the pilots gave Stanislav and me a wordless command to stay in our seats. They descended the helicopter's steps to the ship's deck, and then proceeded to walk towards the approaching crewmen.

"Apparently, everyone wants us to stay in our seats." I said to Stanislav. I held out my wrists. He unlocked my handcuffs. "You know how to fly one of these?" I asked him.

He dropped the handcuffs on the floor and nodded as he rubbed his wrists. His eyes, and mine, then became glued to the scene on the deck.

What happen next occurred so quickly that I could barely comprehend it, even though it took place right before my eyes.

When the two crewmen had come within five feet of the pilot

and co-pilot, each pulled handguns out from behind their backs and shot the two pilots in the head at point-blank range. Their bodies slumped to the deck like discarded rag dolls. A second later, the ship's bridge was illuminated by flashes of muzzle fire that could be seen through the windows of the steel structure.

"Oh, Mother of God!" Stanislav exclaimed.

Chapter 83

"You get on floor and stay," Stanislav said as he unbuckled me and pushed me down.

I replied, "Last time you said something like that I had to rescue you."

That comment got me a really mean stare. He repeated, "You get on floor and stay."

Stanislav moved quickly towards the open cabin door and, as he stepped out, I expected to hear a blaze of gunfire fill the void at any moment, but it never came. I poked my head up, peered out of the window nearest me, and saw Stanislav talking with the two men dressed as crew members, the same ones that had just popped the pilots. All three of them had smiles on their faces and were shaking hands. Then, they all turned and walked towards the open door of the helicopter.

The first one on-board, one of the shooters, gave me a big, friendly smile. He introduced himself, through a German accent, as Gunter. His blond hair, blue eyes, and sharp jaw reminded me of Dudley Do-Right. After his introduction, he took a seat up front, behind the controls in the cockpit. Then Stanislav entered and sat down in a seat in the front of the passenger cabin. "Relax," he said, "they good guys."

What a relief.

The last guy to come aboard was tall, with dirty blond hair, a brown goatee, and a slim, athletic build. His gray eyes seemed to sparkle with recognition when he caught sight of me.

"Nice shooting," I said.

"Thanks."

"Is it safe to assume that they weren't working for the Pope?"

"Yes, you may safely assume that." He said with an American accent.

"So, who were they?"

"Bad guys."

I certainly hope so. "How bad?"

"The worst." He held out his hand. "Hi Tony, good to see you again, pard-ner." I did not recognize the southern-drawl laden voice, but he was oddly familiar. Nevertheless, I could not remember where I'd seen his face before.

"What did you say your name was?" I asked.

"I didn't," he laughed. "It's Bob Vandenberg."

"I don't remember your name, but I do remember your face."

"You should. We spent two months together in the same dorm room, at Stony Brook. Howard Tucker. Remember?"

Holy shit! I just stared at him, slack-jawed and wide-eyed, as all three of them had a good laugh at my expense. *Ha, ha.*

"I don't understand," I said.

"It's simple, really. I'm with an organization based in a place called Langley, Virginia. Howard Tucker is one of my aliases, what we call a legend. The next question you're going to ask is; what was I doing at Stony Brook pretending to be your roommate? The answer is that you were my very first assignment."

"A CIA agent assigned to me? Why?"

He sat down in the seat across the aisle from me and directed me to the seat next to him, and I sat. "Well, I wasn't exactly there for you. I was there for Mario, or Crazy Nunzio, as we used to call him. It was right after that thing with your dad. Remember? Barella came to us with some crazy theory about this mad-monk squad," he said pointing with his chin to the other men in the cabin. "We thought he was nuts. But when we check it out the pieces started to fit. So, we figured we'd better get a bead on these folks and try to figure out what their real intentions were. And, the best way to get close to them, was to get close to you. So, I became Howie, your roommate. Then, after Mario left, my assignment was over, so I left too. Things were quiet for a while, until this shit started a couple of weeks ago. Lucky, we happened to have your friend Billy Hoffenberg on the payroll, so we dropped him on the scene to keep an eye on things."

"Billy worked for you?"

"Yeah, great guy too. It's a shame that we lost him."

"Maybe you should've thought about that before you dressed him up in that ridiculous park ranger outfit and dropped him into the frying pan."

Vandenberg shrugged, "Shit happens."

On that note, I considered raising the subject of *bullshit,* which, according to McKeown, is what this guy was shoveling in my direction on the subject of Billy just happening to be an employee of the CIA, rather than him being recruited from the ATF seven months ago by the CIA, specifically for this mission.

Instead, I asked, "So all of that stuff about your pilgrim ancestors, and getting up early, and the snooty manners... that was all bullshit?"

He nodded. "A Pilgrim descendant? Me? No way! Those people were way too anal-retentive. It was just part of my legend. As for getting up early, I hate it, but how else was I going to explain my absence during the 6:00 a.m. off-campus briefings with my supervisor? As for my real ancestors, they were Dutch."

"Dutch?"

"Yeah, came to America and settled in New Amsterdam,

present-day New York, before the idea of boarding the *Mayflower* even came into the Pilgrims' heads."

I considered my new, old friend, Bob Vandenberg for a moment. With the exception of some facial features, he seemed to have nothing in common with Howard Tucker. Howie was an introspective nerd who wouldn't harm a fly. This guy, on the other hand, had just put a bullet in a man's head at point-blank range, and he didn't even skip a beat. I wondered how someone could be such a convincingly jovial liar, and a cold-blooded killer, at the same time. And I could also see how someone like him would be annoyed by those preachy, anal-retentive pilgrims.

"The Dutch tolerated everyone," he continued. "Well, almost. They hated the Swedes for some reason, made them live in New Jersey, poor bastards. But the Dutch tolerated just about everyone else. Didn't like 'em, only tolerated them, just like New Yorkers today. As for being snooty, I'm from Texas, son. Which means that while I have every reason to be snooty, there ain't a snooty bone in my body."

I guess my confused stare and stunned silence got my message across.

He said, "Hope you can forgive me for being a little yackety. My adrenaline is still pumpin'. It's the wet-work. What a rush! But I don't have to tell you about that, right? Anyway, so that's the Howie story. I was there to scope out Mario, and you were the honey for the bee, or in his case, the grizzly bear."

I recalled that Howie was pretty yackety at times too. What was his excuse back then, I began wondering. I tried to remember if there were any reports of murdered or missing faculty or students, when a fourth person boarding the helicopter interrupted my thoughts.

Bob Vandenberg said, "Speak of the devil."

Mario entered the passenger cabin with a broad grin below his large, walrus mustache, and bowed gracefully. "Hello Tony, my friend. Good to see you safe and sound."

Vandenberg interrupted, "It's about time, pard-ner. Best get this bird in the air before our friends blow this monster."

Mario gave him a quick, sloppy salute and then took his place in the pilot's seat. In a moment, the machine came to life, and the loud drone of the engines, and the drumming of the rotor blades, once again drowned out the sound of the sea.

Vandenberg leaned towards me and spoke over the noise. "That Navy SEAL team, the one you came in with, they're going to send that big boat to the bottom. You see, the bad guys' plan was to load this helicopter with high explosives and fly it into the middle of the capital of Malta, a town called Valletta, with you in it, kamikaze-style. Boom!" he said, making an exploding gesture with his hands.

I still hadn't recovered from the shock of my reunion with my former roommate, so I just sat there and listened, trying to get my head around this latest shovel-full of clandestine cloak-and-dagger crap.

"They decided to include you in the package at the last minute," Vandenberg continued. "Their little way of saying 'fuck-you-very-much' for that firefight at the beach - you know, the one where you kicked their collective asses. Then, a little while later, when the place is swarming with people from the military, rescue services, police, hospital personnel, spectators, and lots of television cameras, the assholes drive that big bitch down there into the main harbor and, *Kaaa-boooooom*!"

He pointed down at the oil tanker. "It's loaded with thousands of tons of high explosives, ammonium nitrate, aluminum, magnesium and ferric oxide powder, plus hundreds of tanks of compressed hydrogen, and about a million gallons of diesel fuel. And if that's not enough to make your asshole pucker, these fine gentlemen rigged a two-stage detonation. First one sends the entire cargo a few hundred feet in the air. The second detonates the lot of it. They used something similar for the 1993 New York Trade Center attack, and also the Beirut barracks bombing back in '83, except this one is much, much bigger."

I looked down at the tanker and tried to imagine what a bomb that size could do to a city.

"It's called a thermobaric bomb," Vandenberg continued. "We used a similar device in Nam, the Blu-82. Called them daisy-cutters. Nice, friendly name, don't yah think? But they would cut a helluva-lot more than daisies; we vaporized miles of tropical jungle with them. And if a company of enemy infantry happened to be in the jungle at the time: poof! Gone. Nothing left except some bone fragments and sometimes little bits of charred meat. But they were firecrackers compared to that thing down there. We estimate it would have been more powerful than the bomb dropped on Hiroshima. Half the people on the island would have been incinerated or killed by the shock wave. And, if they pulled it off, there wouldn't have been a building left standing, or a heart left beating, in Valetta."

I watched with relief as the tanker rapidly faded into the distance.

"Now, if our SEAL friends down there get it just right, they'll put just enough plastic explosives on the hull to sink it. Too much and... well, either way, it's gone for good."

"Why?" I yelled back over the noise of the rotors.

"Because the damn thing is too dangerous to take back into any port, even disarmed. But, I asked them to do me a solid and let us have thirty minutes to get the hell outta Dodge, just in case they screw the pooch. But if you see a big flash, better hold onto your balls and kiss your ass goodbye." He laughed.

"No," I said. "I meant, why would anyone go through this much trouble to blow up a town that no one ever heard of, and that's sitting on an island in the middle of nowhere?"

"You never heard of it, and I never heard of it either, but the wackos have, and they have very long memories. These A-rab fellas were on an eight-hundred-year winning streak until they lost at Malta. After that, there were still lots of battles to fight, and lots of blood to spill, but they never regained the initiative again. Sorta-like Gettysburg during the Civil War, or Midway and Stalingrad during World War Two. The war was basically over; it just took some time for everyone to realize it. So, the point of them blowing up Malta was to announce the start of a rematch: the rematch of all rematches, in fact. It would have been their first, big, symbolic victory in the new war, in the same exact location of their greatest defeat, in the old one. And to these people, symbols like that matter a lot. They originally planned to do it on May 18, which is the 436th anniversary of the beginning of the Great Siege of Malta. They had to move up the date, thanks to you. How's that for a psychopathic fixation on symbolism? These are some very crazy, and very dangerous people."

I was almost tempted to laugh at that, coming from this guy, but I began wondering what the first part of that comment was about.

"Thanks to me?"

"Yeah, it's complicated." Vandenberg changed the subject abruptly. "Take a look at the future down there, Tony. We always thought these clowns were like the gang that couldn't shoot straight. All we really worried about was keeping them away from the nukes, chemical weapons and biologics. Hell, any idiot could wipe out a city with that stuff. But that thing down there... that's some dedicated shit. If they can figure out how to hit us with floating and flying bombs, then we're really in deep doo-doo. You see, it's hard to get your hands on a nuke. But it's really easy to get your hands on fertilizer, diesel fuel, a big boat, and civilian aircraft. Hell, even the high explosives are not particularly hard to get. You can find that shit everywhere, or even make it in your kitchen. It's putting it all together, developing a plan, and executing that plan: that's the hard part.

And clearly these guys are ready, willing, and able to do that now. And do it all, they claim, in the name of God. So, now we're at war with this latest "-ism" nightmare, Islamism, and if that's not depressing enough, there are well over a billion Muslims in the world, and none of them really like us very much."

"Maybe," I said. "But the nut-jobs in the black pajamas are only a tiny percentage of them. None of the others even know who these guys are, or what their plan is, and if they did they probably wouldn't care."

"Maybe, but consider this. The last time the century turned, there was another nightmarish *ism* brewing. But a hundred years ago, almost no one knew or cared about Marxism either, and certainly no one ever heard of Stalinism. It wasn't even a blip on the screen in 1901. The future hordes of commie-fanatics, that would later help turn the twentieth century into the most deadly and bloody period in human history, never heard of it either. All they knew was that they were angry and hungry and, at least as far as they were concerned, the current system sucked. They also knew that there had to be a better way. None of them knew what that better way was, at least not until they discovered this new thing called Communism, which when you think about is kind-of a nice concept, at least on paper. You know, everyone plays nice in the sandbox together and shares all the toys. Right? But thirty years later, human nature combined with Marxism mutates into Stalinism, and everyone was soon finding out what fun that was. And, if you happened to live in the U.S.S.R., you most definitely knew what it was, assuming it hadn't already killed you. So, at long last, when everybody begins to see that maybe this 'new way' might be worse than the 'old way'- did they admit it? Did they stop it? Hell no, they didn't even try. Instead, they spent years, decades, making excuses for it, and all the while the bodies were piling up by the tens of millions. So, it doesn't matter what a small percentage of people know, believe or agree upon in the beginning of these things; what matters it what they believe or do later, after they get the change and the political control that they want, or think they want. But, by that time, the thing has a life of its own and the folks that were there in the beginning suddenly discover that, regardless of the ugly truth, they either get with the program or they get this." Vandenberg said as he made a slashing motion across his throat. "You watch, if we fail to kill this thing in the cradle, you'll see the same thing happen during this century that our grandparents saw in the last, only worse, because we live in a world filled with nukes, weaponized chemicals, and some very nasty little bugs that actually make nuclear war seem humane by comparison."

The apocalyptic picture that this guy was painting was either the dark vision of someone who was pathologically paranoid, or it contained just enough truth to cause someone else, like me, to believe it. So, I thought it was my turn to change the subject.

"When did we team up with them?" I said pointing to Stanislav's back.

"Very recently, when we caught wind of the plot to wipe these guys out. They're called the Brotherhood, and there are some sisters too, but you already know that. We believe Saddam, or one of his sons, was leading the charge. They wanted payback because the Brotherhood screwed up their plan to whack Bush in Kuwait, in '93. They probably also concluded that the Brotherhood would be a threat to any of their new plans in the future. Well, duh! We don't exactly know what else they have planned, but we know they're up to something big. We didn't really know how big until we uncovered this. So now, we're scouring the history books, looking for the next big psycho-terrorist-anniversary date in hopes of predicting when that next big thing might happen. We have a few dates, but we've narrowed it down to one with the highest probability."

"When?" I asked.

"You're a smart guy," he said. "Can you guess? I'll give you a hint. It has to do with one of your ancestors."

I wasn't really in the mood to play this game, so I ignored his question.

"Don't want to play?" Vandenberg said as he looked out of the window and stared into space. "We think it's the anniversary of the day the Muslims quit Malta and went home, defeated and dejected - thanks to your ancestor, Sebastiano. Logical, right? That date is about five months from now: September 11th, to be exact. The problem is, we're not sure where and how it's going to take place. And that's where our new friends up there come in. They pulled our president's bacon outta the fire in Kuwait, and we've just helped them save their mother ship on Malta. Besides being an act of enlightened self-interest, it also makes us even, and it makes us allies. We knew we needed them, and now they know they need us. So, we're working together to head off the next big one."

"What about Kennedy?" I asked.

I noticed a momentary look of surprise on Vandenberg's face, and then the stupid grin reappeared. He shrugged. "What about him?"

"What about him? These people, your new friends, murdered him."

"You win some, you lose some."

For a moment, I was too dumbfounded to reply rationally to that comment, so I just stared at him. First Barella, and now this guy. I took a deep breath and said as calmly as I could, "The thirty-fifth President of the United States gets assassinated by a bunch of madmen from the Vatican, and all you can say is, 'you win some, you lose some'? Did I miss something? I thought you said you were an employee, and presumably a loyal citizen, of the United States?"

Vandenberg rolled his eyes. "Now you sound like Barella. He wanted all of these guys on the business end of a lethal injection. The man spent nearly forty years hunting these people down. And the bitch of it was, he didn't even like Kennedy. So, I asked him once why he did it. He said it wasn't about the man, it was about the office and about the law. What a Boy Scout." Vandenberg laughed. "Man, was he pissed when he heard about the plan for an alliance with these people."

"He was right to be pissed," I said, as much as I hated to admit that Barella was right about anything. "You can't just forget about what these people did. You can't just sweep a presidential assassination under the carpet!"

"Son, that's a pretty strange thing coming from your mouth."

"What does that mean?"

He changed the subject again. "Look, Tony, Dallas is my home town, and everybody in Dallas felt real bad about what happened, even people like my folks, who didn't even vote for the man. But, what can you do? Besides, its ancient history, at least how we measure history in the good ole' USA."

Oh my God, the man is certifiable. I started looking around to see if I could find a door and a spare parachute. *Why does this keep happening to me?*

Chapter 84

"Tony, you payin' attention, son? It's not the last forty years we need to be worried about, my friend; it's the next forty. We're about to enter the big ring for the fight of our lives, and we've spent the last three decades systematically decommissioning our human-intelligence capabilities. Did you know that? Did you ever hear of the Church Committee?"

The Church Committee? Sounded like the people that plan the annual parish picnic. "No, what's the Church Committee?" I asked reluctantly.

Vandenberg informed me, "It was a group of fine senators, from both sides of the aisle who, back in the mid-seventies, looked at the stuff that the Kennedys tried to pull with assassinating Castro, and LBJ with Vietnam and Operation Phoenix, and the Nixon people - who were just plain inept morons - and came to the incredibly stupid conclusion that our very own highly trained and highly capable intelligence services were more dangerous to American citizens than to our enemies abroad. So, they gutted it. All of it. Can you believe that shit? And if that's not bad enough, those same assholes thought we could replace those boots on ground with birds in the air. We put all of our eggs into the techie-propeller-head basket and hoped for the best. Now, we have the best techie shit on the planet. Hell, we've got satellite technology that can read the label on your underwear before you unzip your fly. Unfortunately, the best satellites in the world can't read minds or tell you what your enemies' intentions are. For that, you need human intelligence. But our human intelligence infrastructure has become a joke. In fact, for large swaths of the globe, it's gone altogether. The United States of America is like one of those bodybuilders, flexing his muscles at the beach: all brawn and no brains. All it takes is one sneaky kick in the balls, and we'll be down for the count."

Vandenberg stopped in mid-sentence, reached into his shirt

pocket, and placed a cell phone to his ear. He placed a finger into his opposite ear and strained to hear over the noise from the rotors.

How the hell can he get a cell phone call in a helicopter over the middle of the Mediterranean, when I can't get one on a Long Island beach?

"Okay, thanks for the update." He said as he snapped the phone shut and then placed it back in his pocket. He returned his attention to me, but before he could ask I said, "Sneaky kick in the balls."

"Right. So now, at long last, some of the idiots in Washington have finally woken up and, as they say, smelled the coffee. Not all of them, mind you: just some of them. In fact, the information that we used to prevent Malta from becoming the largest human funeral pyre since Nagasaki, mostly came through unofficial channels, an accidental meeting at a place called Elaine's."

Vandenberg didn't even bother to wait for me to ask the question.

"No, that's not a code word for some futuristic super-spy center. It's a watering hole on the Upper East Side of Manhattan. You see, as the rules are presently written, there's an information firewall between the CIA and the FBI. The American people have been brainwashed into thinking that the heads of these all-knowing and all-seeing, Orwellian federal organizations have regular meetings in smoke-filled conference rooms, in some spooky Washington inner sanctum, and that they sit there in front of a 3D, computerized model of the planet, puffing on fat cigars, listening to Wagner and devising new ways to fuck over Joe and Jane Citizen: you know, listening to their private phone conversations and watching sneaky videos of them on the john taking a shit. All they worry about, apparently, is how much of their personal information these mysterious spooks are passing across the table. But it never occurs to them to think that we not only can't share information about their personal lives, we can't even share information about the people from all over the planet who are trying to kill them—assuming we even have that information. And you know what? Most of the time we don't. And if we did, we couldn't share it because we'd go to prison. Yeah, that's right: things have become so twisted inside that former swamp we call the nation's capital, that it's illegal for the FBI to even talk to the CIA, and vice-versa. So the people who are paid to protect Joe and Jane Citizen are reduced to passing little coded, handwritten notes, like a bunch of school girls, at places like Elaine's."

He continued. "And while our human-intelligence capabilities were degraded to the point where we didn't know about the collapse of the Soviet Union until we saw the report on CNN, a group that calls themselves Al Qaeda has been infiltrating the US and Europe and has been quietly establishing sleeper cells here, there, everywhere."

Something suddenly struck me. Why are people, like Barella and Vandenberg, telling me stuff that no one without top-secret clearance should know? Did they really think I would just promise to keep it all to myself? Then a disturbing thought came to mind, a very disturbing one: dead men tell no tales. I could feel the sweat starting to form on my brow.

"Tony? You okay? You look a little pale. There's a puke bag in the seat pouch in front of you, if you need it."

"I'm fine."

"Good."

"Sleeper cells."

"Okay. So, these people, our new friends in the Brotherhood, have kept the faith, and they've perfected their human-intelligence capabilities for over four hundred years. And thanks to that promise they made to your great-great-great-whatever-granddaddy, they have the skills and the infrastructure that we desperately need, and need now, to survive long enough to rebuild ours. Hell, they've got sleepers like you all over the goddamn place, and you don't even know you're a sleeper until you get a wake-up call. It's enough to give the guys at Langley a hard-on just thinking about the possibilities. So now, we're on the way to a big powwow on Malta to make a deal, a second Covenant of Malta, sorta-like the first one with your granddaddy. Except this one involves us covering their backs, while they cover ours. The enemy of my enemy is my friend—my friend."

I was really starting to miss old Howie. I said, "I'm just a software developer from some little Long Island town no one has ever heard of, but I managed to put away nine of the assholes in the black pajamas, so I'm having a really hard time understanding what the problem is for you CIA guys from Langley. If I can do that, this should be easy shit for big-shot killers like you, right?"

I was expecting Vandenberg to get a little pissed-off by that comment, but instead he gave me this creepy smile, and said, "Your count is eleven."

"What?"

"You got eleven of them, not including the three assists."

Three assists? What is this, the NHL? "Whatever. The point is that these guys can't be that much of a threat if a guy with a computer science degree can kill so many of them... so quickly."

Vandenberg nodded. "You have a point. But I think you may be missing something. It's not that they weren't good, they most definitely were, it's just that, somehow, you're that much better, sort of a natural-born killer."

"Oh, please, don't give me that shit."

"It's not shit, Tony. There's a lot you don't know about yourself, not yet, anyway. You can put a computer keyboard in front of a pit bull and teach it to use it. Hell, you can even dress it up in a suit, but it doesn't change the nature of the animal."

"Fine, whatever you say," I said with a dismissive wave of my hand. "In any event, it sounds like your people got what they needed from me and my family. You used us to find these guys, and now you have them. So, what am I doing here?"

"It's complicated. But I can tell you that of all of your relatives, the Brotherhood has a very special interest in you. They insisted that you come along."

"What does that mean?"

"I'm not supposed to tell you that. Besides, if I did, it might make your head explode."

"Try me."

"Forget it. You won't be happy, trust me."

Trust you? "Bullshit! You and the rest of these clowns, like Barella and the idiots from the Brotherhood, live in a world of make-believe. You wouldn't recognize the truth if it bit you on the ass. I think you all need to be locked in padded cells."

Vandenberg digested that for a few moments, and then he grinned and said, "Okay, if you insist, but don't say I didn't warn you. Let me start by saying that one of the first lessons I learned at Langley was that nothing is what it appears to be. I think that's a concept you need to get really friendly with, pard. First, there's some story about a prophecy." He stopped and laughed. "Can you believe that shit? A prophecy! It's like a bad movie. There's always a prophecy, right? Anyway, the story is that your father is from some Norman, Sicilian line, like Barbarossa or some shit, and your mother is from some Greek, Sicilian line, some warrior-king called Hieron, from Syracuse, or something. Turns out, they're the same two lines that the original guy, Sebastiano, came from. So, the way the Brotherhood interprets the prophecy, is that you may be the new Sebastiano: the new head honcho. Understand?"

"Prophecy? Head honcho? Is this some kind of bad joke?"

"Nope, not according to them. They believe that you were born specifically to lead us in our current hour of need," he said with a condescending smirk. "But who knows with prophecies, right? I mean, you ever read that Nostradamus gobblely-gook? Who can figure out what that shit means? Anyway, the weird thing is, if that isn't weird enough already, is that it was an accident."

"What was an accident?"

"Your mother and father getting together."

"What are you taking about?"

"You see, what started out as a relatively straightforward agreement to protect your granddaddy's descendants turned into something a little different. At some point, it became, essentially, a warrior-breeding program. So, for about four hundred years the people running this organization have been matchmaking, essentially selectively breeding people like you in preparation for, I don't know, someday like this, I guess. But in your case, well, you were kind of an accident. They didn't even know about your mother's lineage when the Brotherhood assigned her to your father's protection detail. And she was forbidden to get emotionally involved with your father, in any event. Her cover was as an investigative reporter for a local newspaper. Well, I guess she did a little more investigating than she was supposed to when it came to your dad."

"What the hell are you talking about?" I repeated.

"Sorry, that last comment was out of line; didn't mean that."

"My Mother? One of them? Are you nuts? She doesn't know which end of a gun to hold. She wouldn't even step on bug, for Christ-sake."

"Hey, I warned you. Look, I don't really give a shit about any of this prophecy stuff, and I don't care if you do either. But you, of all people, at this stage in the game, should start getting your head around this. I mean, shit, son, did you think your secretary, Marcella, was a bodyguard when you hired her - that she was a trained killer who was there to keep a four-hundred year old promise made by the Pope to some old guy? No? How about your old college roomie, the WASP named Howard Tucker, or your friend Billy? Did you know that they were agents with the CIA? No? Well, maybe your head is going to explode, but the truth is this: your momma has been watching over little Tony since the day you were born, like any momma, I suppose. But in her case, she was armed to the teeth, locked and loaded, and ready to rock and roll if anyone even looked at you cross-eyed. In Texas we call a woman like that hot and spicy. Goddamn, son!"

"You're completely insane. Are you aware of that?"

"Hell, I've been called worse things, and you just may be right, in any case. But like they say, facts are stubborn things, and the facts are that she was the one who put down the two guys who tried to kill your dad. Two shots, two kills… at thirty feet, right between the eyes," Vandenberg said, pointing his index finger to his forehead for emphasis. "I can tell you that there are not a lot of people in the business who could have made those kills."

I knew someone who could: Marcella. But I said, "My dad shot those guys, and he got a medal to prove it."

"No, Tony. Your dad was down before he ever got a shot off. And when Mommy was finished eliminating those two threats, she saved your daddy's life by giving him one of those injections with that special sauce. It kept him alive long enough for him to make it to the hospital. There was no mysterious EMT guy. Just your mom, doing her job. And when the shit hit the fan on Fire Island a couple of weeks ago, the Brothers called her out of retirement. She hopped the next flight out of Miami and was the first one on the firing line while Gunter up there was in the NYPD lockup, and Bill and Marcella were down, and the rest of us were still trying to figure out what the hell was going on. She covered your back during that fight, called in the Mounties, and then stood guard over you until help arrived. And she did it all without being detected by anyone, including you—like she was a ghost. She's not just good, she's fucking supernatural: a spook's spook. She was also the one that got Marcella the hell outta there... Oops, didn't mean to tell you that last part. Forget that."

"She took her body? Or was Marcella alive?"

He looked away. "I don't know. You have to ask them. But your new reality is this: those people - you know, the ones that you said you wanted to punish for the past, they're people like your mom, and your girlfriend, and you're one of them, too. So, I wouldn't be too preachy about what happened to JFK, if I were you."

"Is Marcella alive?" I demanded.

He stared at me, but said nothing.

Chapter 85

The helicopter flew through the night sky as I thought about Vandenberg's rants and revelations. First Barella, and now this guy. What was it about government service, I wondered? Did the work drive these people nuts, or was paranoid schizophrenia just part of the job description? How much of this could be true? And how much was misinformation designed to… what? Confuse me? Obfuscate the truth? But why? Why tell me any of this in the first place? And what if it was true? My God. I closed my eyes and put my head back on the seat. So, how many other rabbit holes were there? I wondered.

I asked him. "What were the official channels?"

"What?"

"The information about the attack on Malta; you said before that it mostly came from unofficial channels. What were the official ones?"

To be honest, I didn't expect any response to that question. In fact, I was expecting him to say that if he told me, he would have to kill me - or something to that effect. But his response, assuming I got one, might help me decide if anything this guy had just told me was true. I mean, how plausible is the notion that the CIA and FBI have national security meetings in a New York restaurant? That had to be bullshit. Right?

Vandenberg took out a pack of cigarettes and offered me one. I pointed to the nearest illuminated 'No Smoking' sign. He smiled, shook his head, and lit up.

"His name was Henkel." Vandenberg said. "He was a friend of mine. We didn't understand what he had until after the Elaine's meeting."

Vandenberg blew smoke toward the ceiling. "Langley sent him in to meet with someone in Afghanistan, a warlord named

Massoud. Henkel had some experience with Muslim culture from a stint in Bosnia, and even knew some Arabic. He was half Jewish, so when he grew a beard, and got a little sun, he could almost blend in." Vandenberg looked at me. "Then they sent him into the fucking lion's den alone, because everyone else was a blue-eyed, blond-haired, all-American, who didn't understand a word of Arabic, and knew more about comic books than the Koran." He shook his head in disgust. "Like I told you, our human intelligence assets are pretty thin. Henkel knew that, and he knew his chances of making it back were pretty thin, too. But he went anyway. Bravest, smartest, son-of-a-bitch I've ever met. And he almost made it too. He was on his way back when he was captured. All we knew then, was that the information he had for us was pretty hot."

Vandenberg pulled a silver flask out of one of the pockets of his coveralls, and took a gulp. He handed it to me. I shook my head.

"The assholes that killed him sent us a video. They cut his head off with a butcher's saw. Fucking animals!" He spat out. "In fact, the guy doing the sawing was one of the pricks that you wacked at that beach, the one you practically cut in half with that machete. Poetic justice for that son-of-a-bitch. Thanks for that, by the way."

I just nodded. What could I possibly say?

"So in the video," Vandenberg continued, "Henkel is kneeling there, knowing he's going to die very soon, and he's praying. Understandable, right? He's reciting the Lord's Prayer, loud and clear, over the rants of the prick with the knife, while he's staring into the bright lights of the video camera. Our analysts studied every frame of that video, trying to find a message – Morse code in his eye blinks, and that sort of shit. But they found nothing. So, since we didn't even have the man's body to return to his family, we thought about editing out the worse stuff and taking the tape to them. In fact, I got that shit-duty myself."

I tried to imagine Vandenberg sitting with the grieving family in front of a television, and collectively watching the image of a man who knew he was about to die a horrible death.

"At the last minute, the brass canned the idea," Vandenberg said. "To be honest, I was relieved. But a week later we get a call from his dad, who demanded to see it. Turns out, his old man was a retired Army Intelligence officer. Guess he found out about the video through the old-boys network. So, the brass changes their minds again, and I find myself sitting with his dad watching this fucking tape. Again. His mom had passed away, and his dad didn't want the rest of the family to see it, so it was just the two of us."

"As we're watching it his father comments that it's a strange prayer for him to say. When I asked him why, he told me that his wife was Jewish, which I knew, and that she raised their son in that faith, which I also knew. Everyone else at Langley knew it too, because his religion was listed in his personnel file, but it never quite registered on anybody. Hell, even if it did, what good would it have done? The guy was probably tortured for days, no food, no water, he's probably delirious, and if he's aware of anything at all it's that he's about to die, he knows that, and he's praying. What fucking difference does it make what prayer he's saying!"

Vandenberg sighed, then smiled, "In fact, I remembered having a conversation with him once. We're all told that taking any sort of religious symbols or books into the Islamic badlands was ill-advised. If you're a Muslim, and they catch you with a Koran, they shoot you immediately as a traitor to your faith. If they find anything Jewish on you they'll torture you, then shoot you, because, well, you're Jewish. If they find Christian items, they get pissed, but strangely, they usually gave you pass, like you're just confused or stupid, but not hopeless. When they caught Henkel he was carrying a King James Bible."

I said, "I guess no one gets a pass now."

Vandenberg nodded. "So one day, Henkel shows me this Bible. And he tells me that it was a gift from his grandma, his father's mother, a good southern Baptist, who wasn't really that happy about him being raised Jewish. Henkel said that his mother told him to take it and keep it with him, out of respect for grandma, but just to read the Old Testament parts." Vandenberg stopped and laughed again. "But one night we got drunk, and Henkel confessed that sometimes, when no one is looking, he sneaks a peek at the New Testament." Vandenberg stopped laughing, and took another drink, swallowing hard this time. "He told me he liked reading Paul. Said he was probably the smartest Jew in either the new or the old Books." He cleared his throat. "They cut Paul's head off too." Then Vandenberg went silent and rubbed the stubble on the side of his face.

He resumed his story. "So, we're watching the video, and I'm trying to hold it together, seeing him kneeling there, helpless and waiting to die, and I was so relieved when it was finally over. I just wanted to get the hell out of there. But then his father asked me to play it again. I thought that maybe the poor old guy was losing it, but he didn't even have a tear in his eye. I played that thing four more times. Then his father informed me that his son loved to play word games with him when he was a kid. Cyphers, puzzles, cryptographs; old spy stuff like that. Then he looked at me and said that his son wasn't the sort of man to say a prayer and get it wrong. He told me that his son knew that prayer, that his grandma had taught it to him when he was a boy - but the words in the video were wrong. He told me to take the video back and have someone study it more closely, because his son was sending a message. That's why he chose a Christian prayer in the first place, to get our attention, to make us understand that he had something to report."

"So, I did, and he was right. Can't believe we almost missed it. It was an obvious code. He used the number of syllables in the sentences to indicate the words of the alphabet; one syllable for 'A', thirteen for 'M', etcetera."

"So, what did the message say?" I asked.

"He gave us three locations. We already knew, from our unofficial meeting with the FBI at Elaine's, what we were looking for. We also knew its port of origin. What we didn't know was the target it was heading for. The first location Henkel gave us was M-A-L-T-A. So, naturally, when we put it together, we figured out where they were going to strike first. We began a radius search pattern starting at Malta and kept going until we found the tanker. Actually, we found four tankers. Without Henkel's message it would have been like searching for the proverbial needle in the haystack. It's a big ocean, and there are lots of tankers in it. So then, we just had to narrow down the selection to one. We were working on that when you and Stanislav helpfully arranged that ride that put us right on the deck."

"What about the other two locations?" I asked him.

Vandenberg looked at me for a long time, then he said. "NY and DC."

"You think they're going to try to pull this same shit in America? In New York and Washington?"

He nodded slowly. "Looks that way."

I thought about an oil tanker, out there somewhere, filled with enough explosives to level a small island, and on its way to New York or Washington. Or both. Then I thought about Henkel. What a combination of brains and balls that guy must have had to devise and send a message like that, while he was waiting to have his head cut off.

Vandenberg broke into my thoughts. "You getting the picture now?"

I nodded.

Chapter 86

I looked to my left as the lights of what I assumed to be Sicily came into view and soon passed, fading into the distance and the darkness behind us. The wheels in my head were spinning like the rotor on the machine I was flying in, trying to make sense of all of the new information that just got dumped on me by Vandenberg, and I hadn't even finished processing the crap from Mario and Barella yet.

I finally gave up and redirected all of my thoughts, excluding everything, except a single focus: Marcella. My mom told me, when I was in the hospital, to find Marcella and bring her home. I realized now that what I thought was her hopeless confidence was actually something else. She knew Marcella was alive, because she found her and took her to safety. Mom was probably also the one who planted the note in the bathroom, the thing that finally got my ass in gear. *Jesus! It was right in front of my face, and I missed it.*

But why wasn't Marcella waiting for me at the castle in Pavone, like the note said she would be? And where was she now? And why is everyone refusing to tell me anything about her?

Vandenberg interrupted my thoughts. "There's Malta."

I looked down at the lights of the island.

"Okay." Vandenberg said, "Tighten your seat belt and hang on; it's time for a little creative flying!"

"What?"

"There might be some of those guys in the black pajamas down there watching our approach," Vandenberg replied. "They're expecting a suicide dive into the heart of the town, remember? And when they don't see it, they'll conclude that their mission was blown, and they might just decide to put a heatseeker up our ass. Besides, they really want you dead, you know."

I asked, "How is it that these guys even know I'm in Italy?"

"That's a good question." Vandenberg said, frowning.

Just as he was about to start his next sentence I felt the seat drop out from under me. If not for the seat belt, I would have hit the ceiling.

"You ever do this before?" I yelled over the high-pitched scream of the blades.

"You mean fly like this? Yeah, sure. But never in the dark. Hell, I've never even *heard* of someone doing this kind-a-shit in the dark."

What?

Vandenberg yelled directly into my ear. "Pucker up, pard!" Then he looked at me with a big, toothy grin. "Yee-hah!"

The helicopter began a series of sharp, fast, zig-zag banking and descent maneuvers that caused my stomach to ball up into a knot. It felt like the worst roller coaster ride I'd ever been on, times ten. I sank my fingers into the seat back in front of me and tried to keep my ass, now fully puckered, on the seat cushion.

You didn't have to be a military expert, or work for the CIA, to understand what the purpose of this type of landing approach was. And you also didn't need to be an aviation expert to figure out that one tiny miscalculation by the man at the controls would result in a burning oil slick on the surface of the water. I started praying that my crazy friend Mario was also an insanely good pilot.

"Apparently some people from Italy like to fly."

"What?" Vandenberg yelled back.

I managed to push myself back and down into my seat and began scanning the horizon through the window, peering into the dark for the sight of an approaching missile, while also contemplating the capacity of the barf-bag in the pouch in front of me. Suddenly, the craft took another wild, banking turn to the right, leveled off, and a moment later the dramatically lit walls of a massive stone fortress came into view.

The ramparts rose in steep steps from the harbor and soared high above us, as we flew just a few feet above the lit surface of the water. Then we began what I hoped was our final approach toward the landing zone.

"Hey Tony!" Stanislav yelled back to me between the seats, "Welcome to Saint Angelo. You think you be safe in this place?"

I didn't respond, but I thought I might be, assuming I survived the landing, and also assuming that there wasn't a missile heading for us, or another explosives-laden oil tanker out there somewhere and heading this way. *How the hell did I get into this mess*?

I turned my attention back towards the brooding mass of the citadel, which grew with each passing moment. I remembered that once, when I was a kid, my parents took me on a visit to some Revolutionary War fortress in upstate New York. I remember feeling like an ant in comparison to its massive fortifications. But nothing I had ever seen or imagined compared with this thing. The size and shape of Saint Angelo made it appear more like a work of geology than of men.

The helicopter continued to fly fast and low, passing a wharf filled with large luxury yachts, and then the nose flared up and it suddenly decelerated to a near stop. We landed a few moments later, touching down gently in a seaside courtyard.

Two large, black SUVs sat waiting on the edge of the landing zone. We exited the helicopter, and as we did, our pilot and copilot, Mario and Gunter, stood by the door and thanked us for flying Air Brotherhood: *We know you have a choice and we're glad you chose us.* Actually, they just gave me a friendly wave as I passed, but I was too busy trying to keep my legs steady and my stomach contents down to return the gesture, so I just smiled and nodded. *Great job!*

The two of them followed us to the waiting vehicles. On the way, Vandenberg gave me a quick salute and told me that he would buy me a drink later, after his meeting and my meeting. I didn't even know I was here for a meeting.

Stanislav and I got in the first SUV, and the others climbed into the second one. We drove from the landing zone up a stone ramp and around a series roads that snaked through and around the massive fortifications until we finally drove through the gates of the citadel.

Jesus, this place made that upstate fortress look like an ant hill. At some point we turned right and the second SUV disappeared to the left. Our driver stopped the SUV in a dark alcove. Stanislav left the vehicle and I followed him through a wooden door into a nearby stone portico, entering what appeared to be a small chapel. Stanislav proceeded up the center aisle to the altar, while I hung back. When he reached it he knelt, bowed his head, and made the sign of the cross. A glance back at me indicted his expectations for me to follow. And so, trying to recall my best Sunday-school etiquette, I followed him and did the same. Then we both stood and proceeded through a door on the right side of the chapel.

We entered a broad corridor that was brightly lit. It felt cool and dry and smelled old, like a museum. The sound of the door, closing behind us, echoed loudly.

The floor was made from multi-colored marble, inlaid with a large, circular depiction of a coat of arms that consisted of a blue background, a gold shield, and several crosses in the middle. It was all topped off with a golden crown. Evenly spaced along the walls were lamps that illuminated standing displays of suits of armor, as well as paintings on the walls and ceiling depicting people, places, and events, none of which I recognized.

Stanislav led me up a series of spiral stairs. I was amazed at how fast he was moving, given the fact that he nearly died yesterday. I began to huff and puff pretty badly after about five flights. When we reached the tenth flight, we exited through a wooden door to the right. As I gasped to catch my breath, I made a mental note to start on an exercise program when I got home.

Stanislav looked back at me and smiled. "You okay?"

I nodded.

The door opened into yet another large stone room, this one furnished more elaborately and in a style that can best be described as early Vatican chic: red drapes and carpets with inlaid gold leaf everywhere on the darkly stained wood and furnishings. On the wall at the front of the room was a fabric tapestry consisting of what I immediately recognized as a white, eight-point Maltese cross encircled by what appeared to be blue beads. A white cape formed a larger backdrop, and all of it was capped by a blue and gold crown topped by yet another cross. Closer to the center of the room was a white marble altar, and sitting upon it was a large gold crucifix.

I whispered to Stanislav, "Nice to know the collection plate money is being put to good use."

Stanislav replied with an expression that indicated that he did not appreciate my humor, which was odd, considering that I stole the line from his colleague, Mario. He placed his index finger over his lips and then pointed it ahead towards a figure who seemed to have materialized out of thin air.

"That is not very funny, Anthony," a deep voice commented with a thick Spanish accent. I made another mental note: don't make smart-ass cracks in large, echoey stone rooms.

"Call me Tony," I replied.

The man was facing away from me and appeared to be looking up at the crucifix, then turned, approached, and proceeded to circle and examine me as if I was some sort of lost dog that had just returned home. He wore white robes fringed with elaborate red and gold trim. On his head was a white pointed bishop's hat adorned with the same colorful pattern. On his chest, suspended by a gold chain, was a medallion, and in the center was the Maltese cross.

"It is good to see that you are safe and sound," he said.

"Thanks, it's good to be safe and sound."

The man's face appeared ancient, his leathery skin revealing deep grooves and age spots. He nodded at Stanislav, and without a word, Stanislav made a graceful bow and disappeared behind a door at the side of the chapel.

I watched Stanislav leave and was tempted to follow. The old man gave me the creeps, and the last place I wanted to be was in a dimly lit room, alone with this guy.

"I understand you have many questions, young Anthony."

I was tempted to remind him again about calling me Tony, but concluded it would be a waste of time. "I would say that's an understatement," I replied. "Let me start by asking two very simple ones: Who are you, and why am I here?"

The old man smiled broadly. "I am consistently bemused and exasperated by Americans' brashness. What is it about that land that makes you so… " He search for a word, but I decided to fill in the blank.

"Annoying?" I asked.

"Not exactly the word I was searching for, but it will do for now."

I tried again. "So, who are you?"

"I am Bishop Pietro Montagne. Stanislav and our brothers Mario and Gunter work for me. I work for the Vatican. One of my jobs is to help keep that promise to protect you, the one that you have heard so much about, apparently. However, as important as that job is to me, my first priority is to defend the faith and the faithful. Maintaining the promise to your ancestor is directly derived from that first, and most sacred, mission. As for why you are here, well, perhaps you can explain that to me."

I stared at him and said, "Unfortunately, I don't exactly qualify as one of the faithful. So, I'm not here for that reason. In fact I can't recall the last time I went to church or made a confession. And I certainly never signed up for this protection crap, either. I'm here, Bishop, for only one purpose, and that is to find Marcella."

He absorbed the words, then asked, "And why, may I ask, are you looking for her?"

"Because I love her. Why else would someone travel four thousand miles, surrounded by lunatics, and dodging bullets, bombs, missiles, and exploding tankers along the way?"

The old man turned away suddenly and said, "I am sorry, Anthony, I cannot help you with that request."

"You can't help, or you won't help?"

"I cannot and I will not. It is forbidden."

There was that word again. "It's forbidden? What the hell does that mean?"

"It means exactly what it sounds like it means, young man."

"So, Marcella is alive."

The bishop placed his head in his hands and shook it. "Whether she is alive or dead, the matter is closed! You can never see her again!"

"Oh, you're wrong there. Let me tell you something, Bishop. If you really believe that my ancestor was this great warrior-hero, and if you really believe that I have even a drop of that blood in my veins, then you better believe this: I *will* find her. And anyone—and I mean anyone—who tries to stop me will not be long among the living!" By the time I reached the last word my voice was loud, harsh, and trembling, which reverberated in the chapel.

The bishop took a deep breath and let it out slowly. "Very well, Anthony, you have made your position clear. Let me give it some thought. But in the meantime, there is something I want you to see, and someone I want you to speak with."

Before I could reply, he smiled and waved his hand towards the first row of pews, indicating that he wanted me to sit down. I surprised myself by obediently finding a seat in the first row, folded my hands in my lap, and tried to regain my composure.

My own words came back to me and blended with the feelings and longings I had for Marcella. The intensity of the feelings made my heart pound, and I bit my lip until it hurt. The logical part of my brain was working hard, trying to restrain my urge to grab this guy by the neck and shake the truth out of him. I knew that it would be a waste of time and energy, but I was getting tired of being screwed around with. I wanted to see Marcella, and I wanted to see her now!

Chapter 87

Two massive gilded doors in the rear of the chapel swung open, and I watched over my shoulder as a procession of five men started down the aisle. My first reaction was disappointment, not because of who I saw but because of who I didn't see, the only person I was here for.

The first man, a priest in plain black robes and carrying a tall staff crowned by a gold crucifix, was followed by four men in double ranks. They wore martial uniforms, from the fifteenth or sixteenth century, if I were to guess. These colorful costumes consisted of red pants and shirts adorned with gold stripes. On their chests' were ornamental armor plates shined to a mirror finish and overlaid diagonally with a red silk ribbon. Around their necks', above the flared armored collar, was a white frilled fabric that folded up and under their jawline. Each of them also carried a feather-adorned helmet tucked under their left arm and a sheathed sword that swung at their side below it.

I had no idea what this was all about, but it was definitely too early for Halloween, and too late for Mardi Gras, so I assumed I was being treated to some solemn ceremony or other by the Bishop - perhaps as a way of eliciting my cooperation, or as a means to impress me.

Then I noticed a sixth and last man, bringing up the rear of the procession. He was taller than the others, covered in a white cape adorned on both sides with a large, red Maltese cross, and a white linen hood that fitted loosely over his bowed head and concealed his face. He seemed not to belong, somehow. I'm not sure, but I think it was something about his walk, which appeared very twentieth century, and in fact, very American.

The procession moved slowly and solemnly towards the bishop at the front of the chapel, each step timed in rhythm with a chanting chorus of deep voices coming from somewhere in the darkness above, in the high, vaulted ceiling.

The priest took his position at the side of the bishop and the four men in armor took theirs on each side of the altar. The man in white then stood in the middle, directly in front of and facing the bishop. He knelt and removed his hood, revealing a round, red cylindrical hat on the center of a thirty-something-year-old head, covered with thick, black, wavy hair. He had a handsome profile with a sharp, curved nose, and a strong jaw line, that I immediately recognized.

One of the armored men to his right drew a long, menacing-looking sword from his scabbard and handed it reverently to the bishop. The bishop held the sword, blade down, at the place where the blade met the hilt, thereby forming a cross. The Bishop lifted the heavy object high above the head of the kneeling man and began chanting something in what I recognized as Latin.

When the old man had finished his incantation, he brought the hilt of the sword down and kissed it. Then he lowered it towards the younger man, who kissed it in the same way. The man then rose as the bishop took a cup from the priest and placed a small wafer from it into his mouth. One of the armored men at his side then removed the younger man's white cloak to reveal a uniform that consisted of a red, gold-trimmed jacket, along with similarly adorned black trousers.

Now, all of them took ceremonial bows in unison, followed by an exchange of hearty handshakes, along with congratulations, spoken in English, to the younger man.

The bishop gave a single wave of his hand, and just as suddenly as everyone had appeared, they all left the room. All except the tall, younger one. The bishop whispered into this man's ear, then sat in a throne-like chair near the altar. The younger man nodded, bowed, turned, and came towards me, taking a seat in the pew next to me.

"Hello Tony." he said in a low voice.

"Hello, Agent Castro."

"My first name is John, but my friends call me Jack."

I replied, "Since I'm not a friend, I don't know what I should call you."

"Well," he said, "you're family, so Jack works."

"So you're the guy, the one with Bush in Kuwait that Barella told me about. Right?"

"Yes, I was part of his Secret Service detail."

"Then it was you the Brotherhood was trying to protect, when they accidentally saved Bush."

"Yup, that's me. I guess you can say I was just doing my job, you know: saving the president from certain death. Unfortunately, I had no idea at the time that I was doing it. In fact, I didn't find out until years later."

He waved his hand around the chapel. "These guys are that good. I thought I was part of the most professional protection service in the world, but these folks have forgotten more about the job than we ever knew."

I nodded. "Is that a Californian accent?" I asked.

"Yeah, San Diego."

"So what's the connection with my family?"

"The short version goes like this. The Pope promises the old man, Sebastiano, that he's going to protect all of his sons. But after Malta he discovers that, in the small print, the deal only covers the ones residing in regions under the Church's dominion. Translation: the sons of his Muslim son, the one he was forced to kill on Malta, are on their own. As with Real Estate, the deal was all about location, location, location. But, the old man didn't like that very much, so he spent most of the rest of his life bringing his second, Muslim family - at least the ones he could find, out of the Muslim world and setting them up in various places in Italy and Spain – regions under the protection of the Church. There's some pretty exciting cloak-and-dagger stories during this period, as a result. There's actually one where he goes right into the heart of enemy territory and gets some of us out, right under the nose of Suleiman. Unfortunately, he is captured. So, he's being held in a fortress prison awaiting execution, when he's rescued by some of his friends in the Brotherhood, who use that stuff in the little black capsule to put him into a deep sleep. Everyone thought the man was dead. So, out of respect, Suleiman agrees to hand over the body for burial on Sicily." Jack laughed. "Almost didn't work. The old man woke up too soon. But all's well that ends well."

"So, that's where my family comes from," Jack Castro concluded. "He planted us in Spain, away from his other family, for obvious reasons. Then some of my family moved to the New World, just like yours did a few centuries later. We were some of the original Californians, when it was still part of the Spanish Empire. But, we're sort of the black sheep of the clan." He smiled. "Some converted to Christianity, some didn't. Sebastiano didn't care. That wasn't part of the protection deal. He just had to relocate us."

I changed the subject to the present. "Something of an irony that your name is John."

"I should say so. My mom was, as they say, a child of the Sixties. She named me after him. My full name is John Fitzgerald Castro."

"I assume she has no idea what an irony that is."

"No, of course not, and she never will."

I thought about that and then said, "Never? Unless she's dead Jack, sooner or later, she's going to find out. Someone is going to leak this out to the rest of the planet. No secret this big ever stays secret for long."

Jack started to laugh and shook his head. "You know, that's

exactly what I would have said not so long ago. Now I know better. If the story of our common ancestry proves anything, it proves that the really big secrets can last a very, very long time." He sighed. "You want to know how it happened, Tony? I can tell you in exquisite detail; how many shooters there were, where they were positioned, how many shots were fired, and in what sequence. I can even show you one of the weapons, if you'd like. You want to know who? Well, you've just met one of them," he said, nodding his head in the direction of the old man who sat quietly in front of us. "You see that wrinkled right index finger, the one with the gold ring? That's the finger that pulled the trigger that dropped the hammer on the rifle that made the head shot."

I looked at the Bishop's finger, and as I did, a series of images from the Zapruder film started playing in my head: fuzzy, colored images of the motorcade gliding slowly and silently to that moment when Kennedy's skull blew open. I closed my eyes and tried to push the images away as Jack continued to talk.

"But you know what? In the end, nobody really cares about how and who. In the end, all anyone cares about is why. And that's where this whole thing hits a brick wall. You try telling someone that the thirty-fifth President of the United States was killed by a secret organization that works for the Vatican because of a promise made four hundred years ago to some guy from Sicily. You go ahead, but I promise you, even the wackiest conspiratorial jerk-off on the planet will think you've blown a gasket. You probably couldn't even convince our crazy cousin in Havana, and he's been scratching his head about this mystery for forty years. He knows he didn't do it."

"How did you find this out?" I asked.

"Barella approached me about a year ago, and laid out his theory for me. I thought he was completely gone," Jack said, wagging a finger at his temple. "But eventually, I started to believe it. All the pieces seemed to fit, but they didn't all come together until the recent series of events with you. Then we both knew he had it right. Too bad he won't see the fruits of his long labor."

We both sat there a while, staring in the direction of the bishop, before I broke the silence. "I don't understand this," I said, pointing to the man on the throne who was watching us. "I thought Barella was out to get these guys because of what they did to Kennedy?"

"He was. But things have changed, couz. If you've been keeping score, we had the Trade Center bombing in New York and the attempted assassination of Bush in '93, in 1996 there was Khobar, then the embassy bombings in '98, then the USS *Cole* last year, and now this Malta thing that we just stopped from happening. We also know they've got other major operations coming down the pike; we just don't have all of the details yet. The Islamists are on the move again, just like four hundred years ago. And our family history is on a collision course with the present. And, just like four hundred years ago, most of the Christian world is asleep at the switch. As for the U.S., we have the best intelligence technology the world has ever seen. But without old-fashioned human intelligence, it's nearly worthless."

"Yeah, I know. I got that speech from Vandenberg," I said.

"Yeah? What else did he tell you?"

I relayed the details Vandenberg gave me about the mission to stop the tanker headed for Malta. Most of it, Jack Castro seemed to know. But some of it he seemed not to. Like the part about Henkel. I concluded, "I don't understand why people keep telling me things I probably shouldn't know. Isn't this stuff top secret, or something?"

Castro shrugged. "Yes, but it's not a problem if they recruit you."

Or I'm dead.

I asked, "So you think that Barella and Vandenberg wanted to hire me?"

"Maybe."

Work for Vandenberg? Not in a million years!

Castro must have noticed the unpleasant look on my face because he asked. "So what do you think of Vandenberg?"

I replied, "At first I thought he was certifiable, and he definitely didn't do anything to enhance my opinion about the people from the great state of Texas. But now, I'm not so sure. Maybe he just needs a vacation, or a little couch-time with a shrink."

Jack Castro laughed. "He's not the only one in that organization who needs a shrink. As for being from Texas, I wouldn't take that to the bank either. The man is a chameleon. Next week he might tell you that he's from Minnesota and that his family emigrated from Norway. Secret Service people have worked closely with the CIA on this project for some time. But we never assume anything they say is the truth. Worse than that, they have this amazing ability to edit their words in a way so that everything they tell you is technically true, but taken as a whole it's all a lie."

"That sounds pretty complicated," I said.

"Not really. Here's an example. Vandenberg probably led you to believe that he caught up with our friends here as a result of that incident in New York with you two weeks ago, right?"

"Right."

"And that's technically true. What he didn't tell you was that the timing wasn't a coincidence. He and his people at Langley intentionally precipitated the incident."

The look on my face was the only response Jack needed to understand that I was completely clueless about what he was talking about.

Chapter 88

Jack Castro said, "They kept tabs on you and your family after that incident with your dad, once Barella told them his theory. Like I said, everyone thought he was nuts. But just in case he wasn't, they kept an eye on you to see if they needed to start keeping an eye on Them, assuming there was a Them," he said, pointing his chin towards the bishop. "Langley was starting to get bored with it until things started heating up with a Middle Eastern group we now know as Al Qaeda. Then, people in Washington started to get a little panicky when they finally realized that, hey, maybe we do need human-intelligence capabilities, after all. So, someone in Langley gets the clever idea that we need to hook up with the Brotherhood, assuming they really exist, and you're elected as bait."

"Why me? Why not use you? You're a member of the clan, and a government employee."

Jack laughed. "Yeah, that's why I make the big bucks, right? The reason is that Barella wouldn't let them. He didn't think that the CIA had any idea of what they dealing with, and he wasn't going to let one of his own hang his ass out there to prove him right. So they rigged up that little piece of work with the key man life insurance scam, and hung your ass out instead."

"I thought that was Jan's and Kyle's plan?"

"Nope, it came directly from Langley. Jan was a plant, and Kyle... he was just greedy and stupid."

"Jesus Christ. So the CIA started this whole mess? They're responsible for all of this mayhem and death?"

"Hey, mayhem and death is part of their mission statement. It's all in the name of the greater good, of course. In fairness, it wasn't supposed to get as crazy as it did. And obviously, they weren't as ready as they thought they were, just like Barella warned them. So, one day, Jan has a meeting with this three-time loser to set up the hit on you, and the next day, she's dead. They weren't really going to let the guy kill you, of course. In fact, they chose him because he was a half-wit who probably couldn't kill a fish in a bowl. But the Brotherhood took him very seriously. Next thing you know, after both Jan and the dopey assassin dude are dead, everything went to shit."

Christ, isn't anyone or anything what I thought it was? "I guess that was a little embarrassing for the conniving pricks at Langley, huh?" I said.

"Boy, I can tell you that there was some serious shit coming down at the debriefing on that one. In fact, one genius suggested we drop the plan and go after the Brotherhood. He thought they were more dangerous than Al Qaeda. Vandenberg, who was running the op, told them that was exactly the point. He said we needed them because they're really dangerous, smart, and wired all over the place. So, Vandenberg prevails and they proceed with the plan. But, what no one knew at the time was that Saddam and company were trying to smoke out the same organization, and had been trying to do so since the Brotherhood screwed up their plans for Bush's assassination in Kuwait, in '93. So, when the murder reports on Jan and Dopey show up on the police networks—the ones describing the powdered bullets in their heads and the oily crosses, etcetera—a mole flags the info and passes it on to Saddam. He, in turn, dispatches the guys in the black pajamas, including the guy that Marcella whacked across the street from your office."

"Wow, great plan, CIA guys," I said. "And these are the idiots guarding the gates?"

"Unintended consequences, man. They're a bitch. Saddam's initial target, we think, was Marcella and the rest of the Brotherhood. You and I and our families were next. But then you and that big horse on Fire Island got involved and really messed up their plans."

"You heard about that?" I asked.

"I surely did, and someday I want you to tell me all of the gory details over a beer. I'll buy the first round."

"I'm happy I could help out a little."

"You helped more than you know. Those guys you took out on Fire Island were supposed to be part of the team that delivered that little floating surprise to Malta."

"You mean the exploding oil tanker?"

Jack nodded. "Because of you they had to recruit new people for the project, to replace the ones that you... retired. That's how Vandenberg found out about the plan. When the conspirators tried to recruit the replacement operatives, one of them happen to be an FBI informant. That was the first lucky break. The second one was the FBI guy who broke the rules and passed the information to Vandenberg."

A picture came to mind of two tough guys at some place called Elaine's, passing a note under a table like a pair of school girls.

"Then we got a third break," Jack continued, "when you also retired the replacements with that big bang at the little cottage in Italy. All we needed to do then was to fill in the empty seats on the helicopter with that SEAL team, that you met earlier. They were going to be there anyway, they just came in by helicopter rather than a parachute." Jack smiled. "The team leader asked me to thank you for the comfortable ride."

I thought about all of this and considered how unlikely that series of events was. Jack seemed like a straight shooter, but I couldn't avoid being skeptical.

"By the way," He said to me, "that was a crazy-dangerous mission that you volunteered for. You have a reckless streak that you need to get under control, couz."

"You mean the oil tanker thing? It was nothing. I just sat there and watched."

"It was nothing, huh? That was a suicide mission for those Al Qaeda clowns." Jack pointed to his knee. "Mega-bomb trigger." He then showed me his hand. "Hand of suicide asshole." He slapped his hand on his knee. "Vaporized Tony Mascelle. They could have blown that ship the instant they realized that they were being attacked. That's how close you were to being dead."

Not reckless, just stupid. "Well, you should have warned me it was going to be dangerous."

Jack shot me an angry look.

"I'm kidding. But next time try to be more convincing. Tie me up, throw me in the trunk, and just drive me to the airport."

"I'll take that under advisement." Jack Castro replied. Then he said, gesturing toward our babysitter up front, "He's been hearing a lot about your handiwork, especially the Fire Island, thing. You really got his attention on that one."

"What do you mean?"

"It's another long story."

"You don't mean that prophecy crap, do you?"

"Yeah. To the extent that any of it is understandable, as far as they are concerned, at least at the moment, you seem to fit the bill. The bottom line is that they are really impressed with you, and they started to become really cooperative with us after that Fire Island incident. We weren't sure why at the time, but we know now it was you."

Yeah, right, the prophecy. What lunacy.

Jack continued. "So, what started out as a nice, neat little CIA plan that was supposed to lead to an introduction, and maybe an alliance, turns into a small war, just like that. Anyhow, the CIA catches some breaks, uncovers the plan to blow up Malta, and, with your aforementioned help, Langley pulls the proverbial rabbit out of the hat. Now, Langley and Malta are new best friends."

I asked Jack, "Does being a part of this make you feel good? I mean, is this what they taught us in civics class? Is this what America is all about? Are these the rules we're supposed to be playing by: making unholy alliances with people like this? Vandenberg tried to convince me that I'm one of them. But that's bullshit. This whole mess makes me sick to my stomach, just thinking about it."

Jack Castro contemplated that question. "If it's any consolation, Tony, I can tell you that these guys really hated that operation, the one with Kennedy, that is. Especially him," Jack said, motioning to the bishop. "Their job is to protect the faith, but they were forced to keep their pledge and save Fidel Castro, a man who once called the leaders of the church scribes, Pharisees and Fascists. And they were forced to save him by killing another man, a Catholic man, who was by no means a saint, but by all indications was at least trying to do the right thing for the world. I think that mission left some deep and lasting scars on this organization, and I suspect that saving Bush in Kuwait was as much about their penance, as it was about saving my life."

"I can't say that I take any consolation from that at all." I said. "In fact it sounds like a massive rationalization that you and the rest of the people you work for, and with, are using to justify what is not justifiable."

Jack's relaxed Californian style became a little tense. "To tell you the truth, Tony, I'm not interested in getting your understanding or approval, and I'll also tell you that this whole thing scares the shit out me. But just like Vandenberg, I want to get those nut jobs that tried to pull that shit in Malta, and that are planning new attacks as we speak. These Al Qaeda people are like nothing we've faced before. They are extremely dangerous, extremely motivated, and now they have someone on their side, like Saddam, who can provide the resources, operational capabilities, and training that they need to make their sick dreams into our worst nightmares. As for me, whatever needs to be done to protect my country, I'll do it: no apologies, no excuses. But I'll tell you something else; in the final analysis, this thing is bigger than that. Much bigger."

He turned and gave me an intense look with his gray-green eyes. "All of these Islamist assholes are gathering in the hills of these third-world shit-holes. Most of these people have never even seen indoor plumbing, for Christ's sake. They're still living in the sixteenth century. And yet, when they get their balls up and they team up with some competent leadership, they can do some serious damage. That's obvious. Right?"

"Now just think about this scenario. One of these groups gets their sweaty little hands on two or three nukes, and they set them off in two or three of our cities. Millions are dead or dying, the US economy collapses, and for the first time in living memory, children in America are dying from starvation and diseases that we thought disappeared a long time ago. In the meantime, the rest of the Islamist pricks are dancing in the streets. They finally knocked off the Great Satan. Right? Wrong!"

"What do you think happens next? You think the American people are just going slink away somewhere and go lick their wounds? Or maybe they'll want to have a friendly little chat with these folks to figure out just what their problem is with us, and see if we can resolve our differences over a nice cup of warm milk and cookies, and then we'll all sing Kumbaya. Right? No way, José. If and when such an attack occurs, the game will move to a whole different playing field. The gloves come off, the Marquis of Queensbury rules go out the window, and these assholes are going to see something they can't even imagine yet."

"Think about 300 million Americans with their balls up, in a rage that's deeper and more vicious than anything those clowns in the caves have dreamt of in their worst nightmares. We have the most deadly arsenal ever assembled on the face of the earth, and America is going to demand that we use it. You think that some moderate voices in Washington, or the left-wing media in New York, or the useless pricks at the UN, are going to stop that rage from playing out? Nope! And if any of the usual clowns get in the way, this time, they'll be shot in the streets, or will be hanging from light posts along Broadway or Pennsylvania Avenue. You mark my words; you'll see it with your own eyes!"

"Nothing will stop what happens next. The American people are going to demand payback, which means the next casualty is going to be the Republic. The Constitution, the government, the courts, everything we've deluded ourselves into believing are permanent components of our political and social lives will disappear, just like they did in Rome. And they'll be replaced by someone or something that gives the people what they want: security, and revenge."

"And what happens next is going to be total, no-holds-barred war on a scale we've never seen before. The contestants? It'll be the assholes with the AK-47s, and the body bombs, in the toilet-less bat-caves - versus the USA with the ICBMS, stealth bombers, satellites, nuclear submarines, aircraft carriers, and enough nuclear warheads to set the atmosphere on fire. And that's to say nothing of a twenty-million-man, all-volunteer American army with a really bad attitude."

"Five years, fifty years, five hundred years... it won't matter. Whatever it takes, they'll do it. What happens to Islam? It's gone; there is no Islam. Because of a few maniacs, who claim they're fighting a holy war, hundreds of millions of innocent Muslims will pay the price. There won't be anything left standing on this planet that even resembles a mosque, when this is finished."

"So, in a strange way, Tony, I'm not only fighting to protect my country; I'm also fighting to save these Islamist maniacs from themselves. Do I like the rules we're playing by today? Maybe I do, maybe I don't. But sometimes, bad rules are better than no rules."

I replied, "What is it with you guys? This is the third crazy speech I've heard in twenty-four hours. Have all of you gone insane?"

Castro shot back, "Barella, Vandenberg, and I all have the same thing in common, even though guys like Vandenberg would never admit it: we're all scared shitless, waiting and wondering when the next shoe is going to drop. So if we seem a little off in the head, or a little crazy at the moment, that's why."

I asked him. "Do you really think that Americans are capable of throwing away everything they believe, everything they stand for, and doing something like that?"

Jack Castro informed me, "Do you think that the Nazis, Imperial Japan, or Stalin's USSR collectively woke up in the morning one day and said, 'today we're going to be evil assholes'? No, of course not. No matter how outrageously evil they were, they somehow managed to justify their deeds, at least in their own minds, as being for the greater good."

"We're not the Nazis, Jack."

"Yeah, and the Nazis didn't think they were the Nazis either, Tony. I'm not here to debate the topic of American exceptionalism, if that's what you're alluding to. In fact, I think America is exceptional, and because I think that, I'm willing to lay down my life, like a lot of other people are ready to do, to defend her. You know: the ones who you think are crazy. America is exceptional, but there are at least two ways to view American exceptionalism, in my opinion. The first one goes like this: we're great, we've always been great, and we'll always be great, no matter what anyone says or does and regardless of what happens. In other words, we wear blue tights and a red cape and the bullets will just bounce off. But that's the way a ten-year-old would define the term, not an adult that has an even passing acquaintance with history."

"Look," I said, "I know a little history myself, and I don't think we're going to throw it all away, our whole way of life, to go on a vengeance bender."

"Really? Why? People have been doing that for millennia. Why not us? There's this amazingly ignorant, to say nothing of dangerous, idea floating around out there that government by the governed is somehow the default condition of the human species. Nothing could be further from the truth. Representative government is hard and messy, and so it's extremely rare, because very few people or societies like hard and messy. Most people like easy and neat. And they also like what they know, what's familiar and comfortable. Every human being on this planet spends the first two decades of his or her life in the control of a benevolent dictatorship known as the family. And you know what? Most of them just want to keep on living with Mommy and Daddy, but just replace them with someone called the Great Leader, and let them take care of the tough decisions, from cradle to grave. They don't really want the responsibility of making those decisions themselves and then having to deal with the consequences. Now, this approach to government would be all fine and good if the world was full of truly enlightened and benevolent despots. But, unfortunately, those people are really hard to come by. What's it been, maybe once every thousand years or so, one shows up? And then, just like that, they're gone again. Nonetheless, every few years, someone, somewhere claims they found another one and hands them the keys to the kingdom."

"Okay," I said. "You know that, and I know that, and I'd like to think that most of the rest of the people in the States knows that, too."

"Well, I'm sorry, Tony, but that sounds a lot like a ten-year-old's view of the world," Castro retorted. "An adult, on the other hand, should be capable of perceiving America and our system for what it is: the most rare and endangered species on the face of the earth. So, here's another view of American exceptionalism: yes, we're exceptional, but nobody is really clear on exactly how that happened, why it happened, or why it happened in this particular place and at this particular time. I mean, it's never happened before. Even Greece and Rome, the so-called models of democracy, didn't last very long—not as democracies, anyway. And when they had democracies they sucked, in any event. Only a tiny minority of people could vote, and most of the rest were slaves. So, by some miracle, two thousand years later, we developed this incredibly messy, difficult, and complex system called the United States of America that seems to work better that any other system that's ever been created, and it's worked for well over two hundred years. So, lots of other people in lots of other places, who also have no clue why, try to copy it, because it seems to work really well. But does that mean it's indestructible? Does it mean that simply because it's lasted this long that it's going to continue to last forever? Not if you look at the historical record, it doesn't. I have. So, the first thing I do in the morning, and the last thing I do at night, is to thank God that it's managed to survive just one more day. And if the day comes when it ceases to exist in America, the very next day it will cease to exist everywhere else. People will move on to the next thing, and only God knows what a nightmare that'll be."

I said, "Don't you think that what you're doing, and what these people are doing, is going to threaten the very thing that you're trying to protect?"

"Every single day! And there, my friend, is the rub, isn't it? How do you protect something so fragile, something you love so much that you would die for it, from the millions of people on this planet who apparently want to kill it, and do so without killing it yourself? You figure that out for me, cuz, and I'll buy you another beer."

The conversation ebbed at this point, and we both sat there and stared ahead into space as I thought about this latest version of the Apocalypse. I also began thinking about how much I missed being the CEO of an Internet startup that was going bankrupt.

It occurred to me that Jack, his motivations, and his view of the world, were obviously different from Vandenberg's. Vandenberg seemed to love the thrill of the game - the hunt and the kill. Jack, on the other hand, was playing the game because he had to, out of his dedication to a cause, and it was clear that he was just trying to do the best he could with the shitty hand that he was dealt. But there was more to it than that. When this conversation started, it was a difficult distinction for me to make, but it wasn't any longer.

If I allowed myself to think the unthinkable; Jack's scenario with the nukes going off in American cities; I could imagine a scene in the aftermath. A massive, outraged mob rampaging through the streets. In front of them would be a guy like Jack with his arms outstretched, trying to calm the mob down, reminding them that they were Americans, and then being promptly torn to shreds as he was explaining the advantages of the rule-of-law.

A guy like Vandenberg, on the other hand, would be standing in the middle of the mob, and helpfully passing out lengths of rope preconfigured with hangman nooses, as well as an enemies list, and maps indicating the locations of the strongest light poles, from which to hang someone. If the worse ever did happen, these guys would definitely not be standing on the same side of the barricade.

The bottom line was that Jack Castro was an honorable man. I may not have felt comfortable with his methods, or even his conclusions about his fellow citizens, but there was no denying that he seemed to be one of the good guys, someone I was glad to have met, and to call my cousin.

I looked at him and said, "You know, it's hard for me to take anything you say very seriously."

He seemed to be searching for a retort when I continued, "I think it's the red beanie. I just can't take a guy who wears a hat like that very seriously."

Jack's face softened and he smiled. "Yeah, I know."

"I liked the white cape though."

He laughed. "Yeah, and it had that cool hoodie-thing, too."

"So what was this ceremony all about?" I asked.

"Well, according to the people in my organization; my special situation by birth, and my Secret Service training, make me an excellent candidate to function as a liaison between Malta and Washington. Just call me Sir Jack. Besides, someone has to keep an eye on these guys."

"The guys from Malta, or from Langley?"

Jack smiled. "Now you're getting the idea."

I said, "Vandenberg told me about the program that these people have been running for the past four hundred years. The one about breeding us as warriors. I got to tell you, hearing shit like that really makes me want to kill something. I still don't understand how you can work with these people."

He shrugged. "Sometimes you have to do things you don't like for the greater good. Besides, how much worse can they be than Vandenberg and his ilk?"

I laughed. "Actually, I wouldn't be surprised if Langley started developing their own selective breeding program." Then I asked seriously, "So you think that it's true, that we've been bred like pit bulls, or something?"

"I think guys like that think its true," he replied, looking towards the bishop. "The thing is, people like him have been trying that same bullshit forever. If it was true, the world would still be run by a bunch of inbred emperors, kings, aristocrats and robber-baron families. But it's not. Most of the products of human selective breeding are more rejects than regal. If you want a purebred, get a nice poodle or a Chihuahua. For my money, I'll bet on the mutts any day, which is what America is - an empire of mutts. Besides, no one planned who the original guy's parents were. Sebastiano was a bastard, as were many of his ancestors. You'd think these people would figure this out, but apparently they haven't."

I asked, "So, what happens next?"

"That, cuz, is a very interesting question. I understand that there's a girl problem."

"Well, I hope there is, but I can't even get anyone to give me a straight answer when I ask if she's alive."

He smiled. "Dude, if she was dead, we wouldn't be talking about her, would we? So, what's the deal with her? Do you love her?"

"Yes."

He looked at me with an odd expression. I detected something, but it was hard to discern. Doubt?

He asked, "How much?"

"More than I thought possible. More than I want to admit in front of another guy."

"Sounds serious."

I nodded.

"Well, you have a little problem, then."

"Yeah, I've been told, it's forbidden."

"Yes and no."

"What does that mean?" At that moment, a thought entered my mind and it made my stomach turn. I said to Jack, "She's not a nun or anything like that, is she?"

"Oh, God, no. What a creep-show that would be."

"So, what is she to these people?"

"This is a highly structured institution, Tony. They all have their titles and their specific roles to play. Marcella is a Donat."

"A donut?"

Jack smiled. "Not donut; Donat, with an 'A'. They're laity who join the organization in various ways. Most often they're displaced people or orphans that the Brotherhood takes in and cares for as children. At some point, they choose to become one thing or some other thing. Marcella chose to be a Protector, who are sort of-like the palace guards. Protectors are forbidden from becoming personally involved with the people they are protecting."

"But what about my mom? She married my dad."

"Oh, you know about that? Well, she was a Donat, too, and she was also the exception to the rule that gives you the ace up your sleeve."

"Look, I really don't care about all this hocus-pocus, and cloak-and-dagger crap. Can't Marcella just quit?"

"Yeah, quit the job, become a housewife, pop out a few puppies, right?"

"Something like that."

"Well, it's just not that easy. First off, these guys are very highly trained killers. I mean, from the time they're teenagers they are learning how to do the job. Secondly, they take their job, their loyalty, and their religious vows very seriously, and it's for life. Even if she quits and then you two... well, you know. You both go to hell."

"You must be kidding."

"I kid you not. This may sound like a bunch of bullshit to a couple of guys from the US of A, but these people have been running this entire operation for over four hundred years out of a belief and respect for both a heaven and a hell. It's what makes them who and what they are. So she'll probably never agree to see you again, because she would rather suffer missing you for the rest of her life, than risk having the both of you face eternal damnation. And you know what? Even if she decided to break her vows and go with you, she wouldn't be the same woman you fell in love with. Her heart and soul would be torn out of her."

"This is bullshit!" I said, raising my voice loud enough for the bishop to come to attention.

"Yes, cousin, it is most definitely that. But now that I've told you what they wanted me to tell you, I'll tell you something else they don't want you to know. In fact, they don't know I know it yet, which takes us back to that story about the prophecy. In their eyes, you're some kind of golden child, right?"

"Yeah, whatever the hell that means."

"It means that there is a way around this. Part of my job is to get intimately familiar with their traditions, rules, and mindset, and I'm a fast learner. So I can tell you that there is a way, but this may be something that you don't want to do. . ."

"Tell me what it is."

"Okay. Marcella can't leave the order and go with you as long as you are under the protection of the Brotherhood. But you can leave the protection of the Brotherhood anytime you want, so that you and she are no longer under that commitment or are required to comply with those rules."

I looked at him. "Are you kidding me? All I have to do is tell them to go away, and I can have Marcella? I've been trying to make them go away since this crap started."

"Well, first off, you can be pretty sure they won't let that happen. I mean, you're too important to them, so they don't want you to tell them to go away. But you're going to have to convince them that you're going to, or it won't work. If you make the bluff, they'll probably make an exception for you, just like the one they made for your mother."

"Why did they do that for her?"

"Because by the time they found out about your parent's affair, she was already pregnant with you." Jack looked at me for a few seconds. "Sorry about having to tell you about that part of the story... I mean, under these circumstances."

I looked at him in disbelief. "You mean about my mom being pregnant with me before she was married?"

Jack nodded and shrugged.

I wanted to tell him that, with all of the unbelievably weird shit I'd heard over the past twenty-four hours, this revelation was actually comforting. Also comforting was the knowledge that no one but my mom and dad picked who my parents were going to be. I said, "Its fine. So, what happened to her after they found out?"

"Normally, they would have brought down a shit-storm on her head. But, around that time they started thinking that you might be the person in the prophecy, so they didn't do anything. And now they seem convinced that you're this guy, so it's not likely they'll do anything about you and Marcella, either. In a strange way, you started giving these people the bird, to say nothing of a bad case of heartburn, even before you were born. So, they're probably getting used to you by now."

I looked Jack directly in the eyes and said, "I want Marcella. Tell the bishop whatever you need to tell him. I want her."

"I'll tell him, but suppose he decides to let you go? Look, Tony, you need to think about this. If you do this, you may get Marcella, but you could lose the Brotherhood's protection, and so do your sons and their sons, forever. They'll cut the cord. You need to consider that without these guys, you would probably be dead. In fact, you probably would never have been born. It's a big move, dude."

I said again without hesitation. "Tell him."

Jack smiled. "Are you going to invite me to the wedding?"

"Not if you come dressed like that, I won't." We both started snickering.

He held out his arms. "What? I thought I looked good in red."

"Maybe it'll work for a Halloween party. You bring the costumes, I'll bring the coffee and the Donats."

We both covered our faces trying to stifle our laughter. I asked. "Is he looking at us?"

Jack looked up at the Bishop. "Yeah, and he doesn't look happy."

"Do they still whack you with rulers, like the nun's in Catholic school?"

"They whack you alright. But with bullets, not rulers."

There were tears in our eyes by this time, but we eventually got ourselves back under control. Jack wiped his eyes. "It's been a while since the last time I laughed like that. With all of the shit going down lately, the pressure has been so intense, you dare not even smile."

"Hey, what are friends for, if not a few laughs?" I said.

He looked at me and nodded. "Okay, I'll deliver the message. I'll see you around. Take care of yourself, cuz."

"You too, Jack... and thank you for this."

"No problem. That's what family is for."

Jack Castro got up and walked to the bishop, who remained seated. Jack bent over and whispered into the bishop's ear. As he did, the bishop's expression changed from pensive confusion to shock, and then anger. He growled something at Jack that I couldn't hear. Jack straightened up, shrugged his shoulders, smiled, and said loud enough for me to hear, "Hey, what can I say? The man is in love."

Jack turned and walked towards the door at the side of the chapel. He gave me a little salute as he passed, which I returned. I then refocused my attention on the bishop as I listened to the side door open and then close.

The both of us sat there in silence for what seemed like a very long time. He was giving me an angry stare, like a parent who was upset with his offspring.

For my part, I gave him the best "screw-you" look that I could muster, and hoped he was getting the full effect. Then, just as I was about to get up, walk over to him, and demand that he give back my employee, my girl, and my future wife, he nodded his head at someone behind me.

The sudden sound of a door opening at the back of the chapel broke the silence, and a moment later I heard another sound, one that made the hair on my neck tingle. It was the sound of my name coming from Marcella's mouth.

"Tony?"

I stood and quickly turned towards the source. I saw a woman. She was in her fifties, stern-faced and dressed in a nurse's uniform. She appeared to be pushing something, which was blocked from my view by the high backs of the pews. Then she turned left into the main isle and began walking towards me.

"Marcella?" I called, momentarily doubting my own ears.

"Yes, I'm here." Marcella's voiced replied, this time quivering.

Then I saw her, in front of the nurse. She looked so small and helpless, as she was pushed along in the wheelchair.

Her eyes were tearing, but her face was lit up with that beautiful smile, the one that I thought I would never see again.

I swallowed hard, trying to clear the lump in my throat.

"Marcella!" I croaked, as I moved rapidly up the aisle.

Chapter 89

Ahmed Shakir watched the bloody demonstration without emotion. The victim's screaming had subsided to the barely audible breaths of the unconscious. The only other sounds in the room was that of the whoosh made by each vicious pass of the blood-soaked stick, on the way to its target on the falaqa, then the wet thud on contact, and the grunting of the man who wielded the stick as he wound up to take another savage swing.

The last impact sent an especially large spray of blood and tissue from the bottom of the unconscious man's feet into the air, some of which traveled across the room and landed on the left side of Shakir's face near the long scar on his jaw. The man with the stick, Uday Hussein, stopped mid-swing and then smiled in Shakir's direction. He reached down and grabbed a clean white towel that was steamed and fragrant, tossing it to Shakir who used it to wipe away the gore.

Uday Hussein examined the stick in his hands and addressed the unconscious man. "Adib! Look at this mess you've made." Uday laughed and threw the stick into a pail that contained two others in the same bloody condition. He grabbed another steamed towel, wiped his face and threw the towel into a stainless steel basket. Tucking his blood-spattered dress shirt into his expensive western jeans, he suddenly turned toward Shakir. The smile was gone. "What the fuck happened?" he asked Shakir through clenched teeth.

Shakir straightened in his chair and replied, "Things did not go according to plan."

"Things did not go according to plan? Really? You fucking idiot, nothing went according to plan! I trusted you with my best men and a blank check, and you delivered nothing! Not a single one of those bastards from Malta is dead, and their fortress is still there, untouched, and ready to undermine this entire project!"

Shakir said, "We're not done with them. We have devised a

new plan that we will implement right after we strike at the heart of the Americans with our next operation. Even our recent failure has succeeded in this one respect. We wanted to distract the Americans, convince them that we were focused on foreign targets. We accomplished that. They will never suspect where we will be striking them next."

Uday turned and reached for a basket with fresh sticks. He drew one out and smacked it hard across his palm, flinching with the impact. "And suppose *this* operation is a failure? Suppose the Americans find out that we are behind it. If your operatives are captured, the Americans will eventually obtain enough information to lead them back to us."

"It will never happen," Shakir said. "If the operation is not completed as scheduled, all of them will be silenced. And if it is completed, the operation itself will serve the same purpose."

Uday said, "The Americans may still suspect us."

"They will not; we already have many misinformation assets in place. We will weave the yarn that Saddam would never ally himself with either the religious radicals based in Afghanistan, or our sworn enemy, the Iranians. The Americans, or at least enough of them, will believe it. They are weak, fat, and stupid. So they will retreat in confusion behind the safety of their ocean borders, and as they sit there, licking their wounds, we will drive another dagger into their hearts."

Uday began stretching with the stick over his head. "You'd better be right," he said as he looked toward his victim on the falaqa. "This is my favorite hobby, did you know that? Leave me now, and do not come back until there is death in the streets of America." Uday stopped stretching, picked up a half-empty bottle of Hennessy cognac, and took a long swig.

Ahmed Shakir stood up and walked to the door. As he did, he heard Uday start to laugh. "Come, Adib, wake up! You are ruining my fun."

Shakir opened the door and turned back towards Uday just in time to see him pour the contents of the bottle over Adib's bloody feet. The man on the falaqa released a wild scream and tried desperately to free himself.

"That's better," Uday said as he wound up with the stick again.

Shakir left the room and closed the door on the sound of the animal-like screams.

EPILOGUE

THE ISLAND OF MANHATTAN
Tuesday, September 11, 2001
7:58 a.m.

"He's baaaaack!" Joe Mascelle yelled down the hall.

Sean McKeown replied with a broad grin. "Joe? Hey, how the hell are you?"

"Hi, Sean!"

"What brings you down to the Lucky Thirteenth? Slumming it?"

"You didn't expect me to miss you on your first day back, did you?"

"Well, technically, yesterday was my first day; but between the body exam, the head exam, and the paperwork— Jesus, the paperwork!" McKeown laughed. "There would have been less paper work if that son-of-a-bitch killed me." McKeown's levity was interrupted with a wince of pain.

"Still hurts?" Joe Mascelle inquired.

McKeown nodded. "Only when I breathe."

"Well, follow me. I got a break in the case that will take your mind off of your pain."

"A break in what case? The Malta thing? What break?"

"You won't believe it unless you see it for yourself."

Joe led Sean to one of the large conference rooms, opened the door and stepped aside. "Check this out."

The moment Sean step into the doorway a sudden roar assaulted him. "Welcome back!" The room was packed with blue uniforms and gray blazers, and in the middle of the conference table was a large sheet cake decorated with a bulls-eye and a chalk outline of a murder victim's body.

Sean looked back at Joe, red face beaming and eyes glistening. "Dirty trick, Mascelle. I'll get you for this."

Mascelle laughed. "Welcome back, partner. The people around here apparently really missed you. Can't figure it out for the life of me."

"Me neither. Thanks, Joe."

Joe waved his hand across the room to a big, brown face. "Not me, thank that big pain in my ass over there."

Chief Jack Sachel snapped a smart salute in McKeown's direction, and despite his best efforts at maintaining a straight, stern face McKeown noticed a smile peek through Jack's lips.

Sean walked over to Jack and held out his hand, which was immediately engulfed. "I'm tempted to give you a hug," Jack said to Sean, "but I don't want that lung of yours to start whistling again."

Sean said, "Save it for Christmas, I should be ready for it by then."

McKeown made the rounds in the crowded room, shaking hands, patting shoulders, and accepting an occasional peck on the cheek. Gradually the cake shrank and the room emptied.

About thirty minutes later only Jack, Sean, and Joe remained.

"Where's Sandy?" The words had barely left Sean's lips when he noticed the looks on his friends' faces. "What's up?" He asked, this time with concern.

Jack cleared his throat, glanced at Joe, and said. "She's been having a rough time for the past few weeks, Sean. She's really been out of it."

"Out of what?"

Joe chimed in, "She's been sick—not physically... well, that too—but mostly up here." Joe said, tapping his forehead.

"Alright, what's going on?" Sean said impatiently.

Joe Mascelle said, "She looks like shit, she hasn't been eating or sleeping, and she barely says a word to anyone. Most of the time, she just stares off into space. When you try to get her to talk about it, she just breaks down in tears. It's bad Sean; she looks like she's got cancer or something, but the docs say she's fine—at least physically."

"Where is she now?"

"I put her on sick leave," Jack said. "I told her she can't come back until she gets cleared."

Sean knew what that meant, another psych-leave until further notice. "She didn't talk to anyone about it? That's not like her."

Both men shrugged, and Joe said, "She won't talk to us. We thought about calling you, but we figured you had enough on your plate."

"I'll take a ride over to see her this morning. I'll get her back on track, Chief, don't worry," Sean said, trying to make light of it, despite his deep concern about his friend. He changed the subject and asked Joe, "So, how's your nephew?"

"Tony's fine. Still on Malta. I think."

"So, when are he and Marcella going to tie the knot?"

"We've all been waiting for a date and a location, but every time I talk to him he just tells me he's working on sorting things out with her people."

"What does that mean?"

"Who knows? But he's got a new gig in the meantime. He's working for the Feds."

"Doing what?"

"Techie stuff, I guess. What else would he be doing?"

"Which Feds?"

"No idea. He probably doesn't even know himself. But, can you believe that shit? A Mascelle working for the Feds?"

"Yeah, right, what's the world coming to?"

Just then Mascelle's beeper went off. He read the words on the LED. "It's a message from my wife. She says Tony has been trying to reach me— says' it's urgent."

"Sounds like that wedding date has finally been set," Jack said.

"Maybe. Weird. He's been doing that lately. It's like he knows when we're talking about him."

Sean said, "Yeah, well, he's with the spooks in Fed-land, now. They probably have a special X-ray satellite looking down on us right at this moment, reading our lips." Sean McKeown looked up at the ceiling and then raised his hand with a single, middle finger extended. "Read this, buddy." The other two men laughed and imitated his defiant gesture.

A movement in the doorway caught Sean's attention. He turned and looked, but it took a while for his brain to process the image. He recognized the face, but at the same time, it was that of a stranger. Her hair was stringy and her skin pale-white, nearly gray. She had apparently attempted to put on makeup, but the results were almost comical. Lipstick was spread on one side of her mouth, and the rest of her makeup was distributed in a strange patchwork of pink blotches. However, it was her eyes that really startled Sean. They were deeply set, surrounded by dark, puffy flesh, and they seemed lifeless. "Jesus, Sandy." Sean whispered.

Jack Sachel and Joe Mascelle both followed Sean's startled gaze to its target. They were startled as well, but it was from something Sean had not noticed yet. She was holding her service piece, low at her side, and it was pointing right at Sean's chest. As Sean made a movement towards her, she lifted the gun and pointed it at his head. Sean froze.

Sandy then waved the gun at all three of them. "Move, over there." She said pointing the barrel at the wall on the far side of the room.

The three men started to move cautiously towards the wall as Sandy reached behind her back and closed the door to the conference room. Jack Sachel said. "Sandy, what the hell is this about, girl?"

"I'm sorry Chief, I can't explain it. You wouldn't understand." Sandy's lips began to quiver and tears formed in her eyes. "I can't lose you; I can't lose any of you. I won't allow it."

"Sandy, this is Sean. What's up, honey? Tell me."

Sandy's face seemed to lighten momentarily at the sound of Sean's voice, and she replied with a sad smile. "I missed you so much, Sean. I can't, I can't do that again. I won't let you go."

"Sandy, I'm not going anywhere. I am right here. Put down the gun and tell me what's on your mind. You can tell me, I'll understand. Whatever it is, I'll understand."

Sean made a movement toward her and her smile disappeared. She brought the gun up and placed the end of the barrel against her own temple. "You won't understand, Sean. I've seen it. You leave me and never come back. You all leave me. I won't let you do that. Not again, not ever. I'd rather blow my brains out than relive that."

Suddenly her body began to tremble and her eyes rolled back in her head. "Here it comes," she whispered. "Do you hear it?"

There was a moment of utter silence as each of the men's minds came to the same helpless and gut-wrenching conclusion: Sandy Taylor was about to put a bullet in her brain, and there was absolutely nothing any of them could do to stop her in time. Their thoughts were suddenly interrupted by a roaring sound coming from outside of the room. It was all around them, almost like a slow-motion explosion. They could feel the vibration in the floor through the soles of their shoes. The rumbling soon faded, but was transmuted into a piercing shriek, a sound that was now coming from inside the room, from Sandy's wide-open mouth. Her wild eyes were staring into the void in front of her face and she was screaming in horror, as if something terrifying was approaching. A moment later, her body went stiff and she fell over, both the gun and her body hitting the floor hard. The men rushed to her, and just as they reached her side, they felt the building tremble and heard the window panes rattle.

Sean reached Sandy first. "She's got a pulse."

"What the hell was that sound, Jack?" Joe Mascelle asked as he watched Sean check Sandy's pupils. "What the hell is going on?"

Jack said, "Sean, you stay with Sandy; Joe, get an ambulance, and I'll find out what that sound was."

The men nodded and then Jack said, "Sean, put your cuffs on her, just in case, okay?"

Sean was about to protest, then thought better of it and

reached for the handcuffs on his belt.

Just then, a female officer opened the door.

"What was that noise outside, Helen?" Jack asked.

Helen was staring at Sandy's body and at Sean as he fumbled with the handcuffs.

"Helen?" Jack Sachel repeated.

She looked up at Jack. "We think it was a low-flying plane. And we just got a report that it might have flown into one of the Towers."

"What? A low flying plane in the middle of Manhattan?"

"Yes, someone just called it in. Said it looks like a private pilot may have hit one of the Towers, with a Cessna or something."

"Cessna, my ass," Joe Mascelle said. "That was no small aircraft. That was something big and loud, like a passenger or military jet."

Jack Sachel said, "Joe, get out there and see if you can find out what's going on. Helen, please call an ambulance for Sandy."

Sandy's eyes suddenly opened and darted around the room. "Don't you leave me! Don't you leave me, Joe!" She screamed as Sean and Jack tried to restrain and comfort her at the same time.

Jack made a motion with his head towards the door. Joe left.

Sean, holding her with one arm, placed his hand gently over Sandy's unkempt hair. "Sandy, calm down. Take a deep breath and try to control yourself. These things that you're seeing are just images in your head, they're not real, honey. I'm real, Jack is real, this room is real, but the images are just dreams. They can't hurt you, and they can't hurt us."

Sandy looked at the cuffs on her wrists and shook her head. "Not dreams, Sean. Not dreams." She looked at Jack. "You know that I love you, right?" Jack Sachel nodded, trying hard to hold back his tears. She looked back at Sean. "And you Sean. Do you know how much I love you?" Her voice was like a little girl's, pleading, begging to be heard.

"Yes Sandy. I know honey, and I love you too. That's why I need you to calm down. Help is on the way. We'll get you right. I promise. Okay?"

Helen returned and said. "I can't find an ambulance. They're all headed for the Towers."

"Keep trying, Helen." Jack Sachel replied.

Joe Mascelle passed Helen as she left.

"Did you find out what's going on down there?" Jack Sachel asked Joe Mascelle.

"I don't know, Jack. The reports indicate a small aircraft accident, like Helen said. But I'm looking at what's coming in on the tube, and whatever it was, it wasn't small. It's a mess down there. I don't even want to think about the casualties. It's going to make the '93 attack look like a day in the park. We've been ordered to get down there in force, Jack, everyone. The dispatcher said that if it walks, rolls, or flies it's ordered to report at the Towers."

Sandy sat up and began flailing. "No Joe, no! Don't go down there, please, please listen to me. Don't go, don't go." Then she stopped flailing and began to sob uncontrollably.

Sean wrapped both of his arms around her. "Calm down, Sandy." He whispered in her ear. "I'm here, and I'm going to stay with you. Calm down."

Jack nodded his head at Joe and looked back at Sean. "I'm putting you in charge, Sean. I need you to hold down the fort. You stay here with Sandy. The rest of us are heading down to the Trade Center. I'll leave behind a skeleton crew for communications and logistics, and I'll try to get an EMT for her as soon as I can. When we know what's going on down there we'll give you a call."

Sean nodded. "Be careful, guys."

Sandy started to shake her head wildly. "No, no, no, no!"

The men left, leaving the door of the conference room open. Sandy resumed her struggling, but Sean managed to hang on. "Sandy, you need to calm down. My lung, honey, it's not fully healed. You're going to open my wound if you keep flailing around like this."

Sandy slowed her movements and looked up at him. "You don't understand, Sean. Joe and Jack are going to die if we don't stop them. Do you remember those dreams, the ones you asked me about? I know what they mean now. It's all clear. But it was too late. If only Tony had stayed, he would have understood, he could have helped. But it's too late now. All I can do is save my friends. You, Jack, Joe. You're all I have. And two of you are already walking straight into hell. I've seen it, Sean. It's the worst thing you'll ever see, the worst thing you can imagine."

"I know Sandy, I believe you." Actually, Sean did not know what he believed, and in any event, he didn't know what else to say to her, or what else to do. A part of his brain told him to trust her. She had earned that. But another part of him just couldn't accept it, couldn't grasp the idea of someone looking into a crystal ball and seeing the future, not even Sandy. Not even after all the inexplicable things he had witnessed her do with his own eyes. It was just too much, too unreal. And there was another part of his brain that couldn't accept the scale of the calamity she was describing, either. When he got up this morning, it was a beautiful September day. By the time he stepped into the precinct the sky was a brilliant blue and the sun was warm on his face. A perfect day to be still among the living. When he saw Joe in the hall, he was suddenly reminded about how much he missed the job and the people he worked with. They were his extended family, and after a long absence he was finally home again, and everything was normal like he hoped it would be. The sights and sounds of his friends around the table, and that stupid cake, made him forget the surreal events of the past months, including the one event that nearly ended his life. Especially that one. It was so good to be back to normal. He did not want to leave normal ever again. But it did leave, and he would soon understand that it would never return again.

Sean could hear a perfect cacophony of sound coming from the other room through the open door. Someone had channeled a radio receiver into the intercom system, and the building was filled with the squawking and crosstalk of radio traffic coming from the people on the scene at the World Trade Center. A small group of men and women, comprising most of the remaining crew still at the precinct, were gathered around a television set that was hastily set up on one of the desks. Their bodies were blocking the picture, but the volume on the television was set high, and much of it was also reaching Sean in the conference room. The combination of sounds from the intercom and the blasting television should have been enough to drive a person mad, but he noted the near trance-like composure of the group assembled around the television as they watched and listened.

Sandy had stopped moving, and Sean had assumed that she was as exhausted by her flailing as he was holding onto her. Then she said to him, in an unnaturally calm voice, "It's not over Sean. You believe me, don't you? Please tell me you believe me, and that you won't go down there. Not today. Tomorrow, you'll be the only one I have left. If you're gone I'll have no one. I can't live like that, Sean. I can't live with all of you gone, especially knowing how, and that I couldn't stop it. Please stay. I'll do anything, just tell me you won't leave me today, please."

"I'm not going anywhere Sandy. I'm right here, and you're not going to lose anyone. Joe and Jack are going to be fine, you'll see."

Sandy started weeping. "I love you guys. I'll miss you so much." Her body began to tremble again, this time violently. Sean released his grip and tried to place her down on the floor, but then her eyes moved back under her lids, her back arched, and she went completely stiff. He reconsidered, deciding to hold onto her instead.

At that same moment, Sean heard a collective gasp come from the men and women standing around the television. Then a strange thing happened. All of the voices in the room, and over the radio, and on the television, suddenly, and all at once, ceased. He wondered if he had gone deaf. Then the building shuddered again. The voices resumed. Loud, angry voices.

"You sons-of-bitches," Sean heard one cop say in the room next door.

"You fucking animals," From another.

At the same time, disembodied voices came in over the intercom. "Did you see that?" one voice asked over the open airwaves.

"Jesus Christ almighty," said another: stunned, disbelieving.

Sean called out from inside the conference room. "What the hell is going on?"

One of the officers turned away from the television screen and said to him. "A second plane just hit the other tower. This is no accident, this is an attack; it's like Pearl Harbor. Our Pearl Harbor. Those motherfuckers are attacking us with our own passenger planes. They've just slaughtered thousands of civilians."

Sean felt Sandy's body relax for a moment and then stiffen again. She reopened her eyes and looked up at him with a tortured face. Then through quivering lips: "Oh my god, Sean. Screaming, blood, parts of people everywhere. So much death, so much pain. Burning, crushing, horror. Unspeakable. The fire. The smell. No way out. The heat, the heat. No escape."

Sean lifted Sandy into his arms and, holding her as close as he could, began gently rocking her as tears began rolling down his cheeks.

"Shhhh, Sandy, calm down honey, calm down."

He was thankful when he felt some of the tension in her body begin to fade again. Soon she was entirely limp. The expression on her face was now peaceful. Then a calm, almost happy, girl-like voice came from her lips. "Fly away. Fly away."

Over the intercom, Sean heard a man on a radio, "Do you hear that, those thumping sounds?"

"Yeah, what the hell is that?"

Then another voice, with a sickening response, "Oh God, no, please God, no."

"What?"

"They're jumping. Mary, Mother of God, they're jumping."

"Move everyone away from the base of the building. Now!"

Sean heard one of the women in front of the television start to scream.

THE END

AUTHORS NOTES

Many readers might consider an intelligence or military alliance between the United States and the Order of St. John (a.k.a. The Knights of Malta) highly unlikely. However, multiple independent sources provide fuel for such speculation.

In a 2007 editorial, published in the United Arab Emirates daily Al-Bayan, entitled *"The Knights of Malta – more than a conspiracy"* Jordanian MP Jamal Muhammad Abidat suggested that such an alliance does exist and that it has played, and continues to play, a key role in the Middle East and in the conflicts in Iraq and Afghanistan. Abidat was quoted as saying:

"The painful saga of modern Arab-Muslim history evokes the battles fought in Crusades of the 11th century – when the Knights of Malta began their operations as a Christian militia whose mission it was to defend the land conquered by the Crusaders. These memories return violently to mind with the discovery of links between the so-called security firms in Iraq, such as Blackwater, that have historic links with the Order of Malta. You cannot exaggerate it. The Order of Malta is a hidden government or the most mysterious government in the world."

The Pulitzer Prize winning, and highly controversial, investigative journalist Seymour Hersh went even further, alleging in a 2011 speech given in Doha, Qatar, that the U.S. military's Joint Special Operations Command (JSOC) *"are all members of, or at least supporters of, the Knights of Malta"*, whose mission is to *"change mosques into cathedrals"*.

The backstory for this novel is set in the sixteenth century, a time of great tumult for both Europe and Christianity. The fall of the Eastern Roman Empire, to Islamic conquest in 1453, cleaved both Europe and the Church in half leaving what remained, in Western Europe, highly vulnerable in the century that was to follow.

This book describes two pivotal battles that occurred during this period, The Great Siege of Rhodes and The Great Siege of

Malta. But these events, while epic in scale and outcome, were just two of the many critically important sixteenth century engagements that determined the fate of Europe's history and, by extension, that of the New World. Others, including the Battle of Mohács, Hungary (the first one - 1526); the Siege of Vienna, Austria (also the first one - 1529); the naval battles of Preveza, Greece (1538); Djerba, Tunisia (1560); and finally, the Battle of Lepanto, Greece (1571), were all unprecedentedly large and bloody battles between the forces of Islam and Christianity, and each was fought on a scale that would not be seen again until the nineteenth century.

The fourteen-hundred year-old history of conflict between Christianity and Islam is a highly complex one. It's filled with villains, cruelty, conquest, slavery, and an enormous amount of bloodshed - along with some highly unlikely heroes, alliances, acts of compassion and friendships - on both sides. But it has become mired, through ignorance or propaganda, in misinformation that attempts to simplify and amalgamate all of these conflicts under the catchall heading of the "Crusades". This word has become the mother of all politically-correct terms, and has for decades been used as a code-word to blame Europe, and the West, for all of the ills and conflicts, past and present, in the Middle East.

However, the historical facts paint quite a different picture. Prior to the nineteenth century, the vast majority of the conflicts between Islam and Christian Europe were battles of conquest initiated by Suleiman, his predecessors or successors, in the attempt to absorb all of Europe, as well as most of the known world, into a global Islamic Caliphate. The Europeans did not want to be absorbed, so they fought back. Simple self-defense, right? Well, not when you hear it told by many contemporary pundits and so-called historians.

During this same period, Western Europe and the Church would also be confronted with destructive forces tearing it apart from within. The Reformation, and the religious civil wars between Catholics and Protestants that it spawned over a period of two centuries, would cumulatively cause as much, or more, death and destruction as the aforementioned Islamic battles of conquest. Some of the most violent of these internecine conflicts were, perhaps somewhat surprisingly, between different factions of Protestantism, which resulting in the destruction and depopulation of entire cities and towns in northern Europe. Most of the early settlers, in what would become the United States, were refugees from this violence. They chose probable death on the untamed frontier of the New World, over near certain death, in the old one. All in order to realize their simple ambition to worship as they chose.

It is probably not an exaggeration to say that the confluence of these two destructive forces, one external and the other internal, could well have resulted in the demise of Christianity and Western European culture in Rome and Western Europe, just as the same forces had largely expunged Eastern European culture in the former Christian capital city of Constantinople (today's Istanbul) and much of the former Eastern Roman Empire (regions now comprising all or parts of the Balkans, Turkey, Egypt, Iraq, Saudi Arabia, Syria, Jordan, Israel, Libya, Algeria and the surrounding regions).

One of the most significant events, helping to prevent the West's demise, was the Protestant exodus from Europe to the New World. These waves of emigration served the vital function of spreading western culture to a new continent, and also acted as a social "relief valve" permitting at least some of the animosity, and thereby the bloody religious conflicts between Christians in Europe, to be diffused and thereby subside over time.

The massive influx of wealth, from the New World into Europe, served an equally vital role by providing the resources required to defend what was left of Christian Europe from Islamic domination. Somewhat predictably, the Christian civil wars, as well as the countless conflicts arising out of the competition for the treasure and resources found in the New World, ultimately caused dramatic advances in weapons technology. This was especially the case for shipborne warfare. Many Western naval innovations, ones that would lead to dramatic improvements in naval tactics and capabilities in the seventeenth and eighteenth centuries, were first developed in the sixteenth century in response to these potent historical events. The mountains of gold and silver that arrived from the New World also provided the West with the resources needed to build the navies, and armies, which ultimately put these innovations into practice.

It was a combination of these factors, most of them resulting directly from the discovery of the New World, that enabled the West to eventually halt the Islamic conquest of Europe and ultimately leave the Islamic World, as well as much of the rest of it, centuries behind in terms of military capabilities and economic resources - and to, eventually, enable the West to shift to an offensive posture. It is this dramatically successful turnaround; from the near extinction of Western Civilization, to global domination by it, which lies at the center of the angst associated with the term *Crusades*.

Although historically inaccurate, it is somewhat understandable that commentators from the Islamic World would try to promote this one-sided perspective of these historical events. However, for someone from the West to concur with this myopic interpretation of history requires, one would think, a sincere dedication to historical ignorance, or at least to cultural self-flagellation. This is not to dismiss, or make excuses for, the various abuses committed by Europeans, and later, by Americans. But there are, as always, at least two sides of a story, and they all deserve to be told, and understood, in the context of the time and place in which they occurred.

One example of this pseudo-history is the often made accusation that the "Christian Crusaders" have, and some say still are, trying to defend their conquered Islamic lands, or more inflammatory, turn mosques into churches – or in the case of Israel - into synagogues. Those who make this argument seem to have their historical facts and timelines somewhat askew.

If defending conquered lands from reconquest is in some way the hallmark of the crusader-aggressor, as suggested by Jordanian MP Jamal Muhammad Abidat, then it's not the so-called Christian (or Jewish) Crusaders who are the primary aggressors. *"Islamic Crusaders"* have been defending conquered lands for thousands of years, territory that they conquered from Christians and Jews. For example, one of the oldest Christian churches in the world is located in Saudi Arabia, near a place called Jubail. It was built in the 4th century, three hundred years before the birth of Islam. This region, once almost entirely inhabited by Christians and Jews, was one of the first places to fall to Muslim conquest during the seventh century. The Jews and Christians living there were either killed, forced to convert to Islam, or banished. To this day, Christianity and Judaism are effectively outlawed in all of Saudi Arabia, and the Saudi government hides the Jubail Church from locals and bans foreigners from openly visiting it. Even archaeologists are denied access.

If the destruction or conversion of holy sites is the act of a crusader-aggressor, as Seymour Hersh suggests, then consider the history of just one example, presented in this novel; the Cathedral of Toledo, Spain. It was built on the site of an ancient Catholic church that was completed circa 587. Following the Islamic conquest of Spain, this original church was torn down and replaced by a Mosque in 784. With the Christian reconquest in 1085 the site was *converted back* to a Christian church, the current cathedral, in 1087. This cathedral is among hundreds of example of the continuous "deck-shuffling" of holy sites that has occurred between Islamic and Christian conquest and subsequent reconquest. And yet, some contemporary commentators seem intent on promoting the idea that this type of activity was solely the domain of depraved "Christian fanatics". This point of view clearly does not represent either an accurate, or fair, interpretation of the historic facts.

In any event, Western Europe, Christianity, and what we now refer to as Western Civilization, could very well have been extinguished during the sixteenth century, were it not for the discovery, exploration and settlement of the New World that began at the dawn of this century.

However, even Columbus' discovery, and the subsequent settlement, of the New World has entered the bizarre realm of *western-cultural-sadomasochism* - at least in the past few decades. Substantial numbers of people, claiming to embrace western culture and values, are at the same time intent on rejecting this rather amazing accomplishment of their forbearers, and in so doing seem to reject the very basis of their own current existence.

In 1892, on the 400th anniversary of Columbus' discovery, cities and states throughout the country competed ferociously to hold the most spectacular commemorations in honor of this accomplishment, and of all of those that followed. The most spectacular was held in Chicago, at the Columbian Exhibition, which open the eyes of the world to the amazing advances, and the unbounded potential and optimism, of the United States of America. One hundred years later, in 1992, the 500th anniversary of Columbus' discovery was met principally with apoplectic protest, pathetic apologies, and absurd accusations. Accomplishments, such as discovering and settling new worlds, along with the countless others, is the very basis of what has allowed western culture to survive and thrive. Somewhere along the way, we seemed to have forgotten that. It makes one cringe at the thought of what the 600th anniversary will reveal about the then flaccid state of our culture, assuming it exists at all.

Whatever the reader may think about the improbability of the seemingly superhuman displays of courage, and unimaginable lopsided scale of the victories, described here as fiction, I can assure you that they are mere shadows of the genuine people and events from this period of history. Fictional superheroes have become very popular in books, movies and television, of late. But these real people, from our own real history, were the genuine thing. The historical accounts of the Order of the Knights of Saint John (a.k.a. Knights of Rhodes and Knights of Malta), from its founding in 1023 as a charitable organization, by merchants from

Amalfi and Salerno, to the climactic events of the sieges of Rhodes and Malta, some five hundred years later, provide numerous examples, in many written accounts, for those readers interested in exploring the history of some of the truly remarkable people and events from our past.

The Great Siege of Malta was one of the bloodiest and most fiercely contested in history, and also became one of the most celebrated events in sixteenth century Europe. The Ottoman armada of 250 ships, with an army comprised of approximately 50,000 Islamic warriors, arrived on May 18th. Defending the island were some 6,000 Christian Knights and soldiers. The desperate fighting went on for four months until finally, pressed hard by a counter attack from a recently arrived relief force of eight thousand volunteers from Sicily, the Ottoman Turks fled to their ships and left the island on September 11th, 1565. This final engagement was a far more gruesome conclusion to the siege than that depicted in this novel, however. In the end, approximately 30,000 Ottomans were killed or wounded. After four months of fighting in the sintering Mediterranean summer sun, with a vanishing supply of food and water, as well as enduring the bombardment of 130,000 cannon balls - approximately 4,000, of the 6,000 original Christian defenders, survived the siege.

The French writer, historian and philosopher Voltaire later commented that, *"Nothing is better known than the siege of Malta."* Its significance to the survival of Western Europe was not lost on the contemporaries of the event, either. This understanding was probably most clearly and succinctly summarize by Queen Elizabeth I, who wrote: *"If the Turks should prevail against the Isle of Malta, it is uncertain what further peril might follow to the rest of Christendom."* Elizabeth was said to have kept a painting, depicting The Siege, in her chambers until the end of her life.

With their victory on Malta, European confidence in their ability to defend themselves grew significantly. But the bloody contest between Christendom and Islam would continue for centuries.

Many readers may be unaware of the pivotal role a fledgling United States of America played in this distant, and seemingly endless, conflict. Thomas Jefferson, that uncompromising revolutionary firebrand that helped birth a new nation, was no less uncompromising when it came to Islamic terrorism. His rejection of the European policy of appeasing the shipborne Islamic raiders from the Barbary Coast of North Africa, through the payments of ransom and tribute, was based largely on his revolutionary principles. He believed that; having thrown off the tyranny of European rulers, the United States should never again subjugate itself to tyranny of any kind, including that of terrorists. Many of his contemporaries considered this policy both extreme and impractical. At least they did until, as President, Jefferson sent a tiny American armada to destroy the once invincible fleets of Tripoli, Algiers and Tunis, which finally resulted in the eradication of the centuries-old practice, once and for all. One could argue that, in so doing, he embedded these beliefs as part of the founding principles of U.S. foreign and domestic policy, with regards to kidnapping and terrorism. To this day, the United States is one of the few nations in the world to maintain a standing policy of no compromise, and no ransom payments, to terrorists, under any circumstances. For those who are interested in learning more about this subject, I recommend Joseph Wheelan's "Jefferson's War: America's First War on Terror 1801-1805".

The reader will note that the two sieges described in this novel, Rhodes and Malta, were separated by forty-two years. As such, they might reasonably be wary of the fictional account in this book, in which a man participates in both of these battles - first as a very young man, and later as an old one. I refer those understandably skeptical readers to the real life story of Jean Parisot de la Valette. He fought during the siege of Rhodes as a young knight and, as the Grand Master of the Order, engaged in hand-to-hand combat during the siege of Malta. He was seventy years old by that time, fully ten years older than the fictional character described in this book. Following the victorious outcome of the siege, he apparently became restless and bored.

So, at the ripe old age of seventy-one, he decided to occupy his spare time building the capital city on Malta that now bears his name. You really can't make this stuff up.

It may also come as a surprise to many readers that Sicily was, for the better part of three millennia, often at the epicenter of events in Europe, Northern Africa, the Levant, and in fact, the entire Mediterranean basin. In addition, throughout the region's history, Sicily has often also been at the center of the arts, sciences, and political progress; and serving as a model for the entire region. From Archimedes, who is considered one of the greatest mathematicians of all times, and who has been credited with the invention of the world's first computer (the Antikythera Mechanism) more than two thousand years before IBM's founding, to the *first Reconquista,* that took place on Sicily and began turning the tide of the invasion of Europe by Islamic rulers - this island has been one of the central players in the development of Western Civilization.

In 1062, the Norman reconquest of Sicily helped provide the men, resources, and tactics necessary for the conquest of Britain four years later, which was an event that profoundly shaped Anglo-Saxon history, and by extension, the history of America.

The Holy Roman Emperor, Frederick II, was a direct descendant of these same Normans who conquered Britain in 1066. He was born on December 26, 1194, to Constance of Sicily and the House of Hohenstaufen. He began his rule at the age of three and eventually became one of the most powerful and admired emperors of the Middle Ages. The political and cultural power and influence of his royal court, in his beloved city of Palermo, stretched through Sicily, Italy, Germany, and as far east as Jerusalem. Historians have searched for superlatives to describe him, as in the case of Professor Donald Detwiler, who wrote: *"A man of extraordinary culture, energy, and ability—called by a contemporary chronicler stupor mundi (the wonder of the world), by Nietzsche the first European, and by many historians the first modern ruler—Frederick established in Sicily and southern Italy something very much like a modern, centrally governed kingdom with an efficient bureaucracy."*

Speaking six languages (Latin, Sicilian, German, French, Greek, and Arabic), Frederick II was an avid patron of the sciences and the arts. He also played a major role in promoting literature through what would later be called the Sicilian School of poetry, which is credited with the invention of the sonnet. This poetry had a profound influence on Italian literature, and on what was to become the modern Italian language. The Sicilian School, and its poetry, were saluted by no less a giant of Italian literature than Dante, who credited it with providing the foundations of the Tuscan idiom that would eventually become the dialect of Italy's elite.

Tragically, Sicily's nearly three-thousand-year history—from its central influence as part of Magna Graecia (Greater Greece) at the height of Greek power and influence, through its cultural and strategic impact on the Roman Empire, its profound contributions to the arts and sciences during ancient times and the Middle Ages, and right down to its central role in the unification of Italy in modern times—has been systematically subsumed by the (very oddly popular) mythology surrounding a small, latter-day band of organized criminals. Reducing the social, scientific, cultural, political and historical contributions of the inhabitants of Sicily to that of the Mafia is roughly equivalent to claiming that America's contribution to the world is limited to rap music, graffiti, and McDonald's. Only a complete ignoramus, entirely devoid of even the slightest inkling of the historical facts, would present or promote either claim. Do I sound bitter?

One of the earliest descriptions of the Muslim sect known as the Assassins was given by Marco Polo, the Venetian merchant who authored *De Mirabilibus Mundi,* now generally referred to as *The Travels of Marco Polo*. In it he described his far-flung travels in the East between 1271 and 1291. According to Polo:

"The Old Man [Hasan Sabbah] kept at his court such boys of twelve years old as seemed to him destined to become courageous men. When the Old Man sent them into the garden in groups of

four, ten or twenty, he gave them hashish to drink. They slept for three days, then they were carried sleeping into the garden where he had them awakened. When these young men woke, and found themselves in the garden with all these marvelous things, they truly believed themselves to be in paradise. And these damsels were always with them in songs and great entertainments; they received everything they asked for, so that they would never have left that garden of their own will. And when the Old Man wished to kill someone, he would take him and say: 'Go and do this thing. I do this because I want to make you return to paradise.' And the assassins go and perform the deed willingly."

It doesn't require a great stretch of the imagination to see the parallels between Hasan Sabbah, and his tactics, and those of Osama bin Laden. In both cases, not only are the methods of exploitation of impoverished young men the same, but the identical tactics of murder-suicide against both Muslim and Christian leaders are nearly identical. Both men also share a common background of privilege, and the same fanatical belief in themselves as the incarnation of a just ruler. These parallels have not been lost on contemporary Muslim scholars and commentators. Salim Mansur, a professor of political science at the University of Western Ontario wrote:

"Osama bin Laden and his band of fanatical warriors are a contemporary version of Hasan Sabbah and his Order of Assassins. Mr. bin Laden's hideout in the mountains of Afghanistan is a reminder of Sabbah's mountain stronghold. Like Sabbah, Mr. bin Laden has raised his warriors from boyhood to accept death for a political program dressed in religious slogans that set him apart from mainstream Islam."

Thankfully, for both the Islamic and Christian worlds, and just as I was completing these notes, it was announced that Mr. Bin Laden had been unceremoniously dispatched into the oblivion of history, by a few brave U.S. Navy SEALs.

After discovering that some of the early readers of this manuscript were often unfamiliar with the more contemporary historical events referenced in this story, I decided to include the following notes to help provide some illumination on these topics.

Documents that have recently become available verify that the U.S. government withheld information regarding the events surrounding the assassination of JFK, from both the public and congressional investigators, until *at least* the late 1990's. An operation, called AMWORLD, was just one of the many revelations to emerge from the declassification of hundreds of thousands of documents following the 1992 passage of the *JFK Assassination Records Act.* AMWORLD was a massive program, under the direct control of Attorney General Robert Kennedy. Its goal was to kill, or overthrow, Fidel Castro in an operation that was to commence on or about December 1st of 1963. This operation was aborted 9 days prior due to the assassination of JFK on November 22, 1963 at 12:30pm, in Dallas Texas.

The AMWORLD coup plan was so serious, and far reaching, that in the days and weeks before Dallas, Robert Kennedy had a secret committee making plans for dealing with the possible "assassination of American officials" if Castro found out and tried to retaliate. Historians and journalists are only beginning to understand the extent of this operation, and the related subterfuge and cover-up, as more documents trickle out of the Nation's classified archives.

Generations of Americans have grown up wondering *what could have been* if JFK survived to be reelected. The lamentations of some members of the Baby Boom Generation are particularly poignant in this regard. The flip side of this decades-long mourning process is a rather unreasonable, and sometimes ugly, tendency to ignore the shortcomings of the Kennedy administration and lay the blame for every national misfortune on previous or subsequent administrations.

For example, the unquestioned tendency to lay the debacle of the Vietnam War entirely at the feet of LBJ and Nixon, now standard fare in the mainstream media, as well as in many history books, continues despite the vast amount of new information that paints a much clearer, and less complimentary, picture regarding the Kennedy administration and its policies. As alluded to in this novel, this nightmarish war began, and rapidly grew, under JFK.

If it's possible to blame any single individual for such a cataclysmic event, most commentators seem to agree that Vietnam can best be characterized as *Robert McNamara's War.* Secretary of Defense McNamara, one of Kennedy's so-called Whiz-kids, was also one of his most trusted advisers. According to Kennedy's Special Counsel, adviser and legendary speechwriter Ted Sorensen, Kennedy regarded McNamara as the "star of his team", calling upon him for advice on a wide range of issues beyond national security, including business and economic matters. After Kennedy's death, McNamara continued on as Secretary of Defense in the Johnson administration, which largely adopted the same policies towards Vietnam developed by McNamara during the JFK years.

As such, it seems a somewhat dubious proposition that, if reelected, JFK's second term, at least with respect to the Vietnam War, would have been any different than LBJ's first term, which saw a continuation of the same policy of rapid escalation of U.S. involvement in Southeast Asia begun during the Kennedy administration. Sorry Oliver. Really.

As a somewhat interesting side note, a direct link connecting Operation Mongoose and AMWORLD, with the attacks that occurred on September 11, 2001, can reasonably be made.

In 1975, the *United States Senate Select Committee to Study Governmental Operations with Respect to Intelligence Activities,* known commonly as the *Church Committee,* was convened by U.S. Senate committee chair Senator Frank Church (D-ID). It followed closely on the heels of the Watergate scandal, but had a much larger focus on the numerous abuses by various administrations, and intelligence services, especially the CIA, which had occurred over the previous twenty years. The attempted assassination of Castro, and the successful assassination of the Diem brothers in

Vietnam during the Kennedy administration, were primary topics of discussion and concern. Unfortunately, as is often the case in Washington, an otherwise rational attempt at reform turned into a full-blown witch-hunt. According to testimony before the Committee, given by CIA director William Colby:

"These last two months have placed American intelligence in danger. The almost hysterical excitement surrounding any news story mentioning CIA or referring even to a perfectly legitimate activity of CIA has raised a question whether secret intelligence operations can be conducted by the United States."

According to some, Colby's testimony somewhat understated the scope and ultimate goal of the Committee. Robert Ellsworth, Assistant to President Nixon, the Deputy Secretary of Defense under President Ford, and a former Congressman from Kansas, stated:

"They [The Church Committee] were very specific about their effort to destroy American intelligence [capabilities]. It was Senator Church who said our intelligence agencies were 'rogue elephants'."

Ellsworth, and Presidential adviser Donald Rumsfeld (under President Ford), are credited with preventing the committee from dismantling the CIA, and other intelligence organizations, entirely. But what did emerge from the work of the Church Committee was the *Foreign Intelligence Surveillance Act of 1978*. The bureaucratic policies and procedures developed under FISA lead directly to, among other things, the *information wall* between domestic and foreign intelligence services. It was precisely this *wall* that was blamed for the failures of the CIA and FBI to successfully track and foil the terrorists that carried out the 9/11 attacks.

Even after this immense national trauma, it required six long years, and many proposed and defeated bills, to finally reform FISA. This was accomplished under the *Protect America Act of 2007*. The bureaucratic overreach contained in FISA, which excessively weakened national security, is directly linked with the type of intelligence abuses that occurred during the Kennedy administration (and others), such as Operation Mongoose and AMWORLD.

What remains to be seen, however, is if the next swing of the *intelligence pendulum* will continue to follow this pattern of extreme gyration. Having spent decades at one abusive extreme, and then subsequent decades at the opposite extreme, which resulted in the worst terrorist attack on American soil in history - will it finally settle in a *safe and competent center*, or will it continue its wild swings? Perhaps this is a naïve question, but we can hope. Can't we?

Regarding the connection between Saddam Hussein and both of the attacks on the World Trade Center, as well as the attempt by some members of the United States government to conceal that connection, Laurie Mylroie gave the following testimony on July 9, 2003, before the National Commission on Terrorist Attacks upon the United States:

"Prior to the February 26, 1993, bombing of the World Trade Center, it was assumed that major terrorist attacks against the US were state-sponsored. But that bombing is said to mark the start of a new kind of terrorism that does not involve states. That notion is dubious. Rather, the claim that a new, stateless terrorism emerged with the 1993 Trade Center bombing was a convenient explanation in that it required no military response. Once promulgated, it was hastily accepted even before much progress had been made in the investigation of that attack itself."

Mylroie holds a doctorate degree in political science from Harvard University and was employed by Harvard's Department of Government. Later she became an associate professor at the US Naval War College and was also, ironically, an Iraq consultant for the Clinton administration during his 1992 campaign for President. But, despite her rather impressive credentials, her testimony was attacked by various pundits as being everything from misinformed to delusional.

Five years later, in March 2008, the Pentagon released its study of some 600,000 documents captured in Iraq following the 2003 invasion of that country. It reported that Saddam was directly supporting several of Sheik Omar Abdel Rahman's Islamic groups, the same ones that were behind the 1993 World Trade Center attacks. I guess Mylroie wasn't as crazy as some of the pundits thought, after all. Despite this, the historical record has never really been corrected, at least not in the general public's mind. Oddly, Mylroie's critics don't seem interested in discussing it any longer. She later wrote:

"America's leading lights, including those in government responsible for dealing with terrorism and with Iraq, made a mammoth blunder. They failed to recognize that starting with the first assault on New York's World Trade Center, Iraq was working with Islamic militants to attack the United States. This failure left the country vulnerable on September 11, 2001. Many of those who made this professional error cannot bring themselves to acknowledge it; perhaps, they cannot even recognize it. They mock whomever presents information tying Iraq to the 9/11 attacks; discredit that information; and assert there is 'no evidence.' What they do not do is discuss in a rational way the significance of the information that is presented... Following the February 26, 1993, bombing of the World Trade Center, senior officials in New York FBI, the lead investigative agency, believed that Iraq was involved. When Clinton launched a cruise missile attack on Iraqi intelligence headquarters in June 1993, saying publicly that the strike was punishment for Saddam's attempt to kill former President Bush when he visited Kuwait in April, Clinton believed that the attack would also take care of the terrorism in New York, if New York FBI was correct. It would deter Saddam from all future acts of terrorism...But if the entire 1991 Gulf War did not deter Saddam for long, why should one cruise missile strike accomplish that aim?"

We now know that a mysterious Iraqi intelligence operative named Ahmed Hikmat Shakir, also known as Shakir el-Iraqi, was present at the now-infamous January 2000 meeting in Malaysia that kicked off the 9/11 plot. Shakir was later arrested in Qatar, six days after the 9/11 attacks, in possession of contact information for several high-ranking Al Qaeda terrorists. These contacts included Zaid Sheikh Mohammed, the brother of Khalid Sheikh Mohammed, the operational planner of the 9/11 attacks, and Musab Yasin, an Iraqi and the brother of Abdul Rahman Yasin, who mixed the chemicals for the first World Trade Center attacks. Shakir was also known to US intelligence because he had received a phone call in 1993 from the safe house where the planning for the first WTC bombing took place. Following his 2001 arrest and release in Qatar, he was arrested and questioned again in Jordan. He eventually returned to Iraq after Saddam pressured the Jordanian government to release him. He has never been seen or heard of again.

On September 1, 2003, The Washington Times reported in an editorial entitled *Bill Clinton's Failure on Terrorism*:

"The president did not want to hear about bad news — such as our terrible losses in October 1993, when Black Hawk helicopters were shot down in Mogadishu, Somalia, or the even more terrifying losses in New York. That would require a strong response which might upset some of the strange group of advisors and officials Mr. Clinton had collected. So it was with all the other missed opportunities to get bin Laden. CIA Director James Woolsey rarely had any meetings with Mr. Clinton. The president never supported Mr. Woolsey's urgent request for Arabic-language translators for the CIA in 1994."

This editorial also quoted Richard Miniter's book, *"Losing bin Laden: How Bill Clinton's Failures Unleashed Global Terror"*. The author charges that:

"The Clinton foreign policy was to get re-elected. Therefore, anything that might be controversial had to be avoided. So, from the beginning to the end of the administration, the Clintons' demanded absolute proof before acting against terrorists.' This high bar guaranteed inaction. At the beginning of his term, after the attack of Feb. 26, 1993, Mr. Clinton refused to admit that the World Trade Center had been bombed. Later, he referred to it only as 'regrettable' and 'treated the disaster… like a twister in Arkansas.' Earlier, he had urged the public 'not to overreact to the 1993 World Trade Center bombing."

Michael F. Scheuer, a former CIA intelligence officer who served for 22 years, and whose assignments included being the Chief of the Bin Laden Issue Station (aka "Alec Station"), from 1996 to 1999, served with the Osama bin Laden tracking unit at the Counterterrorist Center, and as a Special Advisor to the Chief of the bin Laden unit from September 2001 to November 2004; stated the following during a September 2006 CBS interview:

"The former president (Clinton) seems to be able to deny facts with impunity. Bin Laden is alive today because Mr. Clinton, Mr. Sandy Berger and Mr. Richard Clarke refused to kill him. That's the bottom line... The Clinton administration had eight to ten chances (to kill bin Laden) that they refused to try."

Henry Crumpton served in the CIA's Clandestine Service starting in 1981. For most of his 24-year career he operated in the foreign field, including assignments as Chief of Station. In Washington, he served as Deputy Chief of the International Terrorism Operations Section (1998-1999) and later led CIA's Afghanistan campaign (2001-2002). In a May 2012 interview on 60 Minutes he stated: *"We saw a security detail, a convoy, (near Kandahar) and we saw Bin Laden exit the vehicle, clearly... The optics were spot on, it was beaming back to us, CIA headquarters. We immediately alerted the White House, and the Clinton administration's response was, 'Well, it will take several hours for the TLAMs, the cruise missiles launched from submarines, to reach that objective. So, you need to tell us where bin Laden will be five or six hours from now.' The frustration (at the CIA) was enormous."*

In the same interview he characterizes the attitude of the Taliban towards the U.S. with regards to the potential American response to the 9/11 attacks: *"They expected that we would not respond in any meaningful way. The enemy thought the U.S. was weak. The last thing they thought is that we would drop commandos, CIA and Special Forces, behind their lines."*

On July 19, 2004, it was revealed that the US Justice Department was investigating Sandy Berger, Bill Clinton's longtime National Security Advisor, for the unauthorized removal of classified documents in October 2003 from a National Archives reading room prior to testifying before the 9/11 Commission. It was reported that he stuffed "code-word"- class secret documents into his pants, sneaked them out of a secure review room at the National Archives, and "inadvertently" destroyed them. The *Washington Post* later reported that Berger purloined all draft revisions of a key critique of the government's response to the millennium terrorism threat, a document that detailed Administration knowledge—and inaction—regarding Al Qaeda's presence in the US in 1999 and 2000. Stolen also were crucial notes in the margins of these drafts that reveal the thinking and the agendas of the Clinton Administration relating to the mounting terrorist threat.

The first man to investigate the crime, Inspector General Paul Brachfeld, concluded that Berger may have withheld key information about the Clinton Administration's anti-terror strategy and efforts from the 9/11 Commission. Following his investigation, Brachfeld remained silent for more than two years, but in March 2007 he stated, *"I'll spend the rest of my life going to bed at night wondering, 'Did he take more?' The American people should go to bed every night wondering if he took more. We'll never know; only Sandy Berger knows."*

A Congressional report entitled *Sandy Berger's Theft of Classified Documents—Unanswered Questions,* released in January 2007, mirrored Brachfeld's comments, concluding, *"The country may never know the full effect of Berger's misconduct. His deliberate, calculating actions to remove highly classified documents compromised the national security of this country in more ways than one."*

Berger eventually pleaded guilty to a misdemeanor charge of unauthorized removal and retention of classified material on April 1, 2005. Berger was fined $50,000, sentenced to serve two years of probation and 100 hours of community service, and stripped of his security clearance for three years. On May 17, 2007, Berger relinquished his license to practice law as a result of the Justice Department investigation. By giving up his license, Berger avoided cross-examination by the Bar Counsel regarding the details of his theft.

A man by the name of John Patrick O'Neill was the one-time chief of the FBI's counterterrorism department and a top anti-terrorism expert during the Clinton years. He was well known for his frequent, late-night rendezvous with his colleagues from the other US security services at an upper-east-side New York restaurant known as Elaine's. In 1993, following the first Trade Center bombing, he began an intensive study of Arab terror networks. He later assisted in the capture of Ramzi Yousef, one of the operational leaders of this terrorist attack who was later identified as an Iraqi intelligence officer. O'Neill was also directly involved with the 1996 Khobar Towers bombing investigations, was in charge of the investigation of the 2000 USS *Cole* bombing, and was one of the first to identify Al Qaeda and Osama bin Laden as serious security threats to the United States.

Unfortunately, during the year that preceded the second World Trade Center attack, O'Neill became the subject of a smear campaign orchestrated by senior officials inside and outside of the FBI. As a result, he took an early retirement from the FBI in August of 2001. Later that same month, on August 19, he became the head of security at the World Trade Center. Nineteen days later, at the age of 49, he was killed in the 9/11 attacks. He died, along with thousands of his fellow citizens, the victim of an attack many believed he could have prevented if his investigative work and his reputation had not been undermined by his superiors in Washington.

In 2002 O'Neill became the subject of a *Frontline* documentary describing his efforts to warn the Clinton administration of the impending danger that the nation faced from Osama bin Laden and Al Qaeda. The title of the documentary is: *"The Man Who Knew"*.

In October 2010, Gen. Hugh Shelton, the former chairman of the Joint Chiefs of Staff during the Clinton administration, published his autobiography. In it he provided a detailed account of how President Bill Clinton lost track of "the Biscuit", a credit-card-sized piece of plastic containing special codes that allow the president to launch a nuclear attack. The codes are a key part of America's nuclear protocol. They allow the president to open a special briefcase, called the "football," that contains instructions for a response to a surprise nuclear launch against the United States. The commander-in-chief is supposed to keep the card with him at all times.

"The codes were actually missing for months," Shelton wrote. *"This is a big deal—a gargantuan deal—and we dodged a silver bullet."* Analysts say the case of the missing codes marks one of the most serious security breaches in American nuclear history.

The 1993 World Trade Center bombing, and the Iraqi attempt to assassinate former president Bush during his visit to Kuwait using a Toyota Land Cruiser packed with explosives, occurred within two months of each other. The assassination plot went completely undetected by the Secret Service until it was reported to Washington, some weeks later, by representatives of the Kuwaiti government. It is still unknown how the presidential party managed to escape this well planned assassination attempt.

Well, that's actually not entirely accurate; somebody knows.

I hope you enjoyed this novel.

www.ingramcontent.com/pod-product-compliance
Lightning Source LLC
Chambersburg PA
CBHW030429310726
48979CB00009B/1682/J
9780989423304